DEFIANT PASSION

The water was only waist high, Kelsey realized as she swam beneath the piling of the boathouse and then surfaced. Salford still wouldn't let go of her hand. He broke the surface when she did. She tried to jerk her hand back, but couldn't.

"You did that on purpose!" she blurted out. "Of all the insufferable, irritating—"

He grabbed her and kissed her, cutting off her tirade. She beat on his chest, but he squeezed her tighter. She stopped fighting him, knowing it was useless.

His lips softened. All she could think about was the warmth of his mouth, the feel of his tongue running along her lips, the wet warmth of his face melding with the wetness of her own flesh. Her lips parted, and his tongue plunged inside. She tasted the bittersweet flavor of whiskey in his mouth. Her arms wrapped around his neck, and she grabbed a handful of his hair, pushing his face closer to her, urging him onward as every part of her came alive, crying out for his touch. . . .

<u>BOOK YOUR PLACE ON OUR WEBSITE</u> <u>AND MAKE THE</u> <u>READING CONNECTION!</u>

We've created a customized website just for our very special readers, where you can get the inside scoop on everything that's going on with Zebra, Pinnacle and Kensington books.

When you come online, you'll have the exciting opportunity to:

- View covers of upcoming books
- Read sample chapters
- Learn about our future publishing schedule (listed by publication month *and author*)
- Find out when your favorite authors will be visiting a city near you
- Search for and order backlist books from our online catalog
- Check out author bios and background information
- Send e-mail to your favorite authors
- Meet the Kensington staff online
- Join us in weekly chats with authors, readers and other guests
- Get writing guidelines
- AND MUCH MORE!

Visit our website at
http://www.zebrabooks.com

My Darling Duke

Constance Hall

Zebra Books
Kensington Publishing Corp.
http://www.zebrabooks.com

ZEBRA BOOKS are published by

Kensington Publishing Corp.
850 Third Avenue
New York, NY 10022

First Printing: July, 1998
10 9 8 7 6 5 4 3 2 1

Printed in the United States of America

To Norman, Daniel, and David, the loves of my life

One

Kelsey Vallarreal blew back a long, thick strand of dark hair that had escaped the ribbon at the back of her neck. She bit her lip, heaved a bucket of coal aside, then opened the chamber door. The door squeaked on its rusty hinges. She didn't bother seeing if the noise disturbed her father, but went directly to the hearth and plopped down the heavy burden with a loud clunk.

Her father groaned.

This brought a wry smile to her face. Scooping out a shovel of coal, she threw it onto the grate. The solid clamor of coal against metal elicited another groan. Her grin broadened. She wiped her hands down the front of an old paint-stained smock, rose, then strode over to the threadbare curtains in the room and flung them back.

Sunlight hit Maurice Vallarreal square in the face. Tiny wrinkles at the corners of his eyes deepened in a pained expression. He shielded his eyes with his hand and moaned, "Go away."

"Time to get up, Papa. It is almost noon, and you have a sitting." Kelsey grabbed the empty bottle of rum lying near her father's side and set it on the table by the bed.

He flinched and held his temple. "Oh, *ma chère,* I can't, I'm dying here." He rolled on his side, then buried his head beneath a pillow.

"Mrs. Watson will be here any moment for her sitting." Kelsey could not keep the desperation from her voice. "I've prepared your palette and all is ready in the studio."

"Mon Dieu! That woman has the face of a crow. I cannot look upon it so early in the day. Tell her I am dead."

"I shall do no such thing." Kelsey crossed her hands over her chest and eyed him like a recalcitrant child, but the look was lost on him.

"You finish the portrait, *ma chère.* You paint as well as I— perhaps better."

"I have finished most of it, but she did not come here to have a mere assistant paint her, and well you know it, Papa. She wants you. You are the famous French artist Vallarreal, not me. All you have to do is put the finishing brush strokes on the canvas and sign your name."

"Tell her an *artiste* cannot work unless driven by creative juices. Tell her my juices dry up when I look at her. Tell her—"

"There is nothing dry about you—if only there were. Now you must get up." Kelsey grabbed the pillow off her father's head. Teasingly, she hit him on the backside, several times for good measure.

When he did not move, she tried a different assault. "Papa, that was the last of the coal. And the larder is empty save for a few turnips and two eggs. We need a new roof. And if you do not get up and finish this painting, we will starve, and you"—she poked him in the side and had the pleasure of seeing him jump—"will not have money for your rum, for not one bottle is left in the cupboard. You will also have to forgo your visits to your—" Kelsey caught herself before she said *whores,* then thought of the epithet her father used when speaking about them, and she added, *"Ladyloves.* And you know that the monthly allowance you get from Uncle Bellamy is gone. You spent that the first sennight after receiving it."

At the mention of his pleasures being curtailed, his swollen lids opened and a pair of bloodshot gray eyes peered at her. The years of abuse Maurice had put his body through had done nothing to destroy his looks. For a man of fifty, he was still handsome, with thick dark locks peppered with gray. His strong, chiseled features could charm a smile from the opposite sex whenever he stepped into a room, but he was not going to charm anyone that morning. No, he was going to get out of bed.

"Don't stare at me so, *ma chère*. It makes me want to cry. I know you are unhappy with me." He looked at her forlornly.

"Oh, Papa, I'm not angry with you." The firm resolve melted from her face and she bent down and kissed him on the cheek, wrinkling her nose at the sour odor of rum on his breath. She stood and placed her hands on her hips. "I just want you to get up, please."

"There is no need to get up." He decided after all. "I have a far more lucrative commission."

Kelsey grabbed his arm, attempting to yank him out of bed, but she paused. "What did you say?"

"I said I have a far more lucrative commission . . . to the tune of three thousand pounds." He smiled proudly at her now, the radiance of it lighting up his face, making him look ten years younger.

"Three thousand pounds?" She narrowed her eyes at him in disbelief.

"It's true, *ma chère*. The Duke of Salford wants a fresco restored in his ballroom."

"The Duke of Salford!" She blurted out the name so loud, Maurice cringed and held his head.

"A care, *s'il vous plaît*. My poor head . . ."

"How could you, Papa?" She stepped back from the bed and turned toward the window, unable to look at Maurice any longer.

She gripped the windowsill. Her hands trembled slightly from the pressure of her fingers digging into the pine. Stillmore, the duke's rambling castle, loomed atop the brow of a hill. The moat, drawbridge, and battlements had long since been done away with, but the four flanking towers and the original keep had remained untouched when it was remodeled. That should have softened the castle's appearance, but it did not. It was without warmth or welcome, an impregnable medieval fortress. The crenelated battlements appeared like bared teeth smirking down upon the poor village inhabitants from every angle. And more so today.

Maurice stared at the petite frame of his daughter, standing so grave at the window. He took a very long look at her, as if seeing her for the first time, and felt a stab of conscience. Her long, thick curly black hair was caught at the back of her neck and flowed down her back in wild disarray. If she had combed it that morning, it wasn't noticeable. The pocket on her paint-stained smock flopped over, ripped at both seams. She wore a pair of his old breeches she'd taken in. One of his old white shirts, faded to a dingy yellow, hung down to her thighs. She had a boyish thinness, adding to her haggard and pathetic look.

Where had the years gone? He had failed her miserably as a father. Tears stung his eyes. He surreptitiously blinked them away, then forced his legs over the side of the bed, feeling the room spin as he moved.

"We can live comfortably on that, *oui*." He tried to sound upbeat as he stood and waited for the room to stop spinning, then he pried her small hands from the window frame and held them. Her head barely reached the top of his shoulders, and he had to lean down to look into her large green eyes. He rubbed his thumb across the top of her hand.

"Don't be angry, *ma chère*. I only want to do what is right for you." When she opened her mouth to protest, he put his finger against her lips. "Look at your hands, all red and cracked from housework. Your mother's hands were like this, and it killed me to see them so. I would sell my soul to the devil not to see your hands this way."

Her dark arched brows drew together and she jerked her hands from his grasp. "If you took a commission from Salford, then you have, indeed, sold your soul to the devil, Papa."

"It doesn't matter. I want to buy you a new wardrobe and deck you out as you should be. I don't want to see my daughter looking like a ragamuffin." He pointed at her. "Look at you. You are twenty now, a beautiful young girl . . . a petite spring flower ready to be plucked by some deserving man. I want you to look and dress like the beautiful woman you are."

"I'm not beautiful, Papa. Griffin says I'm shaped like a drain-pipe and that I have calf eyes."

"What does Griffin know? He is like a brother to you. To wed you would be an honor for any man."

She raised her chin to a stubborn angle. "If I have to dress finely for a man to notice me, then I'd rather be a spinster. And I would gladly wear rags the rest of my life than see you lower yourself and work for Salford."

"I know, but pride will not feed us, *ma chère,* or provide for you as I wish to do." Maurice looked deep into his daughter's enormous green eyes and reached out to touch her shoulder, but she stepped back.

"Your intentions are always well meant, but we both know you will only spend the money on drink and—"

He raised his hand to stop her. "I know what you were going to say—nothing you have not lectured me on before. I know my own vices, *ma chère,* but I'm a Frenchman." He emphasized Frenchman as if it were the final justification for all his foibles.

He watched her profile. As he expected, her lips hardened with annoyance. Ignoring it, he turned toward the pitcher on his dresser and poured some water into a bowl. He sluiced his face, then groped for a towel. Kelsey jumped to get it for him, and he smiled to himself.

When he'd dried his face, he put his arm over her shoulder, then frowned at his reflection in the mirror. He patted the loose flesh beneath his square jaw and made faces in the mirror. "Ah, ten years can do terrible things to the face, *oui* . . . and can do much to ease the memory."

"Salford was responsible for Clarice's death. Can you forget that so easily?"

He spoke to Kelsey's reflection in the mirror. "I'll never for-get it, but it sours a man to carry animosity within him." His next words sounded like a lament. "Somehow I always knew

Clarice's life would end in tragedy. She was nothing like your mama."

"Then why did you marry her, Papa? Why did you love her more than Mama? I don't understand."

Kelsey's frank question wasn't surprising. He had raised her to be uninhibited. A free spirit. He never knew what would come out of her mouth, but they'd never discussed this delicate subject before. He chose his words wisely so as not to hurt her. "Your mother was beautiful, gracious . . . a proper lady. I loved her in my own way." He smiled sadly, gulped down the dryness in his throat, and continued pensively. "It was a complaisant and comfortable love. Loving your mother was like slipping on a pair of old slippers, I always expected them to be right where I left them . . . until she died."

He fell silent for a moment. The reverence and sadness left him, and his eyes sparkled as he thought of his second wife. "Then I met Clarice. She was wild, untamed. She was heaven and hell to me. She loved with such fire in her soul. And I know I was burned by it, but"—his voice grew soft with emotion—"God help me, I shall never be sorry for it. I hope you will know that kind of fire when you fall in love and marry."

Kelsey remained silent for a moment, the reflection of her large, expressive eyes boldly studying him in the mirror. If he had hurt her, it didn't show in the liquid green depths of her eyes. He was thankful she understood. Perhaps she understood too much. He frowned at that thought.

"You may be able to forgive him, but I cannot." Her voice held no accusation, but was delivered in her usual direct tone.

He pushed back an unruly lock of curly hair that had fallen down the center of her nose, then looked into her long-lashed green eyes. "If I can forgive him, *ma chère.* you can too."

She looked as if she were about to speak, but the sound of a carriage pulling up made her glance toward the window. "Oh, Mrs. Wilson is here."

"Show the crow"—he saw Kelsey's scowl, and said—"lady to the studio and drape her. I'll be there in a moment."

She hurried to the door, but paused with her hand on the knob. "Papa, don't take the commission. You may have forgiven him, but I'm sure a man like him couldn't care less about gaining your favor. I doubt he has a conscience at all. He probably has some perverse reason for wanting to hire you—probably to laugh in your face." When she saw his crestfallen expression, she added, "I'm sorry, Papa. I had no right to say that, but I can't bear the thought of you working for him." She opened the door and was about to close it, but her father's words stopped her.

"He didn't ask for me, but for you."

"What?" Kelsey's jaw dropped open, and the color drained from her face.

"He must have wanted to spare both of us from embarrassment. He has asked that you paint his fresco. His carriage will arrive in the morning to convey you."

"I think three thousand pounds is a cheap price for your forgiveness—" She opened her mouth to say more, but the rapping at the door stopped her. She flashed her father such a scornful look that he took a step back and bumped into the dresser behind him. He jumped when she slammed the door in his face.

A wide grin spread across his face. He knew his Kelsey. She would never pass up so much money when they needed it so badly. She would go to the duke.

The next morning the butler at Stillmore pushed the massive mahogany door closed, its iron hinges creaking. The door slammed shut, blowing a gush of cool air past Kelsey's face. The musty odor of ancient stones filled her senses, and not a shaft of the bright midday sun penetrated the confines of the foyer's ancient darkness. She glanced around, feeling closed off from the outside world, swallowed by the medieval aura that pervaded the castle.

The only light came from the candle the butler held. It reflected off the broadswords, axes, pikes, and maces mounted on the gloomy stone walls. Twelve suits of armor stood guard on either side of the foyer, their shimmering silver forms melting into the impenetrable shadows of the room. They looked ready to come to life at any moment, grab one of the weapons from the wall, and defend the castle against modern intruders. She felt like an intruder.

The butler cleared his throat.

Remembering she wasn't alone, she turned to look at him. He was as tall and willowy as a blade of grass, and his head was almost totally bald. A pinched look about his mouth made him look like he'd just taken a bite out of a lemon. His expression grew markedly disapproving as he eyed Kelsey's breeches and paint smock.

Her father had begged her to wear one of the two dresses she owned, which were faded and worn and ready for the rag heap, and in her opinion not any more presentable than her work clothes, but her rebellious nature won out. She'd worn exactly what she wanted. Why should she wear a dress, or alter her appearance, to please someone as contemptible as Salford? She told her father that too, and the blistering way she'd said it sent him scurrying from the cottage. And she wasn't about to be intimidated by Salford's haughty butler either. She let him know this by fixing him with a rapierlike smile and a bold gaze. As if to explain away her appearance, she said, "I'm Miss Vallarreal. Lord Salford is expecting me."

The butler said nothing, the pinched expression failing to leave his lips. He stared absently at her mouth, a blank look on his face, as if he hadn't heard a word she had said.

She shouted now, carefully enunciating each word, "I-am-Miss-Vallarreal! The artist! The-duke-is-expecting-me!"

"No need to yell, miss, I can hear you well enough. I'm sure the corpses beneath the chapel floor heard you."

Kelsey smiled at the quip, then blushed when she realized how oppressive the silence seemed inside the castle, her own

breathing loud in her ears. Surely, Salford had heard her screaming.

"I'm sorry," she whispered. "I thought you were deaf."

"Just admiring your teeth," he said in a faint murmur that
matched her own. "They are remarkably straight and white."

"My father has good teeth, and so did my mother. It apparently runs in the family." His acerbic expression must be from
having bad teeth, not from a sour disposition, she thought.

Some of the pinched look melted from his mouth. "You are
fortunate, miss." He took the case that held her brushes and
sketching supplies from her and set it aside. "His grace is expecting you."

Kelsey followed the butler. Their footsteps reverberated off
the stone walls of the entrance foyer like cannon blasts. The
dank bleakness, the stifling silence, caused the air to vibrate
with a suffocating feeling. She inhaled deeply and rubbed her
arms, trying to rub away the eerie sensation.

She followed the butler down a long, dark hallway. Rows of
stag horns hung on both sides of the walls, jutting out like claws
from the stones. She frowned and looked up, her eyes watching
for any sign of their reaching down to grab her.

A sound like fingernails scraping slate made her glance over
her shoulder. Total darkness shrouded the end of the hallway.
The hair-raising sound emanated from the gloomy shadows.
She gulped hard, quickening her pace until she was alongside
the butler.

"Did you hear that noise?"

"No, miss."

"I heard something."

"Stillmore has a lot of creaks and groans. You will get used
to them."

Get used to them? She drew her brows together at the butler's
stiff profile, unable to dismiss the feeling that someone, or some
thing, was behind her, watching from the darkness, enjoying
her fear. *Scrape-screech*. It came again. She looked over at the
butler. Oddly, he didn't even flinch, didn't raise an eyebrow, so

Kelsey pretended not to hear it either, though she felt her flesh crawl. She stepped closer to the butler's side.

He appeared not to mind that she was so close to him that her arm bumped against his sleeve as they walked—or he had too much dignity to show it.

"Is it true what I've heard about the fifth duke decapitating his wife and her lover in her own bed?" she said, whispering and glancing behind her as if he might be the one lurking in the shadows.

"That was a century ago, miss, I wouldn't know about such things."

"Well, what about the second duke? I heard that some of his guests never came out of the castle and perished here."

"I'm afraid, miss, you've been listening to far too much gossip in the village."

"Please don't think I believe in such nonsense," Kelsey said, trying to sound indignant. "I've heard so many stories about Stillmore being haunted, I just wondered if any of the tales were based on fact. That is the only reason I asked." She felt like a fool and made a vow never to listen to Griffin's ghost stories again. The sound she heard must be from her overactive imagination.

The butler cut his eyes at her, then paused in front of a door and opened it. "Miss Vallarreal, your grace," he announced to the room.

Kelsey wiped her sweating palms down the front of her smock, tried to still the pounding of her heart, then stepped into the room. . . .

The door slammed abruptly behind her.

She jumped, realizing the butler really hadn't slammed the door at all; it only sounded like it in the wasteland of silence clinging to everything.

She glanced around the long, massive room. Shafts of light shone through two small windows near the top of the ceiling. Clouds of dust motes danced between the thick oak beams there. Centuries of black smoke had turned the beams black, making them appear as petrified as the rest of the castle. The windows afforded very little light for such a large room, but it was enough to see the row upon row of tomes lining the walls. The lending library in South Shields was not one-fourth as large. Part of the village could fit comfortably in this one room.

"Don't just stand there, Miss Vallarreal. You may be seated."

She started at the deep, commanding voice that reached out at her and scraped against every nerve in her body. She turned and glanced down the length of the room. Even though it was the middle of June, a fire burned in the grate, the flames flickering in a hearth that was big enough to roast a boar. The room needed the warmth; it felt as gloomy and forbidding as the rest of the castle.

She rubbed the gooseflesh on her arms and saw two chairs facing the hearth. Before one of the chairs, a pair of long legs were stretched out toward the fire. Light danced along shiny black Hessians. Long human arms reposed on the arms of the chair, and two large hands grasped a book. A face was hidden by the back of the chair. She felt his palpable, engulfing presence that made the room feel terribly small now.

"You can come closer," he said with bored civility. "I won't bite, Miss Vallarreal."

"I have reason to suspect otherwise."

"If you are afraid of me, I wonder that you are here."

"I'm not afraid of you. My father accepted this commission before consulting me," she said in a composed tone that belied the quivering in her stomach.

When he said no more, she cautiously moved toward the wing chair opposite his, but his voice stopped her.

"That is far enough. You may sit in the chair behind me."

She glanced at the hard-backed chair, sitting at a discreet angle behind his chair, as if it had been purposely placed there. She felt like a naughty child who had been made to sit in a corner for punishment. She crossed her arms over her chest, then made a face at the back of his chair.

The crinkle of paper broke the silence in the room, sounding like distant thunder. Her gaze fell on the long, slender fingers in the wing chair as they turned a page in the book. She fidgeted in her chair, watching him continue to read as if she were not in the room. It was a mistake to have come. She knew that now. Three thousand pounds wasn't a large enough inducement to be humiliated like this. She stood, ready to leave, but his voice stopped her.

"Sit down, Miss Vallarreal."

She stiffened. "Do you expect me to sit here for the rest of the day, waiting for you to condescend to speak to me? I have better things to do, *your grace.*"

"Sit down." The order was uttered softly, yet the threat behind the words was unmistakable.

She stared at his large, strong hands, still clasping the book, and knew he could easily overpower her. She sat, keeping her eyes on him, ready to leap up again should he come after her. He didn't move, the muscles in his thighs relaxed. She let out the breath she'd been holding.

"Since you will be here for some time, I suggest you curb your insolent tongue, Miss Vallarreal."

"I'm sorry that my plain speaking offends you," she said, anger quickly replacing her apprehension. "Hopefully, our meetings will be infrequent and of short duration—if at all."

"I think that would please us both." His long fingers poised on the corner of a page.

"Yes, it would, and while we are being so poignantly honest, let us come to an understanding straightaway. If it were not for the generous sum of money you're offering, I wouldn't be here—but I have a feeling you already know that. There's something else you should know. Frescos are not easily restored. If the damage is acute, I may suggest that the fresco be taken down and a new one painted. If I find the present design disgusts me to repaint it, then I will leave and let you find another artist. I can't paint what I can't envision or what my heart cannot like."

"So you think the present design might be so sordidly perverse and darkly wicked that it will disgust you."

Her brows rose at the satiric amusement in his voice. "People surround themselves with art that mirrors their souls. I doubt you will surprise me."

"Your opinion of me must, indeed, be very low."

"How could it be otherwise? Your conduct in the past and the insult you heaped upon my father by importuning him to send me here is all the proof I need of your character. You must have known he couldn't refuse the sum of money you offered."

When he didn't answer her, the tension in the air grew so taut she could walk on it. She decided to change the subject. "By the bye, how did you know I painted?"

He hesitated a moment, then said, "It was obvious that your father is . . . shall we say . . . not very dependable. I know that you are his assistant and that you do most of the work for him without taking credit for it and that you keep house for him. I know that you and your father survive on very little, and that he claims to be a great French artist, but in truth he was never very well known in France. In fact, he migrated to England after Waterloo because he'd lost what few clients he did have and couldn't support himself. Unfortunately, the aristocracy here have never solicited his services either, his only clients are the nouveau riche who have amassed their fortunes in trade. I also know your father receives a monthly allowance from a distant uncle in France, and your father spends it unwisely."

How did he know about the allowance from Uncle Bellamy? The rest was common knowledge, all except that she did the painting for her father, and he could have guessed at that. "You know an awful lot about me," she said, annoyance dripping in her voice.

"I have a certain interest in you."

"Why is that? Could you possibly be feeling remorse over cuckolding my father, making him a laughingstock in the village, and being responsible for Clarice's death?" Kelsey paused, clenched her fists tightly, and waited for his response.

He said nothing.

His silence felt like a slap in the face. She could endure it no longer. Unable to keep the bitterness out of her voice, she said, "I assure you, Clarice's death was no loss to me, for she wasn't a loving stepmother"—she paused and glared at the back of his chair—"at least to me—that is. But . . . my father loved her. The scandalous circumstances surrounding her death destroyed him—in fact, *you* destroyed him. I'll never be able to forgive you for that. So, please, don't take an interest in me. I don't need your pity—if you are capable of such a tender emotion."

She blinked back the tears that threatened to fall from her eyes, then sat on her hands to still the violent trembling in them. Her arms remained like rigid supports at her sides as she fought for control of her emotions.

He didn't reply right away, obviously fighting to rein in his temper. She glanced at him. He had not moved, his arms and legs so still, they could be made of marble. The average person might not have noticed the barely perceptible tension and strain of the small muscles in his hands as he clutched the book. But she noticed. And she knew what self-mastery it must be costing him to appear calm. An effigy of complete control. A veritable tower of reserved ice and stone. His frigid voice broke the silence, making her jump.

"After you see the fresco and if you decide to paint it, I will leave the subject matter to your discretion. As long as you are here, you must follow the rules in this household. I like my privacy and will not have it disturbed. A room has been set up for you near the ballroom. You shall take your meals in that room and sleep in it. You needn't leave that part of the house. I expect you to stay there. If you wish to take a turn in the gardens, do so from eight to ten in the morning. No visitors are allowed during your stay here, but you can write as many letters as you like. You may use the library, but enter it only between twelve and two in the afternoon. If you play the pianoforte, you may use the one in the music room, but only from three to four in the afternoon. Do you understand the rules?"

"Quite." She stood, then rolled her eyes at the back of the chair. "I'm to take my meals in my room. The gardens from eight to ten and the library from twelve to two. If I play, I may use the pianoforte from three to four. No roaming. No breathing." She had said it to make him angry, but when she heard his infectious, rich laughter, she grinned in spite of herself.

She straightened her face and stared at the long, graceful lines of his fingers. Wonderful specimens. It surprised her that she felt an urge to draw them. Dismayed, she said, "Are there any other rules I need follow?"

"Yes, I may come to view your progress, but when I do you will leave the room." Frigid aloofness had replaced the mirth in his voice. "I'll have Watkins inform you of my visit ahead of time."

The sadness, the loneliness lying just beneath the autocratic facade in his voice, touched a compassionate nerve Kelsey didn't think existed. The smile left her lips and she asked softly, "Tell me, do you keep these rules to protect my sensibilities or to protect your vanity?"

"I'll not answer that." His voice grew defensively low. "As long as you are abiding under *my* roof, you will follow *my* rules and not ask questions. Is that clear?"

"Quite." Kelsey intended to say no more, but couldn't resist adding, "Please allow me to reassure you that if it's for my benefit that you have established these rules, then you need not. My father made sure that I was well educated in every art form. I have seen things that would make Dante's hell look like heaven. Most excitable young ladies would have swooned dead away if they'd seen what I have seen. I can stand before you and with utter honesty say that I never once swooned in all my life—even when my father insisted I learn to draw human anatomy and dragged me to London to view an autopsy."

Kelsey frowned at the memory and continued. "I gave up my accounts all over the front of his shirt, but—I did not swoon.

It's common knowledge that you were deformed when Clarice was killed. I feel sure that's the reason for all these rules, but you need not hide your appearance from me. The sight of you will in no way sway my opinion of you, or provoke even a gasp of horror out of me."

He slapped the book shut and drew his long legs toward the chair. She thought he was going to stand and face her, but he said, "You are dismissed. Watkins will show you to your room."

Kelsey frowned at the chair back, turned, then walked toward the door. If he were incensed by her or laughing at her, she was unable to tell, but a hint of emotion was in his voice, a quality she hadn't heard thus far. She wasn't sure she was comfortable with it yet, or with this newfound sympathy she felt for him. Perhaps now she might be able to speak civility to him when they were forced to be in the same room. Perhaps.

Two

When Kelsey closed the door, Watkins was waiting for her. He looked flustered, as if he'd been listening at the door.

"Your room is this way, miss." He turned and started down the hall, his posture as stiff as a wire brush. "I suppose you know about the rules?"

She followed him and said in her usual candid manner, "You should know they were pointed out to me, since your hearing is excellent."

Some of the brittleness left Watkins's voice as he said, "Since we're speaking in such frank terms, miss—"

"Then I hope you'll drop the 'miss' and call me Kelsey."

"Ah, yes, Miss Kelsey." He said her name as if it were painful for him, then he continued. "Allow me to take the liberty of telling you that I haven't heard his grace laugh in years. I thank you for that."

"Don't thank me, I was trying to make him angry, as you well know. And I'm sure you know I dislike him for all the pain he's caused my father."

" 'Forgiveness is better than punishment; for the one is proof of a gentle, the other of a savage nature.' "

"I cannot believe this! My mother used to spout that quote at me all the time—that, and Proverbs. Epictetus and Solomon haunted my childhood until I decided I'd had enough, and"— she smiled—"my mother found me burying my Bible and a book of Epictetus's quotes."

"What did she do?" A hint of amusement played in his voice.

"Not much when my father applauded my deed. It caused many an argument in my home. You see, my father and mother were always at odds over my upbringing. He disagreed with her puritanical ideas, and she could not abide his bohemian logic. But it never stopped her. After the book burying episode, she started quoting Pope's 'Moral Essays' and the Book of Psalms to me."

"Your mother must have been a very fine lady."

"Oh, yes, very fine." Her voice grew solemn. "My mother's father was the third son of Lord Brittlewood, and he chose the church as his occupation. My grandmother's father was a squire. I never knew my grandparents. They didn't approve of my father and disinherited my mother when she ran away and married him."

"Oh . . ." His voice trailed away. He grew pensively silent afterward.

Watkins turned abruptly down another hallway. Wallpaper and paneling covered the walls there, evidence that they were in a newer wing of the castle. She wrinkled her nose at the bright yellow and cranberry paisley paper. It was horrible, but she was glad they had left the shadows and the creaks and groans back in the older part of the castle.

He turned again and they entered a portrait gallery. Struck by the beauty of the room, she slowed her pace. Sunlight streamed in through ten large windows that stood in a neat row on one side of the room. Strategically placed settees sat beneath each window. Gold carpet stretched the length of the long room, its coloring matching the gold swags on the windows and the cushions of the settees. On the other wall, portraits of the duke's ancestors hung in intricately carved gilded frames.

She strode past the solemn powdered faces of Salford's relatives, noting among them the styles of Gainsborough, Rubens, Lely, and Van Dyck. She rarely got the chance to view such exquisite artwork, so she paused before a painting by Sir Henry

Raeburn, an artist she knew well by his rich color and broad, vigorous brush strokes.

The man in the portrait stood beneath an oak, holding the reins of a horse. His dark brown hair was cropped short. He had smooth, aristocratic features with high cheekbones that gave him a hawkish appearance. The rugged strength of his jaw added to the overall arrogant authority in his countenance. His eyes, the color of black onyx, twinkled with an innate keenness and rakishness, captured with astute clarity by Raeburn.

Next to the gentleman hung a portrait of a beautiful woman in a long gown, also a Raeburn. The sadness in the woman's eyes drew Kelsey. She stepped in front of the portrait and studied the tall, beautiful woman. She was very young, probably as old as Kelsey, but the way Raeburn had captured the loneliness and melancholy in her eyes made her look much older. Golden curls framed her pale face. By the slight curve of her shoulders, the modest tilt of her face, she appeared unassuming, aloof, and hating every moment of the sitting. A martyr in the making.

"I see you've found the portraits of the master and the late duchess."

Kelsey jumped at the sound of Watkins's voice so close to her. She grabbed her throat and said, "You startled me."

"I'm sorry, Miss Kelsey."

His monotone didn't sound at all contrite. She smiled at him, then glanced at the painting of the slim-hipped, broad-shouldered gentleman. "So this is Lord Salford?"

"Yes, when he had just come into the title," Watkins said, his voice beaming proudly.

"I should have known it was he." She frowned now, growing thoughtful, the faded memories coming back. "I used to see him driving through the village at breakneck speed, with some pretty young lady at his side. But it was so long ago. . . ." Before the scandal, before she hated him.

She quickly glanced away from Salford's portrait and looked at his wife. She touched the bottom of the gilded frame, feeling the smooth edge with her fingertip. "She looks very sad," Kelsey said, trying to change the subject.

"It was painted on her wedding day."

"Not a very happy occasion, I take it." She studied the misery in the woman's face, feeling a profound sense of pity for her. Being forced to marry Salford must have been worse than a life sentence in the Tower of London.

"It was an arranged marriage."

"Is that a polite way of saying there was no love between Lord Salford and his wife?" She turned to look at him.

He nodded. "I'm afraid so."

Her mother told her ladies never gossiped with the servants, but since Kelsey didn't consider herself a lady—ladies were wealthy, privileged, pampered individuals, not daughters of poor artists—she didn't hesitate to ask, "Did the duchess really kill herself because of the scandal, Watkins?"

"I couldn't say, Miss Kelsey." Watkins straightened his spine and said no more, obviously too loyal to Salford to give his opinion.

"Her suicide must have fueled the scandal broth that Clarice's death had already created," she said, continuing to probe.

"I suppose so, but it's not my place to speculate about such things."

"I see." She sensed that was Watkins's way of saying the subject was closed. The duchess's death still mystified Kelsey, but she knew Watkins wouldn't divulge anything further. It was common knowledge in the village that Salford's wife had committed suicide, but the particulars were never known. Kelsey decided it might be better if she didn't know—there were some things one was better off not knowing.

An image of Salford and Clarice rose unbidden in her mind. Two clasped bodies behind the coal shed. They thought no one saw them, but Kelsey's room was in the attic and she could see them perfectly from her window. Clarice kissing him, grinding her hips against him in a feral, primitive undulation . . .

She squeezed her eyes closed, willing the haunting image

away. She had seen them only that one time, but it had haunted her deepest, darkest dreams for years. Always it was Salford in her dreams, kissing her. And when she woke, she was drenched in sweat, trembling, and filled with a deep emptiness that was quickly replaced by self-loathing for letting a man she despised make love to her in her dreams. Watkins's voice brought her back to the present.

"You look pale. Are you well, Miss Kelsey?"

"I'm fine, really. Just had an unpleasant thought," she said, rubbing her hands together, feeling the sweat on her palms. He looked worried, and she added, "Truly, 'tis gone now, I feel fine."

"If you'll follow me, then."

Kelsey gave the woman in the portrait a final look of sympathy, then hurried to catch up with Watkins. They went through a maze of halls, made several more turns, then finally he paused before two large doors. "This is the ballroom."

He leaned over to open the door, but a commotion erupted from inside. He paused, his blue-veined hand on the door, and murmured, "Brutus."

"Brutus?" Kelsey stepped behind Watkins's back, positive that Brutus must be an Irish wolfhound that ate anything handy—especially people.

"You needn't worry. He's vicious only if you try to touch him." Watkins pushed the doors open.

Kelsey peered around Watkins's shoulder. The largest orange tabby cat she'd ever seen slapped and hissed at a springer spaniel. The dog cowered and growled, then backed farther into a corner. Blood oozed from claw marks on the dog's nose.

"Brutus is our resident bully and rat catcher," Watkins said matter-of-factly. He walked over to the cat and flapped his thin arms. "Go on with you, leave Trusty alone."

Brutus hissed at Watkins, then softly padded out of the room, his tail swishing, his muscular sleekness moving with the predatory grace of a dominating king.

The dog saw his chance for escape and took off running. He shot past Kelsey's legs as he flew out of the room.

She laughed, then stuck her head around the stanchion, watching Trusty gallop down the hallway, his tail tucked between his legs. "I suppose Brutus likes dogs as well as he likes rats."

"We don't have any rats. I'm sure there will come a day when I wake up and find Trusty absent as well." Kelsey smiled, surprised by Watkins's wry, unexpected sense of humor. He continued, his voice growing sterner. "Brutus is very unsociable. If you should encounter him, stay well away from him."

"I'll remember that," she said, stepping into the ballroom.

It was immense and must have been, at one time, a very grand place, but now the room was empty, the chandelier covered, an aura of stark bareness pervading it. Along the walls, couples twirled and whirled in seventeenth-century costumes. Musicians, servants, and tables of food filled in the bare spots. They weren't the lewd frescos she had expected to find in Salford's ballroom. The tameness of the subject matter surprised her. After seeing the way he had kissed Clarice, she had imagined explicit love scenes between Greek gods and goddesses with naked nymphs running around them.

"Down there is the spot his grace wishes you to paint." Watkins motioned toward the wall at the far end of the room.

They strode across the marble floor, their footsteps ringing vacant and hollow in the empty room. A scaffold had been placed near the wall, she guessed, for her use.

Watkins paused beside a metal support beam. He placed his hands behind his back and straightened his shoulders until his back became as rigid as the support beam he was standing near. Intently, he observed her, his head tilted in her direction, apparently waiting for a reaction.

Kelsey shot a covert glance at him, then ducked beneath the metal supports. A long, slender fracture ran from floor to ceiling. She ran her finger along the inside of the half-inch crack, feeling the uniform depth, then flicked off several loose pieces of plaster with her finger. She recoiled at the crack, then glanced at Watkins. His mouth had shrunken inward, his lips no longer visible, and he appeared enthralled by the patterns in the marble floor near his feet.

"I cannot restore this fresco. The crack is too wide and deep. How did this happen to the wall?" She dusted her hands, then walked out from beneath the metal supports of the scaffolding.

He didn't look at her as he spoke. "I—I couldn't say. It appeared there not too long ago. His grace said it must be from settling."

"Settling?" Kelsey crossed her arms over her chest, then raised her dark brows at him. "I was under the impression the remodeling of the castle took place during the end of Queen Elizabeth's reign."

Watkins hedged, weighing his answer carefully, then he said, "I believe you are correct, Miss Kelsey."

"Hmmm. That would make this new edition some two hundred years old. Does it not seem odd to have settling in such an old structure?"

"I wouldn't know."

"Have you noticed any other cracks anywhere else?"

"Only this one."

"I think it wise to inform Lord Salford that he may need an architect to come and inspect the crack. This new edition may come crumbling down around him. I hope he doesn't use this room very often." A smile hovered in Kelsey's voice.

"Hasn't been used in years, Miss Kelsey. His grace's mother used it when she was alive, but she's been dead over seventeen years."

"I wonder that Lord Salford bothers repairing the wall at all. Seems an awful large expense for an unused room."

"Oh, he's a stickler when it comes to keeping the castle in perfect condition."

"I see." When she observed how guilty and uncomfortable Watkins appeared by the conversation, she said no more. Even if she pressed him, he wouldn't admit what really happened to the wall.

He looked relieved and let out a breath that released his lips from inside his pinched mouth, then he motioned toward a door near the end of the scaffolding. "Your room is this way. Please follow me and I'll show it to you."

Kelsey sighed deeply and watched Watkins's rigid back as he walked toward the door. Obviously, someone had deliberately damaged the wall. But why? She really didn't care as long as she received three thousand pounds for fixing it.

She would paint Salford's wall and keep every cent of the money. She would never again let her father sign his name to her work—not after the underhanded way he had accepted this commission without even discussing it with her. Men might dominate the art world, but with the small fortune from this commission, she meant to live comfortably at the studio, dole out the money to her father as she saw fit, and make a name for herself. She could advertise in London. Perhaps even move in polite circles and make connections. She had visions of ladies and gentlemen begging to be painted by her. But what price did she have to pay for her dreams? Would it be too high?

A door opened at the far end of the ballroom. Kelsey glanced up from her sketch pad. A young girl pushed her hip against the door and maneuvered a tray into the room. She was thin, her uniform hanging loosely on her frame. Her bright red hair was covered by a maid's cap. She blew out a long, tired sigh, and the cap flopped around her face as she lifted the tray a little higher. She didn't notice Kelsey, who was snuggled into the far window seat at the opposite end of the room. The girl headed toward the door that led to Kelsey's bedroom chamber.

Kelsey glanced down at the hands she'd drawn, then frowned at them. She'd meant to sketch ideas for the motif of the wall. The old design was too plain, too drab, she wanted to do something new and spectacular, something that would stand out as her own work, but she couldn't get the image of Salford's elegant, aristocratic hands out of her mind. Like a ninnyhammer, she had wasted time drawing them. She slapped the cover of the sketch pad closed, then stood.

The maid pivoted. Her eyes widened and stared at Kelsey as if she were a ghost. The rosy color drained from her cheeks, then she dropped the tray and screamed.

Kelsey hurried toward her. The girl's hysterics didn't stop, but grew worse as Kelsey approached. She grabbed the girl's shoulder and shook her. "It's all right. I won't hurt you. I'm Kelsey Vallarreal—the artist. I'm supposed to be here. I arrived earlier this afternoon."

The maid stopped screaming and stared at Kelsey, blankly at first, then recognition dawned in her eyes. She grabbed her heart as she spoke. "Ay, miss, you gave me a fright, you did. I wasn't expectin' you to be in here yet."

"I'm sorry I scared you." Kelsey bent down to pick up the tray.

Splattered food on the tray's bottom made it stick to the floor. She tugged on it and heard a sucking sound as the bottom came free. The motion propelled Kelsey backward, and she hit the floor. Her bottom landed on a piece of almond cheesecake, and she slid a foot before she finally stopped.

"Ah, miss, did you hurt yourself?" The maid grabbed Kelsey's arm, helped her up, then knocked the blob of cheesecake off her rear with her hand. "You should o' let me clean this mess up. I'm so sorry. Are you hurt?"

"Nothing but my pride is stinging." Kelsey smiled at her.

"Oh, lordy, miss, I'm glad you can see the mirth in it. Some wouldn't, ya know. Oh, dear, and this bein' your supper tray. You must be starvin' and so good-hearted about it." Tears gleamed in the girl's eyes as she bent and used the napkin from the tray to wipe the floor.

Kelsey squatted beside her. "It's just a little mess, certainly nothing to cry over." She picked up a piece of roast veal near her foot, then flipped it onto the tray with a comical flick of her wrist. It landed on the tray with a loud flop, making the girl sob and giggle at the same time. "What's your name?" Kelsey asked, grinning to herself.

"Me name's Mary . . . Mary Simpson."

"Well, Mary Simpson," she said, imitating the girl's Scottish brogue, "I'm Kelsey Vallarreal."

"Pleased to make your acquaintance." Mary grinned shyly at her, then used the end of her apron to dab her eyes and wipe her nose. "I don't know what came over me . . . it's—it's this room. It makes me skin crawl."

The smile left Kelsey's face as she picked up a spoon, scooped up a large mound of bread pudding, then dropped it onto the tray. "What's wrong with this room?"

"Oh, I shouldn't be tellin' you this, they having set up your room so close. . . ." She motioned toward the door that opened into Kelsey's bedchamber. Mary lowered her voice to a conspiratorial whisper. "Well, you've a right to know, don't you. You should know. I don't think it's fair they haven't told you."

When Mary didn't go on, Kelsey wanted to shake her, but she said, "Tell me what?"

"That this was the room the late duchess hung herself in." She pointed to the chandelier. "They found her swinging from that . . ."

Kelsey glanced up at the draped chandelier and conjured up the scene in her mind. The sad, beautiful young lady in the portrait gallery, swinging by her neck from the ceiling, her golden curls falling down around her pale face . . .

Abruptly, one of the many crystal tears tinkled in the chandelier, a slight sound, but the impact of it froze the breath in Kelsey's chest. Her heart pounded, forcing its way up into her throat. Mary noticed it too, her face as white as a new snow.

"What is this?" The voice echoed through the ballroom.

Kelsey jumped and grabbed her heart. She glanced down the room at Watkins, standing in the doorway, then sighed aloud with relief. She realized Watkins must have opened the door, and the slight draft made the chandelier move. She forced herself to relax so the lump in her throat would leave.

"What have you done, Simpson?" Watkins said as he strode toward them, moving with more vigor than a man of his years should possess.

"Don't blame Mary," Kelsey said. "I overturned the tray."

"Oh." Some of the wrath left Watkins's voice. "Simpson, get another tray at once. Clean this mess up later."

"Y-yes, sir." Mary gathered up the tray, bobbed a curtsy to Watkins, one to Kelsey, then practically ran out of the room.

Kelsey glanced into Watkins's face. The shrewd look in his eyes suggested he had guessed the truth. She stood, then said, "Don't be too hard on her."

"I shan't as long as you don't believe the nonsense she put in your ears about this room."

"Like I said before, I don't believe in ghosts," she said, realizing she'd added far too much emphasis to her words. "Do you, Watkins?"

"No. Only the living haunt Stillmore Castle."

Kelsey glanced upward at the chandelier once more. One of the teardrops moved, she thought, but then . . . she had a vivid imagination. She'd already suffered from the effects of her imagination when she'd first arrived and heard the strange noises in the hallway. Watkins must be correct, the only thing that haunted Stillmore was the present duke himself.

She looked into the young boy's eyes, saw the smile in them, then crawled up into his lap. It felt good when he wrapped his arms around her and hugged her. He loved her. And she loved him better than anyone else in the world.

"Will you marry me when I grow up?" She ran her fingers through Rabbit's soft fur.

A smile lit his face. "You sure you don't want to marry that rabbit instead?"

"No, only you. Rabbit will watch us be married in a fine chapel." She laughed and shook Rabbit up and down playfully. "Won't you, Rabbit?"

Someone entered the room. Seconds later she was ruthlessly pulled out of the boy's arms. She kicked and cried and reached out for him, but he'd vanished into a ghostly gray mist. . . .

Kelsey woke with a start from the recurring nightmare, a dream that had plagued her since her earliest childhood. It wasn't like one of the lurid dreams that Salford haunted; this dream always left her feeling as if her heart had been ripped out. She pressed her hand against her chest, felt the rapid beats against her palm, then forced herself to breathe deeply. She wiped the tears out of her eyes with the back of her hand.

That's when she felt another presence in her room. . . .

The memory of someone or something lurking in the shadows when she arrived at the castle that afternoon gripped her again. Her eyes flew open. Two green, devilish orbs glowed back at her. They hovered above the bed. Kelsey's mouth opened, her throat worked, but she couldn't scream, only tremble. She felt the gooseflesh rise along her skin, felt a drop of sweat as it trickled down her brow, felt her tongue move over her teeth, but she couldn't scream.

She had left the curtains open in the room. The moonlight, though not bright, lit enough of the room to silhouette the hunched outline of a small feline figure standing on the foot of her bed.

"Brutus?" she whispered, feeling the paralysis of her body easing, her pulse slowing. "You scared the life out of me. How did you get in here?" She raised her hand out to him. "You can come closer, kitty, I'm as lonely as you are."

She thought he might stay, but he jumped off the bed and disappeared into the shadows of the room. The chamber assigned to her was an anteroom off the ballroom. It was obvious the room had been hastily put together for her arrival. The plain pine bed, wardrobe, and drawing table clashed with the golden French wallpaper, the gilded mirrors, and a delicate settee covered in gold silk that sat beneath one of the windows. She didn't mind the thrown-together look, it was still far nicer than her own bedroom. And luckily, the room wasn't large enough that Brutus could easily hide from her.

She threw back the covers, got down on all fours, then lifted the bedskirt and peered into the blackness beneath the bed. "Here, Brutus. Come here, kitty, kitty."

Creaking floorboards above her head answered her.

Distracted by the noise, she dropped the bedskirt, leaned back on her heels, and glanced upward. It sounded like someone was pacing above stairs. Her room was in the east wing of the castle, a part she assumed was unused. So who was in the chamber over hers? And who was so rude to be pacing in the middle of the night? Surely not the duchess's ghost.

Once again, she reminded her overactive imagination that ghosts did not exist. The sound of a carriage coming along the drive drew her attention away from any thoughts of ghosts.

She strode to the window that faced the front of the castle and pulled back one of the golden brocade curtains. The moon peeked out from behind scudding clouds, affording her a clear view of a barouche, the ducal crest stark against the shiny black-lacquered sides. A team of spanking grays pulled the carriage. The driver's dark form hung over the front of the box, the whip in his hand looking like a fishing pole in the moonlight as it tauntingly dangled over the backs of the grays.

Who would visit the castle in the middle of the night? She watched as the carriage sped up the circular drive that led to the front of the castle. It veered to the right, taking an alternate route that wound around to the back of the castle, toward the servants' entrance. She turned away from the window and noticed that the pacing had stopped.

Against her better judgment, against the dire "rules" she was supposed to follow, she lit a candle, then quietly slipped out the door.

The ballroom was hidden in shadows. She purposely kept her gaze from the chandelier as she hurried across the large marble floor, feeling the coldness of it against the soles of her bare feet. She went to the door Mary had used, confident it would take her toward the kitchen and the servants' entrance.

At the end of the long hallway she heard approaching footsteps coming from an intersecting hallway. Quickly, she blew out her candle, set down the candle holder, and pressed her body against the wall. She sucked in her breath, feeling the wooden paneling poking her back through her thin nightrail. Candlelight danced shadows on the walls as the person came closer.

Watkins appeared, then he paused in front of a door. He seemed oblivious of Kelsey's presence in the opposite hall. One turn of his head would expose her. She squeezed her eyes closed, heard the door open, then he said, "His grace is expecting you."

Kelsey opened her eyes and saw him escort a woman inside.

The woman patted Watkins's cheek and said in a husky voice, "I'm sure 'e is, honey."

Kelsey caught a fleeting glimpse of the woman's indecently low-cut décolletage, the full breasts about to fall out of it. The dress hugged the woman's hourglass figure, the thin red crepe leaving nothing to the imagination. Thick blond curls were piled on top of her head, and one long curl hung enticingly over one shoulder. Her lips and cheeks had so much rouge on them that she would have looked ridiculous if she weren't so beautiful. Abruptly, Kelsey thought of Clarice. That was the kind of gown Clarice liked to wear. Clarice was blond too. Beautiful too. Clarice looked very much like this woman; they both resembled she-dragons. So this was Clarice's replacement.

Kelsey glowered at the end of the now-empty hallway. She ought to go back to her room, but had she ever done anything she ought to do? It pricked her to think that Salford would allow this brazen piece of work to see his face and not herself. She waited until their footsteps faded, then she skulked down the hall, following after them, darting behind furniture, keeping to the shadows. Up a flight of stairs. Along a corridor. The prying eyes of Salford's ancestors watched her every move from shadowed gilded frames, but she paid them no heed, nor could they sway her present course.

Watkins and the woman paused in front of a chamber door. Kelsey stopped dead and pressed her back against a wall. She realized they were still in the east wing. By her calculations, the duke's chamber was directly above her own room. Salford had been the one pacing. Now she knew why.

"Your grace, your visitor has arrived."

The woman strutted past Watkins, her fists on her hips, her breasts bouncing as her rounded hips swayed. "Thanks, sweetcakes," she said, then blew Watkins a kiss.

Kelsey bit her lip to keep from laughing at Watkins's expression. He looked like he'd just caught a whiff of the kitchen midden. With more force than was needed he closed the chamber door, then his lanky form disappeared down the hall.

Having been left in the dark with only the light beneath the duke's chamber door to guide her, Kelsey crept closer. The velvety edge of Salford's muffled voice drifted from behind the door, the woman's deep, sensuous laughter followed. She got down on all fours, trying to peek in the keyhole. She could see nothing. She edged her knees closer to the bottom of the door, then placed her ear against it.

It happened so fast, she wasn't quite sure how it all transpired. One minute she was leaning against the door, then suddenly the door opened and she fell into the room.

Three

Kelsey stared down at the flower pattern on the Turkish carpet, mortified, unable to move. Thankfully, her hair had fallen over her face, covering the blush that burned down to her scalp.

Raucous laughter came from somewhere in the room. She realized the prostitute was laughing at her. She squeezed her eyes shut, wishing she could shrivel up and die. At least then she'd be out of her misery.

"This is not funny," Salford's menacingly soft voice drawled, then said more forcefully, "get out!"

She knew by the vehemence in the last order that it was directed at her. It galvanized her into action. She scrambled to her feet, then flew out of the room without looking back. She ran down the hall, the prostitute's convulsive laughter ringing in her ears. The dark shadows in the hall turned blurry and misshapen behind her thick tears.

Inside the chamber, Edward James Huntington Noble, the Eighth Duke of Salford, tried to thrust Samantha aside, but she wrapped her arms around his waist. "Let the silly chit go," she cooed in his ear while she ran a hand beneath his dressing gown. Her fingers closed around his erection. "She was just curious. Ain't gonna hurt the young miss to know about a man's desires. My bet is, she already knows about such things. Her papa's

always visiting my girls, and she just had to see for herself."
Samantha smiled, showing the tiny gap in her teeth.

"I've got to go after her. She already thinks I'm the devil
himself. I can't imagine what she thinks now." Edward thrust
her hand aside and rolled out of bed.

"What do you care what the little miss thinks?"

Edward sat and pulled on his pants. With casual indifference
he said, "If I didn't know better, I'd think you were jealous."

"I just don't like getting all heated up and ready, then have
my man leap out of the bed to go chasing another woman. And
one such as her. She's as small as a child." Samantha pouted
and tossed her silken blond hair back over her shoulder, exposing one full breast to his view.

"I'll be back." Edward smiled wryly at her, then pulled on
his shirt. He bent down and kissed the swell of her breast.

"Go on, then." Samantha sounded indignant as she sat up on
her elbows. "If you think that little piss-in-the-wind can take
care of you, you're mistaken. She'll take one look at that *pretty*
mug of yours and drop clean away." She gazed at him raptly,
obviously waiting for his reaction.

He ignored her and continued to button his shirt.

"I know her type," she went on doggedly. "Don't think I
don't. If you're thinking of starting up a slap-and-tickle with
her, she won't be up to it."

"You don't know her at all." Edward recalled the story Kelsey
told him about the autopsy. In spite of Samantha's snide remark
about his face, he grinned to himself. Kelsey could probably
look a Cyclops in the eye, then laugh at it.

"Oh, I do and all. Don't think I'll stay here and wait for you.
Don't mind calling me back 'ere neither, 'cause I won't come
out again tonight, *your highness.*"

Edward turned, giving her such a ruthless piercing look that
she clamped her mouth shut. "You'll come if I summon you,
my sweet. I pay an enormous price for you to be at my beck
and call." He had the distinct pleasure of hearing Samantha's

indignant grunt as he picked up his boots and headed for the door.

Kelsey didn't stop running until the stitch in her side doubled her over. Each breath came like a stab in her ribs. She clutched her stomach, felt her pulse throbbing in her temples, felt a queasy feeling rolling in her stomach.

When she caught her breath, she stood, brushed back the hair sticking to her sweaty brow, then wiped the tears away from her face with the back of her hand. The fecund odor of plowed earth filled her senses. She noticed now that she was in the middle of a field of wheat. The golden silks swayed in the moonlight around her. A shaft of light gleamed from a whitewashed cottage beyond the field. Its high-pitched thatch roof, the wide cobblestone chimney, the tiny beds of daisies along either side, were familiar to her. She had spent many an hour huddled near the warmth from its fire. She'd run almost three miles to Griffin's house.

She staggered through the rows of wheat, then ran the rest of the way to the front door. The McGregors were probably asleep. The thought of waking them made her frown. She could throw a stone at Griffin's bedroom window, but he slept like a log. He probably wouldn't hear her even if she broke the window. After a moment of hesitation, she pounded on the door.

It took several minutes and another pounding before the door swung open. Alroy McGregor, Griffin's father, stood in the doorway. He was a huge, brawny man, built like a tree. His nightshirt bunched up around the waist of a pair of hastily donned breeches, which made him look even larger. His nightcap listed to one side, his thick red hair, mussed beneath it, stuck out at all angles. He shoved the cap back from his face and raised a lamp toward her.

He looked angry, perturbed, then his eyes widened in surprise as he recognized her. "Be gads, Kelsey girl, what you doin' out this time o' night and in nothin' but your nightclothes?"

She remembered that she had on only her nightgown. Before she could blush, he wrapped a beefy hand around her arm and pulled her inside. He set the lamp down on the mantel above the hearth, then looked uncomfortably about the small dining room cum sitting room. He grabbed an old blanket from the settle near the fireplace, then wrapped it around her shoulders.

"There now." He looked more at ease, but the worry lines didn't leave his wide brow as he walked over to the hearth. He stirred the ashes as he spoke. "Have a seat, child." His usual kind, self-assured manner was back in his voice.

She sat on the settle, stretched her hands out toward the fire, then stared at the flames, unable to look at him. Alroy McGregor was like a second father to her. She'd known him all her life. Still, she couldn't explain to him why she'd turned up on his doorstep in the middle of the night, barefoot, wearing her night-clothes, without dying of mortification. But she guessed he deserved some sort of explanation.

She glanced over at him as he squatted near the fire. "I—I'm really sorry for waking you. I—I shouldn't have bothered y—"

"Stuff and nonsense. Where else would you go if not to us? You know you're part of the family." He stood, took one look at her, then said, "I'll get the missus up and get her to put on a pot of tea."

"Oh, no," she pleaded, lowering her voice. "Please don't wake Edith." She knew if Edith McGregor got up that she would probably wake everyone else. Edith possessed the kindest heart in the world, but she was brusque and boisterous, not the type to tiptoe around the house. Kelsey didn't want to face all seven of Griffin's siblings at the moment, so she added with pleading in her voice, "I don't want to be a bother to anyone, but if—"

"I know who you want." Alroy's eyes glistened knowingly as his bushy red brows rose toward his hairline. "I should have figured you'd want to talk only to that son of mine, thick as thieves you've both been all yer lives. Before I go wake him, if there's anythin' I can do for you, all you need do is ask." A sympathetic smile touched his lips. He reached out and squeezed her hand.

"Yes, I know that. Thank you . . ." Kelsey squeezed his hand back, a tightening growing in her throat.

Mr. McGregor appeared ill at ease with her obvious distress and quickly dropped her hand. In a businesslike tone he said, "Well, then, that said, I'll go and pull our Griffin out o' his bed. But," he added, teasing, "you might have to throw a bucket of water on him to wake him up fully. You know how he sleeps once his noggin hits the pillow for the night."

Kelsey nodded, then watched him pick up the lamp and stride toward a staircase at the back of the room. It led to the loft Griffin shared with his brothers and sisters.

She listened to the heavy tread of Mr. McGregor's footsteps on the stairs and rubbed her arms, huddling nearer the warmth of the fire. She glanced about the tiny room. A long dining table and chairs sat near the hearth and settle. Dark stains and rings gleamed beneath many coats of yellowed wax, evidence of long use and hastily eaten meals. Initials were carved before each chair, designating where each child took his rightful place at the table. She smiled at the bold G.M. etched before a chair directly to the right of where Alroy McGregor sat. A place of honor for the eldest son, Griffin.

She glanced toward the sitting area at the opposite end of the room. A round braided rag rug circled the thick plank flooring, and two hard-backed chairs and a rocker faced a settee, covered in worn damask—the only piece of furniture that Griffin's mother refused her children. "For company only," Edith McGregor would say. Even Kelsey wasn't allowed the privilege of using it, which made Kelsey happy, since it made her feel more like part of the family.

A handmade table sat beside the rocker. On it, a small tin box holding Edith's sewing supplies gleamed in the firelight. A small cross-stitched sampler with the children's names and birthdays hung above the rocker. Still lifes, presents from her, filled the rest of the walls, along with a portrait of Griffin that

Kelsey had painted of him on his sixteenth birthday. The room was plain, utterly void of expensive knickknacks, which made it feel warm and cozy. It wasn't that Griffin's mother didn't like clutter about her, she did, but the McGregors, like many tenant farmers who rented from Salford, paid outrageous rents. That was another strike against Salford in Kelsey's eyes.

She shuddered at the thought of Salford. She wrapped the blanket tighter around her, letting the tranquility, the love, in the little cottage envelop her as she did most times when she was upset. This little cottage and the loving family in it had been a balm against all the unhappiness in her life: her parents' ceaseless arguments, her mother's death, Clarice's malicious treatment—Clarice resented her, never failing to demean her when her father wasn't around.

Clarice had threatened her too. When her father was away working, Clarice always brought home men from the village. She'd made love to them, then dared Kelsey to whisper a word to her father. Her father must have known about Clarice's indiscretions, but he always turned a blind eye toward them, which only increased Kelsey's feelings of anxiety and bitterness toward Clarice. Then the desire to run away would set in. Kelsey always ran to Griffin's house, staying for days, until her father came and brought her back home.

After Clarice died, Kelsey's life worsened. Her father went on drinking binges, sometimes for days. The loneliness swallowed her at times. Her father had always drank and caroused with whores, even when her mother was alive, but it had become an obsession after Clarice's death. The scandal had caused a sensation in all the London papers. After Salford's wife committed suicide shortly thereafter, it was all anyone could write or speak about.

Her father had hidden in the house, drowning his sorrow in rum, while Kelsey, then only twelve, cared for him through untold bouts of crying, ranting, then crying again. Her father was never quite the same after that, and Kelsey had aged a lifetime in those few months. If Griffin had not been her friend, she might have run away from home and joined the Gypsies—a threat she used often as a child. It never worked on her mother, who would only say, "All right, dear, but make sure they bring you home before dinner."

The creak of the stairs brought Kelsey from her musing. Alroy McGregor appeared first, then she could just make out the top of Griffin's head behind him. Amazingly, Griffin was even taller than his father, just as brawny too.

Alroy paused and waited for Griffin to walk past him, then handed him the lamp. "Here, laddie, you'll be needin' this." He smiled at Kelsey. "And if you can persuade her to stay, I'm sure your ma wouldn't mind her beddin' down on the settee."

Kelsey smiled at that gracious untruth. After a concerned look at both of them, Alroy exited through a door that led to his and Edith's bedchamber.

Griffin took one look at her, then ran his hand through his thick shock of flaxen hair, making the straight, disheveled spikes stick out even more. Kelsey would have laughed if she didn't feel terrible about getting him out of bed.

"I'm sorry, Griffin," she said softly, then leaned her head back against the settle and closed her eyes.

"Don't pretend to be sorry, 'cause I know it ain't so," he said in his usual bantering tone.

Something broke inside her. She couldn't hold back the tears any longer and buried her face in her hands.

"Aw, Kell I'm sorry. What's wrong?" He quickly set the lamp on the floor, sat beside her, then enfolded her in his burly arms.

"It's terrible, just terrible." Kelsey sobbed on his shirt. "I never cry, do I? I feel like a fool—I'm getting your shirt all wet." Kelsey pushed away from him, then used the end of the blanket to wipe her eyes.

"You wanna tell me what's the matter and why you're bawling your eyes out?" He suddenly sounded tired. He clasped his hands behind his head, stretched out his long legs in front of him, then crossed them at the ankle.

Kelsey stared at his bare feet, then noticed he hadn't bothered to button his shirt all the way, nor had he tucked it inside his pants. She stared at his shirttail hanging down around his sinewy thighs as she spoke. "I've just come from Stillmore."

"Stillmore?" Griffin sat up now, his deep blue eyes widening incredulously at her.

"Yes, I didn't have a chance to tell you, but Papa accepted a commission there to restore a fresco on a ballroom wall."

"So what are *you* doing there?"

"Salford didn't want Papa, he wanted me."

"You?" Griffin's golden brows rose.

"You needn't look so surprised. I can paint just as well as my father—"

"You know I wasn't thinkin' that. It just seems strange that his mighty *lordship* would ask for you out of the blue. After him and Clarice tried to run off together and she was killed in that awful carriage accident, seems to me, he wouldn't be able to face your pa and all. . . ." Griffin's jaw tightened and one lip moved over the other. His long-held hatred for Salford glowed in every taut muscle in his face.

Griffin's loyalty to her was part of the reason he disliked Salford so much, but he also resented Salford's miserly high rents and the way his family struggled to pay them. Griffin wouldn't need an excuse to take up a battle with Salford. But she wasn't about to let him do it for her, so she didn't tell him about the dubious crack in the wall, or that it looked as if Salford had ruined it for a reason yet unknown to her. She twirled a strand of her long hair around her finger and stared into the burning embers of the fire. Silence hung between them. Finally he broke it.

His gaze locked on her hand as she twirled a dark curl around her finger. "What is it? You're not tellin' me somethin'. You always do this"—he grabbed her hand, stilling it—"when you're trying to hide somethin'. Tell me what it is."

Kelsey took a deep breath and carefully tried to hide the lie in her voice. "It's nothing really, just that I probably wouldn't have minded painting his wall if my father hadn't accepted the commission without discussing it with me. And, well . . . I couldn't refuse after I learned he was offering three thousand pounds—"

He whistled between his teeth, then dropped her hand. "Three thousand pounds? That's a bloody fortune."

"I know, and Papa won't get his hands on it. I intend to keep every penny." A calculating grin reached her eyes. "That's why I went, but you wouldn't believe all the *rules* I have to follow."

"Rules?" He looked perplexed and annoyed at the same time.

She rolled her eyes. "Tons of them. You know how he became a recluse after the accident. The rumors must be true about him being deformed from the accident. He doesn't show his face to anyone. He's concocted all these rules so we shall never meet unexpectedly. I suppose he thinks I'll swoon from the sight of his hideous face." Amused, she grinned slightly. "I tried to tell him I didn't swoon, but he still wouldn't show me his face, and, well—" She paused, her cheeks reddening now at the thought of what she'd done.

"Well, what did you do? I know you did somethin' foolish, Kell, it ain't like you to follow rules." A grin teased the corners of his wide mouth.

"I committed such a humiliating folly, Griffin, I hate to tell you. It makes me sick just to think about." She squeezed her eyes closed.

"Come on, tell it. It couldn't be all that bad."

"It's bad enough." She paused a moment, then told him all that had transpired, how she'd fallen through Salford's chamber door, how she'd run from the house—she left out the part about the prostitute's mocking laughter. She finished, then waited for one of his ready comments. When he didn't offer one right away, she turned to look at him.

He shifted uneasily beside her, then glanced at her. His face contorted as if he were in pain, but a smile gleamed in his eyes. A rumble of laughter rose up in his throat until it burst from his mouth.

Kelsey hit his burly arm. "Some best friend you are, Griffin

McGregor. I pour out my troubles to you and all you can do is laugh."

"I can't help it," he said, trying to catch his breath. "I can see you falling in the room now—you gotta agree, it's better than watching crazy old Aggie from the village walking her pig on a leash."

Incensed now, she jerked the blanket around her and stood. "Fine, fine, have your laugh at my expense," she said, whispering. "I'll go now before you wake up the whole house. All I need are your brothers and sisters laughing at me too."

Griffin grabbed her hand, easily jerking her back down on the settle. He wiped the tears in his eyes. "Ah, Kell, when did you become so sensitive? You know I'm funnin'. Sit down, you ain't goin' nowhere."

"I've got to go back." Kelsey frowned at that idea. After what happened, she'd rather face the devil than Salford again.

"You don't have to go back." The laughter left his expression. He grew pensive, as if an idea had just struck him and he was trying to get used to it.

"I have to. Three thousand pounds is too much money not to go back—that is, if he still wants me to paint his wall after I broke the *rules*."

"You don't need the money, Kell, you can stay here."

"I'm sure your parents would love another mouth to feed. And where would I sleep, in the cow byre?" Kelsey grinned now in spite of her dread of facing Salford. It had to be done sooner or later. Now that she'd talked about it with Griffin and heard him laugh about it, she realized how absurd and ridiculous the whole thing seemed. She could face Salford. She could.

He grabbed her hand, then squeezed it. Griffin had held her hand thousands of times, but something about the penetrating heat of his wide palm and the possessive pressure of his fingers, coupled with the odd gleam in his eye, disturbed her. She tried to jerk her hand back, but he held it fast.

"You could sleep with me, Kell."

"Sleep with . . ." Kelsey couldn't bring herself to say "you."

She sat there, her jaw gaping, staring at her best friend. A person she knew better than she knew herself—or thought she knew.

"You can close your mouth, Kell." He touched her chin, lightly pushing her jaw closed. "I'm not proposing anything wrong," he said, a blush rising to his cheeks. He hesitated a moment, looking torn, then, as if the words were being dragged out of him, he rubbed the dark blond stubble on his chin and said, "I want you to marry me."

Kelsey stared at him a moment, then she grinned at him. "I see now, this is one of your jokes, isn't it?" When she saw the light go out of his blue eyes and a mask of hurt cover his face, her smile slipped away. "You're serious?"

"Serious as a hangin' noose." He didn't grin at the quip. When she started to say something, he raised his hand to stop her. "Don't. Let me explain. I want to marry you. I know I'm just a farmer's son, and you bein' from the gentry and all, and it's only on your mother's side. You've never cared about that anyway, and I sure as hell don't. People might say I'm trying to be an upstart, mind, but it ain't like that—we're both poor as tinkers, so I figure it don't matter. And I think Ma and Pa have always expected that we'd marry. I can build onto the cottage and you can paint till your heart's content. We could be happy together, Kell, and you need not ever go back and face Salford."

"But we don't love each other that way." Kelsey sighed and gently pulled her hand away from his.

"We could grow to love each other." Griffin rested his elbows on his knees and clasped his hands between his legs, then he looked hopefully at her.

"You don't know what you're saying. What about Laura? You told me you were in love with her a fortnight ago. And what about Veronica before that, and Sharon before that—"

"You can stop anytime."

"Why should I?" Kelsey teased him with a smile.

"Because they didn't mean anything to me, and you know it. I didn't propose to them."

"Admit it, you came close to proposing to Veronica."

"That's not all I came close to." A smile lit up his face and his eyes twinkled with a male look that Kelsey knew well.

She didn't comment on what he meant. She'd wrung all the lurid details of their lovemaking out of him when the affair happened a year ago. Veronica was the rector's daughter. In spite of her father keeping a close godly eye on her, it wasn't close enough. Her reputation equaled that of Clarice's.

"It's a good thing the rector found that sailor," she said, "or you would have been leg-shackled to her."

"I wasn't the babe's father."

"I know, but knowing you, you would have married her anyway."

"I'm not that stupid, Kell."

"No?" A smile stretched across her face. "What would you call a person who believed himself in love with Laura when her mother died, and Veronica's baby brother had died when you started paying court to her, and, let me see . . . I believe Sharon's dog had died—"

"What are you saying?"

Kelsey touched his large hand and felt him stiffen. She said carefully, "I'm saying where women are concerned, your inestimable gallantry goes a bit far. That's why I won't marry you. I know you asked me to marry you only out of pity. You know yourself you don't want to marry me. We're friends, true friends, and that's all we'll ever be. Anyway, we should never get along together, and you know it. We'd end up killing each other."

Griffin stared at her for a moment, then he grinned at her, the teasing lilt back in his voice. "Afraid of losing your heart to me too?"

Kelsey shook her head, sending a mass of long, dark curls over her shoulder. "If that were the case, Sir Galahad, it would have happened a long time ago. And if it had, I certainly wouldn't have stayed your best friend all these years. Now that I think on it, I'm sure there's a law somewhere that says best friends and love never mix."

"Well, there's never been any real love a'tween us."

"You're so right. Do you remember the first time we met? I was painting the picket fence around the cottage and you threw an apple at me, and I threw the paintbrush and hit you in the face." Kelsey smiled proudly at him.

"Aye"—Griffin's chuckle rumbled deep in his throat as he lightly slapped the side of her cheek—"but I threw the bucket of turpentine on you and got in the last lick."

"I smelled like turpentine for weeks after that. My mother scrubbed my head until I thought she would scrub my hair away. I never forgave you for that."

"You got me back."

"I did, didn't I?" Kelsey thought about the rock she'd given Griffin and smiled. She'd painted it to look just like a piece of taffy.

"I still got the chip in me tooth for that trick." Griffin laughed at the memory and touched his chipped front tooth.

Kelsey's expression grew serious. "Thank you, Griffin, you've made me laugh. I feel so much better after talking to you. What would I do without you?" Kelsey leaned over and placed a chaste kiss on his cheek.

Griffin had the grace to blush, then a self-satisfied grin turned up the corners of his mouth. She knew he felt the same way about her but would never say it. The sound of hooves drawing up outside the cottage made her pull back from him.

Someone pounded on the door.

"I wonder who that could be at this time o' night?" He frowned as he looked over at her, then he got up to answer the knocking.

She peeked around the settle toward the door, but she couldn't see past Griffin's wide shoulders.

"I saw the light burning," a man's voice said, sounding apologetic. "Have ya seen a young miss by the name of Kelsey Vallarreal hereabouts?"

Kelsey's body tensed at the sound of her name.

"Why you askin'?" Griffin said, his massive shoulders drawing up.

"Me master's been combin' the countryside lookin' for her."

"Well, you can tell your master she's safe here with me, and I'll be bringin' her back when she gets good and ready."

"Can't do that, bloke. Now, give her to me and I'll see she gets back safe"

"I can't do that. . . ."

Kelsey saw Griffin's hand tighten on the edge of the door, his muscles straining against the back of his shirt. In another moment he would pounce on the man. She jumped up and ran to the door.

"Let him in, Griffin, I'll go with him," she said resolutely, but her hands trembled as she clasped the blanket tighter around her.

Edward was waiting on the drive that led to the cottage. He sat on his black stallion, Dagger, slapping his riding crop against his palm. The horse sensed his impatience and pawed the ground, bobbing his head.

He patted the sleek animal's neck, feeling the muscles ripple beneath his fingers. The wind picked up and whipped Dagger's long black mane over Edward's hand. Abruptly the moonlight disappeared, turning the night murky black. The saddle leather creaked as he straightened and looked up at the sky. Not a star shone, the moon's dim blue haze barely visible behind an ominous cloud. A drop of rain hit his shoulder, and he glanced toward the cottage again. His fingers inadvertently tightened around the riding crop as though he meant to strangle it.

He heard voices carry on the wind, then he saw the door open and a shaft of light beamed from the doorway. Grayson, one of his grooms, emerged first, then another man came behind him. He wondered who the young man was. Since the accident, Edward hadn't visited his tenants. He left that to Morely, his steward. But he knew that McGregor and his family still lived in this cottage. This man must be one of McGregor's sons. He made a mental note to inquire after the McGregor boys when next he met with Morely.

McGregor's son stepped aside and Kelsey appeared. He sucked in his breath at the sight of her. The skinny little urchin he remembered had certainly changed. He'd stolen glances of her as a child, but he never saw any signs of beauty in her, save for those enormous, direct green eyes that had a way of looking into a man's soul and capturing it. He didn't get a good glimpse of her when she fell through his chamber door, but he could see all of her now. She had definitely changed—for the better. Very much for the better. Beautiful, in fact.

Dark, thick curls fell down to her petite waist like a thick mantle. Her pitifully old nightgown was only partially covered by the blanket that hung down to her hips. The silhouette of her shapely legs was clearly visible in the light. His scowl deepened.

She turned and faced young McGregor in the doorway. She bent forward, said something to him, then they walked hand in hand toward the horse. Young McGregor helped her mount in front of Grayson, giving Edward a clear view of his face. He was handsome—a damn blond Adonis was more like it.

McGregor touched Kelsey's exposed ankle, then playfully slapped the bottom of her foot. It was a familiar gesture, something a lover would do. Edward cursed and slapped his riding crop against his boot, fighting an overwhelming urge to jump down and teach young McGregor a lesson he wouldn't forget.

As if McGregor could read his thoughts, he walked back into the cottage, then closed the door. Grayson turned his mare toward the drive. Edward quickly pulled the hood of his cape over his face. His hand strangled the reins as he waited impatiently for them. He saw that one of Grayson's arms was wrapped around Kelsey's waist, while the hem of her thin nightgown intimately touched the legs of his trousers. Unknowingly, he jerked back on the reins. Dagger shook his head and snorted at the unexpected tug.

When Grayson reined in beside him, Edward ground out, "She'll ride back with me."

Grayson winced at the tone in Edward's voice. "Aye, yer grace." He bobbed a curt nod, then grabbed Kelsey's waist to set her on Edward's horse. "Here, miss, I'll help ya across."

"I'd rather ride with you." She knocked Grayson's hands away.

Edward lost his patience and jerked on the reins. Dagger reared. She screamed as Edward caught her around the waist and plopped her down in front of him. Dagger's hooves pawed the air, then came down, barely missing the flank of Grayson's mare. The mare nervously stepped to the side. Grayson fought to steady her. An expert horseman, Edward already had Dagger under control, but his own temper was still raging.

"You can ride ahead, we'll manage," he said to Grayson.

After a sympathetic glance at Kelsey, Grayson kicked the mare into a gallop and rode toward the castle without looking back.

"You're insane," Kelsey hissed between her teeth. "You could have killed that man."

"His life was never in any danger," he said with menacing softness, "but I could not have vouched for yours if you had fought me."

Kelsey tried to turn around and look at his face, so he kicked the stallion into a gallop. She fell back against his chest and clung to his arm, which was still clamped around her waist.

"Take me home," she yelled above the pounding of the stallion's hooves. "I won't paint your cursed wall."

He bent near her until his lips almost touched her ear. "We have a deal." He felt a shiver go through her before she haughtily leaned her head away from his mouth. He smiled ruthlessly. "I have the contract your father signed. You're coming back with me, or would you prefer your father spend time in prison for breach of contract."

"I hate you!"

"Do you think I care?" He laughed, a bitter sound even to his own ears.

"Why did you come after me? You should have stayed with your *whore.*"

"If you had obeyed the *rules,* none of this would have happened." When she said nothing, he continued mercilessly. "Since you did not, and you are an employee in my home, I am responsible for you. If I had known you had run to your lover, I wouldn't have left my bed and spent hours combing the damn countryside looking for you."

"I don't see what business it is of yours where I go or what I do." She stiffened in his arms as his fingertips dipped deeper into the soft flesh at her side. She smacked his arm. "Must you hold me so tightly?"

Feeling vindictive, he let his arm drop. She gasped as she lost her balance. He grabbed her before she fell and drew her back against him, but he used more force than he meant to and her back slammed against his chest.

She stiffened, trying to pull away, then a crack of lightning lit the sky and she froze. Thunder rolled. Hard drops of rain turned into blinding sheets.

Some of the ire left him as he felt her snuggle against his chest. One side of the blanket had slipped from her shoulders. He reached down, grasped it, then wrapped it tightly around her. The stiffness left her spine as she nestled against him. Driving rain blew past his hood, rain pelted his face and shoulders, but the added stimulus could not help him keep his mind off her. He was keenly aware of the supple warmth of her thighs next to his, the feel of her bottom pressing tantalizingly against his groin, the softness of her hair as the stubble on his chin brushed against it. His body responded to her womanly softness. He adjusted her in his arms so her head was not right beneath his chin, though there wasn't much he could do about the position of her body.

When they reached the stables at Stillmore, the thunderstorm had petered out into a fine mist, but Edward had a full-blown case of lust. The tightness in his groin ached as he dismounted and tossed the reins to Grayson, who had been nervously awaiting his arrival.

"Make sure Dagger gets a warm rubdown," Edward said sharply.

"Aye, yer grace." Grayson bowed, tipping his hat.

Normally, Edward would have stopped and spoken to his groom. He liked the young man—but he didn't wait for Grayson's reply as he swept Kelsey into his arms. He ignored her surprised gasp and strode toward the servants' entrance.

"I can walk," she said, sounding provoked.

"So you can, but since you have no shoes, you might not like the mud squashing between your toes."

This silenced her. She huffed under her breath, crossed her arms over her chest, then turned her face away in a haughty manner. She appeared willing to allow him to carry her the rest of the way.

She hardly weighed more than a child, but nothing else about her was childlike. The soft roundness of her hip pressed against a sensitive spot on his abdomen, and the velvety flesh of her thighs rested on his arm. Her body heat melted through her thin, wet nightgown, burning his skin through the sleeves of his own damp shirt.

"Thank you, you can put me down now." Her voice was no longer haughty, but soft and pleasant.

"Of course," he said, realizing he was in the ballroom, standing in front of her door.

When he released her, he couldn't resist letting her wet body slide along his own. This impulse was dangerous, but he didn't know how dangerous until her hipbones glided along his abdomen. His corded muscles tightened into hard knots. The slight pressure as her fingers moved down his body. Then her hips met his, pressed against his erection, and slid downward, along the sleek length of him. He moaned softly.

"I'm sorry, did I hurt you?" she said.

He felt her trembling and grinned in the darkness. He placed his lips on her forehead and murmured, "Only if pleasure can kill a man." He lowered her the rest of the way to the floor, ending his torture—but not quite, he couldn't bring himself to drop his hands from her waist.

"Pleasure? What do you mean?" She tried to step back from him, but he tightened his arms around her small waist, a waist so tiny, he could span it with his fingers.

He pulled her closer. "Come, my dear, you sound like a virgin."

"My innocence, or lack of it, is not something I care to discuss with you," she said, her voice breathless.

Very little light penetrated the ballroom through the windows. The cover of the darkness made him bold. He bent down until he could feel her hot breath on his lips. "We need not discuss anything, Kelsey. I know you want me as much as I want you, I can feel you trembling in my arms."

He ran his fingers lightly over her full lips and felt a shudder go through her. "See, you cannot deny us both this pleasure. It would make us both miserable." He grinned sardonically down at the dark outline of her face as he eased the soaked blanket from her shoulders.

She gasped. "You cannot deny misery has some merit."

He laughed at her, then carelessly stripped off his own cloak, tossing it to the floor. "Perhaps it does on the battlefield, but not between a man and a woman."

She started to say something else, but he buried his fingers in the thick wet hair at her nape and brought her face up to meet his. When their lips met, her body stiffened in his arms. He was barely aware of her hands pushing against his chest. Without breaking the kiss, he moved her toward the door until her back was against it.

He pinned her wrists above her head and wondered if this attempt to tease him was a little game she liked to play with young McGregor. He hadn't wanted to make love to her, but that was when he thought she was a virgin. Now the challenge of possessing her, of seeing how long she could resist her own passion, and his, drove him with a need that he'd never felt before in his life.

He deepened the kiss, moving his lips across hers until he felt her mouth soften and her body grow pliant. He ran his tongue along her lips, then a little deeper, along the perfect ridges of her teeth, coaxing her mouth to open for him. She parted her lips. He dove deep into the riches of her mouth, tasting the warm, heady sweetness.

He slid his palms slowly down the insides of her arms, feeling the warm, velvety sleekness of her skin searing his splayed fingers. When he reached her palms, he laced his fingers with hers and opened her thighs with his knee, fitting his hips against her. He rubbed his throbbing erection against her soft flesh and ached to bury himself inside her. But it was too soon. Her breathing was ragged, as if she were still fighting to resist him.

He placed kisses along her jaw. Lower still. Along her thin throat. "You're holding back, Kelsey," he murmured, feeling the delicate pulse at the base of her throat against his lips. "Give yourself to me, love. I want all of you."

"No . . ." She moaned feebly as she let her head roll back against the door.

"Yes . . ." He trailed his tongue along the soft flesh at the base of her neck. Her skin tasted hot and delicate and delicious. The high, prim collar of her nightgown brushed against his chin as he moved his tongue lower.

He let his tongue nestle in the hollow of her throat. Small shudders went through her. He bent down and took one of her nipples in his mouth. He teased the hard little nub between his teeth. The thin wet material of her nightgown brushed against his tongue. When he began to suck, she arched her back, whimpered, then her trembling fingers surrendered their stiffness and they locked with his. She squeezed his hand as tightly as he was squeezing hers.

Her surrender was the most erotic thing he'd ever felt, for it wasn't just her body she was surrendering, but her will. Never had he been so keenly aware of a woman, nor wanted one so badly.

"God, you're beautiful," he gasped against her quivering breast. He felt the slick burning where their palms met spreading down his arms, through his body, searing him.

He found her lips again, thrusting his tongue again and again into her mouth, matching the hungry undulations of his hips. The dampness of their clothes intensified the heat of their bodies until he wanted to drown both of them in it. Her hips started to move against his, and she moaned in his mouth. It was his undoing. He grabbed the collar of her gown and ripped it down the front, unable to stand one bit of clothing separating her from him.

She stiffened. Something hard met his face. He was dumbfounded for a moment, until he felt the sting on his cheek and realized she had slapped him.

"I won't be used like you used Clarice or that whore of yours." A sob caught in her throat. "I always knew you were a cad, a blackguard, a devil—"

"You have said quite enough, madam. I thought you wanted this as much as I did. We were both mistaken." He stepped back as if he had been burned. "You need not fear that I will come near you again. Just do your damned job and follow the *rules*." He turned, grabbed his cape from the floor, then quit the ballroom, the sound of her crying echoing in his ears.

Four

Tears blurred Kelsey's vision as she groped in the darkness for the handle of the door. She found it, opened the door, then stumbled into her room. She fell back against the wood, hard and unyielding. Her heart's erratic beat warred with the deep gasps coming from her mouth.

Every nerve ending still throbbed from where he'd touched her. She wiped the tears from her eyes, keenly aware of the cold air in the room hitting her wet flesh. She glanced down at the front of her body, exposed now from where he'd torn her gown.

"Oh, God!" She jerked the ends of the wet gown together, hating the sight of her own nakedness. She gently banged her head against the back of the door as she moaned, "How could I let him use me like he'd used Clarice and his paramour? How could I be so stupid?"

She felt the door's hard planes against her back. Immediately, memories flooded her mind, him standing over her, a dark, faceless shadow, the lover in her dreams. It felt like a dream when he pinned her hands to the other side of the door, drugging her mind with his mouth, his body, making her want his touch until she ached.

Then he'd torn her gown, and the image of him kissing Clarice flashed in her mind. She struck him, hating her own idiotic weakness more than she hated him. He obviously had no scruples when it came to his base instincts. Any woman nearby was fair game. He'd never get another chance—at least where she was concerned.

Her hand still hurt from the stinging blow. She glanced down, saw her bright red palm, then her fingers tightened around the gown, squeezing the wet material until it bunched within her tight fist. The dampness soothed her burning skin. She hoped that his face was stinging as badly as her palm. It was less than he deserved.

And to think, he of all people had questioned her innocence. He must have seen her with Griffin and assumed he was her lover. Preposterous, of course, but let him think what he liked. Maybe he wouldn't come near her again as he promised.

You know you want him to.

I don't. I hate him.

A rustling sound brought Kelsey back from the battle with her conscience and made her aware of the room. Someone had left a candle burning. In the dim flickering light, she noticed Brutus walking along the drawing table that stood beneath one of the windows.

"Where have you been?" Kelsey walked toward him, clutching her gown closed. When she drew close, he hissed at her, baring his razor-sharp teeth, then he jumped down and disappeared beneath the bed. "I wonder that you keep coming in here if all you want to do is hiss at me."

Determined to befriend the feline, she started to go after him, but something dark caught her eye and she paused. She glanced at the drawing table. The bottle of black ink she used for sketching was lying on its side, empty. A large black blotch covered the table. Her drawing quills had been broken in half and the sketches in her sketch pad had been torn into tiny shreds and thrown about the desk like confetti. Who could have done this? She thought of Brutus, then shook her head. Too much destruction even for Brutus.

Kelsey bent down and picked up several shreds of torn paper. She held them in her palm while she studied the ripped edges. Her first thought was of the duchess's ghost. But would a ghost be so petty? She doubted it. A more reasonable explanation was that Salford must have come down to find her after she'd fallen in his room. When he didn't find her, he took out his frustration on her work. She ground her teeth together so tightly, her jaw muscles hurt.

A knock on the door startled her.

"Yes," she said, dropping the papers and grabbing her torn gown. The thought that Salford might have come back made her take a step back and bump into her drawing table.

"It be me, miss."

Kelsey breathed a sigh of relief at the sound of Mary's voice. She went to the door and stuck her head through the crack, careful to hide her wet, torn gown behind the door. "Yes, Mary?"

"Beggin' yer pardon, miss." Mary bobbed a curtsy.

When she rose, Kelsey noticed that she didn't have on her apron and that her cap was askew. Strands of red hair fell down over her eyes as if she'd hastily donned her cap. Her cheeks were stained red, and she sounded breathless, as if she'd run all the way to Kelsey's room.

Alarmed, Kelsey asked, "Good Lord, Mary, what is it?"

"The master said to give you this. . . ." Mary shoved a nightgown at Kelsey through the opening in the door and continued to babble. "It belonged to the duchess, it's very fine, miss—never been used. I dug it out of a trunk in the attic. 'Tis a shame such nice clothes have been sitting up in the attic when others need 'em. I'm glad you can use it. I'm also to see if you'll be wantin' a warm bath, miss."

She stared at the expensive-looking nightclothes. Her fingers tightened on her own torn gown. Surely the whole house knew she'd run away in her nightgown and that Salford had brought her back and seen her in it. Did they know what he'd done to her? Kelsey stared at Mary, feeling her face grow hot. How could he get Mary out of bed in the middle of night and send her down here with a nightgown, bringing further attention to what had happened? She wanted to strangle him.

Kelsey tried to keep the anger out of her voice as she pushed Mary's hand and the gown back out the door. "I don't need it, nor will I inconvenience you in the middle of the night to have a bath. Go back to bed, Mary. I can't believe Lord Salford woke you just for this. Good night." As Kelsey closed the door, Mary shoved her hand through the opening, the gown and robe flapping in her hand.

"Please take it, miss." Mary sounded desperate. "He'll be angry if you don't, and I'm to report back to him. And if he don't like my answer, well . . . I'm afraid what he might blame me for you not taking it. He was steaming like a teakettle when the order came."

Kelsey accepted the gown only to placate poor Mary. "Very well, I'll take it—" Kelsey paused, her expression turning inquisitive and thoughtful. "Tell me, Mary, you said Salford gave you the order. Does he let you see his face?"

"Oh, no, miss. Never. If I speak to him, it's behind closed doors. Usually Watkins relays the messages. He's the one who told me I was to quick go to the attic and find you something of the duchess's to sleep in." Mary mimicked Watkins's stuffy tone. "Per his grace's orders. And report back to him immediately." She grinned, mischief gleaming in her blue eyes. When Kelsey chuckled, Mary continued.

"I knew I could be frank with you, miss. You ain't stuffy like some of them. I knew that when you tried to take the blame for spilling that tray, when you knew it was my fault. I thank you, miss. It was a stupid thing to do, dropping that tray. And Watkins would've boxed me ears, don't think he won't. It ain't that I don't like Watkins, but he's as stuffy as a cooked turkey and contrary as one too. Cook says it's cause his teeth ache him. And I ain't to blame one for aching teeth. Lord, I've had enough of those in me day, but I think he shouldn't take out his orneriness on others. And he treats us maids like stepchildren."

"How many maids are there?" Kelsey asked, trying to slip in a few words.

"Only two of us. Can you believe that, just two us for this

big, rambling place." Mary shrugged, then said proudly, "I'm the only upstairs maid. It's hard work, mind, and I work me fingers to nubs, but the pay is good. And I understand why the staff is so small, the master being sensitive about his face an' all. Watkins says he don't like women ogling him—not that I'd ogle anyone. I do me work and that's all. If you want to know the truth, I'm glad I don't have to look at his face. Cook says the last maid, afore me, went in to clean his room when she wasn't supposed to, and he was in there and, well . . . she fainted clean away, that's what. They fired her the next day. I felt so sorry for the girl. It warn't her fault she fainted. Even when I clean his room and he ain't in it, I get to sweatin' and shaking—but I think it's more from the fear of him walking in on me and being fired than me seeing his face. I'm sure no one's face can be that bad. I seen a man once at a carnival that had two heads. Can you believe that? And there was a freak there that was half man and half woman—"

"Yes, yes, terrible," Kelsey interrupted, trying not to sound impatient, but she was freezing in her wet gown and her teeth were starting to chatter. "That's very interesting, but I—"

"I'm sorry, miss." Mary's face colored up. "Me maw says once I get started, I rattle on worse than a carriage with no springs." She bobbed her head. Several more strands of red hair escaped her cap. "Is there anything else I can do for you, miss? Can I get more coals for your fire?"

"No, no, Mary." Kelsey paused, then said, "There is one thing. I'll be taking my meals in the kitchen with the rest of the staff from now on."

"I don't know about that, miss." Mary's eyes grew wide. "The master is particular about his orders, and he said you were to eat in your room."

"Since your master never goes into the kitchen, I doubt he shall find out if we don't tell him. I'll speak to Watkins about the matter." Addressing herself more than Mary, Kelsey said, "Lord Salford could not have been thinking when he made that particularly odious rule. He can't expect me to stay closed up in this wing, alone, for weeks. I'm not a solitary creature. I need society, and taking my meals in the kitchen will certainly be less bother on you." Mary opened her mouth to protest further, but Kelsey tactfully said, "Good night, Mary. See you in the morning." She closed the door.

Kelsey listened to Mary's bustling footsteps as she hurried from the ballroom. With Mary around, no one could want for conversation. And that's just what she needed to keep her mind off Salford.

She glanced down at the white nightrail in her hand and wondered if forgetting Salford was at all possible while staying in his home. Everything seemed to lead back to him. Even this nightgown belonged to his deceased wife. It was very prim, with only a little lace around the high neck, made of very fine lawn. She had never felt such expensive finery against her skin. Perhaps he was trying to be thoughtful when he'd asked Mary to bring her the gown. She hoped he wasn't waxing gallant on her. It was much easier to dislike autocratic libertines who made maids swoon with just one look.

Frowning, she quickly slipped out of her wet gown and donned the new one, then she ran a comb through her matted hair, plaited it, and slipped into bed. Exhaustion finally caught up with her. She blew out the candle, then snuggled down beneath the covers.

That's when it started. *Creak creak creak.*

She sat up in bed and rolled her eyes at the ceiling. If she had something to throw at it, she would have. Why was he pacing? Obviously, the harlot wasn't with him. In a huff, she lay down again and jerked the pillow over her head.

"Lord, help me!"

The shriek brought Kelsey straight up in her bed. She rubbed her eyes and saw Mary staring down at the black blot of ink on the desk. The morning sun streamed in through a window and bathed Mary's thin figure in a halo of light.

"What happened here, miss? It's a mess. Watkins will surely plague me heart out if I can't clean it. I don't know what—"

"Just tell him Salford did it, that ought to pacify him," Kelsey said curtly, not the most jovial of souls in the morning—especially after she'd been kept up half the night by Salford's pacing; the other half she spent dreaming of him, kissing her everywhere, touching her everywhere, making love to her in every room in the castle.

"I couldn't do that, miss." Mary bent down and picked up the tiny bits of paper strewn around the desk.

"Tell him the ghost did it, then. That's the only other explanation I can think of. Brutus was here, but I know he didn't tear up my sketches into little pieces. He might be ferocious, but some things are beyond him."

"That old, hateful tabby. He doesn't make mischief like this. He did shred a curtain in the library once, when he was after a mouse, but he couldn't have done this."

"I know. It was like this when I got back to my room"—Kelsey paused, carefully choosing her words—"after visiting a friend last night."

"It's all right, miss," Mary said, sounding distracted as she stood. One lip moved tightly over the other, and she nervously shoved the scraps of paper into her pocket. "It was an old desk from the schoolroom anyway. Don't give it a thought." She strode over and poured water into a pitcher, then laid a towel by it. "Cook has a nice breakfast waiting for you. She tried to box me ears when I told her you wanted to eat in the kitchen. She said guests at Stillmore never ate in the kitchen."

"I'm no guest. I'm an employee just like the rest of you." Kelsey threw back the covers and crawled out of bed.

"Still, miss, I got the wrong end of her tongue for it."

"Don't worry, I'll inform her of the new arrangements."

"You do that, miss. I'll tell Cook you'll be along directly." Mary went to the door and looked relieved when she bobbed a curtsy and closed it behind her.

Mary seemed nervous about something. Kelsey stared at the

door, wondering what that was all about, then it struck her how blessedly silent it was in her room. Glancing up at the ceiling, she listened for any signs of life from the lofty regions.

It was so quiet, she could almost hear her head throbbing from lack of sleep. She stared at the ceiling for a moment longer, rubbed her temples, then a broad, impish grin spread across her face. Wearing a resolute expression, she crawled out of bed and snatched up the poker and the empty coal shuttle from the fireplace.

The first bang made her wince, but the more she banged, the more accustomed she grew to the noise. She even yelled at the top of her voice, a very freeing feeling, so she didn't stop until her ears were ringing and her voice was raw and she was sure Salford was either awake or deaf. The silence was thick in her ears as she dressed in her painting clothes, ran a comb through her hair, then quit the room. She slammed the door not once, but thrice. As loud as she could.

"What the hell was that?" Edward sat up in bed, then jerked on the bellpull by his bed. He folded his arms over his chest and waited with more patience than he felt after a night of fitful sleep. Dreams of ripping off Kelsey's clothes, of kissing her, sucking her breasts, making love to her, tormented him most of the night. The painful bulge beneath the sheet and the ache in his loins were proof of his torment.

Watkins bowed his way into the room. "Yes, your grace."

"Can I not have a moment's peace in my own home?"

The uncustomary bellow sent Watkins back a step. "I don't know what you mean, your grace."

"The noise, man. The noise."

"The noise, your grace?"

"The bloody noise!" Edward threw back the covers and shot out of bed, unmindful of his nakedness.

Watkins kept his eyes lowered, gathered up a dressing gown,

then hurried to help Edward into it. His lips disappeared in his shrunken mouth as he said, "I—I didn't hear a noise."

"Then you're deaf."

"Yes, your grace," Watkins readily agreed.

Edward turned and pinned Watkins with one of his stares. "You know you're not deaf."

"Yes, your grace." Watkins bobbed his head, then turned toward the wardrobe, amusement glowing in his eyes.

"Are you going to yes-your-grace me to death?"

"I hope not, your grace."

Edward stared at Watkins's back for that remark. The look didn't penetrate Watkins's thick skin as he opened the wardrobe and his head disappeared behind the door.

"When you are done fingering my clothes to death, I want a full accounting of who was making that infernal noise. It sounded like it was coming from the ballroom."

"Yes, your grace."

After a barbed glance in Watkins's direction that was totally lost on him, Edward turned and strode into the washroom. He poured water in the bowl, then doused his face. He grabbed the towel. "I'm sure whoever it was woke up Miss Vallarreal. I won't have guests in my home disturbed. Fire that person promptly, Watkins, but first send them to me—yes, send them to me. I wish to have a word with them." Edward dried his face as he strode back into the room.

"I'll see to it, your grace."

Edward still had the towel in his hand. He threw it on the bed as he said, "Is all ready for my cousin's visit?"

"I've had the blue room readied for Lord Lovejoy, your grace."

"Very good. And what about Lady Shellborn's visit? Are we ready for her?"

"When she arrives next week, we will be ready. I wrote a letter to her housekeeper and found out what dishes the lady prefers. I've readied the pink room for her, your grace."

"And flowers, do we have enough in the hothouse?"

"Enough to fill every room in the castle, your grace."

"Very good." Edward walked over to the window and jerked back the curtains. He leaned against the stanchion, rubbed the dark stubble on his chin, pensively staring out the window.

"Riding this morning, your grace?"

"Yes, yes." Edward waved his hand in a dismissive manner. Watkins turned, laying a black riding coat, a white shirt, and a pair of tan buckskin riding breeches on the bed. He methodically smoothed away any creases with his hand.

Edward glanced back out the window, scanning the grounds, looking for any sign of that head of glorious black hair he'd buried his fingers in last night. "Watkins, has Miss Vallarreal called for her breakfast tray yet?"

"I wouldn't know, your grace. Shall I go and check?"

"No, no." Edward turned away from the window and saw Watkins standing near the bed, his lips pursed, the skin stretching over his bony cheeks. The veins in his thin skin popped as he clasped and unclasped his hands in front of him. In a more patient tone than he had used thus far with the old retainer, who had served his father before him, he asked, "What is it, Watkins? You want to tell me something, but you're uncertain. Reticence has never put a spoke in your wheel before now."

"Well, your grace, I was just informed that Miss Vallarreal wishes to take her meals with the staff."

"With the staff?" Edward raised his dark brows.

"It appears she wishes to have company during her meals."

"Don't look at me like that, Watkins, you know I'm not having her at *my* table."

"Allow me to point out that you eat alone, your grace."

"I know I eat alone. I like it that way." Edward blasted a look at Watkins that could have knocked him out the window, but the shrewd old man wouldn't meet Edward's gaze, thus it went right over his head, out the windowpanes that still trickled with morning dew, and landed somewhere above the trees on the south side of the castle.

"I thought the society would do you good, your grace," Watkins persevered with tactful impertinence, as he always did. "Allow me to say, Miss Vallarreal is a fascinating young woman."

"So, she's got you under her spell too, eh?" Edward looked at Watkins from below dark, narrowed brows. The image of young McGregor rose up in his mind. He tried to quell the unexpected pang of jealousy gnawing at his gut.

"I suppose you could say that."

"I know what you're trying to do, Watkins. Matchmaking doesn't become you. Anyway, Miss Vallarreal is already in love with someone else, and she hates me. She pointed it out quite plainly last night." Edward rubbed the cheek she had slapped.

" 'She is a woman, therefore may be woo'd; She is a woman, therefore may be won,' " Watkins said with the air of a sage.

"Good God! Quoting Shakespeare now, Watkins. What? Have you run out of your usual platitudes?" Edward couldn't keep a straight face and grinned slightly.

"It appears so, your grace."

"Let us hope not, I prefer your platitudes to hearing you quote sappy Shakespearean love prose." Edward turned serious, using the tone he always reverted to when Watkins became more of a nuisance than a loyal, respected servant. "In the future, confine yourself to the providence of the castle—leave my bloody love life to me."

Watkins's lips thinned slightly, the only indication that he was annoyed. He turned, heading toward the door. In a voice with far too much deference in it, he said, "Yes, your grace," then quit the room.

Edward shook his head at the door, wondering how many other impudent butlers there were in the world and if they plagued the lives of other noblemen like Watkins plagued his life.

He pivoted, then walked back over to the window, then to the door, then back to the window. He paused, leaning against the stanchion. He had always liked the view from this room. The windows faced west, providing a spectacular view of the gardens, the lake, and the thick forests beyond the village. His great-great-grandfather had planned this suite of rooms when the castle was remodeled. For years he had looked out this window, surveying all he owned. It always gave him a sense of peace, of belonging, of being lord and master, but for some time now he'd felt only a nagging desire for a change of scenery, something to break the self-imposed monotony in which he had lived for the past ten years.

At times the restlessness felt like it might devour him—especially after last night, when Kelsey had rejected him. He regretted that moment of insanity. Now Watkins was trying to pair him up with her. Good God! He needed to get away.

Edward rubbed savagely at the dark stubble on his chin, then he turned and resumed pacing again. He would never allow another woman in his life. He touched the patch over his left eye and knew he'd never ask a woman to be tied to him. He could ask that of no one. To be wife to a beast. A grotesque deformity. To subject her to the blatant stares, the dawning expressions of horror that followed, then the sympathy. God, he hated the sympathy worst of all. Never!

Edward picked up an Oriental statue from the mantel and hurled it at a mirror on the wall. He watched the distorted image of his face crack, then dissolve as the pieces of glass fell out of the gilded frame.

Kelsey was whistling when she pushed her way through the swinging door to the kitchen. A young woman as large as she was tall dropped the rolling pin she'd held and gasped. It hit the counter and rolled to the edge. Another woman, as small as the other was large, had just taken a pie out of the oven. When she stared at Kelsey, she let go of it.

From years of having helped her mother cook, then having cooked for her father, Kelsey reacted out of habit. She grabbed up the hem of her smock and caught the pie, using the material as a hot pad. She smiled at them as if nothing had happened, then set the steaming pie pan back on the wooden counter with the other eight pies that were cooling there.

"Something smells delightful in here," she said, smiling.

The two women looked at each other for a moment, at Kelsey, then back at each other. The larger of the two was the first to come to her senses. She picked up the rolling pin and said, "Miss, when that rattletrap Mary told me you was to eat in the kitchen, I thought she'd gone plum daft. I told her so too." The woman didn't wait for Kelsey's reply, but turned on the little woman beside her, whose thin face was now stained with bright color. "Agnes, you scatterbrained twitterfist. You've done it again. If you'd dropped me pie, I would have boxed your ears. It's lucky the miss is quick with her hands is all I can tell you."

Agnes stiffened her spine, appearing not at all cowed by the much larger woman. She threw down the oven mitt. It landed in the middle of the dough on the counter. "If you'd boxed my ears, I would have scratched your eyes out. That's what, miss lah-de-dah."

"That'll be the day." The large woman shook the rolling pin in Agnes's face. "Oh-ho, that'll be the day."

"It'll come, it'll come."

"Not as long as I got me wits about me." The large woman picked up the mitt and threw it across the room.

Kelsey ducked as it sailed over her head.

"I'm sick of you, Alice. You think just 'cos you're me big sister and you made cook here ahead o' me, you can boss me around. Well, it ain't so!" Agnes dove her hand in the flour tin and threw it at Alice's face.

Alice didn't seem to expect that affront, and her mouth dropped open. Her enormous breasts swelled over her protruding belly as she sucked in her breath. Her small blue eyes disappeared within the white wrinkles of her round face as she narrowed them at Agnes. She looked around for something to throw, saw the dough on the counter, then picked it up and ground it in Agnes's face. "Take that, you skinny, worthless drainpipe."

To Kelsey's surprise, Agnes didn't flinch, standing her ground like a granite statue. Calmly, she pulled the dough out of her eye sockets, then let it drop from her fingers. She glared at Alice. "I'd rather be skinny than big as a cargo ship!"

"You're just jealous 'cos Charlie married me and you wanted him yerself. At least he knows a woman when he looks at her. Do you think he'd o' married a"—Alice's eyes cut across Agnes's thin person—"slimy, slithering, cheeky one with a body like a snake."

Agnes looked down at one of the pies on the counter, then she reached for it.

Kelsey was relieved when the door squeaked on its hinges and Watkins entered the kitchen. Agnes's hand paused near the pie. Both the women turned, staring at Watkins. It took only one look from Watkins, then they quickly turned, flustered, and pretended to be busy with their chores as if nothing had happened. This seemed ludicrous to Kelsey, for flour covered Alice's face and bits of dough hung from Agnes's chin. Kelsey couldn't quell the laughter rumbling up inside her chest. It burst out of her mouth.

All three of them glared at her.

Kelsey shrugged, then snorted a few times as she tried to stop laughing. When she'd gained back a modicum of composure, she said, "Please, forgive me for laughing."

Watkins finally found his voice, addressing Alice. "What is the meaning of this?"

"Nothing, sir, nothing."

Kelsey couldn't help but feel that the altercation was partly her fault for eating in the kitchen, so she quickly jumped in. "They were just showing me a new way to make pie crust. Is that not right?" She surreptitiously raised a brow at the women, signaling them with her eyes.

The anger in their faces melted behind tremulous smiles. "Aye, miss, that's it," Agnes answered for both of them.

Watkins's mouth pursed as he stared at the women, then at Kelsey. Skepticism beamed in his voice as he said, "It seems when you are near the staff, disasters follow you."

"Yes, it does appear so, doesn't it?" Kelsey put her hands behind her back, staring up at the pots hanging above the long counter, avoiding his shrew, faded eyes.

"I think as much as you'd like to learn this new technique, I'll ask Cook to wait until such time as I can also observe this process with you. How does that sound, Miss Kelsey?"

Kelsey saw the anxious expression on Alice's and Agnes's faces, and she said, "I suppose I can wait, since I won't be cooking for a while, but I doubt Alice and Agnes would want you present. This is a highly kept culinary secret. She and Agnes happened upon it in a fit"—Kelsey glanced at both women— "of experimentation. The crust is supposed to be so flaky that it melts in your mouth. I bribed them for the recipe. I told them I'd paint their portraits if they would allow me to watch the process."

"Paint their portraits?" Watkins raised his bushy gray brows at Kelsey, his lips disappearing as he fought to keep an austere expression. Something close to amusement danced in his keen eyes as he said, "Very well, I'm sure they're flattered, even if it was a bribe." He glanced toward Alice and Agnes, his voice deepening with curt authority. "Now that you shan't be conducting cooking instruction, I suggest you clean up this kitchen." Watkins waved a finger at them. "And get your faces clean. Need I remind you we'll have a houseguest dining with his grace this evening? I hope you have things in order."

Alice bobbed her head, the three chins hanging from her jaw jiggling. "Yes, sir. We've prepared almost everything. I got a nice roast and Lord Lovejoy's favorite—"

Watkins waved his hand, cutting her off. "Very well. Have you seen to Miss Vallarreal's breakfast?"

"Have it right here." Alice quickly wiped her face off with the hem of her apron, then hurried over the stove, hefting a large cast iron skillet. She slapped a piece of ham, a mound of scrambled eggs, and boiled farina on a plate.

Agnes pulled the strings of dough off her chin, then drew out several slices of bread from the oven, slapping fresh churned butter on them.

"Watkins, I hope you don't mind that I take my meals here." When she saw the censorious look on Watkins's face, she added, "It will be less trouble this way. And I'll enjoy the company."

Watkins pursed his lips for a moment while he appeared to consider this radical notion. He opened his mouth to speak, then he seemed to change his mind, clamping his lips closed. He graciously motioned toward a long trestle in the middle of the kitchen. "If that is your wish, then please sit, Miss Kelsey."

"Thank you." Kelsey watched him walk toward four enormous china cabinets lining the walls. Three of them held gold-rimmed china plates—enough to feed an army. What must have been a fortune of silver serving dishes gleamed on the shelves of the other cabinet. It was this one that Watkins paused in front of, then opened one of its drawers. Kelsey could see the silverware gleaming in it.

Curious about this new houseguest, she sat, asking casually, "Who is Lord Lovejoy."

"Oh, he's his grace's cousin," Alice said, plopping down the plate and a tall glass of milk in front of her. "He's a lovable creature, that one. Always pleasant. Always smiling. Doesn't put on airs. Even comes in here and always compliments me on me cooking. He is—"

Watkins turned and cut her off with one of his keep-to-your-place glances. Alice closed her mouth, then hurried back behind the counter. She picked up a knife and helped Agnes peel apples.

. Watkins strode back to her side. Before he laid down the silverware in his hand, he examined it closely. His lips wrinkled as he examined the handle of the spoon. He must have found a speck, for he breathed on the silver, then polished it with his sleeve.

"There you are, Miss Kelsey." He set it down for her.

"I don't deserve such royal treatment," she said, accepting the spoon with a grin.

He bent over, whispering near her ear, "I think you do, Miss Kelsey. Anyone who can fabricate lies like you deserves more than the royal treatment, but you must learn to be less obvious about it."

She grinned shamelessly at him. "I thought I did rather well." She scooped up a mouthful of eggs and ate them.

"Your delivery needs work." Watkins stood, paused, then seemed to remember something. "Were you awakened by a noise this morning?"

Kelsey almost choked on the eggs as she swallowed them. "No, why do you ask?"

"His grace complained about being awakened by it. He felt sure it disturbed you as well."

"Me? I didn't hear a thing," she said, keeping her gaze on her plate and taking great care in cutting off a piece of ham.

"Hmmm! Just as I thought." Watkins shot a knowing glance at her. "Well, if you'll excuse me, I have other duties to attend to."

"Yes, of course." She watched his stiff stride as he headed toward the door. He was rubbing his jaw as if it ached, and one side looked swollen.

Alice and Agnes both gave a loud sigh when the door closed behind him. Agnes spoke first. "Lord, old Watkins is cross as crabs today."

"I thought he was rather pleasant," Kelsey remarked, then she looked thoughtful. "I think he has a toothache."

"You're right there, miss," Alice said. "His jaw did look a little swollen. Guess those teeth of his are acting up."

Kelsey made a mental note to see to Watkins's toothache after she met Griffin. Last night he'd made her promise to meet him at the front gates to Stillmore that morning. He looked worried, so Kelsey had promised to meet him at ten o'clock. It must be close to that time now. She wolfed down her food.

When Agnes brought over a plate of pastries, she turned and

asked, "Do you think I could have some of these for a friend? His parents, the McGregors, are tenants of Lord Salford's."

"O' course, miss. I've told Alice more than once 'tis a shame the way there ain't a lady to call on them and see how they're doing. The master don't ever go—'tis a shame, that. Not having a lady around to show them a bit of kindness. I always say it's only the neighborly thing to do, and a visit from the castle keeps up good relations. Lordy, miss, here, you can take a pie along as well." Agnes found a basket and dumped the pastries in it.

"Take a hunk of cheese and all too," Alice said, stuffing in the cheese and pie.

By the time they were through, Kelsey could hardly carry the basket as she walked down the drive. It was a long, curving lane flanked by a row of ancient elms. The sun peeked through the canopy of leaves overhead, casting long halos down to the ground. The air smelled thick with moisture from the previous night's storm.

A squirrel stopped in the middle of the drive, chattering at her for disturbing its territory, then scurried up the trunk of an elm to her right. With her attention on the squirrel, she missed the sound of the hooves until they were right on top of her.

Five

All Kelsey could see was a thousand pounds of horseflesh bounding through the elms. Frozen to the ground, she clutched the basket to her breast, fear draining the blood from her face, making her light-headed. The horse galloped past. The thunder of the hooves vibrated in her chest. *Whoosh.* A wake of air from the horse blew past her face.

Relieved to still be alive, she let out the breath she'd been holding and fell back against the thick trunk of an elm, her knees still weak, her heart pounding so hard, she thought it would knock her down at any moment. She realized the horse hadn't been as close as it seemed. A good four feet had separated her from being trampled. If not for the rider's expert handling of the horse, she knew she would have been killed. The rider must not have seen her until the last moment, then veered away. She glanced toward the retreating rider's back.

At that moment the cloaked rider called over his shoulder, "Breaking the bloody rules again, Miss Vallarreal."

The sound of Salford's voice grated against her. She swiftly found her composure and yelled as loud as she could, "I didn't know there was a rule against taking a walk!"

Salford hadn't bothered stopping, but went riding off across the lawn, his huge stallion churning up clods of green grass high into the air. Enthralled by her first sight of him in broad daylight, she couldn't take her eyes off him. He had on the same cloak he'd worn the night before. It covered his head and body, but it couldn't hide the broad shoulders beneath it, or the wide, stiff back. The black cloak flared out around his riding boots and blended into the sleek blackness of the stallion, making them both appear as one dark ominous entity, growing smaller . . . smaller. She watched them disappear behind a knoll.

She stared at the rise, her heart still hammering. What if he came back? She waited. When he didn't appear, she realized she'd been crushing the basket against her chest.

She set the burden down near her feet, then sighed, not knowing whether she felt relieved or disappointed. A part of her was morbidly curious about his face, another part didn't want to get anywhere near the shadowy seducer, the faceless phantom whom she had dreamed about. He'd touched her in places no one had ever touched her, made her body ache for that touch. She remembered how he'd pressed his hard body next to hers, the feel of his long, sinewy thighs between her legs, rubbing that secret place until she thought she'd go mad. Heat began building in her belly again at the lurid memories.

A scorching blush crept into her cheeks. She took a deep breath, then wiped her sweaty palms on her painting smock. Her hands trembled as she bent down and picked up the basket again. She had to forget what happened last night. He had only used her like he used all women. She mustn't forget that she hated him.

Liar! He could eat you alive and you'd let him.

Go away!

"Are you all right, Kell?"

Startled by Griffin's voice, she turned to see him running toward her. "I was waitin' at the gates and heard you yellin' at someone, and I came runnin'."

"I'm all right. Salford was out riding and didn't expect me to be on the lane. We almost collided. If he wasn't such a good horseman, I might have been mincemeat."

"Didn't the bloody bastard stop to see if you were all right?"

Griffin drew himself up, his huge fists clenching and unclench-ing at his sides.

"No. I suppose if he'd run me over, he might have stopped."

"Which way'd he go? I'll beat the vinegar out of him, I will that. Someone needs to teach him some manners."

It might be Griffin that received a lesson. She remembered how broad Salford's shoulders looked on his horse and how he towered over her, the barely restrained strength of his hard body pushing against her own. She said tensely, "No, no, the incident was my fault. I broke the rules again, you see. I think I was supposed to be in the garden only between eight and ten."

"You sure yer all right? You look a little flushed."

"I'm all right." Kelsey hefted the basket and shoved it at him. "Here. Something from the women who work in the kitchen. Tell your mother I would have brought it myself, but I really should get back to the castle. I want to do my work and leave this place."

"I know what you mean. I don't like you being here. Was everything all right when you got back last night? He didn't touch you?"

"No, no." Kelsey stifled the urge to look away. Griffin would know she was lying if she did. Delivery. Watkins said she must work on it, and she did that now. She kept her face impassive, her eyes focused on Griffin's long, fair eyelashes. "He brought me back and behaved as a gentleman. It surprised me, really."

"Well, it surprises me too." Griffin looked at her from be-neath lowered brows. "Didn't he scold you for leavin' like you did? I'm sure his high-an'-mightyness didn't like leavin' his nightbird and goin' out lookin' for you."

"Well, he did scold me. My ears are still burning from it."

"He wasn't rough with you?" His brows straightened again, a sure sign he was mollified by her answer.

"No, no, nothing like that. He made it plain that I have to follow the rules."

"Oh." Griffin was pensive for a moment, then said, "Is there a rule against you meetin' me again tomorrow? Say at the oak, by the creek. Let's say after supper, about seven."

"I really should be working."

"You can't work all the time, and I want to hear how things are goin' in there." He motioned his head toward the castle. "I can't believe your da let you come here with no chaperon. And all the rules and such and you not allowed visitors, sounds like Salford's up to something."

She pursed her lips at him and rested her hands on her small hips, a stance she used often when she was miffed at him. "Listen here, Griffin McGregor, you know good and well I don't need a chaperon. Naturally, my father trusts me—which is more than I can say for my best friend." She took a step toward him.

He took a step back. "I didn't mean it that way, Kell, and you know it. It ain't you I don't trust, it's Salford."

"I can take care of myself. You should know that better than anyone, Griffin McGregor."

"I—" He never finished his sentence. The back of his heel caught on a protruding tree root. His legs flew out from beneath him as he fell backward.

Kelsey reached out to grab him, but was too late. He made a courageous landing, holding the basket above his head with both hands so the contents wouldn't spill. Unfortunately, his bottom took the brunt of his weight. Pain distorted his brow, and hovered in his eyes.

"Are you all right?" she asked, bending over him, her anger forgotten. She grabbed the basket out of his hands, then helped him to his feet.

"Never felt better," he said, rubbing his behind, the rosy tint of a blush staining his cheeks.

"Let this be a lesson to you." The words were chiding, but her tone was gentle with worry. Teasing, she said, "Next time you'll watch where you're going." She handed the basket back to him.

"I would've if you hadn't been blubberin' at me. Woo, Lord, I pity Salford if he did try anything—I do that." Griffin grinned at her, his dimples beaming. "I'll have to tell him to beware of curly-haired imps bearin' gifts of food—though I'd like to see his face when he bites into a rock, I would that."

They shared a laugh, then Kelsey sobered. "I have to go. I will meet you tomorrow night, but at your house. I'll come by after I check on Papa. And not one word to me about Salford."

"Not a word." Griffin shook his head, sending a curly blond lock down over his forehead. He looked very immature and boyish at the moment, not at all twenty.

"Tomorrow, then." Kelsey turned, thinking she had handled that rather well. Griffin couldn't possibly know what had happened last night or that Salford was the object of her wanton dreams. She felt Griffin's eyes on her and turned to see him watching her, his arms folded over his chest, a curious assessing expression on his face.

The look faded as he waved, then turned around and strolled down the lane. She wondered if he had somehow read her mind. They were friends, after all. Sometimes she could tell what he was thinking just by looking at him. Could he know that she had lied to him about what had happened last night? Lord, she hoped not.

Kelsey strode back into the ballroom, then stopped, her gaze locked on the floor. Tiny pieces of torn material formed a little trail leading to her chamber door. It was as if someone meant her to follow it. She bent down, picked up one of the torn shreds, then rolled the fine lawn between her fingers, feeling the softness. It was the nightgown Mary had given her last night.

She followed the path of ripped material to her chamber, afraid of what she might find behind the door. Her hands trembled as she hesitantly entered the room. She paused on the threshold, looked at her bed, then her jaw dropped open.

When she recovered from the shock, her legs finally moved. She ran to the bed, thrusting her hands down into the pile of shredded material in the middle of it. She opened her hands, watching the tiny pieces of material slip through her fingers. Her clothes. Every stitch of them. Shredded—even her under-clothes.

"Of all the mean, common, spiteful, petty things . . . Oooh! How could he?" Tears blurred her vision. Her fingers snapped shut on the pieces left in her hands. She turned on her heels, storming from the room.

She didn't take the back entrance to the kitchen, but stomped out the front hallway, through the picture gallery, through the ugly paisley-covered hall. She paused in the dim gloominess of the foyer, hands on hips, chest heaving like a bellows. Mary and another young girl were on their hands and knees, scrubbing the floor. They both glanced up at her at the same time.

"Where is Lord Salford?" Kelsey's voice echoed through the gloomy silence.

"I—I don't know, miss." Mary dropped her scrubbing brush in the bucket, then sat back on her knees, wiping her hands on her apron. "What in the world's the matter?"

"The matter?" Kelsey trembled now as she tried to control her rage.

The girl on her knees beside Mary, a plump girl with a round, pink-cheeked face, looked at Kelsey as if she'd gone mad. Kelsey assumed this was the other housemaid in residence. She really didn't care how she looked at the moment, she wanted to strangle, to maim, to see justice done.

Watkins appeared in the foyer with a polishing cloth in his hand. He surveyed Kelsey's livid face. With his usual stately composure, he said, "What is it, Miss Kelsey?"

"Where is Lord Salford? Take me to him this minute."

"He's breaking the fast in the dining room, Miss Kelsey." Watkins's bushy gray brows rose, touching the middle of his shiny brow. "Is something amiss?"

"You could say that. I need to speak to him. He'll just have to be disturbed. Please take me to him."

"He does not wish to be disturbed." Watkins lowered his voice, adding calmly for her benefit, "You know . . . the rules."

"If he's afraid I'll look at his face, I'll walk in there backward, but I *will* speak to him. Now."

Watkins hesitated for a moment, looking unsure of what to do, then he stuffed the cloth in his pocket, picked up a candle, and said, "Follow me."

Watkins didn't seem inclined to speak. Kelsey could only clench her jaw and think of things she wished to do to Salford. Like ripping his clothes to shreds. Better yet, burning them. In silence they walked down the plain corridor that led to the library. Instead of stopping at the library door, he paused at the next door. Angry voices came from behind the door.

"You'll do as I say, or I'll send you away again."

"Where would you send me? No one will have me."

Kelsey listened to the woman's voice, his mistress's face rising up in her mind. The thought of facing Salford and his mistress together again dissolved some of her need for blood. She grabbed Watkins's hand as he was about to knock on the door.

She whispered, "Don't disturb them."

"Are you sure?" Watkins whispered back, almost sounding as if he wanted her to disturb them.

"No, no. Will you give Lord Salford a message?"

"Of course." Watkins nodded.

"Here . . ." Kelsey lifted Watkins's frail hand, depositing the pieces of her clothes in his palm. "This is what's left of my clothes—that's not true, there's more. There's a mound of shreds on my bed."

"Shreds?" Watkins asked, sounding nonplussed.

"I found them like that when I came back from meeting a friend. I really didn't mind him tearing up my sketches last night, but my clothes—well, that is beyond trifling. All I did was walk along the drive. He was the one who practically ran me down. I know I was supposed to be in the garden, but if he wanted to give me a set-down, he could have done it like a normal, sane person, he didn't have to tear my clothes into shreds. It was despicable, something only an imbecilic bounder would do. Don't you think so?"

"Oh, yes, very despicable, but are you sure his grace did this?"

"Of course he did it. I'm really starting to wonder if he's sane."

"I can vouch for his sanity, Miss Kelsey," Watkins said with certainty, a spark of amusement passing over his eyes.

"Well, I can't. For that very reason, and others—which I will not go into at the moment, I wish you to inform him that I have made a rule of my own. Since his rules have confined me to the ballroom and my chamber, I consider that my providence. Forthwith, he's not to enter the ballroom or my room at any time. From now on I'll be locking all doors—and another thing, the price of the fresco has gone up five hundred pounds. And if he decides to have another temper tantrum and destroy anything else that belongs to me, the price will continue to go up. Perhaps he might learn a little self-control if his finances are involved. If he wishes to discuss this new rule as an intelligent adult, then tell him I'll be in the ballroom, working. I'll see him with prior notification. Thank you, Watkins." Kelsey patted Watkins's arm, letting him know she wasn't upset with him, then turned in a huff and flounced down the hall.

Watkins shook his head, watching her walk away. His master's voice rose to a loud roar. Watkins glanced at the dining room door, a full-blown devious smile pulling at his mouth.

Several hours later Edward sat at his desk, going over his correspondence, having a devil of a time concentrating on it. His mind kept wandering back to Kelsey's sensuous body. He frowned down at the letter in his hand from his accountant, unable to recall what he'd just read.

A knock sounded on the door.

"Enter." Edward didn't bother glancing up from the letter. He knew by the succinct knock that it was Watkins.

The door closed and Watkins cleared his throat.

"Yes, Watkins?"

"I've investigated the noise, your grace."

Edward laid the foolscap down on his desk, leaned back in his chair until the leather creaked, then glanced up. "Well, where is the culprit?"

Watkins hesitated, his lips clamping tightly one over the other. "Working, your grace."

"I thought I gave you an order to bring them to me so I can dismiss them."

"You did, your grace." Watkins took out a dusting cloth from his pocket, then began dusting the edge of his desk.

"If you don't stop that infernal dusting, Watkins, and tell me what the hell you're hiding, I may just wrap my hands around your neck and be done with you."

Watkins didn't look at all frightened by the threat; he merely moved to the dry bar in the room, dusting the crystal decanters as he spoke. "Very well, your grace, you have forced it out of me. I have reason to believe it was Miss Vallarreal who made the noise. I did not think you wished to dismiss her."

Edward felt an abrupt pain in his neck. He reached back behind his head, massaging the sore spot, then frowned as he said, "So it was that little termagant?"

"Yes, your grace."

"Did she tell you why she did it?"

"She was not so open about it, your grace."

"So she lied about it." A slight grin turned up one corner of Edward's mouth.

"You could say she denied it, your grace."

"How did you know she was lying?"

"She's not very good at it, your grace."

"Ah! I suppose that's something in her favor." Edward felt the pain easing, then dropped his hand.

"Yes, your grace, though . . ." A decanter had moved slightly during the dusting. Watkins remained silent while he bent down and took great care repositioning it back in line with the other bottles, then he continued. "I would not have you believe this is a common failing of hers. I've observed that Miss Vallarreal rarely lies unless it is to protect someone else."

"Whom has she been protecting?" Inadvertently, he picked up the letter opener on his desk, running his finger along the blade.

"Only the staff, your grace. A tray was dropped and she took the blame for that, then we had some trouble in the kitchen. She assumed the blame there too."

"Oh," Edward said, unable to disguise the relief in his voice.

"There is one other matter we must discuss about Miss Vallarreal."

"Yes," Edward said, wondering what he'd hear next. He impatiently stabbed a stack of papers on his desk with the letter opener again and again, watching Watkins's back, waiting for him to continue.

"Well, she has made a rule of her own, your grace. She bade me to inform you of it."

"Really?" Edward said, sounding intrigued and perturbed both at the same time. He dropped the letter opener, then drummed his fingers on the top of his desk. "I'm almost afraid to ask what it is."

"She has informed me that you are not allowed in her room, or the ballroom, without informing her first. She also said she will, in future, keep all doors locked in that part of the castle."

Edward's expression darkened. He didn't have to ask what prompted that rule. She must have seen his face when he almost ran her down that morning. After last night, she probably couldn't bear the thought that he'd touched her.

He brought his fist down hard on his desk. "Who is she to make rules in my own home?"

Watkins grabbed two of the papers that had sailed off the desk. "She also told me to tell you that the price of the fresco went up five hundred dollars as well."

"The audacity of the little baggage!" Edward banged his fist down on top of his desk again.

Watkins grabbed the papers before they went sailing. "And she said the price would increase if you broke her rule again."

"The bloody hell you say!" Edward stood up this time. He was unaware that his chair had fallen over backward. "Tell her I wish to see her in the library, Watkins. Now!"

"Yes, your grace." Watkins hurried from the room. He stuck his hand in his pocket, fingering the pieces of shredded cloth Kelsey had given him earlier. A self-satisfied grin broke out on his face.

"Tell him if he wishes to see me, he'll have to come here. I'm working." Kelsey pounded the hammer down on the chisel with a loud bang. A large piece of old lime plaster cracked and jutted away from the ballroom wall. She pulled off the large chunk, then tossed it down onto the cloth-covered floor, barely missing Watkins's foot.

He took a step back, and stared up at the scaffolding. "I think you should see him, Miss Kelsey. He was very upset when I told him about the rule and the added expense of five hundred pounds."

"I'm sorry to hear it." With more force than before, Kelsey banged on the chisel. Shards of plaster went flying across the room.

Watkins ducked, dodging the projectiles. "Please, you should come, Miss Kelsey."

"No, I think not, not this time. If he wishes to see me, he can come here." Kelsey grabbed a corner of the plaster, tearing a large hunk away from the metal lath on the wall. She let it fall off the scaffolding and down onto the floor.

"I can't convince you, Miss Kelsey?"

"No, as I said, I'm much to busy here. I have to get this old plaster off the wall so I can put the new plaster on. If he's afraid I might stare at his face, tell him I have no intention of ever looking at him again."

Watkins relayed these very words to Edward, who was pacing in the library. When he heard them, he raced out of the room.

Edward stormed into the ballroom. He spotted her up on the scaffolding. Her back was to him, her long, dark braid hanging down her back. An old scarf was wrapped around her head, the torn edges sticking out on either side of her thick braid. A droopy smock and pants hid the shapely curves of her figure, the shape of which he knew intimately.

Vivid memories drew an instant response from his body. He shifted his stance to accommodate the tightening in his groin, then averted his gaze to her gloved hands. She pounded away at the old plaster as if she meant to kill it. He walked toward her. She must have heard him, because she stopped pounding.

"Do us both a favor and don't turn around, Miss Vallarreal."

"I had no intention of it. The less I see of you, the better." Bang! She drove the chisel into the wall again. Plaster flew.

Many women couldn't endure the sight of him, but none had ever been so bold about their aversion, confronting him outright with it as if he had no feelings at all. Edward's fists clenched at his sides. He was about to vent his indignation, but a hulking piece of plaster sailed over her shoulder, right at him.

He ducked and stepped to the side. The plaster crashed down onto the floor not a foot from him. He stared at the broken pieces on the tips of his boots, fighting the urge to climb up on the scaffolding to teach the little saucebox a lesson she wouldn't easily forget.

"Did I forget to say watch out below? You should be careful, it can be dangerous in here. Perhaps we can talk about this later."

"We'll talk now, while I'm still alive." He stared down at the plaster, then up at her back. "While you are in my house, you will not make the rules, is that understood, Miss Vallarreal? Only I make the rules—which you defy at my every turn."

"You seem to have forgotten that life goes on outside this castle and the strictures of your little set of rules." She whacked on the chisel again. "In the future I'll try to plan my life accordingly around them and be in the exact spots designated, but only if you will show me the same courtesy. I am giving you only one rule to follow, unlike the many you enforce upon me so you will know exactly where I am every moment of the day."

"This is my house, I follow no rules." Edward felt the veins in his neck throbbing as he ground out the words between his teeth.

"Oh, but there you are wrong. The rules you have established govern your every move. You are as much a prisoner to your own rules as you've made those around you. And I don't see how one small rule of my own can be so burdensome. All I ask is a little privacy and security against your tantrums."

"Tantrums!" When he saw her flinch, he realized he'd yelled at her. He never raised his voice. He prided himself on his iron self-control. What was she doing to him?

"Yes, tantrums. You seem to be on the verge of another one," she said causally, laying down the chisel and hammer. She worked at a large slab of plaster with her gloved hands as she spoke. "Which is preferable to me. I'd rather get my ears chewed off by a tongue-lashing than bear the brunt of your other devious forms of revenge."

"Pray, what forms of revenge am I to have executed?" He splayed his legs, crossed his arms over his chest, and glowered at her back.

"Surely you remember. Last night, well"—she shrugged— "a bit messy with the ink, but I can re-sketch my design. I overlooked it because I admit it was my fault for disturbing you and your . . . paramour. And I can understand your anger. But what you did this morning was unforgivable. If you had wanted to upbraid—"

"Wait one moment. I'm a little lost on what I was supposed to have done last night."

"You must know, or do you lose your memory during your tantrums?" She shook her head as if to pity him.

"Nothing is wrong with my memory, Miss Vallarreal. I remember touching your breasts, the way they filled my palms,

the taste of your mouth, and the soft little moan that came from
your lips when I touched you." He had the pleasure of seeing
her spine stiffen.

"So you're not senile *yet,* just given to fits you can't remember." Edward noticed her hands were trembling as she picked
up the hammer again, pounding at the wall.

He grinned in spite of his anger. "The only person having
fits last night was you, madam."

"I suppose you mean the slap. You have to admit you deserved that."

"Admitted," he said, holding back a grin. He felt some of his
anger dissolve at her unexpected candor.

She laid down the hammer, then pulled a chunk of plaster
away from the wall. It was as tall as she was. She hefted it aside,
this time letting it fall over the opposite side of the scaffolding.
It crashed to the floor with a loud bang, well away from where
he stood. Diminutive she might be, but she had the strength of
a man twice her size. He wondered if she made love with the
same kind of vigor. The possibilities made him grin, until he
thought of her lover, young McGregor. His lips hardened, the
grin vanished.

"Well, I'm glad you're willing to acknowledge some of your
faults," she said, as she turned back to the wall.

"I know them all too well, Miss Vallarreal. Do you know
your own?"

"Intimately." Some of the hauteur left her tone. She bent to
pick up the hammer and chisel again. "I can give you a full
discourse on them, but I'm sure they won't interest you."

"You'd be surprised at what interests me." He stared at the
rounded curves of her cute little derriere as she bent over. God,
he wanted her. It was torture just being in the same room with
her. He forced his gaze down to the thick workboots on her
feet.

"I'm sure I wouldn't be surprised in the least." A hint of
censure lingered behind her words.

"I know what you think of me, Miss Vallarreal, you said it

all last night." The truce between them appeared over. He frowned at her back as he said, "We've strayed from the subject. Just what exactly did I do last night during this tantrum?"

"Since you don't remember, I'll tell you. You shredded my sketches and spilled ink in my room."

Edward said nothing as he raised his brows thoughtfully.

"And this morning, I suppose you've forgotten that also."

"I'm afraid so."

She clucked her tongue, then hit the chisel with the hammer. "You really should see a doctor about your memory lapses. I thought since you had a tantrum just this morning, you'd remember, but you don't, so I'll have to tell you; you cut all my clothes into little shreds. You must have had a stroke of inspiration, for you drapped the shreds in a path that led to the door to my chamber—as a sort of arrow I was to follow. When I went in my chamber I found a large mound of shreds on my bed."

"A mound on the bed?" His frown deepened.

"Yes. I was very angry with you when I saw it, but that was before I learned of your condition. I think I can forgive you for destroying my clothes, since you have no recollection of it, but you really must see the necessity of my rule. I have to keep my door locked in case you have another fit and try to cut me into little pieces instead of my clothes. As far as the extra five hundred pounds, let's make it fifty pounds, since my clothes can be easily replaced with such a sum. You probably need the money anyway for a good doctor."

"Very fair-minded of you," he said in a distracted tone, then he turned on his heel, calling over his shoulder as he strode across the ballroom, "Watkins will see that your clothes are replaced. I'll take my leave of you now. I have an important matter to attend to. One more thing—you will stop working on that infernal wall before you do yourself a harm. I'll hire some men to demolish it. We'll talk about this rule of yours later. Good day, Miss Vallarreal."

Kelsey turned at that moment. She saw a fleeting glimpse of

his profile as he disappeared around the doorway. It was the same handsome face in the portrait, as far as she could tell. His hair was longer, pulled back in a queue, but it was still the same face. She blinked at the empty doorway, wondering if his face was scarred at all. Perhaps the carriage accident had caused his madness and that's why he chose to live like a recluse. She could almost forgive him for everything—except he did remember seducing her last night. She couldn't forgive him for that. She sighed, shook her head, then turned. In spite of his command that she stop working on the wall, she raised the hammer and pounded on the chisel.

Six

Forgetting himself, Edward strode into the library. The two maids, who were dusting the shelves, glanced up from their work. One of them, a thin redhead, opened her mouth and stared at him. The other, a plump, earthy-looking girl, standing on a ladder, took one look at him, then her face drained of color and her eyes rolled back in her head.

"Damnation!" Edward rushed to the ladder, catching her as she fainted. When he remembered that it was one o'clock, that he was not supposed to be in this room but in the conservatory, he cursed loudly.

He strode over to the settee, depositing his burden. The other maid had not made a move, but looked as if she'd turned to Italian marble. "Don't just stand there, ring the bell! Be quick about it!" He shot the girl a look that could curl her hair.

"Y-yes, y-your grace." She scurried across the room to do his bidding, then stood there afraid to approach him. She stared down at the floor, ringing her hands.

Watkins appeared with his usual punctuality. If he were at all astonished to find his master in the library, bending over an unconscious maid, it didn't show in his expression or address. With his usual poised gate, Watkins reached Edward's side, then took over fanning the young woman's face. "I'll see to her, your grace."

Edward stood and noticed the other maid was staring at his

face. He motioned toward the door with his head, then growled, "Leave us, and close the door behind you."

She curtsied, almost tripping over her own feet, then practically flew out of the room. He strode over to the dry bar, poured three fingers of bourbon in a glass, then downed it, feeling it burn all the way down his throat.

"You should have told me you'd be in here, your grace, and I could have seen that the room was empty."

"I'm sick to death of creeping around my own home." Edward poured a separate drink, topped off his own again, then walked over and handed the glass to Watkins. "Here . . . see if you can get some of this down her."

"Will you be breaking the rules again, your grace? I should like to know so I can prepare the staff."

"Yes, perhaps, if the mood strikes me." He downed his own drink. "I'll let you know ahead of time."

"Very good, your grace." Watkins sounded pleased as he raised the girl's head, forcing some of the bourbon down her throat.

She coughed and spit, then blinked. "Ohhh . . ." She moaned and brought her hand up to clasp her brow.

"Are you all right, Dorkins?"

"Aye, sir . . ." At that moment her gaze landed on Edward. Her jaw dropped open again.

The scarred side of his face was to her. He started to turn away, but too late . . . her eyes rolled back in her head again. "Bloody hell," Edward mumbled.

"Perhaps you should leave the room, your grace, before we try to rouse her again."

"I think you're right, but before I go, I'd like to find out if you knew that Lizzy was playing some of her tricks on Miss Vallarreal." Edward ran his finger along the rim of his empty glass.

"Yes, your grace, I knew." Watkins continued to fan the girl's face.

"Why didn't you bother informing me?"

"I thought in conversing with Miss Vallarreal that you'd find out for yourself. She's very straightforward, your grace."

"You are right there, Watkins." He laughed derisively. "She thinks I'm mad. She thinks I'm the one who's been tormenting her."

"I hope you informed her of her error, your grace."

"No, I'll leave her to deduce that on her own." He rubbed his chin, a perverse feeling settling over him.

"Then you mean to be in her company, your grace?"

"Don't sound so pleased with yourself, Watkins." His brows knitted at Watkins's back. "In spite of your matchmaking schemes, I don't intend to spend any more time with Miss Vallarreal than is necessary. Now, do you know where Lizzy is?"

"I haven't seen her since this morning, your grace. You know how she is when she doesn't want to be found."

"Yes, I do. If you should happen upon the termagant, tie her up, then send her to me."

"Yes, your grace."

The maid started moaning again. Edward backed away and left the library.

Kelsey glanced over at one of the windows in the ballroom. Darkness had settled behind the panes. Candlelight reflected off the glass in flickering waves, turning her reflection into something distorted, ghoulish. Even the distortion couldn't hide the tired shadows below her eyes. She crawled down from the scaffold slowly, barely able to lift her feet. It had been a long day. A thick film of gritty plaster dust covered her. She could even taste it in her mouth.

When her feet hit the ground, she grabbed her sore back and bent over to stretch it. She felt exhausted, but it was a good kind of exhaustion. She'd sleep well tonight. Those dreams of Salford wouldn't haunt her.

She didn't hear the eerie groan at first, until she stood. She paused, rested her hands on her hips, then said loudly, "All right, your grace, if that's you, show yourself this instant. I'm too tired for this tomfoolery."

Again the groan.

"If you think to scare me, you can forget it. Now, go away, you're breaking my rule. That's rather unsporting of you." Kelsey put her hand on her chamber door, about to open it.

Abruptly, the huge doors to the ballroom slammed shut.

A whoosh of cold air brushed past her. The candles that she'd left burning near the scaffold blew out. Darkness engulfed the room.

The unearthly wail echoed through the room again.

"Can you not find some other form of entertainment?" Kelsey said, all the patience gone from her voice.

She heard the crystals on the chandelier tinkling. The groan grew into a moaning sob that seemed to fill the whole room. She realized the feminine sound was much too high-pitched for Salford to have made. The hair rose on the back of her neck. Could it be the duchess? *Ghosts do not exist.*

She swallowed the growing lump in her throat, felt her heart banging so hard against her chest, it hurt to breathe. She couldn't force herself to glance up at the chandelier.

The morbid moan grew to a banshee cry.

Ghosts do not exist.

But, dear God, something was making that sound. Ghost or not, she was not about to stay around to find out what it was. She flew across the ballroom and ran out the door, the sound of deep, throaty feminine laughter following after her.

Very few of the wall sconces were left burning in this part of the castle, she realized as she ran in the darkness trying to find one. Twice, she fell over something in the darkness, hurting her knees, then scrambled to her feet and kept running.

Thump.

Something blunt hit her head-on, knocking the breath out of her. It felt like a brick wall. Arms appeared out of the darkness and clamped around her. Kelsey screamed, then she did something she'd never done before in her life, she fainted.

* * *

Edward walked into the drawing room carrying Kelsey's limp body, one of her arms hanging at her side, swaying as he walked.

Watkins glanced up from pouring a drink, his expression as cryptically sour as usual. "Trouble, your grace?"

Jeremy Lovejoy, Edward's cousin, bounded out of his chair. "Good God, not another faintee!"

"I'm afraid so." Edward didn't sound at all contrite. Taking great care, he laid Kelsey down on the couch. The warmth of her body clung to his hands as he drew them back. A lock of curly black hair had escaped the rag tied around her head. Without thinking he bent over and gently pushed it off her brow. The dark strand curled around his finger as he said, "I stumbled upon her on my way down to dinner."

Jeremy's hazel eyes lit up as he came to stand beside Edward. He surveyed Kelsey, the dirt smudges all over her face, the rag tied around her hair covered with filth, the dirty clothes, the pants torn at the knee. "By the look of her, you did more than stumble. You sure you didn't trample her?"

"You can save your witty remarks. She's been tearing down the old plaster, which I instructed her not to do." Edward saw Watkins studying him and quickly moved away from Kelsey, mindful of the way he'd just touched her and how it must have looked. He started to pace. "She was hysterical when I found her. I think we all know who is to blame. And when I get my hands on Lizzy, she won't be able to sit down for a week."

"Good luck in finding the little puss," Jeremy remarked as he picked up Kelsey's hand and started to pat it. "I thought she'd come out and at least speak to me, but I haven't seen her." He raised his voice in case Lizzy might be listening. "I suppose I could lure her out, but I didn't bring those taffies she likes so well, I brought chocolate instead."

"If I have to tear this place down brick by brick, I'll find her." After another pensive look at Kelsey, Edward strode from the room with stiff, determined strides.

Watkins gently nudged Jeremy aside, careful not to spill the drink in his hand. "Let's try to get a little of this in her."

Jeremy raised Kelsey's head while Watkins administered the drink.

Kelsey felt something horrible go down her throat. She coughed, clutched her neck, then opened her eyes. Watkins was standing over her, and another man. A stranger. He was handsome, about thirty, with chestnut-brown hair crimped in the latest fashion. The arrogant set of his chin looked very familiar; she had seen the same chin in the portrait of Salford.

The stranger raised her hand to his lips. "Hello there. I'm Lord Lovejoy, Eddie's cousin. Terrible that we should have to meet like this, but I'm glad we have." He smiled at her, a charming smile that touched his whole face.

"I'm Kelsey Vallarreal," she replied, matching his smile with a charming one of her own.

"I have to tell you, Kelsey—I hope you don't mind my frank use of your name— I feel that I should be on a first-name basis with every woman who faints near me." He winked at her. "You have the most astounding eyes."

She stared into the long-lashed depths of his eyes and thought they were by far more astonishing that her own. She forgot what she was about to say, then remembered. "My mother's were very large too, though hers were blue."

"By Jove! I'd for—" He paused and said instead, "Just so, just so."

Kelsey wondered what he had intended to say. She started to ask him, but Watkins cleared his throat and edged his way between Jeremy and her. "If you don't mind, my lord, I really should get her to drink more of this."

"By all means, Watkins. Here . . . let me help her up."

Kelsey could have sat on her own, but she enjoyed the gentle touch of Lord Lovejoy's hand as he slid his arm behind her back. His touch was almost as soothing as her father's, and kindness emanated from him like sunshine. His easy manner made her feel as if she had known him all her life. Now she knew why Agnes and Alice liked Lord Lovejoy so much.

Watkins cleared his throat and gained the attention of both parties. "I think you should drink the rest of this, Miss Kelsey." He gave her another sip.

Kelsey coughed again and made a face. "What is that?"

"Sherry, Miss Kelsey."

"I've tasted better turpentine."

Jeremy burst out laughing. "A beautiful swooning damsel with charm and wit. What a diverse pleasure you are."

"I may be diverse, sir, but as far as charm and wit, I'm sure once you get to know me, you'll think otherwise. Shame on you, sir, you're laughing. You don't believe me. Well, you'll soon find out I'm no swooning damsel." To prove it, Kelsey pushed away the glass Watkins was holding out to her, then swung her feet down to the floor and stood up. The room started to spin.

Jeremy caught her arm, steadying her. "I think in this case you must allow your weakness so that I may play the gallant. I get so few chances at it." He grinned at her.

"That's a cawker if I ever heard one," Kelsey said, using one of Griffin's terms.

"Ah! You've found me out."

"You're not that hard to see through, Lord Lovejoy." She grinned impishly at him. "I'm sure you have the ladies swooning wherever you go."

He chuckled. "Not as many as my cousin, I'm afraid."

The bantering grin disappeared as Kelsey remembered the steely arms that went around her. She groaned aloud and shook her head. "So it was Lord Salford whom I bumped into in the dark?" She had said it more to herself and was surprised when Jeremy answered her.

"Yes, I'm afraid so. I always said he has eyes like a cat.

He walks around in the dark all the time, scared me out of my wits a time or two. I'm just the opposite—night blind. Can't see a thing at night without a candle."

Watkins cleared his throat again. "I think Miss Kelsey should retire."

Her heart started to pound at the thought of going anywhere near the ballroom. Maybe in the morning, in the light of day, she could do it. She bit her lip and tried to think of an excuse that wouldn't make her sound as mad as Salford. She couldn't tell them she'd heard a ghost.

Watkins stared at her a moment, then as if he read her mind, he said, "The yellow room is available, Miss Kelsey, if you would care to sleep there tonight. I'll show you the way."

She stared at him and wondered if he could, indeed, read her mind. "Thank you, Watkins," she said, her gratitude evident in her voice.

"I'll escort you, my dear."

"Don't trouble yourself on my account," she blurted out, pulling her arm from Lord Lovejoy's grasp. "I'm quite capable of following Watkins."

"Are you sure?" He looked worried.

"Very," Kelsey assured him. "How else can I convince you I'm no swooning maid if I don't prove it now?" Her tone grew more serious. "Thank you for your kindness. It's been a pleasure meeting you, Lord Lovejoy."

"And a great one for me," he said. "Call me Jeremy, won't you."

She nodded, then turned, following Watkins out of the room, up a flight of stairs. The paisley wallpaper in the hallway looked familiar. Portraits of Salford's ancestors hung along the walls; they were the same ones she'd passed last night on her way to Salford's room. She asked hopefully, "Watkins, aren't we going in the wrong direction?"

"No, Miss Kelsey." He paused at a door she knew was next to Salford's room.

She took a step back, her hand out in front of her as if to ward off something detestable. "I can't sleep here. Have you no other room for me?"

"No, Miss Kelsey."

"But this room is next to Lord Salford's."

"Yes, but it's the only guest room that is available. All the other rooms are closed and have been for years."

"But this must have been the duchess's room." A shudder went down her spine as she thought of sleeping in the late duchess's chamber. It wasn't the idea of her ghost haunting the chamber that made Kelsey's pulse race, it was the fact that Salford might have made love to his wife in that bed.

"Lady Margaret never used this room, Miss Kelsey. Her rooms were in another wing of the castle."

"In another wing?" Kelsey raised an incredulous brow at Watkins's back.

"Yes." He didn't offer anything further, only opened the door, then gave her a patient look as he waited for her to enter.

She hesitated a moment, then stepped past him. It was an elegant room, much larger than her own. Bright striped yellow wallpaper lined the walls. Three large windows almost filled one whole wall. Brilliant yellow satin drapes matched the wallpaper. A four-poster sat in the middle of the room, a yellow counterpane covering it. A white lacquered writing desk stood against one wall, and a dressing table that matched it was placed near it. The mantel was covered with yellow and white porcelain figures. A large mirror hung over the fireplace, its gilded frame antiqued with white and gold. Yellow canaries were woven into the white background of the lush carpet on the floor.

"It's beautiful," Kelsey said, awed by the room.

"His grace decorated it before his marriage, but sadly, it was never used by the duchess." Watkins walked to a door and touched it. "This is the closet. I took the liberty of filling it with a selection of clothes for you after you'd informed me of what happened to your own. I sent Grayson all the way to London to find premade gowns. I hope they please you."

"I'm sure they will." Kelsey looked astonished as she said, "How did you know I'd be sleeping here?"

"I did not know, but it is a more comfortable room than the one that was temporarily set up for your use off the ballroom. I had hoped that if you saw this room, you might prefer it."

"I'd prefer not to sleep in the castle at all."

"I understand, Miss Kelsey," he said, "but necessity demands that you sleep here, thus you should be comfortable."

Comfortable. She didn't think she'd ever feel comfortable as long as Salford was nearby. She glanced at Watkins's back as he crossed the room to another door at the opposite end of the chamber.

He paused with his hand on the door. "Through here is the washroom, beyond that is a door that leads to his grace's apartments." He touched the key in the lock. "The locks work, if you wish to keep your rules, Miss Kelsey. I'll have a bath and supper tray sent up to you." Watkins strode toward the door, his expression more sour than usual.

"Thank you," Kelsey called to him. She saw him touch his cheek and grimace. She remembered that she was supposed to make a potion for him. "Watkins."

"Yes, Miss Kelsey?" He turned, the pain evident in his eyes.

"You're in pain?"

He nodded, his thin cheeks coloring at his obvious embarrassment.

"Come now, Watkins, we know each other well enough not to be distressed by a toothache."

"Yes, Miss Kelsey."

"Good, then I can say I meant to fix you a potion earlier, but I never got around to preparing it. I'll give you the recipe and you can make it before you go to bed. Take one cup of water and add a good pinch of salt to it. Warm it and let it sit in your mouth as long as you can."

"Salt and water, Miss Kelsey?"

"Yes. An old remedy my mother used to force on me when I had sore throats. My mother grew up in South Shields. She learned the secret from my grandmother's maid. She used seawater, but my mother found that if she dissolved salt in water, it was as good as seawater. It really does heal all sorts of maladies of the mouth. It's wonderful for sore throats—and aching teeth."

"Thank you, Miss Kelsey, I'll try it."

"Good, let me know if there's an improvement." She watched him bow his way out of the room. She waited until he left, then hurried over, locking the connecting door that separated her room from Salford's room, but she didn't stop there. She locked the door that led to the hall too.

Jeremy was already seated when Edward entered the dining hall. The enormous room was in the older part of the castle. Two huge hearths blazed at either end of the room. A large wood and cast iron chandelier hung from the ceiling by a thick chain. Medieval weapons and multicolored pennons, bearing colorful coats of arms, covered the bare brick walls. It was a tradition in medieval times that every knight gracing the table at Stillmore must leave his standard for the present Duke of Salford. A gesture of courtesy. The standards were mounted on poles and hung in an even line along the top of the room. Edward had always liked this room. But tonight it seemed empty, isolated, and bleak.

Jeremy must have heard Edward's boots on the stone floor, for he glanced down the long length of the table and grinned at him. "You're late. Food's probably cold by now."

"Then I'll eat it cold," Edward snapped back.

"No luck?"

"Not a jot." Edward stepped to the head of the table and sat down next to Jeremy.

"I told you you were wasting your time. Lizzy will come out eventually, but she'll probably wait until you've calmed down a bit."

"Perhaps she'd better. I feel like strangling her right now." Having dispensed with hovering servants long ago, Edward thought nothing of picking up the cover of one of the chafing dishes and slapping a piece of roast beef on his plate.

"You really should do something with her."

"Do you have any suggestions?" Edward plopped a mound of boiled potatoes beside the beef.

"Give her a tour of the Continent."

"And who would chaperon her, you?" Edward took pleasure in seeing his cousin flinch as if he'd just hit him.

"Oh, no, not me." Jeremy took a long swallow from a glass of wine.

"I thought as much."

"Can't you send her back to the convent for a year? It might give her time to mature, perhaps she'd change her ways."

"The convent won't have her back. The reverend mother called her a child of the devil. She washed her hands of Lizzy this last time, when she almost destroyed the convent, then ran away." Edward picked up a roll, squeezed it to see if it was fresh, then set it on his butter plate.

"Almost destroyed it, you say." Jeremy shook his head as he cut off a piece of beef, then ate it.

"One of her classmates dared her to ring the cathedral bells at one in the morning. She did, of course. They found her and locked her in her room for punishment. But it appears she'd somehow smuggled gunpowder into her room. She blew her way out and came home."

"Good God!"

"My exact words when I heard about it," Edward said, scowling down at the slab of roast beef on his plate. "Of course, I had to pay for repairs to the dormitory. She'd blown away half of a wall."

"Where did she get the gunpowder?"

"I've never been able to get that out of her, though I suspect she got it from a regiment stationed near Cherbrough."

Jeremy looked astounded, then his ready sense of humor took over and he grinned. "Perhaps you should buy her a commission. I hear they're looking for good weapons men."

Edward frowned at Jeremy for the quip, then he took the cover off another chafing dish. He plopped some candied carrots onto his plate. "I have another commission in store for Lizzy."

"What is that?"

"Marriage."

Jeremy almost choked on a swallow of wine. He coughed several times, then blurted out, "Good God! You can't mean to foist her on some unsuspecting fool."

"That is exactly what I mean to do. If her belly is full with a child, it might tame her. She is eighteen now. It is high time she found a husband. I've asked Lady Shellborn to come here."

"The Dragon of Almack's?"

"The very one. She was a particular friend of my mother's. I cannot see her denying to sponsor Lizzy's come-out."

Jeremy looked dubious. "Have you spoken to Lizzy about all this?"

"I have. I gave her an alternative, she could either impress Lady Shellborn with her polite deportment and biddable meekness, or I would personally lock her up in the tower until she turned gray."

"Did she agree?"

"No, she said I'd have to lock her up."

Jeremy chuckled—until Edward shot him a look. Then Jeremy quickly straightened his face. He stabbed a carrot on his plate and ate it, his expression sobered as he stared pensively down. "You know, perhaps you should take Lizzy to London. I doubt even the Dragon can handle her. It's been ten years since you've left this place. The society would do you a world of good."

"I cannot face London again. Have you forgotten what happened last time?" Edward's fist tightened on the handle of his knife.

"I have not forgotten, but you didn't give the *ton* time to get used to you. It's like riding a horse, you have to get back on when you get thrown."

"Dammit, Jeremy, I won't invite humiliation." He pounded the edge of his knife down on the table. "Unless you want to take Lizzy out in society, keep your helpful suggestions to yourself."

Edward knew he'd been overly harsh with his cousin when he saw Jeremy frowning down at his plate. Jeremy was his only friend. Edward knew Jeremy's comments were born out of loyalty; a kinder or a better human heart did not exist in all of England. But he was in no mood for a tedious scold, or Jeremy's well-meant kindness, so he didn't say anything more to ease the tension between them. What he did do was glower down at his own plate.

A long silence followed. He ate the lukewarm roast beef. It tasted like a dry scone in his mouth. He chewed, watching Jeremy nurse his hurt feelings by draining his wine and pouring another glass.

Jeremy was the first to speak again. "I suppose your life has changed a great deal since Miss Vallarreal has come."

"Yes, she does have a way of bringing about changes."

"Seems like a sweet girl to me."

"You haven't seen her angry, then." Edward pensively rubbed the cheek she'd slapped. When Edward saw Jeremy studying his expression, his grin dissolved and he tried to assume a bland mask.

"No wonder, old boy," Jeremy said, buttering another piece of bread. "You treat her like the help. I spoke to Cook before dinner. She told me that your guest was taking her meals in the kitchen."

"Fraternizing with the help again?"

"Putting in a kind word for you, cousin, just a kind word." Jeremy grinned, then added, "But you'd be surprised at the gossip you can pick up from the staff." Edward shot Jeremy a censorious look. Jeremy shrugged it off. "Well, you never tell me anything. How else am I to learn what goes on around here?"

"You know quite enough, it seems."

"Not if it was left up to you. I would never have known Miss Vallarreal was dining in the kitchen if I had not heard Cook commenting to her sister on it. Do you intend to make her eat in the kitchen?" Jeremy asked, sounding incredulous.

"Yes," he said emphatically, stuffing another piece of cold meat into his mouth.

"Then I suppose you'll have to forgo my company, for I intend to dine with her."

"Stay away from her, Jeremy." His hand tightened around the handle of his knife, and he felt it bending in his grip.

"Why? Do you want her?"

"No." Edward's hand trembled slightly from the pressure he was exerting on the knife. "She's in love with someone else."

"Really." Jeremy pushed his plate away, then lit a cheroot, his hazel eyes twinkling devilishly.

"I won't let you trifle with her."

"You wound me, Eddie. You know I'm not in the habit of seducing innocents." Edward made a dubious face at the word *innocents,* but Jeremy missed it as he continued to speak. "Speaking of innocents, have you told Kelsey why you brought her here?" Jeremy took a draw, blowing a smoke ring out of his mouth.

"No, I haven't, but I shall when the time is right." Edward raised his fork to take another bite of meat, but he looked at it, then set it back down on the plate. When Kelsey found out about her past, she would be devastated. He wanted to spare her the pain as long as he could. Then there was the money. She'd certainly go away and start a new life. He wasn't prepared to let her go yet. Having her at the castle had brightened it somehow.

"There is no right time, in my opinion," Jeremy said, breaking the silence.

"I'll tell her when she needs to know."

"You'd better do it before she turns of age and the solicitors come knocking on her door and tell her she is an heiress."

Edward scowled down at the cold food on his plate, suddenly losing his appetite.

Seven

Kelsey watched the boy's lips as he read to her. They were smooth, wet lips, and such beautiful words came from them, always kind words. She longed for kind words. His words.

He stopped reading and glanced down at her. "You're not paying attention."

"I am, I'm watching your lips move."

"Watching my lips is not paying attention. You are supposed to be listening to the story."

"I'd rather watch your lips move."

"You'd better be careful or they'll move all over you."

The boy growled at her and bared his teeth, then he tried to bite her neck. He was playing, and she knew it, and she giggled as she scurried away, laughing. And when she turned to find him, he'd vanished. She called for him, then screamed for him. But he was gone. . . .

Loud voices woke Kelsey from her dream. The darkness disoriented her for a moment. She lay in bed, trying to recall where she was, then she remembered. She frowned up into the inky shadows and brought a trembling hand up to her brow, wiping away the film of sweat there.

The voices grew louder. Salford's chamber walls muffled the din so she couldn't hear exactly what was being said, but she could hear the throaty bawl of a woman. He must be having a row with his "nightbird," as Griffin called her. This brought a perverse smile to her face. She lit a candle, got out of bed, saw that it was two o'clock in the morning by the mantel clock, then tiptoed over to the connecting door. She pressed her ear against it. . . .

As if to tease her, the yelling abruptly stopped. She grimaced, cursing her luck. A door slammed, making her jump. Someone stomped down the hall, then another door slammed.

She shook her head, blew out the candle, then crawled back into bed and snuggled beneath the covers.

Moments later the first booming chords of Mozart's *Rondo alla Turca* brought her straight up in bed. Mozart would have turned over in his grave if he'd heard how someone was murdering his sonata, playing it with such force that it was a wonder the keys stayed put on the pianoforte.

She stared at the connecting door. "Salford," she said between her teeth. Was this another tantrum of his? Perhaps the argument with his paramour brought it on. She laid back down, shoved the pillow over her head, and doubted if the pianoforte would still be standing after he was done taking out his anger on it. The feather ticking did nothing to dull the sound. She squeezed the pillow tighter to her ears.

The song finished.

Surely, he'd stop now. As she pulled the pillow off her head . . .

Bang bang bang. This time Beethoven was to be crucified. He struck the notes of the *Moonlight Sonata* as if he meant to either kill the moonlight or break his fingers.

Knowing she'd never get back to sleep now unless she pointed out the impudence of his playing like a maniac in the middle of the night, she lit the candle again, threw the covers back, and leapt out of bed. She stomped to the closet, found a robe among the clothes Watkins had left for her use, donned it, then snatched up the candle and unlocked the connecting door. She flounced through the small room which she had used earlier to take her bath, then crossed to the opposite door and tried the knob. The door was open.

She flung back the door, then looked for Salford. The room

was empty. There was no doubt that this was his chamber. An enormous mahogany bed sat in the middle of the room on a raised dais, and a candelabrum had been left burning on a table by the bed. Huge ancient pieces of carved furniture stood around the room, all finished in dark, dreary hues, just like the posts and headboard of the bed. Dark burgundy curtains and wallpaper added more gloom.

Bang bang bang.

The hammering of the music emanated from behind a door at the opposite side of the room. She felt sure it led to a sitting room of some sort. Her quarry would certainly be there. She took a deep breath, squared her shoulders, then marched across the room and opened the door. She stepped inside, then, without thinking, slammed the door behind her.

Silence.

The abrupt quiet and the momentary glimpse of him seated at a pianoforte on the other side of the room startled her. She dropped the candle in her hand. It hit the floor, dousing the flame.

Utter black silence throbbed against every nerve in her body. Abruptly, she regretted storming into his den. That's what it felt like, a den of darkness. His lair. She glanced over where she'd last seen him before she dropped the candle. His grim presence hovered on the right side of the room like thick steam from a boiling kettle. She remembered distinctly what happened the last time she'd been in total darkness with him.

"What the hell are you doing in my private chambers?" The words were spoken softly, but they made Kelsey jump.

She fell back, hitting her spine on something large. Her hands groped in the dark, then met a hard surface. She grabbed it, steadying herself. When she felt soft material beneath her fingertips, she realized she'd bumped into a sofa or chair of some sort. The pain galvanized her, making her blurt out the first thing that popped into her mind, "Do you always sit around in this stupid manner in the dark?"

"It's none of your business what I do. Now, get out."

"But it is my business. You have no consideration for others. How am I to sleep, when all I can hear is you defiling Mozart and Beethoven?"

"Are you saying my playing is disturbing your sleep?"

"Absolutely."

"Among your other talents, you must possess an extraordinary sense of hearing if you can hear me below stairs."

"If I were below stairs, I would probably still hear it—the floors in this old place are not half as substantial as one would think—but that is beside the point, since I'm not below stairs, but trying to sleep in the chamber next to yours—"

"Next to mine." This was growled.

Kelsey's fingernails dug into the edge of the piece of furniture she'd fallen against, afraid of what he might do during one of his fits. It occurred to her she should have thought of that consequence before she entered this room. Now she felt like a lion tamer without a whip, without even his pants. She tried to control the apprehension in her voice. "Yes, Watkins gave me the room temporarily, but if it bothers you, I'll certainly move. It's probably for the best anyway. I'll go right now. . . ." Kelsey felt around in the dark for the doorknob.

"Wait!"

"For what? So you can growl at me in the dark? I'm really much too tired for all that, and it only upsets you anyway." Kelsey continued to grope for the knob. She found it, was about to open the door, but his voice made her freeze.

"If you leave this room, Miss Vallarreal, you will certainly regret it when I'm forced to come after you." His voice was lower, controlled, velvety with warning. The playing started again, but this time it was very soft, hardly audible. Beautiful, in fact, for the song he'd chosen, Beethoven's "Für Elise," was meant to be played with such delicate subtlety.

She swallowed hard, feeling trapped by the hypnotic notes of the song and the man playing them. If she left the room, he would certainly follow through with his threat. He would never

hurt her, if her intuition was correct, but she had no doubt he
would try to seduce her again. She couldn't let that happen.

She had never dealt with an insane person, but she thought
that humoring him might be a good start in getting out of the
room unscathed. "That sounds lovely. You are quite accomplished."

"Are you sure I'm not defiling it?" he said, smugness dripping in his voice.

"No, I think once you calm your nerves you play very well.
You really should try to stay calm. Perhaps the fits wouldn't
come so often."

He laughed, a deep, throaty sound that echoed in the darkness, but he never missed a note.

"You may find mirth in your sickness, but I do not."

"Do you not? I thought you would."

"Why would you think that? Do you think I'm so callous
that I would laugh at your illness?"

"I had the impression you hated me, thus you would be
amused at my flaws."

"You really don't know me at all. It doesn't please me to find
flaws in others. I rarely look for them."

"You look for flaws only in me."

"I do not." Kelsey realized she'd lost some of the restraint
in her voice. She took a deep breath, then, using the most serene
tone she could muster under the circumstances, she said, "I
resent you saying that."

"But you have to admit you hate me."

"I don't hate you." Kelsey's admission surprised even her,
and she added, "Hate is not a good word to describe what I feel
for you, it's more dislike."

"That's only a gracious term for hate."

"All right, then, I hate you. Are you satisfied now?" Losing
the thin hold on her patience, Kelsey stomped her foot at him,
stubbing her toe against something. She groaned as a pain shot
up to her ankle.

"Are you all right?" The playing stopped. His footsteps came toward her.

She limped backward, holding up one hand in the darkness. "Don't come near me, I'm all right."

Too late. His arms clamped around her and she was swept off her feet. "What are you doing?" she asked, squirming in his arms. "Put me down."

"Don't worry, I know my touch disgusts you, so you need not worry that I will force myself on you again." He gently set her down in a chair.

She jumped when she felt his hands touch her aching foot, then asked, "How did you know which foot I stubbed?"

"Because I saw you trip."

"I don't see how. It's so dark in here, I can't see a thing."

"I'm used to the dark."

"You must be a mole if you can see in here—but then, everyone knows moles are blind." She heard him chuckle, knew she was babbling like an idiot, but she had to do something to take her mind off his hands touching her. The image of his beautiful hands rose up in her mind. She envisioned them on her leg as the roughness of his palms glided down her ankle, over the top of her foot. When his fingers touched her toes, a tingle shot up her leg, mingling with the warmth that was beginning to glow in her belly.

She fidgeted in her seat. Her voice lacked conviction as she said, "Really, it's fine now. It was just my toe, it's quite all right now—aches a little, that's all." She tried to pull her foot away, but he wouldn't let it go.

"Hold still, let me see if you've broken it. Which one is it?"

"My little one, but it's not broken. I know what it feels like to break a toe. I broke my big toe once when I jumped down from the roof. I'll never forget the pain." She felt no pain now as his fingers moved over her little toe, massaging it. Even the ache was gone, lost in the sensation of his hands and the hot sparks moving up her leg, past her belly, pooling in her breast.

"Nothing seems broken." The torture ended. She heard him

rise, then the cushion beside her shifted beneath his weight as he sat. He was so close to her, the heat of his arm burned her skin through her robe and nightgown.

She felt the warmth from his hands still clinging to her foot. No part of him touched her now, but his nearness was so invasive that it felt as if he were lying on top of her. She jumped up. "I really should go to my room now."

"I never took you for a coward, madam, but you are certainly acting the part now."

"Pray, what do you mean by that?" Kelsey turned toward him.

"Just what I said, you are a coward."

"I'm no coward."

"Prove it, then. Sit down and talk to me for a moment."

The loneliness in his voice reached out to her. She hesitated, unable to fight a premonition that she'd regret what she was about to do, but she sat down again anyway. She rested her head on the back of the chair, staring up at the darkness, listening to his breathing, sharing the utter silence with him, knowing that he needed to feel someone near him. She felt close to him, closer than when they had kissed. Without the physical sensations in the way, she felt the pain, the despair, radiating from him. She lifted her hand to reach out to him, but changed her mind at the last moment, letting it drop back down into her lap.

"Afraid to touch me?"

Kelsey started at the sound of his voice. She had forgotten he could see her. It disturbed her to know he'd been watching her in the dark. She tried to hide her distress by teasing him. "You have an unfair advantage. You can see me but I can't see you."

"You are avoiding my question." The emotion intensified in his voice. "Are you afraid to touch me? I want an answer."

"Yes—no . . . I don't know what I mean." Kelsey squirmed uncomfortably in her seat.

"What are you afraid of?" His voice grew heated with impatience.

"Nothing."

"You are a liar!" He grabbed her shoulders and shook her.

"All right, all right! I'm afraid of you!" She knocked his hands away, then stood, her body trembling.

"I don't know why, you can't see my face," he said, bitterness dripping in his voice.

"You don't understand at all. Do you think I'd be afraid of your face? There's nothing wrong with your face. It's here." Kelsey pounded on the region above her own heart. "It's what's in your heart that frightens me, your callousness, your disregard for everyone's feelings but your own—"

"You think me such a monster, perhaps you should get the whole picture." His fingers clamped down on her wrists.

"No! Leave me alone!" Kelsey tried to fight him, but he was pulling her across the room. She dug her heels into the carpet. It was useless. He was ten times stronger than she, pulling her like a rag doll.

He opened the door, dragging her into his chamber, then over to the candelabrum, where candles were still burning. She saw only his broad back, the long, dark hair hanging down around his shoulders. He was dressed in a white shirt and black pants.

He swung her around, then shoved his face into hers. "Now you can get a good look at the monster!"

Frightened of what he might do if she took her eyes off him, she stared at him, afraid to breathe, afraid the wrong sound or least movement might give away the shock and abhorrence she was trying desperately to hide. She wanted to turn away. But that's what he wanted her to do. Turn away. He wanted the whole world to turn away from him. She fought the urge, staring straight at him.

His mahogany-colored hair hung loose around his face and shoulders. One side of his face was perfectly untouched save for the severe fury and bitterness that marred it, though some semblance of the handsome face she had dreamed about was still there. But the other side was hideously scarred.

She blinked, swallowed past the tight knot in her throat, then looked upon it. One large scar started in the middle of his brow, slashing its way across his right eye socket. It disappeared beneath a black patch, then curved down to the top of his high cheekbone. Another raised scar began near his ear and arched down to almost touch the corner of his mouth. Smaller scars branched out along the lower scar, turning the side of his face into rivulets of thin white branching scar tissue.

She took a breath, forcing the air down into her lungs. It hurt as the air passed out of her mouth. Her ragged breath sounded loud in the silence. She felt his hot breath on her lips as his one dark eye stared into her face, watching for her reaction. She waited for him to say something, knowing anything she said would send him over the edge.

When he said nothing, only bored through her face with that one black eye, she could stand it no longer. "I'm sorry . . . I had no idea." Instinctively, she reached out to lay her palm against the scarred side of his face.

"I do not need your goddamned pity! I would rather have your hatred." He thrust her aside.

Kelsey fell back against his bed, grabbing one of the posts to keep from falling. Her hair had fallen in her face and she shoved it back, her chest heaving. "Well, you have my hatred, but it's not from seeing your face. And I'll tell you something else, I'm not sorry for you. You deserved what you got for trying to run away with Clarice and for hurting my father! I won't feel sorry for you! I won't!" She turned and bolted through the connecting door.

"Don't break the rules again, or you'll regret it," he bellowed.

She fled into her room, slamming the door, his words ringing in her ears. She fell back against it, panting, her heart pounding against her ribs. Tears flowed freely down her cheeks. Groping in the dark, she found the lock and twisted the key in it, her hands shaking so badly, she could hardly hold the key. She snatched it out of the lock, ran to her bed, then buried her head in her pillow so he couldn't hear her sobs.

It was sometime later that Kelsey heard the yowling at her

door. She'd tried to go to sleep, but it was impossible. She'd heard him throw some sort of fit, crashing things left and right in his room. Finally, he'd settled down. All was silent now, almost too silent. The yowl came again.

She crawled out of bed. Cautiously, she opened the door that led out into the hallway. She heard a hiss, then glanced down to see Brutus. When he saw that she had opened the door, he strode into the room, his orange-ringed tail swishing from side to side.

"Well, hello to you too." She watched him jump up on the bed. He yowled again, rubbing his back against one of the posts.

"You smelled the milk, eh?" Watkins had left her a cup of warm milk to help her sleep, and since she hated warm milk, she'd left it by her bed. She emptied the milk out into the saucer, then set it down on the edge of the bed.

"There. And if you hiss at me, I'll take it away." She crawled back in bed and watched Brutus attack the milk. After he'd finished, he sharpened his claws on the counterpane a few times, then curled up on the end of her mattress. His green eyes watched her as Salford's had done. She knew if she tried to touch him that he would lash out at her just like his master. In a lot of ways they were alike. She fell asleep watching the end of Brutus's tail curling and uncurling.

"Good morning, miss."

Kelsey put her pillow over her head. "Go away, Mary," she grumbled.

"Oh, miss, it's past three in the afternoon. Lord Lovejoy bade me to wake you. He's been waiting all day to talk to you."

Kelsey pulled the pillow off her head. "Do you know what he wants?"

"Don't know, but I think it might be about the master." Mary went to the closet and stepped inside. "And what a row must have gone on in the master's chamber. Never seen such a mess. Porcelain figures smashed. He must have thrown a regular temper tantrum in there last night. It ain't like him a'toll. But Lord knows, I'm lucky to have me job, after yesterday—I am that. Poor Dorkins got the ax. She fainted dead away after seeing the master's face. He came in big as day into the library yesterday, scowling like the devil himself. What a row he caused." She came out of the closet with a blue muslin day dress in her hand. "He had to catch poor Dorkins. She was on a ladder, minding her work when he came in. She fainted dead away. Never seen the like of her. I saw his face, but I didn't faint. Must have been her fainting that caused him to have such a temper. You usually don't even know he's been in a room."

Mary took a breath, and Kelsey said, "Where is he now?"

"Been down at the lake all day. There's a boathouse down there that he sometimes goes to. Watkins seems upset about him, but he don't say nothin' to no one, he just keeps looking out the windows down at the lake. Lord Lovejoy went down, but he came back with a scowl on his face. Something's up, you can bet on that."

Kelsey bit her lip, feeling more than a little responsible for Salford's latest fit. She should never have gone in his room last night. Or was it a good thing? She saw him as he really was, not the rogue who had tried to run away with Clarice and destroyed her father's happiness, not the phantom lover who had plagued her dreams for years, but a scarred madman wallowing in self-pity, doubt, loneliness, and bitterness. He was a man to be pitied.

She regretted blurting out those horrible things to him last night, but she had given in to her anger. It probably pleased him, for he must have known he was goading her into it. He had wanted to push her away, and she let him. But not anymore. Last night the perverse side of her decided never to let him provoke her again. The riotous desire he aroused in her must be controlled. Henceforth she would treat him with complete, utter indifference. Mary's voice brought her back from her thoughts.

"You're not listening, miss. I asked if this ain't the prettiest dress you ever did see." Mary held up a light blue morning dress with dark blue velvet sleeves. She didn't wait for Kelsey's reply, but continued to ramble on. "All these clothes arrived late yesterday. Watkins had me put them in here. All of them are new, and there's fancy silk underclothes to go with it. And I'll fix your hair if you let me. I'm right handy with a comb— you wouldn't know it to look at me own hair, but you got curl in yours, and it could be very pretty."

Kelsey glanced at the dress, in awe of Watkins's efficiency. "I can't work in that dress. I'll ruin it."

"Don't think you'll be getting much work done today. It's just about gone. Anyway, there's two men in there taking down the rest of the plaster and cleaning up. Watkins hired them yesterday. They came bright and early this morn. Not much you can do until they get done. And Lord Lovejoy is waiting on ye in the parlor."

"Oh, then I should be quick about it." Kelsey listened to Mary drone on incessantly about any and everything while she helped her put on a mulberry-colored dress of glacé silk, then plopped Kelsey down in front of a dressing table and went to work on her hair.

When Mary was done, Kelsey stared at her reflection in the mirror. The rich color of the dress brought out the green in her eyes, fitting her body to a T. It made her seem taller, showing off her thin waist and full breasts to advantage. She stared at her face and a stranger looked back at her. The full red lips, large green eyes, the small oval face, were still the same, but her thick black hair that she usually haphazardly pulled back from her face any old way that was convenient—usually a braid—was now swept up on top of her head. Many strands had been left to curl whimsically around her temples, brow, and along her neck, framing her face.

She smiled at Mary's image in the mirror. "Well, Mary, it has taken you forty-five minutes to make me look as if I've been blown about in the wind."

"Ah, miss, you look fetching, you do. Like a right and tight lady, you do. You're beautiful. When Lord Lovejoy gets a look at ye, he'll be drooling."

"Do you think so?" Kelsey asked, her mind not on Lord Lovejoy's good opinion but a certain brooding madman's opinion.

She was still thinking about Salford when she stepped into the library. Jeremy was pacing impatiently before the hearth. He wore a fine tailored yellowish-brown waistcoat, sage-green trousers, with a brown paisley frock coat. A ruby pin winked from his cravat. Kelsey realized he was a tall man, almost as tall as Salford, but not as broad-shouldered. He slapped a pair of gloves against his thigh as he turned to pace in the opposite direction. He noticed her and paused.

"Miss Vallarreal, I'm glad to see you. You must allow me to say you are looking perfectly beautiful this afternoon." He bestowed a warm smile on her, contradicting the worry in his eyes.

"Thank you." Kelsey blushed slightly. "What is this I hear about Salford?"

Jeremy's smile faded. "Such a sad state of affairs. I've never seen Edward like this. Even after the accident he was not this bad. I hate to burden you, but I had hoped perhaps you might try to talk to him. When Watkins told me he'd been down there all night, I went to talk to him, but I couldn't convince him to come up to the house with me. Watkins said you might have some influence over him. You're my last resort. I know it is an awful imposition."

"Watkins has far too much confidence in me. I don't know how much influence I might have over him, but I would be glad to speak to him," Kelsey said, growing worried.

"I'll accompany you, of course."

"No need. I think I might do better alone with him."

"I thought perhaps I should be with you if you should happen to see his face."

"I've seen it." Kelsey suppressed a grimace.

"Oh . . ." Jeremy frowned down at the gloves in his hands,

shaking his head. "Terrible thing, that. He used to be so different before the accident. It's such a pity."

"Yes, but save your pity, he pities himself far too much. He's been spoiled by it, I think. What he needs is a good kick in the rear. Now, if you'll excuse me, I'll go see he gets one."

Jeremy watched her flounce out of the room, his expression going from worry to amusement, then back to worry again.

The lake was picturesque. The sunlight created thousands of blue diamonds along the surface. Weeping willows swayed near the bank, the slender fronds dangling at the water's edge. Butterflies fluttered about a row of daffodils that circled the lake. A small island rose up in the center. In the middle stood a gazebo, masses of trailing roses curling along the white columns, showering the gazebo with red sprays of vivid color. The benches in the gazebo looked deserted.

She glanced to the lake's opposite shore. Amid green cropped grass and more daffodils stood a small white building that looked like a boathouse. Salford was probably there, sequestered behind the privacy of the walls, drowning in his sorrow. After seeing his face, she understood his torment. She could even sympathize with him, but until he moved past the self-pity and anger, he would never gain the self-esteem he'd lost. He would live his whole life in misery, hiding from the world in a prison he'd created for himself. Her worst enemy—if she had one—didn't deserve such a fate. She decided to try to help him. Someone needed to.

With her resolve firmly in place, she started to walk around the lake to the boathouse, but a small rowboat near the bank caught her eye. It looked pleasantly inviting. Not wanting to soil her new clothes, she took off her shoes and silk hose, then pulled her dress and petticoat up between her legs. She secured them around her hips with the sash of her dress, making a loose pair of trousers, a trick she'd learned when she was little and her mother made her wear dresses. She pushed the boat out into the water, feeling the mud on the lake's bottom squish between her toes, then she climbed inside.

Soft ripples trailed behind her as she rowed across the water. The few clouds overhead swiped the blue sky with thin, almost transparent streaks of white, as if an artist had painted them there with white watercolor. The mossy scent of the water, the peaceful swish of the oars, followed her across the lake to the opposite shore.

When she neared the boathouse, she rowed toward shore. She stowed the oars, glided up onto the bank, then hopped over the side of the boat. The grass felt like velvet against the soles of her feet as she strode toward the boathouse. When she stood at the entrance, she opened the door and scanned the inside. It was perfectly plain, with wooden benches along one side. The back of it opened out onto the lake. A rowboat was docked inside, making a lapping noise as it rocked in the water. Several pigeons cooed softly from the wooden eaves overhead.

She turned, thinking Salford wasn't there, but she heard a thump, then a curse from the rowboat. She turned back around, walked past the benches, along the pier that jutted out from them, then leaned over and stared down into the boat.

Salford was there, a bottle of whiskey in one hand, while his other arm hugged an oar to his side. He was lying on his left side. His head was propped against the starboard seat, his hair, loose, falling over the good side of his face. He wore the same shirt and pants he'd had on the night before. He was so still, she thought he might be asleep, but he raised the almost-empty bottle to his lips and took a swallow.

"You look very uncomfortable," she said, crossing her arms over her chest.

He didn't flinch, didn't even bother looking at her, only set the bottle back down on his hip, some of it sloshing down into the bottom of the boat. "Get the hell out of here."

"If you want to feel sorry for yourself," she said, ignoring his command, "you should do it in a more comfortable place, perhaps in bed with your whore. I know that's where my father likes to do most of his bemoaning and drinking."

"You never cease to amaze me with what comes out of your mouth."

"I see nothing wrong with honesty."

"Bluntness is more like it." He thrust the oar he was holding aside as if it were bothering him.

"All right, bluntness. Let me be more blunt. If you wish to make a fool of yourself, it would be less trying for your cousin if you would come inside and go to your own bed—though I don't know why he should care a fig about you, the way you've behaved in this depraved manner. I am willing to try and patch things up with your paramour, perhaps she will join you there."

"You would fetch my whore for me and make sure my bed is warmed? Your thoughtfulness knows no bounds."

"You can save your snide remarks. I was only trying to do you a favor, since having her with you might brighten your outlook—it always does my father. And since I heard you bawling at her last night, I thought I'd try to make amends for you, but if you prefer to wallow around in the bottom of a boat like a drunken fish, then I'll leave you to it." Kelsey turned, walking back along the pier.

"Wait."

"Wait for what?" she said, pausing, her hand on the door that led outside.

"Wait for me. Help me up and I'll go with you."

Kelsey turned, casting a surprised glance at him. He sat up, causing the boat to rock in the water. He grabbed the sides, waited for it to grow still, then brushed back the long hair hanging down on his forehead, exposing a widow's peak in the middle of his forehead that added a certain sinister look to his already scarred face. She hadn't noticed the widow's peak the night before.

He glanced up at her. Their gazes locked.

He stared at her as if seeing her for the first time. His gaze slowly raked her from her new coiffure all the way down to her bare toes. "You look charming with your dress tucked up between your legs. You surprise me, you have shapely flesh on those short little legs of yours. Did you wear your dress that way to tease me and lure me out of the boathouse?" He raised a dark, satirical brow at her. "I'll warn you now, I tend to forget I'm a gentleman when I'm teased by such womanly wiles."

She had forgotten her dress was tucked up between her legs. Her cheeks burned as she jerked the hem of her dress down in a huff. She slapped at the wrinkled folds, wishing it were his face. Her pride was still stinging from that comment about her short legs as she glared at him and said, "You know I wore it this way to keep it from getting wet."

"That's too bad, I had hoped otherwise." His gaze lingered on her breasts now, glinting with a sensual hunger that seemed to eat right through her clothes.

She crossed her arms over her chest, feeling her traitorous body responding to his gaze as if he were actually touching her. She gazed at his mouth, wanting to slap it even as she wondered what it would feel like to have him kiss her again.

One side of his lips quirked in a grin, as though he knew what she was thinking. Kelsey felt her face burn down to her neck.

His grin quickly faded, the severe mask back as he held out his hand. "Well? Are you going to stand there all day, or will you help me?"

She glanced at his proffered hand for a moment, the long slender fingers, the wide-open palm. He would know he unnerved her if she refused to touch him. If she was going to try to help him gain his self-esteem back, she must somehow hide her physical attraction to him, or he'd find a way to use it to his advantage. She walked toward him, armored with a resolve of indifference.

She slipped her hand into his. His fingers tightened around her hand. She recalled an earlier time when their palms had touched. He had held her arms pinned against her chamber door, while he sucked her breasts and had done wicked things to her with his hands. She fought the urge to snatch her hand back.

He clutched her hand, using it for support as he stood, never taking his gaze from her face. She strained against his weight, feeling his fingers tighten over her's, the roughness of his skin slick against her sweaty palm.

"You'll have to pull harder." He made a move to step out of the boat.

She grabbed his hand with both of hers and yanked.

The boat teetered. She ground her heels against the planks of the pier, but it was too late. He wouldn't let go of her hand. She caught a glimpse of the wicked grin on his face as he fell backward and she tumbled in behind him.

Eight

The water was only waist high, Kelsey realized as she swam beneath the piling of the boathouse then surfaced. Salford still wouldn't let go of her hand. He broke the surface when she did.

She tried to jerk her hand back, but couldn't. She started to order him to let go but succeeded only in choking down the water in her mouth. With her free hand she pushed aside the hair sagging in her face and glared at him.

"You did that on purpose!" she blurted out. "Of all the hateful, belligerent, insufferable, irritating—"

He grabbed her and kissed her, cutting off her tirade. The kiss crushed her lips against her teeth with punishing intensity. She beat on his chest, but only hurt her hands. He squeezed her tighter, until she couldn't breathe. She stopped fighting him, knowing it was useless.

His lips softened. All she could think about was the warmth of his mouth, the feel of his tongue running along her lips, the wet warmth of his face melding with the wetness of her own flesh. Her lips parted, and his tongue plunged inside. She tasted the bittersweet flavor of whiskey in his mouth. Her arms wrapped around his neck, and she grabbed a handful of his hair, pushing his face closer to her, urging him onward. Every part of her came alive, crying out for his touch.

He rubbed his hands up and down her spine, then cupped her buttocks and pulled her closer. His fingers kneaded her bottom while he deepened the kiss. She felt his erection through her wet clothes, the thick, hard shaft pressing against her abdomen. Moving lower . . . achingly slow . . . pressing against the tender flesh between her legs.

Her muscles tensed in her belly as the yearning grew unbearable between her thighs. Those wicked throbbings he'd awakened deep inside her seemed to have a mind of their own. She felt her hips stirring against his erection.

He growled deep in his throat, then suddenly stiffened as if he'd gained control of his passion. He pulled back from her and glared down at her, drops of water falling off his chin, the patch over his eye making him look like an avenging pirate.

"I warned you about breaking the rules, now I've shown you. I don't need you interfering in my life, especially where my bed is concerned—unless, of course, you wish to warm it with your own body. Not that there's much to it. . . ." His gaze roamed lazily over her. "And you're not blonde. As you know, I prefer blondes."

"I did not know you had preferences. I thought anything with two legs and a skirt would do for you," she said, her tone as snide as his.

"You may be right there." He raked her body with his gaze again, then sneered at her before he shoved past her and waded to shore. He called over his shoulder, "And keep your damned dress around your ankles, where it belongs—unless, of course, you mean to take if off, but I suppose you do that only for your lover."

"I certainly wouldn't do it for you," she said, shaking her fist at his back.

He ignored her as he stalked up the shore, leaving a trail of water and his footprints behind on the muddy bank.

"Oooo! Hateful, hateful man!" She smacked the surface of the water with her open palms, then grimaced when it stung.

She rubbed her stinging flesh with her thumb and watched him walk off. She wanted to look away, but the predatory grace of his stride held her gaze. He strode through the middle of a row of daffodils, his wet shirt clinging to his stiff back and broad shoulders, dipping inward at his waist. His dark pants stuck to his slim hips, his powerful thighs rippling as he walked. Something soft brushed against the side of her ankle, making her aware that she was still in the lake, watching him like a simpleton.

She trudged to shore, echoing his words under her breath. ". . . Unless, of course, you wish to warm it with your own body. Not that there's much to it. As you know I prefer blondes." She knew she wasn't remaining indifferent. How could she remain dispassionate with someone she wanted to kick in the backside?

Forgetting she had on a dress, she tried to climb the bank without lifting the hem of her skirt. She tripped and fell forward on the muddy bank. She wiped the mud out of her eyes, then noticed her face had landed right in Salford's muddy bootprint. She ground her teeth together, tasting the gritty mud, then beat the ground with her fists.

Edward strode up the path and saw Jeremy leaning against the trunk of a tree, puffing on a cheroot, obviously waiting there for someone.

Jeremy glanced up at the sound of Edward's approaching footsteps. He casually tossed the cheroot away, ground it out with his boot, then his gaze roamed over Edward's dripping clothes and face. The worry that had been in his eyes was instantly replaced by a wide, amused grin.

"Don't you have some skirt to chase?" Edward said, pausing in front of him.

"I'm chasing one now." A determined glint lit Jeremy's eyes. "I was waiting for Miss Vallarreal in case she needed me, but I see it was you who needed help."

"Stay away from her." Edward's fists tightened at his sides.

"I thought you had no claim on her."

"I don't."

"Then you cannot object to me paying court to her."

"But I do object—" Before Edward knew it, he drew back his fist then slammed it into Jeremy's face. He regretted the moment his knuckles connected. It was a hard punch, one Jeremy didn't see coming.

Jeremy fell back a step, clutching his bleeding nose, his hazel eyes blazing with bemusement. "That wasn't very sporting of you, Eddie."

"I don't feel very sporting, or indulgent. Stay away from her!" Edward stepped past him and started toward the castle.

"You can't say that and walk away." He grabbed Edward's arm, swung him around, then slammed his fist into Edward's ribs.

Edward braced his feet, taking the punch, then stared at Jeremy as if he hadn't been hit. "All right, I deserved that one. We are even now, let us leave it at that."

"I see you still have an iron gut," Jeremy said, shaking his fist, an amused gameness twinkling in his eye. He raised both fists, taking up a boxing stance. "I'd like to soften it up a bit for you."

"I don't want to fight you."

"Then you shouldn't have thrown the first punch, old boy. And since you have thrown down the gauntlet and I have no wish to meet you at dawn, we had better have it out right here." Jeremy came at him with a swift right.

Edward ducked.

Jeremy did some fancy footwork and moved back. "You're getting slow. You used to be a lot faster when we were younger. All this sedentary brooding finally made you soft?"

"Not as soft as you think . . ." Edward faked left, then followed with his right, hitting Jeremy's jaw, but not with the full force of his strength.

Jeremy fell backward, surprise in his eyes, then he dodged to the left and came across with a right.

Edward saw the fist coming and ducked.

"What are you two doing? Stop it this instant!"

At the sound of Kelsey's voice, Edward looked over at her. He caught a fleeting glimpse of her mud-covered face, her flashing emerald eyes, before Jeremy hit him in the eye. Edward swayed on his feet, waiting for his vision to clear.

Jeremy lunged.

They fell to the ground. Edward blocked a right, then hit Jeremy in the ribs, hearing the crack beneath his knuckles. Jeremy groaned, then doubled over as he rolled off Edward. Edward fell back on the ground and closed his eyes, catching his breath.

To his surprise, Kelsey knelt down beside him. She leaned over him and laid her palm against his scarred cheek. "Are you all right?"

He was so surprised by her reaction that he didn't answer her right away. Not even Samantha had ever touched his scars. She touched every other part of him, but she made it a point to avoid his scars. Kelsey didn't seem to mind. He reveled in the feel of her warm, soft skin against his scarred flesh.

"Oh, God! Are you breathing . . ." She leaned farther over him, then laid the side of her face against his chest, listening for his heartbeat.

He felt her breasts against his arm, felt her face and lips pressed close to his heart. His muscles clenched, his breathing became ragged. Visions of her naked, those shapely white legs wrapped around his hips, made him instantly hard. The vision disappeared when he felt her draw back. He started to reach for her, but Jeremy groaned like a felled bear beside him. Edward cursed inwardly, wishing he were alone with Kelsey.

He opened his eyes. She looked charmingly disheveled with smudges of mud on her face, her coal-black hair falling down over her shoulders in wet strands. She was staring at him, behind long, dark, spiked lashes. Her large eyes gleamed like liquid emeralds behind a thick layer of tears. The sight of those tears made him reach out and grasp her hand.

"Were you frightened for me?" he asked, unable to suppress a grin.

"Certainly not! After the way you've behaved, who could worry over you?" Kelsey jerked her hand out of his as if his touch had burned her.

"I say, I feel ill used," Jeremy said, a hint of jealousy in his voice. "I'm just as wounded as my cousin here."

She appeared surprised by the sound of Jeremy's voice, as if she'd forgotten he was there too. She glanced over her shoulder at Jeremy, who had landed spread-eagle in the grass. Blood oozed from his nose, and one of his eyes had swollen and turned purple. He held out his hand so Kelsey would take it.

"Tend your own wounds—both of you!" She slapped Jeremy's hand, then scrambled to her feet. "Next time I'll leave you two to kill each other! I own, you both deserve to be put to bed with a shovel." She turned and flounced down the path toward the castle, blades of grass sticking to the hem of her wet dress.

Edward couldn't suppress a grin as he sat up, watching the sensuous sway of her rounded hips. She wasn't voluptuously molded as he liked his women to be, but she had enough luscious curves on that petite body to tempt any man. Including her lover. His grin faded.

"I'd say the lady was angry," Jeremy remarked.

"Really, I hadn't noticed a change in her."

"She's not like that around me, thank God. It must be you, Eddie, but you always did bring out the best in women." Jeremy grinned until he rolled on his side, then he groaned and clutched his ribs. "By Jove, you've cracked my bloody rib."

"Nothing more than you deserved." Edward got to his feet, then helped Jeremy stand.

"It is not my fault you looked at her when I hit you." Jeremy smiled innocently, then grimaced when he tried to take a step. "We are even now."

"Yes, we are even." Edward grinned, then tasted blood in his mouth. He winced as he wiped a trickle of blood off his lip with the back of his hand.

"I think we should find Miss Vallarreal." Jeremy took a step, swaying on his feet, clutching his middle.

Edward frowned over at Jeremy, then put his arm around Jeremy's waist to support him. "I think you had better lean on me and forget about running after Miss Vallarreal's skirt for the moment."

"You might be right there." Jeremy was silent for a moment and appeared busy concentrating on putting one foot in front of the other. Then he said, "What did we just do? Hell, I like a round of fisticuffs as much as the next fellow, but we cannot do this every time I mention her name. You cannot be this unreasonable. We have to settle this here and now and be done with it. I'm in earnest when I tell you I have every intention of courting her properly. I give you my word of honor that I have no intentions of seducing her. Dammit, Eddie, I need to know here and now if you want her."

"If you are as serious as you sound"—Edward paused, forcing the next words out—"then take her, but if you hurt her—"

"I won't. This is different. I've never felt this way about a woman."

Edward glanced down at the front of his shirt. The muddy impression of Kelsey's cheek was still there, over his heart, where she'd listened to see if he was still alive. He frowned down at the spot, seeing the tears in her eyes again, hearing Jeremy's words echoing in his own ears, *I've never felt this way about a woman . . .*

The image of Salford's smug, sardonic grin materialized in Kelsey's mind as she stomped up the path. He'd laid there like an oaf, letting her believe he was hurt. To think she'd almost shed tears over him after he'd dunked her in the lake on purpose! Oh, yes, he'd insulted her too with that comment about her inferior body. She should have kicked him. How would she ever face him again?

Adding misery to her indignation, Kelsey felt her wet silk drawers and petticoat sticking to her bottom. The mud on her face was starting to dry and itch. She stormed up the path that led past the garden and stables and would eventually take her to the servants' entrance at the back of the castle.

The path narrowed slightly as she came to an ancient row of boxwoods that bordered the garden. She had seen the beautifully groomed garden from the window in her new chamber. Typically English, the garden had an intricate maze made of neat towering hedges. Two fountains, bordered by multicolored flowers, filled each end of the maze.

Feminine laughter cackled from the other side of the tall hedge, then grew convulsive, as if the person couldn't control her mirth. Salford's blond paramour must be laughing at her again. She'd taken all she could stand from this woman. She locked her shoulders, clenched her fists, then her feet pounded the ground as she stalked the sound. She felt like scratching the woman's eyes out, but she'd settle for giving her a piece of her mind.

It didn't take long to find an opening in the hedge. She ducked inside the maze, listening intently to the throaty laughter. She took first one turn, then another, growing angrier by the moment. Closer now, she was almost upon the woman. Kelsey ran now, down another long lane of hedges. . . .

Abruptly, the laughter stopped. The woman must have heard Kelsey's approaching footsteps.

She gave up the pretense of a surprise attack and said, "I know you're there, so you might as well come out and face me." Kelsey tried to peer through the hedge, but it was so dense she couldn't see through it. "We need to have a chat about your sense of humor."

No answer.

"Going to be shy, are you? It's a little late for that, don't you think?" Kelsey ran down the end of the hedge as she spoke.

The woman's retreating footsteps were nearby, but not as close as Kelsey thought. She paused and listened. The sound growing fainter . . . fainter . . . until she was left in total silence.

She glanced up at the tall wall-like hedges towering on either side of her, then she realized that blond witch had made a fool of her again.

She had no idea how to get out of the maze.

Six hours later, Edward and Jeremy sat in the dining hall, staring down into their glasses of port, neither speaking, which was unusual for Jeremy. Edward had seen his cousin silent only once before in his life, when he was twenty and thought himself in love with a widow ten years his senior. That was quickly dispelled after he walked into her London town house unannounced and found her making love to another man. Jeremy's silence could mean only that he was pining over a woman. Kelsey.

The thought made Edward tip up his glass. He set the empty goblet down so hard, the stem broke. Edward stared down at the broken stem in his hand, then at the thin stream of blood trickling down his palm.

Jeremy glanced over at him, then nonchalantly pulled a handkerchief from his pocket. "Better take care of that, here . . ." He tossed the handkerchief to Edward, looking as if his mind was on Kelsey, not on Edward's cut.

Edward wrapped the linen around his hand, tying it as he spoke. "You needn't act so concerned."

"Sorry." Jeremy looked over at Edward with his full attention now.

When Jeremy stared at him for what seemed like hours, saying nothing, Edward broke the silence. "Do you mean to stare the blood away?"

"I'm just wondering what has you in such a surly humor?"

"I'm not surly."

"What would you call it then, cheerful?" Jeremy grinned, then glanced at Edward's hand. "Any more cheer from you and you might have cut off a finger."

"I would rather bleed to death than sit and watch you moon over Miss Vallarreal."

"So that's it." Jeremy took a sip of port, then eyed Edward over the top of the glass. "You do not want her, but you do not want me to have her either. Well, you cannot have it both ways, old boy. You cannot hoard the cheese and not expect the rats to come around." Jeremy smiled now, a white-toothed grin.

Edward had known Jeremy long enough to recognize he was being cleverly goaded, so he leaned indifferently back in the chair, stretched his long legs out in front of him, resting his hands behind his head. He said casually, "I do not want her. Like I said earlier, go to it."

"Are you sure?" Jeremy looked skeptically amused as he tapped the top of his glass with his index finger. "I am not blind. I have been thinking about the way she reacted toward you today. She did not know I was alive—"

"She was distraught at the violence." Edward glanced down at the spot over his heart where she had laid her cheek. He felt his chest tighten.

"It didn't look that way to me." Jeremy's golden brows rose to meet his hairline.

"Well, that is all it was." Edward realized he'd added too much emphasis to his words.

"All you have to do is say the word, and I'll give way."

Edward looked askance at him. "Aren't you being a bit premature? You talk as if she is already in love with you."

"I know you said she loves someone else, but I am sure I can persuade her to forget him."

"I find that highly amusing since she'll not speak to you at the moment."

"She's just brooding in her room. I can't blame her. We really shouldn't have acted like such brutes earlier. She'll get over it before we do." Jeremy frowned down at his ribs. "Anyway, I don't feel all that slighted. I'm not the only one she is not receiving. She has not answered the door for Watkins either. He tried to take in a tea tray for her, but she would have none of it."

Edward remembered how he'd stayed in his room all afternoon listening for a sound of her in the chamber next to his, but he'd heard nothing. A nagging feeling clawed at him as he said, "I'll have Watkins open her door." He stood to ring the bellpull. His hand paused on the cord when he heard Watkins's voice out in the hall.

"You cannot go in there. His grace is dining."

"I'll go where I bloody well please! Now, where is he?" Edward recognized the man who appeared in the doorway. It was Kelsey's lover, McGregor's son. McGregor stood there, his chest heaving, his fists clenched, a hostile set to his square jaw. When his gaze landed on Edward's face, his jaw slackened. His expression went from disbelief to stricken, then to amazement.

Watkins appeared behind McGregor, his mouth unusually pinched. "I'm sorry, your grace, I tried to tell this gentleman you were dining, but he insisted he see you—"

"It is all right, Watkins," Edward said without taking his eyes off Kelsey's lover. He wanted to wrap his hands around the young man's neck, not because of his blatant disgust at the hideous face before him, but because he'd used Kelsey's body and she let him. McGregor had probably never received a slap from her. His hands shook as he forced them to stay at his sides.

"I'm standing before you, man, what do you want?" he asked.

McGregor clamped his jaw together, moved his lips one over the other, then strode into the room. "Where is Kelsey? What have you done with her? She was supposed to come by the house, but she didn't show. She always keeps her word."

"Who are you?" Jeremy demanded before Edward could

speak. He stood up, clutching his ribs, then stepped up to McGregor until they were nose to nose.

"I'm Griffin McGregor, Kelsey's friend, that's who. Who are you?" McGregor didn't back away.

"I am Lord Lovejoy," Jeremy said, "*also* Miss Vallarreal's friend."

If he hadn't been worried about her, Edward might have enjoyed watching these two lovesick calves come to blows over Kelsey, but he stepped between them. "Look here, McGregor," he said, using his most intimidating tone, "I was just going to send Watkins to check on Miss Vallarreal. She has been in her room all afternoon and not answering her door."

"That don't sound like her," McGregor said. "Kelsey ain't one for broodin'. She usually shrieks at you when she's mad, then she forgets about it."

"I'll go check on her, your grace."

"No, Watkins, I shall go." Edward knew he'd get to her room quicker than Watkins. "Jeremy, you will be so kind as to show McGregor into the library and wait for me there."

Edward didn't wait for a reply, but hurried to Kelsey's room. He tried the door, expecting it to be locked, but he was surprised when the knob turned in his hand. He thrust open the door and peered inside the room. A dim beam of light from the hallway sconces met the dark interior of the room. It afforded enough light that he could see the empty bed, still made, not a wrinkle in the counterpane, as if she hadn't even sat on it.

He slammed the door and was out of breath by the time he reached the library. He found Jeremy and McGregor in a heated argument as they stood at either end of the hearth.

"By the looks of your face and the high-and-mighty one's fat lip, I'd say you did something to her and she had to protect herself."

"I told you, we had a round of fisticuffs earlier!"

"Don't look that way to me. If something's happened to her, I swear, gentlemen or not, I'll have your blood on this one."

"How do we know you did not hurt her? You had as much opportunity," Jeremy said, the patience in his voice long gone.

"She is not there." Edward strode into the room and stood between them.

"My God, where could she be?" Jeremy started to pace.

"I suggest we start a search. McGregor, you check her father's cottage in the village. She might have gone there."

"Aye, aye, I'll do that." McGregor bobbed his head.

"If you find her, send word back here."

"Aye, I will." After a hostile glance at Jeremy, then at Edward, McGregor quit the room.

Edward turned to Jeremy. "Come with me. You can search the east side of the property, I'll take the west."

"Your grace." Watkins appeared in the library door, his usually stately air marred by a grimace.

"Yes, Watkins."

"I spoke with one of the maids, your grace. She said that Miss Kelsey did not come back into the castle this afternoon when she went down the lake. She said she waited for her in her chamber in case she needed attention, but she never entered her chamber."

"She had to disappear between here and the lake. I saw her go up the path." Edward spoke his thoughts aloud.

"There is one other thing, your grace."

"What?" Edward asked impatiently.

"I spoke with the undergardener. He said he saw Miss Lizzy run out of the maze this afternoon." He paused, then added, "And she was grinning, your grace."

Edward felt his gut clench as he turned to Jeremy. "Check Lizzy's room and see if you can find her. If I find her, I will not be responsible for what I do to her."

"All right, I will look for her," Jeremy said, not sounding enthusiastic. "If I find her, do I have your permission to take a strap to her?"

"Yes, by all means. I'll search the garden while you're looking for her."

"Good luck, your grace—Lord Lovejoy." Watkins frowned at the backs of both men as they left the room, the worry never leaving his faded eyes.

Kelsey was having a nightmare. Salford was in it, so was his blond paramour. They had bound her and left her in the ball-room, to be haunted by the duchess's ghost. The duchess's spirit sat atop the chandelier, laughing, plucking off the chandelier's crystals and throwing them at Kelsey. The only part of her body not covered by the crystals was her face. She couldn't move, could barely breathe with the weight of the crystals on top of her. Salford and the blonde's laughter mixed with the ghost's, growing louder and louder. . . .

"Kelsey!"

She opened her eyes at the sound of her name. Disoriented, she stared up at the stars in the sky, then at the dark shadows around her. Tall, looming shadows. She glanced down at the iron bench she was stretched out on, saw no glass crystals on top of her, then remembered that she'd been lost in the maze.

"Kelsey!" The frantic bellow came again.

"Lord Salford?" Kelsey called to him as she sat up.

"Keep talking so I can find you. And my name is Edward, use it."

"All right, *Edward,*" Kelsey said, hating the name on her lips. "I'm near a fountain. I can't tell which one. I got lost in here. When I couldn't find my way out or climb out, I fell asleep. It wasn't very comfortable." Kelsey rubbed her aching shoulders as she continued to talk. "I want you to know something, Lor—" She caught herself and said, "Edward. If I get my hands on that paramour of yours, I intend to do her a harm. She lured me in here on purpose. If—" Her mouth was still open as she felt him sweep her up into his strong embrace.

He kissed her soundly. Then she felt Salford's shoulders shaking as if he were laughing at her. She wedged her hands between them, pushed on his chest, finally breaking the kiss. She raised her hand to slap him, but he caught it.

"Not this time," he said, squeezing her fingers tightly as she tried to pull out of his grasp.

The moon was behind him, casting his towering form into brawny shadows and hard planes. She couldn't see his face clearly, but she knew he was smiling.

"How dare you laugh at me!" She tried to squirm out of his grasp, but his arm clamped tighter around her.

"I am not laughing at you, but at what you said about my paramour," he said, straining to keep his voice from breaking.

"You may find it funny, but had it been you stuck out here all afternoon, you wouldn't find the mirth in it."

"It wasn't my paramour that lured you out here."

"It wasn't?" Kelsey stopped struggling in his arms.

"No, she hasn't been here since the night you fell into my chamber."

"Then who was that woman I heard laughing in here?"

"That was Lizzy."

"Lizzy?"

"Yes, she's my younger sister."

"Oh," Kelsey said, a degree of anger leaving her voice. "Why have I not met her?"

"I can never find the little hellion to introduce you to her— probably for the better. Lizzy takes some getting used to."

"I see." Kelsey was silent a moment, then she asked, "Is she the one who tore up my sketches and my clothes?"

"Yes."

"So you're not really insane?" The warmth rose in her cheeks when she remembered what she'd said to him about being mad.

"Did you really think I was?" Gently, he brushed the hair away from her cheeks, then tilted her face up so she'd have to look at him.

The roughness of his warm palms against the soft skin on her cheeks sent waves of sultry sensations down her neck. Her voice wavered as she asked, "Do you want my honest opinion?"

"I did not think your scruples capable of anything but honesty," he said softly, his mouth inches from hers.

"You're right, of course." She grinned tremulously, feeling his hot breath brushing against her mouth, his callused thumb rubbing along the edge of her jaw. "I did think you were mad."

"And you, Kelsey, are you quite sane?"

"I was sure of it until I came to stay in your home."

He threw back his head and laughed. The freeness of the deep, vibrant sound went straight to Kelsey's heart, warming her all over.

"Tell me," he said, sobering, "was the display you made today when you found my cousin and me in a round of fisticuffs part of your newfound insanity?"

"Do you mean the way I made a complete fool of myself by running to your side and shedding tears over you?"

"Yes." He bent his head closer and whispered near her lips, "But I would not call it foolish."

"No? I suppose you're right. It's no more foolish than the way you keep kissing me every time you're near me." Her breasts quivered against his rigid chest. Her voice was soft, ragged with emotion as she said, "Wouldn't you agree, it's a fair assumption to say we are both very foolish . . . or very mad."

He started to kiss her but veered away at the last moment, crushing her tightly to his chest, hugging her. She felt him bury his hands in the raven curls that hung loose down her back. His strong arms encompassed her with a strange kind of possessiveness she'd never known or felt before—even his kisses had seemed tame compared to its power. She felt his whole body trembling, as if he were fighting his feelings for her with every fiber of his being.

Afraid for the closeness to end, she returned his embrace, clinging to him, burying her face in the fine linen of his shirt. He laid his lips against the top of her forehead as they swayed on their feet, neither of them speaking. It felt so right to be in his arms. So familiar. Like she belonged there. As if to seal her destiny, a nightingale cooed somewhere in the garden and its mate answered.

Lost in the sounds of the night, the warmth of him, Kelsey didn't hear the approaching footsteps.

Nine

"Am I disturbing something?" Unfamiliar irritation rang in Jeremy's voice. "I could not find Lizzy, so I came to see if you had any luck. It looks as if you were more successful than I."

Instantly, Edward dropped his arms, then stepped back from Kelsey. She bemoaned the loss of his closeness and glanced over at Jeremy. Like Edward, his face was hidden in shadows. She couldn't see his expression, but she could feel the sudden tension emanating between the two men.

When a long silence followed, neither of them speaking, she tried to lighten the moment. "You weren't disturbing a thing, Jeremy. I don't know what got into me. When Edward found me, I had been asleep. I felt disoriented for a moment and he gave me his arm."

Edward turned, glancing at her. His face was in the moonlight now, a "that's a blatant lie" expression clearly written on his face. A cynical smirk curled up one side of his mouth.

She quickly glanced down at her feet, wondering if she would go to hell for all the lies she's told since she came to Stillmore.

"I'll leave you to show her the way back to the house," Edward said with cold reserve, then he turned and strode down a path of boxwoods.

"Wait!" Kelsey called after him.

He turned. "What is it?"

What was it? She couldn't tell him she wanted to run to him, to cling to him, to feel his arms around her again. Instead, she asked, "Will you not walk with us?"

"No." His reply hung in the air, cold and aloof, cloaked in a wall of reserve.

What had caused this sudden barrier of coldness in him? Puzzled, she watched him turn around, then she followed the primitive sway of his broad shoulders in the moonlight as he disappeared into the shadows of the hedges.

"I can see you safely through the maze," Jeremy said, his wounded pride coming through in his voice. "I played in here as a boy. I know it as well as Edward."

"I'm sure you do." Kelsey tried not to sound disappointed as she accepted Jeremy's arm.

For a moment neither of them spoke as they walked through the maze. She listened to the crickets' night song humming beneath the hedges, a lonely hollow trill that seemed to echo how she felt at the moment.

He broke the silence. "May I ask you something personal, Kelsey?"

"Of course."

"Who is this Griffin McGregor to you?"

"Griffin . . . oh, no!" She tapped the side of her head with the edge of her palm. "He must be worried. I forgot that I was supposed to visit him."

"He came here looking for you."

"I suppose he was worried."

"Yes."

She rolled her eyes heavenward, shaking her head. "His whole family will be worried. I really have to go to them and assure them I'm unharmed."

"I sent one of the servants to do that."

"Oh." She couldn't keep the disappointment out of her voice. She needed to be someplace where she felt completely at ease, away from Edward, so she could sort out her feelings for him.

"Are you and Mr. McGregor"—he cleared his throat—"friends?"

"Are you asking me if I love him?" She was unable to suppress a smile.

"Well, yes." He guided her out of the maze, then they started across the lawn toward the castle.

"I thought so. And to answer your question, yes, I love him." She felt the muscles in Jeremy's arm tense, and she quickly added, "I love him as a friend. We've always been friends. Nothing more."

"I see." He sounded relieved.

"Now I must tell you something of a personal nature."

"You can tell me anything."

"I hope that you were not asking about Griffin because you harbor some feelings for me. I must be completely honest with you and tell you, I'm not looking for a romantic attachment. I have decided never to marry."

"I hope that you would not dismiss all of us out of hand," he said, a hint of amusement in his voice. He covered her hand with his, pressing her fingers against his forearm. "I would beg you not to judge all our kind by Edward."

She marveled at the lack of sensation she experienced from Jeremy's touch. It was nothing like she felt when Edward touched her. "I assure you, I made that decision long before I came here and met Edward."

"Then it is up to me to change your mind." He didn't sound at all daunted.

"I implore you not to try."

"Would it distress you if I did?"

"You are the most likable man I've ever met, but I wouldn't want to encourage you."

"Too late, I was encouraged when I first met you." He squeezed her fingers gently.

The seriousness in his voice disturbed her. She was glad when they reached the veranda at the back of the castle. "Thank you for escorting me." She gently pulled her hand from beneath his. "I can find my way now."

"Good night," he said as he walked over to the edge of the veranda and sat down. "I think I shall stay out here for a while."

"All right. Good night." She watched him pull a cheroot out of his pocket, then she turned and glanced through the glass doors for some sign of Edward. He was nowhere in sight. She desperately needed a glimpse of him.

The candlelight flickered across Kelsey's hand as she moved the quill across the page with quick, precise strokes, shading in the shadows of her drawing. She stared down at the sketch of Edward when she'd found him down by the lake, lying in the boat. Frowning critically at the page, she set the quill down on the nightstand by the bed, then thumbed through her previous sketches: Edward kissing her, Edward wading through the water, a close image of just his mouth, a sardonic grin twisting one side of it, his handsome profile, the curving, long, dark lashes and strong jaw. On the opposite side of the page, his scarred profile with the patch over one eye. Lastly, an angry Edward, his thick, dark brows meeting in the middle of his forehead, his jaw tensed, his lips stretched taut over his teeth.

Kelsey sighed deeply, then set the sketch pad aside. She had tried to work on an idea for the ballroom wall, but the myriad sketches of Edward were all she had to show for hours of work. For the hundredth time that night, she glanced toward the connecting door and held her breath, listening for a sound from his room.

It was as silent as a mausoleum.

She glanced at the mantel clock. It was close to eleven. She wondered if he had retired for the evening. Jeremy had knocked on her door earlier and begged her to play a game of two-partner whist, but she hadn't felt much like playing cards—especially with him. If Edward had asked her, she would have played, but he was ignoring her, isolating himself behind the same wall of icy reserve he had erected when they'd first met. She knew he was trying to push her away because, like her, he had felt something happen between them in the maze, during that magical moment when they'd embraced.

Putting a name to what happened frightened her. Not in her wildest imaginings had she ever dreamed she could grow to care about a man whom she had hated for years. But it had happened. *God help her, it had happened!* Denying it would be ludicrous. Perhaps it was his loneliness that reached out to her. Whatever it was, it wasn't pity, as she had first thought. No, it was something much deeper. Something she should try to forget.

She stopped twisting her hair around her finger, then rose from the bed. She checked the locks before she blew out the candle. Now that she knew Lizzy was the one playing mischievous pranks, she didn't want her paying a visit in the middle of the night. She crawled back into bed and pulled the covers over her head, hoping Edward wouldn't invade her dreams.

Before she fully fell into a deep sleep, something much worse plagued her. The muffled creak of the floorboards beneath the rug brought her fully awake, making her keenly aware that she was not alone in the room.

Her eyes flew open. The figure was at the end of her bed. Hovering. A white specter, glowing in the dark. An eerie yellow light flowed out from the middle of its white, tattered robe. It had no face, no arms, no legs. Just a macabre waving glowing mass.

"Leave . . . this . . . castle." The specter flapped its arms.

Kelsey recognized Lizzy's voice from the ballroom. She frowned and folded her arms over her chest.

"Doooo yooooou heeear?"

Kelsey couldn't help but grin.

"Answerrrr meeeee!" Lizzy stepped closer to the end of the bed. Her foot hit the bottom of the bedpost. "Dammit!" Lizzy cried. It looked as if she might lose her balance, then she grabbed the railing and hopped up and down.

Kelsey laughed, then said, "Nice touch with the lantern,

Lizzy, but if you're going to wear a sheet, you have to put holes in it so you can see where you're going."

"Damn you! I'll teach you to laugh at me." Lizzy dropped the lantern she was holding, then dove across the bed and landed on top of Kelsey.

"I hate you." Lizzy grabbed Kelsey's throat.

Kelsey tried to pull her hand from around her neck, but Lizzy's fingers tightened around her windpipe. Lizzy was too strong. Kelsey coughed, but only a strangled sound came out of her mouth. The sheet was still over Lizzy's head. Kelsey grabbed it and twisted it.

Lizzy released her throat, then yanked the sheet out of Kelsey's hands and off her head. "I'll get you," she said, grabbing a handful of Kelsey's hair and yanking.

Kelsey cried out, feeling as if Lizzy were pulling her scalp from her head. She grabbed Lizzy's arms and thrust her away. Lizzy was lying near the edge of the mattress, and the push sent her over the side. She grabbed Kelsey's arm on the way down, yanking her along too. They tumbled to the floor. A table crashed as they fell.

Kelsey landed on Lizzy's back. She wrestled her arms down to the floor, then pinned them there with her knees—a move she'd learned from Griffin. Lizzy was bigger than Kelsey, maybe even stronger, but Kelsey had the need for revenge behind her now. Lizzy twisted and bucked, but Kelsey held her down with sheer determination.

She realized someone was banging on the connecting door, then . . . a loud crash, as if the door had been forced open.

"What the hell is going on in here?" Edward's bellow echoed around the room.

Out of breath from the recent exertion, Kelsey said in between pants, "Nothing really, I've just caught a ghost."

Lizzy growled beneath her, still struggling to pull her arms free.

Kelsey tightened her hold on Lizzy's wrists, digging her knees deeper into the back of her arms. She knew it was painful.

Griffin had done it to her many times, but she was past caring if she hurt Lizzy. She needed to be taught a lesson.

Edward lit a candle and flooded the room with light.

"Well, well, the elusive Lizzy. I'm glad to finally meet you," Kelsey said, staring at the girl's back as she kept her pinned to the floor.

"Yes, you stupid cow! Now get off of me!"

"I will if you tell me how you got in here. I locked the door."

"Doors can't stop me. Now get off of me!"

Kelsey fought the urge to jab her elbow in the middle of Lizzy's back, but she didn't. She had made her point. She rolled off the girl. Edward reached down and helped her to stand.

Kelsey looked over at him and noticed that his hair hung loose around his shoulders. He wore a dressing gown that exposed a deep V of bare flesh on his chest, revealing a thick patch of dark chest hair. A blush burned her cheeks as she glanced back at her assailant.

Lizzy stood up, rubbing the backs of her arms. "You are crazy. You could have broken my arms."

"You're lucky I didn't." Kelsey's green eyes met Lizzy's flashing golden ones.

Lizzy looked about ten and eight. Her tall, slender form was hidden behind an ill-fitting black plain dress that could rival one of Kelsey's old dresses. Her straight umber-colored hair was pulled back in a braid. Her square chin, though smaller, favored Salford's, and it was raised at a haughty angle. She could have been beautiful, but for the intense hostility in her face.

"You won't get the chance again." Lizzy's golden eyes bored into Kelsey's face.

"Then I assume that means you'll stay out of my room."

"This is my home. I'll go where I want." Lizzy plopped her fists on her hips.

Edward grabbed Lizzy by the arm. She winced as he spoke. "You apologize this moment, Lizzy."

"No." Lizzy threw out her chin and crossed her arms over her chest. "You can't make me."

"Can't I?" Edward hauled her to the door.

"Leave me alone, you brute! I hate you! I hate you!"

"Wait! I don't want an apology," Kelsey blurted out, not wanting Lizzy punished on her account. She'd already punished Lizzy when she pinned her to the floor.

Edward turned, freezing Kelsey with a dark, quelling look. "Stay out of this, Miss Vallarreal. It is high time Lizzy learned some manners. I will not have her treating our guests in this infamous manner."

He thrust a fighting, clawing Lizzy out the door, then slammed it behind him.

"Leave me alone! I won't apologize! You can lock me up, but I won't! I won't . . ."

Kelsey grimaced at the door, listening to the sound of Lizzy's protests growing fainter and fainter. Lizzy would probably blame Kelsey for being punished, not a very promising start for an acquaintance. She wasn't angry with Lizzy for her harmless escapades. She herself had been just as mischievous when she was younger. Before Griffin became her friend, pulling pranks on him was one of the ultimate pleasures in life. Lizzy's spunk was admirable.

She wanted to somehow become her friend. In a way, she felt sorry for Lizzy, being cooped up all alone with no company but Edward—he didn't seem at all companionable. Sighing heavily, she walked to the door. She was about to close it, but a flash of orange stripes whipped past her as something furry touched her feet. Startled, she jumped back and watched Brutus as he slowed, padding past the foot of the bed.

"You're a bit late to be of help. Somehow I didn't take you for a coward."

Brutus paused, sniffed at the broken cup and saucer on the floor by the bed, then he bent, touching his tiny pink nose to the spilled milk on the carpet. He looked up at her, his tail swishing as if it were her fault the milk spilled.

"I'm sorry about that. Capturing ghosts is a messy business. I suppose you'll have to go without your snack tonight." She bent down to pick up the broken pieces of china.

Startled by the sudden movement, Brutus hissed at her, then he retreated under the bed.

"No need for all that spitting, I've no intention of petting you until you come to me." Instinctively, she glanced at the connecting door that separated her room from Edward's. The wood was splintered near the lock, rendering it useless. The door hung unevenly on its hinges where he'd burst into the room. It didn't worry her that the lock was broken. She had a feeling Edward would never enter her room uninvited.

The image of him wearing only his dressing gown formed in her mind, the barely leashed power of his muscular body, the patch of dark hair on his broad chest. . . .

Something sharp pierced her hand. Glancing down, she saw a trickle of blood on her pointer finger. She set down the broken piece of china, then sucked on her finger, chiding herself for not paying attention to what she was doing. But how could she concentrate with so many wanton thoughts of him swimming around in her head? She doubted she'd ever really be normal again, not after the way they had clung to each other in the maze. The thought made her frown and suck harder on her finger.

At four in the morning Kelsey decided to get out of bed. Sleep had evaded her most of the night. It was the deafening silence coming from Edward's room, the awareness that he was in there, only a door separating them, that had kept her awake. Since she was no longer afraid the duchess's ghost would haunt the ballroom, she decided to inform Watkins she wanted her old room back. Perhaps she might be able to go to sleep there, knowing, at least, that a whole floor separated her from Edward.

That thought drove her as she quickly dressed in another new gown, a bright green muslin with puffy sleeves and a low scooped neck. After trying to fix her hair like Mary had done, she gave up, braided it, then wound it into a tight bun at her nape. She slipped out of her room, closing her door as quietly as possible.

The ballroom was empty when she entered it. It was too early for the workers Edward had hired to be there. Sunlight was just starting to peek over the horizon. A soft beam of light filtered through the tall windows, giving the white marble floor a pinkish hue. Her footsteps rang hollow in the room as she walked to the wall, then paused. The men had stripped the old plaster down to the metal lathing save for a few jagged pieces remaining on the corners and the edges.

Kelsey crossed her hands over her arms and made a moue at the bare wall. Turning her head first one way, then the other, she studied the bare spot for over ten minutes, then her lips burst into a grin as the design for the wall appeared in her mind. She would paint a mirror image of the room, making it appear as if the ballroom went on forever.

Excited now, she went in search of breakfast. She didn't expect to find anyone in the kitchen this early in the morning. It startled her when she opened the door and almost ran into Agnes. She was standing on tiptoe, hefting a huge pot down from an iron rack. She glanced over her shoulder at Kelsey. "Morning, miss."

"You're up 'fore the roosters," Alice said, glancing up from a pot of porridge she was stirring.

"I suppose so." Kelsey walked farther into the busy room, surprised to find Watkins there as well.

He had a silver tray in his hand. He spoke as he walked past her toward the door. "Good morning, Miss Kelsey. Did you not sleep well?"

"Not well at all, I'm afraid."

"I'm sorry to hear it, Miss Kelsey," he said with his usual toneless civility. "You'll pardon me, I must take this to his grace immediately."

"Yes, of course." Kelsey watched Watkins leave the kitchen.

"Well, that makes two of you who didn't sleep well, miss." Agnes paused from peeling potatoes, then glanced over at Kelsey, a mischievous grin on her thin face.

"Oh?" Kelsey tried to sound disinterested as she watched Agnes slicing potatoes into the pot, her hands moving so quickly, she could hardly see them.

"Aye, miss. You would o' thought with all the commotion yesterday down by the lake, and what with you gettin' lost in the maze, and Lady Elizabeth throwing her tantrums, that his grace would have slept better than he did. He don't ever get up this time of the morning, but there he was, ringin' the bell at dawn. I never seen Watkins move so fast." She grinned, belying her next words. "I pity him having to deal with his grace."

Was there anything the servants didn't know? Did they also know that Edward had kissed her in the lake? Heat crept into Kelsey's cheeks.

"Stall that runaway tongue of yours, Agnes, 'fore I jam this spoon down your throat," Alice said, waving the spoon at her sister's pinched face.

"You do, and you'll need a new fat face." Agnes shook her knife at Alice's chin.

"Please, it's all right," Kelsey said, wondering if they wouldn't kill each other one day. She quickly changed the subject. "Tell me, Agnes, where is Lady Elizabeth?"

"She's locked in her room, miss. I took a tray in last night to her. She tried to brain me with it. She's hateful to the bone, that one."

"From what the old cook afore me said, she's got reason to be the way she is," Alice said.

"What happened to her?" Kelsey asked.

"Well, miss, the master's parents died—he was but a lad then, fourteen, I think—and his guardian, an old solicitor, sent Lady Elizabeth off to live with an aunt and uncle when she was but a babe. Some folks ain't meant to be parents—if you know what

I mean." Alice cocked her head and put her fist on a plump hip. "I ain't sure what went on there, but the poor thing was sent away to boarding schools when she was just a wee one. When the master turned of age, he brought her home, but she was such a hellion by then that he couldn't control her either. After the accident, he sent her to a convent, hoping they could do something with her.

"They couldn't, she broke out of the last one and came home. She was living here for a month before any of us knew she'd come home, sneaking around, stealing food from the kitchen. But Watkins found her prowling around the castle one day. His grace has some fine lady from London coming in hopes of giving Lady Lizzy her come-out. I suppose he hopes to get a husband on her so she'll behave herself, but knowing her the way I do, I don't think even a husband can rein her in."

Kelsey's dark brows came together as she stared down at the table and envisioned Lizzy, raised by negligent nurses, probably never receiving love from anyone, not even her own aunt and uncle. Now Edward wanted to force her to find a husband because he couldn't be bothered with her. She shook her head and said, more to herself, "What a shame."

"Yes, miss." Alice stopped stirring and glanced at Kelsey. "What would you like for breakfast?"

"The porridge smells good."

"You should have something else. Something that'll stick to yer ribs."

"The porridge is fine. I really should hurry and eat. I want to visit my father, then the McGregors this morning. Do you think you might be able to spare a bit of breakfast for my father?" Kelsey knew he probably hadn't eaten since she left him.

"O' course, miss."

Kelsey didn't taste the food as she ate, her mind on Lizzy the whole time. She made a mental note to speak to Edward about her as soon as she could.

* * *

Edward was dressed when Watkins entered his room with the tray. Watkins looked surprised to see him attired, but he quickly hid it behind his impenetrable expression. He nodded and said, "Good morning, your grace."

"I know what you're thinking, Watkins, I am capable of dressing myself. As you well know, that is why I gave up the pretense of a valet a long time ago."

"Yes, your grace." Watkins set the tray down on the edge of the bed.

"I'm going riding now." Edward picked up his riding crop. "I'll forgo the morning coffee."

"Yes, your grace, but isn't it a bit early? You never ride until nine."

"So I'm breaking a rule, Watkins. This is my house. I am allowed the privilege of breaking my own damn rules." Edward smacked his riding crop against his thigh.

"Of course, your grace. I'll inform the staff."

"You do that." Edward started for the door, but turned. "One more thing. I heard Miss Vallarreal get up. Where is she?"

"In the kitchen, your grace. I believe she may be eating breakfast." Watkins picked up Edward's dressing gown from where he'd thrown it on the floor.

"I see. And Lady Elizabeth, have you checked on her this morning?"

"She has not rung the bell, your grace. I don't think she's awake." Watkins hung up the dressing gown in the wardrobe.

"I'll check on her before I go."

"A very prudent idea, your grace." Watkins turned from the wardrobe. "She was not in the best of tempers last night."

"That's putting it mildly," Edward said derisively as he closed the door behind him.

He remembered having to fight Lizzy all the way to her room last night. The threat she had made still rang in his ears: "You can't make me apologize to that little stoat. I won't! I won't! I don't want her here. You only brought her here to seduce her like you did her stepmother."

"You'll never speak to me that way again, Lizzy!"

"The truth hurts, doesn't it!"

His patience snapped, then he did something he'd never done before. He grabbed her, pinned her across the bed, and spanked her until his palm felt raw. When he was done, he let her go, his chest still heaving with fury.

She stood and glared at him, her eyes gleaming with hatred and defiance. "I've been beaten so many times, I've got calluses on my arse. So go ahead, beat me, it won't change me." She crossed her arms over her chest and raised her chin haughtily. "And I won't have her here. Get rid of her, Eddie, or I'll make her wish she had left. . . ."

Edward knew if he stayed in the room, he might wrap his hands around her rebellious little throat and strangle her, so he had left the room and locked the door behind him. He hated losing his temper with Lizzy, but since Kelsey had come to Stillmore, he'd lost his well-schooled discipline. Rational thinking had left him the moment he'd felt his first stirrings of lust for Kelsey.

He still couldn't understand why Lizzy hated Kelsey so much. He suspected Lizzy's pride had been hurt when Kelsey wrestled her to the floor. And she was still angry with him for forcing her to have a come-out. By God, he'd find her a husband and get the little hellion off his hands.

Grinning now at the thought, he recalled how frightened he'd been when he'd heard the noise and how relieved he felt when he saw Kelsey's petite little body expertly pinning Lizzy to the floor. The sight of her slender, bare calves exposed beneath her nightrail, her thick, dark, curling hair, a cloud of disarray around her back and waist, lingered in his mind. That image had haunted him all night. He still felt the effects of it. He grimaced as he stared down at the throbbing rock in his breeches.

The pain hadn't subsided when he unlocked Lizzy's chamber

door. He walked quietly inside, expecting to find her asleep, but the bed was bare, the covers torn off the bed and thrown on the floor as if she'd had a fit in the room. Lizzy's words came back to haunt him.

"Get rid of her, Eddie, or I'll make her wish she had left. . . ."

Edward turned, then ran out of the room. He was panting when he reached the kitchen. A large woman gasped when she saw him. The thin woman next to her put her hand over her mouth as if to stifle a scream.

Watkins was seated at the table, eating. When he noticed Edward standing in the doorway, he rose right away, swallowing a mouthful of food. "Your grace?"

"Where is Miss Vallarreal?" Edward asked, squeezing his riding crop in a white-knuckled grip.

"Left, your grace."

"Left where?"

"She went to visit her father in the village, I believe."

"On foot?"

"Yes, your grace." Watkins's brows drew together as he asked, "Is something amiss?"

"Lizzy has escaped from her room again. I think she means to do Miss Vallarreal harm." Edward ran out the door, cursing himself for not locking Lizzy in one of the towers.

Watkins watched him go, then leapt forward and caught Agnes as she fainted dead away.

It was an unusual morning, not a cloud in the sky. Kelsey glanced up at it through the canopy of leaves overhead, admiring the pure cerulean sky, stark against so much vivid green. Instead of taking the front drive, which would have added another half-mile to her walk, she'd chosen the shortcut through the woods. It would put her at the east end of the village, near the cottage.

She and Griffin used the shortcut regularly when the wild blackberries ripened near the quarry. "Pilfered blackberries always taste better in a pie," she could hear Alroy McGregor saying as he polished off a piece of his wife's pie. It always made everyone in the McGregor household laugh, including Kelsey. She had to agree with him. She grinned, thinking it would soon be time to raid the blackberry patch again.

The air redolent of rotting leaves and rich, dark earth filled her senses. She liked the feral, uninhabited smell of the forest. Breathing in deeply, she reached a clearing where the trees gave way to a steep, rocky hill. Her leg muscles strained as she climbed the winding path. She was out of breath when she reached the hill's crest.

She paused, trying to catch her breath, and glanced at the quarry. Blue water glistened in the bottom of the massive, cone-shaped cavity. It hadn't been mined for thirty years, and nature had begun to reclaim the land where the workers had stripped it bare. A thick stand of trees covered the east side, while a row of blackberry bushes stubbornly grew along the west side, hiding the hundred-foot drop to the bottom.

Her heart raced as she picked her way along the bushes. Every time she climbed to the top of the quarry, she had to overcome a recurring fear of falling. Griffin always teased her about her fear when they picked the ripe fruit. She usually ended up bombarding him with berries for it, and he'd go home with black spots all over his shirt. She usually had a few too. Smiling now, she remembered one of their more vicious battles that stained his hair for a month. A loud hum intruded into her thoughts.

The sky suddenly turned dark and moving. Buzzing. Swarming. She caught a quick glimpse of a conically shaped hornets' nest on the path, as if someone had dropped it there and stirred up the hornets in anticipation of her approach.

The hornets quickly found her. One stung her hand. Another her neck. She screamed, dropped the basket of food she was carrying to her father, then ran blindly into the blackberries as she tried to protect her eyes with her forearm. She felt the thorns pulling at her ankles, her dress, the bees stinging her, then . . .

The ground gave away under her feet. She tripped and rolled down the quarry, the cliff's jagged face tearing at her body.

Ten

Lizzy stood at the top of the quarry, leaning over the side, a worried look on her face. When Kelsey's body hit the water at the quarry's bottom, she held her breath and waited for her to surface. But she didn't.

"You're not supposed to die, you stupid twit," she said under her breath as she stumbled down the rocky incline, holding the hem of her black dress up with one hand, using the other to steady herself against the jutting rocks. The water was clear, enabling her to keep her gaze on the woman's head in the water.

When she reached the water's edge, she dove in. The roaring silence below the surface throbbed in her ears as she swam across the quarry toward the limp body in the water. She had always been wiry, tall, as strong as a reed, so she easily grabbed Kelsey beneath her armpits, bringing the dead weight up to the surface.

She kept Kelsey's head above the water as she dragged her to shore. The shore was but ten feet away, Lizzy discovered as she pulled her burden up on the bank. Kelsey's hair had come loose, the braid slashing across her face. Lizzy pushed the dark braid back and listened to Kelsey's chest.

Nothing.

Frantic now, Lizzy pulled her up into a sitting position by her arms. Kelsey's limp head fell forward. Lizzy pushed it back as she began smacking Kelsey's face. "Wake up! Wake up! Come on!"

Kelsey's head lurched, water spewed out of her mouth, then she coughed, thrusting Lizzy's hands away.

"Back with the living finally?" Lizzy said in her most sarcastic voice.

Kelsey stopped coughing and opened her eyes. The haze cleared as her eyes widened and she blurted out, "You! You put those hornets on the path! I'll ring your neck. . . ." She reached for Lizzy.

Lizzy jumped to her feet before Kelsey could touch her. She plopped her fists on both hips, then stared down at Kelsey. "Is that any way to talk to someone who saved your life?"

"Saved my life?" She reached out, grabbing at Lizzy's leg, then froze and grimaced. Her face contorted in pain as she clutched her arm. "You nearly killed me."

"I didn't mean to kill you, only scare you away." Lizzy sounded hopeful as she asked, "Have you been scared away?"

"Why do you want me to leave? Did I wrong you in any way, Lizzy?"

"I don't like you."

"Why?"

"I've already gotten one beating because of you."

"You sure it was because of me? You weren't very pleasant last night. Could it be that you pushed your brother a little too far?"

"You're the only one pushing him." Lizzy picked up a small rock, rolled it between her fingers, then skipped it across the water's surface. "I've seen the way he looks at you and kisses you."

"You spied on us?"

"Of course." She turned, giving Kelsey one of her wicked grins. "What else is there to do to amuse myself?" She picked up another stone.

"You could try to make yourself useful to your brother." Kelsey pulled her feet up beneath her wet dress, rested her elbows on her knees, then stared up at Lizzy and looked content to sit on the rocky bank and talk for the remainder of the day.

Lizzy frowned at her for being so agreeable. The twit should be screaming her head off, angry with Lizzy for trying to kill her, but what was she doing, being bloody amiable, trying to give her advice. Why couldn't little meddling artists behave the way they were supposed to?

In her best curt tone that always managed to stir Edward's ire, she said, "Why should I put myself out by being useful to my brother? He's never had any use for me." She skipped the rock in her hand across the water. "He's trying to force me to marry some tiresome Tom-fool with a title."

"I'm sure you're wrong. He wouldn't do that."

"I own, you are the most naive person I've ever met—not even those neophytes in the convent were as guileless as you."

"I don't think wanting to believe the best of someone is naive," Kelsey said, sounding defensive.

Lizzy checked Kelsey's face. She didn't look angry, only hurt. "I suppose you're right," she said, not knowing why her tone was suddenly congenial. "It's all how you look at it."

"Have you met this Tom-fool Edward's forcing you to marry?" Kelsey raised a dark brow at Lizzy, an amused gleam in her eye.

"Not exactly." Lizzy picked up another stone, then skipped it with so much force, the rock hopped all the way over to the other side of the quarry before it fell to the bottom. "You see, Edward's threatening to ship me off to London for the season with Lady Shellborn. She'll parade me around at the balls like a Thoroughbred mare in front of the eligible studs of the *ton*. I suppose he thinks one of them will pick me, but if he makes me go, I'll run away. I hate being put on display, expected to smile and simper and generally act like a jell-headed debutante."

"It sounds horrible," Kelsey said, shaking her shoulders in a feigned shiver. "I've never been to a ball, though my mother used to tell me about the ones she attended during her come-out. They sounded awful. I think she did a lot of smiling and simpering, but she never told me the secret to acting like a jell-headed debutante. I suppose the simpering has a lot to do with it."

"Go ahead, make fun of me, but you should be glad you've never been to a ball. They are more irksome than listening to one of Edward's long-winded jobations. I just want to stay here in peace. I have no wish to go on in society. I'm certainly not going to look for a bloody husband in London—especially one I'm forced to marry because he has a title and wealth. When and if I marry, I'll pick the man not because of his rank in society but because I love him."

"I wouldn't have taken you for a romantic, Lizzy. You surprise me."

Lizzy felt a blush coming on and kicked a rock with the toe of her boot, sending it out into the water. She stared pensively down at the blurry image of the quartz bedrock below the water's surface, not looking at Kelsey. Everything about her irritated Lizzy at the moment; she could wrestle like a man, made Edward and Watkins infatuated with her, had an uncanny control over her temper, even made Lizzy say things that she'd never say to another human being. Lizzy wished the bothersome creature would go back to the village where she belonged.

"I'm sorry, I've embarrassed you. I didn't mean to." The sincere tone in Kelsey's voice made Lizzy look over at her. "Maybe if you made yourself a little more agreeable to be around, you might be able to sway Edward and get him to change his mind. Maybe he'll send you next season."

Lizzy remained silent, brooding over the possibility, staring back at the water.

Kelsey continued, the teasing tone back in her voice. "If you can use that devious nature of yours to practically kill me, surely you can come up with some way to change your brother's mind. I have every faith in you. In fact, if we were at war with the French again, I'd want you on our side. You would definitely frighten away Bonaparte—that is, if he should decide to rise from his grave and take up arms."

Lizzy looked at Kelsey. She wanted to glare at the woman,

wanted to say something cutting, but she found herself grinning and extending her hand. "Can you get up?"

"I think so."

Kelsey took her hand and groaned as Lizzy pulled her to her feet. She was a little shaky on her feet, so Lizzy grabbed her elbow. "Are you sure you're all right?"

"Yes, only minor bruises and a few stings. I have to commend you on the hornets. Ingenious really. Highly effective too. How'd you do it?"

"The nuns kept bees at the convent. I knew that smoke calms them, so I climbed a tree, lit a piece of burning wood, then plucked the hive from a limb. It was easy."

"You should know." Kelsey grinned at her, her green eyes gleaming. "If you ever try anything like that again, I'll pay you back double."

"I suppose that's only fair," Lizzy said, looking at Kelsey with more respect than she previously had.

"Kelsey!"

They both glanced up at the sound of Edward's deep bellow. He stood at the top of the quarry, staring down at them, his face a mask of fury as he took in their wet clothes. "What is the meaning of this? What have you done, Lizzy?"

"He'll kill me now," Lizzy said under her breath. Her hands went to her sore bottom, and she grimaced. She really didn't want another spanking, even though she'd lied with bravado and told him differently last night. Then again, he might do something even worse. She knew how far she could push him, but he seemed to have a shorter fuse these days.

"You could grovel," Kelsey said lightly as she waved to him. She raised her voice and called to him, "Everything is fine—no, no, don't come down. We're coming up."

"I'm groveling. I'll be your slave for a month—no, two months, if you don't tell him."

Kelsey slipped her hand into Lizzy's as if they'd always been friends. Lizzy felt the urge to draw back as they climbed the quarry, but she didn't. She never allowed people to touch her, but she was beginning to like Kelsey in spite of wanting to hate her. So she really didn't mind holding Kelsey's hand and helping her up the slippery rocks. Kelsey hadn't answered her, obviously prolonging the distress, Lizzy was sure, on purpose.

Kelsey waited until they had made it almost to the top before she spoke. Edward was pacing near the edge, so she kept her voice low as she said, "A slave for two months? Sounds fair, but there is another thing."

"Anything."

"You have to promise to be agreeable for that time as well."

"Well, all right, but you must know it will kill me."

"I'm sure of it," Kelsey said lightly, grinning, then she added, "and no more spying."

"All right."

When they reached the top, Edward helped them up. He stared at Lizzy, then back at Kelsey. His gaze snapped over Kelsey, taking in her torn clothes, the bruises and scrapes on her arms, then both his hands went to her shoulders. "Are you all right?"

"Of course. I owe my life to Lizzy." Kelsey cut her eyes at Lizzy when Edward wasn't looking. "Tell him, Lizzy, don't be modest."

Lizzy hesitated a moment, then said, "It's true, I saw her fall down into the quarry, and I jumped in to save her." Lizzy saw the skeptical look in her brother's eyes, so she crossed her finger over her heart and added, "I swear it."

"It's true. A hornet was chasing me, I wasn't thinking and took a tumble down into the quarry. I'm quite fit to walk on to the village."

Edward didn't look at all convinced as he scooped her up into his arms and strode toward his horse. "You're coming home with me. I'll get a doctor."

"No, really, I must insist you don't. I'm quite all right. I've only a few bruises and a couple of bee stings." Kelsey chewed on her lower lip.

"I won't allow you to walk to the village. My carriage will convey you when you are able to go."

"Miss Vallarreal is quite capable of walking. She's getting you all wet," Lizzy remarked as she walked beside Edward.

Edward scowled over at her. "Don't start with me, Lizzy. I know you had something to do with this, and when I find out what you did—"

"Oh, dear." Kelsey put her hand to her head, feigning a moan that was better than any Lizzy used when she was pretending to be the duchess's ghost. "Could you not yell so loudly?"

"What is it?" Edward said, his anger momentarily diverted.

"It's my head. I think I should lie down for a while. Perhaps I was hurt. You will hurry and get me back to my room." Kelsey surreptitiously glanced at Lizzy beneath her hand, giving her a look that said, "Remember your promise."

Lizzy frowned back at her, then rolled her eyes.

Edward carried Kelsey to his horse, easily mounting with her in his arms, his face contorted with distress, the scars more hideous than Lizzy ever remembered them being. She had never seen Edward look so worried. He shot a look at Lizzy that could fry an egg, then kicked Dagger in his sides.

Lizzy glowered at her brother's back, watching him ride away, feeling something between hate and filial affection for him. It had always been that way between them. A deliberate grin spread across her face as she stared at his back, saying under her breath, "If you force me to go to London, I hope she breaks your heart. You might learn that you can't control everyone's life—including your own."

As if Edward had answered her in a perverse way, a hornet began buzzing around her head, then more followed. She thought they had finished swarming, but as a cloud of hornets surrounded her, she realized that was not the case. Swatting at the persistent creatures, she ran back down the steep quarry and dove into the water, cursing her luck and Edward.

* * *

"Edward," Kelsey said, fighting the urge to snuggle against his neck. She felt terribly comfortable riding in his arms, even though she could feel the anger at Lizzy oozing from him.

"Yes, what is it?"

"Can I say something about Lizzy?"

"The subject of my sister is not open for discussion. I thought I made that perfectly clear last night." His jaw clenched, the veins in his muscular neck protruding.

"You might have said that, but it pains me to see both of you arguing."

"I told you I don't wish to discuss this."

"Well, I do. I want to understand Lizzy. I know she had to live with an aunt and uncle that didn't love her after your parents died, but I don't understand why you treat her with such callous indifference."

"I don't treat her with indifference."

"Of course you do. She doesn't want to go to London. You shouldn't force it upon her. It will only cause more dissension between the two of you."

"She's been speaking to you, hasn't she?" He grunted under his breath. "She's good at manipulation. Believe me, I'm doing only what's best for her. Lizzy needs authority over her, or else she'll run wild like a savage for the rest of her life. I've tried to change her, but I cannot seem to reach her. I think a husband could do more with her, if she let him."

Some of the ire left his voice as he said, "You don't know what it's been like raising her. My aunt Augusta was a shrew and made Lizzy what she is today. She berated Lizzy constantly, then she sent her away when Lizzy started to rebel. I even wrote to her when I knew she was old enough to read, but my aunt didn't give her my letters. She wouldn't even tell me what school Lizzy was attending—though she never stayed at one over six months. She was proficient at getting expelled. Lizzy never knew I existed until I came into the title and became her guardian."

"How awful. Why was your aunt so horrible to her?"

"She was my mother's half sister by a previous marriage and had always resented my mother because she was favored by their father. She took out her hatred on Lizzy. When I came of age, and found out about it, I went to see the solicitor who had acted as our legal guardian with the intent of ringing his neck." The side of his lip twisted in a shameless grin. "I pointed out to him that he should never have given Lizzy to our aunt, but as I had my hands about his thin little neck, he convinced me that he'd interviewed Aunt Augusta thoroughly. She had put on a loving facade, eager to be a mother to Lizzy, so he felt confident my sister was in good hands."

"Is your aunt still alive?"

"No, she died three years ago." He was silent for moment. His hands tightening on the reins, then, as if he needed to get it all off his chest, he said, "I thought it would be so different when I brought Lizzy here to live with me"—his voice thickened with emotion—"but I had a ten-year-old hellion on my hands, who resented me when I tried to discipline her. After she went through five governesses, I was forced to send her to a convent in France—she'd been expelled from every boarding school in England, none of them would have her." He grew silent, as though he'd abruptly realized he'd said too much.

Kelsey listened to the steady clop of the horse's hooves and watched the animal's ears twitch as a fly irritated its head. After a moment she carefully chose her next words. "I know you think you are doing only what is best for Lizzy, but forcing her to marry will just cause her to rebel. It's very evident to me that she is quite as stubborn as you. You'll never bend her to your iron will by forcing her to do something you feel is right for her. A little kindness and understanding might help her to see things your way."

"I've tried that; it does nothing," he said, his voice growing razor-sharp.

"Perhaps you have not tried hard enough."

"I don't need your meddling opinions concerning my sister. I'll do what I like with her, I'm her guardian."

"That is true, but you haven't been successful so far. You're too busy wallowing in your own self-pity to be aware of how to get on with anyone else in your life." She realized he had goaded her. She had vowed never to let him do that again. No doubt she'd regret what she just said, but it had felt good when she had said it.

He remained silent as they reached the front of the castle. Maybe that was a good thing, for his face had turned red and he looked ready to pull her hair out, or his.

He jerked the horse to a halt. Kelsey's shoulder slammed into his hard chest. In one smooth motion he caught her, swung his long legs over the side of the saddle, then dismounted with her in his arms.

Watkins met them at the door, the usual pinched look around his mouth. Only the concern in his eyes gave him away. "How are you, Miss Kelsey?"

"She claims to have stumbled into the quarry—at least that seems to be the story she's telling at the moment." Edward narrowed his good eye at her. With the widow's peak on his forehead and his dark hair pulled back in a queue, he looked like a one-eyed hawk.

"I believe Watkins was addressing me," Kelsey said, still irritated with Edward for goading her, but more annoyed with herself for allowing him to do it. She glanced at Watkins. "I'm fine, Watkins, please don't worry."

"Send for the doctor, Watkins."

"Right away, your grace." Watkins turned to leave.

"Don't send for the doctor." Kelsey watched Watkins turn back around, his expectant gaze on her. She smiled woodenly back at him. "All I need is a hot bath, Watkins." She wiggled in Edward's arms. "Put me down, I'm quite capable of walking on my own. And I will not be manhandled by you."

Edward didn't loosen his hold on her. If anything, it tightened, his fingers biting into her side and thigh.

"Put me down this instant!"

Ignoring her, Edward walked down the hallway and said over his shoulder, "Send for the doctor, Watkins."

"Don't send for the doctor." Kelsey tried to look over Edward's broad shoulder at Watkins, but she couldn't see him, so she spoke into Edward's shirt. "If a doctor comes to my chamber door, I will not let him in. Do you understand me, Watkins?"

"Yes, Miss Kelsey."

"You *will* let him in," Edward growled near her ear.

"We'll see about that." Kelsey crossed her arms over her chest.

"I look forward to it."

"I'd hate to ruin any anticipation of yours." Kelsey couldn't let him have the last word.

It turned out he had the last word, for sometime later, after Edward had dumped her on her bed and stormed from her room, the doctor arrived. Kelsey had finished soaking in a hot tub and Mary was in the process of helping her into her petticoat, when the knock came at the door.

"Kelsey, it's old Dr. Jamerson, at your service."

Kelsey recognized her family doctor. He was such a kind, dear man that she could not, just to make a point to Edward, keep him standing outside her door. She quickly donned a dressing gown and said to Mary, "Please, let him in."

"Right away, miss." Mary bobbed a curtsy, opened the door, curtsied to the doctor, then let herself out of the room.

Dr. Jamerson lumbered into the room. He was a round man with a ruddy, moon-shaped face that matched his protruding middle. He wore a pair of wire rectangular spectacles down on his nose and an ancient white wig from a bygone era.

He pursed his lips, looked through his spectacles at her in that disconcerting way of his, then said, "What mischief have you done yourself, my dear child."

"Nothing that should have need of your attention, Dr. Jamerson." Kelsey threw up her hands in frustration. "I tried to tell Lord Salford that, but he was insistent."

"Well, our resident duke can be insistent. It goes with the

title, my dear." Dr. Jamerson smiled at her now. "I hear you've turned the castle upside down since you arrived. Is that about accurate?"

"Now, where would you hear such nonsense?"

"I'm a doctor." He set down his little black bag on her bed. "People confide more than their ills to me—too much sometimes."

"You've been playing chess with Mr. McGregor, haven't you?"

"Yes." The doctor chuckled, his belly jiggling like a Christmas pudding. "You've found me out."

Kelsey sighed, then her shoulders drooped as she sat on the bed. "I suppose the whole village has heard that I ran out of the castle in the middle of the night."

"Yes, you'll be happy to know they lay the blame on Salford. They are saying some pretty damning things about him."

"Are they? Well, I'm inclined to believe he deserves everything they say about him."

"I wouldn't be so quick to judge him, my dear. He is a very lonely man. One cannot blame him for his disposition. He really has no prospects with that countenance of his."

"There is nothing wrong with his countenance." Kelsey added too much emphasis to her words, realized it, then said in a more bland tone, "I mean, one gets used to his face, it's his dark heart that gives offense."

"I'll tell you something which might prove useful in understanding his darker side. He tried to step out in society once—after the accident. I remember it very well. It was a disaster by all accounts." The bed creaked beneath his great weight as he sat beside her.

"He did?" Kelsey toyed with the sash around her dressing gown.

"Yes. Sad affair, that." He shook his head, sending the ends of the wig flapping against his chubby cheeks.

"What happened?"

"Went to London—he owns a town house there, you know.

It was the height of the season. Invitations came to him at once—somewhat of a curiosity for polite society— the rumors about his face, you know. Well, the first ball he attended was an utter disaster. Debutantes fainted at the sight of him, the musicians couldn't play for staring at him, the waiters dropped trays of drinks. There was a grizzly account of it in the *Gazette* the next day. He quickly left London and retreated here to the country." The doctor shook his head. "Poor devil, never left here after that, shuns all society or contact with people. He'll never regain his life again. He's lost a great deal. I can't help but feel sorry for the man. I know that he hurt your father, but I also know how forgiving you can be, my dear." He squeezed her hand.

"I didn't know," Kelsey said softly, fighting the growing lump in her throat.

"Well, you wouldn't, my dear, you were a child at the time." A warm smile touched his lips. "Now, shall we have a look at you, just to please our surly duke? I believe he's down in the library, pacing with worry over your condition."

"Is he?"

"Yes, my dear." He raised his nose and glanced at her behind his spectacles.

"All right, I suppose it couldn't hurt," she said, feeling like she wanted to crawl in a cave and let the bats have at her. She deserved it, didn't she? She winced, remembering every poignant word she had used to demean Edward for caring more about his own deformity than he did about Lizzy. If anyone had the right to be selfish, God knows, it was Edward.

Dr. Jamerson touched a spot on her back. She yelped and jumped.

"Hmmm, I see you've got a nice bruise on your spine."

"Probably not anything I don't deserve."

Dr. Jamerson stood up straight, then frowned down at her, the curiosity in his bright gray eyes magnified by his glasses. "What have you been up to, my dear?"

"Don't ask, it's better you don't know," Kelsey said, then

jumped as Dr. Jamerson touched her arm. "My temper always gets me into trouble. You would think I should have learned by now to control it."

"Life would be boring if our backsides didn't get singed by a little fire every now and again. It breaks the monotony, you know." He winked, then smiled at her as if he had guessed what she'd said to Edward.

She wondered if his healing talents allowed him to read minds as well.

Eleven

Edward was in front of the hearth in the library, pacing, when Dr. Jamerson entered the room. He saw the doctor and walked up the room to meet him.

"Well, how is she?"

"No more than a few bruises." The tension in Edward's neck relaxed at the news. "She'll be fine, but I wouldn't let her do anything strenuous for a day or two."

"I'll see to that."

Dr. Jamerson glanced at Edward through his spectacles, then moved one lip over the other. "I wish you luck on that score. Kelsey has never been a biddable child—her father has seen to that."

"I suppose he did." Edward remembered his manners and said, "Please take a seat. Would you like a drink?"

"No, no, none for me. My gallbladder's acting up. Nasty business, that. I really should be going, but before I go I was wondering if you told Kelsey about her inheritance."

"No, I haven't. I—"

Kelsey breezed into the room, looking radiant, every bit the highborn lady she truly was. Her raven hair was swept up on top of her head, then cascaded down, falling over one shoulder. Her gown was a deep green, fitting her hourglass curves to perfection. Her eyes, so large, so bright green, they seemed to light up the very room. She didn't look at all as if she'd taken a tumble into the quarry.

She strode toward them. "I'm sorry for interrupting. I wanted a word with you, your grace, but I can come back later."

"No, no," Dr. Jamerson perked up. "I really must be going. Good-bye, my dear." He squeezed Kelsey's hand, then gave Edward a "get on with it" glance before he lumbered out of the room.

Edward couldn't keep his eyes off Kelsey's breasts, so he turned and strode over to the wet bar, then poured out two fingers of whiskey into a glass. "You shouldn't be out of bed."

"I feel fine. Anyway, I had to speak to you."

"You can save your breath if it's about Lizzy."

"It's about Lizzy—I mean, it's not exactly about Lizzy, but the terrible thing I said to you when I was talking about Lizzy." She hesitated, her brows coming together in serious contemplation. "I'm sorry, I had no right to say the things I said. You must hate me for it."

"I could never hate you." Edward's fingers tightened around the decanter. He turned to look at her with the decanter in his hand. "To what do I owe this sudden apology? Ah, yes, Dr. Jamerson's been plying you with stories of my wretched life. He's very proficient at soliciting sympathies on my account."

"I don't know why, you seem to have enough sympathy for yourself to last a lifetime—there I go again, letting you goad me. You really are a belligerent creature." Green fire lit up her eyes as she plopped her fists on her hips. "Can't you accept a simple apology? No, I guess you can't. You think any kindness shown you must be from sympathy. Well, let me tell you, if I had any sympathy for you, you've ruined it. You're not only belligerent, you are self-centered too."

"Are you quite through giving me a dressing-down, madam?"

"I think I've said all I care to, thank you very much."

"I'm glad." He looked at her, amazed that he wasn't annoyed with her. No woman had ever spoken to him with such passionate fury. Margaret, his wife, rarely spoke more than two words at a time to him, and when she was angry she said nothing at all. She'd sit in a chair like a pale gravestone, not breathing, showing no emotion at all, about as stimulating as a wet towel. And his mother, God rest her soul, couldn't be bothered enough to get angry over anything he did.

"Now you have me worried. You're not growling back at me. There might even be a ghost of a smile on your face. Can I add *perplexing* to your list of irritating qualities?"

"If it pleases you," he said in a more subdued tone than he'd used thus far. "Has anyone ever told you your eyes turn black when you're angry?"

"No. I don't think anyone has ever irritated me as much as you do. My father has come close, but you do a much better job of it."

"Well, I suppose that's something in my favor." He glanced down, realizing he was still holding the decanter. He asked, "Would you like a drink?"

"I don't drink spirits of any kind."

"Ever?"

"Not ever, especially in the morning," she said with censure in her voice. "I made a vow never to touch the stuff. I've seen what alcohol did to my father."

Edward winced at the word *father*. Very soon he'd have to tell her the truth about her father. He poured more bourbon in his glass than he meant to, then turned around and asked, "How is your work progressing? Have you decided on a design?"

She was silent a moment, biting her lip as if she were unsure about speaking, then she said, "Yes, I have, but since you said you didn't care what I painted on your wall, I decided to let it be a surprise."

"I've never cared for surprises." He took a drink of whiskey and eyed her over the rim of the glass.

"That's too bad, you could use some in your life."

"Do you have any in mind?" His gaze strayed to her breasts again, lower to her small waist and the flare of her hips.

"Not exactly, but I'm sure between Lizzy and me we could

manage a few for you." She smiled at him now, a siren's smile, while her eyes twinkled perversely with a guileless gleam.

He wondered if she used that charming, seductive, enigmatic look on her lover, McGregor. His voice grew caustic as he said, "You don't need Lizzy's help, you are much more resourceful than she could ever be."

"Is that a compliment? I couldn't tell, you were frowning like the devil." Her smile broadened, her straight white teeth gleaming. "If it is a compliment, I'm astonished, I never thought I'd hear one coming from you."

"I didn't think a compliment from me would be worth much in your eyes." He looked away from her smile, feeling the warmth of it reeling him toward her like a hook.

"I don't hate you, Edward."

Something in her voice made Edward look at her. He shouldn't have looked; now he couldn't stop staring at her. She didn't appear able to look away from him either. Her eyes were full of soft emotion, no pity, just warmth, all directed at him. He wanted to set his drink down, go to her, and drown himself in them.

He didn't know why it mattered to him, but he asked, "How do you really feel about me, Kelsey?" His whole body grew taut as he waited for her reply.

"You have your tolerable moments, I suppose, especially when you kiss me—yes, I think I even liked you when you kissed me in the maze last night." She cocked her head at him, that siren's smile back.

"You are a wicked tease," he said, polishing off his drink in one gulp without taking his gaze off her.

"Not any more than you are. You kiss me one minute, then you act like I don't exist the next. I thought something happened between us in the maze last night, but you purposely ignored me the rest of the night. You have been staring at me since I came into this room like you wanted to kiss me again, all the while goading me. Really, I'm at a loss to know what you want from me."

"Don't you?" He looked askance at her. He stared at her full, rosy mouth, visions of all the sensual pleasure she could give him with it rising to torture him. He wanted to take her there, right then, in the library.

"No, I don't know what you mean," she said, looking so naive, he wanted to choke her.

"Don't look so bloody innocent. I may look like a monster, Kelsey, but I'm a man, and I want the same things you give freely to McGregor. You might think this is some sort of game you're playing, but it's a dangerous game to tease a man. I'm not a young puppy like McGregor, and I don't like games. If you're not prepared to give your body to me, then stop telling me you want me with your every look and word. Do you like playing the coquette around men while you stay loyal to your lover, McGregor? Is that it? Are you waiting for me to touch you so you can slap me again? Well, I won't stop at one slap this time." He glared at her, hoping to get his point across.

The color drained from her face as if he had actually slapped her. She blinked at him, her emerald eyes like unveiled gateways to her soul, the hurt bubbling up and out of them.

"Edward, have you seen Kelsey? I've been looking—" Jeremy came into the room and paused. He looked from Kelsey to Edward, then back to her. "I'm sorry, did I interrupt something again?"

Edward glared at him. He wanted to smash something, or Jeremy. What he really wanted was a piece of McGregor. What he should do is apologize to Kelsey for taking out his ire on her. He had meant to warn her, not hurt her. He stepped toward her. "Kelsey, I—"

"No." She stepped back from him, her bottom lip trembling, and held up her hand. "You have said more than enough, your grace. We have nothing more to say to each other." She turned to Jeremy and smiled, her lips so wooden, they looked like two small red lines drawn across her face. "I believe you came into the room at a very appropriate moment."

"I was worried about you," Jeremy said. "I ran into Lizzy in the hall." He turned toward Edward. "She looked awful, sopping wet and had bee stings on her hands. You really shouldn't let her run wild, Eddie."

"Did she really have bee stings?" Kelsey asked, faint amusement mixing with the distress in her voice.

"Yes, several, looked awful, like a hive attacked her." Jeremy walked toward her and held her hand. "She told me what happened to you. Are you all right?"

Edward felt his whole body strain as he quelled the urge to fling Jeremy out the library doors and have Kelsey all to himself.

"Perfectly sound. So sound, in fact, I'm going into the village to call on my father, then I'm going on to the McGregors." Kelsey turned and glared at Edward. "I'm sure Griffin is eager to see me. He was supposed to teach me a new game."

Edward felt the full meaning of her words. She was flinging his own words back in his face. He must not have hurt her as badly as he thought. It didn't take her long to get her saucy mouth back. He smiled sardonically at her, then said, "I'll have the carriage sent around for you." He strode toward the bellpull.

"No need for all that," Jeremy said, not taking his besotted eyes off Kelsey. "I was going driving myself. Got a new pair of grays I want to put through their paces." In a low, reverent tone, he said, "It would be my honor if you let me drive you."

Kelsey hesitated a moment, then she said, "Of course, I would enjoy your company." She glanced at Edward as if to say, "It must be preferable than my present company," then she turned back, bestowed a blinding smile on Jeremy, and linked her arm with his.

Edward watched them stroll out of the room. She didn't look back at him, even though he willed her to. He was afraid to move, afraid that he might go after her and drag her back to his side so he could kiss that impudent little mouth of hers. He waited until their footsteps died away, then he strode out of the library, grinding his teeth.

* * *

Kelsey listened to the steady clip-clop of the hooves hitting the road and stared at the backs of the grays, their sleek coats glistening in the midday sun. Jeremy held the reins tightly, holding them back. She knew he was trying to prolong the carriage ride to be alone with her. The bruises on Jeremy's face had faded from where he'd fought Edward, and he appeared to glow with good looks and a pleasing disposition. A little too handsome and pleasing for Kelsey at the moment. Perversely, her mind was centered on a scarred face and a nasty disposition.

How dare Edward say such cruel things to her, and how could he think Griffin was her lover? She was too hurt by what he'd said to immediately inform him of his mistake. Perhaps she had flirted with Edward. She was, after all, drawn to him. More than drawn, she had to admit. But he could be so infuriating. Sometimes she wanted him to kiss her and touch her, then at other times he made her so angry she wanted to slap him again.

"You're frowning, Kelsey," Jeremy said, breaking into her thoughts. "I own, there isn't a better felicity in the world than to be driving with a handsome lady at my side, but I would rather she look as if she were enjoying herself."

"I'm sorry." She tried for a smile. "Something else you should know. You have no lady at your side, Jeremy, only a poor painter with little to recommend her. I don't even own the clothes on my back." Kelsey sighed, then looked at a row of wild primroses growing along the ditch.

"But of course you are a—" He hesitated, then blushed as he added, "I meant to say, you are everything that is a lady."

"Why did you hesitate just now?" She turned to look at him. "What were you going to say?"

"I was just going to say I don't think one must have consequence to be a lady. I have seen women poor as church mice that were ladies."

"I don't think that is what you meant." Kelsey's eyes glinted at him shrewdly. "But since you probably won't tell me the truth, I'll have to thank you for the compliment." She grinned at him.

He laughed, his dimples winking in his cheeks. "You needn't thank me, you deserve every compliment I can give you." His grin dissolved, his expression turning serious. "Kelsey, I have to ask you something."

At the somber overtones in Jeremy's voice, she knew he was about to ask her something that she would rather not hear. She shaded her eyes with her fingers and craned her neck at the road ahead. "Look!" she cried, feigning excitement and pointing. "Is that not the village before us? I do believe it is. Yes, I'm sure of it. You truly have a fine pair of grays to have gotten us here so quickly."

"Yes, I picked them out myself." He sounded disappointed by the abrupt turn in the conversation.

She prudently kept him talking about horseflesh until they reached the village. The carriage rolled past the tiny shops lining the streets. The sidewalk buzzed with the inhabitants of the village. All faces turned to stare at her and Jeremy as they rode past in the open carriage.

Kelsey saw the rector's wife, Mrs. Stevens, and Mrs. Morris, the butcher's wife, as they stood talking in front of the posting office. She waved to them. Their jaws dropped open at the shock of seeing her in a new dress and riding with a gentleman. She could not have made more of an entrance if she'd been Lady Godiva riding into the village. After they had gotten their eyeful, they quickly glanced away and ignored her.

"That was a right-out snub, Kelsey," Jeremy said, staring hard at the two ladies' backs. "Do you want me to stop the carriage so I can back it up and run over them?"

Kelsey laughed, not because he had said it to be funny but because he'd sounded so serious. "Dr. Jamerson told me there was a rumor in the village that I was sharing Lord Salford's bed. I suppose the snub has something to do with it. The good folk of Jarrow don't approve of upstarts or whores."

"But you're not a whore." Jeremy's face turned red with indignation. "I vow, someone should teach these people to stop spreading malicious rumors."

"They'll never change. I have never cared for their good opinion. Anyway, they have never really liked me."

"Why is that? I cannot believe such a thing."

"It's true." Kelsey shrugged, saw the puzzled look on Jeremy's face, and added, "You see, they never have approved of my father's flagrant lifestyle. He has always been open about the fact that he visits the local prostitutes every Saturday night, unlike most of the men in the village, who try to hide it. Then they get up and go to church the next morning." Kelsey smiled. "At least my father does not do that. I have always admired his open convictions concerning life. He is no hypocrite, nor will he ever be."

Jeremy stared at the reins in his hands, looking guilty, as if he had been one of those hypocrites in church the next day.

Kelsey touched his arm. "Oh, dear, I didn't mean to offend you."

Jeremy's face blushed slightly. "No offense taken. A man has to watch every expression around you, doesn't he?" He grinned.

"Not really, I'm no Miss Nancy. I am well aware that gentlemen have their mistresses, and goodness knows what else they do." Kelsey rolled her eyes. "My father has taught me that all men have sexual yearnings that cannot be repressed. I have always felt 'tis better they are agreeably engaged in such pursuits than to have them making wars. Don't you agree?"

He threw back his head and laughed. He wiped his eyes as he said, "You really are a treasure. You're not like any lady I've ever known." Jeremy's hazel eyes gleamed with awe and blatant desire.

"You must know that you cannot flatter someone like me. I'm jaded in that area as well." She grinned, then realized they had reached the end of the village and were stopping in front of the cottage.

Jeremy secured the reins, then rose to help her down from

the phaeton. She touched his arm. "Please, don't bother. I'll be only a moment."

It didn't seem to bother Jeremy that she hadn't invited him inside. He merely smiled tolerantly as he watched her get down, then handed her the basket of food she had brought along for her father. She would have invited him inside, but she wasn't sure in what condition she would find her father.

"Thank you, I'll be back shortly." Kelsey hurried through the white picket fence and up the flagstone steps to the front door. She tried to open the door, expecting to walk right inside, but it was locked. Her father never locked it. Concerned, she walked around to the back of the cottage and went in through the kitchen door.

"Papa!" She set the basket down on the kitchen table.

Silence answered her.

"Papa! Where are you?" Feeling that something was wrong, she ran past the small parlor and up the steps that led to her father's chamber. She thrust open the door and saw that the bed was made and had not been slept in. The room looked spotless, no empty rum bottles, no clothes left strewn about as he usually left them.

"Papa!" She turned and ran into the studio. The scent of turpentine and oil filled her senses as she paused in the doorway.

Light streamed in through overhead windows, bathing the high-ceilinged room in north light. She glanced toward the couch, expecting to find him passed out there, but it was empty save for the burgundy velvet drape he used for his subjects. The table beside his easel, which usually held his oil paints and brushes, was bare. Out of the corner of her eye she saw a wrinkled slip of foolscap tacked to the top of the easel.

Her hands shook as she grabbed the note and read the broad, flourishing strokes:

Dear chérie,
  Do not worry about your papa, I am fine. Uncle Bel-lamy swears his heart is giving out, and since I have not

*seen my brother in years, I decided I should go back to
France. I know how you worry, but do not. I will be fine.
Try not to be angry at my hasty departure. I had to leave
at once. I knew you would be in good hands with your
duke.*

*I pray that you have found it in your heart to forgive
him. I know you can brighten his life as you have mine.
I shall write and give you my direction.*

Your adoring papa

Dumbfounded, Kelsey stared at the note. She could not see
her father nursing anyone in their deathbed. Death disturbed his
sensibilities; he did not even attend her mother's or Clarice's
funeral. And what did he mean by *your duke.* Edward was not
her duke.

Something was amiss. Her father had left England suddenly
for a reason, and it was not to visit Uncle Bellamy on his deathbed. Her father never even mentioned his brother until he started
receiving an allowance from him after Clarice's death. And
when she had asked her father about Uncle Bellamy, he gave
her vague answers. Sometimes she had wondered if her father
knew him at all. So where had her father gone? Kelsey sighed
deeply, then stuffed the note in a pocket inside her petticoat. Of
one thing she was certain—he was not at Uncle Bellamy's bedside.

Twelve

When they reached the narrow lane that would take them to the McGregor farm, Jeremy glanced over at Kelsey. "Something is the matter. You have not said a word since you left your father's house, and you've wound your hair so tightly around your finger, you have cut off the circulation."

Kelsey pried the hair from around her pale finger and smiled nervously at him. "I'm worried about my father. He left a note informing me he has gone to visit a sick brother in France."

"Is this uncommon behavior for him?"

"Most definitely, the sickbed and death are not his province. He goes out of his way to avoid them. I feel he has gone somewhere else and doesn't wish to tell me. I can't help but think he's gotten into some sort of trouble and is running from it."

"If you would like, I know of a Bow Street Runner whom I could engage on your behalf."

"Would you?" Kelsey laid her hand over the top of his and squeezed it. "I would be most appreciative. It would ease my mind if I knew where he was."

"At your service, my lady," Jeremy grinned gallantly, flashing his heartbreaking eyes at her.

"Thank you. You are a good friend." Something in his grin made her emphasize the word *friend* and move her hand back from his.

"I hope that you will one day think of me as more than a friend, Kelsey," he said tenderly.

"Jeremy, I thought we have been through all this. Really—"

"I won't give up on you. We need to spend some time together. You'll see, we were meant for each other."

Kelsey was glad when they reached the McGregors' cottage. Edith McGregor came running out to meet them, her ample breasts bouncing over her rounded stomach. She pushed aside the wisps of straight brown hair that had fallen in her face and exclaimed, "Lord, 'tis you, Kelsey me dear. I didn't recognize you at first, all decked out as you are." She appeared flustered as she noticed Jeremy and bobbed a curtsy. "How do, sir."

"Allow me to introduce Lord Lovejoy," Kelsey said. "And this is Edith McGregor, my adoptive mother." She smiled at Edith. Edith's face lit up with pleasure, then she said to Jeremy by way of explanation, "Kelsey is like one of me own. Always has been."

"The pleasure is all mine." Jeremy smiled winningly and tipped his beaver.

"Lord bless me." Edith waved a pudgy hand through the air. "We don't stand on circumstances round here, me lord. You'd best save those fine manners for me girls. They'll eat you alive when they see that pretty mug of yours. Come in, come in. I was just baking some apple tarts, you'll stay and have one."

"Of course, apple tarts are my favorite dessert," Jeremy said, jumping down, then walking around and helping Kelsey debark.

Edith guided them into the parlor area and made sure Jeremy sat on the settee. Kelsey sat in the rocker next to it. She noticed that Mrs. McGregor's square face was unusually red and that she seemed nervous about something. Edith wasn't the type to get nervous very often, so Kelsey said, "Is everything all right? You seem upset about something."

"I am that." Edith wiped her hands down the front of her apron, then wrung her hands.

"What is it? Has something happened to Griffin?" Kelsey stood up.

"No, child." Edith put her hands on Kelsey's shoulders and eased her back down into the rocker. "I'm worried about my

Alroy. He went to see his grace. There was an awful row here. Morely came." Edith's voice grew taunt with hatred. "He said his grace was upping the rent. We can hardly pay it now. My Alroy got mad and threw him out o' the house. Morely threatened to have us evicted. My Alroy's just gone to his grace about the rents. I'm afraid he'll throw us out for sure. My Alroy don't have a lot patience when he gets riled. I sent the boys along of him, but Griffin and John got tempers as bad as their father."

"Morely won't get away with this." Kelsey jumped up from her chair.

"Oh, me dear, I shouldn't have told you." Edith shook her head. "I can tell by that look in yer eye you mean to get involved. Don't, please. My Alroy will give me a blessing out for sure, and you working for the duke. No, no, I can't let you ruin yer job there. Griffin told me you'll be making an awful lot of grub. I won't have you losing it on my account."

"You know this family means more to me than all the money in the world." Kelsey saw the tears in Edith's eyes and hugged her. "It will be all right, you'll see."

Jeremy stood. "I'm sure my cousin would never turn these people out of their home."

"Oh, he would, me lord," Edith said angrily, stepping back from Kelsey's embrace. "He turned out the Allisters for not paying their rent. Lord knows how they're faring with their twelve—probably in the workhouse by now. And he turned out the Jenkins's too."

"His grace couldn't know about this," Jeremy said, defending his cousin.

"I don't know nothin' about that, all I know is that Morely works for him and it's Morely who turns the people out. That tells me his grace does know about it."

The McGregor girls burst through the cottage door, yelling, "We saw the carriage, Ma!"

They saw Jeremy and fell into one another. Hannah, the oldest at four and ten, stared openmouthed at Jeremy. She was a pretty girl who favored Griffin in coloring and looks. Sarah clung to

Hannah's shoulders and stared at Jeremy as if she'd never seen a man before. She was two and ten, and though not as pretty as Hannah, she had the promise of beauty. Johanna, the baby of the family, only six, was all big, wide gray eyes. She had a braided ring of daisies in her hair and looked like a little cherub.

"Where are yer manners, girls?" Edith snapped at them.

In unison the girls curtsied and said, "Pleased to met you, my lord."

"Lord Lovejoy, allow me to introduce Hannah, Sarah, and Johanna McGregor," Kelsey said, grinning at the amazed looks on the girls' faces. Not one of them could drag their eyes away from Jeremy long enough to notice that she was in the room.

"Ladies," Jeremy bowed slightly.

"I'm sorry, Edith, but we can't stay."

"Won't you stay for a tart?" Edith said, sounding disappointed.

"No, we'll pay a call tomorrow," Kelsey said. "I have to get back and see that Lord Salford does the right thing in this matter." Kelsey saw the crestfallen look on the girls' faces as she strode to the door. She said, patting Hannah on the arm, "Cheer up, I'll bring Lord Lovejoy back."

"You promise?" Hannah said, her gaze glued on Jeremy.

"Yes, she promises," Jeremy said, winking at Hannah.

Hannah looked ready to swoon, but Sarah grabbed her arm. Kelsey might have laughed if she weren't so angry at Edward. How could he be so miserly and raise the rents again?

Edward was in his study, trying to compose a letter. He stared down at the blank page, then slammed his pen down on the desk. How could he write a bloody letter, when Kelsey kept creeping into his mind?

A knock on the door drew him from his thoughts. Watkins poked his head in the door. "Mr. Morely to see you, your grace. Shall I show him in?"

"Yes, by all means," Edward said, scowling down at the

empty paper before him. A vision of Kelsey formed on the page, her large eyes gleaming back at him like the little temptress she was. When he heard Morely's footsteps coming down the hall, the vision vanished. He shook his head, balled up the blank paper, then threw it in the wastebasket by his desk.

"Your grace." Morely bowed in the doorway. He was a hard-faced man with leathery, tanned skin and eyes as cold as marble. He had the estate books under his arm.

"You're two weeks late with the books. I thought we agreed that you'd bring them on the first day of every month."

"I'm sorry I did not get here sooner, your grace, but my job is never done. There is always something to be seen to."

"Spare me the excuses. Sit." Edward watched him plop down in the chair, then Edward grabbed a letter from a stack of correspondence on his desk and stared down at it, then back up at Morely. "Would you mind explaining this letter?"

"W-well, your grace." Morely shifted uneasily in his seat, then appeared unable to meet Edward's unwavering gaze and looked down at his hands. "I thought it was self-explanatory."

"It is, but I don't understand why you've asked to raise the rents twice in one year."

"We need it, your grace. Stillmore isn't making a profit. It's the only one of your estates that isn't. Since you refuse to irrigate the land, we have to make up the loss somehow to pay the taxes."

Edward narrowed his good eye at Morely. "I find it a bit strange that Stillmore has not made a profit since I employed you as my estate manager two years ago." Edward smiled sardonically at him, then said, "New tailor, Morely? You must let me know whom you use. And the silk of your waistcoat, that's very expensive cloth, is it not?"

"Ah . . . yes, your grace." Morely said, pulling at his cravat as he shoved the books across Edward's desk.

After a brief look at Morely that made the man squirm in his seat, Edward found the current month of June and carefully scanned the pages.

"I need to speak to you about Alroy McGregor, your grace."

Edward glanced up from the page. "What about him?"

"He's three months late on his rent."

"I find that odd," Edward said, giving Morely a sidelong look. "McGregor has been a tenant at Stillmore for thirty years. He's never been late on his rent."

"Well, he's late. I went to see him today, and he refuses to pay his back rent. I'm going to have to evict him—"

"You cannot go in there!" Watkins's stern command boomed from the hallway.

Abruptly, the door flew open and banged against the wall behind it. Alroy McGregor filled the doorway, his broad chest heaving.

"I'm sorry, your grace," Watkins said flatly from behind McGregor's back. "I tried to stop him."

"It's all right, Watkins." Edward rose to his feet and met McGregor's gaze. Some of the anger left his tenant's expression as he took in Edward's scarred face.

"I'm sorry about barging in on you, your grace, but I needed to talk—" McGregor paused when he saw Morely, then he blurted out, "You bastard!"

McGregor lunged for Morely and grabbed him by his cravat. He pulled Morely up until they were nose to nose. McGregor was a tall man, and Morely had to stand on tiptoe to keep from being hanged by his cravat. "I suppose you've been spinning some of your lies, 'ey, Morely?"

"You're going to be evicted, McGregor," Morely said, sneering.

"Well, if I'm goin', then I'll get a bit of pleasure out of it...." McGregor drew back his powerful fist.

"Don't do it, McGregor." Edward's voice held enough menace to give McGregor pause. "I suggest you rein in your temper and we'll discuss this."

McGregor gritted his teeth, struggling to control his temper. After a moment he dropped Morely's cravat. Morely stumbled back and hit the edge of Edward's desk. He cried, "You'll be put out for this, McGregor, and I'll see you never rent another farm for miles around."

"One more word from you, Morely, and I might be forced to silence you myself. Is that understood?" Edward said in a voice dangerously low. "Now, *sit"*—he turned to McGregor—"you too."

McGregor didn't look happy about it, but he sat in a chair opposite Morely's.

Edward strode back behind his desk and sat. He leaned back in his chair and gave McGregor a severe look. "Is it true you haven't paid your rent for three months?"

"That's a bloody lie!" McGregor stood, his fists clenched, his whole body trembling with indignation.

"Sit down!" Edward narrowed his eye at him. The look sent McGregor back down in his seat. Edward continued again. "Now then, Mr. Morely tells me differently."

"Mr. Morely is a liar. I paid the thirty pounds I owed and I been paying it."

"Thirty pounds?" Edward said, not sounding surprised in the least.

"Aye, your grace. Thirty bloody pounds. I'm just about done-for paying it, but I been paying yer rent."

Edward glanced down at June's ledger, then back up at Morely. In an ominously repressed tone he asked, "Would you mind telling me why the books show that Mr. McGregor is paying only fifteen pounds a month?"

Sweat dripped from Morely's brow, and he took a handkerchief from his pocket and shook it out. He dabbed at his brow and said, "He's lying, your grace."

"On me mother's grave, he is the liar. You can ask me wife. She watches me give the money to him."

Morely leapt up and tried to make a mad dash to the door, but McGregor jumped out of his seat, drew back his fist, and hit Morely square in his face. The blow knocked him out cold, and he tumbled to the floor with a loud thud.

"Anyone ever tell you you have a hell of a right, McGregor," Edward said, staring over his desk at the fallen man.

"No, I rarely have to use it, your grace," McGregor said, grinning now.

"I owe you a debt of thanks for exposing a liar and a swindler. I found out that he was cheating me a month ago and I was about to have him packed off in irons, but I needed proof. You have given me that. How about a drink and we'll talk about this back rent that is coming to you."

"Aye, your grace. Ye won't mind me telling you something, will ye?"

"I am all ears." Edward poured two brandies.

"I hope you'll be paying more attention to your tenants, your grace, like you did afore the accident. You can't be trusting yer affairs to the likes of someone like Morely."

"I see that now," Edward said, then turned and glanced pensively at McGregor.

Lizzy had changed her clothes, put salve on her bee stings, and was on her way to the stables, when she heard loud voices coming from the entranceway. She strode down the steps and saw a thin, frail Watkins trying to deter three giant males at the door. He wasn't having much luck at it.

Eager to even the odds and jump into the fray, Lizzy bounded down the steps. "What seems to be the matter here?" she said in her best intimidating tone.

"These young men are trying to find their father. I told them they must wait here," Watkins said.

"Well, they can just turn around and leave and wait for him outside," Lizzy said, glowering at the three in question and slapping her riding crop in her palm.

They stared at her like openmouthed simpletons. Two of them were blond and blue-eyed, they looked about twenty or younger. The shorter of the two looked seventeen, more her age, and had bright red hair and freckles. Since she despised boys her own age, she addressed the oldest-looking one.

"Don't just stand there, you dolt. *Leave.*"

"We ain't leaving," he said arrogantly, crossing his arms over his chest. "We come for our da, and we ain't leaving till we see him."

"You can't talk to me like that," Lizzy said, jamming her hands down on her hips.

"Oh, can't I? Well, I'm doin' it."

"You'll regret it."

"Really, Miss Breeches," he said, staring insolently at her riding breeches.

"Do you know who I am?"

"Nope, and I don't wanna know."

"Well, I'm telling you." Lizzy raised her riding crop and shook it in his face. "I'm Lady Elizabeth."

"Don't look like no lady to me. Does she look like one, Ever?" the red-haired one said, punching his older brother.

"Nope, and she don't act like one neither," the one called Ever said.

"Now, you two hold yer wagging tongues. You might offend her delicate sensibilities." This from the eldest one.

The other two burst out laughing.

Fuming, Lizzy raised her riding crop to strike the eldest one, but he grabbed her hand and wrenched it loose.

"Why, you . . ." Lizzy attacked him with both her fists.

She didn't take into account he was a head taller than she and broad as a barn until he grabbed her arms and threw her up on his shoulder. She beat his back. "Let me go, you, you lack-brained oaf!"

Lizzy felt the first whack on her backside with her own riding crop. "Now, Miss Breeches, I suggest you calm down, or I'll give you another lick."

"You do and I'll have you drawn and quartered, you insolent, maggot-headed stump!"

Another whack.

This one was harder than the last and brought tears to her eyes.

"What is going on here?"

At the sound of Kelsey's voice, Lizzy yelled, "Get the magistrate! I mean to see this man hanged before the day is out! No, wait! Get my brother's dueling pistols, I'll kill him myself."

Lizzy felt the man's shoulder shake against her belly as he laughed.

"Put her down this instant, Griffin," Kelsey said.

Abruptly, Lizzy was dumped on her feet. She turned on Kelsey and pointed at the still-smiling giant. "You know this ignoramus?"

"I do indeed. He is my best friend, and these are his brothers, Everard and Jacob."

"Well, I pity you having such friends." Lizzy saw Jeremy standing beside Kelsey; he also, had a grin on his face. "Some cousin you are. Are you going to let him get away with treating me like this?"

"I'm sure you did something to deserve it, puss."

"Lizzy, try to calm down," Kelsey said.

"Calm down?" Lizzy was so angry, she had to close her eyes to keep her body from trembling.

"Griffin's not so bad once you get to know him." Kelsey gave Griffin a look of reproach.

At that moment Edward strode into the entrance foyer, another giant following him. "We heard you yelling, Lizzy," Edward said. "What is the matter?"

Lizzy looked at the one Kelsey called Griffin, gave him a smug look, then turned to her brother. "This boneheaded jackass manhandled me."

"She attacked me with this." Griffin handed him the riding crop.

"That's the truth," Jacob said, staring at Edward's face.

"Who asked you, carrot top!" Lizzy said.

"Lizzy, apologize this moment."

"But I didn't do—"

"Apologize," Edward said in a tone that would brook no argument.

Lizzy felt Kelsey's gaze on her and Lizzy glanced at her. Her eyes were hard, reminding Lizzy of her vow to be agreeable. "I'm sorry," Lizzy said, each word giving her pain as she spoke them.

"I'm sorry for my sister's behavior. She has yet to learn how to go on in the civilized world. I hope one day she will." Edward shot Lizzy a threatening glance.

"No harm done. We did tease her," Griffin said, grinning wickedly at Lizzy, then he addressed the man standing behind Edward. "Is all well, Da?"

"Aye, lad. We'll be going now. You'll come and pay us a visit soon, your grace?"

"Yes, soon." Edward nodded.

"What about the eviction? You can't allow it," Kelsey said anxiously to Edward.

"I have no intention of evicting my new estate manager."

"Estate manager?" Kelsey said with a thoroughly confused look on her face.

Edward smiled wryly at her. "I knew Morely's been stealing money from me, and since I'm in need of a new manager, I asked Mr. McGregor if he would take the job—which reminds me, Watkins, Morely's bound in the study. See that Grayson goes for the magistrate."

"Yes, your grace," Watkins said, walking away.

Lizzy noticed that Kelsey couldn't tear her gaze away from Edward, and Jeremy couldn't tear his gaze away from Kelsey, and Edward was glaring at Jeremy.

"We'll be off, then," Mr. McGregor said, herding his sons out the door.

The four giants left, and Lizzy, after frowning at the love triangle, slipped away from the entrance foyer unseen. The closest window was in the library, and she hurried to get there. She pushed the rolling ladder beneath the windows, then swiftly gained the top with her long, lithe legs. She rested her elbows on the sill of the small window, pressed her nose against the glass, and searched the front lawn for the one they called Griffin.

His bright flaxen hair was easy to spot. He was walking down the drive, next to those oafs he called brothers, slapping one of them on the back as if he might be enjoying a good laugh. She watched the cocky sway in his stride, and wondered if he was laughing at her. It didn't matter, of course. She hated him. After another moment of watching him, she realized he was by far the most handsome of the three oafs. He also fascinated her like no other oaf had ever done.

That afternoon, Kelsey was sitting on the scaffolding, her sketch pad in her lap, drawing a representation of the room. The two men Edward hired had finished cleaning off the plaster and had disposed of the refuse. She was alone in the room now.

She heard the echo of footsteps and glanced up to see Jeremy striding toward her. "Well, hello. I thought I'd find you in here," he said. He paused below the scaffolding, then glanced up at her.

"You find me earning my wage." Kelsey laid down the quill on the sketch pad and looked down at him.

"Should you be working after the fall you took?"

"Sketching is not work for me, it's pleasure."

"My pleasure would be watching you sketch." He splayed his legs and clasped his hands behind his back, taking up a comfortable stance to watch her.

"Don't. I must call you a liar, my lord, and a silver-tongued devil." Kelsey grinned down at him.

"You wound me." He placed his hands over his heart. "Me a liar? You must believe that watching you would give me the keenest pleasure in the world."

"I cannot see any man sitting idle for hours—especially gazing at a creature like me." Kelsey glanced down at her paint-stained smock and breeches. "Surely you would be better entertained by watching the beggars in the village."

He threw back his head and laughed.

"See, you're laughing because I speak the truth, and you know it."

His expression turned serious. "You don't know how wrong you are, my dear."

Kelsey picked up her quill again. "I hate to be rude, but you must go away so I can finish my sketch."

"I am going away. I came to say good-bye. You'll be rid of me for a day or two."

"Oh." Kelsey tried not to sound pleased.

"Do you not want to know where I am going?" He sounded hurt that she hadn't asked.

"Of course. Where are you going?"

"To London to hire that Runner for you."

"Thank you."

"Would you mind coming down here and facing me while you thank me? I've got a bit of a crick in my neck from looking up at you."

"All right, I suppose that was rude and insensitive of me." She laid down her tablet and started to get up.

"Here, I'll catch you. Hop down." He held up his arms to her.

The scaffolding was so high, he couldn't reach her even with his arms extended over his head. She hesitated, looking down into his handsome face, then at his well-manicured hands.

"What's the matter, don't trust me?"

"I trust you." Kelsey leaned forward and jumped.

He caught her around the waist and set her on the floor, but he did not take his hands away from her sides. "You are so petite, I barely felt you in my arms."

"I was there." Kelsey tried to step back from him, but he pulled her forward and kissed her.

Kelsey stood there allowing Jeremy to kiss her, measuring

his kiss against Edward's. She felt nothing other than a desire for it to end.

"I see I'm disturbing something."

Kelsey and Jeremy broke apart. She glanced over to see Lizzy, emerging from behind a hidden panel in the wall. So that was how she had haunted the ballroom.

Kelsey saw the dark censure on Lizzy's face and immediately felt her cheeks color up. She took a step back from Jeremy, then said, "It's not what you think."

"Oh, no? A simpleton could deduce what you two were doing."

"It was nothing, puss," Jeremy said. "I was just kissing Kelsey good-bye. Now, come here and I'll kiss you good-bye."

"Don't you come near me, you libertine!" Lizzy screeched as he chased her around the room, then he caught her and placed a chaste kiss on her cheek.

"Let me go!"

"Of course." Jeremy dropped his grip on her. "I'm off, then."

"Where are you going?" Lizzy asked, brushing the sleeves of her drab black gown as if to brush off Jeremy's touch.

"To London for a few days. Will you miss me?"

"Like I'll miss a bellyache," Lizzy said, giving him an irritated look.

"I suppose, then, I'll have to look to Miss Vallarreal to miss me." Jeremy turned toward Kelsey, who was still blushing.

She was too embarrassed to speak, and remained silent, not smiling. And seeing the glower on Lizzy's face made her discomfort intensify a hundredfold.

Jeremy finally broke the awkward silence and bowed to her. He looked suddenly uncomfortable by Kelsey's silence, but he covered it with a smile as he said again, "I'm off, then."

Kelsey curtsied to him and watched him walk down the room and disappear through the doorway.

Lizzy waited until his footsteps died away, then she plopped her hands on her hips and said, "What kind of mischief are you up to? First you kiss Edward, now I find you with Jeremy. You'd better make up your mind which one you want, or you might have them dueling over you. You'd like that, wouldn't you?"

"You're wrong, I wouldn't like it," Kelsey said, hurt and frustrated by the attack.

"Of course you would. You're a tart, that's what you are. Why don't you leave this place. I hate you!" Lizzy turned and ran back through the secret panel door.

"Wait, Lizzy!" Kelsey ran after her, wanting to explain to her that Jeremy had stolen the kiss.

She saw Lizzy grab a lantern off the wall, then she disappeared behind a corner. "Lizzy, wait! Let me explain!"

Kelsey followed the dim, swaying light, then a door slammed and she was left in total darkness.

Thirteen

Kelsey was forced to put one hand in front of the other to keep from bumping into the walls.

"Lizzy! Answer me!"

At the silence, Kelsey moved forward, abruptly bumping into a door. When she pushed on it, it opened suddenly, and she fell into a dank stairwell. It smelled ripe with centuries of stale air and damp stones. She heard the rhythmic pad of Lizzy's footsteps echoing from above. Glancing upward, she saw a winding stairwell, the dim light of Lizzy's lantern as she ran up the steps.

"Lizzy! Wait!"

She ran up after Lizzy. The steps were angled so that each step was treacherous. To keep from falling, she had to slow down. This must be one of the flanking towers in the castle, the stairs built in that manner to keep early invaders from penetrating the castle tower with ease. They must have been effective, for she had to concentrate on each step she took. The angle didn't seem to bother Lizzy. She took them like she had wings on her feet.

Kelsey finally reached the top, out of breath but ready to do battle with Lizzy. The stairs opened into a small circular room as wide as the tower. A plain rope bed sat on one side and a weathered desk stood on the other. An old bookcase was beside it, filled with books. A round braided rug covered the floor. Two pigeons cooed on the sill of a slender, almost nonexistent window in the room. She spotted Lizzy in front of the desk with her hands on her hips.

"Get out of here!"

"I'm not leaving until you listen to me. Do you expect me to endure your insults and let you run away? Well, I won't. And I'll have you know, I didn't throw myself at Jeremy. He stole that kiss. I never invited it. As a matter of fact, when he declared himself, I told him straightaway that I wasn't interested in him, but he doesn't seem to listen."

"Why should I believe you?"

"Because it's the truth. Do you think I look like a seductress in these clothes?" Kelsey pulled at the hem of her baggy smock.

She saw Lizzy try to maintain her scowl, but her expression softened. "I suppose not, you don't dress much like a tart." Lizzy turned, scooped out a cup of cracked corn from a small tin on the desk, then spread it on the windowsill for the pigeons.

"I see you've got quite a room here."

"Yes, I like the solitude up here."

Kelsey saw an open book on the desk and leaned over to read it. "You write poetry?"

Lizzy slammed the book closed. "Yes, and my work is private."

"I see." Kelsey turned and read the titles of the books on the shelf. "Shakespeare . . . Milton . . . Keats . . . Scott . . . Shelley. You like some of the same authors as I do."

"You don't have to make polite conversation." Lizzy turned, clasping her poetry book to her bosom. "I detest it."

"You're not being very agreeable," Kelsey said as she strode over to the bed and sat on the edge of the mattress.

"This is as agreeable as I get. Why don't you be agreeable and tell me if you care for my brother."

"All right, I'll be honest with you. I think I like him very much." Kelsey rested her hands in her lap and steepled her fingers.

"How much? Would you consent to be his mistress?"

"Absolutely not," Kelsey said indignantly.

"You should know, he told me he'd never marry again."

"I don't know why you're telling me this, it doesn't matter to me." Even if it did, Kelsey wasn't about to admit it. "I've no wish to marry him. As soon as I'm done with the ballroom, I mean to take the money your brother pays me and go to London and start my art career."

"You never answered me. Do you love him?"

"You really are as infuriating as your brother, Lizzy. Some things I will not answer, and that is one of them," Kelsey said, getting to her feet. "But I will tell you this, I'd like to somehow help him recover his self-esteem. If he'd stop living like a re- cluse and go back out into society, I'm sure he'd be able to get on with his life."

Lizzy laughed so hard, it made Kelsey frown at her. Lizzy set the book she'd been holding down on the desk. "If you think to play the heroine and try to change Edward, then you had better forget it. It's too bad you love him—"

"I never said I loved him."

"You don't have to say it." Lizzy rolled her dark eyes. "I see just by talking to you now that your eyes sparkle when you mention his name. I didn't see it before, but I do now. You love him scars and all." An ironic grin spread across her face. "Be careful that you don't get hurt. If I were you, I'd stay away from him."

Kelsey couldn't do that, but she wasn't about to tell Lizzy that. Edward needed someone to help him gain his self-esteem back, and she decided to be that person. She stood. "It's time for me to leave."

"One more thing before you go."

"What?"

"What do you know about Griffin McGregor?"

"Why do you ask?" Kelsey looked at her slyly.

Lizzy turned away from Kelsey's gaze and petted one of the pigeons on the head as she spoke. "He's such a rag-mannered curiosity, is all. I was merely trying to understand what makes such a brute tick."

Kelsey grinned at Lizzy's back. "Well, I suppose I know what makes Griffin tick, I've been his best friend for years."

"That puzzles me exceedingly. Why are you friends with such a crude, stupid person?"

"He's really charming once you get to know him. Those who know him don't find him crude or stupid at all—especially the village girls."

"He's a libertine and a rake, then?" Lizzy turned, pleasantly enthralled now, her dark eyes gleaming like onyx.

"Not really." Kelsey tapped the side of her cheek. "I wouldn't call him a rake." She saw Lizzy's hopeful expression fall, and added, "He's courted just about every pretty girl in the village though. I guess he could be considered a rake."

"Oh." Lizzy looked interested again.

"Yes, women fall all over him. His problem is that he thinks he loves every woman he courts, but it's really only pity. He's much too gallant when it comes to women, and they seem to know it, for they prey on his good heart, though none have caught him yet. He thinks he's much too wise for that."

"Does he really?" Lizzy turned, a thoughtful gleam in her eye.

"Would you like to go with me when I call on the McGregors tomorrow morning? I promised Mrs. McGregor that I would come back and sample one of her apple tarts."

"Will Griffin be there?"

"Probably."

"I don't think I can be agreeable to him or his odious brothers," Lizzy said petulantly.

"They can be irritating at times. I won't expect you to be agreeable to them, just civil."

"I suppose I can manage that."

"I never doubted you couldn't." Kelsey smiled serenely at her, then said, "I guess I should get back."

"Wait! I'll take you back."

"No need, I can find my way. I would beg a candle from you though."

Lizzy lit a candle, then handed it to her. "Do be careful. There are miles of tunnels beneath the castle. The Second Duke of Salford had the tunnels put in so his captives could not escape this tower. Some of them lead to dead ends and others lead to the oddest places, like to several wine cellars, and the dungeon, and one actually leads to the chapel. When Stillmore was remodeled, my great-great-grandfather decided it was a good joke, and he built secret passages throughout the new wing that led directly to the tunnels."

"So that's how you came into the ballroom."

"Yes."

"And that's how you got into my room when the door was locked."

Lizzy shook her head, looking amused.

"From now on knock on the door."

Lizzy laughed. "I will. Here. . . ." She handed Kelsey the candle holder. "Be careful. I got lost once when I was small." She grinned. "It took Edward two days to find me."

"Yes, I will. I'm sure I remember how to get back."

Kelsey waved to Lizzy as she descended the long, winding stairs. Going down was much easier than coming up. She stepped through the thick oak door, then started down the passageway. Abruptly, she saw Brutus leap out of the shadows.

"Hello, you old mouser. Why did you follow me?" She squatted down and reached her hand toward him. Right before her fingers touched him, he took off running down the tunnel.

"Brutus, come back!"

Kelsey was afraid he would get lost and not find his way out. "Brutus!"

She raised the candle high into the air and ran after him, barely able to keep him in the light. She ran into a cobweb and almost dropped the candle as she tore it away from her head.

She raised the candle again to find Brutus, but he'd disappeared. "Brutus! Kitty! Kitty! Come here!"

She ran ahead, turning left and right, desperately searching for him. Feeling as if she were going around in circles, she paused, the silence in the corridor ringing hollow in her ears.

"Lizzy!" Kelsey screamed at the top of her lungs, feeling suddenly panicked.

After what seemed like hours but had been only minutes, she gave up on Lizzy coming to her rescue. The stone walls were so dense, Lizzy probably couldn't hear her anyway. She tried not to panic and reminded herself the tunnel she was in had to lead somewhere. The marked downward slope of the floor told her she had not been in this particular direction yet. She left a trail of candle wax on the floor as she moved ahead, just in case she had to backtrack and find another way out.

Abruptly, she reached a door. Cobwebs hung around it as if it hadn't been opened in centuries. "Please let this be the chapel," she said to herself. Her hands trembled as she beat away the cobwebs and forced back the iron latch on the door. She threw her weight against the door. It creaked as it opened.

She raised the candle higher. Rack after rack of bottled wine filled the room. The damp coldness went straight through her bones. She shivered as she stepped down the two steps into the wine cellar, then drew closer to one of the wine racks. She brushed aside the cobwebs and dust on one of the bottles. It was labeled 1491. She picked up the bottle and stuck it under her arm in case she couldn't find her way out right away and needed some fortification, which seemed highly likely.

Out of the corner of her eye she spotted an ancient corkscrew hanging from the end of one of the wine racks, and she slipped it into her pocket. Her heel hit something when she turned to leave. She glanced down and saw a fully clothed skeleton leaning against the end of the rack, a fleshless hand still clutching a bottle.

She opened her mouth to scream, but nothing came out.

* * *

Edward looked up from his desk and glanced around his study as if he'd heard something. The knock on his door distracted him. "Enter," he said.

Jeremy stood in the doorway, his hat in one hand and his driving gloves in the other. "Just thought I'd say good-bye before I left."

"Where are you going?"

"To London."

"I thought you were avoiding London these days."

"I'm sure the scandal has died down by now. I have important business there."

"What business could force you there after you shot Lord Britterwood. I would think you'd want to stay clear of the man."

"It's his wife I wish to stay clear of." Jeremy grinned roguishly. "And I have no intention of running across her in town, unless she is looking for another victim on Bow Street."

"What are you going to do on Bow Street?"

"As to my business, I've been charged by Miss Vallarreal to hire a Runner for her."

"For what reason?" Edward started to leap to his feet, but he didn't want to give himself away in front of Jeremy, so he remained in his chair, trying to look indifferent.

"Her father has gone missing and she wishes to find him."

"I sent him to Bath." Edward leaned back in his chair and clasped his hands behind his head.

"Whatever for?" Jeremy bristled and slapped his riding gloves against his thigh.

"To dry out. I thought it was the best place for him."

"You're afraid he'll tell her the truth. If he hasn't done so by now, he won't. She is worried about him. You have to tell her where he is."

"I shall, in my own good time."

"You'll do it in a sennight, Eddie, or I'll do it for you."

"Is that a threat?" Edward stood up, his fists clenched at his sides.

"Yes, it is." Jeremy jerked on his driving gloves. "This farce has gone on long enough. I mean to propose to her, and I won't do it knowing that you haven't told her the truth." Jeremy turned on his heel and left the room.

Edward stared at the empty doorway. *Propose.* The word reverberated through his mind. Would Kelsey accept him? She could have her pick, McGregor or Jeremy. The walls felt as if they were closing in around him, his restlessness clawing at him. He ran his hands through his hair, jerking it out of the queue at the back of his neck, then he slammed his hand down on the desk. *Propose . . . propose . . . propose.* The litany went through his mind as he rose from his desk and stalked out of the room.

Sometime later, Kelsey's candle had burned out and so had she. She flopped down on the floor of a tunnel, hungry, freezing, and thirsty. The sight of the skeleton still burned in her memory. She pulled the cork on the wine.

"I suppose it's all right to drink in dire circumstances such as these," Kelsey mumbled before she turned up the bottle. Her first taste was a small sip. It wasn't bitter as she thought it would be. It tasted almost sweet.

She turned up the bottle again, and again, until her head started to spin. Sighing, she thrust the empty bottle aside and listened to it roll across the stone floor. She batted a cobweb out of her face, then leaned her head back against the stone wall, feeling the icy coldness pressing against her spine.

"So this is what it feels like to be in a dungeon," she said to herself.

Suddenly something cold and hairy touched her hand. She screamed, thinking it was a rat or mouse. Then she heard the yowl, a very familiar yowl. Something hairy brushed against her arm.

"Brutus! You horrible wretch." Kelsey picked him up and clutched him to her breast, hugging him tightly. She realized he was allowing her to hold him, and tears stung her eyes as she buried her face into his soft fur. "You're letting me pet you now, are you? What a price I had to pay. Have you been hiding all alone, playing games with me. What do you say you show me the way out of here? I promise you a whole barrel of warm milk if you do it." She scratched him behind his ears and heard his loud purring.

"You won't mind if I put a little leash on you, will you? Too bad if you do. If it wasn't for you, I wouldn't be in this mess." The worn and faded piping on her smock came off easily, and she used it as a leash, tying it around Brutus's neck. Her hands were clumsy and it took her two tries to tie it. "There now, show me what a gallant cat you can be and rescue me."

She slowly got to her feet, feeling her head spin. In spite of her dizziness, she managed to stagger behind Brutus. Up, up, up. Brutus paused. Kelsey took off the leash, then picked him up. She ran her hand over the stones and found a long crack. A cool draft brushed against her fingertips.

"Good, kitty. This must be a door. All I need to do . . ." She shoved and the door opened.

She stumbled out onto an altar and realized she'd found the chapel. Even with her wine-dulled senses, she felt the aura of ageless silent solitude in the building. Her own heartbeat sounded thunderous in her ears. She glanced up at the nave, at the thick black beams spanning it. A quaint circular stained glass window shone with dim light over the chapel doors. By the dull blankness of the window, she knew the sun had already set.

The pews drew her gaze now—one in particular as Edward stood up from it. He wore a black coat, black pants, and no cravat. The top button of his shirt was open, and she couldn't help but stare at his exposed chest hair. She wondered what it would feel like to run her fingers through it.

"What are you doing in here?" he said, looking irritated enough to chew her head off.

"I could ask you the same thing." Kelsey stopped staring at his chest and swayed on her feet, hugging Brutus.

"I come here often to meditate. Why are you unsteady on your feet? Are you ill?" He came toward her.

"No, no, I'm a little bit inebriated." She gave him her best drunken grin.

"You never cease to amaze me." He paused near her, towering over her. "What are you doing with Brutus in your arms? He's wild. He'll bite you."

"No, we are friends. You wouldn't do that, now, would you, Brutus?" Kelsey scratched Brutus behind the ear after she found his head, which took two tries. "Must you scowl at me like that, Edward? I hate it when you do that. Don't you believe me?"

"I'm not scowling."

"Now you're yelling. I may be drunk, but I can still hear quite plainly and"—Kelsey lowered her voice to a whisper—"your deep voice carries in here. I do have a reason for holding Brutus and for being in this state."

He crossed his arms over his broad chest and his scowl deepened. "Really, I'd like to hear it," he whispered back to her, his voice silken with irritation.

"I was lost for quite some time in the tunnels below the castle. Did you know there's a skeleton in a wine cellar below?"

"I'm sure that's not the only one."

"Really?"

"Yes, the Second Duke of Salford liked to punish his enemies by locking them in the tunnels. Some of them were found after they starved to death. The lucky ones found the wine cellars and drank themselves to death before the end."

"I see you get your sense of fair play from them." A lazy grin spread across her mouth.

"I suppose I do."

"That poor bag of bones below scared me half to death. The stories I've heard in the village about your ancestor must be true, but he could've had the decency to have located his enemies and given them a proper burial."

"I'm sure they got far less than they deserved, but if you'd like, I'll have the body brought out and properly buried."

"That would be prudent—'specially if another person gets lost down there. Thank God for my friends here—no, no, there's only one feline in my arms, but I see two." Kelsey giggled and hugged Brutus tighter. "If not for him, I would still be lost down there in the bowels of the first Stoop of Salmore's hell." Kelsey laughed at her twisted words and Brutus jumped out of her arms. She went to grab him and fell forward.

One minute she was falling. Then she was in Edward's arms. She grinned up at him. "See, you can be amiable if you try. I like you much better this way, instead of always growling at me."

"I should do more than growl at you." He strode out of the chapel with her.

"The question is what would you like to do?" she said tauntingly.

"For a start, I'd like to gag you."

"Very well, consider me gagged." She bit her lip to keep from talking and felt the crispness of the night air as he carried her out into it. She took a deep breath, felt her head clear a little, then glanced over his shoulder at the moon. She kept her eyes on it as he walked. Her head lolled backward over his arm, and she smiled at the huge round sphere from her upside-down position.

"Sit up before you break your neck."

"You should try looking at the moon upside down. It's singularly beautiful from this angle. I don't think I've ever seen it—"

He pushed his arm up and her head fell forward. "Do you

enjoy anything?" she asked, still dizzy from the sudden movement of her head.

"Silence and solitude."

"That is not true. If that were true, you wouldn't have a paramour."

"I have a paramour out of necessity."

"Necessity?" She looked baffled for a moment, then grinned. "Oh, yes, male necessity. I know all about it. Sure you're not French? My father says Frenchmen have a great need for necessity."

"Does he?" His mouth twisted in a grin.

"See! I knew your face wouldn't break if you smiled. You really do have an intriguing face when you smile. Anyone ever tell you that?"

"Not recently," he said flatly, the smile fading.

"It is so very different, yet seems so familiar to me. Would you let me paint you one day?" Mesmerized, Kelsey traced the line of his proud jaw with her eyes, the hard lips, the deep cheekbones, the widow's peak on his high forehead.

"Why would I want a portrait of myself, when it sickens me to look in the mirror?"

"You can't see what I see, for it doesn't sicken me at all. Quite the contrary. This is your best side." She touched the scarred side of his cheek and felt him tense. She grinned to herself and said, "Do you want to know why I like it best?"

"No."

"I'm going to tell you anyway." She ran her finger over the long scar that slashed downward from his cheek. "I like this side for the simple flawed beauty there, hiding nothing from the world. But this side . . ." Kelsey moved her hand to his perfect profile. She rubbed her fingers over the stubble on his chin, feeling his tense jaw muscle pulse beneath her fingertips. "This side frightens me in all its dangerous perfection. It gives away nothing and hides everything behind a severe, controlled mask—"

"You sound like a drunken fool."

Kelsey grimaced at him, then dropped her hand from his face. It plopped down on his chest. "Perhaps I am a drunken fool, but I'd still like to paint your face."

"It will never happen."

"Never say never. You may eat those words. I don't need to see you to paint your portrait. I've memorized it."

"You're going to do nothing but go to bed."

A dark strand of hair fell over his forehead and caught her attention. Feeling playful, she flicked it with her finger, watching it fall back down over his brow.

"Stop that."

"You really are too sensitive."

Kelsey was suddenly on her bed. She looked around. "How did we get in my chamber?"

"I brought you."

She felt him pull off her shoes, then lift her and pull off her smock, then he unbuttoned her shirt. She grinned at him. "Are you undressing me?"

"Yes."

"I may be drunk, but I do know I'm supposed to keep my clothes on."

"I'm not going to molest you."

"You're not?" Kelsey couldn't keep the disappointment out of her voice. "I guess you only molest your paramour—well, molest isn't the proper word, is it? You can't molest a fallen woman, now, can you?" She laughed.

"No, you cannot." She watched his lips widen in a grin. "I'm just taking off your clothes so you'll be comfortable."

"That's very thoughtful, but I'm quite comfortable with my clothes on."

He was holding her beneath her armpits while he pried her limp arms out of the shirt. He let go of her to throw the shirt aside, and the upper half of her body flopped backward. She landed against the pillows and giggled, until she felt him unbuttoning her breeches.

She grabbed the front of her breeches. "Really, taking off my clothes won't sober me."

He knocked her hands away, then yanked off her breeches, leaving her in a chemise and drawers. He kept his eyes on her face, pulled the covers up to her neck, and said, "Go to sleep."

He was past her bed, heading toward the connecting door, when Kelsey grabbed her head. Using her most pitiful voice, she said, "You're not going, are you?"

"Yes."

"You can't."

"Why?"

"Because I feel like I'm going to be quite sick."

"I'll get the chamber pot."

"No, just rub my feet. It always worked when I was a child. My mother would rub my feet. It would take my mind off being sick."

"All right." He sounded skeptical, but he pulled her feet from beneath the covers. She felt the mattress sink as he sat on the end of the bed. He laid her feet across his hard thighs.

When his warm hands starting massaging her foot, she closed her eyes and groaned. "Ohhh! That is lovely, really. I'll have to do it for you when you overindulge and get sick."

"No, thank you."

"You like suffering, then?"

"Be quiet and perhaps you'll feel better!"

"I will if you answer one question."

"What?" he said impatiently.

"Have you ever loved a woman?" He started on the other foot. She felt the warmth spreading up her legs from his expert hands. "Ahhh! That feels especially good." When he didn't answer her, Kelsey said, "Well?"

"Well what?"

"Did you ever love anyone?"

"There was a girl a long time ago that I loved."

"Why didn't you marry her?"

"Because I was betrothed from my cradle to the woman I married."

"The duchess who took her own life because of you."

"Not because of me." His massaging grew painful.

"That hurts . . ." She tried to jerk her foot away, but he held it tightly and softened his touch. "That's better. I'm sorry, I just assumed she committed suicide from the scandal with Clarice."

"She killed herself a week before the scandal. She loved another man and her father forced her to marry me."

"Where was her lover?"

"The man had been making his fortune in the East Indies and hadn't learned of our marriage until it was too late. He shot himself a month before Margaret took her own life."

"How tragic."

"Yes, he never spoke to Margaret before he killed himself, or he would have learned that we had not consummated the marriage."

"I'm sorry it was not a happy marriage for either of you." Kelsey heard the sadness and regret in his voice, and it seeped over her and made her want to hold him.

"I didn't know until our wedding night that she despised me. I had no intention of forcing myself on a reluctant bride, so I left her alone. I had even contemplated the scandal of having the marriage annulled so Margaret could marry her lover, but when she heard of his death, she hung herself."

"Why did you marry her if you loved another?" Her voice grew softer as she gave over to feelings of languorous sadness.

"It was my father's fondest wish that I marry Lord Pemberton's daughter. He was my father's oldest and dearest friend. They drew up a marriage contract while we were both in our cradles. I had to honor it when I turned of age, so I did. I was young, I didn't care whether I was in love with her. I wanted to get an heir from her, then we could go our own separate ways."

Edward waited for Kelsey to fire another probing question at him, but after several moments of silence he heard her deep, even breaths and knew she had fallen asleep. He leaned over and kissed the top of her feet, then tucked them beneath the covers and rose from the bed.

"Sleep well, my dear Kelsey," he whispered, then he leaned over and kissed her.

Her breath smelled bittersweet with wine. She moaned softly, her lips a mere flutter against his mouth. Fighting the overwhelming desire to taste her mouth again, to awaken her and make love to her, he strode out of her room.

Edward had left the connecting door open just in case Kelsey grew sick in the night. He lay on his bed, listening for her, hearing every rustle of the covers, every creak of the bed when she moved. He could still feel her soft skin against his scarred face where she'd touched him earlier. She was drunk, of course, but it was all he could do not to make love to her, to feel her touch him all over, to melt in her warmth and sweetness. God! He ached with wanting her. . . .

"Come back! Don't leave me! Please . . . come back!" Kelsey cried out in the next room.

Her voice went through him like a rapier. He jumped up from his bed and ran into her room. She was sitting up in bed, rocking back and forth, covering her face with her hands as she sobbed. She looked the picture of a frightened little girl.

He sat down beside her and wrapped his arms around her. "Shhh! What is it, Kelsey?"

"I couldn't find the boy. He went away . . . I couldn't find him. I want him back." She clutched at his neck, clinging to him, burying her face against his bare chest. "Make him come back . . . make him come back."

"You've had a bad dream. It's all right now." Edward stroked her hair and felt her trembling all over. He held her closer, feeling the warm wetness of her tears against his chest. He leaned down, placed his cheek against the top of her head, then continued to stroke her soft hair, whispering soothing things in her ear.

Her sobbing finally subsided and she leaned back to look up at him. Her enormous green eyes glistened at him in the darkness, those sensitive, giving windows to her soul. At that moment he could have denied her nothing, not even his heart if she had asked for it.

"You won't leave me, will you, Edward?" She sounded so forlorn, her voice soft and pleading.

"I won't leave you," he said in a ragged whisper, then before he knew it, he was burying his fingers in her thick hair and bringing her face up to his for a kiss.

Fourteen

When Kelsey's fingers dug into his bare skin, she realized Edward was naked. She hugged him tighter, feeling the warm, slick film of perspiration on his skin. She let her fingers slide along the taut, rippling sinews of his back, unable to get over the newness of feeling the male body. The male form had always intrigued her, exquisite in all its grace and angular strength, but viewing it from afar was nothing like actually touching the hardness, feeling the muscles ripple beneath her fingertips. She would never draw the male body quite the same way after touching Edward.

She wanted to feel all of him, and lowered her hands to his buttocks. He groaned like a dying man. Abruptly, she drew her hands back, afraid she had hurt him.

He broke the kiss and leaned back to look in her eyes. Dim moonlight streamed in through the window, and she could see the wounded expression on his face.

"If touching me disgusts you so much, why don't you go and find McGregor or Jeremy to comfort you," he said, then dropped his hands from around her and rose from the bed.

"I don't want them. Please, don't go." Kelsey grabbed his hand.

"I think it's best." He jerked his hand free, then strode toward the connecting door.

Kelsey leapt out of bed and followed him, talking to his back. "You misunderstand. I thought you didn't want me to touch you. You groaned like you were dying." He paused and turned to look at her. Kelsey continued to babble on. "I don't want Jeremy or Griffin. I love touching you. You're a beautiful specimen."

He was standing near the window and the moonlight hid nothing from her view. Her heartbeat grew rapid as she gazed at his body—his broad shoulders, his perfectly formed biceps and pectorals, the corded muscle along his flat stomach, his long, granite thighs. Her mouth fell open when she saw his erection.

He pulled her into his arms and hugged her. "Is that all I am to you, a specimen?" He grinned down at her.

"There could never be a finer one," she said tremulously, feeling his bulging erection pressing against her abdomen. She knew the mechanics of intercourse, but she was starting to doubt everything she'd learned. It seemed physically impossible after having seen the size of his phallus. Her heart pounded erratically in her chest. Her palms grew sweaty.

"You're trembling, Kelsey. You need not be afraid, I hope I'm as good a lover as that McGregor pup. . . ."

She started to tell him Griffin wasn't her lover, but he bent down and kissed her, cutting off her words. His hands closed over her breasts, kneading them through her chemise.

She forgot all about mechanics and impossibilities and Griffin as she arched her back, waves of fire searing her entire body. He teased her nipples into hard nubs with his fingers, while he leaned her back against the wall and opened her thighs with his leg. He moved his hand down inside her drawers, then splayed his hand over her flat belly, letting his fingers move slowly downward to the swell of her hips. She sucked in her breath, her muscles tensing as his fingers moved through her dark triangle of hair, then lower still, to cup her moist flesh.

"Oh!" She stiffened and her thighs tightened against his hand.

"No, no, my sweet, let me touch you. . . ."

He kissed her until she felt dizzy. Her knees grew weak and

she melted against him, her thighs relaxing against his hand, her body yearning for his touch. He stroked the soft velvety folds between her thighs with such deftness, it made her writhe and moan and grip his arms.

"Does that feel good, my sweet?"

"No—yes, I don't know. . . ."

"It will soon feel better." He opened her and his finger slowly slid inside. She gasped, feeling her flesh tighten around his finger. He withdrew his finger slowly, prolonging a yearning agony building inside her.

"Please . . ." She dug her nails into his shoulders.

"Yes, my love. Soon. You are so tight, so hot. I can feel your sweet honey. Do you want me, Kelsey?" He moved his finger inside her again, deeper this time.

"Yes, yes, I want . . . I need . . . you." She clutched at his shoulders, trembling.

He withdrew his finger again, painfully slowly. Her hips moved against his hand, and a muffled cry left her lips. His breath grew ragged as he found her tiny bud of pleasure. His finger was wet with her dew, and he stroked her while he slowly entered her again. She went up in flames and cried out, clinging to him.

"That's right, my love, give yourself to me. . . ."

He crushed her mouth, thrusting his tongue deep inside. He moved in and out of her, the rhythm of his tongue matching the thrusts of his finger. Her breathing grew rapid as her hips ground against his hand. She felt as if she might burn up from so much delicious torment. She screamed out his name in his mouth as she exploded with pleasure.

He withdrew his hand from her drawers, then swept her up into his arms.

"Where are you taking me?" She could barely speak past the throbbing still in her body. She rested her head on his shoulder and breathed in the intoxicating masculine scent of him.

"To my bed, where I can savor your body before I take it." He nibbled her ear as she spoke.

Now was the time to save what was left of her dignity, but she could not. He needed her as much as she needed him. If he had asked her to follow him to the moon, she would have gone. And as they entered his room and he laid her down on his bed as if she were a delicate piece of china, she thought he would probably take her to the moon and beyond it.

He bent over her, kissing her as he loosened the ties on her gown. With one quick, skillful movement he eased off her garment. When she was naked, he stood and stared down at her. She blushed under his scrutiny, feeling suddenly shy. The room was lit only by moonlight, but she knew he could see her clearly even in the dark.

"You are so beautiful, my love. . . ."

He lowered his body over hers, then kissed her, his lips gentle yet urgent. The heat of him scorched her. The sensation of him touching her everywhere made her want to melt into him. He kissed a line down her neck. He placed a kiss over the pulse point at the base of her throat, then he took one of her dusky peach peaks in his mouth and sucked. Her nipple was already hard, and he teased the nub between his teeth, rubbing his tongue over it. She arched her back, feeling waves of scalding tingles shooting down past her chest and pooling in her belly. She grabbed handfuls of his hair as she pushed his mouth closer to her breast.

He moved to her other breast, giving it equal attention, driving her mad with his mouth. He raised one of her legs and settled himself against the secret nub he'd touched earlier, then his hips began to undulate. She lowered her hands to his buttocks, feeling the rock-hard muscles pulsing beneath her fingers as he moved. She locked her legs around the back of his thighs, pushing his hips closer, moving with him.

"Touch me, Kelsey," he said in a ragged whisper.

She reached up and ran her fingers along the scars on his cheek, feeling the small, uneven ridges. A shudder went through him. She marveled at the power her touch had over him. Her pulse raced as her hands moved down the hard contours of his chest, then she splayed her fingers in his chest hair and massaged his nipples as he had done to her. He bent down and took her lips in a demanding kiss. Her hands tangled in his thick, dark hair as she dipped her tongue into his mouth, boldly entwining her tongue with his.

He groaned, then lifted her hips and plunged into her. She cried out and hugged his neck, feeling the thick, foreign hardness painfully deep inside her. He froze, then cursed, every muscle in his body hardening. He broke the kiss and stared down at her, heaving, his breath coming in great hot gasps against her face. His body was like granite on top of her, taut from the control it was taking him to remain still.

"You're a bloody virgin."

"You needn't sound so surprised."

"Why didn't you tell me?"

"I told you Griffin wasn't my lover. You should have known I was a virgin."

"I should have known?"

"Don't yell at me."

"Good God, Kelsey! I wouldn't have hurt you had I known."

The uncomfortable throbbing between her legs prompted her to say with resignation, "Perhaps it is for the best that we don't proceed. I think it is impossible. You are so very large and I am way too small. It's impossible to put a square peg in a round hole."

He glanced down at her. A sardonic male grin spread across his lips. "Never doubt it can be done."

"No, no, I don't think so. We had better stop."

"There's no turning back now, you feel too good. . . ." He kissed her again, then he started to move slowly inside her.

She forgot about the pain as his thrusts grew stronger and more rapid. The heat was building inside her again. She gave over to it, matching the rhythm of his thrusts with her hips. Liquid fire poured through her and devoured her. He took her soft scream into his mouth as she found her release. He thrust deeply, touching her womb. She felt his seed fill her, then he shuddered.

He kissed her, then collapsed on top of her.

Tremors still rippled through her, and she clung to him, waiting for them to subside. She could feel the pounding of his heart keeping time with hers. The musky smell of their love-making filled her senses. She was happy. Nothing could equal this sated feeling, this closeness she felt with him.

He rose onto his elbows and glanced down at her as if he had something momentous to say. "Kelsey?"

"Yes . . ." She held her breath, knowing he would declare his undying love for her now.

"We shouldn't do this ever again."

She beat on his chest. "Let me up this instant."

He pinned her wrists to the pillow and grinned sardonically down at her. "Why are you angry with me?"

"That was a wretched thing to say to me after I just let you make love to me. There's not an ounce of tenderness in you. You are all ice. You're about as sensitive as a rutting goat. You were right, this was a mistake. Let me up!"

"I may have ice in my veins, my sweet, but your fire warms my blood. I find I want you again." He grinned down at her. Her mouth opened to spew another retort, but he kissed her. She lay there, feeling his lips moving over hers. It was hard to hold on to her anger as she felt his manhood growing inside her again, completely impossible when he started to move inside her again with slow, drugging undulations. So his lust was all she would get. No, she had to have more. She realized now that he'd said they shouldn't make love again because he wanted to remain safe behind his little wall of aloofness. She wouldn't let him. In her heart she knew he cared about her. Before the night was out, she vowed to hear him say it.

Sometime later, as he made mad, passionate love to her again, Kelsey was the one crying out her love for him. But Edward hadn't said one thing about the subject.

Kelsey stretched like a sated cat. Instinctively, she reached for Edward. All that met her fingers was a cold sheet. She opened her eyes and realized that he had put her back in her own bed and that it was morning.

When she rose from her bed, she felt the soreness between her thighs. She smiled, remembering his sweet lovemaking. He'd murmured his love for every part of her body, but he never said he loved her. "He will," she vowed solemnly under her breath.

A knock came at her door, then Lizzy sailed into the room. "Morning, Kelsey." She sounded more chipper than usual.

Kelsey casually glanced at Lizzy. Not believing what she'd seen, Kelsey glanced at her again. She tried not to stare at the transformation Lizzy had undergone, but it was so astounding, she couldn't draw her eyes away. Lizzy's hair was swept back from her face, and several long curls hung over her shoulder, a very becoming style for her slender face. The ugly black dress was gone and in its place was a pink frock that flattered her thin figure.

"You can stop looking at me like I'm a ghoul with two heads." Lizzy strode over to Kelsey's bed and sat down on the edge. Lizzy's long, coltish strides had disappeared beneath the pretty dress, and she carried herself like a regal queen. "Well, you can say something," Lizzy said, slapping the folds of her dress as if she could barely tolerate it.

"I don't know what to say, Lizzy, but that you look quite lovely. To what do we owe this transformation?"

"Just being agreeable. I've come to ask you to join me for brunch. I intend to dine with Edward this morning, but I really can't stand to see him scowl and grumble through the whole affair like he usually does." Mimicking her brother, Lizzy's face contorted into a horrible scowl, and she grunted aloud several times.

Kelsey laughed. "You are terrible but, you do favor him when you do that."

They both laughed.

Lizzy stood. "You'll join me, then?"

"Yes, thank you."

"Be ready in thirty minutes."

She listened to the rustle of Lizzy's gown as she floated out of the room in a cloud of pink. Kelsey had a suspicion as to what had brought about this transformation, but she would wait and see if her suspicions were correct.

She found out later as she strode into the dining hall behind Lizzy. Kelsey couldn't see Edward because Lizzy was so tall, but she felt his presence. Her heart pounded with anticipation of seeing him.

Lizzy turned and walked over to the sideboard where the food was laid out in chafing dishes, and Kelsey saw Edward sitting at the head of the table.

Their gazes locked. He stared at Kelsey, surprise and delight in his face, then a slow, lazy smile spread across his lips. At his suggestive smile, Kelsey remembered all the things he had done to her the night before. Blood rushed to her cheeks and she grinned sheepishly back at him.

"I hope you don't mind, but I invited Kelsey to dine with us," Lizzy said offhandedly while she ladled eggs into a plate.

"I don't mind." His gaze slid over Kelsey, caressing her breasts, her small waist, the slight swell of her hips.

Kelsey had chosen the most seductive gown in her wardrobe, a low-cut day dress of cream silk with lace overlays on the bodice, which made her breasts appear larger than they were. She still meant to hear him admit he cared for her. If she had to drive him crazy with lust to hear it, then so be it. The dress worked like magic on him. Desire burned in his gaze for a moment, then, catching himself, a mask of indifference slid over his face and he glanced back down at his plate.

Kelsey fought an overwhelming urge to go to him and kiss his apathy away. Later, she promised herself. She picked up a plate and followed Lizzy down the rows of dishes, feeling his gaze on her back.

Edward glanced at Lizzy now and said, "I'm sure it's going to snow today. I haven't seen you at table in a month and you're wearing pink. I haven't seen pink on you since you were a babe."

Lizzy gave him a sour look. "You can save your comments."

He studied her quizzically. "I can't say that I don't admire this transformation, Lizzy. It comes at a very opportune time. I've received word that Lady Shellborn is due to arrive this afternoon."

"Is she?" Lizzy said, gritting her teeth. She frowned as she walked to the end of the long table and sat at the opposite end from Edward.

"Yes, and I expect you to be on your best behavior when you receive her."

Lizzy glared at Edward. "I'm not receiving her. You invited her here, you receive her."

"You *will* receive her, Lizzy," he said in a low, threatening tone.

Lizzy glanced down at her plate, looking like she wanted to throw it across the table at Edward. He stared at her as if he wanted to catch it and toss it back at her.

Kelsey was forced to sit in between them. The silence in the room grew so volatile, she was sure it would explode at any moment. She knew they cared about each other, but their filial relationship was odd in the extreme. On the surface they acted as though they could barely tolerate each other. She wondered if this was the kind of relationship all brothers and sisters who were raised among wealth and nobility had. She thought of Griffin and his family. They might be poor, but love abounded in their home. No children were ever loved more than Griffin and his brothers and sisters. She had a feeling that neither Lizzy nor Edward had ever felt loved.

The silence forced Kelsey to say, "What a beautiful room this is. It makes me feel as if I've been transported back to medieval times." She glanced upward at the pennons hanging on the walls, pretending to analyze the colorful patterns while she chewed on a piece of buttered toast.

"It should. Nothing has been touched in this dining hall since the castle was built in 1392." Pride replaced the anger in his voice.

"It's a cavernous old room," Lizzy said. "I hate it. You freeze in it year-round."

"I wonder that you should have an opinion of it, since you rarely eat in here," Edward said with censure in his voice.

Edward's and Lizzy's gazes clashed. The tension between them grew palpable. Lizzy was deliberately provoking Edward. She was not being agreeable. Kelsey cleared her throat and gave Lizzy a sharp look, reminding her of her promise.

A tight smile spread across Lizzy's face as if she could read Kelsey's mind. She pushed a raisin scone around the edge of her plate, then said, "I'm sorry. I didn't come in here to provoke you, Eddie." Edward looked shocked by the apology, which made Lizzy grin perversely. "I'm feeling terribly affable, I'll do anything you want me to do." She turned to Kelsey. "Are we still going to call on the McGregors this morning?"

Kelsey's jaw was still open from watching the sudden change in Lizzy's disposition. She had a feeling seeing Griffin might have something to do with it. She smiled inwardly. "I had forgotten, I'm glad you reminded me."

"Good."

"Will you join us, Eddie?"

"I don't think—"

"You promised Mr. McGregor that you would call on him. What better time than with us? And he is your steward now, I'm sure you have a lot to discuss with him. You ought to call on him." Lizzy looked over at Kelsey for support. "He did promise, didn't he?"

"Yes, I heard you distinctly."

Kelsey felt Edward's gaze on her and she looked over at him. He was scowling, his brow wrinkled over the dark lacing of the black patch covering his eye, his expression more severe than it usually was. She noticed his hand clenching and unclenching the end of a spoon. In spite of his forbidding demeanor, she stared boldly back at him, issuing a challenge with her eyes.

An impish grin twisted her lips. She baited him on purpose, hoping he would stop hiding his face from people and make that first step back out into the world. She was sure once he took that first plunge, it would get easy for him. She held her breath and waited for his answer.

After a moment of contemplative silence, of looking down at the ham on his plate, then back up at Kelsey, he finally said, "I'll drive you."

"Very good," Lizzy said, looking pleased and almost proud of her brother.

Kelsey didn't look at Edward for fear he would see the delight on her face and regret his decision. He had already pushed his plate away, as if the apprehension had taken his appetite away.

"Wait until you see Edward handle the reins, Kelsey. He used to drive to an inch, but I wonder if he still can. He hasn't been in an open carriage for years." She glanced at Edward, a smirk on her lips.

"I don't think I've forgotten how to handle the reins," Edward said tonelessly.

"We shall see." Lizzy stuffed a spoon of eggs in her mouth.

"I look forward to it." Kelsey hoped Edward wouldn't disappoint her and change his mind. She bit off a piece of buttered toast and chewed it, feeling his gaze on her.

"If you'll excuse me, I'll get dressed. I hope both of you can be ready in half an hour."

Kelsey and Lizzy nodded together, unable to speak for their full mouths. Edward stood. Kelsey watched the sway of his large shoulders and his long-legged, regal stride as he walked down the length of the dining hall. He was so tall, virile, and handsome, it brought an ache to her breast. She wanted to follow him out of the room and feel him hold her again, feel his lips on hers. . . . The sound of Lizzy's voice brought her thoughts back to the table.

"Kelsey, you're not paying attention and you look like a besotted fool."

"I'm sorry," Kelsey said, looking down the table at Lizzy. "Was I so obvious?"

"Like an open book. You must really love him."

"Yes, I'm afraid I do."

"Then you're contemplating being his mistress?"

"No, I won't be his mistress." Kelsey frowned down at her plate, wondering if she wasn't already his mistress.

"What about last night?"

Kelsey looked at Lizzy now and saw the smug grin on her face. "You spied on us again?"

"I didn't. I came to your room late last night and found it empty. I couldn't help but hear the noise in Edward's room." She raised an ironic brow at Kelsey.

Kelsey's blush started in her cheeks and went all the way down her neck.

"You're not going to get missish now. So Edward took you to his bed. You won't be the first to share it. I'd rather see you as his mistress than that cow Samantha he has coming here every now and then. I think you are good for him. I've tried for an age to get him to go out somewhere. I think he agreed to go with us because of you."

"I think your provoking him had something to do with it," Kelsey said, flashing her eyes at Lizzy. "And don't think for one minute that I'll stay here and be his mistress." She wouldn't let him use her like he had used Clarice or Samantha. If he wouldn't propose to her, then she would go to London as she planned and pursue her art career and forget all about him.

"I think he cares about you," Lizzy said with a devious smile on her face.

"He hasn't said he does."

"He will." Lizzy's smile broadened, and she looked very happy.

"You weren't being very amiable to him this morning," Kelsey said, trying to change the subject.

"I know, it's our way."

"I hope you're going to be pleasant when we get to the McGregors."

"It all depends."

Kelsey saw the wicked gleam in Lizzy's eye, and she almost pitied Griffin. But if any man could handle Lizzy, Griffin could. All Lizzy needed was to feel loved and all Griffin had ever done was fall in love with women who had a need of some sort. She was sure no two people were more suited for each other.

Above stairs, it was Watkins's custom to check his grace's room in the morning before the maid cleaned it—especially since Miss Kelsey was sleeping in the adjoining chamber. He was there now, studying the blood on the sheets, when something on the floor caught his eye. He held his back and bent over, scooping up Kelsey's chemise and drawers. A broad smile pulled the wrinkles around his mouth taut.

The smile drew in as the door flew open.

"I need a cravat, Watkins, and my driving gloves and a hat."

"Driving gloves, your grace?"

"Yes, I'm taking Miss Vallarreal and Lady Elizabeth to the McGregors."

"Very good, your grace."

"And have the curricle put to immediately."

"Yes, your grace."

"What the devil are you holding, Watkins?"

Watkins held up Kelsey's underclothes. Even though there was censure in his voice, his eyes twinkled as he said, "I believe these are Miss Vallarreal's. I was just returning them to her chamber, your grace."

"Dammit, Watkins, can you not mind your own business?" He jerked the articles from Watkins's hand.

"It appears not, your grace." Watkins lifted up the top sheet and stared down at the small spot of blood on the bottom sheet. He made sure his grace saw him doing it.

"Now what?" He started to pace, Kelsey's underclothes still

hanging from his hand. "Do you think because I took her maid-enhead I should marry her? Well, you can forget it, Watkins. You know my feelings on marriage."

"Yes, your grace, but we should get rid of the evidence before the maid comes. Gossip can get nasty." Watkins pulled the sheets off the bed and wadded them up into a tight ball.

"Don't think you can pray on my conscience."

"No, your grace, I wouldn't dream of it."

"I can't marry her."

"Yes, your grace." Watkins walked to the wardrobe and pulled out a starched cravat and quoted, " 'There is nothing more difficult to take in hand, more perilous to conduct, or more uncertain in its success, than to take the lead in the introduction of a new order of things.' "

"I'm sorry, this one escapes me."

"Machiavelli, your grace."

"Ah! Getting desperate, hey, Watkins. Well, there'll be no new order of things. Things will stay just the way they are. I've no intention of marrying her."

"Yes, your grace."

"But there is one thing you need to do, hire more staff. You're doing too much around here."

"Yes, your grace, I'll see to it right away. Shall I inform them of the rules?"

"Damn the rules! Send them to me before you hire them. If they can't stand the sight of my face, then we'll know from the start. They'll be no more rules in this house. Is that under-stood?"

"Yes, your grace." A grin tweaked the corners of Watkins's lips. He checked it as he found the gloves and the hat and turned to see the Duke of Salford standing by the window, his head bowed, his face buried in Kelsey's underclothes. Watkins shook his head at his employer's back. He laid the articles on the bed, picked up the sheets, and quietly slipped out of the room, leaving his grace to his conscience and his enthralling musings.

Edward didn't hear Watkins leave, he was too busy remembering the way Kelsey had clung to him, whispering to him that she loved him. He threw back his head and stared up at the ceiling, crushing her underclothes in his hands. His hands trembled from the grip on the clothes. He took a deep breath, wiped the memory from his mind, then turned and threw her clothes on the bed as he stormed from the room.

Edward drove them in a fancy black lacquered curricle pulled by a pair as black as pitch. The horses' coats glistened blue in the June sun as they trotted along the road. Kelsey noticed that Edward had put on a cravat and wore gray driving gloves and a top hat, looking every bit the peer of the realm. He hadn't spoken two words since he helped Lizzy and her into the carriage. She thought he must be apprehensive about the call and that was why he was so quiet.

Edward was sitting between her and Lizzy. Kelsey felt his thigh touching hers, sending hot tingles down her leg. She licked her lips and stared at his long fingers entwined in the reins. She remembered his hands on her body and what pleasure they had given her last night. Desire radiated through her. Her heartbeat grew sporadic. She closed her eyes tightly, willing the light-headed feelings to go away.

The swaying of the carriage slowed, and Kelsey opened her eyes to see that they were turning onto the dirt road that led to the McGregors' cottage. She breathed a sigh of relief, glad that her torture was at an end.

Griffin emerged from the cottage first, his mother and father behind him, then the three girls. The girls' pinafores were so white and full of starch, they shined. Griffin and Mr. McGregor appeared to have washed their hands, which were usually dirty from working in the field. Their dirty sleeves were usually rolled up and their collars unbuttoned, but today they had on clean white shirts with cravats.

"Yer grace." Alroy McGregor looked pleasantly surprised by

the sight of his new employer, and he bowed, wearing a broad smile.

"McGregor." Edward nodded.

Kelsey saw the shock on Edith's and the girls' faces as they stared at Edward. She hoped Edward didn't see it, but he was staring boldly back at them. On the exterior he looked like a paladin of calm invincibility, but she saw his fists clenched around the reins and the anxiety pulling at the muscles of his jaw and neck. She knew what inner strength it cost him to face them and wait for their reaction. Inadvertently, Kelsey reached out to touch his hand, but she remembered they were not alone and dropped her hand back in her lap.

"You haven't met me wife, Edith," Alroy said.

Blood tinted Edith's cheeks as she appeared to catch herself staring, and she ran up beside Alroy and curtsied. "Nice to meet you, yer grace. Forgive me for me rudeness, but we were expecting Lord Lovejoy."

"Sorry to disappoint you," Edward said brusquely as he secured the reins.

"Oh, no, we ain't disappointed. Who woulda thought you'd be paying us a call." Edith's cheeks turned beet red. "I wish I'd known, I would'a done more baking. And I have to thank you for hiring my Alroy as your steward. It was very kind of you. He'll make a good one, I know that. Please, come in, come in. You won't find us all t'home the day. My Alroy sent Everard and Jacob to market with a pig."

"Allow me to introduce my sister, Lady Elizabeth," Edward said, some of the tension leaving his face as he jumped down and helped Lizzy down.

"I knew you had a sister, but we didn't know she was home with you."

"Edward didn't know it either until I ran away from the school and showed up on his doorstep a month ago," Lizzy said proudly, eyeing Griffin, who was openly staring at her with a besotted grin on his face.

Edward helped Kelsey down, and when his hands touched

hers their gazes locked for a moment. He had a remote look in his eye as he set her on the ground, then he glanced away. Puzzled by his aloof behavior and a little hurt by it, Kelsey bit her lower lip and stared at his broad back. She hoped that it was his unease that made him so distant.

"Please, come in," Alroy said.

The girls were still staring at Edward, but one look from Edith and a snap of her fingers sent them scurrying back into the cottage.

Edward and Lizzy were given their rightful seats of honor on the settee. Edith bustled about serving tea and apple tarts, while Edward and Alroy discussed the business of farming and land management. Edward seemed determined to ignore Kelsey; not once did he look at her.

He didn't have any trouble looking at anyone else though. Kelsey caught him several times shooting baleful glances at Griffin. Griffin was oblivious, he was too busy staring at Lizzy's breasts. Of course, Lizzy pretended to ignore him with haughty disdain, while two red blotches stained her cheeks, visible evidence that she knew Griffin was admiring her figure.

Kelsey had hoped Edward and Griffin would grow to be friends, especially since Lizzy was attracted to Griffin. But Edward had been barely civil to her best friend. And Griffin wasn't behaving very well, staring at Lizzy's breasts as intently. Edward could not help but see that. Kelsey cleared her throat to get Griffin's attention, but he wouldn't look at her. Edward wouldn't even look at her.

Kelsey sighed with relief when Johanna flounced into the parlor, her stiff pinafore rustling against her small legs. She stopped in front of Edward and curtsied, then said, "Hannah says you'll bite me head off if I talk to you. I told her you wouldn't."

"I don't normally bite." The hardness around Edward's mouth softened as he smiled at the child.

"Go on with you, our Anna," Alroy said. "His grace don't want you bothering him."

"It's no bother," Edward said, setting his cup and saucer aside.

Johanna stepped closer to him, studying his face with wonder and open innocence. "Yer not as handsome as Lord Lovejoy, but I like you just as well. Sarah said Lord Lovejoy had prettier manners, but I don't believe that."

"There you might be wrong. My cousin is good at wooing the ladies. I fear I am out of practice."

"You wanna see Sheba's puppies?" Johanna took his hand. "Come on, I'll show you."

"Our Anna, you cheeky thing," Edith cried. "Leave his grace alone."

"No, no, it's all right." Edward stood and let Johanna lead him out of the cottage.

Kelsey leaned over and pulled back the curtain on the window and watched them. Edward had picked Johanna up and set her on his shoulder. She was laughing and so was he. He looked so natural with her. He was such an enigma, she would never have guessed he liked children. She felt a deep ache in her breast as she imagined him holding their daughter on his shoulder.

He'll never marry you! Would you have his bastards?

Kelsey shot to her feet, feeling suddenly restless. "Please excuse me, Lizzy, I think I'm going to walk back to Stillmore. I really should be working and I don't want to interrupt your visit."

"Kelsey, wait, I'll walk back with you," Lizzy said, standing.

"I'll go with you." Griffin jumped up.

"Why would she want you to go with her, when she has me?" Lizzy said, cutting Griffin's face into pieces with her sharp, flashing dark eyes.

"I don't know, *Miss Breeches,* maybe she might want someone with her that won't hiss at her and claw her to death." Griffin sounded annoyed, but his eyes twinkled with enjoyment.

"You are the most—"

"Please . . ." Kelsey stared at Lizzy, cutting off what was

sure a scalding tirade. Her look grew stern, reminding Lizzy of her promise.

Lizzy crossed her hands over her chest and huffed loudly, patting the floor with her foot.

"Griffin, why don't you show Lizzy the puppies?" Turning to Lizzy, she said, "I hope you won't be upset, but I'd really like to be alone for a while."

Before Lizzy could answer Kelsey, Griffin grabbed her arm. "Come on"—he leaned closer to her and whispered—"Miss Breeches, let's have a look at those puppies. They might sweeten that temper of yers."

"Unhand me, you . . . you . . . pig-eared beast! I'll see you in hell . . ." Lizzy's voice faded as Griffin jerked her out the door and slammed it closed.

Alroy got up and started to go after his son, but Kelsey stepped in front of him. "Don't reproach him, Lizzy asked for it."

"Still, he ought not treat her like he treats his sisters," Alroy said, turning to frown out the window.

Kelsey followed his gaze and saw Griffin dragging Lizzy across the yard toward the barn, ignoring the pounding of her fists on his arm. "I'm sure she doesn't mind. I think Lizzy likes him—I'll take that walk now, while the coast is clear." Kelsey said good-bye, then left the cottage.

Edith walked over and stood beside Alroy, watching her son drag Lizzy through the barn door. "Would ya look at that. I hope Griffin don't take a shine to that one. She's a handful, that one."

"Aye," Alroy said, looking worried. "And she's dipping low. Salford will never let her marry our Griffin."

"I hope yer right, there. I wouldn't want that wild lady as a daughter. I had my hopes set on our Kelsey and Griffin marrying, but I don't see that comin' 'bout. Did you see the secret looks Kelsey and Salford were givin' each other when they thought the other weren't lookin'. And that gloomy look on her face when she went out o' here—something's stewing atween the two of them."

"I think yer right there." Alroy ran his hand across the coarse stubble on his chin.

"I hope the poor child ain't in love with him. I don't trust him. You know he's got that mistress and you remember what he did to her stepmama." Edith shook her head.

"You know what's wrong with you, Edith, you worry too much. He's done good for us, ain't he? And he came to call on us. He's changin', you can't judge a man by his past. If Kelsey loves him, then I'm sure he can't help but love her back. And she'll be good for him, I know that. Everything will be all right, you'll see."

"I ain't so sure."

"I am." Alroy's eyes sparkled as he wrapped his big, beefy arms around his plump wife. "Speaking of love . . ." He smacked his lips and bent down to kiss her.

She struggled in his arms. "Get away with ya, 'tis the middle of the morning."

"And I'm kissing me wife, what's wrong with that?" Alroy asked as he kissed her until she stopped struggling and melted in his arms.

Fifteen

Kelsey took her time walking, and it was a good forty minutes before she reached the end of the shortcut. A drop of sweat trickled down between her breasts. The morning air was humid, the weight of it hung deep in her lungs. A thrush sang from a bramble near the path. Up ahead, she saw the green lawn of Stillmore at the edge of the path.

Abruptly, the green was blocked out by a pair of shiny black Hessians and familiar corded thighs encased in black buckskin. Her gaze roamed higher, to the flat waist, the broad shoulders. Edward had shed his coat and cravat and his shirt was open at the neck, exposing a thick patch of sable chest hair. She glanced at his face.

He stared at her like a dark, menacing pirate, the patch covering one eye, his arms crossed over his broad chest. The veins in his neck protruded from the strain of a clamped jaw.

"Where have you been?" He strode toward her with stiff strides, a hostile gleam in his eye.

Kelsey stiffened her spine and stood her ground. "I'm surprised you should inquire. You haven't spoken two words to me since last night."

"What have you been doing all this time in the woods?"

"Thinking. That is allowed, your grace, isn't it?"

He paused in front of her and grabbed her chin, his fingers digging into her skin. "Are you regretting our one night together? Is that what you've been thinking about?"

"Yes," she said honestly, tears stinging her eyes. "You couldn't touch me enough last night, but today you ignored me like I didn't exist."

"You will always exist for me, Kelsey. . . ." He drew her against his chest. His lips crushed her teeth against her mouth in a fierce, demanding kiss, stealing her breath and making her knees weak.

She felt the urgency of his kiss, consuming her, creating a burning need in her that matched his. He fondled her breasts and thrust his tongue into her mouth. She jerked his shirt open, ripping off the buttons. They hit the ground around them. The savageness of her own passion made her grin. She ran her hands over his chest, his back, his neck, needing to feel him.

He thrust her back against the trunk of a thick beech tree and yanked her skirts up to her waist. She felt his hands trembling as he jerked down her drawers.

She fumbled with the stubborn buttons on his breeches, then finally freed his erection. Urgently, her hand went to him, and she wrapped her fingers around the thick flesh, squeezing, then ran her finger over the soft, velvety tip.

"Oh, God, you shouldn't touch me like that. . . ."

"But I want to," she said, panting against his chest.

"You drive me mad, Kelsey. I'll never get enough of you. . . ." He parted her thighs and lifted her hips, then thrust deep into her.

Kelsey cried out his name as she felt him fill her. Her head fell back against the tree trunk, and she dug her nails into the thick muscles on his shoulders. Again and again he drove into her with a possessive ruthlessness, as if he meant to take a part of her soul with each deep thrust. Kelsey gave him every part of her, including her heart, until nothing was left but wave upon wave of sheer ecstasy. They climaxed together in a savage melding that left both of them panting and racked with tremors.

She gripped him tightly and dropped her head on his bare chest, feeling weak as a new kitten and trembling all over. The thunderous pounding of his heart throbbed against her eardrum, while his hot, deep breaths brushed against her face.

After a moment she lifted her head and a sultry grin spread across her lips. A dark lock of hair stuck to his sweaty brow. She pushed it back and said, "I thought you said we shouldn't do this again. I'm starting to believe you may not have ice in your veins after all."

A slow, sardonic grin lifted a corner of his mouth. "How can I have ice in my veins when you are near me? I must have been out of my mind when I said we shouldn't do this again."

Her hopes soared. In her mind's eye she felt him clinging to her and heard him whispering, "I love you, Kelsey. Will you marry me?"

He started to kiss her again, and the vision faded.

Kelsey spent the rest of the day supervising the men as they applied the *trulisatio,* or first coat of mortar, over the wall. The second coat, or brown coat, could be applied the next day, so she had sent the men home. She worked alone now in the ballroom, drawing out her design on large pieces of paper.

Frescos could be worked only one section at a time, so each piece of paper represented a piece of the whole design. After the mortar dried enough, the design could be pounced on the wall through tiny perforations in the paper. The final coat of mortar could be applied. Then she could paint that section and move on to the next. As the top coat dried, the pigment would bind into the mortar itself, so that the painting would become part of the wall. Frescos were hard work, but the medium was like no other, providing rich, varied color and dimension. Done properly, frescos lasted for centuries.

Michelangelo had painted the ceiling of the Sistine Chapel in this fashion. She would never forget seeing his work. A distant aunt had died in America, leaving Kelsey's mother a small inheritance, and since her mother had died six months earlier, the inheritance had come to her. Never one to save money when it was in hand, her father gave in to his impulsive nature and insisted they go to Italy on holiday.

They lived lavishly, touring Italy for four months, eating at only the best restaurants, staying at only the finest hotels. She didn't even mind eating turnips for a month afterward, when her father had spent the whole two thousand pounds and came home penniless. He had given her something that was priceless: beautiful memories, and his love for art. They had seen Naples, Venice, Florence, Genoa, Sicily, and finally Rome, the breath of all that is romance, culture, and ageless splendor. Her father took her to the Vatican, where they toured the Sistine Chapel.

She would never forget holding her father's hand as she had glanced up at the ceiling. The scenes from the Book of Genesis impressed her, but one in particular, where God was pointing to Adam and Eve, made her gape in wonder. She squeezed her father's hand and pointed at the image of God, then cried, "Look! Look! Michelangelo has captured your face, Papa. God looks just like you."

Her father's cheeks turned red, for her voice carried in the chapel and other visitors had turned to look at him. He merely shrugged at them, then he bent and scooped her up into his arms. He pecked her on the cheek and said, "How observant of you, *ma chère*. Do you like Michelangelo's work?"

"Yes, Papa, very much."

"Then perhaps you will paint like him one day."

"I'd like that. Can you show me how?" She hugged his neck tightly.

"Oui."

"Shall I paint you on the ceiling of the studio?"

"If you do not, my feelings will be hurt."

From that moment on, nothing would do for her but to study under her father. He had taught her well. She never did do a fresco on the ceiling, but when she was ten and six, she helped her father paint a fresco in a chapel near Newgate and she'd used her father's face as a model for Adam. He was pleased.

The memory made her smile down at the paper before her.

She heard footsteps and glanced up to see Watkins, Griffin following behind him.

"Miss Kelsey, you have a visitor." Watkins sucked in his lips at Griffin. "I told him you were working, but he insisted."

"It's all right, thank you, Watkins." Kelsey got to her feet and wiped her hands on her smock.

"Very well, Miss Kelsey." After a dour glance in Griffin's direction, Watkins left the doorway.

"What's the matter with him?" Griffin motioned toward the doorway. "He acted like he wanted to bite me head off—all I wanted to do was talk to ya."

"He's overprotective, but a very kind man." Kelsey motioned him over to a window seat. "Let's sit over here. What is on your mind?"

Griffin crossed his long legs out in front of him. "I came for two reasons. One is I want to know what's goin' on atween you and Salford."

Kelsey hesitated a moment, then sighed before she said, "I think I've fallen in love with him."

"I suspected as much." Griffin didn't sound pleased.

"I know what you think, so you can save your lecture. I know he's changed, Griffin. He's not the man I thought he was. He can be kind. Look what he did for your father. And I know he cares for me too."

"Have you bedded him?"

Kelsey swallowed hard beneath Griffin's penetrating gaze, then said, "Yes, I have."

"Damn him! He's used ya! I'll beat some sense into the bugger!" Griffin jumped up.

Kelsey grabbed his arm and had to hang on for dear life, then pulled him back down in his seat. "Wait, Griffin! Leave it alone! It was my decision. I let him make love to me. I could have said no at any time and he would have stopped. If you're going to be angry with anyone, be angry with me."

"Has he offered you marriage?" Griffin asked suspiciously, his face livid with anger as he relaxed beside her.

"No, but he will."

"I hope you're right for yer sake. Was he careful with you?"

"What do you mean?"

Griffin looked exasperated and said, "Did he use something to keep you from getting pregnant."

"I don't think so. Is there such a thing?"

"Aye, but it ain't something I care to discuss with you." Griffin glared at her stomach for a moment. "I hope for yer sake that you don't have his by-blow."

Kelsey protectively covered her stomach with her arms. "There won't be a baby, and even if there was, I wouldn't feel guilty about it. I bedded him because I love him. And that's that. Nothing you say can make me feel sullied for following my heart. This is the highest form of hypocrisy coming from you, who has bedded just about every lightskirt in the village. I think you should go now."

"I'm sorry, Kell," Griffin said, some of the anger leaving his face. He saw the tears in her eyes and wrapped his arm around her shoulder, pulling her close to his side. "Don't be mad with me, I'm just worried about ya. It's your life, you have to live it, but if you should need something, you know I'll always be here."

"Yes." Kelsey shook her head, blinking back the tears. "I know that, that's why I love you." She gave him a brotherly peck on the cheek, then he dropped his arm from her shoulders. "Let us forget we had this conversation. What was the other reason you came?"

"Da is planing a jollification. Salford told Da that we was to move into Morely's cottage. It's a lot bigger than ours, and with the salary Salford is paying Da, we can afford to have servants. Imagine that, Kell, servants in the McGregor house." Griffin smiled wryly. "Ma can't believe it."

"I'm so glad."

"Aye, I am too, and I'll be staying on the farm and running it for Da while he's managing for Salford."

"That's what you've always wanted, isn't it?"

"Aye. I guess this means I'll have to be finding meself a wife."

"I guess so." Kelsey grinned to herself as she thought of Lizzy.

"Da's planning a jollification to celebrate his good fortune. That's why I came, I'm to invite you, Salford, and the shrew to it. It's tomorrow night."

"As for me, I'll be there, but I can't answer for Salford or the *shrew.*" Kelsey glanced at Griffin and they both smiled. "She likes you, you know."

"You'd never know it by the way she acts," Griffin said, his golden brows furrowing.

"Lizzy's not like other women you've known. She's more complicated than that. She lashes out at you because she likes you and she's afraid of her feelings. She's never known what it feels like to really be loved, and I think she's afraid of it."

Griffin glanced at her with awe in his eyes. "You always were uncanny in yer understandin' of people. I hadn't thought about why she acts the way she does, I just know it irritates the hell outta me."

"Do you like her?"

"I'd be lying if I said I ain't noticed her, 'cause I have. She's pretty enough. I like the way her eyes flash at me. I know one thing, she'd never bore me. She's got a nice pair of . . ." Griffin paused, catching himself. "I don't think you want to hear about that." His eyes sparkled as he spoke.

"No, I don't want to hear about any part of her anatomy."

After a pensive moment he said, "Aye, I think she'll do well enough, but she ain't for me though, Kell. She's the daughter of a duke. I'm a poor farmer. She could marry a rich highborn gent who can give her everything in the world. What can I give her but a life of drudgery?"

"You can give her something she's needed all her life and never had . . . love."

At that moment the secret panel in the room popped open

and Lizzy emerged, carrying a puppy in her arms. She was wearing a pair of black riding breeches and a white shirt.

"Speaking of the devil," Griffin said under his breath, unable to take his eyes off Lizzy.

She noticed Griffin now and looked pleasantly surprised to see him, but then her expression grew haughty. "Oh, it's you," she said balefully, then strode over to them with her long-legged, coltish walk.

"You needn't look so happy to see me, Miss Breeches."

Lizzy smiled mockingly. "There. Do I look happy enough for you now?"

"Not quite, but it'll do for a start." Griffin eyed her up and down.

"I see Griffin gave you a puppy. Can I see him?" Kelsey asked.

Lizzy laid the Border collie pup in her lap. "I was just coming to ask if you'd like to go out with us for a stroll in the garden, but I see you've got a visitor." Lizzy cut her eyes at Griffin.

Kelsey stroked the puppy's head. "What did you name him?"

"Finly."

"He looks like a Finly," Kelsey said, feeling the puppy's needle teeth gnawing on her finger.

"I'm sorry, Lizzy, but I really should finish my sketches. Griffin will walk with you."

Lizzy snarled her lip at Griffin, then said, "I'd rather go alone. Come on, Fin, let's go for our walk." Lizzy picked the puppy up from Kelsey's lap, then turned and strolled down the room.

Griffin leapt up and ran after her.

Kelsey watched them go, a contented smile on her face, then the smile faded as she glanced down at her belly and touched it. What if she were carrying Edward's baby? What if he didn't propose to her? The thought made her brows meet in a deep frown.

She wouldn't beg him to marry her. Never that. Nor would she use a baby to trap him. If he didn't propose, she would go away and have the child, then raise it on her own. He'd never find out, she'd make sure of that.

Griffin followed Lizzy out into the maze. She was walking quickly and he had to run to stay close behind her. He stared at those breeches now, at her long legs, the sway of her hips as she walked. He licked his lips, unable to draw his eyes away from her cute little bottom.

He knew she was a lady, off limits to someone like him. He shouldn't touch her, but she aroused him like no other woman he'd ever known. Most women fell into his arms with a few courting words and the right come-and-get-me look. Most women were soft and pliable. Lizzy was like dried-up harness leather. He wondered what lay beneath her prickles and claws. What would those claws feel like on his back?

"Can't you go and harass someone else?"

"Nope, yer the only one I want to harass at the moment, Miss Breeches."

"Stop calling me that."

"I would if you'd stop wearing them." He saw her throw her shoulders back and stiffen her spine.

"You really are incorrigible."

"Aye, that's me middle name, incorrigible."

Lizzy reached the maze and ducked inside. Griffin picked up his pace and came abreast of her. "You goin' to a fire?"

"No, just trying to get away from you." Finly must have smelled the grass, for he started to squirm in her arms. She stopped and let him down.

Griffin glanced around at the tall bushes, making sure the two of them couldn't be seen here. He grabbed Lizzy as she stood up.

"Let me go, you . . . you baboo—"

Griffin cut off her words with a kiss. She grabbed his hair and yanked. He was determined not to let her win, so he let her pull his hair while he kissed her. The harder she pulled his hair, the softer he made his lips against hers. He caressed her back with his large, wide hands, moving them along her spine in large circles.

She stopped pulling his hair, then slowly surrendered, melting against him, wrapping her long arms around his neck. He felt the trembling of her body against him and could tell she'd never been kissed before. He gentled the kiss even more, feeling her lips turn to soft velvet against his mouth.

Afraid he might go further, Griffin broke the kiss. When he saw the dazed wonder on her beautiful face, he grinned down at her. "I didn't taste a bit of that vinegar in you, darlin'. You taste sweeter than I thought ya would."

"And you don't taste like a baboon—not that I've ever kissed one, so I really can't judge." She smiled at him.

"Ya know, yer pretty when ya smile, ya ought to do it more often." Griffin ran his finger along her bottom lip.

"I might if I had a reason," she said in an unsure whisper, then shyly touched her lips to his finger.

Griffin gazed into her eyes, saw them turn supple and inviting, but he also saw the emptiness behind them that cried out to him. He knew he was a lost man as he ran a callused finger along her smooth jaw, then brought her mouth up to meet his.

It was a long time before he lifted his head and looked down into her golden eyes. "Lizzy, I need to know what yer feelin' right now, darlin'. 'Cause if you don't feel the same way I do, I'll go away and leave ya alone."

"Yes, yes, I feel the same way." Lizzy gripped his neck, her hold so tight, it almost choked him.

"Are ya sure? 'Cause once we start this, there ain't no turnin' back, and I won't give you up, Lizzy."

"You won't have to."

"Lizzy!" Edward's call came from the garden path.

"Oh, no! Meet me in the chapel tonight at twelve," Lizzy said, looking up at him with the most silken, imploring, eyes he'd ever seen.

Griffin knew he had no business meeting her, but he couldn't say no to those eyes. He nodded and started to run back the way they had walked in.

Lizzy grabbed him. "Not that way, you twit, go this way. Turn left three times, right four and you'll be out. Bye." Lizzy kissed him quickly on the mouth, and watched him sprint down the hedges and disappear.

At that moment Edward appeared from the opposite direction. "Lizzy, I was just looking for you. I thought I saw you and McGregor come in here." He looked past Lizzy's shoulder.

"I came in alone with Finly." Lizzy glanced around for the puppy and found him sniffing at the base of a hedge. "You must have been seeing things."

He looked skeptical. "You don't need to lie to me, Lizzy. I know what I saw. I saw him eyeing you this morning. I'm telling you now, I've turned a blind eye to a lot of the things you've done, but I won't have you involved with McGregor."

"I'm not involved with him," Lizzy said defensively. "Even if I were, it is none of your concern."

Edward grabbed her shoulders. "I'm your guardian, don't forget that. You just turned eighteen and you don't know what you want. That's why I've arranged with Lady Shellborn to give you a season in London. You'll find a man of your own rank—"

"Dammit! I don't want to go to London and meet every fop in town." Lizzy broke away from his hold. "I won't let you rule my life! I won't!"

"You are going to London for the season, Lizzy. That is final!"

"If I go, I'll make such a scandal that it will make yours seem paltry."

"You'll do what I tell you and behave like a lady. And you'll stay away from McGregor." He shook his finger at her.

"How can you stand there and tell me what to do with my life, when you've ruined your own? I know you've bedded Kelsey. Are you planning to marry her, or is this just a pleasant diversion for you?"

Edward's face contorted into rage. For a moment he looked

as if he might lose control. Lizzy knew how far to push him, and she wondered if she'd gone too far this time. She'd never seen his expression so black.

"Get out of my sight, Lizzy, but remember one thing, stay away from McGregor."

Lizzy snatched up Finly. "You're just jealous of him because he's Kelsey's friend. If you want to be jealous of someone, you should watch out for Jeremy. I saw him kissing Kelsey the other day." She fired that parting shot, then left him without looking back.

Edward ground his teeth together and started to pace up and down between the hedges. It was a very long time before he gained enough self-control to venture back toward the castle.

Edward drummed his fingers on the table and stared at the doorway in the dining room. He pulled out his pocket watch, checked the time, then stared at the doorway again. Where was Kelsey? He had informed Watkins that she was to take her meals with him from now on. So why wasn't she here?

As if summoned by his thoughts, Kelsey came through the door, a vision in a green silk dress. The color matched the green in her eyes. Her raven hair was swept back from her small face and fell in long curls over one shoulder. She searched the room for him, and when she looked at him from behind her thick, dark lashes and smiled that glowing smile of hers, his breath caught in his chest. He had never lusted after a woman in his life like he lusted after her. There was no doubt about it, God was punishing him. He'd have only a few more days with her, then what? Jeremy would come back and bloody propose to her. His frown deepened.

"Sorry I'm late." The silk of her gown swished as she walked farther into the room. She stopped and greeted the two new footmen Watkins had hired at Edward's behest.

A flare of jealousy shot through Edward when he saw them admiring Kelsey's creamy breasts. He stood and scowled at them. "We will serve ourselves, that will be all, and close the door as you go out."

They left as Kelsey approached the opposite end of the table. She glanced down at the plate placed there, then her eyes sparkled like two large emeralds as she said, "Must I really sit this far from you, I won't be able to see you for the candelabra."

"No, you needn't sit there if you do not want to." Edward felt some of the jealousy leave him. But Jeremy was still in the back of his mind. The thoughts of Jeremy kissing her had driven him almost mad, and he'd tried to put it out of his mind, but he couldn't.

She set the silverware and glass on the plate, then walked toward him. The creamy white flesh of her bosom was exposed by her low-cut gown, and he couldn't seem to tear his eyes from it, feeling his body responding appropriately.

"Are you in a bad humor? You snapped at those new footmen. I had so hoped to find you cheerful," Kelsey said, bestowing one of her brilliant smiles on him as she placed the plate on the table and reset the silverware.

"Cheer has nothing to do with how I feel at the moment." He stood and pulled out her chair.

"You needn't snap my head off." Her dark brows met over her nose.

He pushed her chair in for her, catching an enticing whiff of lavender. He couldn't help bending down and whispering near her ear, "I wasn't snapping. When I bite you, you'll know it."

He had the distinct pleasure of seeing her shiver and resisted the urge to kiss her luscious bare shoulder mere inches from his lips. She was such a temptation. He stared at the swell of her breasts above her gown and groaned inwardly.

If he didn't put some distance between them, he would have her flat on her back right there on the dining hall table, and take her with the same abandon he'd taken her earlier in the woods. He forced himself to stand and walk back to his chair.

"Let's start again, shall we," she said, her voice straining to be pleasant. "I know you can be nice if you try, and I'm sure there's something here on the table you'd rather bite than me." Kelsey teased him with a glance from her twinkling green eyes.

"Don't believe it," he said, keeping his voice menacingly soft. "If you keep giving me those alluring looks of yours, you might find out just how hungry I am."

"Well, I'm glad to see that at least your appetite is not affected by your mood swings," she said, then pulled the covers off the chafing dishes without looking at him, but he could see the grin on her lips.

Her eyes sparkled as she eyed the roast lamb smothered in onions, green peas, and an array of apricot fritters. "This smells delicious. Alice has outdone herself. May I serve you?"

Edward remained silent, his gaze saying "skip the food, I'd rather have you." When he saw that she knew what he was thinking and blushed prettily, he couldn't help but grin as he handed her his plate. He stared at her delicate hands. Lord, but he loved to feel those hands on his body. He fought the urge to reach for her.

He watched the graceful movements of her hands as she served him. What a domestic picture of bliss she seemed. He had forgotten what it was like to have feminine company, to have a woman at his side, serving his needs and wanting to please him. Margaret had despised him for marrying her and ruining her happiness with her lover. She wouldn't even take her meals with him. There had been mistresses, but somehow it wasn't the same. The only woman that had made him feel special was his mother, and it was so long ago, her memory was a blur in his mind. Grinning, he watched her pile his plate with food and set it before him. He remembered she wasn't ever likely to be his wife, and the grin faded. Then he remembered Jeremy, and his frown came back.

"I saw Griffin today," she said casually.

Edward had taken a drink of wine and choked on it when he heard the name.

"Are you all right?" She set her plate down, then reached over and pounded on his back.

"I'm fine."

"Good—what was I saying? Oh, yes, I was speaking about Griffin. He's invited us to a party the McGregors are having. They're celebrating Mr. McGregor's good fortune in becoming your steward. I'd hoped you'd go with me." She ate a mouthful of cheese soufflé.

"You're going, then?" Edward sawed furiously at his meat, then stabbed a piece with his fork. He used such force that the meat slid across his plate and almost fell onto the tablecloth before he skewered it with his knife.

"Yes, of course, the McGregors are like my own family." Kelsey cut off a piece of meat and ate it, then glanced down at his meat hanging on the edge of his plate, his knife still in the middle of it. "You seem to be having trouble there, would you like me to cut that for you?"

He ignored her question, pushed the meat back in the center of his plate, and sawed it with the knife. "You cannot go alone to this party."

"If you don't go, Lizzy will go with me."

"Lizzy will not go with you." Edward stabbed a piece of meat and jammed it into his mouth.

She looked at him and made a moue. "Why can't Lizzy go with me?"

"I do not like Griffin McGregor and I will not have him around Lizzy. I caught him in the maze with her this afternoon."

"I should think so. Lizzy asked me to walk with her, and when I told her I had to work, I sent Griffin in my place. What is wrong with Griffin?" Kelsey's voice grew defensive.

"I don't trust him."

"You have no reason not to. Griffin is a warm, caring, loving person. If he and Lizzy should ever become attached, he would make her a wonderful husband."

Edward almost choked on the meat as he swallowed it. He meant to keep his voice level, but all his self-control had vanished since Kelsey had come into his life, so he wasn't surprised when he bellowed, "Attached? Have you lost your wits? I won't have him anywhere near Lizzy. She's going to marry someone of her own class. I won't have her tied to a farmer. It would ruin her. She'd be a social pariah. She'd never be able to enter society again. And I saw the way he tried to seduce you, and I won't have him chasing after Lizzy's skirt."

"Griffin is not a skirt chaser. And he has never tried to seduce me. You saw nothing between Griffin and me but filial affection."

"Can you deny he's kissed you?"

"I have no wish to deny it. His kisses have never been amorous, but brotherly, and I resent you implying otherwise."

He stood up now, unable to control the jealous rage eating at him. "And I suppose Jeremy's kiss was brotherly."

For a moment she looked surprised that he'd known Jeremy had kissed her, then irritation veiled her face. "If you think his kiss meant anything to me, then you are a stupid man and I refuse to speak to you while you're like this." She slammed her spoon down on her plate, and it clanked in the silence. She jumped up from her chair and turned on her heel to leave.

Edward grabbed her shoulders and forced her to turn and look at him. "Don't try to play matchmaker with Lizzy and McGregor. I'll never let Lizzy marry him. She is only ten and eight and she does not know her own mind. She has yet to even have a season in London."

"If you entertain the idea of Lizzy marrying an aristocratic dandy, you'd might as well forget it now. You might find one to marry her if you provide a large enough dowry, but she'll chew the poor fellow up and spit him out like stale toast. At least Griffin can handle her and he'll make her happy. And as far as Lizzy knowing her mind, she's not a child you can order about, she's a grown woman. I believe she knows her own mind, more so than you." Kelsey knocked his hands away, then lifted her skirts and ran from the room.

Edward wanted to go after her, but he knew if he did, it would just make matters worse. She obviously cared enough to try and defend McGregor, which irritated him to the bone. Kelsey hadn't bedded McGregor as he'd first thought, for he'd had proof of that. Still, he didn't trust Griffin McGregor to be anywhere near Kelsey or Lizzy with his attractive face and provincial, good-humored smiles. The man was the epitome of a skirt chaser and had honed his skills to perfection. He knew about rakes, he'd been one himself before the accident. One thing was certain, he couldn't stop Kelsey from seeing McGregor. She seemed obstinate in her loyalty to him and intimate with his family, but he could stop McGregor from paying court to Lizzy. And if he ever caught the fellow at it again, he'd make that plain to him.

Sixteen

She was painting at a table. Rabbit was beside her, drawing too. The boy crossed his arms over his chest impatiently, and she frowned at him.

"If you keep moving, we won't be able to paint you."

"I wish you'd hurry."

"Almost done."

"That's a relief."

She painted the last stroke on her watercolor, then grimaced as she looked down at the blurry, misshapen image. The boy came over and stood at her shoulder, then he started to laugh when he saw the picture.

"Stop it! It's not funny."

"Yes, it is."

"It's not! You're not very nice. I don't think I like you."

She grabbed Rabbit and hugged him. Tears streamed down her face. She started to rock back and forth in her chair. She felt his arms go around her.

"I'm sorry, Kelsey."

"You're not sorry, sometimes you like being cruel."

"No, I don't mean to be—not to you anyway. Say you're not mad."

He made a stupid funny face and it made her laugh. She reached out to him, never able to stay mad at him for very long . . .

He disappeared right before her eyes.
"Come back! I forgive you. Come back!"

Kelsey woke from her dream, then sat up in bed. She wiped the sweat from her brow with the back of her hand. The soft melody of the pianoforte invaded her consciousness. She frowned at the connecting door. Edward hadn't come in to her. She was determined not to go to him, even though she ached for him to hold her. He would have to come to her first. She had her pride.

The room was stifling hot in spite of the window she'd left open. Her gown stuck to her perspiring back, and she'd never be able to sleep in the stuffy room knowing Edward was awake and so close. She threw back the sheet and went in search of her dressing gown, then closed the door as she slipped out into the hallway.

The music stopped a few moments later, and Edward entered her room.

"Kelsey . . ." He stood there staring at the empty bed. Had she been so angry that she'd left him and gone home? Or to McGregor? Surely she'd run to him. Edward felt an overwhelming desire to go and kill McGregor with his bare hands. But then, why should he care where she went? Perhaps it was for the better that she ran to him. Edward knew he'd have to give her up and soon. If not McGregor, then it would be Jeremy.

The emptiness of the room reached out to him, pushing against his chest like an iron anvil. No longer able to stand being in her room, he turned and strode back to his own chamber. Inadvertently, he walked to the window and glanced out. The moon was a huge sphere in the sky, so round and close it looked like a ball ready to drop down on the trees and village below and crush it. Edward saw her then, her white nightgown billowing out around her feet as she walked down the path near the garden. She wasn't walking toward the village or toward McGregor's cottage. The weight left his chest as he turned and hurried out of his room.

Moments later he found her nightgown on the bank of the lake. He picked it up, then glanced out at the lake and spotted her. She was across the lake, wading toward the island. Water dripped from her wet, naked body, making it glisten an exotic indigo blue in the moonlight. He watched her from the bank, bewitched by the sight of her.

She reached shore and paused, then pushed back the wet hair from her face with both her hands. Her back arched, thrusting her breasts forward. She kept the pose and stared up at the moon for a moment, unaware of the exotic sight she afforded him. Mesmerized, he followed the sensual lines of her high, proud breasts, the dark peach tips gleaming. He swallowed the saliva in his mouth, almost able to taste them.

His gaze roamed lower still, to her flat stomach, made even flatter by her stance, then to the flare of her small hips and rounded bottom. He clenched his fingers, remembering the feel of her bottom filling his palms. He had never seen anything so erotic in his life.

She moved, breaking the pose. Gathering her long, wet hair with both hands, she wrung it dry, then stood and threw it back over her shoulder. Slowly, she walked up the bank and found a place to sit.

Tearing at his clothes, he watched her, unable to take his eyes off her, afraid his naked water nymph would disappear before he could get to her. God! If he didn't get to her, he felt as though he might be consumed by his own lust. Never had he burned for a woman like he burned for Kelsey. He dove into the water. The cold wetness barely cooled the fire running rampant in his veins.

He reached shore, his pulse throbbing, his breathing heavy. He paused near her feet and stood looking down at her. She was lying on her back in the grass, her head pillowed on her arms, her eyes closed. One of her legs was bent, the dark triangle of hair between her thighs exposed for him.

She hadn't noticed him until drops of water from his body hit her foot. She opened her eyes. "Edward . . ." Her lips trembled as she spoke his name.

"I came to your room to find you, but you were gone."

"Did you really?" She sounded incredulous and pleased both at the same time. "I thought you were still sulking over Griffin. You really should try to like him, he's not as bad as you think."

"Let us not discuss him at the moment."

"All right, if you wish." A slow, lazy smile lit her face as she let her gaze move over his naked body. "Were you naked when you came to find me?"

"I did have clothes, but they somehow fell off when I spotted you." He stared down at her gleaming body in the moonlight. She started to sit up on her elbows, but his voice stopped her.

"Don't move. I want to remember you like this. You are the most sensuous mermaid I've ever beheld."

"Seen a lot, have you?" she said in a husky, teasing voice.

"Not any to equal you, my love. None of them have the power that you have over me." He smiled wryly down at his throbbing erection.

"You shouldn't have told me that. We sea sirens are not above using a man's weak spots for our own gain." Her eyes widened as she glanced at his erection, and she added, "Though, you don't look as if you have a weak spot on you." She looked up at him behind long, dark lashes, looking every bit an enchanting green-eyed seductress.

"I would gladly let you find my weak spots if you stayed naked while you searched for them."

"I don't think I would execute the search any other way." She grinned at him.

He couldn't resist her any longer and fell to his knees beside her. He moved his hands over her legs and slid his fingers along the slippery wet skin of her shins, her knees, her thighs. When he let his hands dip to her inner thighs, he felt her tense and shudder. He smiled at her response, then opened her thighs and lowered his mouth to her.

"What are you doing?" she screeched, and pulled at his shoulders.

"Shhh! There are many ways a man can pleasure a woman, my love. This is but one of the ways." He separated the soft, damp flesh and tasted her sweet dew.

"I don't think it . . ." Her words died as she arched her hips and her breathing became heavy.

He found the tiny bud of her pleasure, stroking it with his tongue. Her thighs relaxed as she gave over to her desire. She writhed beneath him and her hips started to move. He marveled at her uninhibited passion as he brought her to a climax.

Her body was still convulsing when he moved his tongue along her flat belly, trailing a line up to her breasts. He savored the taste of her damp nipple as he sucked, feeling the bud grow hard in his mouth. He felt her hands on his neck, his back, his hips, and he couldn't quell the tiny shudders in him.

"Edward . . ." She moaned his name as she grabbed handfuls of hair and pushed his head closer to her breasts.

"All right, my love," he said against her nipple, feeling her shiver. He rose and kissed her, thrusting his tongue in her mouth, letting her taste her own sweet dew.

Her passion exploded. She dug her nails into his back. When he felt her whimper and move against him, her ardor was his undoing. He'd meant to take his time making love to her, but his body was on fire. Her uninhibited passion had a way of making him burn out of control. He separated her legs and thrust deep inside her, feeling her hot, tight shaft give way for him.

He groaned and drove into her, burying himself in her. "Come, my love, come with me."

"Yes . . ." She wrapped her legs around his thighs and matched the rhythm of his hips.

She tensed and screamed. He spilled his seed as they both

found a release. The power of their lovemaking had him trembling. He collapsed down on top of her.

"Edward?"

"Yes, my love?" He raised his head and looked at her.

She touched the scarred side of his face and whispered, "I love you."

"Don't love me, Kelsey. . . ." She started to say something, but Edward crushed her to him for another kiss. His kiss grew fierce, possessive, the knowledge he'd have to eventually give her up one day driving his lips, his arms, as he wrapped them around her.

Kelsey broke the kiss and stared at him, bewildered. "You hurt me," she said softly, touching her lips.

"I didn't mean to." He ran his finger along her swollen lips, then pulled away from her and fell back on the grass, panting, hating his weakness where she was concerned. He should never have come after her and made love to her again. Now he'd hurt her.

She snuggled next to him. "It didn't hurt very much, just a little. Shall we try it again?" She bent down and kissed him.

Edward wanted to pull away, but he lost all self-control the moment her lips touched his.

Several hours later Kelsey lazily strolled toward the castle, arm in arm with Edward, sated from their lovemaking. She didn't let it bother her that Edward hadn't told her he loved her, she knew in her heart that he did. It had to be enough. Eventually he would declare his love.

A shadow emerged from the path in the woods and slaked across the lawn. She started to tell Edward about it, but she noticed the broad shoulders and the lopping stride and knew it was Griffin. Afraid Edward might see Griffin sneaking into the castle, she grabbed his arm and made him turn to look at her.

"You have a beautiful body, I don't think I've ever told you that." She wrapped her arms around his neck, then pulled his head down for a kiss.

After a moment Edward raised his head and said, "If you don't stop this, we might not make it back to bed." Edward looked pleased by the sudden affection. He had a twisted grin on his lips as he hugged her tighter to him.

"Perhaps you are right. . . ." She moved her head a little so she could peer past Edward's arm and caught a glimpse of Griffin as he slipped into the chapel.

"I don't think I'd mind making love to you again in the moonlight." He ran his hands through her thick hair as he tipped her chin up for another kiss. It was a tender kiss, full of unspoken vows. His kisses had been nothing but tender since he'd hurt her with his forceful kiss.

It was a long time before she regained her senses and pulled back from him. "Come, as much as I like the moonlight, I think I'd like the comfort of a bed better."

He laughed and swept her up into his arms. "Well then, my love, my aim is to please."

An hour later Kelsey heard Edward's deep, even breathing. He was lying on his side, his thigh over hers, his arm resting on her shoulder. Her hair was trapped beneath his arm. She eased it from beneath his shoulder, grimacing as some of the strands pulled at her scalp. She carefully untwined her body from his, inching slowly from beneath him.

"Kelsey . . ." he muttered, then groaned.

She held her breath, hoping he wouldn't wake. He rolled on his back, then his breathing grew even again. She eased off the bed, found her nightgown and robe on the floor, then tiptoed through the connecting door to her own room. She put on her clothes, lit a candle, and went in search of Lizzy and Griffin. If her suspicions were right, Griffin was probably still about. She wanted to warn him to stay clear of Edward.

She went to the chapel in search of them and found nothing but the echoing emptiness of her own footsteps on the granite floor. After a quick look at the extraordinary stained glass window, she hurried back to the ballroom, promising herself a visit to the chapel in the daylight so she could admire the window with the sunlight streaming through it. She slipped through the secret entrance and followed it to Lizzy's tower.

The door was ajar when she reached it. She didn't bother knocking, but pushed the door open. She paused in the threshold and raised her candle. Lizzy and Griffin were lying on the bed, entwined in each other's arms, kissing. Griffin had his hands on Lizzy's bottom.

"My God, what are you doing, Griffin?" Kelsey marched over to the bed, shaking her fist at him. "Lizzy isn't like those village whores you've slept with. How dare you try to take advantage of her."

"Now, wait just a minute." Griffin held up his hands to ward her off. "It ain't what you think."

Lizzy leapt off the bed and stepped in front of Griffin to protect him. Her lips were puffy from being kissed, her dark hair hanging in disarray around her shoulders. "I asked Griffin to come up here," she said. "It's my fault."

"You don't have to protect me, darlin'. Kelsey will understand."

"I don't know," Kelsey said, crossing her arms over her chest. "You'd better do some fancy explaining."

"Lizzy ain't like those other girls to me. For the first time in my life, I'm really in love. I had no idea what it felt like. I thought I loved you, Kelsey, but I realize now it's nothing like I feel for Lizzy." He turned Lizzy around and pulled her into his arms. He lifted her chin and looked into her eyes as he said, "If she'll have me, I want to marry her."

Kelsey couldn't believe what she was hearing and stared first at Griffin, then at Lizzy.

Lizzy looked equally amazed as her jaw dropped open. She stared at Griffin for a moment, then said, "Do you know what you're saying?"

"I know, woman. Now I'm asking you, will you marry me?"

"I'm not the easiest person to live with. Ask Kelsey. I'd make a terrible wife. I'm spoiled and I don't like people telling me what to do."

"We'll have a whole lifetime to work on you," Griffin said, looking into her eyes. He bent down and kissed her again. "Now say yes, or break my heart forever."

"Yes, yes, yes." Lizzy jumped up into his arms.

Griffin swung her around and kissed her.

Kelsey leapt out of the way to keep from being hit by Lizzy's feet. She watched them kissing and felt tears well up in her eyes.

Griffin stopped spinning her, then their kiss turned passionate. Lizzy dug her fingers into his hair, and he pulled her close, rubbing her back.

Abruptly, Lizzy broke the kiss, a stricken look on her face. "What about Edward? He'll never let us marry."

"Then we're for Gretna Green," Griffin said, throwing out his square chin in a stubborn manner that Kelsey knew well.

"When are you planning to go?" Kelsey asked hesitantly, not sure about the idea.

"Tomorrow, after the jollification. If that is okay with my intended?" Griffin smiled down at Lizzy.

She nodded, then kissed him lightly on the lips.

"I'll try to distract Edward, maybe he won't miss you until the morning," Kelsey said, her apprehension coming through in her voice.

"That sounds like a good plan. How can we ever thank you?" Lizzy hugged her.

Kelsey smiled. It was the first show of affection she'd ever had from Lizzy. Kelsey hugged her tightly. "No need to thank me, just don't let him catch you before you get married. I'm sure he'll get used to the idea after the deed is done. Now, come on, Griffin, I'll walk you out." Kelsey picked up the candle and started back down the tower stairs, giving Griffin a few moments alone with Lizzy.

Several moments later she heard Griffin's footsteps behind

her. She waited at the bottom of the steps for him. He was smiling as if he'd just taken a bite out of an apple tart.

"I'm glad for you, Griffin."

"Thank you. I won't forget what you're doin' for us." Griffin put his arm over her shoulder.

"You'd do the same for me."

"You'll come visit us, won't you?"

"Try to keep me away." Kelsey smiled at him, then they walked in silence to the servants' entrance.

When they reached the door, Kelsey bade him good night and watched him walk across the lawn, the moonlight glinting in his bright blond hair. Thoughts of what lay ahead for Griffin and Lizzy made her stomach churn. The part she'd have to play in the deception made her feel even worse. She hoped Edward wouldn't hold it against her once she explained how right they were for each other.

Frowning, she turned and went back up to Edward's chamber.

Pausing at the door, she blew out the candle. The door creaked when she opened it. She bit her lip as she closed it, then tiptoed over to the bed. She set the candle down on a bedside table, pulled off her gown and robe, then slipped back into bed.

"Where have you been?"

Kelsey started when he spoke. She clutched her chest and waited for her heart to stop thudding before she could speak. "Don't ever scare me like that again."

"Tell me where you have been?" he said, his voice tense with impatience.

She couldn't see his face in the dark, but she was sure he was scowling at her. "I—I . . . was hungry, so I went to the kitchen for something to eat. As you recall, I didn't get to eat much of my dinner."

She scooted over to him. When their naked bodies touched, her skin tingled all over, a familiar yearning spreading through her whole body. She laid her head on his chest, then ran her fingers through the dark patch of coarse hair there. "We're not going to argue now, are we?"

"Don't ever leave my bed again unless you inform me where you're going." He wrapped his arms around her and pulled her on top of him.

"Did you miss me?"

"I missed your sweet body when I reached for you and you weren't beside me." He buried his fingers in her hair and brought her lips down to meet his.

He settled her over his erection and eased inside her. Talking about food made her realize how hungry she really was, and she heard her empty stomach rumbling. She hoped he didn't hear it, although thoughts of food flew out of her mind when he began moving with a maddening slowness inside her.

The next day Kelsey made the pigments for the wall, then began painting a small section of it. Edward had been attentive all day. A few times he came into the ballroom and sat in the window seat and watched her paint. Once she caught him staring at her with such a sultry, possessive gleam in his eye that she knew he'd propose to her soon. She couldn't concentrate with him nearby, knowing she was about to go against his wishes and help Lizzy and Griffin run away to Gretna Green. After she had dropped her brush several times, she sent him out of the room so she could work.

An hour later Watkins rushed into the ballroom, his usual stolid aplomb on the verge of dissolving. "Miss Kelsey, have you seen Lizzy? I must find her this very moment."

"What is it, Watkins?" Kelsey set her brush and palette down on the scaffold.

"Lady Shellborn has just arrived, and his grace is looking for her."

"Lady Shellborn?" Kelsey said, sounding lost.

"She is the lady his grace found to sponsor Lady Elizabeth this season."

"Oh, I see." Kelsey wondered if Lizzy and Griffin decided to run away sooner than expected. She saw the worried look on Watkins's face and said, "Have you looked in the garden? Maybe she took Finly for a walk."

"We've checked there, Miss Kelsey."

"Have you checked the tower?"

"Yes, miss, that is the first place I always look for her."

Kelsey shrugged, inwardly cursing Lizzy for running away without telling her. "I don't know, then, Watkins. Would you like me to help you look for her?"

"No, no, Miss Kelsey, but perhaps you can speak to Lady Shellborn while I try to find her. His grace is too angry with Lizzy to be his usual pleasant self."

"Pleasant self?" Kelsey raised incredulous eyebrows at Watkins, then smiled. "I suppose I could try and save the good lady until Lizzy is found." Kelsey thought of Lizzy and Griffin again, then bit her bottom lip as she threw her leg over the scaffolding and climbed down.

Edward was in the parlor, pacing. Lady Shellborn watched him, an amused gleam in her faded gray eyes as her gaze followed him. She patted the side of her steel-gray hair that was pulled back in a bun, an affectation she used often when trying to look annoyed.

To add a bit more fire to the pot—she liked fires—she said, "I've heard about the gal, and I'm not pleased, Edward. I'm not used to be kept waiting by young hellions—I'm not pleased at all." She pursed her lips, stretching her thin, wrinkled skin across her prominent cheekbones. "I'm doing this only because your mother was a particular friend. Thank goodness the poor woman is dead. If she should have lived to see how her daughter has turned out—"

A young woman walked into the room at that moment, startling Lady Shellborn and cutting off her words. Lady Shellborn took in the young woman's paint-stained pants and smock, the smudge of red on her cheek, the huge green eyes that boldly glanced back at her. "The servants' quarters are in the back of the house, gal," she heard herself saying.

"I'm not a servant, madam," Kelsey said, a derisive smile spreading across her face.

Edward had stopped pacing. He eyed Kelsey longer than was proper before he said, "This is Miss Vallarreal, she is painting my ballroom. Miss Vallarreal, this is Lady Shellborn."

Lady Shellborn watched the girl curtsy, thought it was a rusty curtsy at best, then said, "Well, do you know where Lady Elizabeth is?"

"I'm afraid not." There was that bold stare again, but the girl's eyes hid something behind them.

Lady Shellborn was intrigued and said, "Edward, I would that you leave us alone for a moment."

Edward gave Miss Vallarreal a look before he left the room. "Sit down, gal." Lady Shellborn waved to a chair directly across from her. She wanted to be able to see every nuance in the girl's face as she spoke to her. "Now that you are seated, tell me what you know about Lady Elizabeth's disappearance."

Kelsey hesitated for only a moment, then said, "I know she is in love with someone already."

Lady Shellborn wasn't ready for that much honesty to hit her all at once. She opened her mouth, realized it gaped widely, then shut it directly.

Kelsey continued. "Forgive me, madam, but I think it is ridiculous for Lord Salford to send Lizzy to London, when she has found someone who is so very well suited for her. I tried to tell him this, but he won't listen to me. We really can't help who we fall in love with, now, can we? So what if Griffin is a farmer, he's a good-hearted person and he loves Lizzy. And Lizzy needs to be loved. . . ." Kelsey's voice trailed off.

Lady Shellborn pursed her lips, straightened her turban, then said, "I agree with you, gal. I know the aunt who raised the child—a spiteful witch. I never had any use for her, but Lizzy would ruin her life if she were to marry this hay-pitching nobody. It just is not done."

"It all depends on how you look at it, Lady Shellborn. Lizzy doesn't care what society thinks of her, and she has no wish to go on in it. Why can't she be happy? All good society shunned my mother when she married my father, but that didn't stop her. No, my mother knew that she loved him and she married him. And I believe she never regretted marrying my father."

Lady Shellborn knew all about Miss Vallarreal's mother. Her poor grandmother had gone into hysterics when she found out her daughter had run off with an artist, then disowned her. She stared at Kelsey for a moment, then said, "I'm not a romantic, but I know what a hellion Lady Elizabeth can be. So I'm inclined to agree with you, gal, but mind—if this ever gets around, I will personally hold you responsible."

"Oh, I'm so glad you feel this way." Kelsey leapt up. Before Lady Shellborn could stop her, she flung her arms around her neck.

Lady Shellborn grinned slightly as she patted Kelsey's back. "Now, now, that is enough of that." Kelsey backed away. Lady Shellborn took her hand. "You love Edward, do you not?"

"You really are very intuitive, aren't you?" Kelsey smiled over at her.

"Just because I'm in my dotage, gal, doesn't mean I'm blind. I saw the way he looked at you." Kelsey's smile broadened. She really was a fetching little thing, and pretty. "It would be the best thing that ever happened to Edward. Keep at him, gal, and you'll get him. He looks well on the way to being smitten."

"Do you think so?" Kelsey's eyes brightened.

"Indeed. I was as sure about Napoleon invading us as I am about this." Lady Shellborn found herself grinning, something in which she rarely indulged, then she rose with the help of her cane and the girl's arm. "You can inform Lizzy that she can come out of hiding. The Dragon is going back to London now. Tell her I wish her all the best."

"Thank you, Lady Shellborn." Kelsey reached up and pecked her on the cheek.

Lady Shellborn blushed, shook her head at Kelsey, and said, "It's too bad I cannot sponsor you. You would have all the bucks eating out of the palm of your hand. One more thing, I expect a wedding invitation when he pops the question, gal."

"You will get it." Kelsey helped the elderly woman out to her carriage, a massive Berline coach drawn by four smart matching bays with white stockings. Two of the four outriders jumped down, and Kelsey gave Lady Shellborn over to them.

They helped Lady Shellborn into the coach, but didn't do it fast enough for her, and she poked one of the men on the behind with her cane. "Feathers, open that damned door faster. I'm not so old that I can't move."

"Aye, ma'am." He gave her a sour look, then rolled his eyes at Kelsey.

She stifled a grin.

Lady Shellborn nodded a good-bye, then tapped the top of the roof with her cane and bellowed, "Well, any day now."

Kelsey watched the carriage pull away. She was about to turn, but Edward came up beside her. "What the hell have you done? Where has Lady Shellborn gone?"

"She's gone back to London."

"Don't think your meddling will change anything, Kelsey. Lizzy is going to go to London for a season even if I have to pay someone to sponsor her." He turned and marched back into the house, every step stiff with his anger.

Kelsey didn't say anything to him. She knew it would only make him angrier. He'd accept Lizzy and Griffin. He had to. Didn't he?

Kelsey stopped working early to get ready to attend Mr. McGregor's party. She wore a cream silk gown with short puffed sleeves and a low décolletage, covered by tiny ultramarine-blue rosettes. A matching blue sash gathered around her small waist.

The bottom of the dress was covered by more tiny rosettes. A cashmere shawl hung from her bare arms and matched the blue fringe on the dress. Mary had worked her magic again with Kelsey's hair, sweeping it back in an artless, windswept style, leaving curling wisps of hair loose along her neck and face. Kelsey hoped she looked enticing enough to lure Edward to the party. She knew he was still sulking over Lady Shellborn, but hopefully her appearance would cure that too.

She was thinking about him as she descended the stairs, then she saw him at the bottom, his arms over his chest, his broad shoulder leaning against the railing, apparently waiting for her. When he noticed her, his gaze slowly devoured her.

She paused on the last step, directly in front of him, meeting him eye to eye. The height gave her a bit more confidence to face him as an equal, and it came through in her voice. "So this is what it feels like to be tall."

"Where do you think you're going dressed like that?"

"I'll tell you if you stop scowling at me." She wrapped her arms around his neck, pressing her breasts against his chest as she kissed him. If anything could tease the scowl from his face, she knew a kiss would do it.

His arms went around her and he crushed her against his chest as he deepened the kiss. She melted against him, lost in the strength of his arms and the power of his drugging kiss. After a moment he raised his head and stared at her, the hunger for her burning in his gaze. "Perhaps I should take you back up the stairs."

"Oh, no." She pushed at his chest. "I'm going to Mr. McGregor's party and I don't want to be late."

He dropped his arms and stepped back. "You're not going unescorted."

"I certainly am." She took the last step, then turned to look up at him, his height giving him the distinct advantage now. She didn't let it sway her as she said, "This is not a ballroom in London and I'm not a lady bound by the strictures of propriety and etiquette. I'm just the daughter of a simple village painter. It is perfectly all right for me to go alone to this party. . . ." She saw Edward's frown deepen slightly at her words, and she asked him, "What is the matter? If you keep frowning like that, your face will get stuck that way."

"Nothing is the matter but you. And I can't let you go to this party alone." After running a hand through his hair, almost jerking it out, he finally conceded and said, "I'll be your escort."

"If you insist." She reached up on tiptoe and pecked him on the mouth, but his lips were curiously unresponsive. He seemed preoccupied.

"I'll be ready in a moment." He took the stairs two at a time.

She frowned as she watched him climb the stairs. Would she ever understand him? He was like fire one minute and ice the next. It was the cold, indifferent part of him that frightened her.

"Pssst!"

Kelsey turned to see Lizzy standing near the stairs. She moved out of the shadows.

"Lizzy, where have you been?" Kelsey whispered.

"I was hiding so I wouldn't have to speak to that horrible Lady Shellborn."

"She really wasn't as bad as you think. She thinks you should marry Griffin if you love him." Lizzy appeared so stunned, she couldn't speak for a moment, so Kelsey asked, "Why are we whispering like this?"

"I didn't want Edward to see me. I'm not going to the party, Edward probably wouldn't approve. I don't want to arouse his suspicions. Would you give Griffin this note?" Lizzy handed her a folded piece of paper.

"Yes, of course." Kelsey stuffed it in her reticule.

She heard the sound of Edward's footsteps coming toward the stairs. Quickly, she glanced at Lizzy, but Lizzy was nowhere in sight. She had the oddest ability to vanish into thin air.

"Shall we go?" Edward offered her his arm.

"Yes." She took it and smiled tremulously at him.

* * *

The party was in full swing when Edward and Kelsey pulled up in the curricle. The smell of roasting pork filled the sultry night air. Lanterns were lit on the side of the small cottage, and men mulled near the pit where a pig roasted on a spit. Someone played a fiddle while couples danced. It looked as if the whole village was there. Edward doubted the wisdom of having let Kelsey talk him into escorting her.

Kelsey leaned over and patted his hand. "Let's go, shall we? I promise you'll have a good time."

"Don't make promises you can't keep," Edward said as he jumped down and helped her out of the carriage.

The youngest of McGregor's sons came running up to them. "Yer grace. Ya may not remember me, but I'm Jacob." Jacob's red curls bobbed on his head as he nodded, then he slapped Kelsey on the shoulder. "There ya be. Griffin's been waiting all night for ya."

Edward felt every muscle in his body contract at the mention of Griffin.

"I'll see to yer team if that's all right, yer grace?"

Edward nodded. "Yes."

"Come on." Kelsey slipped her arm in his and pulled him toward the party.

Heads turned as they strolled into the middle of the gathering. The music stopped. Everyone stared at him as if he were a specter rising from a grave. He felt their eyes boring into his face. Unthinkingly, he took a step back, but Kelsey gripped his arm tighter.

"It's all right," she whispered.

He stared down at her eyes, so reassuring, so warm, then let her lead him forward.

Alroy had been turning the spit, but when he saw them he hurried over. "There ya are, yer grace. We thought ya wouldn't come. Glad to see ya. Make yerself to home. Kelsey, I think Griffin's here somewhere. Might be helpin' his ma to serve."

"I'll find him."

Alroy McGregor turned toward the staring people. "What's

the matter with ya, this is a jollification, ain't it? Come on, Bones, play that fiddle."

The fiddler was a grizzled, thin man with a long beard. Edward shot him a pointed glance. Bones glanced down at the instrument, then picked it up and began playing. The couples, who stood frozen, moved, and twirled to the music again. But he could still feel their eyes on him. The awkward moment that he had so dreaded around people was over; they had seen his gruesome face. But he still felt the urge to leave.

"Come on, yer grace, come over and we'll talk while I roast this pig. Won't be long now 'fore we eat."

"I'll go and see if I can help Mrs. McGregor in the kitchen," Kelsey said as she gently disengaged her arm.

Edward keenly felt her loss from his side as he watched her stride away.

"Over here, yer grace." Alroy motioned with his hand toward the spit.

Edward followed him as he strode toward the roasting pig.

"Nice evenin' we've got for the jollification. And we've got you to thank for it, yer grace. Ya've done so much for me family and me. I doubt we'll ever be able to repay ya." Alroy walked to a keg of ale, tapped out a mug, and handed it to Edward. "Here you go, yer grace, hope you like ale. . . ."

"That will do." Edward took the proffered mug.

"I'd like to talk to you about the bottom land. I'd like to clear the rocks away and put in crops this fall. . . ."

Edward wasn't paying attention to McGregor's one-sided conversation as he turned and saw Griffin coming out the doorway Kelsey was going through. They spoke for a moment. Kelsey handed him a piece of paper, then she slipped into the cottage.

Last night, when he had found Kelsey sneaking back into his bed, he wondered what she'd been doing. He didn't believe her story about getting something to eat, for he'd heard her stomach growling when they made love. What was she up to? Anything she had to say to McGregor she could say it now. He wondered if Kelsey wasn't playing matchmaker and passing Lizzy's notes to Griffin.

He waited for Griffin to enter the barn, then he turned to Alroy. "If you'll excuse me."

"Sure, yer . . ."

Edward didn't wait for Alroy's answer, but strode toward the barn. Inside he found Griffin standing near a lantern, reading the letter. Startled, Griffin stuffed it in his pocket as he glanced up.

"Didn't know ya'd come," Griffin said, not hiding the chagrin in his voice.

"I suppose you were not expecting me," Edward said in a low voice. He paused, knowing if he drew closer to Griffin he might lose his temper. "I saw Kelsey give you a note. What was in it?"

"Nothing that concerns you," Griffin said, growing defensive.

"I think I know what was in that note, and I'm going to say this only once. Stay away from Lizzy."

"I think that's her decision to make." Griffin widened his stance and crossed his arms over his barrellike chest.

"No, I'm her guardian, and I'm telling you to stay away from her. I know your type, McGregor, and if you put one hand on Lizzy, I'll see you regret it."

"Look who's callin' the kettle black. You don't know my type at all. I ain't like you, I don't ruin innocent girls for pleasure. I tried to warn Kelsey about you, but I was a bit late there. You've already done the dirty with her. There is one difference atween you and me—at least if I'd taken Kelsey's virtue, I would have married her by now." He grinned mockingly. "You plannin' on marryin' her? If so, Kelsey must be keepin' it a secret, 'cause she ain't told me 'bout it."

"That's between Kelsey and me."

"There might be a third party involved if she has your by-blow." The mocking grin faded and his blond brows snapped together.

"I'll provide for her." Edward felt the slender thread holding his patience slipping.

"Sure, you've got plenty of money and your big castle on the hill. You can brush her aside when another bird catches your fancy, but Kelsey's got her pride. She won't be your mistress nor will she take your charity. And I'll tell you something else, you better make your intentions plain to her, 'cause she thinks you love her—she's hardheaded that way. I tried to tell her you ain't changed since you dallied with that whore of a stepmother she had, but she wouldn't listen to me. She's bent on you marrying her."

"Like I said, that's our business."

"It might be at that, but I hate to see Kelsey hurt."

"Kelsey is none of your concern, nor is Lizzy. And I am warning you to leave both of them alone."

"I can't do that." Griffin had a smug expression on his face. "I mean to marry Lizzy. Don't look so surprised, I ain't the kind of man ya think I am."

"I'll never consent to it. I'll send her abroad for her own good before I'd let you marry her."

"For her own good! What the hell do you know about good!" Griffin's composure dissolved. His eyes blazed with furious determination as he said, "She's going to be me wife."

"She'll never be your wife."

"She will, damn you. You won't stop us. . . ."

Griffin lunged at him.

Seventeen

Alroy ran into the barn just as Griffin lunged at Edward. "Here now!" he cried. "That'll be enough of this!"

Being larger than the two in the fray gave him the advantage. He easily shoved Griffin back with one beefy arm and jumped between them.

He glared at his son. "What are ya doin', Griffin? Have ya lost yer mind?"

"I was getting something straight with his high-and-mightiness here." Griffin wiped a trickle of blood off his lip with the back of his hand.

"This ain't the way to do it." Alroy used a tone his son knew well, and it made Griffin glance away.

"Your father is right," Edward said, out of breath, his fists tight at his sides.

"You two want to tell me what this was all about?"

When neither of them spoke, Alroy said, "Uh-huh. Just as I thought, yer fighting over our Kelsey."

"It ain't about Kelsey, Da. It's about his sister."

"His sister?" Alroy felt lost here. Somehow he'd missed something. He thought Lady Elizabeth couldn't stand to be in the same room with Griffin, but then, he'd never understand young people.

"Your son has designs on my sister. I won't have him near her. Lizzy's too young to know her own mind."

Griffin's face turned beet red from the control it cost him to remain quiet. Alroy stared at his son. "That true, Griffin? Have ya been seein' his sister without his knowledge or consent?"

"Yes, Da, but—"

"Don't *but* me, Griffin! I'm ashamed of ya, truly ashamed. Here this man gives me a job and pays me enough to afford servants. He even gives us a new house to live in and ya repay him by actin' like a common rogue. Where have I gone wrong raising ya? Yer suppose to be settin' an example for yer brothers, yer the oldest. Get out of my sight!"

Griffin trudged past Alroy, hurt and anger in his deep blue eyes. Alroy felt the rift between them growing larger with each step his son took. He watched his son until he disappeared out the barn door, knowing that the closeness he'd shared with his eldest boy would never be the same after this. He felt an egg-size lump growing in his throat.

"This in no way reflects on you and I don't hold you responsible for his actions. My offer still stands," Edward said.

"Thank ya for yer kindness, yer grace. I'll see that he don't bother yer sister any longer, even if I have to tie the boy to a post."

Edward nodded, then left the barn. Alroy stared at Lord Salford's stiff back and wondered if he could keep that promise he just made. He knew he'd never convince Griffin that Lady Elizabeth was too far above him, that he'd live a life of torment shackled to a spoiled she-devil like her. Once Griffin got something into his head, it was like pulling a stubborn root to get it out. He'd talk to Griffin, but he knew Griffin would do what he wanted in the end. Why couldn't all children be born when they were forty? Alroy sighed, then walked out of the barn.

Kelsey left the cottage in search of Edward. She couldn't stop worrying about how he was doing, alone, facing all the villagers. She scanned the crowd, didn't see him, then she glanced toward the barn as Griffin emerged. He stomped across the yard toward a keg of ale. She took a step in Griffin's direction, intending to ask him if he'd seen Edward, but Edward abruptly came out of the barn, his face a mask of dark, sulking fury. Then Griffin's father followed, looking grim. Edward must have confronted Griffin about Lizzy, and it didn't go well.

Kelsey was about to go to Edward and try to soothe the rift between Griffin and him, when someone grabbed her arm. She turned and looked into the sneering face of Veronica Stevens, the vicar's daughter. She was a square-faced woman with mousy brown hair, a small, cruel mouth, and darting, keen eyes that missed nothing—especially when it came to men.

"Well, if it isn't the village artist. And look at this fine new gown. What did you do to get it?"

"I won't lower myself by answering that. Why don't you go fly back to your cage, Veronica," Kelsey said, then jerked her arm free from Veronica's grasp and tried to walk past her.

Veronica grabbed Kelsey's arm again, digging her nails into Kelsey's upper arm. "Word has it that you're Salford's whore now, just like your stepmother was."

Kelsey gritted her teeth, determined not to let Veronica harass her. Veronica hated Kelsey because she'd always been jealous that Griffin was her best friend. Veronica had always been in love with Griffin, and had even attempted to trap him with another man's child. Now she was stuck in a loveless marriage with the child's father, a sailor, whom the vicar had forced her to marry. Kelsey thought it was fitting punishment for the way she'd treated Griffin.

"What? Are you ignoring me?"

Kelsey shook her head and said, "You really are to be pitied."

"Don't pity me, you slut, you're the one at whom everyone's laughing. He's already got a mistress, you know. Her name's Samantha. She runs the whorehouse your father visits."

"Do you think I care?" Kelsey tried to sound nonchalant while her insides boiled.

"You'll care when he grows tired of you and sends for Samantha again, though I pity her. Now that I've seen his monstrous face, I wonder how he persuaded Samantha to be his whore. She's not an unattractive woman. I understand how he got you, you've never been anything to look at. . . ."

Kelsey hadn't noticed that Edward had stopped several feet away and stood listening to them, until he grabbed Veronica, forcing her to turn around and look at him.

He stuck his face close to hers and drawled, "I suggest you apologize for insulting Miss Vallarreal's honor, or I might forget I'm a gentleman."

"I—I . . ." Veronica looked too frightened to speak for a minute, then blurted out, "I'm sorry."

Edward dropped her arm. Veronica picked up the hem of her skirt and fled across the yard. He grabbed Kelsey's arm and locked it inside his. "Come on, I've had enough."

"Don't let her comments upset you. She's always hated me. She was saying that about your face only to make me angry."

"I know what my face looks like, Kelsey. Stop trying to smooth it over by treating me like a child."

Kelsey wanted to say something to ease his pain, but the dark, tortured look kept her silent. And Veronica's words still hurt. What if Edward were only using her body? She didn't want to believe it. She couldn't believe it.

He didn't say a word to her the whole way home, or when he left her at her chamber door. Kelsey watched him walk to his room and slam the door.

Tears flowed down her cheeks. The cold, indifferent side of him was winning. She was losing him. With just a few vicious words Veronica had taken away all the self-confidence Kelsey had worked so hard to give him. If she could only reach him through the part of him that she knew loved her. Maybe he didn't love her. She stepped into her room, slammed the door, then collapsed on her bed and sobbed.

* * *

Kelsey woke at the sound of her chamber door being thrown open. It banged against the wall several times. She opened her eyes to see Edward storming toward her. He grabbed her shoulders and shook her. "You knew, didn't you?"

"Knew what?" Kelsey screeched.

"You knew last night that they were running away. That's what the note was all about. How could I have been such a fool?" He dropped her shoulders and staggered from the bed as if he needed the distance to control his temper. His face was a mask of barely restrained fury.

"Are you sure they are gone?"

"Yes, yes, I'm sure. Alroy McGregor was here looking for Griffin this morning. He said he hadn't slept in his bed, then I checked Lizzy's room and her clothes were gone. They left sometime last night."

"I hope they're married by now," Kelsey said, unable to keep the eagerness out of her voice.

"Damn you, Kelsey! You knew I disapproved. You knew I wanted Lizzy to go to London for a season, but you went behind my back and encouraged them." He ground his teeth together, his lips thinning into a tense, angry line.

"They are in love."

"Lizzy will never be happy as a farmer's wife."

"She will, she loves Griffin."

Some of the intensity left his voice. "Romantic notions fade easily when the realities of life intrude upon them."

"How can you have such a callous attitude?" Kelsey asked, feeling the tears well up in her eyes. "Love is stronger than you think."

"It will never be strong enough." He stared sharply at her for a moment, as if the significance of his words were directed at her, then he stalked out of the room.

Kelsey didn't ponder them long, for she threw back the covers, dressing quickly in her painting breeches and shirt. She knew he was going to find them and try to stop the marriage. If he should meet Griffin, they would undoubtedly kill each other. She couldn't let that happen. She felt terrible about lying to him while supporting Lizzy and Griffin, but no two people were more right for each other. Edward would have to accept it.

Kelsey ran out to the stable. The groom, Grayson, stood near the entrance, scratching his curly, dark hair and looking anxious about something.

"Is his grace in there?" Kelsey asked anxiously.

"He's gone, miss. Rode off like a bullet. He was in a foul humor too. Said if you was to come looking for him, I was to keep you here."

"We both know you're not going to do that," Kelsey said, shooting him her best intimidating look. "Now . . . if you'll show me how to saddle a horse, I'll be on my way." She strode into the stable, the smell of fresh hay and horse filling her senses. The aisle between the stalls was wide enough that she could walk between the horses without their noses touching her. Large staring brown eyes followed her progress.

"Which one of these creatures is gentle?" she asked.

"I have to obey orders, miss," Grayson said apologetically as he followed on her heels.

Kelsey whirled around to face him. "If I set out on foot, his grace will be livid when he finds out that you would not give me an animal to ride. Now, do I turn and go out of here on foot, sir, or will you show me how to saddle one of these gentle mares?"

Grayson looked torn for a moment, then said, "All right, but I can't let you go alone."

"Very good, my sense of direction is appalling anyway. You may be helpful."

"Where are we going, miss?"

"To Gretna Green."

"That's a good long way o' here, miss."

"Yes, but we'll make it. Now, for a horse." Kelsey looked down the stalls at the large heads bobbing. A particularly pretty black horse with a star on his forehead snorted and kicked the stall. That one was definitely out.

"We don't have a gentle mare among 'em, I'm sorry. His grace keeps only blooded geldings and stallions."

"I'm sure one of them will do." Kelsey bent over a stall and looked at a pretty bay with four white stockings. He stared back at her with keen bright eyes. She reached out and patted his soft muzzle. He seemed to like the attention. "How about this one here?"

"That's Royal Reeger. He's a tart, but once he's been ridden hard, you can handle him."

"Handle?" The blood drained from Kelsey's face.

"Yes, miss." Grayson raised a curious dark brow at her. "You know how to ride?"

"I've never ridden a horse in my life—never had a need too until today."

Grayson shook his head. "I'll see what I can do in the way of teaching you. All you have to remember is that horses are stupid animals that need a firm hand."

"A firm hand . . ." Kelsey echoed, and smiled nervously at him, her insides churning at the thought of riding a horse. They were marvelous creatures to paint and admire from afar, but the thought of being on the back of one had always frightened her. She started to wonder if she shouldn't walk or go by post.

After she had lost the reins more times than she could count, several times landing in the ditch, twice in the middle of the road, whereby she was almost run over by a carriage, Kelsey finally felt confident on Reeger's back. But the feeling was hard won. It had taken her two days of constant struggle to achieve it. Her bottom ached and she wondered if her teeth were still intact from being jarred constantly. On top of every other misery known to her, it was raining, chilling her to the bone. She didn't have time to pack for the trip and had only the wet clothes on her back. When they found an inn on the outskirts of the village of Brampton, she almost got down and kissed the muddy ground when she dismounted.

Grayson grabbed the reins. "I'll see to the horses, miss."

"I'll get two rooms." Kelsey rubbed her backside as she trudged into the little inn. Watkins, bless him, had come running out of the castle when he saw her leaving and handed her a pouch full of sovereigns for the journey. She must do something nice for Watkins when she got back, she reminded herself.

She walked into the tiny inn, shook the water off her dripping hands, then surveyed the entrance. A stairway was off to her right. A small desk stood in front of her. No one was manning the desk, so Kelsey peeked her head into the taproom. It was a small room with wide, dark beams spanning the ceiling. The room held only three tables. Two of the tables were empty, but Kelsey froze when she saw the third one. Lizzy and Griffin were seated there, eating, their heads bent in quiet conversation. They seemed to feel her eyes on them, for they both turned and looked at her.

"Oh, aye, Kelsey." Griffin motioned her over as if she were expected. "You look like a drowned cat."

"Thank you, I've always wanted to look like a drowned cat. What are you doing here? I thought you'd be in Gretna Green."

"We finished the deed and stopped here to avoid the rain."

"Oh." Kelsey walked over to the hearth and turned her backside to the blazing fire. "Have you seen him?"

"No," Lizzy said, sounding grateful for the reprieve.

The innkeeper came through the door and paused to look at her. He was a short man with greedy eyes and a small mouth. He stared at her wet, paint-stained breeches, then scratched the bald spot an the top of his head as he took in her long, wet hair sticking to her chest, arms, and face.

He frowned at her and said with contempt, "We don't serve your kind in here." The man started toward her with a look on his face as if he meant to throw her out.

Griffin jumped to his feet and stepped in his path. "She's with us, she's my sister."

The man looked incredulous as he eyed Kelsey again.

"Don't worry, I can pay. And I've a groom outside that needs a hot meal and lodgings as well." Kelsey picked out a gold sovereign and flipped it to the man, who caught it in midair. "I hope that will cover all the charges?"

"Yes, ma'am," the man said. He stared at the gold coin, then, not believing it was a sovereign, he bit it with his teeth. When he seemed sure of its value, he turned on his heel and left the room.

"Odious little man," Lizzy remarked. "He gave us the worst room in the inn. The sheets were not even clean."

"Aye, odious, as you say. But dirty sheets didn't matter, did it?" Griffin smiled down at her as he sat beside her, then he put his arm around her shoulder and kissed her on the lips.

Lizzy blushed prettily and seemed to enjoy the attention.

Kelsey took a seat across from the lovers. She was starving and grabbed a piece of bread and buttered it. "So tell me, are you happily married so far?"

"Yes," Lizzy said, smiling over at Kelsey.

"You look happy." Kelsey devoured the bread with three bites.

"Is Eddie very angry?"

Kelsey swallowed the wad of bread in her mouth, feeling it stick in her throat. For a moment she'd forgotten about Edward. She poured a mug of ale from the pitcher on the table and drank a sip before she could speak. "He was very distraught when he found out you'd eloped. He rode out right away to look for you. I had hopes that you had enough lead time to get married before he found you. I see you did."

"He wouldn't have stopped us anyway," Griffin said, doggedly.

"I don't know. He was furious. That's why I followed him, I didn't want him to hurt you, but I'm not a very good rider—"

"Rider?" Griffin grinned from ear to ear. "You were on the back of a horse?"

"Yes," Kelsey raised her chin to an indignant angle, "and I would have you know I'm quite accomplished at it."

"That'll be the day."

"You'll eat those words when you see me in the saddle."

"We'll have snow in June a'fore that happens."

She rolled her eyes at him as the innkeeper came back bearing a steaming teapot and a tray laden with a kidney pie, cauliflower with cheese sauce, boiled turnips, and more fresh bread.

Kelsey dove into the food and forgot all about Edward for the present. After they ate, Lizzy let her borrow a nightgown and Kelsey retired to her room. She missed the warmth of Edward's body next to her and thought of their ride home from the McGregor's party. He had seemed so distant, so cold. The incident with Veronica must have been the reason for it. Just a few offensive, bitter words from Veronica had destroyed all the self-confidence Edward had gained. Her heart ached for him. Would he go back behind his barriers and hide from the world again? And from her? Could he ever forgive her for helping Lizzy and Griffin run away? She wondered where he was at the moment and if he was thinking about her as she was thinking about him.

She didn't have long to wonder. A few moments later she heard someone banging on Griffin and Lizzy's door, then Edward's voice: "All right, McGregor, open the bloody door!" He pounded again.

Kelsey jumped when she heard a thump, then a crash as if the door had been kicked in. She leapt out of bed and ran next door to their room.

Griffin and Edward were punching each other. Griffin was half dressed, wearing only his breeches. Lizzy stood by the bed with a sheet wrapped around her. She had her hand to her mouth and looked pale as a ghost.

"Stop it!" Kelsey screamed and ran toward them.

Edward chose that moment to punch Griffin in the chin. It all happened in a flash, but to Kelsey the world slowed, dragging out every detail. Griffin lost his balance. She collided with his massive back. Air left her mouth in a large whoosh as the breath was knocked out of her, then she and Griffin tumbled backward. Griffin grabbed the stanchion of the door, but she was not so fortunate. Her head impacted with the stair railing. She felt the pain, heard the crack . . . Then everything dissolved into blackness.

"My God . . ." Edward said under his breath as he watched Kelsey's body go limp and her eyes close. He shoved past Griffin, who was just turning to look over his shoulder.

"Oh, no! Kelsey!" Lizzy said, following in Edward's wake.

He fell to his knees beside her. She was deathly pale, her raven hair fanned out around her head. He reached out and touched the tender white flesh on her thin neck.

He held his breath. . . .

The soft, steady beat of her pulse brushed his fingertips. He let out the breath he'd been holding. The tightness in his throat eased. He bent and gathered her into his arms. She seemed so petite, so lifeless, lying limp in his grasp.

"Is she all right?" Lizzy asked, her brows furrowed with worry.

"I think so."

"Where's her room?" Edward addressed Griffin, who stood in the hallway, looking as pale as a piece of parchment.

"There, next to ours."

"Go and get a doctor."

"Aye."

Edward heard Griffin's footsteps as he ran down the stairs, then he heard mumbled voices as he spoke to Lizzy. Gently, he laid Kelsey on the bed. He pushed back the long, black curls in her face, then murmured, "I'm sorry, little one . . . I'm sorry."

A few moments later Lizzy strode into the room, fully dressed. Tears gleamed in her eyes. Edward had never seen an outward show of emotion from Lizzy, and he glanced at her, wondering if Griffin had exacted this change in her.

"I'll sit with her if you like," Lizzy said, lowering herself down gently on the opposite edge of the bed.

"No, I'll stay with her."

"She'll wake up soon, won't she?" Lizzy picked up one of Kelsey's hands. "I've never had a friend before. She was my friend."

"She still is, Lizzy. She's going to be all right," Edward said with more certainty than he felt.

"This wouldn't have happened if we hadn't run away to get married." Lizzy shot him an accusing look. "She came to warn us that you were angry and looking for us. She always thinks about everyone but herself."

"I know," Edward said, brushing the edge of his finger along Kelsey's cheek.

"If she lives, do you intend to marry her?"

"No . . ." Edward abruptly pulled his hand back from Kelsey's cheek.

"I thought you'd say that," Lizzy said, staring at him with anger blazing in her eyes. "It was selfish of me, but I wanted you to fall in love with her so she could hurt you and maybe teach you that some things are beyond your control. . . . But she's the one who fell in love. I'm sorry for it."

"So am I," Edward said, glancing pensively down at Kelsey. He stared at her a moment, then glanced back at Lizzy, his face inscrutable. "Go and pack, Lizzy, you're going back with Grayson. I gave him the order to take you home before I came up here."

"I'm not leaving." She raised her chin, her eyes blazing.

"You will listen to me. This farce of a marriage you've entered into without my consent is at an end."

"It is not. I warn you, I won't give Griffin up. He's my husband. I won't let you or anyone else separate us."

"You married McGregor just to spite me."

"No, I haven't," she said, her voice growing louder.

"I'm still your guardian. I can have the marriage annulled and send you abroad until you come to your senses."

"I'll fight you. We've consummated our marriage and I'll swear it in a court of law. There is nothing you can do, and if you try to interfere in our lives, I'll never forgive you. Never! You hate yourself, you are miserable because of it. You want to make me miserable with you, but I'm not going to let you. I won't let you ruin my happiness like you're ruining your own." Lizzy stormed toward the door, her fists swinging at her sides.

At that moment Edward saw Lizzy not as the spoiled, strong-willed little girl who had plagued him with worry through her childhood, but as a woman bent on getting her own way. He was beating a dead horse and he knew it.

Alroy McGregor filled the doorway, looking disheveled and annoyed. "Where is Griffin?"

"He's gone for the doctor. Kelsey has been hurt," Lizzy said. "And if you think to stop our marriage, it's too late, so you might as well get used to it, *Father.*" Lizzy stormed past him, her face red with rage.

"That true?" Alroy strode into the room, his face a mask of frustration and distress.

"Yes, it appears so," Edward said tonelessly.

"Lord, bless me," Alroy murmured, then paused near the bed and stared down at Kelsey, worry spreading across his brow. "What happened to our Kelsey?"

"An accident occurred and she bumped her head."

"What else can happen in a day, I ask you?" Alroy shook his head and looked defeated as he plopped down in a chair by the bed.

"She might not wake up," Edward said, rubbing a hand over his throbbing brow.

The doctor, a small man with an ashen face and a succinct manner, pulled the covers back over Kelsey. "She has a contusion on the back of her head. I believe your wife has a concussion."

"She's not my wife," Edward said vehemently as he paced beside the bed.

"Forgive me, I thought—"

"I know what you thought." Edward turned and leveled an intimidating glance at the doctor. "Are there any instructions for her care?"

The little man stiffened at Edward's terse reply and slammed his black bag closed in an irritated manner. "None. Keep her warm. She could wake up in a few hours or it might take a day or two. One can't tell in these types of situations. I'll come back tomorrow. I suggest you try and get some sleep." He picked up his bag, then left the room without another word.

Sleep. How could he sleep? Edward began his pacing again, then thought he heard movement from the bed. He turned and glanced hopefully at Kelsey. She lay as still as a porcelain doll. For a moment the weight in his chest had lifted, but now it was back, crushing him. He sat on the edge of the bed and bent, placing a kiss on her mouth.

The cold lifelessness of her lips made him gather her up in his arms and crush her to him. Her words, "I love you," came back to haunt him. He'd never forget their coupling by the lake, when she'd touched his face and vowed her love so sweetly.

He didn't want Kelsey's love. He didn't need it. He was sure this notion that she loved him was born out of pity. But once he told her the truth about her wealth, she would no doubt go out into the world, be courted by handsome gentlemen, and forget this grotesque infatuation she felt for him. And he wouldn't marry her knowing that she'd eventually wake up one day, see his face, and realize she'd tied herself to a monster. He couldn't bear to live with her resentment. He hated to hurt her, but she must understand that it was only lust that had driven him to take her time and again. Only lust. It could be nothing else. She must find a whole man to love her. But first she had to get well.

"I don't know if you can hear me, Kelsey, but you have to wake up, my love," he said past the tightening in his throat that wouldn't go away.

Eighteen

The boy came into the room. He had a sad look on his face. She didn't like sad looks. Sad looks always meant something bad.

"Don't be sad." She took his hand.

He squeezed her fingers. "There's been a boating accident, Kelsey. My parents were crossing the channel and their boat capsized. They are both dead."

"What is dead?"

"They've gone to heaven and they won't be coming back."

So that is what dead meant. "I'm sorry," she said as they both sat down together on a bench.

"I am too. Everything will change now."

"Everything?"

"Yes, I'm going away to school and I won't see you."

"I'll come with you."

"No, you can't."

She felt sad and tears rolled down her cheeks. "I don't want you to go."

"I'm sorry, there is nothing I can do."

She reached out to hug the boy, but he dissolved in her arms. "Come back! Don't leave me yet!"

Kelsey opened her eyes, a horrible feeling of loss pulling at her. Tears streamed down her cheeks. When she lifted her hand to wipe them away, she grew aware of a sharp pain in her head. She turned and saw Edward in a chair by the bed. He was leaning over the edge of the mattress, his head resting on his bent elbows. She reached out and touched the dark, wavy hair spilling down over his face.

Startled, he jumped and raised his head. "Kelsey . . ." he whispered, caressing her name.

"Good morning." She smiled at him, noting the haggard look on his face and the dark stubble on his chin.

He grabbed her and hugged her tightly. He raised his head and was about to kiss her, but he drew back before their lips met. "You had me worried. How are you feeling?"

"I've a pain in my head and a few aches, but other than that I think I'll live."

"The pain is from a bruise on the back of your head. The doctor is supposed to come this morning and examine you." He wouldn't look into her eyes as he laid her back down, then stepped back from the bed.

"Are you still angry with me about Lizzy and Griffin?" Kelsey said, aware of his abrupt aloofness.

"I am angry with you for following me." The softness in his voice belied his words. "I should turn you over my knee for leaving Stillmore on horseback with only my groom. What were you thinking?"

"I didn't want you to hurt Griffin. You seemed so angry, I thought I could stop you from doing something foolish."

"Did you not think about the folly of your own behavior?"

"No, I admit I thought only of you, Griffin, and Lizzy. Speaking of them, where are they? You haven't hurt Griffin, have you?" Kelsey said with worry in her voice.

"No, but I'd like to." Edward turned away from her and leaned against the windowsill as he glanced outside.

"But you won't?" Kelsey asked optimistically.

"No, I won't. I was too late, they have consummated the marriage. McGregor is responsible for Lizzy now," he said, sounding exhausted. "I see now that you were right. My interference at this time in her life will only push her further away from me. I've tried to reason with her, but she seems determined to destroy her life. She's always been headstrong. She jumps in headfirst and regrets it later. I'll have to wait and be here for her when the regrets come."

"You needn't worry, she'll never regret marrying Griffin."

"I'm glad you are so confident of that fact," he said, his voice distant.

"I am." Kelsey slid up in the bed and leaned back against the pillows, staring at his broad back stretching against his white linen shirt. His shirttail was out and hung down around his thin hips. He had on a pair of black buckskin riding breeches. She noticed he hadn't even taken off his boots last night.

"You really are naive when it comes to life." He turned and stared over his shoulder at her for a moment, looking so dark and ruggedly handsome with his hair down around his shoulders that it took her breath away. "I'd forgotten how young you are."

"You talk as if you are ancient. You couldn't be more than ten years my senior."

"I'm lifetimes older than you. Fate has made me so." Impulsively, he touched the patch over his eye, then turned and started to pace at the foot of the bed.

Kelsey sensed that he was about to tell her something that she did not want to hear. She watched his pantherlike strides as he paced. Gently, she leaned her head back against the headboard and braced herself, her heart hammering.

"I can't let you go on believing that our relationship is anything more than it is."

"What are you saying?" She picked up a piece of her hair and started to twist it around her finger while she bit her lower lip.

"I'm saying that if you have any feelings for me, you should wipe them out of your mind. I don't deserve them."

"Of course you do. You'll come to realize that one day."

"I won't. Another mistaken romantic notion of yours gone awry. I never wanted your affections, Kelsey."

"You're just saying this to push me away. I don't believe you—I won't believe you."

"I didn't want to hurt you, but you're forcing me to tell you the truth." He paused a minute, looking unsure of his resolve, then the mask of indifference came back as he said, "I eased my body on you, and that is all."

"I don't believe that."

"You should." He grinned tauntingly at her, letting his gaze stray to her breasts. "You have a sensuous body and your passionate, impetuous nature pleased me. I responded to it. The only thing I felt for you was wild, unabashed lust, my love."

"Why are you lying to me like this? I know you care about me. I won't listen to you." Kelsey put her hands over her ears.

He walked over to her and pulled them away. "Listen to me, dammit! You're wrong. You know only what you want to believe."

"No," Kelsey whispered, drawing back from him until her back hit the headboard.

"It's true." He stood, then folded his arms over his chest, staring down at her. In a bored tone he said, "Since I took your maidenhead, I suppose I should make you an offer. If you would consider sharing my bed with my other paramour, I would gladly consider supporting you. Before you answer me, keep in mind that I may ask you to join Samantha and me in my bed. I am a man who likes variety. And if I am supporting you, I will expect you to do anything I ask of you. I can tell by the look on your face that you don't like the idea, but a threesome in bed can be very stimulating, and you may even grow to like it."

His words stabbed her heart. She couldn't speak past the gripping tightness in her throat. Was he telling the truth?

"What? You mean to stare at me with those large green eyes and not say a word. I've never seen you speechless before." He chuckled derisively. "I hope you know how generous my offer is. I made the same one to your stepmother. She jumped at the chance right away," he said, sounding pleased with himself.

Kelsey squeezed her eyes closed, sure now that this cruelty had to be genuine. No one could be this vicious. She blinked back the tears and grabbed a pewter mug from the nightstand.

"Get out of my sight, you lecherous, perverted swine!" She hurled it at him.

He leaned to the side. It sailed past him and hit the wall, then tumbled to the floor. "I suppose that is a no," he said, sounding disappointed.

"I'd rather die than be your whore! I wanted to believe since the accident that you'd changed. What a fool I've been where you're concerned! It really sickens me to look at your face now! You're hideous inside and out! Get out of my room! I hate you!"

She reached for something else to throw, and found a water pitcher. She hurled it at his head. He thrust open the door and jumped behind it. The pitcher hit the door, barely missing him.

"And don't ever come near me again!" Kelsey screamed at the door, her voice echoing in the empty room. She grabbed her throbbing head, then fell back against the pillows and sobbed.

Lizzy heard the commotion and left Griffin sleeping in bed as she got up and put on her robe. She opened her door as Edward passed it, his expression as dark as a thundercloud. "Wait!" She closed the door behind her and stepped in front of him, blocking his path. "Was that Kelsey I heard?"

"Yes, she's awake, but I wouldn't go in there at the moment."

"Why?"

"She's angry with me." He stepped around her and started down the steps.

Lizzy started to question him about what happened between them, but she knew by the expression on his face that he would just growl at her and say nothing. She leaned over the newly fixed rail and said, "Where are you going?"

"I'm going home," he ground out between his teeth. "There's no need for me to stay here any longer."

Lizzy heard his footsteps hurry down the stairs and fade away. She went to Kelsey's door and knocked on it. "Kelsey, it's me, can I come in?"

No answer.

Lizzy put her ear to the door and heard Kelsey's sobs. She opened the door, then strode toward the bed. Kelsey was curled into a ball, banging her fists against the pillows while she cried.

Lizzy sat on the edge of the bed. "I'm sorry you fell in love with him."

"You tried to warn me," Kelsey bawled. "You were so right about him and I was so stupid. You knew what he was. I thought the accident had changed him, but he's still despicable. Do you know he actually asked me to be his mistress?" She hit the pillows again with her fist as if she were hitting Edward's face.

"Did he really come right out and ask you?" Lizzy said, unable to keep the surprise from her voice.

"Yes, and I won't tell you everything else he proposed, it's too sordid."

Lizzy smiled to herself, remembering how Edward said he wouldn't ask Kelsey to be his mistress. Perhaps Edward really did love Kelsey and he was trying to make her hate him. There might be hope for them yet.

Two days passed before the doctor pronounced Kelsey fit to travel. Edward's black-lacquered barouche with the ducal coat of arms on it appeared at the inn with a driver and two outriders to convey her home. They were new faces, probably recently hired. Since Edward was not in the coach, she gladly accepted the ride home. Griffin and Lizzy rode with her, while Alroy rode on ahead of them.

It was a torturous ride home for Kelsey, watching Griffin and Lizzy kissing, touching, generally acting like young lovers. She couldn't help but feel envious of their happiness. By the time she reached Jarrow two days later, she was glad to be rid of them. They only reminded her of her own pain and disappointment. One thing was certain, she knew Edward was nothing to her now. Nothing.

Still, thoughts of running into him had her stomach in knots as she left the stable yard and walked in through the servants' entrance. Watkins must have been expecting her, for the door opened before she reached it.

"Hello, Miss Kelsey. I am glad you are home."

"Hello, Watkins." She smiled wanly at him as she stepped inside. "I wish I could say I'm glad to be here, but I cannot."

His thick gray brows snapped together. "I'm sorry to hear that, Miss Kelsey."

"Don't be, it is perhaps fortuitous that I find Stillmore a most unlikable place."

"Unlikable, Miss Kelsey?"

"Yes, Watkins, very unlikable."

"You might grow to like it again," Watkins said with a hopeful gleam in his eye.

"No, Watkins, I'm afraid that will never happen. I even entertained the idea of staying at home and walking here every morning from the village so I wouldn't have to stay under this roof, but that would be inconvenient."

"Very much so, Miss Kelsey."

She shrugged, then her eyes widened as she remembered something. "I almost forgot . . ." She pulled out the pouch of coins Watkins had given her and set them back in his hand. "Thank you. The money was a godsend. I will pay you back when Lord Salford pays me for my work."

Watkins's bony fingers closed around the pouch. "Oh, it is not my money, Miss Kelsey, but belongs to his grace."

"Then please tell him to deduct it from what he will owe me."

"Yes, Miss Kelsey." Watkins bowed slightly. "Would you like a bath sent up to your room?"

"No—yes." Kelsey blurted out. She paused and saw the confusion on Watkins's face, then she started again. "I mean I'm going to work and I'd like a bath afterward, but I don't want it sent up to the gold room. I've decided to move back to my old room. Could you have it brought there?"

"You do not find the bed in the gold room to your liking, Miss Kelsey?" Watkins clasped his hands behind his back and scrutinized her with his faded eyes.

"No, and I wish to return to my old room."

"I'm sorry, Miss Kelsey, that is impossible."

"Why?" She turned to glance at him. His face was as enigmatic as usual.

"I gave the furniture to one of the workers who was hired to help in the ballroom."

"Is there not any other room available?" Kelsey abruptly realized that he'd been playing matchmaker when he had put her in the gold room the first time. She didn't want to raise his hopes, so she said, "I suppose I can sleep in the stable if need be. I'm sure Reeger won't mind if I share his stall."

Watkins stared down at his hands, his brow furrowing in deep thought, then he glanced up at her. He hesitated a moment, then said, "There is one room. It is next to the schoolroom."

"Fine. I really don't care where I sleep as long as it's not in the gold room. Please see that my clothes are moved. And I'll take my meals in the ballroom."

"Yes, Miss Kelsey."

"I'll be working the rest of the day if you need me."

Watkins bowed slightly.

Kelsey turned and strolled down the hallway. Watkins sucked in his lips pensively at her back, looking unsure of what he had just done. He raised his hand and took a step toward her. He opened his mouth to call to her, but then he dropped his hand and pressed his lips together. He had a worried look on his face when he turned around and walked down the hallway.

* * *

Kelsey's shoulders ached when she left the ballroom that evening at nine. She had painted for hours, hoping to grow so exhausted that she wouldn't think of Edward. But he was always there in the back of her mind, looming, his perverted words ringing in her ears: *A threesome in bed can be very stimulating and you may even grow to like it.*

Her fingers strangled the candlestick in her hand and she almost dropped it as she stomped up the steps. Watkins had explained how to get to the new room. She reached the top of the steps and started down the hallway. She had to pass Edward's chamber to get to the staircase that would take her to the third floor. As she neared the master suite, she heard the soft melody from the pianoforte, a melancholy song that she had never heard before.

Abruptly, the music stopped.

Her pulse raced. Her palms grew sweaty as she held her breath. She cupped her hand over the candle flame to keep it from going out and hurried past his door.

She heard his footsteps drawing . . . closer . . . closer. His door creaked open. She flung open the door at the end of the hallway, the end that Watkins insured her led to the third floor, and almost fell through it as she slammed it closed. The thought of seeing Edward again terrorized her. Even though she hated him, she couldn't forget their intoxicating lovemaking or her instinctive responses to it. Her body thirsted for his touch every time she thought about him. If he should try to use her body again, she wondered if her willpower was strong enough to resist him. She raced up the narrow stairs and paused when she gained the top.

The door opened at the bottom of the stairs.

Frantic, she ducked into the room closest to her. She eased the door closed, then fell back against it, her chest heaving. She listened for his footsteps but heard nothing but her own pulse pounding in her ears.

She noticed the room now and raised the candle up to peer around it. It was indeed a schoolroom, with a small table in the middle. An easel was sitting in a corner. Beside it, bookshelves covered one wall. Something about the room seemed vaguely familiar to her. She stepped over to the table and set the candlestick down on it, then ran her finger over the ill-formed initials K.W., printed on the table with ink. The initials E.S. were below them. A heart was drawn around both of them. She traced her finger over the wobbly lines, wondering who K.W. was. Probably the girl whom Edward had said he once loved.

A picture on the wall drew her attention. She walked over and examined it. The paper had yellowed from age and the watercolor had faded, but the image of a boy was still clearly visible. The artist must have been a young child, for the boy's body was a stick figure, the head too round and too large, the face simply rendered with dots and a slash for a nose. The hair was black, cropped, and poked out at all angles. She touched the quaint painting with her finger, feeling the rough surface of the paper. An overly familiar feeling flashed in her mind, as if she had seen the painting before.

A dark shadow below the painting caught her eye. She glanced down, seeing a stuffed rabbit sitting on top of the bookcase. She picked it up and held it, then cuddled it to her breast. It was Rabbit from her dreams. Tears flowed down her cheeks as the memories flooded back to her. Vague recollections of being in this room, of being forced to leave this house, of being given over to two strangers—her mother and father, of the boy in her dreams . . .

"Edward." She said the boy's name aloud, remembering it.

"Yes."

Edward's deep, velvety voice behind her startled her. She dropped the rabbit, then turned to look at him. The candlelight flickered off his face, making the sharp, angular planes look sinisterly handsome.

"I'm sorry I frightened you." He leaned over and picked up the stuffed animal. "You remember now?"

"Some . . ." She stepped back from him, the shock of it all

clawing at her insides, making her knees weak. She leaned back against the bookcase for support, biting her lip, tasting the saltiness of her tears.

"I brought you here to tell you about your real identity."

"So you destroyed the fresco in the ballroom to get me to come here?"

"Yes. I wanted to tell you sooner, but I suppose I was waiting for the proper moment."

"The proper moment!" she shrieked, losing control. "Is there a proper moment to learn that my parents are not really my parents as I believed all my life? Is there a proper moment to hear that everything about my life was a lie? Proper moments, indeed . . ." Her words choked away on a sob.

"I know this is a shock . . ." He reached out to touch her.

Kelsey jerked back from him. "Don't touch me! Don't ever touch me! For God's sake, just tell me the truth! All I want from you is the truth!"

"All right, I'll tell you everything." His tone turned coldly detached as he continued. "Your real mother and father died during an outbreak of smallpox. Your father was a particular friend of my father's and he appointed him your legal guardian. You were but two years old when your parents died and you came to live with us. You lived here for two years before tragedy struck and my parents were killed crossing the Channel from France. I was only fourteen at the time and Lizzy was barely six months old. You know what happened after that. I was sent away to school and Lizzy to live with our aunt."

"Why didn't your father appoint Jeremy's father as your guardian?" Kelsey asked, barely able to get the words past the ache in her throat.

With the rabbit still in his hand, he leaned back against a wall and looked up at the ceiling as he spoke. "He did, but my uncle died of heart failure two weeks after my father. My father's solicitor moved into the slot of guardian."

Kelsey leaned back against the bookcase and dug her fingers

into the spine of a book. "And he arranged for my mother and father to adopt me?"

"Yes. The solicitor was an old friend of your mother's parents. Your mother had approached him on adopting a child because she couldn't have one of her own, and he arranged for her to have you."

Kelsey laughed bitterly. "And here I thought I inherited my teeth from my mother and father." She squeezed her eyes closed and felt another wash of tears trickle down her cheeks. After she regained her composure, she said, "And my art talent, from whom did I get it? Certainly not from the man I thought was my father."

"Your real mother was said to be a talented painter, but I've never seen any of her work."

"Oh . . ." Kelsey hung her head and shook it, then asked, "Who were my real parents?"

"Their name was Wentworth. They owned a shipping company and a vast deal of property. When you turn of age on the morrow, you will be an heiress, one of the richest in England."

Silence stretched between them, as she absorbed this astonishing bit of information. She should feel elated, but all she felt was the loss and overwhelming emptiness that came from not knowing her real parents. It was a part of her that she had lost forever. Try as she might, she couldn't even remember what they looked like. She bit her lip to keep the tears at bay.

His voice broke the silence and drew her attention. "I left it up to the Vallarreals to tell you the truth, but they did not. Your father knew you'd find out when you turned of age, and he asked me to tell you."

"That is like him," Kelsey said, unable to keep the mockery from her voice. "He's always avoided unpleasantness. I had rather he told me himself and not thrust the task on you."

"I didn't mind. In a way, I felt responsible for you." He looked at her and some of the hardness left his expression.

"I wish you had not felt anything for me." The resentment and hurt came through in her voice.

"You were my father's ward. I spent many hours entertaining you. I couldn't help but feel some responsibility for your welfare."

"Yes, it is unfortunate though. Perhaps if you hadn't felt so concerned, I might have been spared the humiliation of being made to feel like one of your cheap whores." She watched him flinch as if her words had struck him. Her lips twisted into a sneer.

"I never meant for it to happen, but it did." His fist tightened around Rabbit's belly. The material ripped on one side and some of the stuffing fell onto the floor.

"Yes, well, like you said 'you are a man who likes variety,' I believe those were your words." She stared at the white shreds of cotton falling to the floor as he crushed the rabbit tighter. When she spoke again, she tried to sound indifferent, belying the raging emotions inside her. "I just happen to be accessible and very naive—you said that yourself. And believe me, you broke me in very well, your grace. I'll never be that blind again—especially where men are concerned. Which brings me to another point of deception on your part—the money you sent to my father each month and led me to believe it came from an uncle in France. Very clever there, I never suspected until my father left that note saying he was going to visit him in his sickbed. My father would never visit anyone sick."

"No, a blunder on your father's part. I kept the payments small so you wouldn't know who was sending them. Your father never spent the money on you as I wanted."

"That's not surprising, my father is a self-centered man, but still, I was happy. I knew he loved me . . . that was enough." She glanced up and caught Edward looking at her.

A nameless emotion crossed over his face, then it disappeared behind an icy veneer. He glanced back up at the ceiling, the veins on his neck protruding from his clamped jaw.

"Do you know where my father is? I know he's not in France."

"I sent him to Bath."

"I have to get word to Jeremy, he is hiring a Bow Street—"

"Jeremy knows about it. He's not hiring a Runner. He's known all along about your past."

Kelsey drew back her arm, then used it to lash out at the air in front of her. "Of course, the whole world has known but me!"

"You—"

"Get out!" She cut him off and pointed to the door. "I've heard enough! Just leave me alone before I scream!"

His dark gaze bore into her for a moment, then he threw Rabbit down on the table and left without protest.

Kelsey stared at the mangled rabbit, then picked it up. She hugged it and more of the stuffing fell out into her hand. She glanced down at it, then at the hole in the rabbit's side. Blinding tears came. Sobs racked her body. She collapsed onto the floor, clutched the rabbit to her face, then rocked back and forth.

When Kelsey was numb inside and could cry no more, she ran out of Stillmore with Rabbit in her arms. She had to get away from Edward, away from the lies of her past. The heat of the day still hung in the night air. By the time she reached the village, perspiration covered her. Thank goodness the inhabitants of the village were abed and all was quiet save for the butcher's dog, standing near the shop barking at her as she ran past. The cottage was at the end of the village and she was out of breath when she reached it. She let herself in through the back door, then slammed it behind her.

She started to call out to her father, but remembered that he wasn't home. He wasn't even her father. Her footsteps drifted through the emptiness as she lit a candle in the kitchen, then climbed the staircase to her loft bedroom. The cottage didn't feel like home to her any longer. Where was home? She felt completely lost, as if she didn't belong anywhere.

She clung to Rabbit and walked into her room, then she paused to look around her. The walls were unfinished. The beams and sidewalls left exposed. Her art books rose in haphazard stacks in one corner. The paintings she had done during passionate moments of expression leaned against the base of one wall. She never let anyone see them, including her father, for he was of the old master's school and paintings done *alla prima,* without glazing, were only sketches on canvas. Perhaps they were only sketches of her expression, but she couldn't bring herself to throw them away.

She set the candle on the table by her bed, then placed the rabbit on her pillow. She stripped off her clothes, then undid the braid in her hair as she walked over to the washstand. She bent over the bowl, picked up a pitcher of water, then doused her head, neck, and chest with the cool water. Water ran over her hot skin and she sighed, feeling the coolness wash over her. The intense sensation was reaffirming. She was alive. She could still feel something when she felt so dead inside.

She took a sponge bath, then tossed her head back, throwing her wet hair over her shoulders and down her spine. She grabbed a towel from the stand, dried her face, then hung it around her neck as she walked over to the window and opened the shutters.

The window was small, the bottom of it barely reached the top of her stomach. She rested her hands on either side of the window casing and leaned out as she had done so many summer nights in her life. Tonight the air teemed with the scent of blooming lavender from the herb garden below the window. Every star in the sky shone with a veiled brilliance, as if they, too, held secrets from her. Life teemed with secrets and lies and duplicity. She couldn't help but wonder about her real parents again. Was she wanted? Had they loved her when she was born? Or was she just an inconvenience to be stuffed away in a nursery with a nanny?

A sound from below startled her from her musings. She glanced down at the garden, shadowed by moonlight, then past the white picket fence around it. Something moved near the fence. . . .

Edward! He was sitting on his horse, staring up at her.

Nineteen

Mesmerized, Edward watched her at the window. Candlelight flickered behind her, making her naked skin glow golden. He gazed at the creamy white skin of her thin, swanlike neck, lower still, to the exposed flesh between her high breasts. The towel hanging down the front of her shoulders barely covered her nipples. He could see the bottoms of her breasts.

She must have seen him. Her hands flew to cover her breasts, then she jumped back from the window, breaking the spell, the vision of her gone. He hadn't meant for her to see him, but he had heard her leave the castle and followed her to make sure she arrived at her destination safely. How could he know that she'd come to the window and torture him with the erotic sight of her again?

He ground his teeth together as he turned Dagger and rode back toward home, kicking up clods of dirt as he let the horse have his head. The warm wind blew against his face, and it felt like the soft touch of Kelsey's fingers. He imagined her lips against his, the feeling of her breasts filling his palms, her sweet face when he brought her to a climax, the sound of her husky voice crying, "I love you."

The yearning to bury himself in her tight, hot flesh clawed at his loins until he wanted to cry out from the torture. He thought of riding back to her cottage and making love to her again . . . but he couldn't. He had made sure Kelsey hated him now. He had to let go of her for her own good and his.

He reined in near the lake and jumped off Dagger's back, then ran to the bank. Frantically, he pulled off his boots, then dove in fully clothed. The cool water was a poor substitute for Kelsey's warm, soft skin, and it did nothing to ease the yearning in his body or the burgeoning restlessness eating away at him.

The next morning Kelsey sat in the kitchen, eating a biscuit, fighting a queasy stomach. The sick feeling started last night when she had seen Edward. She couldn't believe he had followed her home and seen her naked at the window. Humiliation and anger stayed with her most of the night, but what kept her awake until the wee hours of the morning were the memories of Edward's kisses, the feel of his powerful body against hers, his wonderful hands and the pleasure they were capable of giving. When would she ever be able to put him behind her? She hated him!

She sighed and nibbled a piece of biscuit. It tasted like dried mud, sticking to the inside of her mouth as she swallowed it. A knock on the door startled her. She almost dropped the biscuit, but caught it before it hit the table. After laying the biscuit down on the plate, she hurried to answer the door.

"Morning, madam." A thin gentleman with a long face and astute darting eyes held the brim of his beaver as he bowed. He stood, ran his hand around the top edge of a severely starched cravat, and said, "Is Miss Vallarreal at home?"

"I am Miss Vallarreal," Kelsey said impatiently, feeling her stomach growing worse.

His gaze moved over her person, taking in her painting clothes, her hair, a frizzy black mass of curls hanging loose down around her waist. He frowned at her. "There must be some mistake, I'm looking for Kelsey Wentworth Vallarreal."

"That is I, sir. I don't feel like standing here justifying my lineage to you. Either state your business or be on your way." Kelsey started to close the door.

"Wait! I am Mr. Bernard Breckeridge, a solicitor with the

firm Jenkins and Jenkins. I have come all the way from London to discuss the terms of the trust your father left for you. As you know, it is your birthday today and you have now come of age."

Her dark brows rose at the mention of her birthday. She had forgotten all about it, what with Edward plaguing her mind. At the thought of him, her stomach tightened, growing sicker. She clutched her stomach and motioned him inside. "Please, come in. I'm sorry for my rudeness, but I've a touch of stomach upset."

"Can I do something for you?"

"No," Kelsey said, showing him the way to the kitchen. After her mother died, her father had long since done away with the pretense of the parlor. Now it held art supplies.

"May I pour you some tea?" Kelsey asked, turning toward the stove.

"Wouldn't dream of putting you to any trouble while you are unwell, Miss Vallarreal."

"It's no bother," Kelsey said, getting the cup down from a hook and pouring the tea. "The employment will give me something to think about besides my stomachache."

"Please, sit," he said, pulling out a chair for her as she carried the tea to the table. "I'll take up very little of your time."

Mr. Breckeridge's manner grew conciliatory over the next quarter of an hour as he explained the vastness of her wealth. She owned a shipping company in London with offices all over the world, an estate in Yorkshire, a castle in the Scottish Highlands, a London town house, a plantation in Brazil, and a villa in the South of France.

"Your income will be a hundred thousand pounds a year, Miss Vallarreal. How do you feel about your newfound wealth?" Mr. Breckeridge took a sip of his tea and eyed her over his cup.

"I really don't know what to think, sir."

"It takes a bit of getting used to. Your life will never be the same." He glanced around the small kitchen as if anything would be better than the life she'd been leading. "Here is a bank draft for ten thousand pounds to start you off. If you need advice, or if I can be of any help to you, I am your servant, madam." He put a card in her hand with the draft, then rose and bowed. His reed-thin body looked as if it might snap in half if he bent over much farther.

Kelsey stared at the bank draft in awe, then showed him to the door. She remembered something and said, "There is one thing you could do for me, Mr. Breckeridge. Would you see that the proper amount of servants are hired to open up the London town house? I intend to occupy it tomorrow."

"Indeed, it would give me great pleasure to see to it." Mr. Breckeridge bowed and looked well pleased to be of service to her.

She smiled at him and said, "Good day, Mr. Breckeridge."

"Good day." He tipped his hat, then with a cranelike gait strolled down the flagstone steps and out the gate. He entered a small gig, then waved as he drove away.

She glanced down at the draft and didn't know if she should leap for joy or go to bed with her stomachache. She slipped the draft into her pocket and was about to choose the bed, when the sound of a carriage's trappings made her glance toward the front gate. Jeremy was just pulling up in his phaeton. His hazel eyes met hers. A devastating grin spread across his face.

"Hello, there!" he called, leaping down from the carriage. He looked like a handsome prince in a fairy tale, wearing a royal blue coat and breeches, with a blue and white striped waistcoat. A bouquet of red and pink roses swayed in his hand.

"Hello yourself," she said, unable to keep the irritation from her voice.

He strode up to her, placed a lingering kiss on her hand, then studied her face for a moment. Worry made his golden brows meet over his nose. "You're as pale as the paint on your fence. Eddie told me you were here, but he didn't tell me he'd let you leave Stillmore when you were ill. I'll have to have a talk with him—"

"No, no, don't! I wasn't ill when I left last night. It started this morning. I'm sure it will be of short duration," Kelsey said, holding her stomach.

"I hope so. I don't think my conscience would allow me to steal a birthday kiss from an invalid." He grinned rakishly at her.

"Don't . . ." Kelsey held up her hand. "I'm in no mood to endure your advances. Anyway, I'm angry with you for not telling me the truth."

"Eddie told you, then?" Jeremy leaned his shoulder against the stanchion, then glanced down at the flowers in his hand.

"Yes, finally," she said with annoyance in her voice.

"Would these help you to forgive me?" His gleaming eyes had a pleading quality in them that was hard to resist, especially while he was holding out a bouquet of roses.

"When you look like a puppy that I'm about to beat, how can I stay angry with you? You really do have your pitiful looks down to an art." She couldn't help but grin at him as she took the flowers.

"Why don't you let me in and I'll show you my whole repertoire."

"Come in, but if you try to kiss me again like you did the last time I saw you, ill or not, I may be forced to fight back—I don't think you'd like that." Kelsey shot a resolute look at him that made him laugh out loud. "This is not a laughing matter, Jeremy," she said flatly, then turned on her heel and walked toward the kitchen. "I like you, but only as a friend. That's all it will ever be."

"I'll never give up hope. I know you have feelings for Edward, but—"

"I don't," Kelsey blurted out too forcefully.

Jeremy smiled. "I'm not blind, Kelsey. I know that you preferred him over me, but Edward is all wrong for you." His voice grew low and somber. "I think you've realized that."

"Yes, I have," she said honestly, knowing she couldn't deny it any longer, "but that doesn't mean I'm looking for a relationship with anyone."

Kelsey watched him pull a small burgundy velvet box from his pocket. Had he bought her a ring? She did a stiff about-face, strolled over to the counter, and found a pitcher in the cupboard for the flowers. She poured water in the pitcher, then arranged the flowers, hoping he would not present the ring to her.

"Perhaps you will look for someone in the future," he said hopefully. She heard the chair creak as he sat down.

"I won't be looking for anyone. Not ever," Kelsey said resolutely, then casually changed the subject. "Would you like some tea?"

"Yes."

An odd moment of silence hung between them. She turned to bring the cup to the table and saw him slip the small box back into his pocket. She breathed an inward sigh of relief, until she noticed the pain on his handsome face.

She set the cup in front of him, then touched his hand as she said, "I'm sorry, I've hurt you. That wasn't very diplomatic of me to blurt out my feelings, but don't you think it is better to be honest than let you believe in something that will never be? I don't deserve your regard. You're dashing, handsome, and everything that is charming and kind. You will find someone who truly loves you—but that person will never be me."

"You are right." He smiled, but it didn't light his eyes.

Kelsey drew her hand back and looked at him as he stared down at the hand she had just touched. She hated hurting him, but there was no other way to make him see reason.

Another knock sounded on the door.

She sighed. "I wonder who that could be?"

"Let me answer the door."

"No, I feel better when I move around. Stay put, I'll be right back."

When Kelsey opened the door, Mary was standing there with a small portmanteau in her hand. Her face was flushed and she looked nervous as she curtsied. "Begging yer pardon, miss, his grace sent me to you. He said you'd be in need of a lady's maid now. I know it's awful me showing up like this, with me clothes and everything, but he fired me right out. Said I was to go to you if I needed 'employment.' Aye, that's the word he used, 'employment'—"

"Well, Mary, I am in need of a lady's maid. How would you like living in London?"

Mary's eyes blossomed. "Oh, I'd love it, miss. I've always wanted to see a big city. The country's nice, but it ain't like the city. Nothing's like the city—"

Kelsey interrupted her again, knowing if she didn't, they'd be standing there for another hour. "Come, Mary, you can have my father's room for the night. I'll show you where it is. On the morrow I intend to pack my things and we'll be on our way to London."

"Aye, miss, I can't wait! Oh, oh—I forgot to give you this. His grace said it was a birthday gift for you." Mary pulled out a small, flat rectangular box from her reticule and handed it to Kelsey.

Kelsey ran her fingers over the black velvet case, then hesitantly opened it.

"Oh, I ain't never seen nothing so pretty, miss."

"Yes," Kelsey said, staring down at the necklace. Twenty-one teardrop-shaped emeralds encased in tiny diamonds hung from an elegant gold chain. She wondered in what spirit the gift was given. Was the necklace a birthday present, or was it a bauble given as payment for services rendered?

A wave of queasiness came over her. She thrust the case at Mary and put her hand over her mouth, then ran out the door and onto the lawn before she hung her head and retched.

"Oh, miss, I ain't never seen anyone throw up their accounts at the sight of somethin' so pretty before. What's the matter, you don't like the necklace?"

Kelsey would have laughed if she didn't feel an overwhelming desire to cry. Tears stung her eyes as she bent over and waited for her stomach to ease.

"Kelsey, are you all right?" Jeremy said, striding over to her side. "Here." He handed her his handkerchief.

"Thank you," she said, wiping her mouth. "I'm sorry you had to witness this."

"I just hope you get well. Let me help you to bed."

"I'll do that, my lord," Mary said, taking Kelsey's arm.

"I feel much better already," Kelsey said, pulling her arm back. "I'm sure this is only a temporary illness."

Two months later Kelsey was in her own London studio, a large building she had bought in Covent Garden. If she looked out her front window, she could see Evans Grand Hotel and a little farther down St. Paul's Cathedral. The foot traffic in this area bustled at all times of the day. When she grew bored with painting, she would go to the window and watch the people. She had a glass domed ceiling installed in her studio, and the north light streamed across the room all day long. It was a nice place to work, with her studio in the back of the building and an art gallery in the front.

She stood back from the painting she was working on, pursed her lips at it, then took up her brush from the pallet and dabbed more yellow ocher on the canvas. She studied the face, a fierce, dark image that was indelibly etched into her mind. Edward's face.

It was like a catharsis for her soul to paint him. Somehow it helped fill the chasm of loneliness that he'd left inside her. Try as she might to hate him, she couldn't forget she had once loved him and the boy he once was. It was the boy that haunted her the most. She still dreamed of him.

The bell on the door tinkled, a sign that someone had entered the gallery. She quickly flipped a sheet over the canvas and wiped her hands on her smock.

"Kelsey, you here?" It was Lizzy's voice.

"Yes, I'm coming." She hurried out into the gallery, past some of her more creative paintings that she'd previously hidden from the world. Wealth gave her the confidence to display them, and the *ton* devoured her work. She couldn't sell her paintings fast enough.

Lizzy walked toward her. A burgundy riding dress swirled around her long legs and added a regal look to her coltish stride. Her dark mahogany hair was swept up beneath a top hat that leaned jauntily to one side of her head, giving her an independent, confident air. Her face glowed like Kelsey had never seen it glow.

"It's good, to see you. Married life agrees with you, I've never seen you looking prettier." She started to embrace Lizzy.

"Oh, no, you don't . . ." Lizzy stepped back from her. "You ruined one of my best dresses the last time I came here and you hugged me." Lizzy smiled and squeezed her hands.

"I bought you another one, didn't I?" Kelsey teased.

"Yes, but I felt terrible about it. You've already done so much for Griffin and me."

"Did you ride all the way from Westmoreland alone?"

"Of course I did, it is barely thirty miles." Lizzy pulled off her riding gloves. "Griffin made me take a groom. The poor fellow is watching the horses. I don't think he liked the neck-or-nothing pace I put him through." Lizzy grinned devilishly.

"I hope you didn't come bearing bad news of my properties."

"No, no. I left Griffin at Westmoreland pulling his hair out in the books."

"He'll get used to it."

"I don't think he likes that part of being a steward."

"No, he's never been one for numbers. Tell him if he needs an accountant to do the books, then hire one. I can't let my estates go to rack and ruin because he's stubborn." They shared a smile.

"He'll muddle through, he always does." Lizzy's dark eyes lit up and her voice held a note of excitement as she said, "I didn't come about business. I have wonderful news."

"I'm so glad. What is it?" Kelsey sat on a bench in the gallery and motioned for Lizzy to sit beside her.

She sat and arranged the folds of her skirt so they didn't touch Kelsey's dirty smock. "You are going to be a godmother."

"That's wonderful news." Kelsey grabbed her hand and squeezed it. "Griffin must be beside himself."

"He won't leave me alone," Lizzy said testily, the grin on her face belying the testy tone in her voice.

"He'll make a wonderful father." Inadvertently, Kelsey rested her hands on her stomach. She felt a tightening in her throat when she thought of her own baby and how it would never have a father.

The excitement left Lizzy's voice as she said, "I suppose we can christen them together."

Kelsey quickly drew her hands down to her lap and tried to sound nonchalant when she said, "Christen who together? Do you have a friend who is having a baby?"

"You know perfectly well you are the only friend I can stomach." Lizzy touched Kelsey's shoulder.

Kelsey felt tears sting her eyes and blinked them back. "How long have you known?"

"Since that bout of morning sickness you had for several weeks when you first came to London. Any fool could see you were pregnant and trying to hide it."

"Does Griffin know?"

"I haven't told him. I'll leave that up to you. What I want to know is when were you planning on telling Edward?"

"I'm not." Kelsey protectively touched her stomach again.

"You have to, Kelsey. You can't keep something like this from him."

"I can and I will. You don't know the callous things he said to me before we parted." Kelsey's voice faltered for a moment, then she said, "He doesn't care about me or this child. Promise me you'll never tell him."

Lizzy hesitated a moment, then shook her head. "All right, I promise, but how do you intend to keep this a secret from him and the rest of the world? You are the reigning darling of the *ton* now. You've got every fop in town dangling after your skirt and your fortune. Everyone watches you like a hawk. You're the only one I read about in the society columns. And Jeremy, have you thought of him? I know he escorts you everywhere you go."

"I intend to go on holiday to my villa in France for two years. I'll tell everyone I was married and my husband died. When I come home with my child, no one will be the wiser."

Lizzy shook her head. "I hope you know what you are doing."

"Certainly I do."

Jeremy had slipped in through the back door, which was his custom when Kelsey was working. He had overheard her speaking to Lizzy about her pregnancy and had paused to listen. Now he moved silently back toward the studio, silently cursing Edward. How could he have taken advantage of her like that? The bastard would do the honorable thing, or Jeremy would make sure he met him at dawn. He silently slipped out the back door and hurried down the alley toward his carriage.

Stillmore looked deserted as Jeremy alighted from his carriage. Not a curtain was open. It looked like the place was in mourning. Jeremy hesitated a moment, fighting a sense of gloom that seemed to hover over Stillmore, then he rapped on the door with the end of his cane.

Watkins answered the door, looking more acerbic than usual. He had a haggardness in his eyes that made him appear ancient. He pursed his lips at Jeremy and bowed. "My lord, I am glad to see you."

"Is he home?" Jeremy handed Watkins his gloves, hat, and cane, then stepped inside the foyer.

"He's here, my lord, but he's locked in the study. Hasn't been out in weeks. He refuses to eat. I'm worried for him."

"I don't think the bastard deserves any of your concern, Watkins. No need to announce me, I know the way."

Jeremy left Watkins, who looked confused and deeply troubled. He reached the study, ready to make Edward see reason or to tie him up and drag him to the altar.

He flung open the door. Total darkness and the smell of stale alcohol hit him. He closed the door. "Sitting in the dark again, Eddie. Can you light a candle? I'd like to see your face while I tell you what I have to say."

"Get out. I don't want to hear it." The words were a growl, but they sounded weak, as if all the life had gone out of them.

He'd never heard Edward sound so despondent. Growing worried, he said, "I'm not going anywhere. Light a goddamn candle, or I'll have Watkins come in and do it."

He heard the chair leather creak, then some fumbling and finally the room filled with dim light. Jeremy started when he saw Edward sitting at his desk. His clothes were rumpled and stained. His eyes had dark circles beneath them, his cheeks looked gaunt from where he'd lost weight. A shaggy beard covered his face. An empty decanter of whiskey sat on his desk, and he held a glass in his hand.

"Have a good look," Edward said contemptuously, then saluted Jeremy as he raised the glass to lips.

"Taking this self-pity a bit too far, aren't you?" Jeremy tried to get over the shock of seeing Eddie and took a seat opposite the desk.

"I don't need a homily from you, I've heard enough of them from Watkins."

"Obviously, not enough."

"What do you want?"

"Want?" Jeremy raised his brows at him. "What I want you already have."

"I have nothing, you fool." Edward lowered his bloodshot eye to the glass and stared at it pensively.

"You've got more than you know." Jeremy felt his temper beginning to get the better of him. "I should call you out for it."

"You'd be doing me a favor." Edward leaned his head back against his chair and closed his eyes.

"I would like nothing more, but I've got a conscience. You see, I can't kill you and leave your heir without a father." Edward looked as if Jeremy had actually shot him. Jeremy felt a brief flash of satisfaction.

After the initial shock, Edward leaned forward, his face a storm of tortured emotions. "Kelsey's with child?"

"Yes, I thought you should know."

Edward leaned back in his chair, the emotion on his face disappearing. He stared blankly up at the ceiling. "What the hell do I care, it's not mine."

"It's yours," Jeremy said, his voice teeming with suppressed anger.

"She's been in London all this time. I'm sure she's found a whole court of suitors."

"She sees none of them. She is two months gone. The child is yours."

"She should have told me. I'll see the child is provided for," Edward said with maddening disinterest. He raised the glass to take another drink.

Jeremy lost his temper and knocked the glass across the room. The glass hit the wall, sending exploding shards of glass out into the room. Jeremy grabbed the edge of the desk to keep from attacking Edward.

"You'd see her ridiculed, mocked, and labeled a whore because you can't get past your own self-pity? I came prepared today to drag your arse to the church and force you to marry her, but I'll be damned if you deserve her. I won't put her through that kind of hell. The child would be better off without you for a father." Jeremy turned to leave, but Edward's words stopped him.

"You've been after her all along. Why don't you give my bastard a name?"

Jeremy lost the thin tether on his patience. He flew at Edward, grabbing him and punching him in the face . . . the stomach . . . the ribs. When he realized Edward wasn't defending himself, he dropped the front of his shirt and shoved Edward back down in the chair.

Jeremy walked out without looking back, slamming the door behind him. He met Watkins waiting impatiently outside in the hall. Jeremy saw the expectant look on Watkins's face and shook his head in a negative manner. "I'm sorry, I can do nothing."

Watkins's expression fell. "I understand, my lord, you tried." Watkins's Adam's apple moved up and down as if he were fighting a lump in his throat. "Here, my lord." He handed Jeremy his hat, gloves, and cane.

"Thank you, Watkins." Still heaving with anger, Jeremy stormed out of Stillmore for the last time and was glad of it. Edward was no longer his friend or cousin.

Back in the study, Edward opened his eyes. His head throbbed as though it wanted to fall off. A vision of Kelsey with his babe in her arms filled his mind. An ache grew in his chest, wrenching his insides until he couldn't breathe. . . .

He heard himself yelling, "Watkins! Watkins!"

The door flew open right away, as if Watkins had been standing by the door waiting for him. "Yes, your grace."

"We're going to London." Edward stood, aware now of the pain in his jaw where Jeremy had hit him.

"Yes, your grace." For the first time in his life, Edward saw Watkins's composure slip, and he smiled.

"I see I've finally done something that pleases you."

"Yes, your grace." The smile dissolved.

"Good. Now perhaps we can hurry. I want to be on the road in an hour. I'll need a pot of strong coffee."

"Yes, your grace, I'll see to it."

He watched Watkins move with more vitality than a man half his age as he hurried out of the room. The thought of marrying Kelsey and making love to her whenever he wanted made a corner of his mouth lift in a smile. Then he wondered if she would marry him. After all, he'd been hard on her and said things to make her hate him. Of course she would marry him once he explained why he did it. She was the most understanding, forgiving woman he had ever known.

The morning sun crept across the white facade of Kelsey's four-story mansion on Upper Brook Street. The black iron railings that curled along the base of every window shone stark against the pristine white exterior. Kelsey sat in the study on the first floor, staring out the window, trying to ignore the mountain of invitations on her desk that she needed to open. Since she'd arrived in London, her correspondence had grown so much that she was considering hiring a secretary.

She sighed, leaned back in the chair, and inhaled the stale odor of cigar smoke that Morris Wentworth had left behind in the room. She had redecorated everything in the town house save for the study. Her natural father didn't seem lost to her when she was there. The leather cushions of his chair had conformed to his body, and when she sat in it, as she was doing now, she felt as if he were somehow close to her and not some enigmatic ghost from her past. She still longed for some memory of him and her mother, but she could remember nothing. She would have given everything she owned for just one recollection of them. All she had left of them was their wealth.

Wealth could be a blessing and a blight, she had discovered. Even though her fortune had gained her immediate admittance into the finest circle of society, she never felt as if she truly belonged there. She had lived too long in the country. Social intercourse in large crowds grew tedious. The coxcombs looking for rich wives were so obvious that they amused and annoyed her. She didn't trust any of them, allowing only Jeremy to escort her. Edward had taught her not to trust any man. She would never again give her affections away so easily. She was jaded. She liked it that way.

A knock sounded on the door.

Startled from her musings, Kelsey glanced up. "Yes."

Fenton, the butler, poked his bald head through the door. He was a short man that reminded her of a nervous Chihuahua. He had yet to grow accustomed to his new position, or to her. Kelsey missed Watkins's profound quotes and unruffled manner.

"Y-yes, m-miss. Sorry to disturb you, but there's a gentleman waiting in the parlor see you."

"Who is it?"

"The Duke of Salford."

Twenty

"Tell him I'm not home," Kelsey said, jumping up from her seat. She realized she was standing, then flopped back down, clutching the chair's arms. "And tell him he will never gain admittance into this house, so he'd need not try calling here again."

"Y-yes, madam." Fenton's head darted back, then he closed the door.

Kelsey tried to concentrate on her mail. With a trembling hand she picked up an invitation to the Swensons' ball. She jumped when she heard Edward's deep voice boom down the hallway.

"I know she's here. I'm not leaving until I see her. Where is she?" Doors started to slam.

"I—I b-beg you not to do that, your grace," Fenton said in his squeaky little yammer that could in no way deter even a rat.

"I'm not going until I see her."

When she heard Edward's voice growing closer, she jumped out of her seat, rushed to the door, and locked it. She fell back against the flat wood and held her breath while her heart tried to pound its way out of her chest.

Bang. Bang. Bang.

His fist hit the door. She felt the powerful vibrations go straight through her back.

"Open the door, Kelsey, I know you're in there!"

"Go away! I don't wish to see you!"

"You'll see me."

"I won't. Now, please, do us both a favor and leave. Whatever you have to say to me, I don't wish to hear it." Kelsey held her breath and prayed he'd leave her alone.

"You'll have to speak to me sometime. I know about the child."

"It's not yours. Whoever told you so is a liar." Kelsey wanted to slap Lizzy at the moment.

"You're the liar. Now, open the damned door!"

"No. I hate you, do you understand that? I won't see you! And I won't have you poisoning my child with your callousness and cruelty. You're not capable of loving either of us. I don't know why you've come about the child, but I know you don't care about it, and I won't let you anywhere near it. If you try to legally claim it is yours, I'll swear I bedded every rake in town and you'll be the laughingstock of England. Now, go away and leave me alone!"

"I can see this is useless, but you won't push me out of your life that easily, Kelsey. I'll be back."

His stiff footsteps faded away. She blinked back angry tears, her whole body trembling with indignation. She walked toward her desk but paused near the window. She pulled back the curtain to peer surreptitiously out at the street. His carriage was there. Grayson and four outriders mulled around the heads of the horses, looking bored.

Edward sprinted down the steps toward the carriage. The sight of him tightened the back of her throat and she swallowed hard. He looked taller than she remembered, dressed all in elegant black. She saw only his profile, his good side. She noticed he had cut his hair and wore a full beard. It made his face look gaunt, his cheekbones more severe than usual. His clothes appeared loose on him. He seemed thinner than she remembered.

The outriders snapped to attention when they saw him. One of them ran to let down the steps of the carriage. Edward put his foot on the first step, then paused. He must have sensed her eyes on him, for he turned and glanced over his shoulder, gazing directly at her.

Their eyes locked for an instant.

She gasped and dropped the curtain, jumping back from the window. When she'd gained control over her breathing and the wild battering of her heart against her ribs, she gnawed on her lower lip and yanked on the bellpull.

"Y-yes, madam?" Fenton said, his voice hardly audible behind the locked door.

"Hire six large footmen, Fenton. Make sure they stand guard on the steps. I do not want another repeat performance from the duke that we had this afternoon."

"Yes, madam."

She placed her hands protectively over her stomach, then strolled back behind her desk. She picked up another envelope and broke the seal, but her hand trembled so violently that she couldn't read the print. The vision of Edward's icy dark glance streaked across the page. She tossed the invitation down on the desk, rubbing her eyes.

Why did he come here? She didn't think he had the courage to face fashionable society. Dr. Jamerson intimated that Edward's last encounter with the *ton* had been a humiliating disaster. Most likely, he couldn't find a third partner for his repugnant pleasures in bed and had followed her to town, believing he could use the child as an excuse to intimidate her into being his paramour.

Well, she wasn't about to agree to his absurd lecherous notions. Goodness knows what sort of odious games he'd dreamed up using her and his present whore. The sooner he learned that she would never speak to him again, the better. Perhaps his fear of people would send him back to Stillmore. She hoped so.

Edward's tall, lean frame moved back and forth behind the shiny panes of a newly polished window. Watkins stood on the sidewalk, his arms folded, watching the duke pace while he supervised the cleaning of the outside of the town house. It was a massive brick structure done in the Georgian style, with wide Palladian windows. Over the past ten years, the house in Grosvenor Square had remained vacant, the outside suffering from lack of care. Watkins meant to see all was put right again now that his grace was back in town.

Watkins glanced at the footman who was standing on a ladder, his hand moving back and forth as he dragged a wet cloth over the windowpanes. He raised a finger at the footman. "When you are done there, the brass on the lantern and the knocker needs polishing. And the shutters could use a coat of paint."

"Aye, sir," the footman grumbled.

Watkins heard the trappings of a carriage and turned to see Lord Lovejoy drive up, looking chipper in a gray suit with a bright pin-striped waistcoat.

He beamed a smile at Watkins and said, "Hello, Watkins. I see you've got the town house sparkling like it used to in the good old days."

"Yes, my lord," Watkins said proudly. "It's nice to be back in town again."

"Is *he* home?" He glanced at the window and said, "Never mind, I see he is. I'll show myself in."

"He's not in a very good humor, my lord," Watkins warned in a low tone as Lord Lovejoy passed him.

"I'm sure being in town will lift his spirits, eventually." Lord Lovejoy affectionately patted Watkins's shoulder, then took the front steps two at a time. A footman flung open the door, and he sailed through.

Watkins watched Lord Lovejoy disappear behind the door, and he subdued a hopeful grin. Then he pursed his lips at the footman's back and said, "You missed a spot in the corner. 'By the work one knows the workman.' "

The footman rolled his eyes at the window as if to say "not another one," then kept to his task, his rubbing growing markedly harder.

In the parlor Edward glanced up when Jeremy entered the room, but he did not stop pacing.

"I see you have finally come to your senses," Jeremy said as he walked to the sideboard and poured three fingers of brandy into a snifter.

"If you're here to gloat, you can leave."

"Why would I be gloating?" Jeremy sipped his brandy, looking both puzzled and amused.

"She won't see me."

"Can you blame her?" Jeremy saluted him with his glass, then took another sip. "You bedded her, then tossed her away like yesterday's *Times*."

Edward stopped pacing, then leaned his shoulder against the mantel and crossed his arms over his chest. He stared broodingly out the window, watching the footman as he cleaned a top pane. "I thought she would at least see me."

"Have you tried all the usual things?"

"Like what?"

"You know . . . flowers . . . baubles . . . perfume."

"I hadn't thought of those." Edward rubbed his beard as he spoke.

"You've been out in the country too long. You've forgotten how to woo the opposite sex."

"I suppose I have," Edward agreed tonelessly.

"It shouldn't prove too terribly daunting. I happen to know she still loves you."

"And how do you know that?" Edward gave Jeremy his full attention now.

Jeremy frowned behind his glass. "Well, there are many reasons. Perhaps one of them is she hasn't fallen prey to the charms of other men—including myself." Edward narrowed his eye at Jeremy and he continued, undaunted. "She leaves every party we attend early. The male populace is not happy with her. She's acquired the nickname the Ice Princess."

Edward's expression brightened at this news.

"And I happen to know she's painting a portrait of you in

her studio. Perhaps she means to throw darts at it." Jeremy grinned at his own jest. "Don't eat me, Eddie, I was only joking."

"I'm glad someone finds the mirth in this. Meanwhile, Kelsey is walking around with my heir in her belly and she won't let me near her."

"Maybe she needs proof of your sincerity. Have you declared yourself?"

"How can I, when she won't speak to me?"

"I'm escorting her to the Jenkins's ball Saturday night. You could approach her there."

"I can't," Edward said resolutely. "I can't go back out into society. I won't face another ballroom."

Jeremy set the empty glass down on the mahogany table with a decided clink, then stood. "You'll go if you want her back."

"I'll have to find another way."

"There is no other way. You said yourself she won't see you."

Edward shook his head. "I won't suffer that humiliation again."

"Your humiliation could be no worse than what she has suffered under your treatment," Jeremy said tersely. "You need to think long and hard about this. I'll leave you to it. Good day." He strode toward the door.

Edward watched Jeremy leave, then walked back to his desk, flopped down in the chair, and brought his fists down hard on the desktop. Damn Kelsey for not seeing him! And damn this uncertainty and restlessness gnawing at him. He couldn't face another ballroom. The sneers. The terrified looks. He couldn't!

Kelsey sat in the blue parlor, one of three parlors in her mansion, staring at the bouquets of roses that filled every available space in the room. Dozens of them arrived daily. No note. No apology. Just the roses. Red, white, pink, and yellow ones. She was starting to hate the smell of roses.

For the past three days, Edward called two and three times a day, requesting to see her. And every day she turned him away. Then the roses would come. She couldn't even go to her studio for fear of seeing him. She had ordered another ball dress from Madame Tulane's, but she didn't dare go to her shop to have it fitted. She knew he had his people watching her house, for she'd seen strange-looking men lurking in the street.

She snapped open *The Times,* then read the society column in hope of getting her mind off Edward. She stared at the print, then her jaw dropped open as she read:

The illustrious Mr. S. has returned to London after a ten-year absence. Rumor has it he is in town to make an offer of marriage. The local hothouses can vouch that he has taken an interest in the wealthy Miss V. Roses are very scarce in England these days, but plenty can be had at Miss V.'s town house. . . .

"Oooo!" Kelsey slammed the paper shut, balled it up, then flung it across the room. It hit one of the slender vases, knocking it over on a table. And like dominoes in a line, the six other arrangements beside it fell. Several crashed to the floor, sending glass flying across the room.

Fenton tapped at the door, then opened it.

"Yes, what is it?" Kelsey spun around, her temper barely in check.

Kelsey's abrupt tone made Fenton flinch. "S-sorry to disturb you, but there's a gentleman on the steps who begs to see you."

"Who is it, Fenton?" Kelsey walked over and started to right the vases. "If it is Lord Salford again—"

"He claims to be your father, miss."

"Papa?" Kelsey paused with two dozen roses hanging from her hands. "Show him in and we'll have tea. And have someone clean this mess up."

"R-right away, madam." He backed out of the room as if he were afraid to take his eyes off her.

Kelsey haphazardly jammed the roses back in the vases, then

her father appeared in the doorway, his smile so bright, it could light up all of England.

"Oh, Papa . . ." She flung herself into his arms, almost knocking him down as she fiercely hugged him.

He chuckled and kissed both sides of her face, then held her cheeks in his palms as he stepped back to look at her. "My sweet *chère,* you glow with beauty. Are you glad to see your papa?"

"Yes, did you think I wouldn't be?"

"I did not know. I thought you would be angry with me for not telling you the truth. And I could not bear the thought of you turning away from me when you found out I was not your real papa."

"I was angry, but now I'm not. Oh, Papa, I could never turn away from you."

He placed a kiss on her forehead. "You do not know how happy that makes me. Since the moment you crawled up onto my lap, I've felt you were my own little girl. I wanted to tell you when you grew older, but your mother wouldn't hear of it. When she died, I didn't have the courage to tell you. All I've ever wanted was your happiness, *ma chère."*

"I am happy now that you have come." Kelsey pulled him over to a Chippendale sofa.

He glanced around the room at the roses. "You have many admirers?"

"Only one plaguing me at the moment. He ran off all my other beaus," Kelsey said flatly.

Her father chuckled and shook his finger at her. "You cannot blame a man for persistence. I got your mother that way."

"Yes, but I know you did not make a fool of yourself with your ardor."

"You would be surprised." He cocked a cheeky brow at her, then the Rubens and the Rembrandt hanging on the wall behind the couch caught his eyes. He remarked, "Very nice, very nice. True masters."

"Yes, they're my latest acquisitions. You must let me give

you a tour of the town house later and I'll show you my collections. I think you will be as proud of it as I am."

"No prouder than I am of you." He gently touched her chin. "I read in the papers of how famous you have become. Was it true the Prince Regent himself asked you to paint him?"

Kelsey shook her head proudly. "I painted him a month ago, Papa. He flirted with me the whole time."

Her father grinned knowingly at her. "And why would he not, you are too beautiful to look upon for hours."

Heat rose in Kelsey's cheeks.

"It is true, I had hoped you'd know that by now." His expression grew solemn. "I think that Lord Salford knew this."

Kelsey was silent. Inadvertently, her hands went to her stomach as she said, "He's an odious man, Papa."

Her father studied her hands on her stomach for a moment, then he said, "Not too odious."

She saw him staring at her hands and dropped them at her sides. "You know?"

"I thought as much when I came in and you had the look of the Madonna about you."

"Oh, Papa." Kelsey laughed at him, then she grabbed his hand. "I've missed you terribly."

"And I you, *ma chère*. Now tell your papa why you have not married Lord Salford. I know he has made the sacrifice of coming to town to find you."

"I won't have him," Kelsey said resolutely.

"You won't have a man that faces his worst fear of being seen to find you?"

"No, I won't. He wants me only for a mistress."

"Has he said that?"

"No, but—"

"My dear child." He reached over and touched her chin again, lifting her face so he could stare in her eyes. "I went to the village before I came here and I can tell you he has severed his relationship with Samantha. He has not seen her for two months. She was not happy about it when I saw her."

"Oh." Kelsey chewed on her lower lip and stared down at the blue embroidered flowers on her dress. "Well, perhaps he grew tired of her. He told me he is a man that likes variety. He's like you, Papa."

"Non, he has lived more like a priest, if the village gossip is to be believed. Rumor had it that he had gone insane and locked himself in his study."

"Well, he seems to have recovered."

"Oui, but for you."

"No, not for me. He cares nothing for me."

"I've kept something from you all these years, but I must tell you now. Do you know that he has loved you since you were small? He knew he couldn't speak to you, but he would ride by our cottage in the village to get a glimpse of you. That is how he met my Clarice."

"That little escapade with Clarice proves the vileness of his character."

"Non, she threw herself at him. He was young, only a man with a man's passion"—he shrugged—"but I know he never took her to his bed. She was insanely in love with him. The day of the accident he severed the relationship. She vowed to leave me anyway. I went to Salford and asked him to speak to her. I thought perhaps he could speak to her on my behalf. He agreed to try."

"But I saw him pick her up in his carriage."

"Oui, but he was doing it only because I asked him to." His voice lowered and the pain hung in his voice. "I knew she would eventually go away and leave me. She grew tired of men easily. She was too beautiful to be tamed or owned by any man. He meant only to try and talk some sense into her and get her to stay with me, but you know how wild she was. When he turned the carriage around to bring her home, she grabbed the reins and caused the accident." Her father's eyes glazed over. "So you see, I caused his disfigurement. It was all my fault. If I had not asked him to talk to her, he would still be a whole man. I never told you about this because I was ashamed of it. My

weakness where Clarice was concerned will plague me till I die. A man should never love a woman so much."

Kelsey couldn't speak for a moment. She saw the shudder go through her father as he started to weep, and she gathered him into her arms, crying with him. During those few moments she wished that Edward were capable of loving her half as much as her father had loved Clarice. The thought made her cry harder.

At eight o'clock Saturday night, Mary stuffed a diamond comb into Kelsey's hair, then stood back and admired her work. "You look lovely, Miss Kelsey."

Kelsey stood and glanced at her reflection in the mirror. The ball gown she wore for the occasion was made of emerald-green silk with velvet trim. The décolletage was low, showing more of her bosom than was comfortable. But it was a new dress and the only one she owned in which she hadn't previously been seen. Her unruly hair was secured back from her face by four diamond combs, then poured down her back in dark, curly tiers.

Kelsey blinked at the mirror and asked, "Don't you think this dress makes me look like a wide-eyed calf?"

"Oh, no, Miss Kelsey. Any woman would kill to have your eyes. You look prettier than most of 'em." Mary grabbed Kelsey's hands and stepped back to look at her. "But you need somethin' . . . a necklace."

Mary dropped her hands and went to the jewelry box. She pulled out a diamond choker. "How 'bout this?"

"No, the emerald one."

Mary picked up the diamond and emerald necklace Edward had given Kelsey and scowled at it. "I thought you said you never wanted to wear this. It made you sick the last time you saw—"

"I've changed my mind, and I won't get sick tonight." Kelsey lifted up her hair while Mary secured the necklace.

A knock sounded on her door. Maurice poked his head in

the room. "Jeremy is growing restless. I've tried to entertain him, but a man runs out of conversation without a lady in the room." He shrugged, then grinned at her. "Look at you. You will outdazzle all the demoiselles at this ball."

"You don't have on one of your new suits. Aren't you coming, Papa?"

"Perhaps later. You do not want me ruining your entrance."

"Oh, Papa, you know I don't care a fig about that."

"Perhaps not, but I do." He blew her a kiss. "I'll see you later, *ma chère.*"

"All right," Kelsey said, trying to keep the disappointment out of her voice.

Mary picked up the shawl and reticule that matched her gown, then handed them to Kelsey. "Here you go, Miss Kelsey."

"Don't wait up, Mary."

"Oh, I wouldn't dream of leavin' you to undress yerself, bein' that way and all." She raised her red brows at Kelsey's stomach. "Oh, no, I couldn't do that. I'd be worried sick. And I don't like the idea of us going to France and havin' the baby. Those foreign doctors ain't right. They ain't. And the wee one should be in his own country when he's born. It gives me the shivers just thinkin' 'bout it."

Mary gave Kelsey a look of reproach. It took only a week of morning sickness for Mary to figure out Kelsey was pregnant, and she didn't scruple to give her myriad opinions on the subject.

"And his da here and all," Mary continued. "Poor little thing won't even know his da. Have you decided to see the duke?" Mary shook her head, her red curls bobbing beneath her cap.

"Not exactly, Mary," Kelsey said, her patience waning, "but if I do, you'll be the first to know." With that, Kelsey left the room.

Jeremy was waiting at the bottom of the steps for her, looking handsome as usual in his black evening clothes. When he saw her, he remained silent for a moment, awestruck. He had never approached her again about his feelings for her, but it was apparent at times like these that he was still very attracted to her.

"Hello, you're early," Kelsey said, the heat of a blush staining her cheeks.

"You look ravishing tonight."

"You say that every time you escort me to one of these tedious affairs. Do you think we can get away before midnight?"

"One would think you don't enjoy my company."

"It's not you, and you know it." Kelsey smiled at him, then took his arm and let him escort her to his carriage.

They did not speak until they were in the carriage. Kelsey watched the flow of traffic as carriage after carriage passed them. The traffic on the streets always grew worse at night. London never appeared to sleep.

Jeremy touched her hand. "I have something to confess to you."

"I'm almost afraid to ask."

"I know you're with child."

Kelsey crossed her arms over her stomach. She frowned over at him. "How long have you known?"

"Since I overheard you and Lizzy talking a week ago. I told Edward about the babe."

"So it was you? How could you!"

"He has a right to know, Kelsey."

"He has no rights where my baby is concerned."

"He is the father. You're carrying the only heir he may ever have. He wants to marry you."

"I won't marry him because he's suddenly grown a conscience over this child. He doesn't love me and I won't marry him just to give my baby his name. Let's not discuss this any longer," Kelsey said in a huff.

She turned away from him and stared out the window. The gaslights and the passing carriages blurred into dark shadows as tears ran before her eyes. She blinked them back and was glad when the carriage finally rocked to a standstill. Jeremy got out first and helped her down. They walked past a crush of carriages lining the street, the silence between them growing palpable before Jeremy broke it.

"Forgive me, I didn't mean to make you angry," Jeremy said softly as they passed an old couple.

"It's forgotten." Kelsey tried for a smile but could manage only a sad grin, then inclined her head at an approaching couple.

Kelsey and Jeremy drew closer to the mansion. Halos of light burst from the ballroom windows. Legions of nameless faces whirled past the glass panes in a country dance. The music melded with the cacophony of voices and drifted out from the mansion. A familiar uneasiness settled over Kelsey. Large gatherings always made her uncomfortable, but it was either go out and try to enjoy herself or mope over Edward. She had done enough of that since her father had told her the truth about Clarice and the accident.

They walked up the steps and were announced, then they greeted Lord and Lady Jenkins. Lord Jenkins was a portly man with a ruddy face and his wife, a thin, beak-nosed woman, stood beside him, wearing a purple turban that made her nose seem even more pointed.

"Glad to see you, Miss Vallarreal—Lovejoy," Lord Jenkins said. A smile spread across his plump cheeks, and he leaned toward Kelsey and whispered in her ear. "I think there'll be someone here you might wish to see tonight."

"Really, who might that be?" Kelsey smiled politely.

Lady Jenkins elbowed her husband in his ribs. "Now, stop that, my lord. He meant no such thing, Miss Vallarreal. Forgive him, he has an obtuse sense of humor."

The next person in line was announced, and Kelsey and Jeremy had to move down the steps. Still puzzled, Kelsey turned and glanced back at Lord Jenkins. He winked at her. What did the wink mean? She didn't have time to ponder it, for they were swept up into the noisy crowd and the heat of the ballroom.

Kelsey spotted Lady Shellborn, motioning Kelsey over with her cane. A group of dowagers sat around her, their turbans bobbing as they gossiped, probably about Kelsey.

"Well, gal, I'm glad to see you here tonight," Lady Shellborn said as Kelsey drew near.

"I could not miss the pleasure of seeing you, Lady Shellborn." Kelsey gave her a brilliant smile, curtsied, then pecked her on the cheek. Kelsey knew the attention would embarrass Lady Shellborn, but she also knew beneath the crusty facade that the elderly lady craved affection. She had become like a grandmother to her. Once a week she had lunch with the grand dame.

Lady Shellborn waved her cane at the dowager next to her. "Move aside, move aside, and let Miss Vallarreal have the seat next to me."

Everyone acquainted with Lady Shellborn was familiar with her abrupt manner and the lethal power behind her cane—in more ways than one. Having been a lady-in-waiting to the poor queen before King George went mad and was forced to turn the reins over to the prince regent, Lady Shellborn could make or break brilliant marriages with the blink of an eye. The dowager next to her must have known this, for the mouse-faced woman merely smiled at Kelsey with icy civility, then scooted over and make room for Kelsey on the sofa.

"There now. Sit, gal." Lady Shellborn banged on the cushion next to her with her cane.

Kelsey sat, then Lady Shellborn leaned over and whispered, "Have you softened toward Salford yet?"

"You know I don't want to talk about him." Kelsey stared at Lady Shellborn's gnarled arthritic hands as she rested them on top of her cane.

"Well, gal, you must talk to him sometime." Lady Shellborn narrowed her faded gray eyes at Kelsey. "You can't avoid him forever. Surely you know he came to town to see you."

Kelsey couldn't bring herself to tell the good lady all that Edward had said to her. She knew only that they had argued. And she certainly couldn't tell her about the babe.

"Let's not spoil the evening by speaking of him," Kelsey said, then she saw the stubborn look on Lady Shellborn's face and added, "Please."

"Well, we shall see," she said with a devious look in her eyes.

Kelsey was about to ask her what was behind the look, but Lord Stevenson came up and bowed low, his blond curls bobbing as he stood. An eager grin spread across his handsome face as he said, "Would you do me the honor of dancing with me, Miss Vallarreal?"

Kelsey opened her mouth to refuse, but Lady Shellborn spoke up. "Of course she will." She pushed Kelsey's arm and said, "You'd better enjoy yourself now, gal."

Kelsey glanced back at Lady Shellborn as Lord Stevenson led her onto the dance floor. The elderly woman raised her brows at Kelsey, an ominous gleam in her eye. Kelsey frowned at her, wondering why she looked suddenly so self-satisfied. And what did that "now" mean? First Lord Jenkins had acted strangely, now Lady Shellborn. Did they know something she should know?

Two hours later Kelsey was extremely tired of dancing and eluding her would-be admirers. She spotted Lord Stevenson's yellow coat and pink striped waistcoat as he strode along the edge of the dance floor. She ducked behind a grouping of potted ferns and crouched there. After they had danced for the third time, he had offered to fetch her a glass of punch. She readily agreed just to escape him; he was one of the more persistent coxcombs who hoped to get his hands on her fortune. She'd heard rumors that his gambling debts were so high that he was in the River Tick and sinking.

He passed by. She separated the fronds and looked for Jeremy. He was on the dance floor with Lady Fulton, a voluptuous blond widow, who, if rumor was to be believed, sampled men like bonbons. And she looked like she wanted to take a bite out of Jeremy at the moment.

The song ended. Kelsey stepped out behind the palms and was about to wrestle Jeremy from the claws of Lady Fulton and tell him she was ready to go home, but she heard a footman's voice carry over the hum of the crowd: "The Duke of Salford."

Twenty-one

Kelsey, along with everyone else in the ballroom, glanced up at that moment. It was so quiet, Kelsey heard the flutter of her eyelashes as she blinked up at Edward.

He took a few steps down the staircase, stared at the crowd, and froze. His face turned as pale as the marble tiles on the dance floor. His hand tightened against the stair railing. The tendons in his hand looked as if they might break under the stress of his grip.

The courage it had taken him to come to the ball was phenomenal. Kelsey's heart went out to him. She took a step toward him, but paused as a footman's voice boomed: "Mr. Vallarreal."

Her father appeared behind Edward. He glanced at the ballroom, taking in the awkward silence, then noticed how terrified Edward appeared. Her father smiled, a charming smile that reached every corner of the room and turned all eyes on him.

He nonchalantly waved his hand through the air and said to the room at large, *"Bonsoir, bonsoir."* He threw a kiss to the crowd as if he were an actor getting a curtain call. "I did not realize I was so well known, but I see that most of you are acquainted with my work. You flatter and humble me. . . ." He bowed low, then walked down the steps and took Edward's arm.

He leaned over and whispered something to Edward. Edward looked at him as if just noticing him, then he allowed Maurice to clasp his arm and lead him down the steps.

Kelsey watched them, thinking they were the two most handsome men in the room. Both of them wore basic black and they complemented each other. She noticed that Edward had not shaved off his beard but had trimmed it. It hid some of the scars on the lower half of his face, but the one that slashed across his patched eye was still visible, making him appear broodingly dangerous and exotically handsome.

The moment was broken. Kelsey heard a titter go around the room. The orchestra started to play again. Couples streamed back on the dance floor, and a throng of people gathered around Edward and her father to get an introduction.

Two debutantes passed Kelsey as they scrambled to get a closer look at Edward. One of them said, "Look at his face. It's positively devilish. He's just how I picture Count Udolpho."

"I think he looks like Blackbeard. Come on, maybe we can get an introduction. I hear there's a scandal attached to the scars on his face, I can't wait to find out what it was. It must be deliciously dreadful."

Kelsey rolled her eyes. London aristocracy ate up anything that was horrific and scandalous. She glanced at her father and saw he was in his element, kissing every lady's hand that came his way and smiling at the gentlemen as if he'd known them all his life. His charisma illuminated the room.

Lady Shellborn fell prey to his charms as well. As her father kissed her hand, she glanced over his shoulder at Kelsey and winked, then motioned with her eyebrows toward Edward, a smug smile on her wrinkled face. Now Kelsey knew what Lady Shellborn and Lord Jenkins had been hiding from her. They knew Edward was coming here.

Lady Fulton edged her way to Edward's side and engaged him in conversation. She touched his arm as if she were intimately acquainted with him. Kelsey crossed her arms over her chest, cocked her head at them, and tapped her foot.

Jeremy strode up to Kelsey's side. "I didn't think Edward would come. He surprised me."

"I find it hard to believe too," Kelsey said, still fighting a wave of jealousy. "I wonder what prompted him to come here?"

"Look, look . . . there's your answer."

Edward was a head taller than the crowd of people around him, and she could see him scanning the ballroom, looking for her.

"I think I should go and rescue him from Lady Fulton before she gets her claws into him again."

"What do you mean 'again'?" Kelsey tried to sound nonchalant, but the jealousy rang through in her voice.

"They were an item when he was at Oxford."

"It's too bad they didn't end up together. They deserve each other."

Jeremy threw back his head and laughed.

Edward glanced over Lady Fulton's head in their direction. He spotted Kelsey right away. His gaze lingered on her face, then slowly devoured her body and moved back up to her face again.

Heat rose in Kelsey's cheeks. She didn't know if she was blushing because of the obvious desire burning in his expression or the fact that her whole body had responded to him and grown uncomfortably hot.

He excused himself and made his way through the crush, not taking his gaze off her. Her heart beat an unsteady tattoo. The room hushed as people turned now to watch them. Kelsey wanted to melt into the floor.

In ten long strides Edward was at her side. He looked down at her, a possessive gleam in his eye. "Hello, my love."

His deep, silken voice moved through Kelsey. It was a moment before she regained enough composure to say, "I'm not your love."

"But you are." Edward grabbed her arm and whisked her out onto the dance floor. He held her closer than propriety allowed and whirled her around in a waltz.

"I really don't want to dance with you." Kelsey tried to pull away from him, but his arm was like a steel bar across the bottom of her back.

"This is not a very good beginning. You should smile a little so the other guests think you are at least comfortable around me."

"If you wanted a willing partner, you should have danced with Lady Fulton . . . or Samantha."

"Do I detect jealousy in your voice?" He grinned, looking pleased and heart-stoppingly attractive.

"You certainly do not." Kelsey raised her chin to a haughty angle.

"I will not give you any reason to be jealous when you become my wife."

"Your wife!" Kelsey had shouted, and the couples dancing near them turned and looked at her. She lowered her voice and hissed at him, "I won't be your wife."

"I beg to differ on that subject. You are already my wife in certain areas." He glanced down at her exposed bosom, then his gaze moved up along her slender neck. "I don't think I've told you how lovely you look in the emeralds, but I'd like to see them on you when you have nothing else on. Do you know how much I've longed to feel your soft skin against my lips and how I've wanted to feel your heat against me and watch your beautiful face when you cry out my name in your passion?"

"Stop it," Kelsey gasped as she leaned closer to him. Her breasts tingled where they touched his chest, and her nipples instantly hardened. A hot sensation moved down her chest and pooled in her loins. She was so aware of him that her skin burned where he touched her back and her hand.

He whirled her around and around until she felt dizzy. Abruptly, the world stopped spinning. The open scent of the night air hit her senses and she glanced around. He had guided her outside onto the balcony.

"We shouldn't be out here." She noticed that her voice didn't sound convincing.

He grinned down at her. "Believe me, it was the prudent thing to do. I would not want to embarrass either of us. If I had stayed in there one more minute with you this close to me, I would have done something rash, like this. . . ."

He swept her up into his arms.

"What are you doing? Put me down this instant! I wish you wouldn't do this." He carried her down the stairs toward the garden. She cried, "If you think you can seduce me and I'll change my mind, you're wrong. I won't marry you because you suddenly want an heir. I won't marry a man that doesn't love me—no, I take that back, you *can't* love me. You're not capable of loving anyone. You're driven only by your base instincts."

He threw back his head and laughed then. Kelsey drew her hand back to slap him. He caught her wrist and set her down on the ground.

"You really must control that desire of yours to slap me. I had much rather feel your lips on my face than the sting of your palm." He pulled her close and captured her arms so she couldn't move.

"You'll feel more than my palm if you don't let me go." She glanced around her and saw they were standing in the dark shadows of a secluded gazebo.

"Listen to me, Kelsey." His voice turned roughly tender. "I want to marry you, not only for the child."

"No." She shook her head. "You don't want to marry me because you love me, you only want an heir. You told me you didn't care about me yourself." Her voice broke and she blinked back tears. "You only used me . . . like . . . like a—"

"I regret hurting you, please believe that." He brought his hands up and cupped the sides of her face. "I said those things only because I didn't want you to be tied to me the rest of your life. You're so beautiful, I wanted you to find a man that wouldn't hide you from the rest of the world, but I can't bear to let you go. Knowing about the babe only made me realize that I can't live without you. I love you. . . ."

Kelsey was silent for a long time, then she wiped the tears from her face and frowned up at him. "Do you mean it?"

"Of course I do. I'm telling you the truth. What can I do to prove it to you?"

"You can kiss me." She smiled at him.

He bent down and kissed her, a soft, gentle kiss at first, then it deepened. She wrapped her hands around his neck and opened her mouth, accepting his tongue.

He ran his hands through her hair. The combs in her hair fell and hit the slate floor of the gazebo. He shook her hair loose and it tumbled down her back.

"Oh, God, I've longed to feel your hair in my hands," he said against her lips, then he buried his fingers in the silky strands. He brought her face closer to his and kissed her again.

The fierce possessiveness of his kiss stole Kelsey's breath and made her knees weak. She wrapped her arms around his neck and felt his hands cover her breasts. She whimpered as his fingers teased her nipples beneath her dress.

"Miss Vallarreal!"

Kelsey moaned softly at the sound of Lord Stevenson's voice.

"Who the hell is that?" Edward grumbled as he stepped back from Kelsey.

"An admirer, I'm afraid."

Lord Stevenson stepped into the gazebo, his yellow coat gleaming in the moonlight. "Is that you, Miss Vallarreal?" Lord Stevenson squinted into the dark shadows at them. When he saw Edward, his eyes widened. "Oh, I beg your pardon. I didn't know you had company."

Edward stepped in front of Lord Stevenson and blocked his view of Kelsey. He towered over the young man. "We are in the midst of celebrating our engagement," Edward said in a tone that sounded much like a growl. "I suggest you go away before you annoy me."

"Oh." Lord Stevenson sounded indignant as he backed out of the gazebo and executed a stiff bow, then took himself off.

When his footsteps died away, Kelsey said, "That wasn't very nice of you."

"I didn't feel much like being nice."

"You really should try to change that surly disposition of yours." Kelsey stepped close to him and wrapped her arms around his waist.

"I doubt it will change until we're married. Even then it may not change, unless I have you all to myself."

"I had hoped you would say that. Can we live in the country? I really don't like the city."

"We can live in the North Pole if that is where you would like to live. I'll be happy anywhere with you. Now, where were we?" He kissed her again.

It was much, much later before they emerged from the gazebo, happy, sated, and lost in each other.

Epilogue

Two years later Edward was in the parlor, on his hands and knees, playing peek-a-boo with his son and heir, Edward James Huntington Noble II. When he heard footsteps, he quickly scooped Edward Jr. up into his arms and sat on the couch, striking a dignified pose.

Kelsey came in. She glanced at the blanket on the floor, then at Edward's mussed hair, at the wool lint from the rug sticking to the knees of his black breeches. She laughed and said, "You had better fix your hair. Griffin and Lizzy are on their way in."

Edward grinned at her, then ran his hands through his hair, smoothing it back. He set Edward Jr. back on the floor, then stood behind Kelsey and wrapped his hands around her waist. "They have the worst timing. How are you feeling?" He nuzzled her neck as he placed his hands over her protruding belly.

"As well as any woman who's eight months pregnant. I think that's an unfair question."

He turned Kelsey around and kissed the pretty pout on her lips. She melted against him.

That's how Lizzy and Griffin found them.

"Don't ya ever let up on her, Salford?" Griffin remarked, strolling into the room with Megan, his daughter, in his arms.

Lizzy and Kelsey laughed at the quip. Edward stepped back from Kelsey and said, "I could ask the same thing of you." Edward stared at Lizzy's bulging belly, then glanced back at Griffin.

Griffin burst out laughing. "Yer right there."

Edward Jr.'s dark eyes glanced up and focused on Megan. He screamed with glee and toddled toward her.

Megan cried out, "E-ddeee!" and tried to wiggle out of her father's arms. Griffin let her down. Megan and Edward met in the middle of the room and stared at each other, then Edward handed her the blanket in his hand.

"They're inseparable cousins," Lizzy said as she walked over to Edward and kissed him on the cheek.

Edward hugged her. "Yes, I think they are."

Kelsey stood back from them, smiling inwardly. Lizzy and Edward had grown close. It made her happy to see them acting the way brothers and sisters should act toward one another.

She glanced up at the painting she'd done of Edward that hung over the mantel, then at the man himself. Edward felt her looking at him and he glanced at her and winked. Love sparkled in his gaze and it warmed his whole expression. The ice was gone forever.

About the Author

Constance Hall lives with her family in Richmond, Virginia. *My Darling Duke* is her first historical romance. Constance is currently working on her next historical romance, *My Dashing Earl,* which will be published in November 1998. Constance loves hearing from readers, and you may write to her at P.O. Box 25664, Richmond, VA, 23233. Please include a self-addressed stamped envelope if you wish a response.

TALES OF LOVE FROM MEAGAN MCKINNEY

GENTLE FROM THE NIGHT*   (0-8217-5803-$5.99/$7.50)
In late nineteenth century England, destitute after her father's death, Alexandra Benjamin takes John Damien Newell up on his offer and becomes governess of his castle. She soon discovers she has entered a haunted house. Alexandra struggles to dispel the dark secrets of the castle and of the heart of her master.
    *Also available in hardcover (1-577566-136-5, $21.95/$27.95)

A MAN TO SLAY DRAGONS   (0-8217-5345-2, $5.99/$6.99)
Manhattan attorney Claire Green goes to New Orleans bent on avenging her twin sister's death and to clear her name. FBI agent Liam Jameson enters Claire's world by duty, but is soon bound by desire. In the midst of the Mardi Gras festivities, they unravel dark and deadly secrets surrounding the horrifying truth.

MY WICKED ENCHANTRESS   (0-8217-5661-3, $5.99/$7.50)
Kayleigh Mhor lived happily with her sister at their Scottish estate, Mhor Castle, until her sister was murdered and Kayleigh had to run for her life. It is 1746, a year later, and she is re-established in New Orleans as Kestrel. When her path crosses the mysterious St. Bride Ferringer, she finds her salvation. Or is he really the enemy haunting her?

AND IN HARDCOVER . . .
THE FORTUNE HUNTER   (1-57566-262-0, $23.00/$29.00)
In 1881 New York spiritual séances were commonplace. The mysterious Countess Lovaenya was the favored spiritualist in Manhattan. When she agrees to enter the world of Edward Stuyvesant-French, she is lead into an obscure realm, where wicked spirits interfere with his life. Reminiscent of the painful past when she was an orphan named Lavinia Murphy, she sees a life filled with animosity that longs for acceptance and love. The bond that they share finally leads them to a life filled with happiness.

ROMANCE FROM JO BEVERLY

DANGEROUS JOY   (0-8217-5129-8, $5.99)

FORBIDDEN   (0-8217-4488-7, $4.99)

THE SHATTERED ROSE   (0-8217-5310-X, $5.99)

TEMPTING FORTUNE   (0-8217-4858-0, $4.99)

ROMANCE FROM JANELLE TAYLOR

ANYTHING FOR LOVE   (0-8217-4992-7, $5.99)

DESTINY MINE   (0-8217-5185-9, $5.99)

CHASE THE WIND   (0-8217-4740-1, $5.99)

MIDNIGHT SECRETS   (0-8217-5280-4, $5.99)

MOONBEAMS AND MAGIC   (0-8217-0184-4, $5.99)

SWEET SAVAGE HEART   (0-8217-5276-6, $5.99)

Elizabeth studied the handsome man next to her.

When had she lost her touch? Most men jumped at the chance to have twenty-five beautiful women fawning over them.

"You owe it to America to be on the show."

"Somehow I think you're exaggerating." Rick chuckled.

She was losing him. He wasn't interested in money, love or fame. What else could he want? She changed gears. "If this is about reliving history, we'll do a better job this time. You won't end up humiliated and alone."

"It must be nice to control the universe."

She reached over and put a hand on his arm, and tried to ignore the skitter in her stomach when she felt his muscles underneath the denim jacket. "Tell me what you want, and I'll guarantee it."

If only she could have what *she* truly wanted.

Dear Reader,

One of my favorite television shows is *The Bachelor*, and I love the idea that you can meet the love of your life on a reality show. Of course, the reality is it doesn't always work out that way, and I wondered what would happen if a bachelor was rejected on live television in front of an audience of millions? How could he come back from that and find a second chance at love? And what if it turned out to be with the wrong woman?

With those questions in mind, I started the story. I named my bachelor after my dad and gave him a lot of my dad's qualities. I discovered that I wasn't only writing a romance, but a story that would honor my dad's memory in a small way.

I hope you enjoy the story as much as I did. And I'd love to hear from you at www.facebook.com/syndipowellauthor.

Syndi Powell

HARLEQUIN HEARTWARMING

Syndi Powell

The Reluctant Bachelor

Recycling programs
for this product may
not exist in your area.

ISBN-13: 978-0-373-36637-8

THE RELUCTANT BACHELOR

Printed in U.S.A.

SYNDI POWELL

started writing stories when she was young, eager to find out what happened after the happily-ever-after in her favorite books, and has made it a lifelong pursuit. She's been reading Harlequin romance novels since she was in her teens and is thrilled to join the Harlequin team. She lives near Detroit with her husband, stepson and a cat and dog who believe they run the household. She loves to connect with readers on Twitter, @syndipowell, or on her Facebook author page, www.facebook.com/syndipowellauthor.

Dedicated to my dad, who I hope can read this book from heaven. I love and miss you. And to my mom, who introduced me to reading Harlequin books in the first place and started the love affair. Thank you both for your love and support.

PROLOGUE

RICK ALLYN TUGGED at the sky-blue tie that had been looped around his neck by one of the production assistants of *True Love,* a dating reality show. Only moments away from proposing to the one woman he'd never believed he'd find, he should feel anxious, right? The butterflies running bases in his stomach only proved his human nature.

After all, Brandy could say no.

But she wouldn't. Not to him. At twenty-five, he was the entire package—looks, smarts and, after his agent worked out the details of his contract, a major-league baseball player.

Lizzie Maier walked toward him. Serious, as always. She was wearing a purple power suit; her long brown hair was tied up in some ridiculous style that only emphasized the sharpness of her cheekbones. And the grass-green of her eyes.

He held up his hands in surrender. "What did I do now?"

Lizzie shook her head and reached up to

straighten his tie. "She's almost ready for you." She didn't look him in the eyes, but kept her focus on his suit and the fit of it. "Are you sure about this?"

Finally she looked up at him. "Brandy's an amazing woman. Beautiful. Smart. What man wouldn't want to be married to her?"

"Right." Lizzie nodded, then tapped her earpiece and shook her head. "They're still not ready. Rick, I should tell you—"

"Lizzie, relax."

"It's Elizabeth."

"Not to me." He winked at her. "I'm going to propose. She'll say yes. Then you're going to throw us the biggest, most romantic wedding that has ever aired on television." Rick rolled his head around his neck to get out the tension. "Now, let's get this show on the road. The rock in my pocket is weighing me down."

"What if she doesn't pick you?"

Rick laughed and shook his head. "She's going to pick Wade? Give me a break. It's not like all of us didn't warn her about him. Brandy's a smart girl. She knows."

"Rick—"

"It's fine. Really, Lizzie." He straightened his shoulders and touched his tie. "I'm getting the girl. I'm winning her heart. And you can print that in the tabloids."

Lizzie tapped her earpiece again. "Okay, they're ready for you." She studied him, then sighed. "You've been a good friend to me during this show. Thanks."

He winked. "Let's go propose on live television."

CHAPTER ONE

FIVE YEARS SHOULD be enough time for people to forget. In a world of thirty-second sound bites and high-speed internet, one person's fifteen minutes of fame should be a distant memory in a few months at most.

But Rick didn't live in a world of shoulds. If he did, he'd be happily married to Brandy. And Lizzie wouldn't be sitting in the stands at the annual Pickle Play-Off game.

Get your head in the game, Allyn. This is for the championship.

He clapped his hands and crouched into a running stance at second base. His line drive had been good enough to get him there, but he needed one more solid hit to get him and the guy on third home to win the game. The young man with Down syndrome up to bat might dampen anyone else's enthusiasm. But not Rick's. Because tonight was his night. He could feel it down to his cleats.

Rick cupped his hands around his mouth. "C'mon, Jeffy. Hit me in, buddy."

Jeffy looked up at him and nodded. He bit his tongue as he got into position in front of the catcher.

The first pitch. "Ball."

Rick stood and clapped his hands once more. "Good eye, Jeffy."

Jeffy swung at the next ball. Missed. "Strike one."

"Wait for your pitch, buddy." Rick put his hands on his knees, rubbing the left one to ease the ache—a remnant of a car accident five years before—then returned to his running stance, ready to make a dash for third if the opportunity arose.

The next ball floated across the plate. "Strike two."

The crowd got to their feet. They could be one pitch away from winning it all. Or losing. They stomped. Shouted. Cheered. Jeffy's mom hid her head in her hands and turned to the well-dressed brunette in a purple power suit beside her.

Why was she here?

Rick shook his head. *Stay focused.* "C'mon, Jeffy. Hit her out of here!"

He held his breath as the next ball pinged off Jeffy's bat and rolled toward first base.

"Foul ball!"

At third base, Tom saw his opportunity and

sprinted toward home before the opposing team could react. He slid safely into home plate and tied the game as Rick reached third base.

One hit was all they needed. One solid hit to get Rick home.

He held his hands up. "Time-out." He started walking toward Jeffy. Time for a pep talk.

THE OLDER WOMAN sitting beside Elizabeth on the bleachers covered her eyes. "I can't look."

Elizabeth looked from the woman to the young man talking with Rick at home plate. "Is that your son?"

The woman turned and smiled at Elizabeth. "You're not from around here, are you?"

"Afraid not." She gripped the handles of her Kate Spade bag tighter. "I'm here on business."

And business was exactly what she should be doing rather than sitting on a hard wooden bleacher, waiting for a chance to talk to Rick. He looked good. Better than good. But five years hadn't changed him. Same brown hair that looked as if he'd run a comb through it sometime that week. Same warm grin that could make a girl's toes curl. And if she could get close enough to see his brown eyes, she knew she'd see the familiar twinkle that played with his good-guy image. Five years and he still didn't see his potential beyond this hick town. Good thing she was there to change all that.

The woman next to her held out her hand. "I'm Martha. Otherwise known in town as Jeffy's mom."

Elizabeth turned her attention back to Martha and shook her hand. "Elizabeth."

"Jeffy loves the game, but because he's slow, coaches won't let him play." She turned adoring eyes back to the two men standing at home plate. "Except for Rick, bless him."

Rick walked back to third base as Jeffy returned to the batter's box. Swung the bat a few times. Hunkered down, ready for his pitch.

Martha squeezed her eyes shut. "Oh, I can't watch."

Elizabeth took the woman's hand in hers. "I'll watch for you." You could get through anything with someone holding your hand.

The pitch. "Ball two."

The crowd let out their breath and clapped. "Jeffy! Jeffy! Jeffy!"

The pitcher glanced at third base, then threw the ball at the baseman. Rick shook his head. "Just pitch the ball, Stu." He turned back to Jeffy. "Nice and easy, now. Just like practice."

Jeffy nodded and tightened his grip on the bat.

The coach from the other team laughed. "No worries, folks. We've got the game. That trophy is as good as ours."

Stu shook off the catcher's first two calls. He nodded and threw the ball.

Crack.

Martha's eyes opened. "He hit it?"

Elizabeth grinned and helped her to her feet as Rick flew toward home and planted his feet on home base. He then stood to watch Jeffy charging toward first base before the ball could get there.

His feet touched the base.

The ball hit the baseman's glove.

"Safe!"

With a roar, fans rushed the field, carrying Jeffy away in their excitement. Elizabeth helped Martha down from the stands, but even his own mother couldn't get to Jeffy through the crowd. Everyone was hugging him. Shouting and crying. All trying to get the chance to put their hands on the young man the other team said couldn't play.

Elizabeth couldn't help but smile. This was better than anything on television.

MARTHA WALKED UP to Rick and hugged him. "Thank you for believing in Jeffy."

"Thanks for letting him play." He patted her back. "You're bringing him to the diner after?"

"He wouldn't let us miss it." She wiped her eyes and turned to find her son amid the crowd.

The opposing coach cleared his throat until Rick turned around and accepted the trophy. "Thanks."

The coach shrugged. "We underestimated you."

"The underdog has to win at least once." They shook hands briefly before the coach walked away.

"Still tilting at windmills?"

At Lizzie's voice, Rick turned to face the inevitable moment. It had been coming since he'd spotted her in the bleachers. She looked good. Too good. Despite the fact that she wore her power suit like armor.

"You've been avoiding my calls."

He started to walk around the bases, picking them up and slapping them together to get off the dirt. "Because they all say the same thing, Lizzie. And my answer hasn't changed."

"If you'd just listen—"

"I don't need to. *True Love* was a onetime shot. I don't need to relive that time of my life. I've moved on." He bent and stuffed the bases into the equipment bags, zipped them shut and hoisted them over his left shoulder. He waved with his free hand to some friends. "See you at the diner," he called after them when they honked their car horns.

"No offense, Rick, but it doesn't look like you've moved much from when I met you five years ago."

Rick turned to observe her. One of television's top reality-show producers stood on a dusty baseball field wearing designer clothes that cost more than what most of the people in this town made in a month. Her haircut, though attractive and stylish, probably cost enough to pay the grocery bills. She didn't have a clue about how his world operated. Yet here she was. Standing on his turf. Trying to convince him to make another mistake.

He opened his mouth, a smart retort on his tongue, but instead stalked off the field toward the parking lot, where two vehicles remained. He glanced at the rental that obviously belonged to Lizzie and shook his head.

"Something wrong with my car?" He could hear the smile in her voice.

He put the bags in the back of his truck but didn't look at her. "It's a convertible."

"I know."

He turned to face her. "In Michigan." She didn't get it. Probably never would, Rick was sure.

Lizzie's smile faded into a frown. "And?"

Rick shrugged and sighed as if to say it was her funeral. "The weather changes every five minutes here."

"But I look good in a convertible."

He sighed. Some things really didn't change. "Always going for style over substance."

"Are you judging me?" She took her sunglasses from the perch atop her head and slid them over her eyes. "I thought we'd gotten past that. I thought we were friends."

Rick swallowed and tried to fight the feeling that he'd messed up again. "Friends who haven't talked or seen each other since I got dumped on television." He took off his ball cap and hit his thigh with it once. Twice. "I apologize, Lizzie. It's still a sore spot."

"And it's still Elizabeth."

Rick grinned and wiggled his eyebrows. "Not to me."

She strode to her car and took a sleek leather briefcase from the front seat. With a few quick snaps, she opened it and retrieved a thin envelope. "Our offer has increased."

He glanced at the envelope, then at her. "You could offer me twice as much and my answer would still be no."

Lizzie fiddled with the contents of her briefcase before placing the envelope back inside. "Rick, this is a chance of a lifetime."

He swallowed. Yeah, like the chance that had made him a joke on every national newscast for a month. "I already had one of those, remember?"

Lizzie sighed and rubbed her forehead. "Could we at least discuss this over coffee?"

He chuckled. "At the diner we only have half-and-half, not that flavored creamer you like." He finished throwing the equipment bags into the bed of his pickup truck before slamming the tailgate closed. Turning, he nearly ran Lizzie over.

"How did you remember the creamer?"

Rick shrugged. "How do I remember that Frank gets pancakes with butter and no syrup every day except on Saturday when it's French toast? How do I know that Miss Maudie wants the crusts cut off her sandwiches and put into a doggie bag to take home to her Yorkie?" He flipped the keys in his hands over a few times. "It's my job."

"I'm not your job."

"But I'm yours?" He glanced at the empty ball field and then back at her. "Why are you here? Why not send one of your interns? Backwater Michigan is a long way from Hollywood for a business call."

"I needed to see you."

He raised one eyebrow. "Interesting."

ELIZABETH TRIED NOT to groan. This wasn't the way things were supposed to happen. She'd come in person to convince him to do the show, which should have impressed him. Instead it seemed to make him even more resistant to the idea. He was supposed to be desperate for her.

Desperate for the show. That was what she meant.

Rick opened the passenger door of his truck. "Convince me. We'll talk on the drive to the diner."

That was more like it. She looked back at the blue convertible. "And leave my car here?"

"It'll be fine." Rick glanced up at the sky. "But you might want to put up the top. It could rain."

Elizabeth looked up. Not a cloud could be seen in the sky. "I'll take my chances."

"Your rental agreement covers water damage?"

"There's no possibility of rain." Besides, when in all of her twenty-eight years had she done something just because some man told her to? She hopped up into the truck, clicked the seat belt into place and turned to Rick. "I don't understand why you won't do the show."

Rick sighed and shifted the truck into Drive. "You're relentless."

"That's why I'm the best." Because she knew which buttons to push to get what she wanted. She only needed to dig a little more. "It's a great opportunity. Aren't you interested in finding love? In meeting the woman you're destined to spend the rest of your life with?" She leaned closer, her voice softer, more intimate. "It can work this time. I know it."

"Why? It didn't back then." He drummed his fingers on the steering wheel to the beat of the Kenny Chesney song playing on the radio. "Call me crazy, but I don't relish the idea of going through that again."

"It will be different."

"How? I'll still be making a fool of myself on TV." He shifted his gaze to her. "Besides, I had more fun talking with you between takes than on any of those fantasy dates you sent me on."

She glanced at him before looking out the window again. "Everyone wants you back."

"Everyone?"

She could feel the heat in her cheeks. "You're the most popular contestant the show has ever had. We get hundreds of letters a week asking us to bring you back." She faced him again. "You owe it to America to be on the show."

"Somehow I think you're exaggerating things."

She was losing him. He wasn't interested in money, love or fame. What else could he want? She changed gears. "If this is about reliving history, we'll do a better job this time. You won't end up humiliated and alone."

"It must be nice to control the universe."

She reached over and put a hand on his arm. Ignored the skitter in her stomach at the feel of his muscles underneath the denim jacket. "Tell me what you want, and I'll guarantee it."

He turned into the parking lot of the diner and parked in the back. "Time's up."

She sighed. When had she lost her touch? Men jumped at the chance to have twenty-four beautiful women fawning over them. But then Rick had never been a typical man. "If you would just give me a chance…"

He scratched his head and replaced his ball cap. "Think that's what I just did." He got out of the truck, then poked his head back in. "See you inside."

Elizabeth watched him walk toward the diner. She could hear the loud shouts from those inside as he entered. She had to make him realize he needed to be on the show. Give him the thing he wanted most, whatever that was.

The perfect cheeseburger. That was what she wanted more than anything. Unfortunately, she didn't eat cheeseburgers anymore. And it didn't help that she sat outside a diner that she suspected must serve them to perfection.

Elizabeth slammed her hand on the dashboard, then tried to shake away the pain. This was crazy. She could have sent anyone else to come out here to talk to Rick, so why torture herself?

Her cell phone sang a Diana Ross tune, and a chill passed over her. "Hi, Mom."

"Bethie, I'm in an awful fix."

Elizabeth closed her eyes. How many times had she heard those same words? "Who was he this time?"

"I didn't know he was married. Honest." Her mom sighed. "And now he fired me."

Of course. They always did. "Mom, I can't talk right now. I'm working."

"I only need a couple of hundred this time." Her mom's voice became whiny, which was not a good sign. "My rent is overdue, and my cupboards are bare. Please, Bethie. You remember what this is like."

The goose bumps intensified on Elizabeth's arms, and she shivered. She couldn't forget, even in her nightmares. "Have you been looking for a job?"

"I've applied at a few restaurants, but you know how this economy is." Her mom started crying. "Who's gonna hire a washed-up waitress when they could hire any of a dozen half my age? What am I gonna do?"

Elizabeth swallowed and closed her eyes, massaging her forehead in circles as if the motion would turn back time. Give her a different mother. A different childhood. "Tell me where to send it. I'll have it there by tomorrow morning."

"You're the best daughter, Bethie."

"Thanks, Mom."

"I love you."

Her phone beeped, and she glanced at the incoming phone number. The head of development at the studio. "Mom, I've got another phone call coming in. Text me with the details later, okay?"

She switched to the other line. "Elizabeth Maier."

"Did he sign the contracts yet?"

She wasn't ready to deal with pressure from the studio. Couldn't he give her a few days at least? "You're always to the point, Devon."

"That's why they pay me the big bucks." He chuckled on the other end. "I don't need to remind you what's at stake. We want Rick."

That had been made abundantly clear. "Yes, sir."

"You got this job because you promised results. Don't let us down."

"I always deliver." Always had. Always would. She straightened her blouse and sat up straighter. "That's why you promoted me."

"Didn't hurt that your boss was having an inappropriate relationship with one of the bachelorettes, either." Devon paused. "The story's been leaked on the internet and hits the newsstands tomorrow."

Just what she didn't need. This could make her job even harder. "So much for sitting on the scandal."

"We need a home run for this show or the studio's pulling the plug, Elizabeth." He let that sink in. "And you promised that Rick would be ratings gold."

"He was last time."

"So get him to sign. Or..."

The threat hung unspoken between them. Elizabeth cleared her throat. "It's like I told you. I always deliver. He'll do it."

Devon hung up the phone on his end. Elizabeth stared at her cell before quietly turning it off and placing it in her bag. So it was Rick and her job or nothing.

A sudden chill made her shiver again, and she rubbed her arms. She couldn't go back to the ways of her childhood. To not knowing where she would live or what she would eat. She'd scratched and clawed her way out of poverty and would never return.

Never.

She needed a new plan. Because more than Rick's future was on the line.

WHEN RICK ENTERED the diner full of folks in bright green uniforms, applause broke out. He held up his hands to summon quiet for a moment. "This is definitely a night to celebrate. And luckily, we know exactly how to do that at the diner."

Cheers sounded around the dining room. Rick walked behind the counter, found an apron and put it on over his softball uniform. His employees looked as if they'd already been taking drink orders, so Rick started at one end of the diner and took food orders. The bell above the front door jingled. Lizzie nodded at him before taking a seat at a table with Jeffy and his mother.

Once everyone had given their orders and food was delivered, Rick drifted over to stand by Jeffy, who smiled around a big bite of his bacon double cheeseburger. Lizzie picked at her chef's salad, dressing on the side, but stared at Jeffy's burger. Some people and their dinner choices. "You doing okay here?"

Jeffy's mom finished her strawberry shake. "Couldn't be better. Could we, Jeffy?"

Jeffy nodded and gave him a thumbs-up. Rick grinned back. "You folks enjoy your dinner. It's on me tonight. Gotta keep my champ happy so he'll play for me next year."

He walked to each table, stopping to chat for a while with team members and their families. That was why the diner sponsored a team every year. Sure, the trophy this year would look great proudly displayed by the cash register. But it was about the friendships that survived off the field year after year. Rick's family was more than just his mom and brother. This team was as close to him as blood. Family forged by sweat.

By the time the last fry had been eaten and the last plate cleared from each table, Rick was ready to collapse on his sofa and call it a night. Unfortunately, an hour remained until closing, and the dirty dishes soaking in the sink called his name. He groaned and rolled his shoulders to loosen them. A clap of thunder caught his attention. His eyes fastened on Lizzie, whose own eyes opened wide in fear.

She rose on one knee and glanced out the window to watch torrents of rain. "My leather seats!"

Gotta love Michigan weather.

Not that he hadn't warned her. The problem was that she had no clue about how his life really worked. And maybe that was his solution to getting rid of her. He supposed if he couldn't get rid of her, maybe he could convince her to do the show his way, in his hometown. If he could gain some control that way, he might agree to it. He approached her table and watched the summer rain pound the parking lot. "That's why you have insurance."

She turned and shrugged at him, but her lower lip still jutted out farther than her top lip. Not that he should be looking at her mouth. Instead, he let his gaze settle on the unshed tears in her grass-green eyes. Man, he couldn't stand to see a woman cry. "Listen, I have an idea."

She brightened slightly. "You'll do the show."

He sighed. *Relentless.* "I can't leave my life for three months while you and the other execs mess with it."

Her eyes narrowed. "You're suggesting a compromise?"

He put one hand on the table and the other on the back of the booth. Leaned in close enough to catch a whiff of her perfume. "I'm suggesting that you spend a week getting to know me. The real me. How my life really works now. And not that Hollywood version you created." He sighed and shook his head. "How can I expect to find my true love if she doesn't meet me where I live?"

Lizzie shook her head and glanced around the diner. Sure, it could use a gallon of paint and even more of elbow grease, but this was home to him. When she turned to face him again, she was still shaking her head. "People want fantasy in their reality TV shows. Ironic but true."

"There is an appeal to small-town living. The pull to lead a simpler life." He leaned in even closer to her. "Give me the chance to prove it to you."

Her eyes sparked with interest. "I give you a week to convince me, and what do you give me?"

He sighed. *Definitely relentless.* "If I can prove to you that we could do the show here, then I'll do it. I'll be your guinea pig again."

"You really mean that?" A smile played around her mouth.

He held out his hand. "You give me a chance, and I'll give you one." They shook on it. Rick nodded. "Good. We'll start here at five tomorrow morning."

The panic in Lizzie's eyes made it all worthwhile.

CHAPTER TWO

ELIZABETH ARRIVED at the diner when the sky was still a dark grayish-blue with only a hint of pink in the direction of the unrisen sun. Even the roosters had enough sense to keep sleeping, but here she stood. Waiting for Rick to come down and let her in to the diner to start their...what had he called it? Small-town education?

She lightly tapped her cheeks in an effort to wake herself. This tired feeling was more than jet lag. She'd dealt with that often enough to be immune to its effects. Maybe it was the déjà vu being in a small town had brought out. She'd grown up in hick towns; her mother worked restaurant jobs with their low wages, meager tips and free food. And the chance that Elizabeth could sit in a booth for a few hours so her mom didn't have to pay a babysitter.

Before she could plumb her past any further, the door opened and Rick stood there smiling at her. He should look as tired as she felt, but instead he beamed at her as he ushered her inside. "Ready for your first look at my life?"

She stifled a yawn and nodded. "Does the first look have to come so early?"

"My day usually starts an hour before this, but I thought I'd give you a break." He leaned toward her, and for a brief moment she wondered if he was going to kiss her. He reached past to turn the sign on the door to Open.

He motioned for her to follow him, and she walked behind him into the kitchen. Savory smells of bacon and sausage assaulted her, making her stomach growl. What she wouldn't give for a sausage patty right now. He opened an oven door, peered in, then adjusted the temperature. When he turned back to face her, he frowned. "Why are you wearing that?"

She glanced down at the outfit she had painstakingly chosen for their day: one of her best power suits in cherry-red and teetering black heels. "I believe you mentioned I'd be meeting people from your town."

He nodded. "And they'll eat you alive wearing that. Don't you own a pair of jeans?"

Denim wasn't exactly a staple in her wardrobe, but glancing at what Rick was wearing told her it was a part of his. She wiped at an imaginary smudge on her skirt. "I'm sure your friends will appreciate good taste."

"The grease will ruin that fancy getup within the hour. Go back to your hotel and change." He turned his back to her and started whisking eggs with flour.

Grease? There'd been no mention of that when they'd made plans for today. What exactly was he planning? "You don't expect me to actually work here, do you?"

Rick turned back to her with a dazzling smile. It was easy to see why the cameras fell in love with him. "You wanted a glimpse into my life, right? Since Mom handed the diner over to me, I'm here twelve hours a day, six days a week. So that's where we're starting."

She crossed her arms across her chest. *Nope. Not happening.* "You don't have anyone to cover for you today?"

"It's the Lake Mildred Pickle Festival. Busiest weekend of the summer. I'm going to be swamped with orders in about ten minutes and won't get a break until after the Ladies' Book Club finishes their last cup of coffee." He continued to whisk and paused only to add more flour.

She glared, hoping that the effect would turn him into stone. "I thought you were the owner and manager here."

"I'm whatever they need me to be. Besides, it's fun."

Sigh. Not her idea of fun. "And I'm supposed to help you out?"

"That's the idea, Lizzie."

She grumbled on the drive back to the bed-and-breakfast to change into the outfit she'd least likely have a fit over if it got ruined. She fumed as she drove back to the diner and parked behind it, where the employees left their cars. And she moaned when Rick threw a clean apron at her and pointed to the stack of dishes that had accumulated in her absence. "Washing dishes? Really?"

Rick started to whistle as he placed slices of bread in a large toaster and pressed the lever. "It's where all good cooks start."

"But I'm not a cook," she muttered under her breath. She couldn't even make toast without setting off the smoke detectors in her apartment.

She wrinkled her nose at the dried gobs of egg and grease on the first plate. There had to be better ways to get Rick to do the show than this. She glanced behind her at the man in question, who cracked eggs onto the hot griddle. If she could just find out why he'd done the show the first time…

"Dishes don't wash themselves, Lizzie."

He threw the eggshells into the large trash can next to him as if they were basketballs and he were Kobe Bryant. He walked over and turned on the hot water, then squeezed a healthy dollop of dish soap into the sink. Pointed to the three sinks, the last full of clear liquid. "Wash. Rinse. Sanitize." He pulled the hose closer to her. "And don't be afraid to get a little wet."

She rolled her eyes and dropped the first dish into the sudsy water.

RICK SWALLOWED A LAUGH as Lizzie glared at him over her coffee cup. She looked like a drowned rat. Her long brown hair was plastered to the sides of her head; her clothes clung to her slight form. Her carefully applied makeup had run two hours ago, leaving her face streaked in brown and blue. "Good job, Lizzie."

She rolled her eyes and forked a bite of French toast into her mouth, pausing to moan after the first bite. "What do you put in these?"

He shrugged. "Little cinnamon. Lots of love."

Again with the rolled eyes. She'd be lucky to end the day without a massive headache if she kept that up.

"So are you done torturing me?"

Torture. Interesting word choice. She'd agreed to get a glimpse of his normal life, and now she considered it inhumane. If only she knew. "You'll probably want to freshen up before the lunch crowd gets here." Panic washed over her face, but he held up one hand. "Don't worry. You're done with the dishes. Jeffy should be here anytime."

Her shoulders relaxed. "Thank goodness."

"But I am short a waitress."

Lizzie stood up and threw her napkin on the table before storming out of the diner. Rick chuckled and took another sip of his coffee. Mission accomplished. Better that she leave now than wait until it was too late.

The bell above the door chimed again. "Ricky."

He glanced up and swallowed a groan at the sight of his older brother, Dan, wearing a suit and tie. If Mr. High and Mighty stooped to grace the diner with his presence, the news couldn't be good. Didn't matter that the diner belonged to the family empire along with the pickle-canning plant and brightly colored cans of pickles on store shelves. Rick knew that the diner didn't even register on Dan's radar.

"Need a cup of coffee?" Rick stood and

retrieved the coffee carafe from behind the counter, hooked a mug with one finger, then joined his brother in the back booth. He poured the coffee into the empty mug before topping off his own. "Still drink it black or should I find the creamer?"

"Black's fine."

Rick nodded and took the seat across from Dan. "What's wrong? Is it Mom again?"

Dan shook his head, then glanced behind him at the customers gathered at the diner. "We can talk here?"

Any news his brother had to share would be sure to make the gossip rounds in Lake Mildred before too long. "Sure."

Dan sighed, rubbing the space between his eyebrows. "I'll be glad when this whole economic downturn is over."

Downturn? Was that what people losing their jobs, homes and lives was? Rick took a sip of his coffee, mostly to keep from saying what he really wanted to say. "Just tell me what you came here for."

Dan leaned forward. "I heard that producer is in town."

Biting the inside of his cheek, Rick nodded. So that was what his visit was about? A pretty face? "Yeah, Lizzie's here. She might be back in about twenty minutes if you want to talk to her."

Dan frowned. "Why would I talk to her?"

"She's cute. All wrong for you, of course. But she does fit your type." Rick poured some creamer into his coffee and stirred it. "Smart. Pretty. No nonsense."

"I'm not looking for a date, Rick." He took a sip of his coffee, then placed the mug on the table. Rubbed his forehead and twitching eye. "She wants you to do that show again?"

He sighed. He couldn't escape the show, not even with his family. "Don't worry. I already told her to forget about it."

Dan frowned and shook his head as if Rick had said the worst thing in the world. "Why would you do a stupid thing like that?"

Wait. His brother wanted him to do the show? "If memory serves, you didn't want me to do the show the last time. Hated it when I left. Then resented me when I came back home."

"I was stupid, okay?" He glanced at his cell phone. "All of Dad's talk about what was good for the family? The company? I think I get it now."

Rick remembered the discussions he and his dad had had over the show. In the end, it had come down to Rick choosing to help save the family company. "You got it five years too late."

"I wasn't CEO then. I didn't realize what a boon that show could be." Dan adjusted the lapel of his suit coat. "Last time, our sales went up almost thirty percent. We got distributors in a dozen more states that sold our product. Business at the diner tripled after they aired your hometown visit." He leaned in closer. "We could use that kind of publicity again."

"No."

Dan shook his head. "What's changed? Dad told you to do the show then. I'm telling you now."

Telling him what to do yet again. Well, Rick wasn't the same little brother who went along with Dan's ideas. He had his own life. His own choices to make. "I'm smarter this time around. I won't do it."

"I get it." Dan jutted his jaw forward, the same way he had since they were kids and he thought he was not only right, but that Rick would be convinced of it, too. "You need to think about it. I'll call you in a few days."

"Call me next week. The answer will still be the same."

Dan stood and placed a hand on Rick's

shoulder. "You've got to think of the family, little brother."

Rick shook his head and bit back a laugh. "I am thinking of the family. You're focusing on the company's bottom line."

"You don't understand the hole we're in. And if we fail, this town will never be the same—" Dan broke off and shook his head. "Never mind. This was a mistake."

Rick got to his feet and leaned in toward Dan. "Why would we fail?"

"Maybe if you read those company reports I send you more than you read the sports pages, you might understand why I'm here." Dan took one last sip of coffee before slapping the mug on the table. "Thanks for the coffee."

Rick was getting pretty good at making people storm out of his diner.

ELIZABETH STARED INTO her suitcase as if a waitress uniform would magically appear. Thankfully, she'd never had to go the same route as her mother. She'd known someone who knew someone offering a job as a page on a studio lot when she turned sixteen, and she'd been into television ever since. It was all that she knew. All she wanted. That was why she had to use this week to convince

Rick to do the show. If that meant washing mountains of dishes and pouring rivers of coffee, she'd do it.

A pair of khakis peeked at her from the bottom of the suitcase, so she pulled them out and found a sleeveless green shell and matching short-sleeved top to go with it. It was better than nothing. Or at least better than the sopping oxford and slacks that hung over the shower curtain rod in the tiny bathroom of her room at the bed-and-breakfast.

She returned to the diner to find Rick barking orders to his cook through the window. He looked comfortable here. As if he knew that he'd be doing this for the rest of his life.

Unfortunately.

Didn't he see that he had so much more to offer? She'd watched the dailies again from the last show he'd done and knew that he was made for bigger things than running a small-town diner. Maybe he didn't want to work for the family company, but he wasn't being challenged here. That was where she came in. She needed to broaden his horizons. Provide him with a better life. Success on the show would mean opened doors for him, and he could write his own future. Be a celebrity chef if he wanted. Get his own cooking show and endorsement deals.

"I'm back." She did a Vanna White impression and turned around. "Will this suffice for a waitress?"

Rick looked her up and down, then grimaced. "You sure you want grease to touch that silk shirt?"

"It's either this or another suit." She put her hands on her hips. "I didn't exactly plan on working at the diner this entire week with you."

"The diner is my life now." He looked at her outfit again. "We'll go shopping after lunch."

She could handle shopping. That thought might get her through whatever he had in store for her. "Is that part of my small-town education?"

Rick grinned and handed her a clean apron to tie around her hips and a blank order pad. "I'll help you with the first three tables, and then you're on your own. Got it?"

She produced a popular television show and made it look easy. How hard could this be? "I think I can handle taking a few orders."

Again with the smile. Why did she get the feeling that there was more to this?

"I'll still help you with the first three. They can be tricky."

Rick chose the first table of two older

women, who chatted with each other more than glancing at their menus. Elizabeth approached them. "Good afternoon, ladies. What can I get you today?"

Talk ceased as they turned to look at her. Perused her outfit. Glanced at Rick. Then sighed collectively. The woman with salt-and-pepper hair spoke first. "Well, aren't you the cutest thing?" She turned to Rick. "Where did you find her?"

Rick stepped forward and clasped his hands behind his back. "She's just helping out a few days for the Pickle Festival. So be gentle with her."

The two women gave each other telling glances. The fading redhead turned to Elizabeth. "What soups do you have today?"

Elizabeth glanced at the back of her order pad, where she'd written them. "Chicken noodle. Clam chowder. And vegetable."

The women resumed looking at their menus. The salt-and-pepper looked up at Rick. "Char's coming in for the festival this weekend, you know."

Rick gave a tight smile. "You must be looking forward to seeing your daughter."

Elizabeth glanced at him. He tugged at the collar of his T-shirt and rolled his head on his shoulders. Clearly not a good topic.

"What she's looking forward to is seeing you again, Rick. Should I tell her to give you a call?"

Rick shifted on his feet until Elizabeth stepped in. "Actually, he'll be busy with me this weekend. Working the festival and all." She glanced at Rick. "Isn't that right?"

Rick sighed and nodded. "Yeah, that's right. It's gonna be pretty busy, Mrs. Stanfill." When the older woman wrinkled her nose, he quickly added, "But I'll be sure to say hello if I see her in town."

Red gave her friend a sideways glance, then offered a big smile to Rick. "Donna will be in town, as well. You be sure to say hello to her, too."

Rick nodded, but he looked as if he'd agreed to pour salt into old wounds. "Elizabeth, why don't you go ahead and take their orders? I've got to check on something in the kitchen."

Rick left her standing alone. She took a big breath. "So what can I get you?"

ELIZABETH WAS CONVINCED that he'd chosen the three most difficult tables to train her on. They all wanted specific orders rather than something off the menu. Maybe he'd put them up to it. Maybe he'd told them to be difficult.

She groaned and hoisted the tray of food for the second table onto her shoulder like Rick had shown her. It was heavier than it looked, and she almost sagged under its weight. A drop of oil dripped from the tray onto her blouse.

Great. She'd definitely need that trip to the clothing store. How did people not have to buy a wardrobe at the end of the day working in food service? If nothing else, she would appreciate how hard her server worked the next time she ate at a restaurant. She promised she'd tip better if she could get through this afternoon.

By the end of the lunch rush, she found herself again at the back booth, her feet up and resting on the seat across from her. She'd developed blisters. She must have the way her feet throbbed and ached. She needed better shoes. New clothes. What else would this glimpse into Rick's life cost her?

"Here." Rick set a plate laden with a BLT and fries in front of her. "My specialty, just for you."

She wrinkled her nose at the bacon but one whiff of the sandwich made her stomach grumble loud enough for Rick to hear. He chuckled.

"Thanks." She laid a napkin on her lap and took a tentative bite.

Mmmmmmmm.

Rick grinned and left, only to return momentarily with his own sandwich. "Mind if I join you?"

"Think the diner will survive without us?" She took another large bite and tried to chew faster to get to the next one.

"I think we have time to eat. You don't have to rush." He looked around the dining room, which held a few stragglers left from the rush. "Shirley's here, so she can take over."

Elizabeth took another bite of her sandwich and groaned again in delight. There was something different about the bacon. "What's your secret?"

"If I told you, then it wouldn't be a secret anymore." He smirked at her. "I bake the bacon rather than frying it. Sprinkle it with Cajun seasonings and brown sugar to give it a little something special."

She wiped her mouth with her napkin. "This is fantastic."

"Thank you."

They ate in silence until Elizabeth pushed her plate away. It held only a few of the fries and a stray piece of lettuce. She patted her very full belly. "I can't eat another bite. What are you trying to do to me?"

He looked her over. "You could use some fattening up."

"Now you sound like a grandmother." Not that she'd ever known one personally. Yet another part of childhood she'd missed.

Rick stuffed the rest of his sandwich in his mouth. They smiled at each other, not saying a word. Not needing to. When he was finished, he wiped his mouth and rubbed his flat stomach. "That really hit the spot."

It felt good to sit. To put her feet up and relax. She almost hated to ask, but she did. "So what's next on the agenda?"

"I show you around town. The Pickle Festival kicks off tonight, so what better way to see it than that? The rides. The food. The people." He winked at her. "You won't be able to resist."

If only that were true. "Even if we agree to tape here, you'll still have to come to L.A. for the live finale. That's a tradition we can't break."

"I'm not asking to break anything. Just change it a little."

Elizabeth nodded, then attempted to get

to her feet, which protested. She sat back down. "As long as we're not talking about long walks anywhere, I'm in."

CHAPTER THREE

SEEING THE NATURAL beauty of Michigan would woo Lizzie, who would in turn convince the suits, so Rick followed the scenic route along the lake. The sun glanced off the smooth dark green surface of the water while boats drifted in the distance. Picturesque cottages and run-down fishing shacks shared the shore, providing its tenants with lake living.

When it was safe to do so, he pulled the truck over to the side of the road and held out his hand to help her down. She groaned as her feet touched the ground, only reminding him that working in his diner had taken a lot out of her. But she was a trouper. Whether it was to convince him for the show or something else, it didn't matter. He admired her spunk.

"I was thinking that this would really look spectacular on film." Though he still had no desire to do the show, the idea of filming here was growing on him. It could be just the boost the Lake Mildred economy needed. He turned back to gauge her impression. "It's amazing here in the spring. Summer. Fall. Even winter with all the snow."

Her eyes widened. "Snow?"

She'd probably never seen a snowflake, much less a foot of the white stuff dumped overnight. "When were you looking to film the show?"

"A live Valentine's Day kickoff. Then live again for the finale in time for the May sweeps."

"So snow, then budding flowers. Nice." He looked out over the lake and took a deep breath. He'd tried the California atmosphere, but he'd been homesick for this the entire time. The clean air. The lap of the waves on the shore. Even the splash of fish, who were practically calling his name to catch them. "We could do a ski fantasy date. Or an ice-fishing expedition. Later in the spring, they could even try out for my softball team."

"You really want us to come here? Disturb the peace of your small town?" She looked around her. "I'll admit this would look good on television. Practically a postcard from Middle America. But we wouldn't leave this place the way we found it."

"Besides bringing your audience a taste of real America, you'd also be bringing local jobs for the time you're here. Jobs that people could really use." He stepped closer to her. "You'd need people to drive. To build. To cater. Sure, you could bring some of those people from L.A. out here, but think of what you could save by hiring locally. You could improve the town's economy."

She looked at him as if he'd suggested that they could cure cancer while they were at it. "We're a television show. Don't give us too much credit."

"Lizzie." He stepped closer. "My dad always told me that with our money came responsibility. I had to give back in any way I could. If I do the show, I want to be able to help the people who have supported me. Will you help me do that?"

She sighed. "You've given me some things to think about, but I'm going to need more than this. Where would I house twenty-four women? As well as a crew of two dozen more. The bed-and-breakfast I'm at is nice, but let's be realistic. We need something a lot bigger."

Rick nodded and considered the issue. "What about some of these abandoned homes? Couldn't you rent one of those?"

"And fix it up with what money? The studio owns a mansion specifically for this show. It works for a reason."

She always had to look on the bleak side,

didn't she? But he could see the wheels turning in her head behind the skeptical expression. She might be throwing up objections, but he could tell she saw the benefits. "What if you don't pay me for my time on the show? What if you instead use that check to do this?"

She turned and looked at him closely. "You'd do that?" She didn't seem convinced.

Rick knew it could work. Bring the show. Put people to work. Keep some kind of normal life while living it out in front of a national audience. It had to work. "To get the show here? Yeah."

She crossed her arms. "Keep talking."

"Consider the tax breaks the state would give you for filming here. The cost of living is less, so you'd be getting bargain prices on the things you take for granted in Hollywood."

"Let's say we could rent a house around here. Two dozen women sharing one, maybe two bathrooms? Even that's a little too real for television."

Rick grinned. "And a whole lot of fun."

Lizzie held up her hands. "Okay. Show me more."

BY THE TIME they got in the truck and headed back to the diner for dinner, Elizabeth was dog tired. She doubted she'd be awake long enough to eat, much less call Devon with an update. And she had to admit the idea of filming here had started to wiggle into her already clicking mind. It would be a change, something that could spark ratings for a show that was starting to show its age. Rick might be onto something.

Instead of going to the diner, however, Rick turned his truck into the driveway of a large Victorian house with a wraparound porch and pulled around back near the lakefront. Elizabeth looked at the manicured landscape outside and frowned. "We're having dinner here?"

Rick wiggled his eyebrows. "First we're going to catch it. Then we'll eat here."

Elizabeth groaned. "You're taking me fishing? Haven't you tortured me enough for one day?"

"Think of it as part of your Michigan experience." He got out of the truck and retrieved fishing poles and a tackle box from behind the front seat. "And you haven't really lived until you've eaten something you've caught."

Elizabeth rolled her eyes. This was not what she had signed up for. Still, she was hungry and she'd agreed to do what was necessary to get Rick for the show. "Fine. But I'm not cleaning any icky fish. You get that job."

"Sure, Lizzie."

"Elizabeth," she muttered under her breath as she followed him to the dinghy tied to the dock on the lake.

Rick held out one hand and helped her step into the boat. She spread her arms to catch her balance before taking a seat on the narrow wooden bench. Rick untied the boat from the dock and stepped inside, pushing off. He took a seat, then pulled the chain for the motor. They putted out to the center of the lake while Elizabeth watched the sun lower in the west behind a wall of magnificent trees. She closed her eyes.

"This place is getting to you."

She opened her eyes. "I'm tired."

"Mmm-hmm." Rick steered them out farther and cut the engine. He handed her a pole. "Have you ever fished before?"

"When I was a kid, my mom took me to the Santa Monica pier. Some guy let me hold his pole while he ran to get a hot dog." She shrugged. "All I did was stand there."

"So you're an expert."

He opened the tackle box and removed a small plastic container. It was full of black dirt and wriggling worms. Elizabeth wrinkled her nose and shook her head. "I'm not putting one of those on my hook."

"Relax. I'll bait it for you."

He removed one long worm and wound it around her hook while Elizabeth squelched a squeal. She wasn't naive. She understood the circle-of-life thing. Instead of allowing Rick to think she was squeamish, she accepted the pole. "Now what?"

"Cast it out toward the middle of the lake."

She looked at him and raised one eyebrow. "Cast is something I hire for a show."

"Ha-ha. Watch me." He swung the rod back slightly, then flicked it forward, sending his line out in a perfect arc that Elizabeth doubted she could repeat.

In fact, she couldn't repeat it. After three failed attempts, Rick cast the line for her. She sighed. "What's next?"

"We wait." He wound the reel in a bit and lifted his face to the sky, his eyes closed.

Elizabeth watched him. He had a boyish charm that the audience had loved. He was also funny and sensitive. Why he was still single after all this time was a mystery to her. He was the type of guy who should be a husband and father. "What happened after you came home last time?"

Rick opened one eye and groaned. "Do we have to talk about that?"

"I'm surprised that some woman didn't snap you up the moment you arrived home, single and willing." She wound the reel a couple of clicks like she had seen him do. "You still want to get married and have kids, right? So why didn't you make that happen?"

Rick rubbed his forehead with his free hand. "Were you not there when I got publicly humiliated?"

"It's been five years. People forget."

"You have hundreds of letters a week that say otherwise." He turned his gaze on her. "I guess no one wanted to date a loser."

"You're not a loser." Elizabeth pulled her pole back slightly, mirroring Rick's movements. "You are a catch. And any woman who doesn't realize that is not only blind, but also not worth your time."

"Then I live in a town full of the sightless." Rick reeled his line in and cast it farther out. "Do you know they had a viewing party at the diner for the night of the finale? All my family and friends were gathered together to watch me propose. Instead they saw me dumped and humiliated."

"I think you're the only one who's not over that already." She glanced at his eyes shadowed beneath his ball cap. "But I do have one question."

"Only one? You're slipping."

"Did you love Brandy?"

He swallowed and adjusted the ball cap again. Then he moved his fishing pole and wound the reel a couple of turns, clearly stalling for time. "Yes." His voice croaked. "And the crazy thing is I thought she loved me, too. Only, she was pretending for the cameras."

"You don't know that."

Rick looked up at her with troubled eyes. "She chose him over me. How else do you explain it?"

She reached out and touched his knee. Then she quickly removed her hand. "You knew she was dating you both. That there was a chance…"

"But it felt real." He shrugged. "That's why I'm conflicted about doing the show. How am I supposed to know what's real and what's for the sake of the cameras? How can I trust my heart to someone else who might be pretending?"

She longed to remove the hurt from his eyes. "That's why you have me. I'll protect you. Like I should have the last time." She glanced out toward the lakeshore. "We were friends. I should have…" She looked back at him. "I want to be friends again. And I'll help you get what you want."

"How do you know what I want?"

"Because it's my job to figure it out. With your help, of course."

He gazed into her eyes until she supposed he could see her soul. If they were any two other people, this would be the perfect moment to kiss. Her lips tingled at the thought.

Rick leaned forward. She closed her eyes. "I think you've got a bite."

Her eyes flew open, and she tugged on the line. Sure enough, something was resisting at the other end. She squealed and stood up. Rick reached out and put a hand on her calf. "Careful. You're going to capsize the boat."

She wound the reel and shouted as a long silvery-green fish appeared at the end of her line. "I caught a fish!"

Rick reached up to steady her, and she threw herself into his arms.

Later, as they sat dripping wet at the campfire, she could point out where she went wrong before the boat capsized. Thankfully, Rick never raised his voice. Unfortunately, he didn't say a word, either.

Elizabeth held out her hands toward the fire to absorb the heat. She looked over at

Rick, who pulled his hooded jacket closer around him. "I'm sorry. Again."

Nothing.

She looked into the fire, hoping to find the right words. "I know you warned me, but I was so excited. I've never caught a fish."

Still nothing.

She sighed. "I'm sorry it got away."

He cleared his throat.

She settled farther into the Adirondack chair. "And that we lost your fishing pole."

His eyes flickered to hers briefly, then concentrated on the campfire again. Elizabeth closed her eyes and rested her head on the back of the chair. Silence was good. They were both tired. And wet.

Her stomach growling broke the silence. Rick's answered in turn.

And they were both hungry.

"I want to make this up to you." She leaned forward. "I'll treat you to the best dinner. Anywhere you want."

"Lizzie…"

She sighed. "He speaks."

"Don't worry about it." He stood and smothered the fire, then walked toward the house.

Elizabeth watched him leave, then rose and ran after him. "We still need to eat dinner."

Rick stopped and looked at his wet clothes, then hers. "No one would serve us like this. And I'm too hungry to change." He turned back and continued walking.

"Where are you going?"

"Mom probably has enough food in her cupboards to feed your entire crew for three months." He grinned at her. "First one there gets dibs."

And with that, he sprinted toward the house. Elizabeth laughed and ran after him.

GREEN OLIVES. Sweet pickles. Crackers and cheese. Leftover pasta salad. It was a feast, and Rick enjoyed every bite.

They sat on stools at the kitchen island while they ate with their fingers. He stopped eating momentarily to find napkins. He handed one to Lizzie, who grinned around a mouthful of salad. He opened the refrigerator and pulled out two cans of soda and placed one at each plate. "You must be thirsty."

Lizzie nodded her thanks and opened her drink. She looked around the kitchen. "Where's your mom?"

Rick popped the top of his drink and took several long pulls. It burned going down, but it was that good kind of burn. "It's the first night of the Pickle Festival, which means she's probably manning the fried-pickle tent." At Lizzie's frown, he continued, "You haven't tasted heaven until you've had a fried pickle. Trust me."

"I heard you mention it before, but what exactly is a pickle festival?"

"Last night's championship game was the kickoff to a weekend full of pickles here. Courtesy of Allyn Pickles, of course." He fished out a sweet gherkin from the jar and handed it to her. "It's a huge deal for the town every year. Financially speaking. Lots of tourists. Family reunions. Homecomings. Everyone looks forward to it."

Lizzie looked down at her clothes. "Speaking of a huge deal, we didn't get any clothes for me. I can't work in your diner dressed in my regular clothes."

"Next town over also has a Meijer, which is open twenty-four hours." Lizzie's mouth gaped, and Rick laughed. "We may be backwater, but we do have some conveniences." He nodded at her empty plate. "So eat some more and then we'll shop."

She stifled a yawn. "I don't know how much longer I'll be functioning. What time are you planning on torturing me tomorrow?"

She did look exhausted. He'd put her through the wringer and had plans for more.

"You did such a great job today, I'll let you sleep in. We can meet at seven."

"That's sleeping in?" she moaned.

He shook his head. "You've had early calls for the show. How is this different?"

"For all you know I complained then, too." She tried to laugh, but it didn't sound right.

Rick frowned. Something didn't add up. "I thought you were a producer. Shouldn't all this be part of your job?" Lizzie stuffed the pickle into her mouth, making talking impossible. His frown deepened. "What aren't you telling me?"

She chewed, then swallowed. "It's complicated."

"You are still on the show, right?"

She nodded. "I'm executive producer. For now."

"For now?" She was about to fill her mouth with crackers, but he stayed her arm. "Tell me."

She sighed. "It's no big deal."

"If you can't tell me, then yes, it is."

She looked down at the plate. Finally, she lifted her gaze to meet his. "If you don't do the show, we're canceled."

CHAPTER FOUR

ELIZABETH POURED the eightieth cup of coffee that morning before returning to the kitchen. Rick turned to beam at her from the dish sink, and her breath caught in her throat. Remind her why this man wasn't taken. She shook her head at the stupidity of the women in this town out in the sticks. Being small-town didn't mean being foolish, but these women needed to get a clue and snap Rick up before two dozen gorgeous contestants descended here.

She paused. Was she really considering moving the show? She shook her head. This place was getting to her.

A bell over the door signaled a new customer. Elizabeth took a deep breath and walked into the dining room, almost mowing down an older version of Rick. He glanced at her outfit. "You're the producer?"

Elizabeth held out her hand. "Dan, right? I'm Elizabeth." She marveled at the strength of his handshake. "And yes, I'm the producer.

But at the moment, I'm a waitress. Can I get you some coffee?"

"He likes it black and strong." Rick joined them and leaned on the counter. "Shouldn't you be checking the floats or bands or something?"

Dan accepted the cup she offered him and took a sip. "It's been done."

Elizabeth frowned. "Floats?"

Rick nodded toward the windows, where people had started gathering on the sides of Main Street. "The Pickle Parade starts at noon. And Dan the man is the grand marshal again."

"That's what I came to talk to Elizabeth about." Dan leaned against the counter. "Ever ridden in the back of a convertible and waved to a crowd?"

Rick stepped in between them. "Forget it. She's busy."

"Pouring coffee and slinging hash? I need her more." Dan sighed and ran his hand through his hair, reminding Elizabeth of his brother. "Miss Brown County can't make it now, and the people need to see someone new. Someone classy." He glanced at Elizabeth. "She'll have to do."

She was sure there was a compliment in there somewhere. "I can't possibly do it dressed like this." She glanced at her brand-spanking-new purple T-shirt and jeans.

Dan grabbed her hand. "Martha's across the street. I'm sure she'll have something that will fit you."

Rick grabbed her other hand. "Dan, Elizabeth never agreed to do it. When are you going to stop and realize that not everyone jumps when you tell them to?"

Dan pulled her closer to him. "She has to do this. It's her responsibility."

Rick tugged her back to his side. "It's your responsibility to make sure that people show up. Not hers."

"Gentlemen." Elizabeth removed her hands from theirs and held them out to separate the brothers. "First of all, I can choose for myself. Second—" she looked between them, then nodded "—I'll help out."

Rick stared at her. "Lizzie, you don't—"

"You wanted me to get to know the community, right?" She smiled wider. "What better way than from the back of a convertible?" She turned to Dan. "So where's Martha? Let's see what she has."

Dan grinned back at her, and she was struck by how good the Allyn boys looked. "I knew I liked you. Come with me."

Rick watched from the sidelines as Lizzie, dressed in a pink sparkly dress, passed by sitting on the back of a red convertible. She even blew a kiss to him. Or perhaps to the kid standing in front of him, but it landed in his general direction. He'd take what he could get.

When the parade ended, he locked up the diner and joined the crowd as they walked down the street to the park, where rides and booths had magically appeared over the past few nights. He found Lizzie still standing near the convertible, surrounded by a group of local men who were trying to get her attention. When she turned and smiled at him, he lost his breath.

Must be the gasoline fumes.

He moved through the crowd and parked himself closest to her. "Madam, I believe we have a date."

She raised one eyebrow. "We do?"

"With a deep-fried pickle. I believe I promised you one?" He put his hand at the small of her back. "I know where they sell the best."

She sighed deeply as they left the crowd. "Thanks for the rescue."

"Part of my service." He steered her in the direction of the large tent at the center of the park. "They're smitten with shiny new things."

She ran her hand down one hip. "Miss Martha does wonders with sequins and a short deadline."

"You look fabulous." He motioned to the open tent flaps. "Now, prepare yourself for a culinary treat that few can top."

He grabbed her hand and walked behind the counters. They skirted past several deep fryers and walked to the far end of the tent. Rick pulled a basket out of one of the fryers and tipped it onto a cloth-covered plate. He held out a golden disk to her lips. "Open."

Lizzie opened her mouth, and Rick placed the deep-fried pickle on her tongue. "Now, tell me that isn't the best thing you ever ate."

She chewed slowly. "It's good."

"Good? It's fabulous." Rick took one and popped it in his mouth. He closed his eyes and let the flavors play on his tongue.

She swallowed the pickle and looked around the tent. "Are you allowed to come back here and help yourself?"

"My question exactly." His mom walked around the tables and poked a finger at Rick's chest. "Who's watching the diner?"

Rick rubbed his chest. "It's closed until five for dinner, Ma. It's fine."

She shook her head, then glanced at Elizabeth. "Miss Brown County?"

"Not quite. Elizabeth Maier from—"

"*True Love.* Yep." Rick's mother glanced at Elizabeth's outstretched hand but didn't shake it. "Thought I recognized you. What are you doing here?"

"Ma…" He should have known his mother wouldn't be happy Lizzie was there. "She's in town on business."

"As long as she's not here to mess with you again." His mom looked back at Lizzie. "Are you?"

Rick put his hands on his mother's shoulders. "It's business, Ma."

"I asked her, not you." She moved around him and walked up to Lizzie.

"Ma…" Not that his mom would take the warning, but at least he could say he had tried. He braced himself for the confrontation.

Lizzie looked down at her feet, then up at his mother. "I assure you, Mrs. Allyn, I have the best intentions."

His mom stared her right in the eyes and gave her the look he'd dreaded as a kid. It meant she knew what he was up to and she wasn't having one bit of it. "And was it your best intention for my son to get dumped on television?"

"No, but it is my intention to find him a wife." Lizzie took a step closer so that she could tower slightly over his mom.

Rick watched as the two women squared off, neither one conceding. "Ma, I'm going to show Lizzie more of the festival. But we'll see you for dinner tomorrow?"

He leaned over and kissed his mom's cheek. Then he held out his hand to Lizzie. "Now that you've tried the fried pickles, you have to taste the dill-pickle soup."

Lizzie wrinkled her nose, but she followed him.

THIS SMALL TOWN could do things to a person. She'd only been in Lake Mildred two days, and part of her was wondering what living there would be like. People smiled and said hello. Acted as if she'd been one of them for years. She didn't feel rushed or anxious. She hadn't thought of her voice mail or email for hours. In fact, she hadn't glanced at her cell phone since the parade two hours before.

Rick turned toward her when she sighed. "It gets to you, right?"

She shrugged and pulled on the hem of her dress. She should have changed after the parade. Or at least after they'd sampled the fried dill pickles, the dill-pickle soup, the gherkin mousse. She should have passed on that last one. But the pickle pâté had been fabulous. The lure of the festival had kept them in the park, enjoying the booths and the people surrounding them. "I guess it is getting to me."

He stopped at the ticket booth and purchased two wristbands, then tied one to her wrist. "Which ride should we try first? The tilt-a-whirl or the scrambler?"

She put a hand over her stomach. "I'd like to keep my lunch down, thanks."

Rick laughed. "Where's your sense of adventure? Your joie de vivre?"

"It prefers not to spend life with my head in the toilet." She looked around at the rides. There had to be something tame. "Why not the Ferris wheel?"

Rick glanced up at it, then grabbed her hand and sprinted toward the line. "You won't believe the view up there. You'll be able to see the whole town."

"All square mile of it? Can't wait."

When they reached the beginning of the line, Rick let her take a seat first before joining her. They got locked into the seat, then took a deep breath as the operator gave a thumbs-up.

The view at the top took Elizabeth's breath away. Trees grew lush and green. The sunlight glinted off the lake and winked with the promise of fun times. Small homes were built around the town square and farther beyond. Cottages lined the lakeshore. Part of her suddenly yearned for a place in this community.

Rick nodded. "I told you it was spectacular."

"You weren't kidding." The camera would love it. She turned to him. "You understand that our coming here would forever change the peace and quiet. We couldn't leave this place as it is now. For months, it would be chaos with the contestants and crew. We'd clog your streets and your businesses, and leave the mess for you to clean up. And then the gawkers would descend."

"What I know is that it would bring jobs and money to people who need both more than you know." He pointed at a home with a tree house in the backyard. "It would mean Steve wouldn't lose his house." He pointed to another with a covered porch. "Or that Shelly could feed her kids this winter."

Elizabeth closed her eyes. She knew what it was like to be hungry. What it meant not to know if there would be dinner that night. "I can't guarantee Devon will go for this idea."

Rick settled back into the seat. "You tell him it's either you have me here or I don't do it at all."

"That's a pretty big threat."

He reached out and touched her hand. "I won't let you lose your job over me, but I won't lose myself in the process, either. I'm not going to lie, the idea of doing the show again is making me quake in my sneakers. But as long as we can establish some ground rules, if we can do it my way, then everyone will be happy."

Uh-oh. His way? She was the producer here, not him. "You ask for a lot."

Rick shrugged. "So do you."

She watched the emotions play over his face. He wanted to save this town, but at what cost to himself? He was a good man. Too good for this business. Elizabeth reached out and touched his face, then snapped her hand back as if he'd burned her. What was she doing?

"Lizzie." The hoarseness of his voice seemed to shock even him.

"Elizabeth."

He leaned back and looked out over the treetops. "Come to Sunday dinner tomorrow afternoon at my mom's."

After the confrontation in the food tent, that was a shock. "Why?"

He turned to her. "Because that's what I do every Sunday. Spend it with my family. And maybe if we talk some more, we can figure this out. Give my mom a second chance. Isn't that what you're offering me here?"

Was it? Elizabeth wasn't sure anymore.

ELIZABETH ADJUSTED her black skirt and straightened her pink linen jacket while wondering for the eighty-ninth time why she had agreed to do this. She'd gone to great lengths to secure contestants in the past, but this topped them all.

She exhaled as she saw Rick come down the back stairs from his apartment to where she waited by her convertible.

"Good morning." He leaned over and kissed her cheek.

She glanced at her watch. "It's technically afternoon."

Rick grinned and shrugged. "Close enough." He moved next to her to lean against the car. "Ready for this?"

Elizabeth's insides vibrated with tension, and she clutched her stomach. "I'm not hungry."

"We'll eat. Talk. Maybe watch a ball game. And have a great afternoon." He bumped her shoulder with his. "My family wants to get to know you."

Why? She was about to change Rick's life again. Maybe coming here hadn't been a good idea. If she hadn't been so worried about her job... Instead of asking, she smiled. "Then I'd love to."

Rick's shoulders sagged in what looked like relief. "Thanks. You'll be saving us from a week of leftovers—roast-beef sandwiches, roast-beef salad, beef pâté."

Elizabeth wiped the sweat off the back of her neck. "Your mother made a roast in this heat?"

Rick shrugged. "She likes to cook."

What would it have been like to have grown up with a mom like that? Elizabeth couldn't even begin to imagine. "Is that where you learned it?"

He nodded. "She taught me everything I know. She's the best."

"Which you obviously use in your job." She turned and looked at him. "Did you know the diner would be your life the last time I saw you?"

He took so long in answering her, she thought at first he hadn't heard what she'd said. At last, he sighed. "No, it's not where I pictured my life passing. I imagined ball fields and team buses. But things changed after the car accident. And the diner stepped in and took the place of that dream. I spend most of my days there because it's easier than looking at my life and wondering what the future holds."

"So what do you want?"

He patted his stomach. "To go to lunch. I'm starving."

She unlocked her car door and stood in the opening while she looked at him. "Should I follow you out to your mom's?"

Rick peered past her to the inside of her car. "Actually, I'll ride with you. Can we put the top down?"

She shook her head. "You're worse than a kid."

He grinned at her, and a punch landed in her stomach. *Wow.*

With his help, they put the soft top down on the convertible and she settled into the driver's seat. He bounced slightly in the seat and tried all the knobs on the dashboard. She playfully swatted his hand, then turned the key in the ignition. "It's a car, not a toy."

He chuckled and settled back in the passenger seat, eyes closed and sun streaming onto his face. "I love Sundays."

"I can tell."

He opened one eye and looked at her. She turned her gaze back to the road. "You don't?"

She shrugged. "In my world, it's just another day. Another day of phone calls, meetings and… Why are you staring at me like that?"

"You really need to find a hobby." He turned his focus back to the road. "Turn left up here, and we'll follow the lake to the house."

RICK HELPED LIZZIE out of the car, then walked around the house to the back door.

He opened the door and popped his head inside. "Mom?" The smell of roasting beef tickled his nose, so he knew she was around somewhere. He turned back to Lizzie. "She's probably changing from her church clothes."

Lizzie looked down at her suit. "Do I look okay?"

He smiled. Always worried about how she looked. He wore his Detroit Tigers T-shirt and favorite jeans. He didn't have to worry. "You're not meeting my family as a girlfriend, so stop worrying. They'll love you."

"Until they find out I'm bringing you back to the show again." She shut the door behind her. "We really need to talk."

He held up a hand. "I know. Later." It was definitely a conversation that could wait.

His mom entered the kitchen and walked over to him. She kissed him on the cheek. "My handsome boy." She turned to Lizzie. Her expression changed from affection to distrust. "I've agreed to be civil, for Rick's sake." Lizzie fidgeted until his mom looked her over and sighed. "Rick's right. You need some fattening up. I hope you're hungry."

Rick took a step between Lizzie and his mom. Better to keep them at a distance for now. "Is Danny here yet? I'm starving to death." He patted his empty stomach again.

His mom rolled her eyes. "Never mind him, Lizzie. He's always hungry."

"Elizabeth."

His mom checked on the roast in the oven, then turned to them. "Rick, you're on table duty. Lizzie, if you'd help me make a salad, then we'll be able to eat once Dan arrives. Now, why don't you tell me more about what's going on with you two."

Lizzie colored as pink as her suit. Rick cleared his throat. "I've agreed to do the show again, Ma."

She stopped pulling vegetables from the crisper and turned to face him. He swallowed and felt exactly like he used to when waiting for his father to come home and discipline him for goofing off in school. He hadn't wanted to blurt it out like that, but it was better to say it now rather than waiting for Dan to start spinning this to his advantage. He watched for his mother's reaction.

She nodded and took a seat at the kitchen island. Rick helped to put the vegetables on the counter and shut the refrigerator. He chuckled, trying to keep it light. "I didn't expect you to be overjoyed, but speechless? Wow."

"Why do you want to put yourself through that, honey?" She put her hands on either side of his face. "Do you think you could handle it again?"

He glanced at Lizzie, who started to peel the plastic wrap from the head of lettuce. His producer wasn't being any help, so he shrugged. "I'm still single. Still haven't found the right woman. Why not open the odds up a little in my favor?"

"It didn't work the last time." She shook her head and buried her face in her hands. "I begged your father to let you off the hook. We didn't need that ridiculous show to survive."

"Mrs. Allyn, the chances of Rick finding

a wife are better this time. He'll be the focus of our show. The one doing the choosing."

His mom turned to her. "I can't believe you're torturing him again with this. You don't know what it was like when he came back. The pain—"

"Ma." She turned back to him. He'd do anything to ease the worry in her eyes. "I know you're trying to protect me. But this time will be different."

"How can you be so sure?"

He winked at Lizzie. "Because we're doing it my way this time."

Lizzie paled but gave a weak nod to Ma when she looked at her. "Rick wants more control this time. We still have to work out the details, but he wants to film here in town."

Rick crossed his arms. "I more than want it. I'm going to have it or there will be no show."

Lizzie accepted the knife from his mom. She started to chop the tomato. "I understand that you want to avoid what happened last time, but there are certain requirements, restrictions, that the show places not only on the contestants, but—"

He held up one hand. "Don't try to produce me right now, Lizzie." He turned back to his mom. "When are you going to stop worrying about me?"

She tried to give him a smile, but he could see what it cost her. "You'll always be my baby."

He hugged her and rubbed her back. "Someday you'll have to trust me to make big-boy decisions."

"What's wrong?"

Rick turned to Dan, who had entered the kitchen, shrugged out of his suit coat and hung it on the back of a stool. "Mom's worried about me doing the show again."

Dan rolled his eyes and crossed his arms over his chest. "So you're really going to do it."

"Yes, Dan. I think so." He glanced at Lizzie, who watched his reaction closely. "I'm almost positive." He turned back to his mom. "I don't want to make the same mistakes, so that's why we're doing the show here. You'll get to know all the women throughout the whole process. And give me advice." He turned to face Dan. "When I ask for it."

"Taping here means that we can showcase Allyn Pickles even more. Make a national audience aware of what we offer." His mercenary brother's eyes glazed over with the possibilities, and Rick sighed and patted his mom's arm.

"I'll set the table, and we can discuss this over dinner. Okay?"

She nodded, but he could tell she wasn't really there. He walked to the cupboard and pulled out dishes and glasses, then disappeared into the dining room. It was mindless work, but that was what he needed to clear his mind.

"What happened after the show last time?"

Rick glanced up from a dinner plate and frowned at Lizzie, who stood in the doorway watching him. "You're supposed to be making a salad."

"Your mom took over, so I came in here to talk to you."

He finished placing the plates on the table and turned to the sideboard drawer where his mom kept the cloth napkins. He folded four and walked around the table, placing them where they belonged next to each plate. "I don't need to talk."

"What happened that's got your mom so scared for you to do this show?"

She stepped in front of him so that he had to look at her or push her out of his way. He chose to look at her. "It's complicated."

"That's my response. Get your own."

He sighed and moved around her to retrieve the silverware from the sideboard. He pulled out four forks, four spoons and four knives, then slammed the drawer shut and braced his hands on either side of him. "It wasn't good."

She placed a hand on his shoulder. "I want you to do this show, but not if it's going to hurt you."

He looked down at her soft mouth. "You want your job. Dan wants his publicity. The town needs the money. Do I really have a choice?"

"You always have a choice, Rick." She dropped her hand but kept her gaze on his. "Tell me what happened last time."

He closed his eyes. "Some people run when trouble comes. Others throw themselves into work." He opened his eyes and saw her watching him, a frown marring her brow. He might as well tell her the whole story, because his family would if he didn't. "I retreated to my family's cottage. Didn't go out. Didn't work. Cut myself off from everybody and everything. I couldn't sleep, wouldn't eat. I became disoriented and got behind the wheel of my car to drive back home. I didn't wake up until I hit a tree. After crushing my knee in the accident, I lost even my dream of playing with the pros." He straightened his shoulders and cleared his throat. "But I won't let it happen again. And you're going to help me make sure of that."

CHAPTER FIVE

By February, Lake Mildred was ready, poised on the brink of either publicity or infamy. Rick poured another round of coffee for his regulars and tried to maintain his good mood despite their incessant questions.

Would the production crew hire local people to help out as they had agreed in the contract? Rick knew they would and had signed papers to make it so. Lizzie had promised, and he knew he could trust her.

Would the show bring more tourists in? Probably, depending on the ratings. If it was popular, they'd want to come experience the place for themselves. If it ended as it had before, they'd want to come gawk at the man destined to be alone.

Would he find a wife? He prayed that he would. There was no other option on this. Either he met the woman meant to be his wife or he'd choose someone who was close enough to his list of expectations and hope that love would grow between them. He wearied of going to bed alone, waking up alone. He didn't want to keep living with only his thoughts.

He replaced the coffee carafe in the machine and leaned on the counter. Ernesto, the cook, came out from the kitchen and joined him. "You ready to give this all up?"

Rick snorted and glanced around the dining room. "It's only for a couple of months. Don't get used to not having me here."

"You're the lifeblood here at the diner. In the community." Ernesto put a hand on his shoulder. "What you're doing for us now is..." His voice broke, and he shook his head.

"I'm not a savior, Ern." Rick pushed himself off the counter and went to stand at the front window, watching as road crews filled in potholes that had cropped up after each thaw. There had been talk of repaving, but it wasn't sound fiscal judgment in the winter.

But it was more than the potholes being filled. Rick had added fancy coffee drinks to his menu, and a bright copper espresso machine had arrived that he'd had to learn and teach his staff to use. Lizzie said it would draw the crew and contestants in like mosquitoes to a bug zapper. Outside the diner, the community task force had repainted benches, shored up docks and ordered more road salt for the snow that hadn't stopped since New Year's Day.

All so he could find a wife and Lizzie could keep her job.

Rick turned away from the window and walked back into the kitchen. Freshly baked cakes lined the stainless-steel counters, cooling and waiting for frosting.

The phone rang, but Rick let Ernesto answer it by the cash register. Probably another take-out order. Or one more reservation for the viewing party on Valentine's Day. While Rick met the future Mrs. Allyn, and twenty-three other beautiful women, at a huge catered party at the Veterans of Foreign Wars hall, the town would gather at the diner to watch it unfold on live television.

Ernesto opened the swinging door and handed him the phone. He stared at it, then put it up to his ear. "Rick Allyn."

"Do you always answer your phone so formally?"

He grinned at the familiar voice. "Lizzie."

"You're never going to call me Elizabeth, are you?" She sighed over the line, making his smile wider. "Do you have plans tonight?"

"If you're here and available for dinner, my schedule is free."

She chuckled. "I'll take you up on dinner.

The plane just landed, and my stomach is demanding real food. We need to go over some things before my crew arrives tomorrow."

His skin warmed, and he held the phone tighter. "You're really here? I won't have to settle for talking on the phone and picturing you hanging on my every word on the other side of the country?"

"We can even sit side by side if you want." She muttered to someone on her end of the phone, then sighed. "They didn't save my convertible for me. Can you believe it?"

"It's winter, Lizzie. Get the four-wheel-drive SUV with heated seats. Trust me." He glanced through the cutout window into the diner, where people tried to catch a peek of him. "You won't believe the changes in town since you were here last."

They hung up with plans to meet at the diner once she had checked in at the hotel where she and some of the crew would stay.

To KILL TIME, Rick buzzed through his apartment, making sure it looked presentable. He'd been raised to keep a tidy room, but it had never been easy for him. He liked his things out and around him. He knew Lizzie wouldn't want to be surrounded by stacks of newspaper with sports stats. His baseball mitt sat on the kitchen table though it hadn't been used in months. The comforter of his bed was dragging half on the floor.

A tapping on the apartment floor brought Rick's attention back to the present. Ernesto's signal that Lizzie had arrived at the diner. He double-checked the tiny space, then took the stairs to the kitchen two at a time. Ernesto motioned with his head to the dining room. Rick took a deep breath and pushed open the swinging door.

Lizzie wasn't alone.

A man stood next to her with a large bag over one shoulder and a camera in the other hand. They didn't hear Rick approach over their discussion about where to set the camera up for the first interview.

Cameras and interviews already? His stomach started to ache. "What happened to dinner with real food?"

Lizzie turned and smiled. "Talk first, eat later. We need to get these one-on-one discussions finished before the live premiere."

He nodded, but the ball in the pit of his stomach grew rather than shrunk. "One-on-ones. I remember those."

"Good." She pointed to the back booth. "We could set up there, make it look intimate. Charlie?"

The guy with the camera looked at the fluorescent lighting in the diner and shook his head. "Intimacy? Not with this lighting. Is there somewhere else we could do this?"

Rick thought of all the cleaning he had done and gave a short nod. "My apartment's upstairs. It's not big, but it would give that intimate feeling you want." He motioned to follow him through the kitchen and up the stairs. He paused only once, when Ernesto bobbed his head to the pie that was cooling on the counter.

Once upstairs, Rick watched Lizzie survey his domain, wondering about her thoughts. It was small but tidy. Exactly what he needed. A worn-out sleeper sofa that had graced the family room growing up. A big-screen television. The place wouldn't win any design awards, but he liked it. This was home.

Charlie set up in the living area so that Rick could sit in the recliner while Lizzie lobbed questions from the sofa. When he left to retrieve more lights from the SUV, Rick turned to Lizzie. "I never liked these."

"I remember." She nodded and started ticking items off on her fingers. "We have a lot to do and less than a week to do it. We've had a crew refurbishing the two houses you found for the women to stay in. As it is, they'll finish them up only hours before the contestants arrive. I have a laundry list of items to locate or buy, interviews to schedule and film, your family to prep." She closed her hand in a fist. "We need to multitask, which means interviews and dinner tonight."

"Didn't you plan on prepping me for this interview?" He shook his head at the edge in his voice. He was disappointed. He'd admit it. Tonight was supposed to be about two friends catching up on the past few months. Not a Q&A in front of a third party. "I was hoping we could relax tonight before the real work starts."

"It's been nothing but work since I landed in L.A. last August." She consulted her clipboard, then set it aside. Fully looked at him for the first time. "Are you okay?"

He shrugged, pretending that it was no big deal. "Honestly? No. I've been nervous since Christmas. Might have to stock up on the pink stuff to calm my stomach." He chuckled. "Other than that, I'm great."

"You'll be fine. Remember—you're the one in charge this time." She picked up her clipboard again and glanced at it. "Except for one tiny thing."

He frowned. "How tiny?"

She looked up at him. "I'm the executive

producer. So I'm really the one who calls the shots." She stood up when Charlie entered the room. "Let's get set up and knock off some of these interviews. Then dinner. And I'll be spending the rest of the evening in the editing bay." She consulted her notes. "I thought we'd tape the segments about your initial impressions of what you're looking for in a true love. Then also discuss what went wrong last time."

"Nothing like ripping off that bandage." He pinched the bridge of his nose. "Fine. Let's get it over with."

ELIZABETH THUMBED THROUGH her cards while Charlie checked the light levels on Rick. She wouldn't show up on camera, so she was worried less about what she looked like. However, this was the audience's first look at Rick since his humiliation five years ago. He needed to look good. Confident. Ready to find love again.

Her schedule had the crew arriving tomorrow afternoon, then a short preproduction meeting followed by a tour of the town and facilities. Party plans needed to be finalized. The female contestants arrived two days after that, which meant making sure the houses were ready. Devon would turn up the day after the contestants for the final walk-throughs and rehearsals, and before she could sneeze they'd be airing live.

She rested her head on the back of the sofa and closed her eyes. She thrived on the adrenaline of getting a show off the ground, but sometimes she wondered what it would be like to have a job that began at nine and finished at five. What would it be like to live a normal life?

"We're ready, E."

She lifted her head, opened her eyes and prayed that this interview would start things off right.

Charlie handed Rick a clapboard with the identifying information on it: take number, scene number, location and producer. It might seem like a cliché to the viewing audience, but it was vital to the editors who pieced the show together from interviews like this. She read off the information, then said, "Roll cameras." She adjusted her note cards one more time. She glanced at Rick. "Ready?"

He couldn't even look at her; he focused on something beyond her against the wall. "Doesn't really matter, does it?"

She held a finger up to Charlie and leaned toward Rick. "Close your eyes." He did after a long moment, but he looked as if he didn't want to. She closed her eyes, as well. "Now, picture the woman you want to spend your life with. Not her physical features, but what she could add to your life. To enrich it. Make it sweeter. What would she be like?"

She opened her eyes and looked at the man before her. She swallowed hard. Those weren't questions she was ready to answer herself. "Okay. Now open your eyes." She caught her breath. "Rick, what are you looking for in a true love?"

"My true love is a woman who believes in me." He smiled. "Even when I'm doing something she thinks is absolutely crazy. A woman who sees me as I am and loves me anyway. Someone who can turn my life upside down, yet make it better. I want a partner. An equal, but someone who's more than me, like a complement to what I'm not. I want us to be a team. An unbeatable one."

Elizabeth nodded and made notes. Ideas for other questions that would further probe his answers. "Have you ever met anyone like that?"

He stared down at his hands, then back at her. "I thought I had, but maybe I was wrong."

"Maybe? Do you mean Brandy?"

He shrugged. "She wanted someone else."

Charlie grunted and kept filming. Elizabeth turned to the next card. "Why do you think that things didn't work out last time? And have you learned from your mistakes?"

"Things didn't work because I was too immature. I didn't know what I really wanted, but I grabbed on to something that looked awfully close." He settled farther into his chair and rested his ankle on his other knee. "I've learned about myself in the past five years. I know what I want. And I also know that I'm willing to work on finding it."

She nodded and made more notes, not really paying attention. Was she setting him up for disappointment? Sure, the show was based on the belief in love at first sight (or at least by the sixth week), and as producer of that show, she believed it. Almost. But she'd seen all the relationships forged on her show end in separation. What did that say for true love?

She turned to Charlie. "Cut." She stood up and moved to the front door. "Let's take a quick break, Charlie. Get something to eat. Rick, you're doing great. Just keep concentrating on the mental picture of your true love." She opened the door. "I'll be right back."

She walked down the stairs and found the cook in the kitchen. He flipped burgers and checked orders without a second thought. He was as attuned to his job as she was to hers. She gave the cook a smile. "Hi, Ernesto."

He nodded at her. "Everything okay?"

"Couldn't be better." She looked around for one of the plastic tumblers and filled it with cold water from the tap. Rick didn't stock his diner with designer bottled water. Or he hadn't until she'd told him he should for the crew and contestants. She strode to the walk-in and found five cases of bottled water cooling on the shelves.

Just another reminder of how she was turning his normal life inside out. But was it for the better?

She turned back and found Ernesto watching her. "Rick get the espresso machine I sent?"

He turned back to his grill. "More buttons on that thing than you need to launch the space shuttle."

"He'll get good use out of it. Especially for the next couple of weeks." She leaned against the counter. Tried to ignore the stomach grumblings that the aroma of the burgers on the grill caused.

"And after that, what happens?"

Elizabeth shrugged. "It's his to keep."

Ernesto and shook his head at her. He

pointed to the aprons hanging up. "Dishes need washing if you got time."

She held up her hands. "They've finally recovered since the last time, but I appreciate the invitation." Maybe she'd offer to buy an industrial dishwasher for the diner, too. "We've got more work to do upstairs."

"Work."

She nodded. "Interviews. Plotting how the show will go once the women arrive. Making plans."

He pointed to a cloth-covered pie. "I made dessert. You take it to him?"

She nodded. "Sure." She started to walk back up the stairs but turned back. "You don't like me."

"I don't know you, but Rick does." He looked up at her. "He likes you."

She thought of Rick and felt her cheeks warm. "I know. He's become a good friend."

"But I don't like people who hurt my friends."

"I wouldn't, either." She took her glass of water and the pie up the stairs so they could finish filming and she could call it a night and return to her room to work. That was what she needed to get through these doubts. More work.

And less thinking.

RICK ADJUSTED HIS SHIRT and glanced at Charlie, who adjusted the lights one more time even though they'd been perfect a moment ago. "So you like the snow?"

The cameraman shrugged. "I grew up in Florida. Never saw much of it."

"That's gonna change." Rick chuckled and thought of how most of the crew would be experiencing firsts here, too. "It's all part of the Michigan experience."

Charlie grunted. Obviously not much for conversation. Rick tapped his fingers on his knee while he waited for Lizzie to return. What was taking her so long anyway? The sooner they finished these interviews, the better as far as he was concerned. "How was your trip here?"

"Fine."

Okay. Thankfully, Lizzie returned with Ernesto's pie in one hand. "I brought some dessert."

Rick stood and took the pie from her. "Dessert before dinner? Perfect. I'll serve."

He found three plates and cut generous pieces, then handed them out. "I could use a break. You guys?"

Charlie accepted his plate of pie and a fork. Took a bite and closed his eyes. "You made this?"

"I wish. I don't have the pie gene." He handed Lizzie her plate and fork. "Ernesto is the genius here."

They ate silently for a moment, reveling in the caramel and apples. Rick stood. "I could make us coffee?"

Charlie held up one hand. "Just water for me."

"I'll take a cup." Lizzie paused in eating. "I'm going to need new clothes if I eat like this every day while we're here."

"You know what my mom would say about that." He chuckled and walked into his kitchen area to fill the coffee carafe. "I only have milk up here."

Charlie looked between the two of them. "Am I missing something?"

"Rick has the bad habit of remembering what everyone likes to eat and drink." Lizzie shook her head. "It may work for the diner, but how am I going to use that to find you a wife?"

"Does everything have to be about that?" Rick scooped coffee into the filter basket, then swung it shut and started the machine. "I'm more than the diner. More than finding a wife."

"Not for the next couple of months." Lizzie balanced her plate of pie on her knee and used her fork to point at Rick. "You need to live, eat and breathe the show. Nothing is more important."

And make his life just like hers? Rick joined them in the living room area. "I'm not saying it's not important. It's just not everything."

"It should be."

Rick crossed his arms over his chest. "Well, I'm not you." He handed the cameraman a glass of water. Okay, so he let the diner consume his life. It was better than being alone. Right?

Charlie cleared his throat as he accepted the drink. "Do I need to be here for this fight?"

Lizzie whipped her head around at him. "We're not fighting. We're discussing."

"Right." Charlie held his hands up in surrender. "My bad." He stayed silent and continued to eat his pie.

Rick chuckled and returned to the kitchen counter. He'd missed this bantering. Missed Lizzie more than he'd realized.

He shook his head and prepared two cups of coffee before turning back to the two, who watched him. "No more discussing. Let's finish these interviews."

Lizzie smiled in response. "Now, that's what I'm talking about."

RICK'S MOM GREETED Rick and the crew when they arrived at the house. He held the door open as they unloaded the van of the lights, cameras and other equipment. He joined them in the family room, where his mom had laid a fire. It looked cozy. Homey. And the audience would want to join the family who lived here.

He adjusted the pictures on the mantel and glanced over his shoulder to find his mom watching him. She turned in a circle. The hem of her dress swished around her legs. "How do I look?"

He walked to her and kissed her cheek. "Fabulous. Like always." He turned in a circle. "And me?"

She patted his cheek and walked into the adjoining kitchen. Took a plate of cookies from the counter. "I made these for the crew."

"They're gonna love you for this." He grabbed one before she could slap his hand. "Are you ready for this? Because I'm not sure I am."

She knit her eyebrows together and let out a big sigh. "Not exactly the time to be having doubts." She put her arm around his waist. "But we can get through this together. We'll find you the perfect wife. And the perfect mother of my grandchildren."

Rick groaned. "Let's get to the wedding before we start discussing kids, okay?" Talk about jumping ahead. Though the thought of a couple of rug rats running around the old house made him smile. He could imagine future holidays surrounded by his wife and kids. "Okay, I'm ready for this."

Lizzie joined them in the kitchen. "Good. Because we're ready, too." She glanced at the plate of cookies. "Peanut butter?"

His mom held out the plate. "Help yourself, dear."

"I really shouldn't." But she took one and bit into it. "These are too good to resist, though. Thank you. The crew will love you."

"That's what I said." Rick took another cookie, but this time his mom did slap his hand. "What? I was going to share."

Lizzie looked between them. "Are you two always like this? Close? Affectionate?"

His mom examined his producer for a long moment. "You wanted natural. That's what you're getting. What is your family like?"

Lizzie shoved the rest of the cookie in her mouth. Rick knew her family life was hardly idyllic, but the avoidance spoke more than actual words might. He put his arm around his mom. "Why don't we give the cookies to the crew and get set up in the family room? Once we finish the interviews, we can have the salads and wraps I brought for lunch."

"And you blame me for trying to fatten everyone up." His mom took the cookie plate into the family room, where she was cheered by the crew.

Rick glanced at Lizzie. "You okay?"

She nodded, but her cheeks burned and the rest of her face paled. "Family is one of those touchy topics."

He placed a hand on her shoulder. "I know." He might not know the details, but he knew her reaction when families were brought up. So he changed the subject. "Dan's been upstairs all morning, trying to decide on what to wear. Suddenly he's nervous about being on camera."

"He's something else."

Dan appeared in the doorway of the kitchen. "Did I hear my name?" He walked forward and turned around. "Did I choose the right suit?"

Rick choked back his laughter as Lizzie stared at his older brother. Dan wore a red blazer, white shirt and navy pants with an American flag tie. He looked as if he was running for office rather than supporting his brother on a reality show. Rick knew he wouldn't wear that on-screen, just like he knew Dan had brought another suit. Lizzie, on the other hand, opened and closed her mouth. Probably trying to figure out the right words to say and the right way to say them. Rick's mom walked into the kitchen and shook her head. "Go change, Dan. We don't have all day."

Rick burst into laughter as Dan winked at Lizzie and left the room. She whirled and glared at Rick. "He wasn't serious?"

Rick shook his head and wiped his eyes. "You should have seen your face."

His mom thrust out a tray with coffee cups, sugar and creamer on it. "Stop torturing the girl and make yourself useful."

He obeyed, taking the coffee to the crew before returning to the kitchen to find Lizzie and his mom chatting about the filming schedule. Dan came into the kitchen wearing a navy suit but no tie. He held the flag tie in one hand, a yellow one in the other. "Tie or no tie?"

Lizzie turned and nodded at him. "Much better. No tie. Let's keep it casual."

Dan glanced at Rick, who wore a light blue sweater and khakis. "Or too casual."

"I've done these before. You're going to

want casual after hours of filming." Rick leaned on the counter. "But the suit looks good on you."

Lizzie sighed. "Why don't we get started? The sooner we do, the sooner we finish." She grabbed the clipboard she'd left on the kitchen counter. "And the sooner we can find you your wife." She walked toward the family room, then turned. "Just think. You'll be meeting your wife in two days."

Rick tried to smile despite the growing knot of dread in his stomach.

CHAPTER SIX

RICK ADJUSTED HIS TIE and winced when Lizzie walked up to him, slapping his hands away. "You're going to ruin all my work."

"I didn't realize being producer meant dressing your star." He tipped his head back so she could get closer to straighten the tie.

"My job is to make sure this all goes the way it's supposed to." She smoothed it down his chest and patted it softly. "There. Perfect."

Rick took her hand in his and let them rest against his chest. "Do you think Mrs. Allyn could be here?"

"Your mother's out there somewhere." When he opened his mouth to protest, she winked and squeezed his hand. "Your future wife is definitely here. What do you think?"

"I hope so." He had twenty-four women waiting in the VFW hall, there for the sole purpose of meeting him. Trying to win his affection. His future wife could be out in that room while he stayed in the kitchen waiting for his cue. He was ready.

Wasn't he?

One of the production assistants entered the kitchen. "They're ready for you in five minutes."

Rick dropped Lizzie's hand and peered into her face. Was that concern looming behind those green eyes? "Showtime already?"

She nodded and grabbed her clipboard from the counter behind them. "We've aired your interview about what you're looking for, and they're finishing each of the women's bios. We'll come back from commercial break, and then you're on."

Rick adjusted the tie once more. "It's hard to breathe with this thing on."

"The tie is fine. It's you that's having problems." She reached up and laid it smooth again. "Your idea about a Valentine's dance with the seniors from the nursing home was inspired. I couldn't have planned it better myself."

Rick felt his cheeks warm. He looked down at his feet, which were covered in uncomfortable leather dress shoes. "I remember how pleased as punch my grandpa was when a young thing paid him some attention after Grandma died."

"Seeing the women in this light is going to really help the audience perception. Maybe give us less drama than the catfights they might expect. But why not show off a better side of humanity, right?" She took a deep breath. "We needed to change the focus of the show after the last producer left, and I think you might be what we need."

"Don't give me all the credit, Ms. Executive Producer." He glanced over her shoulder at the line of studio personnel watching them. "I don't remember all the suits the last time I did this."

She leaned in closer and dropped the volume of her voice. "They want to make sure I do my new job right, I guess. Don't let it worry you. I got this." She winked at him, and the previous nervousness fled from her demeanor. He could tell that she was now in the zone.

He nodded. So was he.

ELIZABETH ADJUSTED RICK'S microphone and checked the levels to make sure it was picking up sound. One of her assistants had already done it, but her job meant that she double- and triple-checked anything and everything. "Talk clearly, but don't shout. The mike is strong enough to pick up even a whisper." She picked up an earpiece from the counter behind her and handed it to him. "Take this.

If you get lost or tongue-tied, I can guide you through."

He shook his head and tried to hand it back. "And I thought we were having a nice moment. No."

She sighed, knowing that she could lose this battle, and she never lost. "Just in case. I'll be your Cyrano."

Again, he handed it back to her. "We're doing this my way. And we're keeping it real."

She groaned and wanted to stamp her heels. Unfortunately, she didn't think that would serve her cause. "Real isn't selling on TV."

"We have an agreement." He closed her hand on the earpiece, and this time she accepted it. "I don't need you, but thanks."

She smiled up into his eyes. "But you do need me. Otherwise we wouldn't both be here again."

"Funny." He took a few deep breaths. "Okay, let's do this. I'm ready."

Charlie walked by them with his handheld camera. "Network says we're back from commercial in ten."

Rick's bravado paled slightly. Elizabeth adjusted his tie again. She wasn't about to lose her star now. "Remember. They're here because of you. They want your attention. They want your love. You don't have to be anything but who you really are." She turned him around, then pushed him through the swinging doors into the hall. "Knock 'em out."

RICK BLINKED at the bright lights and couldn't see one face in the crowd that he knew was gathered in front of them. He held up a hand to shield his eyes from the glare. "I know they talk about the bright lights of fame, but this is a bit much."

He heard a few chuckles. *Score.* "Happy Valentine's Day, everyone. And welcome to Lake Mildred." He'd had a speech all prepared, but the words failed to come to mind. Instead he rubbed his hands together. "Let's get this party going with an oldie but goody."

He turned and nodded toward the director, who started the band playing a slow tune popular when his parents had been young and dating. Good choice. He walked into the crowd and found a woman who had to be eighty years young. "Care for this dance?"

She tittered and blushed as he helped her walk out onto the dance floor and started to sway slowly while she hung on to her walker. "You taught ninth-grade English, right?"

The older woman nodded. "You always were the charmer, Ricky."

A young woman with more hair than dress

approached them. She beamed widely at them. "Mind if I join you both?"

And so the group dance began. Some of the women gathered the seniors to do a slow-moving train around the room, while others rounded them up in groups of two and three to dance. Rick looked around the room. He turned back to his dancing partners. "I think this is the beginning of something special, don't you?"

They swayed until the end of the song, then clapped politely to the band. Lizzie walked out into the hall and called, "Cut. Great job, everyone. We'll be back from commercial in two. In the meantime, enjoy the refreshments and another song from Jimmy's band."

She walked toward Rick and gave him a soft clap of her hands. "Good work. Keep it up." She looked around the room. "Find your wife yet?"

"You should have been a comedian."

She wrinkled her nose. "Not enough money in it. I'd much rather be the lowly producer." She leaned in to him. "Your mom called and said the crowd at the diner loves it so far."

Rick nodded. "Good." He adjusted his tie and tried to swallow.

"Relax." She smoothed his tie. "We're back

in thirty." She started to walk away, then turned and winked at him. "Just act natural."

Natural. Right. He could do that.

As they returned from commercial, everyone started to dance to a faster tune. One of the seniors pulled a young woman onto the dance floor and taught her how to do the hustle. Elizabeth wilted in relief in the kitchen, where they'd set up the production hub. She watched the playback screen as her show sparked to life. Inspired idea, really.

Devon approached her, snagging a canapé from a tray meant for the guests. "So far, so good."

Elizabeth kept her eyes on the monitor. "I promised you ratings gold. And I deliver on my promises."

"So you keep saying." He swallowed the appetizer, then stepped between her and the monitor. "But this Goody Two-shoes act can't last. Not if we want to keep our viewers. They're expecting catfights. Backstabbing. And gossip galore about what's really going on behind the cameras." He glanced back at the monitor. "That's what sells."

"Romance sells. Not smut. But somehow we've forgotten that." She nudged him aside as she watched Rick talking to a few of the women at the edge of the room. They looked young. Happy. Their whole lives ahead of them. "Bob liked keeping it dirty, and the show suffered. We're trying something new."

"We'll see how long the audience buys the Osmond-family vibe before turning on you." He snatched a couple more appetizers. "I'm going back to the hotel."

"You can depend on me, Devon." She turned back to the monitor. "They're going to love Rick. And everything he is."

He grunted in response and left the room, followed by a handful of his assistants who told him what he wanted to hear.

That was fine. She was going to make great television by giving America a bachelor who could run for president if he wanted. A man of character. Integrity. And she'd do it without stooping to the dirty tricks her predecessor had tried. Good television didn't have to mean playing to the lowest common denominator. It could mean showing the best of what the human race had to offer.

While she dreamed quixotically of a better future for pop culture, Rick entered the room. "I think we have a problem. Mr. Jackson's heart stopped."

RICK RAN BACK into the hall with Lizzie close behind him. One of the young women kneeled on the floor next to Mr. Jackson. "Harry, can you hear me?" She checked his vitals and glanced up at them. "He's unresponsive."

Rick marveled at her quick response to help. "You're a doctor?"

"Labor and delivery nurse." The blonde in the navy evening gown began compressions. "Never thought my medical training would come in handy here. Told myself that doing the show would be a nice break." She paused and started to blow into Mr. Jackson's mouth.

Rick kneeled beside her and watched for his chest to move. "What can I do?"

"Time my compressions." She glanced behind them at the wall of people and turned to Lizzie. "Think you can get them to give us some room?"

Lizzie nodded and started crowd control while Rick watched this amazing woman will the old man back to life. She closed her mouth around his and blew air into his lungs. Paused. Blew again. And sighed when the man started breathing on his own.

Mr. Jackson looked up at her. "Are you an angel?"

The young woman shook her head, but Rick had to disagree. He found himself grinning at her.

She moved slightly out of the way as paramedics entered the room with a gurney. Rick stood and held his hand out to her and helped her to her feet.

Here's a woman any man could fall for without hesitation.

"I'm Rick."

"I know. I'm Melissa."

He leaned in closer. "Are you sure it's not Missy?"

She blushed and looked down at the floor. It only made her look more lovely. "Only my dad calls me that."

Rick held out his hand to her again. "Well, Missy, it's an absolute pleasure to meet you."

The moment broke when the paramedics moved them so they could take Mr. Jackson out to the waiting ambulance. Rick watched, debating whether he should go with them. He turned back to Melissa. "I think I should…" He motioned to the door.

She nodded. "You'll let me know how he is."

Rick leaned over and kissed her cheek. "You betcha."

ELIZABETH NURSED a coffee that had long grown cold as she waited in the emergency room lobby for word on Mr. Jackson. A slight dip in the Naugahyde sofa told her Rick had joined her. He sighed. "Some night, huh?"

She nodded and kept her focus on the television tuned to the late show. "We made the eleven o'clock broadcast."

"Already? But it just happened."

Elizabeth shrugged and took a sip of coffee. Shivered at the bitterness. "It happened on live television." Her phone buzzed on the sofa between them. "That's been going off the hook ever since."

Rick picked up the phone and glanced at the caller ID. "It's a local number."

"You could answer it and give them a quote." She turned and finally looked at him. His tie was loosened and askew. His hair looked as if he'd run his hands through it more than once. He looked rumpled. Exactly the way she felt. "They're going to want to know why it took us eleven minutes to get an ambulance. Why we continued to film as a man fought for his life."

Rick groaned and ran his hands through his hair. "I didn't think of the cameras. I was focused on helping Harry."

"That's a great sound bite, but you should be prepared for some backlash." Elizabeth rose to her feet and walked to the trash can to toss her coffee cup inside. She turned back to Rick. "I couldn't have planned what happened. I couldn't have known…"

Rick approached her and placed a hand on her shoulder. "No one could have."

"But I should have. It's my job to prepare for the unknown." She wrapped her arms around her middle. "Tonight I failed."

Rick leaned down to look directly into her eyes. "Mr. Jackson is going to live. That's what's important here. He's going to get another chance."

"Through no fault of my own." She walked back to the sofa and collapsed on it. She rested her neck on the back and shook her head from side to side. "I should have known. I should have—"

"Don't get stuck on the should haves, Lizzie. Stop beating up on yourself." Rick took a seat next to her and held her hand in his. "You did good."

"By casting a nurse?" She shivered again. "My job is not to just produce this show. It's to protect it. At all costs. When you mentioned the nursing home, I should have planned all contingencies. Instead I got caught up on…" She glanced at him. "I wanted to find the perfect wife for you."

Rick gave her a tiny shrug. "Maybe you did."

Already? Elizabeth raised one eyebrow. He certainly hadn't wasted any time. "The nurse?"

"Missy."

She nodded. "She's cute. Sweet. Obviously good at her job." Elizabeth peered at him. "So I'm guessing she'll get the first immunity charm?"

"What can I say? I'm a sucker for a woman who can bring men back to life." He shrugged and leaned back on the sofa. "I'm only sorry we missed the first elimination tonight. Seemed kind of anticlimactic after the medical drama."

"We'll film it tomorrow and air it on our episode next week." She glanced over at the discarded clipboard. "Of course, it makes chaos out of my schedule, but…"

"You going to be okay now?"

She nodded slowly. "Mr. Jackson will be okay. You've found a possible wife already. And my job just got more interesting. What more could I want?"

AFTER THE PREVIOUS night's excitement, the dinner preceding the elimination ceremony seemed tame. Rick mingled among the women, looking into each one's eyes and asking himself if they should stay or go.

The cameras were everywhere, but he tried to ignore them. Better that he concentrate on other things. Like what the petite brunette was saying. "You were really great the last time you were on the show, right? And so I told my mom, 'I gotta meet this hunk.' And here I am."

Rick raised his eyebrows at that. "Hunk?"

The woman blushed and looked down at her hands. "Well, how else would you describe yourself?"

"You're very kind. Thanks." Give her a point for flattery. "So what is it you do in the real world, Becky?"

"I was a teacher before the layoffs."

Rick listened to her talk about how hard it had been. He'd seen enough of that in his town. He'd been fortunate to be born into a family that had become the largest employer in the county. Blessed enough to have inherited his job even after losing his baseball dreams. "It's hard out there."

"Things happen for a reason, though." She shrugged. "Maybe I had to lose my job so I could be free to come here."

Rick felt a shiver of unease. Blame the economy. Or loss of education funding. But don't use him as an excuse. Too much pressure.

A second woman joined them, followed by

a third. Soon he found himself surrounded by a group of beautiful women, only half of whose names he could remember. He glanced across the room and saw Missy watching them. He winked at her and smiled as she blushed. Maybe being the bachelor in charge of this game wasn't so bad.

"BEING THE BACHELOR is hard." Rick frowned at Elizabeth, who scratched another name off her clipboard. "I don't want to hurt any of these women. They're beautiful. Smart. Funny. But they're going to think something is wrong with them if I send them home."

"You're doing fine." She consulted the list. "You've got two more to reject."

Rick groaned and winced. "Exactly. They'll think I'm rejecting them. Think of what I'm doing to their psyches."

"You need to dial back on some of this melodrama, Mr. Allyn. They just met you." She glanced at the crew gathered in the garage of the home where they filmed. She'd spent days converting it into a production room but had failed to consider it wasn't insulated. She shivered and drew her parka tighter around her. "You click with some people and not others. That's how it goes."

"I hate to disappoint them." He peered

at the board with the women's pictures and names while she wondered what he was thinking.

"They'll get over it." She tapped her clipboard. "Two more."

He turned back to Elizabeth, his eyes bright. *Uh-oh.* She knew that look. "Couldn't we do a game and send the losers home?"

She shook her head. "And here I thought you wanted more control."

"I know." He read the names over and pointed to two of them. "I don't think I said two words to either of them." He sighed as if a burden had been lifted. "Now can I go back to my dessert?"

Elizabeth laughed, glad that the hard part was over. "Yes, it's your reward for being a good bachelor."

Rick glanced around the garage. "I'll stay out here for another minute, though."

Was he crazy? Stay out here in the cold? *Seriously. What is going on in his head?* "Don't want to face your adoring crowd?"

"More like wanting a few moments off camera." He shrugged. "Five years makes you forget what it's like to always be onstage. That everything you say and do is being recorded."

She sighed, relieved in a way that it wasn't

more serious. "Take your time, Rick. My crew is filming stuff for filler anyway."

Rick took a seat in her director's chair. "Any drama going on in the houses yet?"

They'd had plenty, and it hadn't been a week yet. The two houses she'd rented were side by side, allowing the women to move back and forth. And some to move again after roommate conflicts began. She crossed her arms across her chest. "I told you that we'd have some with only two bathrooms per house to split between them."

Rick laughed. "I'd love to see that."

"Well, you'll have to wait until it airs along with the audience." She pulled him up to his feet and pushed him toward the door. "Enough stalling. Enjoy your dessert. Then let's send some of them home."

He saluted her. "Fine. You are the boss."

And he'd better not forget it. She chuckled as he returned to the living room.

DESSERT ARRIVED, and they took that with coffee in the great room rather than being confined to their chairs in the dining room. Rick took the opportunity to mingle, smiling and laughing as he darted from one group to another.

He settled himself near the fireplace, mostly

because it was the one corner that was warm. Melissa, in a blue shiny dress, walked toward him. "Could we go outside for a moment?" she asked.

He nodded, then reached out and touched her bare shoulder. "Do you have a coat?"

She glanced around the room. "Not sure where it is right now."

Rick shrugged out of his coat and gave it to her. He opened the door to the patio, where fairy lights lit up the bare trees, and stepped outside. Even with his coat, the woman shivered, so Rick put his arm around her.

She looked up at him. "You really are a gentleman."

It was the way he'd been raised. Always put the other person ahead of yourself.

They sat on a stone bench after Rick wiped off the snow with one hand. He crossed his arms mostly to keep his warmth from completely escaping. He turned to Melissa. "You wanted to talk to me alone?" She shook slightly, her teeth chattering. He put both arms around her. "Is that better?"

"I wanted to let you know I'm here for the right reasons." She leaned in closer to him. "I'm not here for my career. Or to get publicity." She looked up into his face, and he could see the sincerity. "I saw the other show, and

I always felt you didn't deserve to be treated that way."

Rick took the chance to give her more than a passing glance. Her blond hair was cut short and sassy. Her eyes were deep brown pools that shone with trust and sincerity. And she had a small, compact body that told him she took care of herself. He rubbed her arm. "I'm glad you came out here with me, Melissa. I've wanted to talk to you since last night."

She laid her head on his shoulder. "It was pretty crazy."

"I already know you save lives, but what else do you do in your spare time?"

They shared a laugh. Rick thought he could use some of that in his life. Not that his life was joyless or lonely. He had friends. Family. The diner. But he wouldn't mind adding more laughter. Wasn't that part of the reason he was doing all this?

He squeezed her closer. "I hope you want to stay here for a while."

Melissa looked up at him. "I'd like that."

ELIZABETH SHOOK HER HEAD and made notes on her clipboard. She glanced behind her and saw Devon. "I think we found one of our finalists," he said.

"We'll see how it goes." She looked back

at the monitor and continued writing ideas to expand on later when she had some time.

Devon glared at her until she turned back to her notes. "Make sure she stays. They've got chemistry. And I want her in the final three, if not the finale. Got it?"

"We promised Rick that he would choose who moved on and who got sent home." She looked up. "You approved the contract yourself, so you know I can't make him do anything."

Devon leaned in closer to her. She tried not to flinch. "Looks like he trusts you. I'm sure there are ways you could influence him."

Elizabeth frowned. "What does that mean?"

"Am I the only one who thinks he shows chemistry with more than just Melissa?" Devon picked up his jacket from the back of the director's chair. "He likes you, so use it."

She shook her head. "I'm not going to use my friendship to get you what you want."

"You're on thin ice, Elizabeth. I'm not the only one who's noticed you're losing your edge with this one." He shrugged into the jacket and walked closer to her. "Prove to me you haven't lost it."

Elizabeth scowled and returned her gaze to the monitor, where she could see Rick returning to the house and chatting with a group of three women. Jumping through Devon's hoops was growing old. But she'd do it. Because what would she have without this job?

RICK STOOD AT THE FRONT of the room while the women gathered in groups of two and three. He had made a mental list of who would stay, but at the moment he couldn't recall a single name. The cameras ran, recording every word, every movement.

He hated this part of the show.

As a contestant, he'd waited to hear Brandy call his name. Waited to see if she felt the same connection he felt with her. Dreaded going home. Hoped he'd stay.

Now as the bachelor, he hated to dash anyone's dreams. Hated to be the one who would crush them by not calling their name. Dreaded the moment when he'd see the light of hope in their eyes fade.

He held twenty necklaces in his hand. Twenty women who would stay and continue to try to win his heart. Twenty chances to find love in the next three months.

He wiped his forehead. Denise, the makeup artist, added extra powder to his skin with her large pouf. "Sorry. I guess I'm more nervous than I thought."

She gave him a soft smile and continued

putting powder on his face. "Just breathe. You'll be fine."

He turned to Lizzie, who stood at the back of the room. He motioned for her to come talk to him. When she reached his side, he shook his head. "I'm not sure about my list now."

"Yes, you are. You just don't want to send anyone home." She brought up her clipboard and reviewed each name with him. "Can we do this now? You're wasting film."

He nodded and tried to swallow. Found it hard to breathe. He tugged at his tie, but Lizzie slapped his hands away. "Relax. You don't have connections with these four. It's not a judgment against them. It's just the way it is."

"They'll hate me."

"No, they won't." She smoothed his tie. "You bond with some people, not others. Fact of life." She put her hands on his shoulders and shook him slightly. "Let's do this. Like a bandage. Rip it off quick, okay?"

He nodded. She retreated to the back of the room as he cleared his throat. "Ladies, I appreciate your patience." He glanced down at the necklaces with heart charms, each one representing a possible future. "Melissa."

She stepped away from the group and approached him. He held up the necklace. "Will you accept my heart?"

"With pleasure." She dipped her head as he put the necklace around her neck. She kissed his cheek, then returned to the group.

The first necklace had been given out. With each name called, each necklace given out, the task became easier until he only had one in his hand. He glanced around the room and noticed the five women who still had bare necks. They shifted their weight. Looked at the others who already had a necklace with a bit of envy. Or kept their eyes on the floor so he couldn't see the hurt.

He held up the last necklace. "Mona."

A tall, willowy blonde approached him with a smirk. Almost as if to say she had known all along he'd pick her. "Mona, will you accept my heart?"

"Absolutely."

Rick placed the necklace around her neck. He leaned forward to kiss her cheek, but she turned and kissed him full on the mouth. Unexpected. But…kinda nice. He let his eyes drift closed for a moment.

Then stepped back. "Thanks."

Mona winked at him and returned to the group. Rick looked between those who hadn't received a necklace. "You are all beautiful and smart. And I'm sorry we didn't have a connection."

The four going home said their goodbyes and left in the waiting limousines; their luggage was already packed and loaded. Once they left, Rick handed out drinks to the twenty women who remained. He lifted his glass. "Here's to developing friendships. And finding love."

CHAPTER SEVEN

THE SPORTS COMPLEX buzzed with excitement. The regular patrons walked to the changing rooms but craned their necks to get a look at the celebrity surrounded by cameras and beautiful women dressed in softball uniforms. Elizabeth rolled her shoulders and tried to crack the tension out of her neck. She felt warm fingers trying to massage it instead.

"How did the premiere do?"

She closed her eyes and savored the feel of Rick's hands on her neck. It felt really good. She could stay like this all morning if she let herself.

Instead, she shrugged off his hands. "Shouldn't you be getting ready for the game?" She consulted the clipboard and checked off names as more women joined them from the changing rooms.

"Why? I'm not playing." He dropped his hands and walked around to face her. "Are they all here? No one dropped out because of our low ratings?"

"Who told you we got low ratings?" Elizabeth shook her head and muttered to herself. "I don't even have the numbers yet. How did the crew get them already?"

"It was a joke, Lizzie. Relax." He glanced at the cameras that pointed to the floor since they were turned off for the moment. "I don't have to be on-screen during the game, right?"

"We need reaction shots, so yeah, there will be a camera on you. But no microphone." She tapped her earpiece. "Okay, they're ready for us. Now, remember, if there's anyone on the losing team that you want to keep, just tell me. We'll make a deal or something."

Rick frowned. "That's not what we agreed to. Winning team gets immunity for the next elimination. Period."

She tried to keep the sarcasm out of her voice. "And what if Melissa is on the losing team?"

Rick smiled. "I think she's going to be around for a while. Don't you?"

Her bachelor was finding his match. Elizabeth should be thrilled. So why was part of her feeling anxious at the thought? Something to think about later. She glanced at Rick. *Much later.*

Rick flexed his muscles and rolled his

neck. "I don't think I'm sleeping very well. Are you?"

What kind of a question was that? "I'm sleeping fine. Why aren't you?"

"This finding a wife business is intense." He shrugged his shoulders. "And I'm having the strangest dreams. In fact, you were in my dream last night."

Elizabeth gulped and felt her cheeks burn. "Why are you dreaming about me?"

"It wasn't about you. But you were in it." Rick looked at the group of women. "I dreamed that I was on an auction block, and they were all bidding on me."

"Did I bid on you, too?"

Rick laughed and shook his head. "Oh, no. You were the auctioneer." He shrugged. "Guess it's not too far from reality, huh?"

"You've got more input than being sold to the highest bidder." She took a step closer and placed her hand on his shoulder. "This has to be about you and your choices. No one is pressuring you on who to keep around."

He dipped his head and glanced at her sideways. "You sure about that?"

She swallowed. Held her clipboard tight to her chest. "Positive." She patted him on the shoulder. "And don't let anyone talk you out of it. Not even me."

"Thanks." He left her and walked toward the field, where the game would be played.

Ignoring her confusing feelings, she strode into the midst of the chattering women. "Okay. Listen up. We're playing slow-pitch softball. Pinks versus greens. Three innings. Winners get to have dinner at Rick's diner plus immunity in the next elimination. Questions?" She glanced around quickly and, seeing no hands, blew her whistle. "I'll meet you on the field."

RICK SAT IN the bleachers while the teams took their places. He leaned back and tried to get comfortable. It was different sitting in the stands when he'd rather be out in the field. Made him restless. Not that he didn't watch sports. Most of his evenings were spent watching televised games or highlights from them. But he would much rather be the one playing.

Lizzie walked up to the bleachers to where he sat, then continued up two rows past his seat. He'd noticed how some of the contestants treated her as if she was some kind of interloper. He cupped his hands around his mouth. "Come on, girls."

"That isn't sexist at all."

He turned and smiled at her. "I can't exactly play favorites, so I'm cheering them all on."

She kept her eyes on her clipboard, punching things into her cell phone at the same time. Didn't she get confused working like that? "Do you love her?"

He didn't have to ask who she meant. "I don't know her enough yet. But I plan on spending a lot more time with her."

She looked up at him. "You want her to have the first one-on-one?"

He winked at her. "Oh, definitely. And make it superromantic. Over-the-top. You know. Flowers. Music. Good food. The kind of stuff you guys are known for." He looked back to the field as the first woman got up to bat. "And I want a group date, too. I need to get to know more of them better. I'm blanking on half their names."

He could hear the scratch of her pen as she made notes. "What did your mom say about the first night?"

He chuckled at the words his mom had used in describing some of the women. "She has her favorites already, but she's a good judge of character. That's why I wanted her to help me."

"Devon said the viewers like how the family is involved this time around."

Rick frowned and turned back to face her. "When did he find that out? We just aired."

"Hollywood works fast. He called me ten minutes ago with the numbers." She returned to her clipboard and made notations. Didn't look at him. "They're good."

He grimaced. "But not great."

"Do you care?"

He shrugged and turned his attention back to the game. If they wanted his reaction shots, he'd have to actually pay attention. "I know you care. What matters to me is that I meet the right woman."

"You met Melissa."

He considered this. He'd met each of the women for at least five minutes, but what could you tell in that amount of time? Sure, Melissa had intrigued him from the start. He wasn't ready to propose, but he wouldn't mind getting to know her better. See if she could be the right woman. "It's early."

She nodded. "Bachelor Kevin knew the first night which woman he would propose to."

"And how did that end? Right. He dumped her for an actress." He shook his head. "I hope I've learned some things since my last appearance. And I've been watching replays of the previous seasons. Trying to figure out what worked. What didn't."

She cocked her head to the side and peered at him. "Why?"

"It's kind of like a coach watching film of last week's game. Creating strategy for the next one." He clapped his hands, then cupped his mouth. "C'mon, batter."

Lizzie sighed and walked back down the bleachers, where she conferred with her camera operators when the umpire called the last out. The game with immunity at stake had been his idea. A way to spur competition.

He needed to make this time around different. He had to do this right. Had to do the right things to earn not only his true love but acceptance. From the television audience. From his family.

From Lizzie.

ELIZABETH KNEW NEXT to nothing about sports, but she knew what a score meant. The winning team jumped up and down, congratulating each other, while the losers looked dejected, some even pointing fingers at who had caused the loss. She approached them first. This was time to take care of business. Maybe even soothe some bruised egos. "Ladies, I'm sorry. We have a shuttle to take you back to the house, where dinner will be ready. This means you'll be at risk of going home at the next elimination. Again, I'm sorry."

She glanced around the team and sighed when she didn't see Melissa. At least one thing had gone right today. The ratings, however, told her that this was going to be an uphill struggle. They'd been good. Twelve million people had tuned in for the premiere, but they'd lost almost half of the audience after the first hour.

Why had they lost interest? Rick was a good guy. And a good-looking one to boot. He charmed not only the contestants but the audience. What had happened to make things fizzle? Was Devon right and the Goody Two-shoes act couldn't keep interest?

She made sure the losing team hit the showers first, then turned to talk to her winners. Well, Rick's winners. They still celebrated as she approached them and blew a whistle that made even the most ardent hockey fan wince. "Congratulations, ladies. Each of you has made it to the next phase of the competition. We're going to go over the schedule for the next few days. Then Rick will come over and offer his congratulations."

A hand shot up in the back. "Will there be immunity challenges all season?"

Elizabeth smiled. Obviously a fan of the show. "Yes. Rick will form favorites during the next few weeks, but this is to be a competition where hearts are at stake." Man, that sounded cheesy. Like reading from her own promotional copy. She cleared her throat. "After showers and changing, we'll meet at Rick's diner for an early dinner. You'll have free time until Tuesday night's group date. One lucky woman will have the first one-on-one date with Rick Monday afternoon. A box will arrive with her name tomorrow."

She started marking off items with her pen. "Feel free to use your off time to get to know the area. After all, you could end up married to Rick and living here. I have a list of church services if anyone is interested. Also lists of restaurants and shops. A shuttle will be available for a shopping trip tomorrow afternoon. Sign up on the board in the kitchen. Any other questions?"

Seeing no hands, she turned and motioned to Rick, who joined them on the field. He grinned widely and gave high fives to the victors. "That was a great game. Now huddle up." He motioned for them all to come in shoulder to shoulder and place their hands in the center. "On three, we'll shout 'True love.' Okay? One. Two. Three."

"True love!"

Even Elizabeth warmed.

CHAPTER EIGHT

RICK DOUBLE-CHECKED his ski equipment and waited. There was always a lot of waiting when filming a television show, even if the shoot took place on a snow-covered hill at the ski resort one town over. This one-on-one date plan had been Lizzie's. His choice had been tickets to a Detroit Pistons game, but this was still good. He liked skiing. Usually.

A woman dressed in pink attempted to ski toward him, but fell about halfway there. He rushed to help her to her feet again. "Sorry." Melissa looked up into his face. "I've never done this before."

"Then I'm glad I can teach you." He looked over at the crew Lizzie had sent with them. She herself was conveniently absent. Wasn't she supposed to oversee everything on this shoot? Even his first one-on-one date? They hadn't started filming yet, which gave him a few moments truly alone with his date.

Rick helped Melissa adjust the ski poles. "Did they go over everything with you? The microphone? The cameras?" She nodded but bit her lip. He put his hand on her shoulder to reassure her. "Don't worry. Like I said, I'll teach you. We're going to start on the bunny hill."

He helped her move her legs back and forth so that she had forward movement without falling on her face again. He liked that she wasn't afraid to try new things or even to fail. He might have balked at skiing for the first time on television, but Melissa was a good sport.

With cameras rolling, they spent an hour on the bunny hill until she felt comfortable enough to try something more challenging. Rick led her to the chairlift. As they rose into the sky, a camera operator turned in the seat ahead of them and filmed. He got the hint.

He leaned in closer to her. "So why did you decide to try out for the show?"

Melissa snagged a piece of hair away from her mouth. "I'm from a little town in Tennessee. Everyone in my town is either related by blood or marriage. Not many prospects, you know?"

Did he ever. That was one of the reasons he'd done this himself. "But why *True Love?*"

"My mom's a huge fan." She snuggled

into his side, either for warmth or something more, he didn't know. "It was her idea."

"Well, I'm glad you came." He rested his head on hers. "I think you're the first woman I've really connected with."

She tightened her grip and leaned closer. He cleared his throat and faced forward again. "After the last time—"

Melissa placed a hand on his arm. "You don't have to talk about it."

"I probably should. Good for the soul and all that." He glanced at her. "It's taken me over five years to get to the point where I'm open to letting someone in. Brandy…she…" He shrugged even though the camera probably couldn't see it through the layers of warm clothing. "I wanted to believe her. Wanted to trust that she loved me like I loved her."

Why was he going to that place? Hadn't he spent more than five years blocking it out? It was this show. It got to him. Made him think things, feel things. He shook his head and pulled Melissa closer. "I'm glad to have a second chance."

"There's something to be said for starting over." She rested her head on his shoulder.

Rick placed a kiss on the top of her fuzzy hat. "When we get up to the top here, we're going to push off the chair and to the right, okay?"

She nodded, and the spell of the snow and cold was broken. Rick settled farther into the chair. This was going to be okay.

ELIZABETH HURRIED to make sure all the details at the ski lodge were ready before Rick and Melissa arrived. She'd rented out the entire second floor so that they could have some privacy. A fire crackled in the fireplace. Huge overstuffed pillows were placed in front of it. Dozens of red and pink candles flickered. A vase of red and pink roses graced the dining table, where two place settings waited for an intimate dinner. It looked perfect.

So why was she still searching for flaws?

Elizabeth shook her head and consulted the clipboard that seemed to be glued to her hand lately. Even last night when she'd woken from her dream, she'd looked at her hand as if expecting her notes to be there, to tell her what to do next…every moment of her life laid out in black-and-white.

She sighed, wishing she had that kind of control. She tapped her earpiece. "How far out are they?"

"They're on the lift. You've got five minutes, give or take."

She nodded and checked everything again. It looked perfect.

Charlie had set up three cameras to capture the first intimate look at Rick. The one-on-one was more than him singling out a woman who might show up in the finale. It was about letting the audience in, as well. Giving them a taste of who he was and what he wanted.

She turned to Charlie. "We've got four minutes. What am I missing?"

Her cameraman chuckled and tested light levels once more. "I thought you never missed a thing."

"I don't because I ask my crew what I'm forgetting." She looked around the room. "If I was Melissa, would I fall under the spell of this room?"

"It looks perfect, E."

"Exactly. Looks, but doesn't feel." They couldn't pipe in music because that would interfere with editing later. They couldn't serve seafood because Melissa was allergic. She thrived on the couldn'ts of a shoot because she had to get creative. So why wasn't she feeling it this time? What was this scene missing?

Her.

Elizabeth turned as if someone had spoken. She shook her head. She was already losing it, and they still had twelve weeks of shooting and editing, then the live finale in Los Angeles in May. She tapped her earpiece. "How much longer?"

"Relax. They're heading up the stairs now."

She positioned herself in the back, and Charlie stood with a handheld camera near the entrance so they could film the couple's first reactions to the room. Everything was going according to plan.

So far.

Rick entered the room with Melissa, who made the appropriate oohs and aahs. Cliché, but Elizabeth would take it. Being a gentleman, Rick helped Melissa slip out of her coat and scarves, hat and mittens. He even held out a chair for her after they'd taken a tour of the room. Chivalry wasn't dead after all.

Servers immediately appeared with the first course, a steaming vegetable soup to warm the couple from the icy elements. From where she stood, it smelled wonderful. Her stomach growled, and she made a note to order a sandwich in a little bit. If she didn't write it down, she'd never remember.

Melissa reached for her soupspoon and took a tentative sip. "Wow."

Rick snapped his napkin open, laying it in his lap. "They have amazing chefs here."

Elizabeth closed her eyes and pushed her head against the wall. Sure, the couple had chemistry. Even mirrored each other's movements, which was a good sign. But chemistry only went so far. Elizabeth stepped forward. "Cut."

Rick and Melissa looked up at her as if just realizing they were being filmed. Good, but she didn't have time to revel in the fact that they were being natural in front of the cameras. She walked to the table and crouched between the two of them. The smell of the soup still did things to her stomach, but she concentrated on the task at hand. "The audience wants to see something special here. Give them a glimpse of yourself that you usually don't show anyone."

Rick chuckled. "What happened to being natural?"

"Your courtship is condensed into three months. We don't have time for natural." Elizabeth leaned in toward both of them. "Our audience expects to see romance. Sparks. Drama. And it's our job to give it to them."

Rick glanced around the room. "And this isn't romantic enough? All we're missing are winged cupids shooting arrows."

Melissa giggled at this while Elizabeth

rolled her eyes. "Great idea, but out of our budget. I'm being serious."

"So am I, Lizzie."

He dropped his spoon on the table, and it clattered to the floor. Elizabeth picked it up and handed it to one of the servers, who replaced it with a clean spoon. "I'm not asking the impossible here."

Rick thanked the server, then turned back to her. "All I'm saying is that I wouldn't do this in real life."

"Since when has reality TV been about real life?" She shook her head. "Rick, you need to give the audience a reason to care. Because right now? They're turning the channel to see what else is on."

"My love life is not for their viewing pleasure."

Elizabeth chuckled. "You're on *True Love,* so yeah, it is. You signed the contract. You made promises. Let me do my job."

Rick seemed to bristle slightly at this, but his calm composure took over. "You're right, Lizzie." He stood. "I need five minutes."

He pushed past her and out of the room. Once he was gone, she turned to Melissa. "When Rick comes back, tell him what you're hoping this show will bring into your life.

Show him the woman you are and the woman you want to be. Okay?"

Melissa nodded and turned in her seat to look in the direction Rick had gone. "Is he okay?"

"Don't worry. It's not you. It's me." She gave the other woman a reassuring smile, then walked off to find Rick. She waited outside the restroom door until he came out. He seemed surprised to see her.

"Can I have a moment?" she asked.

He crossed his arms over his chest and glanced around the hallway. "No cameras?"

"I told them to take a five-minute break." She sighed. "What's going on here?"

"Nothing's going on." He held up his arms so that they spanned the space around him. "I've given you complete access to my life. You're the one trying to manipulate this competition."

"It's my job to take care of the details. To create an atmosphere that invites intimacy and romance. All the things you asked for." She consulted her clipboard. "Candles. Flowers. Romantic meal. Check. Check. Check. What's your problem?"

Rick opened his mouth, then shut it. Closed his eyes and groaned. "I've been here. I've done this. And I believed it was all true. Only to find it wasn't."

"Melissa is not Brandy." He stopped fidgeting. Elizabeth stepped closer and put her hand on his shoulder. Now it made sense. Her star didn't want to get hurt again. "Is that what this is about? Don't let your past dictate your present."

"Okay, Oprah."

He joked with her, but he didn't appear any more relaxed. Elizabeth leaned in closer. "What can I do to make this easier for you?"

"I wish you could make guarantees, but..."

"I'll do my best." She gave him a quick hug. "I'll protect you as best I can, okay? Trust me."

She could feel him swallow. After a long moment, he nodded. "Okay. Tantrum over. Can I go back to my dinner? I'm starving."

He started to leave her, then turned back. "Thanks, Lizzie. You're a good friend." He returned to the dining cove.

Elizabeth took a moment to calm her nerves. Her heart beat at an alarming rate; her cheeks and chest burned. If she didn't know better, she'd think she was having a heart attack. Instead she inhaled deeply and returned to the room.

Charlie put up a finger and motioned to

the table where the couple sat. *Good.* They'd started filming without her. Melissa was telling Rick about her dreams for the future, which she hoped might include him.

AFTER THE FILMING, a car took Melissa and some of the crew back to the house. Lizzie lingered, settling up with the manager of the ski lodge while Charlie waited at the SUV. Lizzie handed the manager a check and turned to find Rick waiting by the front door, where it was warm. She sighed. "Did you need something else? Because I'm beat and looking forward to a long, hot bath. Room service. And some TV."

A vision of her bare shoulders rising above a tub full of bubbles, damp tendrils of hair clinging to her neck, flashed through his mind. He shook his head and held up his hands in innocence. "Only wanted to thank you for earlier."

She shrugged. "All part of my job. Good night."

He stepped in front of her and blocked the doorway. "There is something I wanted to talk to you about."

She closed her eyes and threw her head back. "I just want today to be over. Is that too much to ask?"

When she started walking past him, Rick reached out and grabbed her hand. "Lizzie. Please."

She stopped and turned to face him. "You have twenty seconds."

"I wanted to say I'm sorry." He looked at her, waiting. "Now is where you say you're sorry, too."

"I really don't have time for this." She walked past him, so he followed her outside.

"You can't try to make me feel things for these women. It doesn't matter how you manipulate the scene or try to invite intimacy." He hurried to catch up to her. "I thought about what we talked about earlier. I want to know it's real and not fabricated for television." He stopped walking and threw his hands in the air. "What do you want from me?"

She stopped, turned and walked back to him. "The real question is, what do you want from me? All I'm asking is that you hold up your end of the deal. Go on these dates. Keep your options open, but don't close yourself off to the possibility that you might meet the woman you're supposed to be with. And let me do my job."

"Not when you're going back on what we agreed."

She pointed at him, slashing the air with

her finger. "We agreed that you would have more input. Not complete control."

He took the few steps that separated them and looked at her. Really looked at her until he thought he was going to implode and cease to exist. The line between friendship and something more seemed to blur for just a moment. He swallowed. "Lizzie..."

She shook her head and walked away. Got in the SUV's passenger side. Didn't even glance in his direction as Charlie backed the car out and drove away.

He felt as if his best friend in the world was leaving. The confusing part was that his heart seemed to be going with her, too.

CHAPTER NINE

ICE FISHING was a logistical nightmare. The shack on ice barely held four people, and that didn't include a camera operator and sound crew. Elizabeth, however, could pull more than a rabbit out of an old hat. She had commissioned three shacks on the ice and a large heated tent on land for this group date. She had enough food to feed not only her cast and crew, but also the locals she'd hired to give authenticity to the scene.

This was going to be the best episode she'd produced.

Or the biggest disaster.

Luckily, the monitors for watching the taping were in the warmth of the tent. She made up a plate of chicken wings to eat while she took notes and barked out orders. Definitely the best part of her job.

She put her feet up on a chair across from her and groaned when someone stepped in front of the camera, where Rick baited hooks for some of the contestants. She tapped her earpiece. "Charlie, move that girl out of the way before I have to come in and do it myself."

He chuckled on the other end. "Why are you so grouchy?"

"I'm not. Just move her." The tension between her shoulder blades eased as the contestant moved.

"Problems, Ms. Maier?"

Elizabeth turned and bit back another groan. Couldn't she have peace for just a minute? "Dan, grab a plate of food and join me." She pushed a chair closer to him. He sat down and unbuttoned his long wool coat, looking every bit as if he'd stepped off the pages of a business magazine. "You're early."

"Thought I'd get the lay of the land, so to speak." He motioned to the monitors. "This is what the audience is seeing?"

"It's raw material before my editors and I cut it down to the most exciting parts." She wiped her fingers on a napkin. "The audience only gets to see about twelve hours of a total of more than a hundred that we shoot."

"So my appearance today...?"

Was he nervous? He didn't appear any different from his usual authoritative self. "Maybe five minutes."

Dan nodded and looked at his fingernails. "And the ad time we bought?"

She patted his arm. "Thirty seconds every episode, plus mentioned as a sponsor in the credits. And we're taping at the diner for several episodes."

"The diner isn't the business, okay? Mom gave Rick the diner, but Dad never meant it to be part of Allyn Pickles." He shook his head. "It's…a restaurant. Hardly a jewel in the company crown. More of a drain. I should probably just sell it."

"Doesn't Rick get any say in that?"

Dan stood and shrugged off his jacket. "Think I'll go check out the buffet."

She watched him leave. This sibling-rivalry drama would add some interest to the show. Help the audience to identify with Rick. She made a note on her clipboard and turned her attention back to the monitors. *Good.* They were having fun. Seeing Rick bait hooks reminded her of their own ill-fated fishing expedition. What would it be like to fish when there was no chance of capsizing?

Someone else entered the tent, pushing the flap aside and scanning the few people inside. The woman walked closer as Elizabeth frantically tried to recall why she looked familiar. She had long white-blond hair and wore a black peacoat with a bright pink beret. Sunglasses covered her eyes.

When she removed the glasses, Elizabeth gasped. *What in the world?* She approached Brandy. Ever the professional, Elizabeth stuck out her hand. "Good to see you again. Or should I say surprised."

Brandy shook hands with her and glanced around the tent. "Is Rick here?"

"Ice fishing on the lake." Elizabeth took a deep breath. "Forgive me for being blunt, but what are you doing here?"

The other woman shrugged. "I saw you were taping the show with Rick, and I thought I might be able to help you out or something."

Help them out with what? Adding to Rick's anxiety? Elizabeth shook her head. "Am I missing something? Did someone ask you to come here?"

Brandy turned her gaze back to Elizabeth. She frowned, marring her complexion slightly. "Mr. Scott contacted me last week. He didn't go over the details with you?"

Devon. Elizabeth frowned. "Sorry, Brandy, I need to make a quick call. Find out what's going on here." She stepped away for a moment, then tapped her earpiece. "Charlie, keep Rick out on the ice. I'm taking care of something back here. Got it?" The last thing she needed was for her star to see their new guest without preparing him. While it might make for good television, she'd promised to take care of Rick. And this time, she was going to keep her word.

With that done, she punched numbers into her cell phone. This was her show. Hers. And she wasn't giving up control to anyone.

Devon picked up on the first ring. "Did my surprise arrive?"

Elizabeth bit back a retort. "Did I miss the memo where this became your show instead of mine?"

He chuckled on the other end. "You said you welcomed ideas. Brandy's mine. And it's pretty fab, isn't it?"

Elizabeth closed her eyes and gritted her teeth. "Did Bob give you this kind of license?"

"You're not Bob."

No kidding. "Obviously. But I won't let you interfere with my job." She opened her eyes and focused on Brandy, who stood at the monitors. Was she hoping for a second chance with Rick? Or was there something more going on?

"Think about it. The old flame comes back to stir up what might have been five years ago? You brought back Rick. Why not

Brandy, too?" He chuckled again. "You want ratings gold? There it is."

She shook her head. Brandy returning would bump up their ratings. But at what cost? "Why didn't you consult with me first?"

"What's to consult? I hold the fate of your show in my hands." There was silence on the other end. "One word to the head of the studio, and we show repeats of our top-rated sitcom instead. Up to you, Elizabeth."

She took another look at Brandy. "I'll call you later."

Brandy looked around the tent, then turned her gaze back to Elizabeth. "Where is he?"

There was no way she was going to let this woman have access to Rick right now. Elizabeth had promised he could trust her. Brandy being there could ruin all that. "Why?"

The other woman looked down at her hands, which Elizabeth noted didn't have the mega-ring the show had bought for her other fiancé to give her. The engagement had lasted six weeks before a public breakup on the reunion show.

Brandy looked back up at her. "I want to apologize. Try to make him understand."

"What's there to understand? You chose someone else." Elizabeth stepped in front of the monitors. "Listen. I need time to figure this out." She gave Brandy a once-over. Five years had certainly been good to her. "Let's talk business for a bit."

Brandy tucked her hair behind her ear and nodded. "I really appreciate this chance. Mr. Scott even said if this doesn't work out for me, I could be the bachelorette again on *True Love*."

Of course he did. "Great." She put her hand on Brandy's elbow and moved them away from prying ears. "I'm thinking we'll do a dramatic reveal of your presence to the other women on the show. That way we get some great reaction shots. And that will make the audience take more notice of you. But Rick... I can't just spring you on him. I need time to prepare him for..." She sighed and glanced over her. "You."

Brandy nodded as Elizabeth made up plans off-the-cuff. Part of her job was being prepared for anything, but this definitely topped the list of surprises. "We'll have to keep you sequestered, away from the other contestants for a while. Problem is that this is a small town. Everyone knows everyone's business."

"She can stay at my mom's house. It's quiet. Remote." Dan approached them and straightened his coat. Brandy turned and seemed to lean closer to him. He gazed down into her face. "I'd be glad to keep her occupied."

Elizabeth shook her head. "You're going to be filming in a half hour."

He didn't look at her; he kept his focus on the other woman. "I can take her to my mom's now and be back in twenty minutes." He grinned wider as Brandy blushed and looked down. "Fifteen if the cop is on break."

One problem solved. Mostly. "Fine. Is that okay with you, Brandy?"

She nodded and glanced up at Dan, then back at the ground. "I wouldn't want to put you through any trouble."

He smiled at the top of Brandy's head. "No trouble at all."

Elizabeth rolled her eyes. This was worse than what she saw on her show. "Great. We'll meet later to go over any questions."

She watched them leave. She'd think about that complication later. She turned back to her crew. "Okay. Major changes coming, people. Let's stay flexible." She stretched her neck and rolled her shoulders. Stupid tension headache.

Two aspirin and a bottle of water later, she was ready for business. Dan even arrived ahead of schedule. The deputy must have been having lunch rather than monitoring the roads for speeders. Maybe, just maybe, things were getting better.

The question was, how was she going to tell Rick about this new development?

RICK WATCHED HIS BROTHER flit in and out of the gaggle of women, checking plates and beverage levels as if he was a born waiter. True, Dad had made them start working for their mom at the diner once they'd turned fourteen. Who knew that all those years of experience would return to Dan in only a few minutes?

Lizzie stayed on the fringes of the party, watching. For what, he wasn't sure. She had something on her mind. Not unusual for her, but whatever this was troubled her. He could tell by the way she kept her eye on him no matter where he was.

He turned back to the woman who was sharing a story of growing up in a small town with four older brothers. Nodded when he should. Laughed when it was appropriate. She was a nice enough girl, but not for him.

He turned and found Melissa in a group of four other women. He hadn't had a moment alone with her since their one-on-one date yesterday. And he wanted to see where it could lead. If the initial connection between them could turn into…something.

She raised her gaze to him, then winked.

He grinned back.

Lizzie stepped forward and clinked her champagne glass with a fork. "Ladies and gentleman." She glanced at Rick. "This concludes tonight's taping. The shuttle will be here to take you back to the house in a few minutes, but feel free to linger as long as you need to. Tomorrow's schedule is up at the house. We'll be leaving at eight sharp. Any questions?" She turned to Rick. "I need to talk to you." She glanced around the tent. "Alone."

Rick said good-night to the ladies, then joined Lizzie outside by the lakeshore. The moon shone down on the icy surface in muted silvery beams. The glow of lights from homes around the lake seemed swallowed up in the dark cold.

He observed Lizzie's back and cleared his throat. "You want to say whatever you've been holding back since we shot the ice-fishing scenes?"

She turned and opened her mouth, then abruptly shut it. "I don't know how to tell you except to just say it."

Possibilities flitted through his brain. "We've been canceled."

"No."

His shoulders sagged slightly, then tensed again. "You're fired?"

She laughed. "Don't get your hopes up just yet." She glanced at the sky. "Brandy's here."

Rick shrugged. "Brandy who?"

Lizzie stared at him until his stomach ached as if he'd been sucker punched. Which was exactly what it felt like. He bent over at the waist and rested his hands on his thighs. "Oh."

"Yeah. Oh. I didn't want to spring her on you even if that's what the suits expected. I thought you deserved to know first, so you can figure out what you want to do."

Rick tried to swallow but found it difficult with the lump growing in his throat. He hadn't signed up for this. Hadn't given them permission to play with his emotions. "Why?"

Elizabeth frowned. "Because I'm your friend. And your producer."

"I mean, why is she here?" Did that mean she still wanted him? That there was still something between them? He groaned. He'd given up on that, hadn't he? Five years was enough time to get over someone, right?

"Because the studio thinks it will add drama. Which means ratings." She took a step toward him. "What do you want to do?"

Rick gazed across the lake, then back at the tent. "What are my options?"

Lizzie closed the gap between them and waited until he looked back at her. "As your producer, it's my job to tell you that you need to get over yourself. That you signed on to do what we tell you."

Not what he wanted to hear. "And as my friend?"

She reached out and put her hand on the sleeve of his coat. "It's been over five years. Don't you want some closure? To finally shut the door on what happened?"

He wasn't sure what he wanted. Other than to run across the ice and get as far away as he could. Forget he signed on to a TV show. Start a new life being the man he'd always wanted to be. But he couldn't start with a fresh slate. His past was written on it in permanent marker, and maybe it was time to take a real look at it. "Why does she want to be here?"

"Devon's promised her her own show if things don't work out with you two."

Rick laughed. "Of course. I get a second shot, so why shouldn't she, right?" He ran his hands through his hair. The burning sensation in his gut intensified. "I never got a chance to find out why she chose him instead of me. Why everything we did turned out to be a lie." Lizzie nodded but didn't say anything. He gave a weak smile, then shrugged. "I don't want her to be here."

"I know."

He believed her. She'd promised to protect him. And she seemed as blindsided as he felt. "But it's not my choice," he said. "I gave that up when I signed your contract."

"True."

She wasn't helping him by letting him choose for himself. In a way, he wanted her to force him into a decision. Might make it easier if it all backfired later. He groaned. "How does she look?"

She shrugged. "Pretty much the same."

Which meant gorgeous. "Who else knows she's here?"

"The crew. Dan. Your mom."

Rick nodded and ignored the empty feeling in his stomach. "And they didn't tell me."

"Don't blame them. I asked to be the one." She held up a hand as if to stop his thoughts when he frowned at her. "It's my fault she's here, so why not be the one to tell you and take your anger?"

It wasn't anger. Not really. More like shock. And an old ache that hadn't healed completely. Maybe that was his answer. "It's not your idea she join us, so why is it your fault?"

"Because this is my show. And everything that happens here is my responsibility."

Rick laughed at her arrogance. "You're taking on an awful lot."

Lizzie shrugged. "It's my job. My life."

Rick sighed and reached toward her. "Lizzie, the show will never be your life."

"I'm executive producer, so you bet it is." The walls around her immediately rose up. He could see it in the way she took a step back and stood straighter. As if holding herself so stiff would make the universe fall under her control.

She didn't get it. "Your life is more than filmed bits that air on television."

"Are you talking as my friend or as my star?"

"It's all the same to me. I'll always be your friend."

Lizzie let out a long breath. "I was afraid that would change because of what I told you."

Rick took her hand in his. "That won't ever change. Friends always." They looked into each other's eyes until he got uncomfortable and glanced away. "All right. I'll do it."

Lizzie nodded. "So then we can bring Brandy on set?"

"Sure. Set up your big reveal." He toed the snow at his feet, turning it from pure white to muddy gray. She could have this, but he wanted something in return. "But I want five minutes with her. No mikes. No cameras. No crew." He looked up at her. "Not even you."

She was shaking her head before he had a chance to finish. "Rick, you know that I can't allow that."

He grinned and leaned in closer. "Not as my producer, no. But as my friend, you'll make sure I have it." He patted her shoulder. "Make it happen."

He didn't give her a chance to respond before he strode back into the tent. Dan walked up to him as soon as he entered. "Brandy's here."

A little too late, big brother. "You should have told me that before."

Dan glanced out at the lake, where Lizzie still stood at the shore. "What are you going to do?"

Rick straightened the lines of his coat. "What's expected. Like I always do."

THE YIPS AND HOWLS of the Lake Mildred Animal Refuge filled the sound track of the show as Rick led his harem into the renovated tire factory. Russell Tires had once been the largest supplier to the Big Three, but it had lain vacant for years until being repurposed. Another sign of the changing economy.

Elizabeth gathered the group around her and held up her hand until everyone quieted. "I've already had several questions about why we're here and not doing a shoot at a more glamorous location." She took the time to look at several of the women. "Rick wants you to get to know his community. By volunteering you'll not only be giving something back to this town, you'll also get a better idea of what life with Rick is like." She held up her clipboard. "I've got you all assigned into one of four teams. You'll each be given a particular task this morning here at the shelter. Feeding, cleaning, walking, whatever. Rick will move between the groups. Any questions?"

One woman raised her hand. "What if we're allergic?"

Already planned. "You're assigned to the front office to answer phones and help with filing. Anyone else?" Seeing no hands, she nodded at her crew. "Okay, we've got a camera assigned to each team. But let's remember why we're here. Volunteers are scarce, and these animals need your love and attention."

She handed out assignment sheets, then watched as everyone did as planned. Cameras whirred. Women chatted. Dogs pranced around at the attention.

Rick approached her, and she grimaced. He looked haggard. "Didn't get much sleep? Still having strange dreams?"

"More like nightmares." He chuckled and attempted to put the microphone on under his sweater. "Maybe Denise can put some cover-up on my dark circles before I go in front of the cameras."

Uh-oh. Here it comes.

"I think you should reveal Brandy after the elimination tonight. Bring her in without telling the other women she's here or why." He shrugged as if it was no big deal. As if he didn't care or hurt. "Make it dramatic. A cliff-hanger for the next episode."

Impressive. "You're talking like a producer."

One eyebrow rose at that; then he grinned. "Guess you're rubbing off on me."

She looked around, then leaned in close enough to smell the lingering soap from his morning shower. "You've got your five minutes." She winced and helped him get the microphone wire connected to the unit on his belt clip. "Well, three because of today's shooting schedule. But you've got it. Just you two."

Rick nodded. "When?"

"After we send everyone to lunch."

He glanced around the shelter. "I remember when this place made the best tires in Michigan. Now it houses those whom others have forgotten."

She nodded and rubbed one arm. Had the temperature dropped? "We've all been in a place similar to this at some point."

Rick turned and peered at her. "What was yours?"

The bench of a bus station holding on to the leg of her well-loved but battered stuffed elephant.

Elizabeth shivered and shook her head to clear the memory. "Doesn't matter. We all have them." She gestured to the group assigned to clean out the cages. "You might want to get your hands dirty, too."

Rick left to join the squealing women, who held trash bags for soiled newspaper shreds.

Elizabeth crossed her arms, trying to stay warm. The director of the animal shelter approached her with a stack of release forms. "Thank you for doing this."

"It was Rick's idea to advertise the pets available for adoption." She took the forms and added them to the back of her clipboard. "We want to help."

The director chuckled. "If that's really the case, I have a finicky kitten who still demands being bottle-fed."

Elizabeth shook her head. She didn't do animals. They represented complications and obligations she didn't have time for right now. Maybe someday. But now? "Thanks, but I have to keep an eye on my show."

The director nodded, but Elizabeth soon found herself sitting on the concrete floor holding a black-and-white kitten that hungrily sucked on a baby bottle. She could imagine taking this little guy with her. Surely a cat could adjust to her bohemian life on set, right?

And for a moment, she could envision a normal life. One where it wasn't all about her job. Where something, or someone, could join her.

The thought warmed her.

RICK HELD THE LEASH of a German shepherd pup that seemed determined to outrun all the other dogs. "Whoa, fella. Why don't we let the girls catch up to us?"

He tugged on the leash, but the pup kept pulling him along. One of the contestants, Vanessa, put her fingers in her mouth and gave a loud whistle. The dog stopped midtrot, and Rick almost tripped over him.

Vanessa caught up with her own dog on a leash, a small Yorkie mix. "He really had you going."

Rick bent over at the waist, trying to catch his breath. "Yes. Thanks."

The other women in their group started to catch up with them at the end of the drive-way. Vanessa glanced back and slipped her arm through Rick's. "Ready to walk again?" she asked and tugged on his arm.

Rick shrugged. "Sure. I take it you want me alone?"

Vanessa tossed her head back and gave a hearty laugh. "You might say that. I'm willing to go after what I want." The look she gave him made him think he was on that list. "Let's take that path to the right."

Rick tugged on the leash so the pup would stay with them. "There's a view of the lake up ahead."

Vanessa nodded and pulled him and her dog along. "I've been hoping to get some one-on-one time with you for a few days. Get to know you better."

He could identify with that. When he'd first been on the show, time alone with Brandy at the beginning had been rare and precious. Maybe he needed to spread himself out more among them. "I'd like to get to know you better, too."

He glanced behind them and saw that the group of women held back but a cameraman ran after them. "I think they want to film this."

"Oh, right." She stopped walking. "It's hard to do this on camera, isn't it? Dating is tough enough without having an audience."

"Life in a small town is kind of like that." He chuckled. "Everyone knows your business and has an opinion."

"Do they approve of this show?"

The camera operator reached them. "Sorry, guys. Can we back up and start over?" Eddie asked. He pressed a button on the camera and walked backward to film them while they made their way down the path with the dogs.

Rick cleared his throat, struggling to find a topic that the audience would find interesting. "So, Vanessa, are you an animal lover?"

She laughed. "My dad's a veterinarian and my brother followed in his footsteps. We always had a bunch of animals around the house. Some injured or sick. Some temporary until they found a permanent home." She leaned down and petted the Yorkie. "I just wuv my animal fwends."

Rick tried not to wince at the baby voice. It seemed a bit much. Maybe she was acting natural, though. He didn't know her well enough to know for sure. But when she began to kiss the dog on the mouth, he fought hard to keep his face neutral. Yeah, he wouldn't be kissing her mouth after that.

Rick glanced at Eddie, who raised his eyebrows and shook his head.

One of the other contestants, Jennifer, ran up to them. "I thought I'd never find you."

Grateful for the distraction, Rick tugged on his dog's leash. "You know, it's getting colder by the minute out here. Why don't we take everyone back inside?"

Rick led the group as they returned to the shelter.

AFTER LIZZIE CALLED for lunch, the hornets in Rick's stomach buzzed louder and angrier. Brandy was near. He could feel it. Always could when they were on set before. Lizzie had laughed when he'd told her, said it was his imagination.

But once the bus had driven the rest of the

production crew and contestants away, he knew she lingered close.

Lizzie tied things up with the shelter director, then joined him by the dog cages, where Rick patted the head of the German shepherd. "You two look good together."

Rick glanced down at the dog. "My life currently doesn't allow room for a pet, but I'm open to the possibility."

Lizzie shrugged. "I know the feeling." She glanced in the direction of the cat room. "But every once in a while, I wonder."

Rick nodded as Lizzie removed his earpiece and microphone; she avoided his gaze. "I'll be waiting in my car." She glanced at her watch, then him. "Three minutes."

He didn't know what to say. Didn't trust his voice.

As Lizzie left the shelter, a familiar blonde walked in and scanned the room before settling her ocean-blue eyes on him.

His heart squeezed but it felt…different. Not like five years ago. Not when he saw a future every time he looked at her. Now he felt as if everything he'd planned on could change in the next few moments. All his plans would turn upside down until he didn't remember what they were in the first place.

He swallowed. *Nope. Not good.*

He walked toward her, but she remained frozen where she was. Was it fear keeping her from moving? He opened his arms then, and she rushed toward him. "Ricky."

When he put his arms around her, she sighed and snuggled closer. "I thought you'd never talk to me again."

He held her out to look at her. She looked good. Too good. Hard to remember she'd once broken his heart. "You look as fabulous as ever."

Brandy blushed and pushed his shoulder. It felt familiar and normal. As if they'd been in touch all this time. "Always the charmer."

"Things don't change much," he observed.

She nodded, then looked at the ground. When she brought her gaze back to his, her eyes were filled with tears. "I'm so, so sorry."

Rick let out a big sigh. *Please, not the tears*. He could handle anything but those. "I am, too."

She shook her head furiously. "But you're not the one who broke my heart."

"But he did." He took her hand and led her to a bench near the front door. The feel of her hand in his was warm. Again, familiar. "I only wanted you to be happy." He looked down at their hands, then back at her. "But I had hoped it would be with me."

Brandy shook her head. "I wanted it to be you so badly. But when it came to that moment, I knew my heart had already chosen someone else."

"Even though we all kept warning you he was a player."

She squeezed his hand. "When it's your turn, you'll understand. You'll know that no matter how much you should choose the perfect woman, it comes down to who's climbed into your heart and made a home there."

"Are you here for a second chance with me or with the audience?"

Brandy peered into his eyes intensely until he could feel a piece of himself starting to come loose and fall away. "Maybe both? I want to make things right with you. And I hope you'll give me that chance."

Rick's cell phone chirped, ruining the moment. "I think time's up." He rose to his feet, still hanging on to her hand. Unwilling to let her go just yet. "Why don't we take things as they come? No promises. No lies. Just whatever happens, happens."

Brandy turned into his arms. "It's a deal."

A BRUNETTE WITH a short blue dress approached Rick after dinner at the house. He had decisions on his mind. Who to send home? Who to keep? How would they take the addition of Brandy to the house? *Distracted* put it mildly.

"Can we talk outside?" the brunette asked.

Always the talking outside. Couldn't they stay where it was warm by the fire? Instead of suggesting that, he nodded. "But let's take our coats."

In the foyer, they both grabbed coats, then stepped out onto the porch. Rick could see his breath as soon as they walked into the cold. He crossed his arms more for the warmth than anything. One of the cameramen turned on lights and gave a thumbs-up before either one said a word. "How are things going, Britney?"

She glanced at the camera, then at Rick. "Um…"

Rick addressed the cameraman. "Eddie, why don't you take a five-minute break? I think we need some privacy." He motioned with his head toward the garage. "I promise you won't miss anything juicy."

"No can do, Rick. Boss lady would have my hide."

Britney shook her head and took a seat on the stone bench. "It's fine. I signed up for this. And it's not something I can't say on camera."

Rick nodded and focused his attention on the young woman. "What's wrong, Brit?"

She stayed quiet for so long that he thought she wouldn't share what was on her mind. Finally, she began, "Rick, you're a nice guy, but—"

Really? That was what she wanted to talk about? He chuckled. "You're giving me the 'It's not you, it's me' speech? Wow."

"I grew up in a town just like this and promised I'd never go back." Britney took a deep breath and shook her head. "I can't do this. Not even for a catch like you."

What was so wrong with his town? Everyone seemed to want to get away from it. But Rick liked it. Loved it. It was friends. And family. It was home. "We want different things is all." He put a hand on her shoulder. "I won't give you a necklace tonight, okay?"

"Thanks, Rick. If it was anywhere else…"

He leaned over and kissed her cheek. "I wish you the best."

Britney threw her arms around him. "You, too." She started to rise. Then she sat back down. "Don't trust Mona."

What? He'd only had a brief conversation with Mona. They certainly weren't picking out china patterns at this point. "Why shouldn't I?"

Britney bit her lip. "I don't think she's in this for the right reasons." She leaned in closer. "None of us do. Just be careful, okay?"

Rick nodded, still stunned. Someone cleared her throat behind them, and he turned to see Lizzie. He patted Britney's shoulder. "Why don't you go back inside and get warm? I have something to take care of."

Once Britney shut the front door, Lizzie stared at Eddie until he turned the camera off and returned to the garage. Rick stood and started to open the door. Lizzie took a step in front of it, barring his way. The hits kept coming. "Liz, I'm freezing. What do you want?"

"Brandy's waiting in the garage until we're ready." She stepped closer to him, touched his arm. "You're sure that you're okay with this?"

He shrugged. "You said it would give me closure, so why not?"

She held up her clipboard. "Want to go over the contestants and narrow down who you're sending home tonight?"

Rick shook his head. "I think I'll do this one on my own."

"Oh." She tried to keep the hurt out of her voice, but Rick heard it all the same. "I only wanted to help."

"I've got to make these decisions on my own eventually." He gave a shrug and a grin he didn't really feel, then opened the door to the house and walked inside.

ELIZABETH COULD TELL that Rick hated the elimination. His brow was damp, his eyes wide. If his coughing was any indication, he had a dry throat, too. No one liked rejection, and he hated being the one who handed it out.

Rick stood in front of the refurbished fireplace with twelve necklaces in his hands. "Ah…ladies?"

Immediately, the conversation dropped to a lull and the remaining contestants gathered in a semicircle in front of Rick. Elizabeth gripped her clipboard. In the past, Rick had discussed the women with her and given a hint about who he was sending home. But this time he'd kept the decision close to his chest, which meant that she was as clueless as the rest of their viewing audience. And she didn't like that one bit.

Elizabeth closed her eyes and mumbled, "Pick Melissa. You like her. So pick her. Please."

On the monitor, Rick looked at each woman a moment. "This is always the toughest part of our time here. Choosing who will stay and who goes home." He cleared his throat. "So…" He took one gold necklace and dangled the heart charm. Glanced at each woman. "Melissa."

Elizabeth went limp with relief.

Melissa walked to stand in front of Rick. He unclasped the necklace and held it out. "Melissa, will you accept my heart?"

The woman smiled and nodded. Dipped her head so that Rick could place the necklace around her neck. Touched the charm to her chest. Leaned in toward him and kissed his cheek. "Thank you."

The ceremony continued until eleven more women had joined Melissa next to Rick. Elizabeth examined them on the monitor. Melissa was definitely the nice girl in the bunch. He'd also chosen two women who had already fought at the house over bathroom space, a loud smart aleck who made him laugh and several who could blend in anywhere. They'd probably be the next to leave.

Rick took the time to say goodbye to each contestant he hadn't chosen while Elizabeth prepared for the surprise. Brandy returning may have been Devon's idea, but it was Rick's brilliant plan to introduce her after the goodbye ceremony. Making it a cliff-hanger for the next episode ensured ratings for both shows.

One of her cameramen hopped up. "We got a crier on the porch. I'm on it."

He ran out of the garage before Elizabeth could stop him. While the crying women often made ratings, she personally hated seeing it happen. She grabbed her coat and ran after Eddie.

The young woman saw them coming and turned away. Eddie already had the camera running before he reached the porch. Elizabeth put her hand on his shoulder and shook her head. "Give us a moment?"

Eddie sighed a little too loudly. "The audience loves these scenes."

"Only because Bob insisted on exploiting them. I'm in charge here now." When her cameraman walked away grumbling about missed opportunities, Elizabeth approached the woman. "Kayla, are you all right?"

She squinted at Elizabeth through tears. "Do I look all right to you?"

Not with those red eyes and stained cheeks. Elizabeth dropped her voice. "Listen, Rick's a great guy, which is why he's on the show, but he's not the only one out there. Just because it didn't work out this time doesn't mean your life is over." She placed a hand on Kayla's shoulder, hoping it would bring some comfort.

Instead the young woman whirled on her. "What would you know about it?"

Elizabeth gave a soft chuckle. "I know plenty about men, good and bad. But I also know that life doesn't stop after a breakup. You're going to be okay."

Kayla shook her head, unwilling to listen. "What if he was the one? I thought that we had a chance...."

"Every woman does. But the reality is that there's someone else out there who is perfect for you. In the meantime, worry less about a prince to rescue you and focus on making the best of yourself."

Kayla glanced at Elizabeth's left hand. "I don't see a ring on your finger, so what would you know about it?"

"My prince is this job. That's what I wake up for every day. It's what saves me from the dragons out there."

Kayla shook her head and walked off the porch. "Whatever."

How many times had she had this conversation with those going home? How many more times would she before someone believed her? She turned to go back to the garage. She spotted Rick watching her. "Kayla was upset."

He nodded and turned his attention to the house. "They're waiting for you before we bring in Brandy."

Back to business. "Right. How do you think it went?"

He turned to look at her. Shrugged, though she knew it took more effort than he had. "I hate telling someone that we didn't click. But that's all a part of life, right?" He gave a soft laugh, but she could tell he took no pleasure in it. "Now, let's go knock the socks off this game."

Elizabeth turned to watch Kayla get in the waiting car. She held up a hand, but the other woman ignored it and slammed the door shut.

From inside, she could hear the murmurs of voices reach a fever pitch. So much for waiting for her to spring Brandy on them.

"But you can't! She can't!"

Here we go.... Elizabeth stepped inside and glanced at the remaining contestants. "Is there a problem?"

Brandy raised her hand from the corner. "I guess that would be me."

"If you want someone to be angry with, pick me." Rick stepped forward. "This show is about second chances for me, and I figured she deserved one, too."

The contestants looked at each other; most of them didn't seem happy about it. Finally, Melissa said, "You're welcome to room with me if you'd like. My roommate, Britney, got sent home tonight."

Brandy nodded but didn't say anything. Neither did anyone else until Rick clapped his hands together. "Well, I don't know about you, but I could use some more of that fabulous chocolate mousse we had at dinner. Any other takers?"

The women slowly followed him back into the kitchen. That man could probably get them to do almost anything, Elizabeth marveled.

Brandy stayed behind. "I didn't think my being here would upset them so much."

"It's a competition. Remember the feud between Wade and Larry? Anything that could get in your way is immediately viewed with suspicion and anger." Elizabeth consulted her clipboard. "I'll make sure your luggage gets moved to the house tonight."

"Thanks." Brandy started to leave but turned back. "Why don't you want me here?"

"I never said I didn't."

"Right."

Elizabeth called after her, "He's a good man. He doesn't deserve to get hurt. By you or anyone else."

The other woman turned and shook her head. "I don't want to hurt him." She shrugged.

"Guess I'll try to get in on some of that dessert, too."

Elizabeth watched her leave and took a deep breath. She needed to get a better handle on hiding her feelings.

CHAPTER TEN

RICK LET HIMSELF into the back door of the house where the remaining women were staying—they no longer needed both places. He'd gotten a key from one of the crew members to plan this surprise breakfast. If Lizzie knew about it, she'd probably have his hide. So the less she knew, the better. This was something he wanted to do for the women, not the camera.

Silence greeted him in the kitchen as he set down the plastic bags of groceries that he'd brought with him. He took off his coat and tossed it on the back of one of the stools. Searching, he found the supplies he needed: whisk, bowls, pans, spatula. As well as a frilly apron that he was sure looked better on the sleeping inhabitants of the house than it did on him.

By the time the coffee had finished brewing, Rick had been joined by two of the contestants, Jenny and Becky. He used some flair to flip a perfect golden pancake onto a plate, then topped it with another. He added a few pieces of bacon to the side. And the first plate was served.

Becky murmured her thanks as Rick started on Jenny's plate. "You guys are up awfully early."

Jenny watched him. "Hard to sleep when the aroma of fresh coffee hits my nose." She took her plate from him. "This looks fabulous. Thanks."

"My pleasure." He winked at her and started preparing another plate. "Everyone else still sleeping?"

The women nodded but continued eating. Rick topped off their mugs of coffee, then poured himself one. He started brewing another pot so it would be fresh for whoever came downstairs next. "So what do you think of my town?"

Becky swallowed. "It's cute. But small." She cut her pancake into tiny bites. "Kind of like me."

Rick raised his coffee cup. "Hear, hear." He heard feet on the stairs and started pouring pancake batter onto the griddle. "Sounds like we have more customers."

When the women saw him standing there, some left to go upstairs and change. Put on makeup. Do whatever it was that women did before facing the world. He thought they already looked beautiful. Rick stopped them. "It's a pj's breakfast. Come as you are."

Soon the kitchen couldn't hold them all, so the women who already had breakfast took their plates into the dining room while Rick brought out more for those who had arrived later as he did at the diner. Sometimes, he couldn't escape it. Once they had all been served, he took a seat at the head of the table. They looked at him as if waiting for him to say something. He stalled and took a sip of his coffee. They still waited. "So what's on the agenda today?"

"We thought you'd know," Brandy said.

She'd been the last to join them, the last at the table. He'd noticed how some had turned their chairs as if to shut her out. He caught her gaze then nodded at her, hoping it reassured her. "I'm as clueless as you. Lizzie usually posts a schedule around here somewhere, right?"

"Yes, I do."

The woman in question stood in the doorway of the dining room. Anger and tension seemed to radiate from her. And the look that she gave him could have scorched the apron off him. "Did I miss the invitation for breakfast?"

Rick stood and held up his hands. "I wanted to do something just for them. A surprise breakfast."

"Oh, it's a surprise, all right." She crossed her arms as she took in the scene. Then she zeroed in on him. "A word alone?"

He poured his producer a cup of coffee, then joined her in the living room.

ELIZABETH COULDN'T believe it. Why was Rick at the house? Where was the camera? The crew? "What were you thinking?"

Rick held out a mug of coffee. "Like I said, I wanted to do something nice for them. What's the big deal?"

"The big deal?" She shook her head. And peeled her coat off and tossed it over the back of one of the love seats. "You're robbing the audience of special moments like that."

"I didn't do it to score points with the audience." He placed the cup of coffee in her hands, then ran his hands through his hair. "I wanted to do this to thank the women who are still here. Just from me to them. Nothing else."

She looked around the room. "How did you get in?"

Rick colored slightly as he dug a key out of his jeans pocket. "Don't get mad."

"I'm beyond that." Elizabeth held out her hand and closed it around the warm key when he placed it there. "I was already dreading holding my meeting this morning, and you being here isn't making my job easier."

"I wasn't thinking about you when I made these plans."

"Obviously." That was the problem. He had only thought about doing something nice for these women. So why was she jumping down his back? Something she didn't want to think about. Not right now. "Any other surprises you need to tell me about?"

Rick dropped his gaze to his feet and shook his head. Elizabeth sighed and touched his arm. "Making breakfast for them was really sweet. But next time can we show it on air?"

"Deal." He glanced at her face. "You look like you haven't slept or eaten. Want me to make you a plate?"

Rather than fight him, she agreed. She joined the women in the dining room and took Rick's spot at the head of the table.

When Rick returned to the dining room with her breakfast, Elizabeth thanked him. "Sweet of Rick to surprise you this morning, huh?" Might as well start things out nice. Because the rest of the meeting wouldn't be.

There was light applause and words of

thanks. Elizabeth smiled at him. "Thank you. Now we girls have some things to discuss without you."

"Dismissed just like that?" Rick chuckled as if to show he didn't care. But the look in his eyes told her he might. "I'll see you all later."

Once he left, Elizabeth pulled her clipboard closer. "Just some quick notes, and then I need to see Mona and Leslie alone."

With efficiency, she laid out the day's schedule and stressed how important it was to explore the town. "Who knows, you could end up living here. Any questions?" No one raised a hand. "Details for those of you going on the trip to the winery this afternoon are posted on the whiteboard in the kitchen. Otherwise, you're free."

They got up and left, and the two she needed to talk to stayed behind. Elizabeth waited until the room was empty, then moved down the table to sit closer to the two women. Mona had her arms crossed already, as if she knew what they were going to discuss, while Leslie kept her gaze on her hands.

She waited for them both to look at her. "Listen. I know space is precious with all of you living here in cramped quarters. But I will absolutely not tolerate any kind of turf war on set."

Leslie frowned and Mona narrowed her eyes at the other woman. "It's hardly a turf war. She's a thief."

"I am not!" Leslie stood. She slowly sat back down as Elizabeth kept her gaze on her. "I didn't know it was hers."

"Regardless, the fighting has to stop." Elizabeth leaned forward. "Although it does get us better ratings on the show, it's not good for you or for the others living here."

"The show?" Mona wrinkled her nose. "She took my necklace, and you're worried about the show?" She scowled at Leslie. "You better be worried about the police."

Every show had one of these meetings. Every bachelor had a group of women who couldn't live together without a fight. Or several. "The necklaces that Rick gives out all look alike. It's a simple misunderstanding."

Mona leaned back in her chair. "She wants me off the show. Her and everybody else in this house."

"Rick decides who leaves, Mona. So can we cut the drama?" She reached for her clipboard and glanced at her notes. "But I think we need to separate you two. Jenny has a free bed in her room. Who wants it?"

Mona stared at Leslie until the woman raised her hand. "I do."

"Good. I'll let you get your things moved."

Leslie rose to her feet, then glanced at Mona. "I'm sorry about the necklace. I thought it was mine."

"Whatever."

Elizabeth let Leslie pass. She turned to Mona. "Now you have the room to yourself. That should satisfy you. So stop the threats." She got to her feet. "Maybe there's a reason they don't want you here. Something to think about."

Mona rolled her eyes. "All I need to think about is that ring on my finger at the end of this show."

Elizabeth left, shaking her head. There was one of those every season, too.

His mom piped lemon filling into the tiny pastry cups, concentration making her tongue peep out at the side of her mouth. "Ma, they're not expecting perfection." He reached out to take one from the tray but got his hand slapped away.

"These are for the ladies. Not you." She started on the next one, looked up at him and sighed. "Fine. But only one."

Rick took one of the first she'd made,

which looked a little lopsided. He bit into it and closed his eyes. "These are fabulous."

She continued filling the pastries. "Of course they are. I made them."

He leaned on the counter and licked off his fingers, watching her for a moment. "Is there something I can do to help you out?"

"Can you count the plates and silverware? Make sure I got them all out?"

Rick pushed off the counter and walked to the kitchen table, where stacks of china and rows of forks and spoons were laid out in precision. "I think it's nice that you're doing this for the ladies," he said.

"And filming it."

He shrugged. "You didn't have to agree to that, you know." He fingered the top of one fork. "But I'm sure Lizzie appreciates it."

His mom placed the last pastry cup on the tray, surveying her work. "I'm doing this for you, not her." She glanced at the clock. "The mini quiches come out in ten minutes. Salads are made." She looked around the kitchen. "Can you arrange the cookies on the trays when you finish? I'll start brewing the tea and making the coffee."

Rick enjoyed working with his mom like this in the kitchen. On holidays, he'd been her little helper, mashing potatoes or preparing salads. In high school, he'd worked for his parents at the diner, then rejoined her staff after the accident that had robbed him of his baseball career. She'd taught him everything he knew, then handed her dream over to him. He loved her for that.

He pulled tubs of homemade cookies from the pantry and started to fill crystal trays with them. He wished he'd inherited her baking gene. It would make life more interesting at the diner. Though Ernesto did have a talented hand with pies. Taking a quick glance to see if the coast was clear, he popped one of the cookies into his mouth. His mom sighed. "At least leave some for your ladies."

"You made enough for them, the crew and the rest of the town if they show up for tea." He continued putting cookies on the tray, then paused. "What do you think of Brandy coming back?"

His mom stopped scooping coffee into the percolator and looked out the window for a moment. "She seems willing to try a second time. Why?"

He shrugged. "I don't know. I thought her coming back might rekindle what we had, but that's gone. Replaced by something…different, I guess."

His mom tilted her head to the side. "Different bad or different good?"

"I don't know. Just different." He resumed putting the cookies on the tray. "I still like her, but I don't trust her. Does that make sense?"

He felt his mom put her hand on his shoulder. Turned to see her watching him, love shining at him. He knew that had never changed. Would never change. He gave her a soft smile. "None of this makes sense, right?"

"Son, I stopped trying to make sense of things a long time ago." He chuckled as she continued, "What matters to me is that you are happy. That you are healthy." She started to walk away. "And that you make me a grandmother."

Thanks, Mom. Nothing like adding more pressure to the process. He cleared his throat. "Can you keep your eyes and ears open today? Let me know what you think? I need help this time. And I'm not afraid to ask."

She walked back to his side, then kissed his cheek. "Of course. Love you." She glanced at the clock on the wall. "Now, finish that tray and get out of here. It's ladies only."

He returned her smile and kept arranging cookies.

ELIZABETH WAS OUT of ideas. Rick wanted to showcase the community more on air, but her creative well had run dry. They'd danced with the seniors. Played with the animals. The only other logistical nightmare left was doing something with kids. And as a rule, she steered her production away from them. Kids might look cute on film, but they were too unpredictable. But then, when had that stopped her before?

Rick sat across from her in the back booth at the diner after a long day of shooting interviews, his least favorite thing on the show besides the elimination ceremonies. He had his arms draped across the back of the booth, head back, eyes closed. She studied him, wondering what else she could do to help him find the right woman. She felt as if she was failing. And he deserved so much more. To be loved and cared for. She reached across the table and smoothed a stray lock of hair that had fallen across his forehead.

He woke with a start and found her staring at him. "See something you like?"

"What do you think about kids?"

"Having them? I'm for it." He stretched his legs out so that his feet rested on the seat beside her. "You volunteering?"

"No way." She shook her head furiously at the suggestion. Her, a mother? What did she know about raising a child? Not as if she had any strong role models in that area. "I meant on the show."

"Don't they say never to work with animals or kids in show business?"

"Only the wimps say that." She drew large circles on her clipboard, willing the ideas to come. Hoping they'd come. Because she needed a lot of them and soon. "I thought you being around kids might raise your appeal."

He leaned across the table. "Aren't I appealing enough?" He held out his arms. "I mean, look at me. I'm every mother's dream future son-in-law."

"You've got some ego on you tonight." She started making X's to match her circles on the paper.

"Must be all this sharing about myself." He stood. "You hungry? I know the diner's closed, but I can whip us up something. A sandwich? Or I think Ernesto has some chicken pie left over."

Elizabeth shook her head, but her stomach growled in response. Rick raised an eyebrow until she sighed. "Fine. But a little piece. I'm going to need bigger clothes the way you feed me."

"That's not a bad thing, Lizzie." Rick disappeared into the kitchen while she doodled some more. They were halfway through filming here, and most of the time left would be devoted to dates. But she'd hoped to have one more group activity. One more chance to make a statement about this town. Maybe some kind of civic cleanup duty? Or volunteer opportunity? Volunteering with kids?

She groaned and rested her head on the back of the seat. Get off the kid track. She closed her eyes and pictured a woman sitting on the couch watching the show. What was she interested in? What did she want to see?

The clink of a plate set before her ended her reverie. That and the heavenly smell wafting toward her. She opened her eyes. "Thanks. I think I ate sometime this morning."

"You need to take better care of yourself." He set his own plate down and handed her silverware wrapped in a paper napkin. "Don't think I haven't noticed the dark circles under your eyes."

"Maybe I should have Denise put makeup on me in the morning, too." She grinned and opened the napkin. Grabbed the fork and speared a thick piece of chicken. Took a bite. "Man, can you cook."

"Can't take credit for Ernesto's potpie, but thanks."

He sat across from her, and they ate in silence for a while. He motioned with his fork to her notes. "Get any ideas?"

"Not any good ones."

"Read them to me. Maybe we can come up with something together." He took a bite of his dinner and spoke with his mouth full. "What can it hurt?"

"Besides your manners, can't think of a thing." She set her fork down and picked up the clipboard. "'Cleanup. Volunteer. Kids.'" She looked up at him. "That's all I got."

He motioned with his free hand for her to give him the clipboard. She ate while he looked it over, waiting for a response. Finally, he sighed and placed the clipboard on the table between them. "It's good."

"That's all you've got?" She grabbed the clipboard and scanned it. "It's good? It's not good. It's reaching." She groaned and rested her head on the table. "I'm better than this."

"You're hungry and can't think." He pushed her plate toward her. "Your creativity needs fuel. Eat."

She lifted her head and sat back up. Took her fork and ate a few bites. When Rick looked satisfied, she stopped. "We haven't had much time to talk lately. How do you think things are going?"

"With the girls, fine." He finished his meal and sat back in the seat. "I'm beginning to see who might make it to the end." He grinned. "I think."

"Melissa?" She mentally crossed her fingers. They had chemistry together. She was a nice woman who was pretty and sweet. She thought of the other woman he had chemistry with. "What about Brandy?"

"Melissa's nice." He nodded, his eyes getting a far-off look. "I can see myself with her."

"But…"

He shrugged. "There is no but." Elizabeth pierced him with her eyes until he sighed and leaned forward. "Okay, there is. I don't feel a lot of sparks with her."

It was her turn to sigh. How many times had her bachelors told her the same thing? How many had believed in the sparks only to find out later that they didn't last? "Sparks are overrated."

Rick shrugged again. "Maybe." He closed his eyes and rubbed his forehead. "Now, with Brandy, there's plenty of sparks."

"But…"

"But I don't know how much I can trust

them. Or her." He opened his eyes and looked at her. "What do you think?"

The big question. Did she think either one of these women deserved Rick or his love? Rather than answer that question, she wiped her mouth and placed her napkin on the table. "Doesn't matter what I think. I'm not marrying them."

Rick laughed. "True." He glanced at their empty plates. "How about some dessert?"

She rubbed her full belly. "No, thanks."

"I've got cheesecake."

Elizabeth groaned and held up her hands in surrender. "Fine. But—"

"Little piece. I know." Rick laughed as he left to get their desserts. He returned quickly with two pieces. "I can make coffee."

"Are you trying to spoil me? This is fine." She took a bite of the cheesecake and moaned. "Your diner will ruin me."

He again took his seat across from her. "It's kinda nice. Just the two of us. No camera. No crew."

She nodded as she finished her bite. "Hard to remember what real life is like without the cameras."

"Exactly." They ate in silence, then Rick asked, "Why aren't you married?"

Where had that come from? She choked on her food. "What? Why?"

He looked her over. "You're pretty. Smart. Successful. Are they blind or just stupid?"

How did they get on this topic? "Doesn't matter. I'm not getting married."

"Ever?"

"Never wanted to."

"So, no kids. No marriage." He leaned forward. "I know you love your job, but don't you want more?"

She searched for a way to change the topic but failed. He looked at her with those warm brown eyes that invited someone to trust him. To tell him everything. She shook her head. "It doesn't matter."

"It does to me. C'mon, Lizzie. What kind of guy could make you change your mind?"

"Why do you want to know?"

"You spent three hours asking me questions, so now it's my turn." He tapped the table. "Fess up. What's your dream guy like?"

She scowled at him. "He wouldn't be pushy."

Rick laughed and leaned back. "Okay, what else?"

It had been so long since she'd thought of this. She couldn't remember anything she used to dream about. Well, mostly. "He'd have a good job. Security. Strong principles."

"Now we're getting somewhere." Rick frowned. "But he sounds kind of...I don't know. Boring."

"Boring can be good." She polished off the last bite of cheesecake. "Thanks for the late dinner, but I've got to get going." She stood and grabbed her clipboard. She turned to find Rick helping her into her coat. It was almost like being on a date. Almost like... She shook her head. "You are a true gentleman. Those are rare."

He turned her around and kissed her on the cheek. "Good night, Lizzie." He put his arms around her shoulders, and they looked at each other.

Too long. Until she flinched and hurried away.

"Night," she croaked, then ducked out of the restaurant.

ELIZABETH'S PHONE RANG from the bedside table. She groaned and rolled over. Peered at the digital clock. Who in the world would be calling her at four in the morning? She jabbed her finger at the offensive phone. "This better be good."

"Have you taken a look outside?"

She frowned. *What?* Slowly getting to her feet, she walked to the curtains that led to the balcony. Opened them slowly. And groaned even louder. All she could see was white. At least a foot and a half of it against the glass doors.

"I knew there was snow in the forecast, but not a blizzard."

Charlie chuckled. "So much for the hockey game in Detroit tonight. Hope you had a plan B."

"And C and D, if needed." She turned on a light and located her clipboard where she'd left it the night before by the television. "Give me a few hours. I'll make some phone calls. Check some websites. We can still make this work."

"It's a little after four. Most people will be sleeping."

"Which makes me wonder why you called me right now. This couldn't wait?" She turned on her laptop and waited for it to boot. Waited for the real reason Charlie had called her. "What else do you need to tell me?"

"I spotted Wally Ray at a local bar last night."

Elizabeth's heart fell into her stomach, and she rubbed her forehead. "Did you talk to him?"

"He approached me. Told me he's on an explosive scoop." Charlie got quiet. "What else is here in this teeny town besides us? He's got some inside story on the show, E. What else could it be?"

No.

No, no, no.

She picked up the hotel phone and dialed Devon's cell phone. "Charlie, I'll call you back with details later." She hung up her cell phone and wrapped her finger around the hotel phone's cord. When Devon didn't pick up, not that she expected he would, she growled, "You'd better call me in ten minutes. *Hollywood Insider* is here investigating us. What is going on?"

She slammed the phone on the cradle and picked up her cell phone. Dialed a friend's phone number. "Jeremy, I need some answers that I know you have. Please call me back."

Without anyone to talk to, she brought up the internet and scanned her list of secondary plans on the clipboard. They wouldn't be able to drive to Detroit in this weather for the game, but could they find one closer to home? A local team perhaps?

Her cell phone chirped. She glanced at the caller ID before answering it. "Tell me what you know about this."

"Elizabeth, sweetheart, there's nothing to know." Devon sounded as if he'd enjoyed too much whiskey. "You're worrying about nothing."

This topped her list of things to worry about. "Wally Ray is in town. He doesn't show up unless the story brings in high five figures. Tell me what you know."

Silence. *Great.*

Elizabeth printed out the new itinerary for tonight's date while she waited for Devon to come up with some excuse. Some reason why a Hollywood reporter would come snooping in their very own backyard. "Is it because we added Brandy?"

Nothing.

"Devon, did you pass out or are you avoiding me?"

"Beth, baby…"

She sighed. "Good night, Devon. I'll put out the fires like I always do. Glad to know they pay you the big bucks for all my hard work." She threw her phone on the bed. Then picked it back up and called Charlie back. "Did he say anything about the story he's on?"

"That's why I called you. It's obviously us, but I don't know the angle."

"Did he say where he's staying?"

Charlie gave her the directions as she pulled on jeans and a sweatshirt. She wasn't going to look the greatest, but this wasn't a time for vanity. It was a time for action. She had to get answers and quick. Had to protect her show. No matter what.

Wally Ray's hotel was definitely several rungs lower than those she'd put her crew up in. She slammed her hand on the door until he answered.

"Beth."

She wrinkled her nose at the smell of him, but moved past him and into the hotel room. Glanced around at the disheveled queen-size bed. The empty bottles on the bedside table. The open suitcase that could hold clues. "You alone?"

"You could have had me anytime, princess. I've been waiting for you to beg." He shut the door behind him and locked it. Lounged against it as if posing for a magazine cover.

She whirled around and stalked toward him. "What's your story?"

"I ain't got one, sweetheart, but if you give me a few minutes, I'll make one up for you." He licked his lips. "For a price."

She pushed him against the door. "Why *True Love?* What have you got?"

"Oh, that story." Wally Ray chuckled and

moved over to the bed. He picked up a cigarette butt from the ashtray and relit it. "Is that what's got you so hot? It's nothing."

"Really? That's not what I heard."

He laughed again and took a long drag. "Even if there was a story, why would I go and spill it to you? Unless you've got a hundred large to outbid my employer."

A hundred thousand dollars. Elizabeth paled. It had to be huge. She switched tactics. "Wally, you know I have a soft spot for you. Maybe we could help each other. You don't get more on the inside than with me."

"You're on the inside all right." He blew out the smoke so that it drifted in her face.

Her cheeks grew warm. "Leave Rick alone. He's a nice guy, not like the others I've worked with."

"Like I said, unless you can outbid my employer…"

Sweet-talking him didn't work. Neither did appealing to any compassion he might have. She shook her head and grabbed the sleeve of his plaid shirt. "You little opportunistic weasel. You're messing with people's lives. There's nothing going on here."

"That's not what my source says."

She let him go and wiped her hands off. "Do what you want. Say what you want. But you'll be hearing from the network's legal department."

"Freedom of the press, baby."

She unlocked the door and slammed it shut behind her. Just what she didn't need.

RICK CHEERED ON the Lightning Bolts as they scored another goal. Although he would have loved to see the Red Wings play, it felt good to be in the stands rooting for his old high school team. The women on each side of him took up the shouting and clapping. Now, this was his kind of date. He glanced at his three dates. "Anyone want hot dogs? Popcorn?"

He took their orders and walked down the bleachers to the concession stand. Charlie filmed him as he ordered their food, but he noticed that the man seemed a little stressed. "You okay, man?"

"Don't worry about me."

Rick paid the cashier for the food. "What about Lizzie? She as tense as you?"

Charlie lowered the camera. Looked around, then nodded. "There's a reporter in town."

"There's a lot of those. So what's different about this one?"

Charlie leaned in closer. "It's *Hollywood Insider*."

Rick accepted the box of food from the cashier and walked away from the stand. He waited for Charlie to catch up. "What's the story?"

"We don't know."

Rick stopped walking and stared at Charlie. "C'mon. Lizzie knows everything. What's the story?"

Charlie looked him square in the eyes. "The former producer's affair with the bachelorette is becoming old news. Now they want something juicy going on set here."

Rick glanced at the food, then up at the stands where his dates waited. "The reporter will go home when he sees there's no scandal." He looked back at Charlie. "And there is no story. Right? We're all playing our roles. Doing our jobs."

The other man nodded and put the camera back on his shoulder. "Glad we could come to an understanding."

Rick returned to his dates. He handed out hot dogs, popcorn and sodas to the women, then settled in between Becky and Jenny. "This is some game, isn't it? And I have a surprise for you all after the game. We're ice-skating."

His dates squealed, and Rick forced a smile onto his face. He would have fun if his life depended on it.

CHAPTER ELEVEN

RICK WORKED LIKE a magician behind the grill, flipping pancakes, scrambling eggs and frying bacon. His two breakfast dates, Mona and Melissa, watched him with huge eyes much like Elizabeth had when she'd first seen him cook. They sat on stools in the kitchen while the rest of the town tried to peek through the windows of the diner to see what was going on with their favorite citizen.

Rick flipped two pancakes onto a plate, then slid three slices of bacon next to it alongside a scoop of scrambled eggs. With a flourish, he placed the plate in front of Mona. "Here you are, my dear. Compliments of the chef."

Mona wrinkled her nose. "You don't have egg whites?"

Elizabeth rolled her eyes and made notes on her clipboard. When Rick placed a similar plate in front of Melissa, she looked up and thanked him. She got a wink from the handsome chef.

The talk during breakfast centered on their morning plans—a sleigh ride through the town. Elizabeth had found a local farmer who owned not only a cutter but two roans to pull her cast through town. It would be a picturesque tour of Lake Mildred, and her audience would love it. Maybe Rick was right and the show would bring in much-needed tourism.

Jeffy showed up to clear the plates and bumped Mona's elbow, sloshing coffee on her lap. "Hey, watch it. These jeans cost more than your life."

Rick's head snapped up, and he frowned at her. "It was an accident."

"Then he should be more careful. If he can't do his job right, then he shouldn't do it at all." Mona mopped at the dark stain with napkins. "I'd fire him."

Jeffy looked at Rick, then ran outside. Rick dropped the volume of his voice. "He is careful. He's also sweet and kind and wouldn't hurt a fly. He's a good employee. And my friend."

Mona suddenly turned sweet under Rick's glare. "It's okay, sugar. I know he didn't mean to."

Rick glanced at Elizabeth, who turned to Eddie. "Let's take five." She ushered the crew out to the dining room. She returned to discover Rick had left to find Jeffy. She glanced at Mona and Melissa. "Everything okay?"

"Everything was fine until he ruined my outfit." Mona still dabbed at the brown stain on her jeans. "Do you know how much these cost?"

Elizabeth rolled her eyes. "And what about the cost of your tirade to that sweet boy?"

Mona gave a big sigh. "I apologized."

Elizabeth raised an eyebrow. "When? I certainly didn't hear it." She turned to the other woman. "Did you, Melissa?"

She shook her head slightly but didn't say a word. Rick returned to the kitchen and slapped the towel on the counter. He glowered at Mona. "I wouldn't get too comfortable here."

She stood up and straightened her sweater. "Don't worry. This town isn't my type, and neither are you. Whatever happened to defending the woman you love?"

"The woman I love wouldn't come down so hard on a kid. She'd be compassionate. Understanding." He narrowed his eyes at her. "Not cold like you."

Mona turned to Elizabeth. "I want to go back to the house." She glanced at Melissa. "He's all yours."

Melissa smiled brightly. "Gladly." She got

up from her chair and walked beside Rick, linking her arm in his. "The man I love would defend those who can't do it themselves." She looked up at Rick. "You're amazing."

He grinned down at her, and Elizabeth fought the feeling that rose up from her stomach. Anger? Jealousy? She shook her head. This was crazy. He was her friend. Nothing more.

Mona stormed out of the kitchen and into the dining room. Elizabeth groaned. "You two couldn't have waited until cameras were on for that display? We could re-create it."

Rick shook his head. "The moment's over, Lizzie. Besides..." He hugged the woman next to him. "It wouldn't be real. I think you're amazing, too, Missy."

Elizabeth turned on her heel and walked out to the dining room, leaving the two lovebirds. That was what she wanted, right? She wanted Rick to find a wife, and if the moment in the kitchen was any indication, he had. The perfect partner.

Eddie squeezed up next to her. "I'll set up the handheld for the sleigh ride." He pulled his coat on and walked out of the diner.

She surveyed the crew left in the dining room and found the SUV driver finishing his breakfast. "Lou, Mona's going back to the house and we'll be done here around noon."

He wiped his mouth with a napkin, then slid out of the booth. "Noon it is." He left the diner without a word to Mona. Obviously, her little fit in the kitchen hadn't gone unnoticed.

Rick and Melissa walked out of the kitchen holding hands. Elizabeth should be cheering, but instead alarm bells started ringing in her head. She watched the couple for a moment, then sighed. "Ready for that ride?"

WHAT SHOULD HAVE been a quiet sleigh ride through the countryside had turned into a slippery, wet mess in a blizzard. Eddie kept wiping the camera lens. Rick felt cold and miserable. If he didn't have the warm woman snuggled against his side, it would be a disaster.

He put his arms around Melissa and squeezed. "Not exactly the sleigh ride you expected, huh?"

"Does it always snow like this?" Her teeth chattering almost drowned out her words.

"Pretty much, from November through April. Do you think a Southern belle like you could adjust?"

She looked up at him and tried to smile.

"For someone I love, I'd turn my world upside down."

Rick held her closer. She said all the right things. She was beautiful and warm and funny. She was perfect.

Wasn't she? Or was she playing for the cameras like Brandy had? How could he tell what was real?

They took a turn at the end of the road, and the frozen lake the town was named after came into view. The ice-fishing shacks still dotted the icy surface. Long tracks beside the road meant cross-country skiers had recently been along this trek. Despite the cold, wet snow, Rick loved it.

He leaned forward past Eddie, who seemed determined to film everything, and shouted to the driver, "Take a left up here. I want to show Melissa something."

Lizzie glanced around them and shook her head. She held up her clipboard. "That's not on the schedule."

"You can't do everything by the book, Lizzie." He leaned back and pulled the quilts higher. "Let's shake it up a little."

When they reached the family home, Eddie was the first to hop out of the sleigh. Rick held out a hand to Melissa and helped her down, then turned to give Lizzie the same courtesy. As soon as their hands clasped, electricity sparked and he brought his eyes up to meet her own startled expression.

Not good.

His mom met them at the front door, holding it open and sending shards of light onto the covered porch. She looked as if she'd been busy with a book; her reading glasses rested on top of her head. "Come in and get warm."

He reached over and kissed her cheek. "Sorry to barge in like this. I thought I'd show Melissa around. If you don't mind."

She turned to Melissa. "Not at all. I'll make us some coffee while you do that. Warm you all up from the inside out."

Rick helped Melissa out of her coat and hung it on the rack near the front door. He took Melissa's hand and led her into the spacious living room. "This is where I grew up."

"I remember from the tea party your mom hosted." She released his hand and walked over to the fireplace, looking up at the framed pictures that graced the mantel. "You certainly were a handsome young man."

"Still am." He winked at her and took down the picture of his parents on their wedding day. "This was my dad. I wish he was still around to meet you. He'd have loved you."

Melissa looked up at him, her cheeks pink,

obviously pleased by his words. "I remember him from the first time you were on the show."

"It was his idea for me to go on." He replaced the picture. Touched the frame. "He said it was for the company, but I think he knew I needed a wife."

"And now?"

Rick glanced at the camera behind him. "Still do. But I'm willing to take the time to make sure I do it right."

She nodded and turned back to the fireplace. She picked up the recent picture of his family, without his dad. "Do you miss him?"

Every day.

Rick cleared his throat and took her elbow. "I'll give you the tour that you didn't get before."

He took her upstairs to the bedroom where he'd grown up. Trophies and posters still decorated the room. The quilt his mom had made him still covered the twin bed. The books on the shelves above the bed were mostly biographies of sports heroes.

He showed her the bathroom he'd shared with Dan. The corner of the tub where he'd hit his head and needed stitches after he'd been horsing around with his brother. Even after his dad had warned them.

Dan's room and the tiny cubbyhole underneath the floorboards that his brother had thought no one else knew about. The journal he'd kept in high school still waited there. He told Melissa how he'd read it aloud one night over dinner. How Dan had paid him back by running a pair of his boxers up the flagpole at school. Typical brother stuff.

He took her up to the third level that entirely contained his parents' bedroom suite. They'd shared almost thirty years of marriage before his dad had died. Clothes still hung in his dad's walk-in closet.

Melissa looked around the spacious bedroom with the large bathroom and his mom's sewing room jutting off of it. "This house is huge. Unlike anything I've ever seen."

Rick nodded. "My dad designed it. If granddad hadn't died and left him the pickle company, I think he might have become an architect. But we all have to give up dreams sometimes to do the right thing."

Melissa put her hand on his arm. "What about your dreams? What have you given up?"

Rick rubbed his left leg and shrugged. "It doesn't matter. We get the life we deserve."

"Or we can take our circumstances and find new dreams."

Where had Lizzie found this woman? Rick reached out and touched her cheek. Noticed the cameraman recording them and cleared his throat. "If you like the house, you'll love the kitchen. It's really the heart of this place."

The tour ended in the kitchen, where he found his mom and Lizzie sipping coffee. His mom sprang to action and poured mugs for both him and Melissa. "It's not fine china, but it's what's inside the cup that counts." She gave him a pointed look.

Rick put cream and sugar in Melissa's mug, then handed it to her. "Just the way you like it."

Melissa took a sip and nodded. "Perfection," she said, looking at him rather than her cup.

Lizzie shook her head and walked out of the kitchen, mumbling about needing to revise their schedule.

THE CONTESTANTS EACH paired up with a preschooler; Rick had his own rambunctious four-year-old to deal with. He tried to get comfortable in the tiny seat, but his knees came up almost to his shoulders sitting that way. He adjusted and moved until little Wesley turned and frowned at him. "Miss Tompkins don't like it when we wiggle."

Rick leaned in and dropped his voice. "How do you get comfy in these chairs, then?"

Wesley scrunched up his face and put a finger to his mouth. Then he leaned in so close that Rick could smell the shampoo from his bath. "We wiggle when she's not looking."

Miss Tompkins must have seen them. "Wesley, do you have a question?"

Rick raised his head. "No, Miss Tompkins. Just waiting for your directions." He turned to Wesley, and they shared a grin.

Lizzie stood in the corner of the room, checking the releases each parent had signed to get their little one on the show. Rick noticed some parents were determined to get their child more airtime, too. Luckily, Lizzie shepherded them out to the other room with the crew. Rick gave a sigh of relief.

Miss Tompkins passed out old shirts and had the adults help their child partners into theirs after putting on their own. She then passed out large pieces of newsprint paper and paper plates with large splotches of paints in bright primary colors. Some of the women paled as they saw the paint and the eager expressions on their partners. Rick chuckled and nudged Wesley. "What are we gonna paint?"

"Miss Tompkins ain't said yet." Wesley

looked at the colors. "Probably another rainbow. Or butterflies. She really likes those."

"And you don't?"

"I like cars."

Miss Tompkins returned to the front of the classroom. "Boys and girls. Ladies and gentleman. I want you to paint what love looks like. Whatever you imagine love is, paint that."

A little girl near the front raised her hand. "Like hearts?"

Miss Tompkins nodded. "If love looks like hearts to you, Ashley, then yes. Paint hearts."

Rick's tiny partner groaned and crossed his arms. Rick ruffled his hair. "Wesley, what do you love?"

"Cars." He shrugged. "And my mom."

"So maybe love looks like your mom driving a new car?" Rick looked up to find Melissa watching him. He winked, then turned back to his painting partner. "I think love is more than just flowers and hearts, too. Sometimes it's the people we care about."

"Like girls?" Wesley wrinkled his nose.

Rick laughed. "Sometimes. But wait until you're older."

Satisfied with his answer, Wesley set about painting a large red car with big blue wheels. Rick peered at his own blank sheet. What did love look like? He closed his eyes and could see his family. His friends. Even the diner.

Funny how none of the women vying for his heart had made it into the picture.

BRANDY'S FIRST ONE-ON-ONE date with Rick took place in his apartment. He'd made dinner for the two of them and created a romantic atmosphere down to flickering red candles and Ernesto's apple pie.

Charlie set up lights and cameras as both Rick and Brandy got their microphones checked and pinned to them. Elizabeth glanced at the clipboard as if the answers would be there. Answers to questions she didn't want to ask.

What was she doing?

Was she falling for someone she was being paid to marry off to someone else?

What if he found a wife at the end of this? Wasn't that what she wanted? Or was she just fooling herself? Had she engineered this whole thing so she could spend more time with Rick?

She shook her head at the last question. Fought the panic that bubbled in her belly. She was here for a job, not a man. That was her life. That was what she planned.

Not some crazy idea that maybe her friendship with Rick could lead somewhere.

"We're ready."

Her head snapped up at Charlie's words. Leave it to her camera operator to keep her on task. He'd done it before and promised to do it again. "Great." She approached the couple, who nervously adjusted their clothes and hair. "Relax. You two have both been here before. This should be old hat."

She consulted her clipboard. "Dinner here. Then a moonlit walk down Main Street. Romantic. Intimate."

Rick shivered. "Freezing."

She crooked one eyebrow at Rick. "The forecaster said we might hit twenty tonight."

"And the weatherman's always right." Rick grinned at Brandy. "But then we midwesterners know how to handle cold, right?"

Brandy chuckled.

"We're all set up, E." Charlie took a spot behind the camera. "Ready when you are."

She clapped her hands once, then gestured at the table that was set for two. "What do you say we start this date?" She held up the clapboard for the camera as they got settled into their chairs.

Rick pulled out the chair for his date, then brought their salads to the table. "I left off the green peppers on yours."

Brandy froze, the fork halfway to her mouth. Her face broke into a grin. "You remembered."

Rick winked at her. "Hard to forget someone like you."

Brandy swallowed and wiped her mouth delicately. "We haven't talked much about what you've been doing the past five years. Do you like running the diner?"

Rick took his seat and placed the napkin on his lap. "After I lost my contract with the major league, it was my lifeline. The reason I got up in the morning. It saved my life a thousand times. I know I don't have to be there from open to close, but I love it. It's my life." He grabbed his fork. "But that's a talk for another time. Let's eat."

They ate quietly for a moment while Elizabeth took a seat on Rick's sofa and pretended to pay attention to the scene in front of her. There was way too much déjà vu for her. She stood and crossed the room to gaze out the front windows that overlooked the downtown strip. What if she were the one sitting across from Rick? What would her life here be like? She gazed back at the couple enjoying dinner. Would she die of boredom? Or would the charm of this town bring new experiences? A new life?

After the salads, Rick brought out the pot

roast with fixings. Elizabeth's stomach grumbled, which made him smirk. He prepared two plates, brought them to her and Charlie, turned back and made two more. Elizabeth accepted hers with a nod of thanks and began to eat while she watched the date continue.

Brandy gracefully sliced her meat and put a bit of gravy on it. She took a bite, and her eyes closed as she chewed. "Oh, wow. Is that rosemary?"

"And garlic, yes." Rick took a bite of his own meal. "Plus a little coffee added to the gravy to make it hearty."

Brandy licked her fork. "Fabulous."

Elizabeth agreed. Who wouldn't want a husband who could cook like this?

Rick laid his fork next to his plate and glanced at Brandy. "Do you mind if I ask you something?" She sighed but waited for the question. He paused a second, then asked, "Why choose Wade?"

Elizabeth held her breath. It was the question the audience would be asking themselves. Why hadn't she chosen the nice guy? Why choose the bad boy who broke her heart instead?

Brandy dabbed her mouth, then laid the napkin in her lap. "I've been expecting that question."

"Do you mind answering it?"

"The heart wants what it wants." She reached out and touched Rick's hand. "I loved you, too, but it was different."

Rick scooted his chair back from the table. "So what's changed now?" He paused, then tipped his head to the side; one lock of hair fell across his forehead at a rakish angle. "Do you think there's a chance for us this time?"

Brandy shrugged. "Before I didn't know what I wanted."

"And now you do?"

Elizabeth leaned forward. Rick was asking the questions America wanted to know, too. She gave a silent prayer that viewers were tuning in to hear Brandy's answers.

Brandy nodded. "I know better now. I'm ready to be better this time."

It was an answer that would be quoted ad nauseam after they aired, Elizabeth knew. One she would make sure was posted on their website. It was an answer that sounded good, despite the fact that she doubted it. Maybe Brandy really did want to be better this time.

And maybe Elizabeth was wrong about the attraction she'd sensed between Brandy and Dan.

Brandy gave a soft smile, then raised her

water glass. "To Rick, a new man with a new mission."

He raised his own glass and clinked it with hers. After they had taken a sip, Rick kept his gaze on hers and nodded. "To second chances."

Elizabeth hoped the same thing for Rick, a man who deserved another chance.

RICK PUT HIS ARM around Brandy's shoulder as they took their moonlit walk down Main Street. The darkened storefronts added a hint of mystery and romance with the glow of the streetlamps lighting their path only a few steps at a time.

Being with Brandy felt comfortable. Familiar. He'd been here before. He could easily fall back into love again. After all, five years could be nothing.

Brandy leaned her head on his shoulder, and Rick pulled her in tighter. "I'm glad you're here."

She sighed, and her body seemed to melt further into his. "I'm glad I came."

They walked to the end of the street, then turned back. Rick could see a dark sedan parked in front of the diner. "Looks like my brother wants to see me."

Brandy's body tensed but remained glued

to his side. She looked away from the car and focused on him. "Dan seems nice."

"He can be. But then he's my older brother so I remember all the lame things he did growing up." He chuckled and pulled her closer. Tried to ignore the fact that she didn't respond as quickly as she had earlier. "Before we get back, I'd like to talk to you about something."

She didn't say anything. Seemed to wait on his next words.

He held out the small jewelry box. "If I give you the immunity charm—"

"Rick, don't." She pushed the box back into his hands and stepped away from him.

He frowned and stopped walking. Waited until she looked up at him. "Don't you want to stay?"

"Of course I do." She bit her lip, a habit that had enthralled and frustrated him before. "But I need to earn my place here just like all the other girls."

Rick held the box out again. "You already have. I want you to have this." She shook her head and started walking back to the diner. Rick had to sprint to keep up with her fast little legs. "Brandy, I want you to stay."

She turned and faced him. "Give the charm to someone else this week."

He thought he understood. He could remember what it was like returning from one of their dates with the charm. It made things tense with the other guys, even those he'd become friends with. He put the box back into his pocket. "Are things bad back at the house?"

She shrugged, then nodded. "They don't like me. Well, except Melissa. She's a sweetheart." She picked at her mittens. "Giving me the charm this week would only make it worse. Please don't."

Rick nodded, then pulled her back into his arms. "Okay. You're the boss."

Brandy giggled, and the heaviness in his heart lightened slightly.

CHAPTER TWELVE

RICK TURNED the open sign and unlocked the doors to the diner. After several weeks playing bachelor, he welcomed the chance to get back to a seminormal schedule.

Last night's elimination hadn't been a surprise to anyone. Mona needed to go home, and he had been more than happy to send her. They were down to six women—Melissa, Brandy, Becky, Jenn, Leslie and Vanessa. The only one he wasn't sure was meant for small-town life was the last. They'd barely spoken except for that moment by the lake with their dogs, but tonight's one-on-one would change that.

The bell over the door tinkled, and Mr. Crosby walked in followed by his pals Mr. Teetum and Mr. White. "Hey, fellas, I've got fresh coffee."

They waved their agreement and took their usual spot at a table near the back, where they'd spend the next four hours discussing sports and politics and drinking coffee. Rick snagged three mugs and the carafe.

Once the men were settled, Rick discovered that Lizzie had called a crew meeting at the front of his diner. Troy, Charlie, Eddie and Nick, the sound guy, perused menus while Lizzie chirped on the phone. He grabbed four mugs and met them at the table. "Gentlemen, lady, can I interest you in some coffee?"

Charlie accepted a mug, as did Nick. Eddie shook his head. "I'll take an espresso, though. Elizabeth told me you got the new machine."

Rick raised an eyebrow and shrugged. "It's been over a month, so it's hardly new. Single or double?"

Eddie grinned. "Surprise me."

Rick turned to Lizzie, who held up her finger at him as she hissed into the phone. Obviously a bad morning. He poured her a cup of regular coffee, then left to get Eddie's espresso order.

When he returned with Eddie's drink, Lizzie had finished her call and was going over notes with her crew. "The set looks dark on air. Charlie, that's your expertise. Brighten it up. Bring in more lamps. I don't care. Fix it."

Charlie nodded and took notes on his napkin.

Lizzie turned to Eddie, who guzzled the espresso, then held his tiny cup out for Rick to refill. "I'm also not happy that you're choosing your own footage. You've got your shot list. Stick to it."

"Then we lose the candid moments." Eddie leaned in. "Like the criers the past few weeks. The audience eats that stuff up, you know."

"So you're producing the show, too, now?" Lizzie shook her head. "Stick to your list. And leave the editing decisions to Troy and me."

"I'm trying to make this tired show into something magnificent." Eddie stood and slammed down his cup. "If you're done yelling, I'm outta here."

Lizzie stood and glared at her cameraman. Rick took a step closer in case she needed him to knock some sense into the kid. She shook her head at Rick and he took a step back. "We're done when I say we're done. And these are just the beginning of the notes I have from last night's show."

Rick passed out menus. "Why don't you order some food to go with those notes? Everybody feels better with some food in their stomach."

Lizzie seemed to sigh in relief. "Thanks, Rick. That's a great idea."

After they had made their selections, Rick left to give their order to Ernesto. The diner was still short a waitress, and Rick had interviews scheduled for later that week. Which gave him an idea.

As he delivered their breakfasts, he leaned against their table. "I've got another great idea."

Lizzie groaned, which made her crew grin. "What's it going to cost me?"

"That's the beauty. Not a thing." He leaned down, inviting them to draw in. "What about putting the remaining six in a waitressing competition? See who's got the stuff to work here, be a true partner."

Lizzie whistled. "When you get good ideas, you really do. I like it." She turned to her crew. "How much of a logistical nightmare would it be to film?"

Charlie glanced around the diner. "Lighting's an issue. Sound might be another story, but it could work."

"Thanks, Rick. We'll schedule it just before the next elimination."

Rick hummed a tune as he returned to the kitchen.

ELIZABETH WAS SMART enough to know when someone had a better idea and to use it. She liked the idea of having the women wearing waitress outfits and being put through the same test Rick had put her through before agreeing to do the show. It was character building. And it made great television. She'd made a list of items she needed to pick up as well as a schedule of what needed to be done and where.

She picked at her cold piece of toast. Her crew had left a few minutes ago, after being given their assignments for the day. Charlie was filming tonight's one-on-one with Rick and Vanessa, while Eddie got assigned the women's house and candid interviews. She reviewed her clipboard, then rose to her feet to find Rick.

He sat at the counter in the kitchen eating hash browns loaded with sour cream and green onions. She wrinkled her nose. "You really eat that?"

Rick motioned her closer and held up a fork. "Taste it first. Then tell me what you think."

She approached him and opened her mouth. The first taste was creamy and tangy followed by the bite and snap of the onion. She closed her eyes and swallowed. "Oh, my, that is good."

Rick smirked and returned to eating his breakfast. "You needed something?"

"That idea of yours is inspired." She leaned against the counter, facing him. "I should listen to you more."

"I do have good ideas every once and a while." He shrugged. "Not that many people listen to them."

Probably thinking of his brother. "Then they're really missing out."

Rick reached up and wiped the side of her mouth with one finger. Her skin tingled at his touch, and her mouth opened slightly.

He held out his finger. "Sour cream."

She wiped the side of her mouth he'd just touched. "Right. Thanks."

A noise outside the kitchen door caught her attention, but no one was there. Probably her imagination. "Good luck tonight. Vanessa might be a hard sell on the whole small-town-living thing."

"Maybe she has reason to be."

"You cut people a lot of slack. Whether they deserve it or not." She stood and adjusted her coat. "That's what makes you one of the nice guys."

"I try." He motioned to the pile of dirty dishes near the sink. "Feel like washing some for old times' sake?"

She held up her hands. "I need these today. But thanks." She laughed and walked out of the kitchen. Made a note to finally get him that industrial dishwasher.

VANESSA LOOKED LOVELY in a red satin dress. The fact that it was strapless and the weather was more suitable for sweaters didn't seem to faze her. Rick glanced at the program. It constantly amazed him that Lizzie could come up with fresh ideas for dates in such a small town. Tonight's date was a play put on by a nearby community theater. It wouldn't be Broadway, but it promised to be entertaining.

Rick leaned closer to Vanessa, catching a hint of orange blossoms. "So you're a dental hygienist?"

She looked up at him and considered him before answering. "Actually, I had to quit to come on the show."

He frowned. Not a smart move in a shaky economy. "Why would you quit a job?"

"Why would you come back on television to find a wife?" She adjusted the top of her dress. "I felt I had no other choice."

He swallowed at the sudden pressure in his throat. Wanted to wipe at the moisture he was sure gathered at his temples. Had they turned up the heat in the theater? "And what if this doesn't work out?"

Vanessa shrugged. "I'll find another job. I might not get another chance like this with a nice guy." She placed her hand on his arm.

"You don't date nice guys?"

She gave a soft smile but it had a tinge of bitterness. "I have the bad habit of dating the wrong ones."

Rick understood. Hadn't he had his own share of dates with women who were definitely wrong? "So what are you looking for in a man?"

She removed her hand from his arm and placed it on his thigh, caressing his leg. Rick didn't move away despite the panic it brought him. "Nice. Good-looking. Someone who makes me laugh."

He chuckled. "Have I told you the one about a duck that walks into a bar?"

Vanessa laughed harder than was necessary. Rick frowned at the response. He was looking for something real, but this wasn't it.

Real was Melissa. Maybe even Brandy.

Or Lizzie.

He welcomed the anonymity of the darkened theater as the production began onstage. Gave him time to consider that last name.

ELIZABETH STARED at the images on the computer screen.

No. Not possible.

Yet there they were. In Rick's kitchen. They appeared cozy. Intimate. She paled as she saw the picture of Rick touching the corner of her mouth. This looked bad.

Her cell phone chirped, but she ignored it. She searched Rick's name on Google and grimaced when six websites came up boasting the same pictures. Headlines of True Love for Producer and Bachelor? and It's Getting Hot in the Kitchen screamed from her computer screen.

Obviously someone had been spying on them and taking pictures. But who? Someone in town? One of her own crew? Wally Ray?

She picked up her cell phone and saw she'd missed Devon's call. So she wasn't the only one who had seen these. Instead of calling him back, however, she grabbed her jacket and headed out the door. Time to talk to the weasel himself.

Wally Ray didn't answer when she pounded on his motel door. A glimpse under the door and through the crack of the drapes revealed no lights inside. She walked back to the parking lot and glanced up and down the street. Wally Ray was a drunk, but he wasn't an idiot. He'd walk to the nearest bar rather than risk driving anywhere farther out.

She found him at the Rusty Nail, nursing a beer and yelling at the television. She stood in front of him, blocking his view. "Hey, I got money on that game."

She stayed where she was and crossed her arms. "Who gave you those pictures?"

Wally Ray took a sip of his beer. "Saw them, huh? They're good. And I got paid coupla times over for them, too." He snickered. "Everyone loves a scandal."

She grimaced and shook her head. "There's nothing going on."

Wally Ray licked his lips. "You sure? 'Cuz it looked like a big something to me."

She leaned down and tried not to tip his chair over. He wouldn't get away with this. "Rick is a good guy. Decent. Leave him alone."

"Is that why you're with him?"

She stood and shook her head. "I'm not. We're not." She ran a hand through her hair. "We're friends."

"I gotta get me a friend like you, then." He started to sip his beer, but she took it from him. "Hey, I paid for that."

"Who took those pictures?" When he tried

to take his glass back, she held it higher. "Tell me and you get it back."

"I can order another."

He held up his hand to the bartender. But Elizabeth waved him off. "Be the nice guy for a change. Where did you get these photos?"

"Sweetheart, I get paid well for those photos. And I get paid more to keep my mouth shut." He stood and looked up at her. "Now, unless you have a nice big figure in mind, I'm gonna find me a drink."

Elizabeth growled and left the bar. Her cell phone sang a Diana Ross song, and she prepared herself for bad news. "What happened this time, Mom?"

But the gruff voice that answered didn't belong to her mother. "Ms. Maier, your mother is in the hospital."

CHARLIE PUT THE CAMERA equipment in the back of the limo, then joined Rick and Vanessa inside. The performance had been good, but hardly prizewinning. Still, Rick made a note to see more of these productions. Support some of the local theater. Might be nice to support someone else's dreams for once.

Charlie's phone rang. While he answered it, Rick glanced at Vanessa. She patted her hair into place despite the fact that it looked perfect. He tried to imagine what a future with her would be like. "Did you enjoy the play?"

She shrugged and gazed out the window. Rick sighed and tried to find something to talk about. "Ernesto made Italian cream cake today at the diner. I've got three pieces with our names on them. What do you say?"

Charlie snapped his phone shut. "Can't. E needs to see you right away."

That didn't sound good. "Everything okay?"

Charlie didn't answer; he leaned toward the driver and changed their destination to the house where the women lived. The rest of the car ride was silent. Rick tried to figure out why he felt as if he were a child waiting for his father to come home and discipline him. Something wasn't right. And he had no idea what it could be.

The driver let Vanessa out at the women's house, then sped off toward the hotel where Lizzie and the crew were staying. Rick turned to Charlie. "Not even a hint about what's going on?"

"E will go over it with you." The cameraman didn't elaborate, but by the grim set of his mouth, it wasn't good.

"Okay." Rick settled back into the seat, gazing out the window as they passed through Lake Mildred. He glanced at his dark apartment and diner, wishing he could end the night alone. Maybe catch the sports report on the news.

They arrived at the hotel, and Charlie quietly escorted Rick to one of the conference rooms, where crew members milled around talking on phones, typing on computers, ignoring them. Rick spotted Lizzie across the room on the phone. He didn't need to hear the words to know that she was upset. She paced. Shouted. Shook her head. Talked with her hands even though the person on the other side couldn't see them.

When she looked up and saw him and Charlie, she stalked toward them. Charlie patted Rick's shoulder and left. Rick glanced at his retreating figure and swallowed at the panic rising in his throat. What happened to sticking together?

Lizzie grabbed a stack of photos from one of the tables and thrust them at Rick. "What do you know about these?"

Rick glanced through them and frowned. "Who's taking pictures at my diner?"

"That's what I want to know." Lizzie pointed to the top one. "Who's trying to sabotage your life and my show?"

"And you think I know the answer?" He stopped at the one where he was wiping sour cream from her mouth. Winced. "This looks bad."

"You think?" She snatched the photos from him and slammed them on the desk. "Who in town needs money bad enough that they would sell these?"

Wait. No one he knew could do this. Would do this. Rick frowned. "You think it's one of my friends?"

Lizzie glared at him, probably hoping it would wither him. Make him confess something. "Hollywood coming to town doesn't happen every day. Maybe someone thought they could make an easy buck."

"No one I know would sell me out." He crossed his arms and looked her over. "But I'm sure you know a few who would."

"This is why I wanted it done the regular way. A closed set. Controlled." She rubbed her forehead. "Those pictures are all over the internet. It's the lead story on tonight's news. I got calls from the tabloids. It's like the scandal with Bob all over again. This is a nightmare."

Rick looked at the pictures again and tried to chuckle. "It's not like they're nude photos."

Lizzie pointed at him. "Don't make a joke of this. They're damaging enough."

She stalked away from him. Rick grabbed

the top photo and perused it. Anyone with half a brain could see they had chemistry together. Even if there was nothing going on, his confusing feelings were now out there in glossy eight-by-tens. He followed Lizzie to a computer and pulled up a chair next to her.

He sighed and folded his hands in his lap. "So what do we do now?"

"We spin it." She kept her focus on the computer monitor. Refused to look at him. "And we hope that a bigger story comes to take its place quick."

Rick nodded. "Sounds like a plan."

"And you stay away from me. We're never alone. We don't even have to talk to each other." She glanced up at him, then back at her laptop. "If we're not seen together, there's no story."

They worked together. How in the world were they going to avoid each other? "But you're my producer."

"Not for the next couple of days." She clicked off her laptop and shoved it into a messenger bag. "I have something personal to take care of."

When she started to step away, Rick grabbed her arm. "Won't it look even more suspicious if you suddenly disappear from the set?"

She shook his hand off. "There's nothing

to see if I'm gone. And it's only for a couple of days. Maybe a week."

Rick looked around the room at the crew, who scurried here and there, answering phones, typing on laptops. "And who's going to do the day-to-day producing when you're gone?"

Lizzie nodded at a young man surrounded by crew members. He held a familiar clipboard. "I've promoted Troy. For now."

Rick shuddered. "That guy rubs me the wrong way."

"At least there won't be incriminating pictures of you two all over the internet." She hitched the bag higher on her shoulder.

"Those pictures only captured innocent moments between friends." He wanted to tell her it was going to be okay. That they weren't going to be driven apart by this. "You're making a big deal out of nothing."

Lizzie looked up at him, tears threatening. "This might be my last season with the show. I'm on notice."

He winced at the tears. He could handle anything but that. "Then you'll get a new show."

She shook her head. "If the network fires me, no one in Hollywood will hire me."

"They're not that powerful." Only in her

mind. Maybe he could help her see that. Maybe he could convince her that there was more to life than the show. The network.

Lizzie snatched the pictures from the table and shook them in his face. "These will ruin any chance for me. Who's going to hire a producer who can't keep scandal away from her show?" She slammed them back onto the table. "This is not a game to me, Rick. This is my life."

He reached out and touched her arm. "It's your job, Lizzie. Not your life."

"It's the same thing."

"Then I feel sad for you." He started to walk away.

Lizzie followed him. Practically stepped on his heels. "You don't get to tell me how to live my life."

He whirled around and faced her. "You've done a pretty good job of telling me how to live mine." He motioned to everyone in the room, who had stopped talking to watch them. "I was fine before you all came here. I had a life before the show, and I'll have one that's just fine after."

Lizzie smirked. "If your life was so great, why did I find you still stuck here after five years? What happened to your plans of getting out?"

Plans changed. Dreams did, too. Rick seethed and gritted his teeth. "When my dad died—"

"Right. He died. Not you."

He opened his mouth to say something. Shut it. Then turned and walked out of the conference room.

CHAPTER THIRTEEN

RICK SAT IN FRONT of the camera and rolled his head from side to side. Rubbed his knee, which had begun to ache. Troy had been doing interviews for the past two hours nonstop. What was he trying to do? Kill the show with boredom?

"Seriously. Can't we plan one of the dates? Or plan the next elimination?" Rick glanced at Charlie, who looked as bored as he was.

Troy shook his head and consulted the clipboard. "The problem with Elizabeth was she focused on the dates, but the audience connects with the bachelor because of the interviews."

"Have you ever watched the show? They love the conflict and the romance." Rick stood and stretched to get feeling back in his arms and legs. "Trust me. They fast-forward the interviews."

Troy frowned. "Well, Elizabeth said—"

"Lizzie's not here." Rick glanced at Charlie. "Sorry, man. I need to stretch my legs or something."

Rick left his apartment and walked down to the diner. The lunch crowd had already thinned out, but he found Jeffy sitting at the counter, eating a plate of fries. Rick took the seat next to him. "Mind if I have one?"

Jeffy pushed his plate toward him. "Mr. Rick, we've missed you."

Rick snagged a fry and dipped it in ketchup. "I've missed you, too, buddy. They keep me pretty busy."

"When will this be over? I want to work with you again."

"A few more weeks." Rick ate another fry, then motioned to Shirley. "Can you get me a club sandwich and fries?"

"Sure, Rick." She wrote his order down and leaned on the counter next to him. "Please tell me this show is almost done."

He touched his chest. "You guys miss me that much? I'm touched."

Shirley groaned and rubbed her lower back. "The lunch crowds are killing me. I deserve a raise."

Rick shouted after her as she left, "You'll get one." He turned back to Jeffy and helped himself to another fry. "So what have I missed?"

"Shirley's feet hurt and make her cranky. Mr. Ernesto is tired." Jeffy bit his lip, then shrugged. "Did Mr. Eddie give you the picture?"

Rick stopped eating the French fry and frowned. "What are you talking about, buddy?"

"He took a picture of you and Miss Lizzie. Said he was going to give it to you. Like a surprise."

Rick closed his eyes. *Right.* "Yes, those pictures were a surprise. Thanks for telling me." He got to his feet and motioned to Shirley. "Can you wrap my sandwich to go? I have a phone call to make."

ELIZABETH HAD ELEVEN missed calls on her cell phone when the plane landed in San Francisco. While in the air, she'd glanced out the window and marveled at the clouds that covered any view of the land below. Too bad she couldn't live up there where problems wouldn't find her. Where temperamental cast members wouldn't make her life miserable. And internet rumors wouldn't make her run away.

As if that was the problem.

The longer she'd thought about it, the more she'd come to believe that the photographer who had started all this was someone she knew. Perhaps someone she'd hired. The fact that they knew who to give the pictures to pointed to someone with inside knowledge of tabloids. Someone who knew the business. Someone who could get in touch with Wally Ray, promising a big story.

She regretted now the way she'd jumped all over Rick. He hadn't deserved that, but he'd been there. Earnest and handsome as ever. She'd wanted to protect him from the press, but it turned out that she needed to protect him from herself.

She searched the concourse for a coffee shop that didn't have a mile-long line. These endless days and sleepless nights were getting to her.

While she waited in line for coffee, she dialed her voice mail and entered her password. She listened to the first three before hanging up and dialing Devon. "I want that weasel off my set."

"Elizabeth, you obviously got my message."

The line moved up one step. If she didn't get coffee soon… "Tell me I can fire him."

"It's not that simple."

Frustrated, Elizabeth left the coffee shop and strode down the hall of the terminal, hiking her carry-on higher over her shoulder. "Eddie compromised the show for a couple of bucks. I should have known—"

"No one knew."

She walked in the direction of the ticket counters. "Well, now that we do, I'm going back to take care of this." She checked her watch and read the signs to see when the next flight back left.

"You have more important things to take care of right now."

"I know." She stopped walking and closed her eyes. "If I didn't have to go take care of my mom, you know I'd be back on the next plane. This is my show."

"Knowing it was Eddie doesn't change the fact that you're getting too close to Rick."

She scanned the crowded hall and lowered her voice. "Rick is a good friend. There's nothing going on. How many times do I have to say it?"

There was silence on the other end of the line. Elizabeth almost felt triumphant to make Devon speechless.

"You're off set for a week, Elizabeth. Let the scandal blow over." He paused while she let her carry-on sag to the floor. "In the meantime, keep doing what you planned. Take care of your mom."

Elizabeth hung up with Devon and massaged her forehead. *Right*. Take care of her mom. Truth was, she had no idea what she'd find once she got to the hospital.

RICK SAT IN one of the booths as the six women raced to serve their tables. Ernesto had mixed orders to see which women could keep them straight and which could handle the stress while staying positive. Melissa appeared to be handling it the best, providing the best service with a smile. Brandy, on the other hand, could spot the switches and change it back to the way her orders read.

If anyone had doubts about who would fit into Rick's life, this competition was clearing any of that confusion.

Once the orders were served, they all joined Rick at the booth. Jeffy brought over plates of salads with little cups of dressing. Rick gave each of the women a wide grin. "You all did very well. My life can sometimes get like what you just did. What did you think?"

Melissa placed her fork on the table. "It would be a challenge to learn, but I think I could adjust."

Rick agreed. She'd handled it really well. He could see her in the diner. He could see

her living with him in the apartment upstairs, too. They'd probably want to find a
house soon after the wedding. The place was
crowded with just him.

Brandy shrugged. "It was fun to do, but
I don't think I could handle working at the
diner day after day. Is that really your life?"

"For now." Rick poured some French dressing over his salad while he changed Melissa
with Brandy in the picture of his future. Even
if she didn't help out at the diner every day,
she could still fit into his world. But then he'd
always seen her here in Lake Mildred. "My
whole life is the diner at the moment. And
that means early mornings and long days. I
wouldn't expect my wife to work here unless
she wanted to, but I do view our life together
as a partnership."

They considered that as they finished their
salads. Jeffy brought out their turkey dinners
and a basket of rolls. "Enjoy."

After dinner, they drove back to the house
for the elimination. Rick didn't have any
doubts which women were going home this
time. Looked as if he was going to pull another surprise out of the bag.

RICK STOOD IN FRONT of the women. He knew
what he had to do. Knew he had to make the

right decision. And that was what this was. The necklaces felt heavy in his hand. As if they knew they meant more than a gold chain with a charm. He looked between them then nodded. "Brandy."

She stepped forward. "Brandy, will you accept my heart?"

She gave him that smile that made him want to drop to his knees and hold on to her. "Absolutely."

He placed the necklace around her neck, then kissed her cheek before she turned and joined the rest of the women. He separated the next necklace. "Melissa."

Melissa also smiled as she approached him. He could lose himself in her beautiful face. No doubt. He found comfort in her. Peace. None of the soul-troubling passion he had once felt for Brandy, but he felt safe with that. As if he wouldn't lose himself by loving her. "Melissa, will you accept my heart?"

She reached up and kissed his cheek. "Yes." After the necklace rested around her neck, they embraced tightly. He almost didn't want to let her go.

He looked at the necklaces in his hand then surveyed the rest of them. He pulled another necklace away from the other two then looked out and nodded again. "Becky."

She practically ran up to him and threw her arms around him. "Yes, yes, yes."

He chuckled at her exuberance. She would be joy and light in his life. She would bring laughter and fun. He put the necklace around her neck and kissed her cheek. "I'm glad you're willing."

She winked at him. "You have no idea."

She joined the rest of the contestants, who watched him. Waiting for the next name. Wanting it to be theirs.

He looked down at the necklaces. "I'm sorry, ladies. I won't be giving out any more tonight." When they protested, he shook his head. "I've enjoyed my time with you, but it would be unfair to drag this out any longer. Each of you is beautiful. Amazing. And deserving of love. But I don't feel that you can find that with me."

He approached them and took his time telling the other three goodbye. Leslie tried to hide her tears, but he could still see them glistening. "You'll find the guy who's right for you. I know it."

She shook her head and walked away from him.

Man, he hated this part of the show.

ELIZABETH APPROACHED the hospital room but paused before entering, unsure of what she'd find on the other side of the door. A nurse whisked past her into the room while she stood trying to decide. In a moment, the nurse came back out. "She's awake if you want to see her."

Elizabeth steeled herself and then stepped inside.

She let out all her air at the sight of her mother hooked up to machines. Both eyes were black with bruises, and a bandage covered her chest from what the cop had said was a slash from a butcher's knife.

This couldn't be happening. Shouldn't be. *No, no, no.*

She took a step forward and clutched the end of the bed. She hung her head and cried silently until the woman in the bed stirred. "Bethie?"

"Oh, Mom." She walked to the head of the bed and collapsed into a chair beside it. Grasped her mother's hand. "What happened?"

"I thought he loved me." Tears squeezed from her mother's bruised eyes. "But this… It's not love."

"No, Mom. It never is." She leaned her forehead on her mother's hand. "When are they releasing you? Do you have somewhere to go?"

Her mother stayed silent. Watching her. Finally, she said, "I was hoping I could stay with you."

Mild panic rose in Elizabeth's chest. With her? Could her mother fit into her life now? They hadn't been close in years. Hadn't lived together since she was sixteen and her mom had wanted to move to Arizona. She shook her head. "I'm not at home right now. I'm on assignment."

Her mother swallowed. "You always are."

"Because that's my life." It was always her life. In the past year, she'd been home a total of thirty-two days. If she didn't need somewhere to go back to, she'd get rid of her apartment altogether and live out of a suitcase. Much like she already did.

Her mom closed her eyes and faintly squeezed her hand. "Oh, Bethie, I wanted more for you than some job."

"This is not some job. This is a major show on network television. This is what I've worked for my whole life."

"And what about love?"

The woman tethered to machines was going to lecture her about relationships? "We both can see where love can get you." Elizabeth winced. "Sorry, Mom. I didn't—"

"I know." Her mother squeezed her hand again. "I haven't been the best example."

"Not even close." Elizabeth swallowed and removed her hand from her mother's. "Why did he always come first?"

"He didn't—"

"I was six, and you left me at a bus station while you went off who knows where doing whatever it was with your new boyfriend." Elizabeth shuddered, pulled her arms closer to her sides and crossed them. Whether to keep out the chill or to protect herself, she wasn't sure. She only felt the need to hug herself. "I thought you'd left me. I thought you were never coming back. I thought you stopped loving me."

"I could never stop that."

"You only call me when you need something. Not to say hi or to find out how I'm doing." She stood. "You call me when your new man dumps you and you have to move out again. You ask me for money when he steals all of yours. You want to move in with me when you have nowhere else to go." The tiny beeps of the machines filled the air between them. Elizabeth shook her head. "That's not love, either, Mom."

"Neither is your job."

"My job makes sure I have somewhere to

live. And food in my belly. Which is more than you did." She hiked her purse higher on her shoulder. "I'm sorry that he did this to you. And I'll pay for your hospital bills. But I can't let you go home with me right now."

Elizabeth's cell phone chirped, but she ignored it. "I can help you find somewhere to go."

Her mom turned away. "Just go answer your phone."

She walked out of the hospital room, shut the door and dialed Troy's number. "What now?"

"You need to come back."

As if she didn't want to. She needed this job even more now. The proof of that was lying in a hospital bed. "I'm dealing with some personal things. What is it?"

"Your boyfriend just changed our entire schedule."

Elizabeth shut her eyes and tapped the cell phone on her forehead. She replaced it to her ear. "Is Rick there?"

A few seconds later, a warm voice came on the other end. "Lizzie."

"Don't 'Lizzie' me. What did you do?"

There was a pause, then a long sigh. "Tonight was the elimination."

No kidding. She may not be on set, but she

was still very aware of what was happening on her show. "Yes..."

"And I sent Vanessa home."

She took a deep breath. "Okay. I had a feeling she wouldn't last."

"And Jenny. And Leslie."

He'd just removed two weeks from their schedule. "Then you ask two of them to come back."

"I'm not doing that."

"We have schedules for a reason, Rick. We have to fill so many weeks with episodes, and when you change it up, we lose whole weeks of programming." She rested her head against the wall. "We're locked into an agreement with the network about how many we'll deliver." She fought to keep her voice calm. "And you just screwed that up."

"You might see it like that."

Might? He had no idea what he'd done. "Because that's how it is."

"Or you could see that I want more time with the finalists. Give me a chance to really know them." He paused. "How can you expect me to know who I want to spend the rest of my life with when I barely know her? I need more time."

"Well, you just got it. Put Troy back on the line." There was an exchange on the other side, and Troy came back on. She started marking things off with her fingers. "Do you have your clipboard? Good. Move the family dinner to this weekend and eliminate the bingo night. It was a logistics nightmare anyway. And I'll figure out the rest. Have you got that?"

"When are you coming back?"

Elizabeth pulled her planner out of her purse and consulted her calendar. "I'll be there by Friday night. Make sure you have a car to pick me up. And, Troy? No more surprises."

She snapped her phone shut and tossed it into her purse. No more surprises at all.

RICK DELIVERED a veggie stir-fry to Troy's table, then took a seat across from him. "Can we talk?"

Troy looked up from his cell phone and frowned. "Is something wrong?"

"You tell me. Lizzie's been gone for days, and I need her." He lounged back in the booth. He'd missed her these past few days. He'd been busy with the show, planning for the family dinner this weekend, but his thoughts drifted to her often. He missed her laugh, her smile, her presence. He rubbed his face. "Why isn't she back yet?"

His producer placed his cell phone on the table and unrolled the napkin surrounding his silverware. Adjusted his water glass. Fiddled with his fork. Stalling.

Rick sighed. "Why did she leave?"

"She'll be back tomorrow afternoon. Then you can make *her* life miserable instead of mine."

Rick rose to his feet. "Enjoy your dinner."

He left Troy and saw Charlie sitting at the counter. Rick took the seat next to the cameraman. "Did you need anything else?"

Charlie looked down at his empty plate and shook his head. "I think I've gained ten pounds eating here every day."

Rick nodded and grinned. "Appreciate the business, man."

"Pretty easy to do when you're one of the only restaurants in town." Charlie picked up his coffee cup and took a long swallow.

Rick rose to his feet and retrieved the coffee carafe, topped off Charlie's cup and poured one for himself. Sure, it was late, but he hadn't slept much the past few nights anyway. He returned to his stool and doctored his coffee with cream and sugar. "Who's going to pick Lizzie up from the airport tomorrow?"

Charlie shrugged. "Probably Troy. They

have some things to go over, and you know how E hates to waste time."

Rick chuckled at that. Very true. "Think I could hitch along on that ride? I have some things of my own to discuss with her."

"I don't think that's a good idea."

Rick turned and looked over the cameraman. "And why is that?"

"Listen, I'm not supposed to know this, but she's feeling fragile right now." Charlie paused, as if to let the words sink in, then shook his head. "Sorry, I shouldn't have said anything. Never mind."

"You can't start talking and then just stop like that." Rick leaned in. "I consider her my friend, too, and I'm worried about her. What happened?"

Charlie glanced around, then dropped his voice to a whisper. "I'm only telling you because she's going to need a friend when she gets back. And you're the best one she has right now."

That meant a lot, especially coming from him. Rick held up two fingers. "I won't share what you tell me. Scout's honor."

The cameraman looked him over, then sighed. "Her mom got hurt pretty bad, and E flew out to check on her, to take care of things."

Rick sat back and absorbed the information. "She doesn't talk about her mom."

"She's got reason not to." He picked up his cup and took a swallow. "And that's all I'm saying."

Rick nodded and toyed with his coffee cup. His heart ached for her. He remembered watching his father in the hospital. Praying that he'd recover, accepting the inevitable when the doctors gave them no hope.

He stood and clapped Charlie on the shoulder. "Thanks for being honest with me, man. Lizzie means a lot to me."

And in that moment, he realized how much. And he needed to find a way to be the one to pick her up from the airport. Because there were some things that needed to be said between them before it was too late.

ELIZABETH SCANNED the luggage-retrieval area for her ride. Lou, Troy, whoever. It didn't matter. She'd told Troy no more surprises, and she'd meant it. And being stood up at the airport didn't work for her.

"Lizzie, over here."

She turned and saw Rick waving. But then maybe surprises were a good thing.

She grabbed the handle of her rolling suitcase and headed in his direction. Once she was a few feet from him, he jogged up and took the handle from her. "Here. Let me."

Always a gentleman.

She handed him the suitcase, and he led her out to the sidewalk, where Lou waited with one of the SUVs. Rick opened the door and helped her inside, then ran to the back and loaded her suitcase. He was being so solicitous. She wondered if he was buttering her up to get something. Probably something she wasn't willing to give.

He opened the door and slid in next to her. Leaned over and gave the driver the signal to leave. Then settled back and fastened his seat belt.

He looked tired, she thought. Puffy eyes. Tension lines in his forehead. Jaw clenched. She reached out and touched his hand. "What's going on?"

He shrugged. "What do you mean?"

"Why are you here instead of Troy?"

He opened his mouth, then shook his head. "I bribed Troy into letting me be the one to pick you up. That's all."

That's all? There was more to it, she was sure of it. "Okay, then." He'd tell her when he was ready. She settled into the seat and turned on her cell phone. Scrolled through her email. Checked her phone log.

Rick sighed. "I know about your mom."

Her eyes snapped up to meet his. She scowled, hating the pity she saw there. "How did you…?"

"Charlie let it slip," he said. "But you should have been the one to tell me."

"It's none of your business." And it wasn't. Never would be. Why did he have to be so comforting, so welcoming? Why couldn't he let her keep her personal problems to herself and not bring them out for everyone to see?

"It is when it takes you away from my show."

Elizabeth chuckled. "Your show? Interesting."

"You know what I mean." He reached out and took her hand. "I thought we were friends. I thought we could tell each other anything. And then you leave town…"

"I had to leave town." She removed her hand from his grip. "Things were getting too…" Her voice trailed off, and she stared out the window at the passing highway. "We needed to put some space between us."

"I don't want space. I want…"

Elizabeth turned to look at him. Saw the different emotions playing in his eyes. She felt a pull toward him. The need to reach out and smooth the hair by his forehead that was sticking up at an odd angle. Instead, she clenched her fists. "You want to find your wife. And I'm here to help you do that."

He swallowed and searched her eyes. "What if my wife isn't one of them? What if she's someone else entirely?"

The air in the truck warmed as they gazed at each other. Finally, she shook her head. "Rick..." Her voice broke, so she cleared her throat. "It's cold feet. I've seen it every season. It gets down to the last three contestants, and the bachelor starts to get nervous. That's all this is. Nerves."

"We both know it's more than that." He leaned forward and touched her cheek.

Her eyes drifted closed, and her breath caught as Rick pressed his lips against hers, so softly she thought she thought she must be imagining it. But the pressure on her lips stayed until she turned away.

"Don't." She rubbed her lips with the back of her hand, trying to stop the tingling sensation his kiss had ignited.

Rick's brow furrowed with hurt. And to build up the wall between them, she gave a bitter chuckle. "My bachelors usually try that about now, too."

She watched him pull away from her. She wanted to call him back, to wrap her arms around him and taste his lips again. She realized now that it was what she had wanted all along. But she knew this was for the best. It was better for him and for the show if she kept her feelings to herself.

She turned and gazed out the window again. Reminded herself that it didn't matter what she wanted. Or felt.

The show had to go on.

RICK STARED OUT the window of the SUV and watched as cars passed them on the highway back to Lake Mildred.

He shouldn't have come. Shouldn't have expected that Lizzie would return his feelings. Because at the moment, all he felt was embarrassment. Well, that and a little confusion.

Okay, a lot of confusion.

He had three women waiting at home for him, each of them beautiful and smart and loving. Yet he was hung up on the woman sitting next to him.

When had it changed? They'd been friends, confidants. He could tell her anything and found himself saving up tidbits to tell her the next time they saw each other. He looked forward to their morning meetings going over the schedule so he could watch the hair fall over her shoulder as she focused on her clipboard. He enjoyed the way her green eyes lit up with excitement during brainstorming sessions. He loved the way she laughed, throwing her head back and giving her entire body over to the joy.

He snuck a glance over his shoulder and found that she stared out the opposite window. She couldn't even look at him after he kissed her.

He had to fix this. The thought of not having her in his life at all left an empty ache in the middle of his chest. But how?

He cleared his throat and reached across the seat to touch her hand. It startled Lizzie, and she withdrew her hand. He looked down. "Sorry, Lizzie. I shouldn't have done that."

"No, you shouldn't have."

Her words were clipped. Short. Her tone icy.

"Maybe you're right. This is cold feet." He searched her eyes to gauge her reaction, but they were wary, guarded. "So help me figure this out. You're really good at that." He took a deep breath. "What do you tell your other bachelors?"

She stared at him for a moment, then seemed to snap out of it. "Why don't we go over what you like about each woman? You must be attracted to them, or you would have sent them home long ago." She flexed her fingers as if trying to reach for her clipboard. "First, Melissa."

"Ah, Melissa." Rick closed her eyes and imagined her. "She's one of those rare women who is gorgeous and genuinely kind. As my wife, she'd be an asset, watching over me and making sure I take care of myself." He could see how wonderful she was, but he wished they had more sparks, more chemistry together.

"And Becky?"

The picture in his mind changed to the brunette with an infectious laugh. "She's funny and makes me laugh." He opened his eyes and glanced at Lizzie. "But are laughs enough to make a marriage?"

Lizzie swallowed and looked away. "I don't know. I'm not exactly an expert on marriage."

"But you are on engagements. What does a couple need to last?"

"You're asking the wrong person."

Rick shook his head. "You're wrong. You've seen enough people getting together to get a sense of who will make it."

"Well, my instincts must be off, because none of the couples I got together have lasted." She sighed. "I must be the world's worst matchmaker."

"It's not like you can control the contestants' hearts or ensure success for the rest of their lives." He shrugged and tried to make light of it. "They make their own choices, and you're not responsible for those."

"Still…"

They stayed silent for a moment. Finally, Lizzie asked, "And what about Brandy?"

Rick's eyes drifted closed and he saw her in his mind. But the feelings from five years ago had changed. "I don't know about her." He opened his eyes and gazed at Lizzie. "I feel as if she's holding herself back somehow. Like she's got a secret that she's afraid to share with me."

She glanced down at her hands. "Rick, I should tell you…"

"She's secretly married to someone else? I knew it."

He shot her a grin, but she didn't return it. Instead, her expression seemed to turn sad. "I knew five years ago that she was going to choose Wade, and I didn't tell you. I couldn't because of my job. But I wanted to." She reached out and touched his shoulder. He warmed at her touch and longed for her to keep it there, but she dropped her hand. "Be cautious with her this time. She's hurt you once, and I'd hate to see her do it again."

He frowned at her words. "Is there something you know and aren't telling me?"

"I don't know anything, but I have this... feeling." She shrugged and laughed it off. "Maybe it's nothing. Maybe I'm wrong."

"You're never wrong."

"Thanks, but we both know that's not true."

They fell silent once more until Rick chuckled. "I like this much better. I've never been able to talk about things with someone like I can with you. It was true before, but it's even more so now."

She returned his smile. "I'll always be your friend. No matter what."

And maybe that was what he needed to hang on to.

He nodded and returned to looking out the window. He'd go back to Lake Mildred and make the best of this situation. Put aside his feelings for Lizzie and try to figure out how he felt for the last three contestants. The finale loomed, and he needed to know who would make the best partner in his life.

RICK WASHED ANOTHER dish and handed it to his mom, who dried it. He glanced out at the dining room, where the three remaining contestants sat talking to Dan. "So what do you think?"

Mom put the dish up in the cupboard, then reached for the next plate he handed her. "I like them."

He turned off the faucet. "But?"

"It doesn't matter what I think. What counts is how you feel."

How he felt. *Right.*

He returned his hands to the soapy water and wiped the remains of their dinner from a bowl. "How did you know that you wanted to marry Dad and not Mr. Henderson?"

She chuckled softly. "Did your father tell you about that?" She took a glass from the counter and dried it. "Your dad was the only one who got my pulse humming. That made me feel alive. Loved. Wanted." She stood on tiptoe and put the glass in the cupboard, then turned to him. "That's what I want for you boys. A wife who makes your life more than you imagined."

Rick glanced toward the dining room again. "There is someone, Mom, but…I don't know."

"You don't know that you love her?"

He shook his head. "It's complicated." He handed her some dripping silverware. "She's unlike anyone I've ever known. But I don't think we can be together."

She put the towel with the silverware on the

counter and approached him. Put her hands on his cheeks. Forced him to look down at her. "Nothing is impossible if you know what you want. Do you love her?"

Lizzie walked into the room with more dirty dishes, and Rick moved away from his mom. He pointed to the coconut cake displayed under the glass dome. "We're just finishing up the dishes. Then we'll have dessert in the family room."

"Great." She smiled at his mom. "Dinner was fabulous, Mrs. Allyn. Rick obviously learned how to cook from you."

"He begged me to show him how to make his favorite pancakes when he was four." She glanced at Rick with a grin. "Been teaching him my secrets ever since."

"Your hard work paid off." Lizzie put the dishes on the counter and returned to the dining room.

Rick followed her with his eyes before turning to his mom, whose smile had faded. "Oh, honey. What have you done?"

Rick frowned. "I haven't done a thing. We're just friends."

He turned back to the dishes and rinsed off a platter. When he tried to hand it to his mom, she reached up and hugged him instead. "Is she what your heart wants?"

"More than my heart, Ma." He peered into his mom's eyes. "What am I gonna do?"

RICK GLANCED AROUND the dining room table at his family, then at his three dates. He stood and held out his hand to Becky. "Want to go for a little walk?"

Becky nodded and took his hand. He hated to do this. Didn't want her to go home yet, but he knew that more time wouldn't change how he felt. He helped Becky into her coat, then took her hand again and led her outside. He waited a moment for Charlie to check lights and turn on the handheld. He gave a nod, so Rick walked with Becky to the end of the dock.

The thick layer of ice that once crusted the lake had thawed into a cracked surface that would soon melt. Winter would be a memory.

He turned to his date. "Becky…"

She took a deep breath. Held it in. Then let it out in a big sigh. "I know what you're going to say."

"I wish things could have been different. You're amazing." He reached out and touched her cheek. "There's some guy out there who's going to be a very lucky man someday."

She backed up slightly so that his hand fell to his side. She turned and looked out at the lights from the houses across the lake. "Time will heal. There are other fish in the sea. It's not you, it's me." She turned back. "Any other clichés you'd like to add to your speech?"

"Becky, I—"

"Don't." She took another step back and crossed her arms over her chest. "I thought we had something special."

He closed his eyes. He knew what she meant. Knew what she was thinking. Hadn't he been saying similar things when Brandy had left him? "I don't think I'm the right man for you. You need someone—"

"Don't tell me what I need, because you have no clue." She shook her head. "If you did, you wouldn't be saying these things to me."

Rick winced. Gone was the sweet, funny Becky. Replaced by a hurt, angry one. "I'm sorry."

"I bet you are." She turned and left, brushing past Charlie and his camera.

Rick glanced at the cameraman. "That went well."

"You know women."

Rick nodded, but in truth he was learning he knew very little. He'd thought Becky would be gracious. Maybe tear up a little but otherwise accept his goodbyes.

He knew nothing.

ELIZABETH WATCHED FROM the kitchen window as Becky stormed to the waiting limousine and slammed the door shut once inside. She consulted her clipboard before Rick could return and they planned their next steps. So the hometown dates would be Brandy and Melissa. Chicago and Tennessee. City and country.

Rick opened the back door and shut it quietly behind him. Elizabeth walked over and rubbed his shoulder. "She take it hard?"

He nodded but didn't explain. He looked around the empty room. "Melissa and Brandy?"

"I sent them back to the house to pack." She held up the clipboard. "We really need to go over these plans."

"Not tonight." He walked past her into the family room, turned off lamps and checked the fireplace to make sure that the fire had been put out. When he looked back up at her, she walked toward him. He backed away. "Seriously, Lizzie. It's been a long night. I've had to break another heart. I'm in no mood to talk about schedules and dates and finales, okay?"

She tilted her head to the side and watched him. "This is about more than Becky going home."

He walked out of the family room and into

the kitchen. Elizabeth followed him closely. "Rick, talk to me."

He turned and faced her. "Why?"

"Because I thought we were friends." She looked into his eyes. "Was I wrong about that, too?"

"What we are seems to go back and forth from colleagues to friends to more." He started to put dishes from the dish rack away in the cupboards. "You made it clear that we need to keep our distance. And yet here you are. Alone. With me." He turned and faced her. "So what is it that you want? For me to open up and talk or to stay away? Because, frankly, I'm getting whiplash with your mood swings."

"Mood swings!"

He shrugged. "You have a better word for it?"

You bet there's a better word. "How about I'm trying to help you? I'm trying to find you a wife." Didn't he get it?

"And keep your job while you're at it."

"I never made it a secret that my whole life is this show." She crossed her arms over her chest. "Especially now."

He stalked toward her. "And maybe my job is to show you that there's more."

He pulled her into his arms and looked

down into her eyes. She wanted this. She didn't want this. Finally, he released her.

Elizabeth bit her lip and struggled to pull her emotions together. She bowed her head and stared at her feet while Rick finished putting dishes away and started to turn lights out in the kitchen. They stood in the dark, silent room. He walked to the back door and opened it. "Goodbye, Lizzie. I'll see you in Chicago."

"Why are you so upset?"

He handed her the car keys. "Drive carefully. It's starting to snow."

"I care about you, Rick." More than she should, if she wanted to admit it. She walked closer and took the keys from his hands. "But you're right. I need to stay away from you."

"Fine."

"Fall in love, Rick. Just not with me." She gave him one last look, then stepped out into the cold night.

RICK LOCKED THE FRONT door and stood quietly for a while. He turned to head to bed, when he saw movement on the porch. The sheriff had mentioned that there had been a break-in a few streets over on Lawn. Well, it wasn't happening on his watch. He whipped open the door. "Gotcha."

Dan and Brandy jumped apart. Rick stared

at them, then walked back into the house and slammed the door.

"Ricky, wait."

He turned to his brother, who stood alone in the foyer. "For what? So you and Brandy can stage a repeat performance?"

"We weren't doing anything."

Rick doubted his words. "Then why act guilty?" He returned to the kitchen and locked the back door.

Dan followed him. "I think I love her."

Rick stared at his older brother. Was he kidding him with this? "I chose her tonight because I thought she and I might still have something." He held up his hands. "But she wants to be with you instead? How did I end up here again?" He shook his head and closed his eyes. Five years was definitely not long enough. "I should have known. Should have seen."

"We didn't even see it until tonight." Dan took a few steps toward his brother, then stopped when Rick backed away. "I thought it was just me. That she couldn't…" He groaned. "I'm not the marrying type, but when I look at her, I see her in a white dress in a church. Heaven help me."

"This isn't helping me."

Dan shook his head. "My plan was to wait until the end. When you picked Melissa."

"What makes you think I was going to pick her?"

"Because she's perfect for you. We all see it."

Rick nodded, not because he agreed but because he didn't know what else to do. "I'm glad you're deciding my life for me."

"Someone has to. Because you seem to be completely willing to sail through without going after what you want." Dan stood taller, reminding Rick of his father. "I know what I want. And I'll go after it. But I'll wait. And then she'll be mine."

"And she feels the same way?"

Dan nodded. "I think so. It's what we were talking about when you interrupted."

Rick leaned against the kitchen counter and gazed at his feet. "How did you know you wanted her?"

"When you know, you know."

THE NEXT MORNING, Rick knocked on the door to Lizzie's hotel room. She'd called him an hour earlier, requesting a meeting. Didn't say why. And he didn't ask. But his damp palms and the warmth spreading across his chest made him think that his life could change when she opened the door.

The door opened, and she ushered him inside. Before she could say anything, Rick started. "Lizzie, I don't know why I'm here, but I have to tell you something."

A second knock at the door stopped him from telling her. He'd been so sure about what he had to say, but Brandy walking into the room changed that. He shook his head and started to leave. "I don't need to be here for this."

Lizzie blocked the doorway. "Oh, yes, you do." She pointed to the bed. "Sit." She turned to Brandy and pointed at the chair by the window. "You, too."

He had no choice but to obey with that authority in her voice. He sat on the edge of the bed and turned to face Lizzie rather than looking at Brandy. Ever since seeing her with Dan last night, he'd felt as he had five years ago. Betrayed. Bewildered. And wondering what was wrong with him. Was he really that bad a catch that she would keep choosing someone else? He'd thought they had something again. And again he'd been wrong. So wrong.

Lizzie looked at them both, then sighed. "Does someone want to tell me what happened after I left last night? Or do I have to fill in the blanks myself?"

Rick glared at Brandy. "Why don't you ask her? She's the one who's been lying this entire time."

Brandy stood and faced him. "It wasn't lying."

Rick stood, as well. "Then what else would you call sneaking around behind my back?"

"We didn't do anything!"

Lizzie stepped between them and held up her hands. "Stop. Both of you." She snapped her fingers, and they both sat again. "Brandy, do you want to continue on the show?"

Rick jumped to his feet. "Why should it be her choice? I'm the one looking for a wife here. She's the one who lied and cheated. Again."

Brandy looked over at him, then down at her hands, remaining silent. Lizzie looked at Rick until he sat back down on the bed. She buried her face in her hands. When she looked up at them, she seemed tired. Ready for this to be over. Rick knew exactly how she might feel.

Lizzie looked at Rick. "If you want to send Brandy home and bring Becky back, we can reshoot the last episode. Make it look as if you had in the first place."

He shook his head. "I sent Becky home because I didn't see a future with her." He turned and glanced at Brandy. "I saw one with you, though. Always thought that's the way it was supposed to be."

"Rick, I'm sorry—"

He held up his hand to stop whatever she might say next. "What if the reason I saw you in my future was because it was supposed to be you with Dan, and not with me?"

Lizzie turned to him and opened her mouth but stayed silent.

He continued, "I'm not saying I'm not hurt. And a little angry. I still feel like you lied to me."

"I didn't think the feelings I had for Dan could go anywhere. I didn't know he felt the same way." Brandy closed her eyes. "I like you, Rick, but maybe I should drop out. Give you a chance to find real love."

Lizzie threw her hands up in the air. "So where does that leave us? Is Brandy going home? Is Becky coming back? How do you want to handle this?" Lizzie looked between them both. "I'd like to hear some suggestions because I'm out of them."

Rick glanced between both women. "I don't think Melissa would like to know she won by default. It's not fair to her or the audience."

He rose and walked toward Brandy. "Would you be willing to stay on? We can pretend for the cameras for the last few shows."

She bit her lip. "But is that fair to you?"

He shrugged. "I guess I'm proposing to Melissa." But even as he said the words, he knew he didn't mean them. If he did, he would be more excited. More certain. If anything, he only felt more confused. "What else am I supposed to do? What do you want from me, Lizzie?"

"I want you to be happy. Does this decision make you happy?"

"The fact that my brother is in love with one of my contestants?" He shook his head. "Nope. Not happy about that. But I can't do anything to change it, can I?"

The room started to close in on him. He held up his hands. "I need some air."

He left them behind.

ELIZABETH WATCHED Rick go. Wished she could ease his pain. Instead, she turned to Brandy. "You should have told him from the beginning about Dan."

Brandy frowned. Almost pouted, which Elizabeth thought was more annoying than anything. The woman shook her head. "I thought my feelings were one-sided. I didn't know he felt the same."

"Then you should have told Rick you were having feelings about someone else. You've done this to him twice, Brandy. Don't take this the wrong way, but I hope he kicks your butt to the curb for this." She walked to the door and held it open. "Unfortunately, Rick is a nice guy, so he won't. He'll forgive you and accept you. And let you get away with it."

Brandy walked through the door, then stopped and turned. "What about the show?"

"That's up to Rick now. But I'd start packing my bags." She slammed the door in the other woman's face.

Her heart reached out to Rick. It was bad enough that Brandy had rejected him before, but now this? Small comfort in the fact that it had been done behind closed doors rather than on live television.

She picked up her cell phone and dialed Rick's number. Wasn't surprised that her call got directed straight to voice mail. She hung up the phone and considered the possibilities.

Without the sense that the proposal could go two different ways, much of the drama and romance would be left out of the last dates. As well as the live finale. If the audience knew who Rick had chosen, why would they tune in?

She sank to the bed, head in her hands. Should she call Becky and ask her to come back? Give them a chance to redeem the show?

Or keep all this quiet and proceed with Brandy and Melissa?

Again she thought of Rick. He didn't deserve to be treated like this. He deserved love. True love. The kind that poets wrote about and singers sang about. The kind that made her show popular.

The kind that just maybe she deserved, too.

She sighed, not wanting to think about that, grabbed her phone and dialed another number. When he picked up, she held her breath. "Will you meet me in an hour at the factory? We need to talk."

DAN MET HER in the pickle factory parking lot, leaning against his car as if the gray skies and melting snow on the ground didn't affect him. She'd asked him to meet her here thinking he'd be more comfortable on his own turf, and since it was Sunday there wouldn't be too many unwanted eyes and ears for their conversation. Elizabeth got out of her SUV and walked toward him. He held up his hands. "We haven't done anything yet."

She nodded and removed her sunglasses to

look at him. "But you haven't made this easy on me. Especially with Rick." She shook her head. "What were you thinking?"

"For once, I was thinking about myself. Not Rick. Or the company. Or the town." Dan turned up the collar of his coat. "I love her."

"I knew it. I could see it happening right in front of my eyes. But I thought I could control it. Just like everything else."

"No offense, Elizabeth, but you can't control love."

She looked at him and slowly nodded. "I think I'm finally realizing that." She crooked her head at the factory. "Mind if we continue this conversation somewhere warmer?"

Dan led her inside the factory, where the hissing and whirring of machines and conveyor belts filled most of the space. He walked her down the hallway to his office and held open the door for her.

She surveyed the room. It was much like Dan. No-nonsense. Neat. Organized. And focused on business. She turned and leaned against his desk. "What do we do about Rick?"

Dan frowned and looked at her as if she'd asked about climate change. "He'll honor his commitment to the show, of course."

"I meant about his heart." She pushed off

the desk and approached Dan. "He's really hurting right now, and I need to find him."

"Well, he's not answering my phone calls." Dan held up his cell. "I've called him every fifteen minutes this morning. No response."

Elizabeth nodded. "I'm worried about him. If he was hurting, where would he go to think?"

Dan considered this. "Our cottage is closed in the winter. Otherwise I'd send you there. He'd be alone." He shrugged. "Other than that, I'd say your best bet is the Penalty Box. It's past Main Street before you get to the lake."

"Thanks, Dan." She left to find Rick. Had to find him. Because he should know he wasn't alone.

RICK BIT INTO another nacho and cheered as someone scored a goal on the television. He wasn't quite sure who was playing, but it didn't matter. At least someone was winning.

The door to the bar opened, and Lizzie walked in, scanning the room until her eyes locked on his. *Great.* The one person he didn't want to see.

Well, maybe there were two or three.

He returned to eating his early lunch, piling the chip with two jalapeño peppers. Bit into it. Welcomed the sting and burn.

Lizzie sat in the seat across from him. Folded her hands and placed them on the table. He nudged the plate toward her. "Want one?"

"No, thanks."

She glanced at his mug and raised an eyebrow. He shrugged. "It's pop. Too early for anything stronger."

She motioned to the bartender to get her a pop, then turned back to him. "We need to talk."

"Do what you want about the show, okay? I don't care." He took a swig of his drink.

"I don't care about the show, either, right now," she said, leaning forward into his sight line. "You're the one I care about."

"Why?" When she raised one eyebrow at him, he winced. "I don't do the wallowing thing very well. But I desperately want to wallow."

"Rick, you're an amazing guy, but you've got to stop acting like a victim." When he started to protest, she continued, "Brandy doesn't love you. So what? Give Melissa a chance. Or find someone else. But don't act like your life is over."

Where was the sympathy? The reassurance? He glowered at her. "Aren't you supposed to be comforting me? Supporting me in my time of need?"

She shook her head and waited as the bartender placed the drink in front of her. She handed him her credit card. "I'm picking up his tab, too." Once he was gone, she leaned in closer. "Is that enough support for you?"

"You don't get it, Liz." He closed his eyes and shoved the plate of nachos away. They sat heavily in his belly, the burn of the spices no longer welcome. "I let her into my life, and she hurt me again."

"So you made yourself vulnerable. What's wrong with that?" She reached out and grabbed his hand. "Part of loving someone means you open yourself up to getting hurt by them. It's a risk. Sure. But isn't it worth it?"

Why did she have to make sense? Couldn't she let him enjoy the pity party before getting back to his promises? "I'm still alone."

She looked at him hard. "Are you really? You have your family. Your friends." She glanced around the bar at the few patrons who watched the game. "You even told me yourself that this town won't let anyone be alone. I'm sure any one of them would join you for lunch."

"I'm tired of going home alone." *There.*

He'd said it. The thing that weighed on him every night as he tried to ignore the ache and emptiness. "I'd hoped that this time would be different."

"And it is different. You still have Melissa."

He looked up at Lizzie. "But is she the one I want?"

Lizzie swallowed and turned her gaze elsewhere. Watched the game for a few seconds. Then she faced him. "I'll support whatever you want to do going forward. But I think you should give Melissa a chance. I know you like her."

He did like her. Which was the problem. He never wanted to hurt her. "But what if I'm not in love with her?"

"Then open your heart and take a chance." She squeezed his hand. "It'll be worth it in the end. I promise."

CHAPTER FOURTEEN

RICK STOOD OUTSIDE Brandy's Chicago apartment, hand raised to knock on the door. Was he doing the right thing? Should he even be there alone? Before he could lose his nerve, he knocked and waited for her to answer.

He should have called first. She might not be home. But he wanted to surprise her so she couldn't run away. They needed to talk. They had to get this thing figured out before cameras started rolling again.

He knocked again. Maybe she hadn't heard the first time.

This was crazy. He could have done this over the phone, but he thought being face-to-face would make the truth easier to see. To say.

He hung his head and debated knocking again. She obviously wasn't home.

He'd turned to leave when the door opened. Brandy looked at him, then up and down the hallway. "You're alone?"

He held up his hands. "I wanted us to talk,

just the two of us. No cameras. No producers. No Dan. Just us."

She nodded and stepped aside, letting him brush past her into the apartment. He looked around. It was on the small side, but she paid more for the address than the space. She still kept things neat and homey. It was a place where he wouldn't mind curling up on the couch and watching TV or cooking for her in the galley kitchen.

He shook his head. He had to stop thinking about Brandy that way. He turned to her. "It's a nice place."

She shrugged and motioned to the love seat. "Can I get you something to drink? I can make coffee."

He shook his head and patted the sofa next to him. "I only want to talk."

She took a seat in a rocking chair across from him. Folded her hands and kept them in her lap. Her casual wear told him that she'd planned for an easy day; her blond hair was pulled up into a messy ponytail. He sighed. Again, he had to stop looking.

"I've told Lizzie that I want you to stay on the show." He watched for her reaction, but she didn't give one. She waited for him to continue. "It wouldn't be fair to Becky to bring her back when I've already decided she's not the one for me."

"And Melissa?"

He thought of the blonde and softly smiled. "I've also asked that they shorten our week together so that I can spend more time with Melissa in Tennessee." He shrugged. "Might as well get to know my future wife, right?"

Brandy rose and took the seat right next to him. "Do you love her?"

"I like her. A lot." He chuckled. "Guess I have to do more than just like her if I'm going to marry her, huh?"

"No one says you have to marry her just because she's the last woman standing." She touched his hand, and he tried not to flinch. "It's just a show. But marriage is your life. Can you see yourself with her?"

Rick shifted on the sofa, then stood and walked to the entertainment center. Brandy had a much smaller television than most, but he remembered she'd preferred spending time out with friends rather than at home. He turned and faced her. "Can you see yourself with Dan?"

Her head shot up, and her eyebrows knit together. "Do you really want to talk about that?"

He'd rather have a root canal, but this conversation had to happen. He noted the boxes stacked by the wall. "You planning on moving?"

"My lease is up next month. I'm ready to make a change." She stood and approached him. "I'm moving to Lake Mildred."

Huh. Hadn't seen that coming. "Does Dan know?"

She shook her head. "We've agreed that we won't contact each other until after the show. But I know this is what I want."

"Dan. You want Dan." He put his hands on his hips and looked at her. "What's wrong with me?"

"Nothing."

He crooked his eyebrow. "Really? Because twice you've dated me, then chosen someone else." He shook his head. "Why couldn't it have been me?"

She shrugged. "I tried, Rick. I really did. You're a nice guy. Everything a woman could want for a husband." She turned and walked to the balcony that overlooked the shore of Lake Michigan. "But when I saw Dan…" She turned back and looked at him. "Sorry."

Rick took the few steps to reach her. "No matter what happened with us, I always wanted you to be happy. That's no lie." He took her hands in his. "If Dan is what makes you happy, then I say go for it. Move to Michigan. Find a future with him. And be happy."

She hugged him, and he let her linger in his arms for a moment. When she stepped back, he put his hands in his jeans pockets. "I should go. But I'll see you tomorrow with your mom and best friend."

She nodded and walked him to the door. Opened it. Waited until he passed through before she gave balm to his hurting heart. "I want you to be happy, too. And you deserve someone special. If that's Melissa, then great. But if there's someone else…"

He shook his head. "Doesn't matter. I can't have her."

RICK MET LIZZIE in the lobby before the limousine would take them to the restaurant. She again wore a suit, this time navy. But her hair looked a bit shorter. He reached out to touch it, but she backed away. "It looks good on you."

She nodded and turned her gaze to the parking lot. "You talked to Brandy alone."

"Thought I should. Had to clear up some things before shooting today's home visit." He sighed. "Believe me, it was not a conversation for the audience to be a part of."

Lizzie gave a short nod. All business. "I've

rearranged the schedule with Melissa. We'll go over my notes on the plane there."

Rick watched her for a moment. "Have I done something wrong? You're ignoring me."

"I'm your producer, so I can't avoid you, can I?" She glanced down at her clipboard, then back out to the parking lot.

"But you're doing exactly that." He stepped closer to her. Put a hand on her arm. Which she brushed off. "What did I do?"

"Nothing. The limo's here." She walked out the revolving doors.

Rick followed her. Took a seat in the limo beside her and gazed out the window. On the ride, Rick relaxed for the first time since this crazy show had started. He didn't have to pursue Brandy because her heart already belonged to another.

Just like his.

Problem was, she didn't belong to him. Never would.

Though his heart was filled with regret, Rick couldn't help enjoying the view of Chicago. He watched as buildings passed, people walked by and other cars tried to get to their destination faster than anyone else on the road. He even caught a glimpse of the El and grinned like a kid. He loved this town.

They arrived at Willis Tower, though in

Rick's mind it would always belong to Sears. He got out of the car, then craned his neck, trying to see the top of the soaring skyscraper. He remembered coming here as a kid with his family. His dad had let Uncle Larry take over the company while they explored Chicago for a week. It was one of the best vacations he could remember. Probably because it was the only one they'd had.

Brandy stood next to a young woman with dark hair and an older woman with dyed blond hair and dark roots. She looked like an older version of Brandy that had been crumpled up and left in a dark corner. Rick approached her and held out his hand. "Mrs. Mathews, it's good to see you again."

"Just call me Rita. Never saw a reason to get hitched myself." She glanced at Brandy. "But this girl has been planning her wedding since she was a flower girl for my sister when she was ten." She looked back at him and perused his face as if trying to place it. "Baby, he's different from the picture you sent me."

Brandy colored. "That wasn't him," she said in a hushed voice.

"Well, you sure are a good-looking man." She put a hand in the crook of his elbow. "Let's go. I'm dying for a drink."

Lizzie had made arrangements beforehand,

so they sat at a table near one of the windows. Salads waited for them as well as a bottle of wine for Rita. Rick passed around the basket of freshly baked bread as they talked about movies, the show. It was a nice dinner.

Until Rita asked, "So you gonna marry her this time or what?"

Charlie turned his camera in Rick's direction. He shook his head. "I can't really answer that question now. There's still one more woman in the picture."

Rita leaned her head on one hand. "But do you think you might? I mean, what's wrong with her?"

Rick sighed as the waiter brought their pasta dinners. As Rita continued to stare, he shrugged. "Nothing's wrong with her."

Brandy nudged her mother. "Mama, just drink your wine."

"My glass is empty and so's the bottle." She held up a hand to a passing waiter who didn't belong to their table. "Another house white."

Brandy leaned closer. "Then maybe you've had enough."

Rita glared at her. "You're right. I've had enough of your thinking you know what's best for me. You don't know. Never have and never will."

Brandy winced. "Mama…"

"Rita…"

Rita stood up, and Brandy's friend Lil took her elbow when she wobbled. "I think I'll take your mom home." She turned to Rick. "Good luck with the show."

Brandy rose and gave Lil a quick hug. "Thanks. You're the best."

After they left, Rick had no idea what to say. And by Brandy's silence, he guessed she didn't, either.

Finally Charlie cleared his throat. Rick sat up straighter. "Right. We have some time to sightsee if you're in the mood."

Brandy nodded but didn't say anything. She kept her gaze on the full plate of lobster ravioli in front of her.

Rick reached across the table and touched her hand. "I'm sure they'll edit it to put our time together in the best light."

Brandy glanced up at him. "She's having a bad day." She tried to smile.

Rick nodded. "I know."

She chuckled glumly. "Actually, she's having a bad life." She put her face in her hands, and her shoulders started to shake.

Rick looked at Charlie and made a slashing movement near his throat. The red light on the camera turned off, and Charlie excused himself. Once he left, Rick took the seat next to Brandy and touched her shoulder. "It's just us now." Brandy looked at him through her fingers. "Families aren't easy, are they?" He reached up and wiped a tear from her cheek. "Why don't you take a moment, okay? Maybe go to the bathroom and freshen up or whatever it is you ladies do in there."

She kissed his cheek before leaving the table. Lizzie walked over and sat in the chair next to him. She took his hand in hers. "She doesn't deserve you."

"Well, she's not getting me, is she?" He took a deep breath and looked her over. "Thanks for understanding about my needing to talk to Brandy alone yesterday."

She nodded. "You were right."

Rick touched his chest and waved Charlie over. "Did you hear that? Ms. Producer said I was right. We should have recorded that for posterity."

Even Charlie chuckled at that. He took a seat next to them and cleaned off the camera lens while they waited for Brandy's return. Rick watched Lizzie, who kept looking in the direction of the bathrooms. He nudged her shoulder. "Do you want to go check on her?"

"I probably should." She stood and put her hand on his arm. "I'm sorry about the attitude earlier. To be honest, I was hurt you didn't include me. But I understand now."

Rick patted her hand as she walked away. He glanced at Charlie. "Does life ever get easy?"

The cameraman stood and switched the camera on. Rick turned and saw Brandy walking back to their table. He stood and pulled her chair out for her. She looked more composed and pulled together. He swore women could perform miracles in the ladies' room.

Once they were seated, Brandy picked up her fork and resumed eating her meal. Rick followed suit and placed the napkin back on his lap. He cleared his throat. "I think after dinner we should go all the way to the top of the tower. You game?"

RICK LOOKED OUT the windows and tried to see if he could catch a glimpse of the Michigan shore. It was a cloudy day, so what appeared to be land on the other side of the lake was probably just fog. Brandy brushed against his sleeve. "Trying to see home?"

He turned and smiled at her. "Can you see where you live from here?"

She grabbed his hand and pulled him to the south side of the building and pointed. "I grew up in one of those houses. But I try not to go there often."

"Hard to go home?"

She nodded. "You saw what my mom is like. Would you want to be around that day after day?"

"She wasn't like that the last time we met."

"It was a good day, I guess. I don't know." She shrugged and wrapped her arms around herself, then stood off to the side. "There's good and bad, and you never know what you're going to get until she shows up."

To break the somber mood, Rick snatched her hand and pulled her onto the glass floor that jutted out over the side of the building and made him feel as if he were walking on air. Brandy squealed and closed her eyes. "I can't look down. I feel like I could fall at any moment."

Rick glanced at his feet and marveled that glass could hold him up all fourteen hundred and fifty feet in the air. He squeezed her hand. "If you fall, I'll catch you."

RICK HELD A BOUQUET of daisies. Lizzie checked him over. "You couldn't have worn something nicer?"

He glanced down at his jeans. "This is my nice pair. Besides, what she sees is what she gets with me. Why dress up to look like something I'm not?"

Lizzie glanced up at the hospital. "My source told me she's working on the third floor today. Cameras are set up to record your surprise visit. She thinks you're not arriving until next week."

Rick nodded as he took in the information. Today's plan to surprise Melissa at work had been his attempt to keep part of this real. Besides, he really wanted to see her. Especially after everything with Brandy. He sniffed the flowers. "Daisies are a nice touch."

"You said she seemed like a daisy girl. Not roses." Lizzie consulted her clipboard, then sighed. "Please give her a chance, Rick. I'm not saying you have to marry her, but open yourself up to that possibility."

"Melissa is a wonderful woman. I'd be lucky to have her. But I need to make sure it's really love before I can promise anything."

"Agreed." She glanced behind her at the camera crew, who waited for her to give the cue to start filming. "We ready for this?"

Rick wanted this to work. Wanted to give her a chance. He'd worked so hard to turn off his feelings for Brandy, but now needed to turn them on for Melissa. She might be his future bride. "Let's do this."

Cameras followed him as he entered the hospital and found the page who would escort him to Melissa's ward. Patients and families gave them odd stares as they got in the elevator and even more when they reached the third floor and started walking down the halls. One woman approached Rick. "You're from *True Love!* Honey." She motioned to a man in the waiting room. "He's from that show."

Rick grinned at her. Held his finger up to his mouth. "We're surprising Melissa."

The woman's eyes got big and she nodded and allowed them to pass down the hallway and approach Melissa's nurses' station. He spotted her walking out of a room and quickly turned away. He held the daisy bouquet over his face as if that would hide him and the cameras, then glanced behind at Lizzie. She mouthed, *Go.*

He ran down the hall. "Missy."

She turned and took a moment to realize it was him. Smiling widely, she ran toward him. They embraced tightly, the flowers smacking Rick in the face as he pulled her closer. "I've missed you." And he realized he meant it. He took a step back and held the bouquet out. "These are for you."

Melissa took the bouquet and held it up to

her face. Inhaled deeply. "Daisies are my favorite. How did you know?"

Rick shrugged. "I guessed." He glanced around at the crowd that had started to gather. "When's your break? Maybe we can have lunch."

She sighed. "Not for two more hours. You're sure you want to wait around that long?"

"For you, I'd wait even longer." He touched the tip of her nose.

A nurse in purple scrubs approached them. "Why don't we switch breaks for today? I'd hate for you to keep your man waiting."

Melissa beamed at the other woman. "That's so sweet of you. Thanks." She glanced at her watch. "Can we meet in ten minutes?"

"Absolutely." Rick rubbed her arm. "I brought us a picnic."

ELIZABETH FOLLOWED RICK and Melissa as they took a seat on the bench in the park adjacent to the hospital. The trees and flowers had budded, and the scent of spring was in the air. Which should make a young man's attention turn to love. Or so the poets said.

Rick opened the basket and brought out the salads she'd ordered for them. He'd told her nothing fancy or over the top, so she'd chosen a simple grilled chicken over greens with balsamic vinaigrette. She'd ordered one for herself and sandwiches for the crew while she was at it.

They talked quietly between bites of lunch, and the cameras filmed every word. Every glance. They looked like a young couple in love enjoying a brief moment together.

This was what she wanted for Rick. After everything else that he'd gone through, he deserved some happiness. He needed love in his life. And if the scene playing out in front of her was any indication, he could find it with Melissa given some time.

Rick wiped his mouth with his napkin. "I know this is short notice, but I was hoping you were free tonight. Maybe we could go see a movie?"

Melissa smiled. "That sounds so…normal."

Rick shrugged. "I could use a little normal right now. Especially before I meet your family this weekend." He reached up and touched a flyaway strand of Melissa's hair. "So what do you say to dinner and a movie?"

"I'd love it." She leaned across to kiss his cheek.

But Rick turned at the last moment so that they kissed on the mouth. Lingered for a moment. Then they sat back and acted as if nothing had changed.

But it had.

He hadn't willingly kissed anyone on camera this season. Had told Elizabeth he wouldn't until it meant something. She should be thrilled that he'd waited for Melissa.

So why did her heart ache?

RICK SHOOK HANDS with each of Melissa's four brothers. By the time he reached her father, his hand and shoulder hurt from the vigorous workout they had received. "Mr. Weskitt."

"Rick."

The two men nodded and shook hands briefly. Rick turned to greet her mom. She was the same height and build as Melissa. "You two could be sisters."

Her mom blushed while Melissa laughed and linked her arm through his. "Mom's putting on our Sunday best for dinner tonight. Fried chicken. Mashed potatoes. Biscuits."

Rick's stomach growled in response. "Sounds fabulous." He turned to Mrs. Weskitt and rubbed his hands together. "Why don't I give you a hand in the kitchen and you can give me some pointers?"

He soon found himself elbow deep in flour and buttermilk as Barbara showed him how to dredge the chicken in milk before adding it to the flour. The pieces turned golden in the oil as they fried.

He peeled potatoes, grated carrots and cabbage, and talked up a storm to Melissa and her mom while Charlie recorded every moment and asked for tastes between takes. Rick felt at home with them. Not for the first time, he felt something for the beauty smiling and laughing beside him. It could be love. It would make life easier if it was. But then he'd usually chosen the road less traveled.

Once dinner was placed on the dining room table, Rick had to admit he could eat a bear if he had the opportunity. The family gathered around the table. Yes, he would fit in here.

But was it enough?

Over dinner, they discussed religion, politics and the show. Her dad brought up Rick's plans for Melissa. Rick deflected by asking about the family business. They didn't lack for topics.

After dinner, Rick helped clear the table, then took a dish towel and dried dishes while Melissa washed. Once the kitchen was clean, he put an arm around her shoulder. "We make a good team."

She nodded and stepped closer. "You make it easy."

"I could say the same thing about you." He tapped her on the nose. "What say you show me how to ride a horse?"

"You never have?"

He shrugged. "I was more a bike rider growing up."

She smiled and took his hand. They went out the back door and followed the path to the stables. With an expert hand, Melissa showed him how to talk to the horse before putting a saddle on it. "You want her to trust you first. Then she'll let you take her anywhere."

Rick pulled her closer. "And what about you? Do you trust me?"

Melissa looked down and took a deep breath. "I want to."

"I want you to, too." He kissed the top of her head. "So how do I climb on?"

They followed a path alongside the river that bordered the Weskitts' land. The landscape glowed in golds and greens as the sun began to set. Rick knew that it would look magnificent on television. And as long as it looked good, everything would be fine.

But inside, nothing was fine with him. He glanced at Melissa, who rode next to him. He could see a life with her. It would be comfortable like a pair of his favorite jeans. He could be happy. Right?

To find out that answer, he pulled his horse up next to hers, then leaned over and kissed her. She brought her hand up to the back of his neck to pull him closer. He sighed into her mouth.

And waited for the fireworks to start.

CHAPTER FIFTEEN

FOR RICK AND BRANDY'S last date, Lizzie had scored tickets to a sold-out concert at the Hollywood Bowl. Before the concert, they enjoyed a picnic on the lawn as the musicians warmed up. They feasted on cheese and crackers, fruit salad and brownies.

After they ate and filmed what they needed to, the crew left so they could enjoy the concert. Brandy leaned back and looked up at the sky while the music flowed over them and out into the stars. Rick nudged her arm. "What are you thinking about?"

She ducked her head and checked to make sure that the crew was truly gone. "Your brother. He'd love this."

"He'd never come out here. Hasn't been on vacation since Dad died." Rick sat up. "Brandy, if you really like Dan, you have to know he's serious about his work. He needs someone like you to show him there's more to the world than spreadsheets and production schedules." He nudged her shoulder. "I think you could make his life magnificent."

Brandy nodded. "I can try."

"I figured you would."

They sat listening to the music for a while. Brandy turned to him. "Have you decided what you're going to do at the finale?"

He swallowed as if something got caught in his throat. "I don't know."

"Melissa is a wonderful woman."

Yes, she was. But she wasn't the one for him. He didn't trust his voice, so he nodded. Perceptive as always, Brandy frowned. "You do love her, right?"

"I think we could have a good life together. But is it enough?"

Brandy took his hand. "I've been there, remember? Always go with your heart."

"Your heart led to you getting dumped."

She sighed. "But for those six weeks I had, it was marvelous." She settled back on the blanket. "And now my heart is leading me to your family. So it can't all be bad, right?"

Rick fell back next to her and looked at the faint stars that tried to break through the lights and smog of this town. "If you say so."

RICK TOOK MELISSA to the Santa Monica Pier for their last date. They ate hot dogs on the boardwalk, then took a ride on the Ferris wheel. Melissa sat next to him and gasped as they reached the top and saw the city dressed in twinkling lights. "They look like jewels in a crown."

Rick pulled her tighter to his side. She was the jewel tonight. He hated to hurt this amazing woman next to him. "Melissa, about tomorrow—"

"I know you can't tell me what you're going to do. But I want to tell you…" She sighed and turned to face him head-on. "No matter what, I love you and want what's best for you. Whatever makes you happy makes me happy."

It could have been word for word what he'd told Brandy on their last date more than five years before. Was this sinking feeling in his stomach how she had felt that night? He shook his head. "What if that means someone else?"

"Then I hope she makes you happy." She put her head on his shoulder. "But I think you should know that I love you. We could be good together. We could make a wonderful life. If you just give me the chance."

She looked up at him, her heart shining out of her eyes. And he couldn't help it.

He touched her cheek and leaned in. Softly kissed her.

And thought maybe it could be her...if he kept his eyes closed long enough.

Once the date was over, Charlie put his equipment in the trunk and glanced at Rick. They'd seen Melissa off in the limo, and just the two of them remained. "Tomorrow's the big day."

Rick rubbed the back of his neck. "What am I gonna do?"

"I've done enough of these shows to know when two people should be together." Charlie slammed the trunk closed, then slipped a piece of paper into Rick's hand. "Don't tell her I gave this to you."

Charlie got in the car and left. Rick looked at the paper in his hand. He unfolded it, unsure what it could be.

Lizzie's address.

ELIZABETH UNPACKED ONE suitcase as she started to pack another. After tomorrow's finale, she was scheduled to fly out to Dallas, where she would begin interviews with the next bachelorette for the show. It would never end. She'd always be working on the show. Sometimes she dreamed of a different job.

A different life.

A knock at her front door startled her out of her thoughts. She needed to stop thinking about changing her life and get more focused. On her career. On the balance in her checkbook. And on the bills waiting to be paid.

She opened the door and found Rick standing there with grocery bags in his hands. She glared at him. "How did you... Never mind. What do you want?"

He grinned, and it almost melted her resolve. "You."

"Rick—"

"You missed my date with Melissa."

She nodded and planted her fists on her hips. "I told you before that Troy was taking over that shoot. I had a meeting with the suits that I couldn't get out of." She looked him over again. "Now, what are you really doing here?"

"I want to make you dinner." He pushed past her into the apartment and whistled. "Now, this is some place."

"It's okay."

Rick crossed the living room to look out the windows into the darkness. "I always wondered how you lived. I bet you have an ocean view."

"More like an alley view." She clenched her

hands and wondered what he was doing there and how he'd gotten her address.

Rick continued to look out the window. "You have the best life, I swear."

"Didn't your mother ever tell you not to swear?"

He turned back to her, one eyebrow lifted at her attempt at humor. "Cute." He lifted the bags. "Where do you keep your pans?"

"Why?"

He walked past her and into the tiny kitchen. "Knowing you, you forgot to eat and now you're starving. Am I right?" He started poking his head through the cupboards.

Her stomach rumbled. Rick chuckled and made himself at home in her kitchen. He searched the cabinets and found her pans. Opened drawers and found her knives. Unlatched her pantry door and found her food stash. He glanced over his shoulder at Elizabeth, who moved in between him and the pantry door, attempting to shield the contents from his view. "Stay out of there."

Rick whistled softly. "That's a lot of macaroni and cheese."

"Don't. Start. With. Me."

Rick glanced back at the shelves of cans and boxes of food. "Are you expecting a food shortage? You could live a year off the stuff in there."

"Eighteen months." Elizabeth crossed her arms tightly over her chest.

"You don't even cook."

"And you don't know what it's like to go hungry." She shut the door and leaned against it—keeping him out of the pantry and that part of her life.

"And you do?"

So much for keeping him out. She bit her lip. "My mom wasn't known for hanging on to a job. And sometimes there was no money. Which meant no food." She stood taller. "I won't go through that again. No matter what, I won't be hungry."

Rick took a step back. "I didn't know."

"No one does. It's not something I brag about." She walked away from the door and away from him. "There's a reason I keep that door shut, Rick. Don't open it."

"If you can't open it with me, then who?" He took a step closer to her. "Who are you going to let into your heart?"

She broke off eye contact. "I thought you were making me dinner."

"Yep." Rick rubbed his hands together. "The way to a woman's heart is through her stomach, right?"

He took packages out of grocery bags and laid them on her kitchen counter. Ground beef. Cheese. Onion rolls. Lettuce. Tomato. Onion.

She glanced at the ingredients. "You're making me a cheeseburger?"

"Not just any cheeseburger. It's my specialty." He motioned for her to step closer. "And I'm going to teach you how to make it."

She shook her head and held up her hands. "I told you before. I'm no cook."

"You can learn just like I did." When she didn't move, he grabbed her hand and pulled her to the kitchen counter. "First wash your hands. Very important."

He led her to the kitchen sink, pumped soap into his hands, then massaged it into hers. Elizabeth swallowed, trying to will her feelings away and hoping that as he turned on the faucet to rinse off the soap, her fears would go down the drain with it.

Rick dried her hands off. He found a mixing bowl in the cupboard and handed her the package of meat. "Put that in the bowl while I get out your ketchup and mustard."

She opened the package and dumped the pink meat into the bowl. Rick squirted the condiments on top, then added chopped onion and shredded cheese to the mixture. He then took her hands in his and helped her knead the mixture together. "Make sure it's mixed well. Then we'll form patties."

His hands on hers distracted her again, but she did as instructed. She took a palm full of meat and flattened it into a round disk. "Like this?"

"Perfect." Rick winked at her and placed his own patty next to hers. "Now we preheat the pan. We want to make it hot enough that it will sear the meat and make almost a crust on the outside to keep the juices inside."

Once their hamburgers were fried and the vegetables sliced, Rick took two buns from the package and warmed them in the microwave. Placed more shredded cheese on each burger. Then began the process of stacking the burgers to perfection. More ketchup and mustard on top. Then placed them each on a plate.

"And that is how you make my cheeseburgers." He held his up in a toast. "To you, Lizzie. You can do anything you set your mind to."

She smiled and tapped her cheeseburger to his. Then took a bite.

Oh, my.

She closed her eyes and chewed slowly, letting the flavors play on her tongue. She swallowed to let her stomach in on the experience. He'd taught her how to make the perfect cheeseburger.

She opened her eyes and found Rick watching her. She set the burger back on the plate, then put her arms around Rick's shoulders and kissed him. The man tasted even better than the burger.

The fact that she shouldn't be doing this started to flare in her mind, but she ignored it.

"Lizzie," Rick said softly against her lips and pulled her body closer to his. He started to kiss her neck. "I think I'm in love with you."

That brought her back to reality. "Don't. We can't." She pushed him away. "What were you thinking?"

"Me? You were the one who kissed me."

She shook her head and crossed the room to the kitchen sink and leaned against it. "This is ridiculous. You need to leave."

"I came here tonight so we could figure out whatever this is." He motioned between the two of them.

"There is no this. You're probably going to be proposing to another woman tomorrow." Elizabeth laughed when she'd rather start crying. "What were you thinking?"

"I'm wondering the same thing about you."

He stepped closer to her, but she retreated to the living room. He followed her. "We have something between us. I know it. And you do, too. Otherwise you wouldn't be so scared."

"There can't be anything between us. That's reality." She shook her head and glared at the ceiling. "I can't believe I'm so stupid."

"The only stupid thing you've done is convince yourself that you don't love me. But we both know the truth. That kiss proved it."

"That kiss was a mistake."

"The best mistake of my life." He stalked toward her and grabbed her shoulders. "I love you, Lizzie. More than I want to. And I know that messes up your plans, but it's the truth. And you love me, too."

"The show—"

Rick groaned. "It's just television. It's not real life no matter how you want to package it. The fact is that I don't love Brandy or Melissa. I don't want to spend the rest of my life with either of them." He looked into her eyes. "You're the one I want to wake up next to every morning. The one I want to sleep next to every night. It's you I want to see across the dinner table. And our baby I want to hold in my arms."

"Rick, don't."

"It's too late. Because I do." He pulled her in and kissed her.

She closed her eyes and pretended for a minute that she could have this. That this could be her life. Then she pushed him away. "I don't love you."

Rick just shook his head. "Right."

"Don't make a mistake tomorrow. It's not just your future it affects, but mine, too. Don't do something we'll both regret."

"My only regret would be proposing to someone who I know is wrong for me."

"I asked you to leave."

He snuck a quick kiss, then winked at her. "See you in the morning."

CHAPTER SIXTEEN

ELIZABETH REACHED UP and straightened Rick's tie. "Are you ready?"

"You feeling the big déjà vu vibe here?" He grinned at her and peered into her eyes. "I'll be making television history again today."

"So you're sure about your choice?" She swallowed at the lump in her throat as he nodded once. "And you still won't tell me if you're going to propose?"

"Is the suspense killing you?"

She gave a half shrug. "Not that I'd let you know."

"Of course not."

She reached up to fix his tie again, but he slapped her hands away. "It's fine."

"I just want everything to be perfect for you this time."

"It will be."

"I wish I was as confident as you." She glanced at her clipboard. "The finale is always a nightmare, but these changes you gave me? I'll be lucky not to find myself without a job in the morning."

"Lizzie, about last night…"

She looked up at him and shook her head. "Nothing happened last night. End of story."

Rick smiled at her again, and her heart caught in her throat. Was she really going to stand back and watch him make the same mistake? "Listen, Rick, what if we forgot all this? You can go back and live your life the way you want to. I won't bother you again. How can you be so certain that you found the one right for you?"

"Sometimes, Lizzie, you just have to have faith."

She rolled her eyes and pushed her earpiece tighter into her ear to hear better. She glanced at Rick. "They're ready for you."

Rick reached out and touched her cheek. "If I don't get a chance to say this later, thank you."

She frowned. He was thanking her for making his life miserable yet again? "What did I do?"

"More than you know."

With that cryptic answer, he stalked away and took his position at the end of the rose-strewn path. Elizabeth thought she was going to get sick all over the red petals and white satin carpet. It would cost big bucks to get it cleaned, but she doubted that she'd care. She had to stop this. Had to keep him from making a huge mistake.

She glanced at the people around her, each waiting to see true love play out on her carefully created stage. And if they believed that, they didn't know what love was, because it certainly wasn't what she'd tried to produce on this show.

And it wasn't watching the man she loved make a big mistake. She should stop him. She should tell him.

Instead, she nodded at Charlie. "Roll cameras."

RICK WATCHED the patio doors open, and the two finalists dressed in their finest walked toward him. He kissed each on their cheek and turned to the main camera.

"Over five years ago, I stood on this stage and made a mistake. I proposed to a woman I now realize was wrong for me. I won't make that same mistake today."

He cleared his throat, mentally reviewing what he'd practiced in the mirror that morning. This had to work. He didn't know what would happen to him if it didn't.

"I found my true love. She inspires me yet

infuriates me. She makes my life amazing and completely crazy. She reminds me of why I still seek something better than what I have. She's moved into my heart and made it her home." He reached into his pocket for the ring and started walking past Brandy and Melissa toward the cameras.

Lizzie whispered, "Follow him."

He stopped in front of her, then dropped to one knee. "Elizabeth, would you marry me?"

Everyone's eyes bulged and mouths dropped. He could hear the whir of the camera trained on him but not a word fell from his beloved's mouth. He gave a quick grin to hide his nerves. "I know. This is sudden. And completely different from what you were expecting. But isn't that what life should be?"

The execs watching the filming stood and started to whisper among themselves. Lizzie glanced back at them and scanned the cast and crew. She turned to Rick. He smiled in encouragement because he knew this was what they both wanted.

Her mouth opened. "I can't."

CHAPTER SEVENTEEN

ELIZABETH POUNDED ON the hotel room door. "I know you're in there. The front-desk clerk said he saw you." No answer. She rested her palm on the door as if she could heal the problem with her touch. "Rick, please. I need to explain."

Still no answer.

She hung her head. What had she expected? She'd turned him down. Live. On national television. In front of an estimated twenty million viewers.

She knocked once more. "Please. I'm so, so sorry."

She heard the chain on the other side of the door move. She took a step back. A deep breath. Which she blew out in a rush at the sight of Rick's mother. "Mrs. Allyn—"

She held up a finger. "Don't." She closed the door behind her and stepped out into the hallway. "I asked you to make sure my son wouldn't get hurt. I begged you to protect him. I didn't realize you were the one I should be protecting him from."

"Mrs. Allyn—"

"I'm not finished." She put her hands on her hips like a schoolmarm scolding a misbehaving student. "When he told me he loved you, I warned him. Warned him that it would only come to pain. I wanted to be wrong, but you certainly proved me right."

"Mrs. Allyn—"

"You can speak when I'm through." She clutched her hands in front of her. "He loves you, Miss Maier. More than he can say. Now, what can you possibly say that would make this better?"

Elizabeth opened her mouth, a thousand retorts in her brain but none that would journey to her vocal cords. She dropped her gaze to the floor. "I'm sorry. I didn't know he would do that."

"Didn't you? You're a smart woman, so I'm sure the thought crossed your mind at least once."

More than once. "I thought it was a crush and he'd get over it." She lifted her eyes to the mother of the man she'd humiliated. "I never expected this. Not a proposal."

"It doesn't make it hurt any less." Mrs. Allyn glanced back at the door and sighed, her eyes closed as if in a prayer. "Go home, Miss Maier. Forget Rick. Let him get over you without having to see you."

She shook her head and held up her clipboard as if that would make things right again. "He still has the reunion show to film. Plus the publicity tour."

"Fine. He'll honor his commitments. But I suggest you find somewhere else to be." She turned, opened the door and disappeared behind it.

Elizabeth heard the decisive click of the bolt sliding into place. What else had she expected? She stared at the door, waiting for it to open again. So she could see Rick. And tell him...

Tell him what? Hadn't she said enough? Maybe Mrs. Allyn was right. She should just stay away, let him get over this. Over her.

She opened her cell phone and dialed Devon's number. "I need to talk to you."

"Good. We need to talk to you, too."

We? That didn't sound good. "Great. Where can we meet?"

"How about the scene of the crime? There's some things we need to take care of."

She stopped walking. "There's nothing to take care of. Because I quit."

ELIZABETH PAUSED OUTSIDE the hospital room. Had she made the right decision? Didn't matter. She was off the show now. Couldn't change that.

And part of her didn't want to. Part of her wanted to see what else was out there besides working all the time.

She walked through the doorway into her mother's hospital room. A month had made a big difference in how she looked. She sat up in the bed, still covered in gauze bandages, but the machines that kept her alive had been removed. "Bethie, you came." Her mom held her arms open.

Elizabeth rushed forward and hugged her. But not too tightly. Still afraid she'd break her mom. "The doctor said they're releasing you tomorrow."

Her mom nodded. "'Bout time, too. Going stir-crazy in here." She turned the volume down on the bedside television with her remote. "Are you doing okay?"

Had everyone seen it? Elizabeth winced. "You watched the show?"

"Never miss it." Her mom patted the side of her bed, so Elizabeth took a seat. "That Rick is something else. Why'd you let him get away like that?"

She couldn't talk about that, not now…

maybe not ever. "Mom, I want you to come home with me."

Her mom looked at her closely. "Why?"

"You have somewhere else to go?" Elizabeth looked around the room. No cards. No flowers. No sign that she had anyone else in the world.

"The last time we talked—"

"I was angry. Upset. Not at you, at least not entirely." She sighed and looked down at her lap. "I'm sorry. I shouldn't have said what I did. Not when you were fighting for your life like that."

"So you're sorry for when you said it, but not for the words you said." Her mom sounded sad, defeated.

Elizabeth stood and walked to the window that overlooked the parking lot. "We can't change our past." She turned back and looked at her mom, who picked at the blanket, not looking at her. "But I'm willing to work on making our relationship better from this point forward."

"Why?"

"Because you're still my mom." She walked back to the bed and took her mom's hand. "And I really need you right now." She started to cry. "I screwed up. And I've lost everything."

Her mom gave a soft smile and opened her arms. Elizabeth crumpled into them. "Bethie. Baby." She rubbed Elizabeth's back and rocked back and forth. "I don't think I've seen you cry since you were a tiny thing."

Because she never had, not in front of her mom. Elizabeth sniffled. "What am I going to do, Mom?"

"You'll find another job."

She shook her head. "I meant about Rick."

Her mom continued to rub her back. It felt good. This was the mother she'd wanted. Craved. Elizabeth didn't know if this closeness would survive beyond today, but she would enjoy it while it lasted.

Elizabeth looked up into her mom's eyes. "I want to know what real love is. And I think I let it go."

"So you'll get it back." Her mom wiped her face with a tissue from the box by her bed. "Love always wins." Elizabeth stared at her until her mom shrugged. "At least it does on television. So why can't you find it out here in the real world, too?"

Elizabeth sighed. That was the question.

RICK CHOKED AS DENISE applied more powder to his face. "Am I really looking that bad?"

"Your dark circles have circles." Denise

dotted foundation under Rick's eyes. "You'll have to check those bags before you fly. Aren't you sleeping?"

"Funny." Rick closed his eyes and let Denise work her magic. Truth was, he wasn't sleeping. His mind kept replaying the events of the past couple of days over and over. What could he have done differently? Said differently? Why hadn't she said yes? Didn't she love him?

When would he stop loving her?

"I'll be with you in two secs, hon. I'm just finishing up here," Denise told someone. Then she sighed. "Even a magician can only do so much with what she's given."

Denise removed the cape from Rick's neck, and he opened his eyes. And saw Melissa on the stool in front of the mirror next to him.

He looked at her, but she didn't meet his eyes. He'd been in her situation. He knew what she felt. Thought. He cleared his throat. "Missy."

She glanced at him, then returned her gaze to her own image in the mirror. "Rick."

He wasn't the only one hurting after what he'd done. When was he going to learn? "I'm so sorry. I wish—"

She whirled around and stared at him. "Don't."

He reached out a hand to her, then dropped

it. "If it could have been anyone else, it would have been you."

"Is that supposed to help?" Melissa shook her head and turned her chair, as if she was unable to look at him.

"I didn't mean to hurt you."

She stood and approached him. Rick backed up and felt the stool hit the back of his thighs. He had nowhere else to go. Melissa poked him in the chest. "It still hurts. And you should know that better than anyone."

She stormed off as Rick watched her. She was right. And he couldn't fix things with her any more than Brandy could have fixed things with him.

Great. Now he had regret and guilt.

Rick ran after her. "Wait. Let me explain." She stopped walking but didn't turn around. He paused and closed his eyes. "I wanted it to be you. Hoped I could make it happen." He opened his eyes and stepped closer to her. "You're an amazing woman, Missy."

She turned, her eyes glittering with tears. "But not amazing enough for you."

"I'm an idiot, okay?" He held out his arms so that she could land a punch in his chest if she wanted. "But I didn't want to settle for something that wasn't real." He dropped his voice. "And neither should you."

Melissa turned away, blinking and wiping the corner of one eye with her pinky finger. "They've offered me one of the next seasons on the show. At first I told them no. But I don't know. Maybe."

Rick nodded. "Lizzie will take good care of you."

She narrowed her eyes. "Didn't you hear? Your girlfriend quit."

After dropping that bombshell, she walked back to the makeup department to get ready for their reunion show. Rick staggered back. She'd quit? Since when had Lizzie ever quit anything?

He'd hoped and feared that she'd be at the reunion. He'd wanted to talk to her. To ask her why. Now he wouldn't get that chance.

Rick walked to the wardrobe department and waited for one of the producers to tell him what to wear, what to do. Without Lizzie, he felt lost in more ways than one.

THE LONG SOLITARY drive north from the airport gave Rick time to think. Which could have been a good thing under any other circumstances. In this case, it only made him more anxious. More wary. What would he find when he came home?

He took the exit off the freeway toward

Lake Mildred, and his anxiety level tripled. What was he doing? He couldn't do this. Couldn't face the town that had stood behind him only to watch him mess it all up.

He'd already done what he had to. He'd done the interviews, answered their questions for the past week. Now he wanted only to go home. Lie in bed and lick his wounds. And wonder where he'd gone wrong. Again.

Better yet, he needed to disappear where no one would find him.

And lucky for him, he owned just the place. He checked the road and made a quick U-turn. It would take him a couple of hours to reach the Upper Peninsula, but it would be worth it.

Peace. Quiet.

And completely alone.

RICK TOOK HIS CUP of coffee out on to the covered porch and took a seat in the Adirondack chair that faced the lake. The only sound to break the silence of the woods was the call of a hawk stalking its prey. He sipped his coffee and closed his eyes.

Aah. Peace.

Which was interrupted by the sound of an approaching car engine. He peeked out of one eye and groaned. If he wasn't answering Dan's phone calls, what made him think he wanted to talk in person? He shouldn't have been surprised.

Brandy getting out of the passenger seat made his eyebrows rise. She walked around the car and held hands with Dan as they approached the cottage. Rick scowled. "What are you two doing here?"

"You've been here for a week. That's enough time to sulk alone. Now I'm going to talk some sense into you and get you back home." Dan planted one foot on the lower step of the porch. "And if that doesn't work, Brandy will."

"There's nothing to talk about."

"You're in the middle of nowhere by yourself. The closest neighbor is three miles away." Dan looked around. "I know you, Rick. You need people around you. You thrive on it. That's what makes you a great manager."

People around was exactly what he didn't want at the moment. "I don't feel so great right now. And I definitely don't want to be around anyone. Now please go."

Brandy stepped forward. "No." She walked onto the porch and took a seat in the other Adirondack chair. "Not till you listen."

"And what has that gotten me? Oh, that's

right. A broken heart." He rose from the chair and looked at Dan. "Now leave."

When neither his brother nor Brandy made a move, Rick walked into the cottage and slammed the front door.

Moments later, Dan walked through. "Kind of hard to keep people out when you don't lock the door."

Rick stared at his brother and wished they hadn't been raised to be so stubborn. "Seriously, Dan, I don't want to talk."

"Good. Then you can listen. And maybe read this over and tell me what you want to do."

He handed Rick a small stack of papers. Rick flipped through them. "You got everyone in town to sign a petition? I'm not going back home just because you got people to sign a piece of paper."

"It's not a petition to get you home. They want you to run for mayor."

Rick frowned and reread the papers. "And why would they want that?"

Dan ticked the reasons off on his fingers. "Because you saw an opportunity to help the town and took it. You brought us jobs and a cash flow with the production in town. You saved Allyn Pickles by putting us in the national spotlight again. And you certainly saved Lake Mildred."

"The show's over. The jobs are gone."

Brandy handed him a second sheet of paper with figures and pointed to a colorful graph. "Tourism is up almost 300 percent. And as the new sales agent for Lake Realty, I can tell you that home sales have doubled since the show ended."

Rick glanced through the figures and shrugged. "That's not enough to make me a mayor."

"No, but your love for the community is." Dan leaned in closer. "When everyone else, including me, was giving up, you fought to keep the town alive. To make our town the way you remembered it. No one loves Lake Mildred like you. And that makes you perfect for the job."

"A job I don't want." He closed his eyes. "The first time I did the show because Dad wanted me to save the company. I did it again to save the town. When is it going to be my turn to do what I want?"

"What do you want, Rick?" Brandy sat closer to him and put a hand on his arm. "What is it you really want?"

"I want the woman I love to stand next to me. A partner who can help me conquer the world. Or at least our portion of it. I want to raise my kids like I was raised. To feel safe. Loved." He opened his eyes. "But she turned me down."

Brandy nodded. "There are other women out there."

"None like her."

Rick rose to his feet. "Thanks for coming up here to check up on me. But I'm okay."

Brandy stood and hugged him. "We know you're not, but we'll leave for now. Seems like you have some thinking to do."

Rick hugged her back, then shook hands with Dan, who pulled him closer. "I love you, little brother. The town needs you. But it's your choice. Your decision. It always has been."

ELIZABETH CLOSED her email program and checked her cell phone for messages. She'd sent almost a hundred résumés and portfolios out to production companies in Los Angeles. So far, she hadn't received any responses. No interviews. No requests to see more copies of the shows she'd worked on. Nothing.

Except silence.

She logged in to her bank account and did some quick calculating. She'd already given notice to her landlord and had a lead on an apartment that she could better afford. If she moved to the Valley at the end of the month, she'd cut expenses and could survive the next three months without a job.

She glanced around her apartment and tried to determine what things she could sell. Her cell phone rang, but she didn't recognize the area code. She was about to let it go to voice mail when something told her to answer it. "This is Elizabeth Maier."

"Ms. Maier, this is Ronald Treeman with WPYT. How are you doing today?"

She racked her brain at the station name. It seemed familiar but not local. "I'm sorry, what station?"

"We're northern Michigan's number one station for news and weather." When Elizabeth didn't say anything, he continued talking. "I heard from a friend that you're interested in a producing job. I've seen your work. I've even had a behind-the-scenes look at how you produce. And we're impressed."

"Um…thank you?"

"I'd like to fly you out for an interview."

Elizabeth waited for the joke to be revealed. "Listen, no offense to your friend, but I'm looking for a job here in California."

"I see. And how is that working out?"

More like it wasn't. She didn't respond.

"Then why not give us a shot? We're not Hollywood. And our budget is only a portion of what you're used to. But I think we might be a good fit."

"And how do you figure that?"

"Because unlike Hollywood, we're not interested in your mistakes." He paused. "We love your triumphs. And *True Love,* despite what they said in the tabloids, was your best work."

Finally someone was recognizing her show. Seeing her. "That show was my life."

"Ms. Maier, it was just a show. But you come out and work for me, I guarantee you'll find a life."

Elizabeth paused. Michigan, huh? "Mr. Treeman, what friend recommended me?"

"Rick Allyn, of course."

CHAPTER EIGHTEEN

THE HUNGRY CROWD cheered as Rick brought out the first tray of turkey dinners followed by Dan, Brandy and his mother with equally heavy trays. They moved quickly, placing a heaping plate in front of each man, woman and child. "Don't forget to pick out a new coat before you leave," Rick told them. "And the church ladies made hats, scarves and gloves."

"Bless you, Rick." The thin woman in front of him placed a hand on his. "I didn't know if we'd eat today."

"I know, Shelly." He smiled at her four kids. "And leave room for pie. With extra whipped cream."

Once everyone had been served dinner and dessert, the family helped their less-fortunate guests choose warm winter wear that would hopefully get them through the coming cold months. Rick greeted each one as they left and reminded them about the Thanksgiving parade the next day. It would be his first as grand marshal, but then being the new mayor brought certain privileges.

After dishes were washed and leftovers delivered to the shelter, Rick's family joined him in his apartment for their own Thanksgiving dinner. They held hands around the table as they said grace, then started to eat. "Mom, this stuffing with walnuts is fabulous."

"It was one of my grandmother's recipes I found in an old cookbook." She took a bite and nodded. "It's just like I remember."

Rick nodded at his brother. "You ready for Saturday?"

Dan reached out and took Brandy's hand. "I was ready the day I proposed, but Brandy's the one who's been keeping me waiting."

She slapped Dan on the arm. "I told you I needed time to put a wedding together."

"Well, here's to the happy couple. I wish you an amazing life of love and laughter." Rick raised his water glass. "To Brandy and Dan."

They clinked glasses and returned to their meals.

"And what about you, little brother? I noticed that Tonya's been eating at the diner every day for a month." Dan leaned closer. "When are you going to finally ask her out?"

A knock at the door downstairs saved Rick. He wiped his mouth with a napkin, then stood. "I'll be right back."

He took the stairs two at a time, then paused when he saw Elizabeth peering into the darkened diner. He considered walking upstairs, pretending he hadn't seen her. But his mother had raised him with better manners. Unfortunately for him.

Her face lit up when he opened the door for her. "Did I miss dinner?"

She'd missed a lot more than that. When would she get the hint? "What are you doing here?"

"Ron told me about the dinner you throw for the less fortunate. I came hoping to get a story." She lifted her handheld camera as she looked around the diner. "I missed it."

Rick stared at her, wondering if it was possible to make her disappear by wishing her away. "Elizabeth…"

She frowned. "You always call me Lizzie."

"Elizabeth, I don't want you here." He walked back to the front door and opened it. "I'm spending the evening with my family."

She walked past him toward the kitchen. "Great. I'd love to see them."

He intercepted her before she could head

upstairs. "You don't get it, do you? You're not welcome here. They don't want to see you."

She pawed through her purse and brought out a familiar purple invitation. "This says different." She glanced at it. "Believe me, I was shocked to open my mailbox and find it waiting for me. But I thought if your family could forgive me, then maybe there's a chance with you."

She took a deep breath and smiled at him, knocking the air out of Rick's lungs. Six months since the finale should be long enough to make him forget his feelings for the woman standing in front of him. Six long months to forget her and the way she could turn his life upside down with a simple smile. "I can't, Elizabeth."

A squeal behind him made them both turn. "I knew you'd come." Brandy rushed forward and hugged Elizabeth. "But you missed dinner. I would have saved the dirty dishes for you if I'd known."

"Very funny." The women put their arms around each other and walked upstairs.

Rick cleared his throat. "Don't I get a say in this? It is my place."

"No," they both answered and disappeared up the stairs.

DESPITE THE WARM WELCOME from Brandy, Elizabeth paused before following her into Rick's apartment. His mother's frown might have had something to do with it. But her less-than-warm welcome from Rick made it perfectly clear that she might be wrong for showing up. She shot a furtive look at Mrs. Allyn. "Sorry I'm late."

Rick brushed past her and started to make a plate for her. He brought a desk chair from the living room and pulled it up to the table. Elizabeth took a seat and thanked him as he placed the food and silverware before her. He didn't glance at her once. Not a good sign.

Rick bristled. Kept his gaze on the table rather than on her. "Thank Brandy, not me."

"I invited her, Rick." Dan shrugged at his brother's glare. "No one deserves to be alone at the holidays."

Rick pointed to her. "It was her choice to be alone."

"Maybe I made the wrong choice." She looked down at her hands. "I've made a lot of mistakes."

"Congratulations. Admitting you have a problem is the first step." Rick took his plate to the sink and stood there for several moments before turning back. "I need some air."

After he left the apartment, Elizabeth glanced at his family. "I'm really sorry."

Mrs. Allyn shook her head. "Don't tell us. Tell him."

"He doesn't want to listen."

The older woman touched her hand. "Do you love him?"

That was the question, wasn't it? She'd listened to Ron's job proposal but had calculated the distance from Rick while she agreed. She'd made a mistake letting him go. She wasn't going to do that again. "Yes, I love him."

"Then why are you sitting here? If you want him, go after him."

She got to her feet, hugged them all, then left the apartment without another word. Main Street wasn't that big, so she could see Rick's dark figure at the far end. She ran after him. "Rick, wait."

He turned and saw her. She was half-afraid that he'd turn away and leave her. Instead, he waited. She ran toward him and wondered why she hadn't grabbed her coat. She'd have to get used to the cold weather if she wanted to spend the rest of her life with the man before her. When she reached him, she was out of breath. "Thanks."

"For what?"

"You waited." It encouraged her.

Rick glanced at the ground. "Elizabeth—"

"I told you, it's Lizzie."

He looked up at her. "Why are you here?"

She rubbed her arms, hoping to get feeling back. Tried to think warm thoughts. "For Thanksgiving. For the wedding."

"Is that all?"

"No." She stepped closer to him, but he took a step back. "Rick, I didn't know who I was without that job. I thought I was the job." She shivered and looked down at her shaking hands. "I had to give it all up to find out I'm so much more."

"I'm happy for you." But his tone said something otherwise.

He turned and continued to walk down the street. Elizabeth followed him. "Don't you want to know what else I found out?"

"No." He glanced at her, then took off his jacket and put it around her shoulders. "When am I going to stop having to take care of you?"

"Hopefully never." She looked at him, hope rising in her heart. "I was wrong to turn you down that day. I listened to my head and not my heart. But I won't do that again."

"So you say."

"I mean it. If you give me a chance—"

Rick laughed, but it didn't sound joyful. Bitter instead. "I've been burned twice. What makes you think I would ever let you get a third shot at my heart?"

She reached out and held his hand. "Because I love you. And you love me."

"That was before, Elizabeth." He dropped her hand, crossed his arms over his chest and rubbed his arms. Started walking back to the apartment. She watched him walk back alone. Then she hung her head and prayed she wasn't too late.

RICK TOOK HIS RESPONSIBILITIES as best man seriously. He had insured that his brother showed up on time and in his tux. He'd held on to the ring until it was time to hand it off to Dan. He had signed the marriage license and posed for the pictures that would be perused for years to come.

He'd pretended he was happy.

Not that he wasn't glad to see his brother happily married. But it only made Rick feel lonelier. And more miserable.

He looked around the room of well-wishers, friends and relatives he hadn't seen since the last family function. He clinked his knife against the champagne flute and stood as the room grew silent.

He took a deep breath, then grinned at the crowd. "I'd like to take credit for bringing my brother and his new wife together. After all, I met her first. Dated her first." He leaned forward and said in a mock whisper, "I even kissed her first."

After the laughter died down, he got serious. "But I discovered that while Brandy was an amazing woman, she wasn't the one for me."

He looked out and found Elizabeth watching him. He looked away from her. "Luckily, she is the right woman for Dan. And he's the right man for her." He raised his glass. "To Dan and Brandy. May you have many years ahead of you. May you find in each other the perfect partner and friend."

Everyone raised their glasses and drank to the happy couple.

Elizabeth stood and approached the head table. She took the microphone from Rick.

Whispers started softly and grew as she stood in front of them. "I can tell by your reaction that you know who I am. What I did." She glanced back at Brandy, who nodded. "But there are some things I need to say."

She took a deep breath. "Weddings bring out some of the best in people. Those who are in relationships feel the bond grow stronger.

Those who aren't find themselves looking for the person who might fit into their lives." She paused. "And those who have loved and lost begin to question the mistakes they made. The opportunities they've missed."

Rick leaned forward and tried to take the microphone from her. "Elizabeth, don't do this."

She held on tighter and stepped away from him. "Don't what? Tell the truth?" She glanced at the videographer. "You confessed your feelings in front of an audience of millions. Why can't I share mine with hundreds?"

Rick walked around the table. She moved farther into the room and continued her speech. "I've watched this man walk out of my life twice. The first time, I missed his friendship. The way he made me smile. The second time, I missed him. The way he made me feel. Made me love."

She turned and faced him, and Rick could feel his stomach start to tumble. He looked around the room and found his mom watching him, smiling through her tears. He turned back to Elizabeth.

"Rick..." She got down on one knee and looked up at him. Gasps sprung up around the room. He shook his head and approached

Elizabeth. Tried to get her to stand. When she didn't, he knelt beside her. She looked into his eyes. "I've loved you since the first time you called me Lizzie. You looked past the Elizabeth who could bark orders and make things happen and saw the Lizzie who could be vulnerable and was looking for a man like you to love her."

Rick reached out and moved a wayward wisp of hair off her forehead. "Lizzie..."

"Because that's who I am." She leaned forward and touched her forehead to his. "I'm your Lizzie. Forever. And I want to make my home in your heart."

Rick swallowed around the lump in his throat and pulled her into his arms. Kissed her bare shoulder.

"But before I do, I need to ask you a question." She cleared her throat. "Rick, will you marry me?"

It was as if the entire room leaned forward, waiting for his answer. He hated to disappoint her. He peered into her eyes and warmed at the love shining out of them. But he shook his head. "I can't."

She frowned and tears glistened in her eyes. He brushed his fingertips over her cheek. "Not until I can find you the perfect ring."

Lizzie smiled through tears. "I don't need the perfect ring. Just you."

Rick leaned forward and kissed her soundly amid the applause.

He'd gone on the show to find true love, twice. This time, he was going to hold on to Lizzie forever.

His heart had found a home in hers.

* * * * *

REQUEST YOUR FREE BOOKS!
2 FREE WHOLESOME ROMANCE NOVELS
IN LARGER PRINT
PLUS 2
FREE
MYSTERY GIFTS

HEARTWARMING™

Wholesome, tender romances

YES! Please send me 2 FREE Harlequin® Heartwarming Larger-Print novels and my 2 FREE mystery gifts (gifts worth about $10). After receiving them, if I don't wish to receive any more books, I can return the shipping statement marked "cancel." If I don't cancel, I will receive 4 brand-new larger-print novels every month and be billed just $4.99 per book in the U.S. or $5.74 per book in Canada. That's a savings of at least 23% off the cover price. It's quite a bargain! Shipping and handling is just 50¢ per book in the U.S. and 75¢ per book in Canada.* I understand that accepting the 2 free books and gifts places me under no obligation to buy anything. I can always return a shipment and cancel at any time. Even if I never buy another book, the two free books and gifts are mine to keep forever.

161/361 IDN F47N

Name _____ (PLEASE PRINT)

Address _____ Apt. #

City _____ State/Prov. _____ Zip/Postal Code

Signature (if under 18, a parent or guardian must sign)

Mail to the Harlequin® Reader Service:
IN U.S.A.: P.O. Box 1867, Buffalo, NY 14240-1867
IN CANADA: P.O. Box 609, Fort Erie, Ontario L2A 5X3

* Terms and prices subject to change without notice. Prices do not include applicable taxes. Sales tax applicable in N.Y. Canadian residents will be charged applicable taxes. Offer not valid in Quebec. This offer is limited to one order per household. Not valid for current subscribers to Harlequin Heartwarming larger-print books. All orders subject to credit approval. Credit or debit balances in a customer's account(s) may be offset by any other outstanding balance owed by or to the customer. Please allow 4 to 6 weeks for delivery. Offer available while quantities last.

Your Privacy—The Harlequin® Reader Service is committed to protecting your privacy. Our Privacy Policy is available online at www.ReaderService.com or upon request from the Harlequin Reader Service.

We make a portion of our mailing list available to reputable third parties that offer products we believe may interest you. If you prefer that we not exchange your name with third parties, or if you wish to clarify or modify your communication preferences, please visit us at www.ReaderService.com/consumerchoice or write to us at Harlequin Reader Service Preference Service, P.O. Box 9062, Buffalo, NY 14269. Include your complete name and address.

HWDIR13R

LARGER-PRINT BOOKS!

GET 2 FREE
LARGER-PRINT NOVELS
PLUS 2 FREE
MYSTERY GIFTS

Love Inspired®

Larger-print novels are now available...